Constable Crime C[illegible]

Also by M. J. Trow

Fiction

The adventures of Inspector Lestrade (1985)
Brigade: the further adventures of Inspector Lestrade (1986)
Lestrade and the hallowed house (1987)
Lestrade and the Leviathan (1987)
Lestrade and the brother of death (1988)
Lestrade and the Ripper (1988)
Lestrade and the guardian angel (1990)
Lestrade and the deadly game (1990)
Lestrade and the gift of the prince (1991)
Lestrade and the magpie (1991)

Non-fiction

Let him have it Chris: the murder of Derek Bently (1990)

CONSTABLE CRIME OMNIBUS 2

The adventures of Inspector Lestrade
Brigade: the further adventures of Inspector Lestrade
Lestrade and the hallowed house

M. J. Trow

Constable · London

The adventures of Inspector Lestrade
First published 1985

Brigade: further adventures of Inspector Lestrade
First published 1986

Lestrade and the hallowed house
First published 1987

All three books first published in Great Britain by
Macmillan London Limited
4 Little Essex Street, London WC2R 3LF
and Basingstoke
Reprinted 1991
by Constable & Company Ltd
3 The Lanchesters, 162 Fulham Palace Road
London W6 9ER

ISBN 0 09 471060 0
Set in Linotron Palatino by
Falcon Typographic Art Ltd., Edinburgh & London
Printed in Finland by WSOY

A CIP catalogue record for this book
is available from the British Library

The adventures of Inspector Lestrade

The man in the Chine

Melville McNaghten pushed the ledger away from him. He buried his knuckles in his eyes and drew his fingers down his cheeks, taking less care than usual not to disarrange his faintly waxed moustaches. Three years' work, he mused to himself. A lot of good men, a lot of panic and in the end – nothing. What was it Her Majesty had said? 'We must improve our detective force.' Five women had died – or was it more? Over two hundred men arrested, hundreds more questioned. He shuddered as he thought of the fiasco of Barnaby and Burgho, the bloodhounds who had not only not caught the murderer, but had lost their handlers in the fog. And that idiot Charles Warren who had wiped the anti-Jewish slogans off the wall. He'd gone back to the army now – best place for him. And who was the buffoon who thought of photographing the dead eyes of Catherine Eddowes in the hope that a likeness of the murderer would appear on the plate?

He was glad at least, he reflected, that *he* hadn't been involved in that lunacy. He was the first policeman on the case – the first real policeman anyway. Again, the four names caught his eye – *his* suspects, *his* deductions. Nothing provable, of course, nothing absolutely tangible. But enough for him. Enough so that if he whispered just one of these names in the street, the vigilantes of Whitechapel would swarm from their hell-holes with noose and zeal. He could practically hear Mr Lusk, their chairman, wringing his hands in anticipation.

A knock at the door brought him back to the present. He snapped shut the ledger.

'Come.'

Under the lamp's flare he saw the trousers of a constable enter the room.

'Inspector Lestrade, sir.'

McNaghten straightened his cravat. 'Show him in.'

The constable's trousers were replaced under the light by those of the inspector. McNaghten swept the ledger quickly into a side drawer of his capacious desk. Lestrade stood with his back against the door, watching every move with a wry smile.

'The Ripper file, sir?'

'What?' the suddenness and volume of McNaghten's reply indicated that he had heard perfectly well.

'The ledger.' Lestrade walked more fully into the light, gesturing to the drawer as McNaghten locked it.

'Er . . . yes.' McNaghten was more reasonable as he sat squarely again in the chair. He swept his hand across his whiskers and straightened his cravat again. Lestrade remained motionless, hands in the pockets of his voluminous Donegal. McNaghten sighed and resigned himself to the unspoken question –

'Lestrade . . .' Too formal, he needed familiarity. 'Sholto . . .' Lestrade felt the avuncular arm metaphorically creeping across his shoulder. 'You know I cannot divulge a word of these contents . . .'

It wasn't enough. Lestrade had not moved. McNaghten read his mind. 'Yes, I know you were on it, but it was Abberlines's case.' It still wasn't enough. McNaghten stood up abruptly and the two men faced each other across the darkening room, their faces lit from below, like the inhabitants of Madame Tussaud's. 'Damn it, Lestrade. It is classified.' McNaghten hated dealing with subordinates, especially those as discerning as Lestrade. He was a thorn in his side, an itch he couldn't scratch. The Head of the Criminal Investigation Department turned to the window. Outside the rain was driving listlessly over the river and the arc lamps below. 'One day,' he talked to the heavy London sky, 'one day they will write about it. One day they will open my files and they will know.'

'I shall be a hundred and thirty-eight,' said Lestrade.

'Damn it, Lestrade,' McNaghten whipped round. He'd

already said that and it weakened his argument to repeat himself.

Lestrade smiled. He raised his hands in a gesture of defeat. 'I understand, sir,' he said. He turned up his collar and made for the night. At the door he stopped. 'Goodnight, sir.' The smile was chill.

The door closed and McNaghten slammed a paperweight on his desk. How typical of Lestrade to want to know. But he could not know. Nobody could. In a hundred years, when they officially opened the file he was about to consign to the archives, it wouldn't matter. He, Lestrade, all of them would be dead.

Lestrade's trousers under the light were replaced by the swish of an electric-blue skirt. 'Father?' McNaghten's daughter swept into the room.

'Ah, my dear,' McNaghten's professional face vanished. He was a family man again, in the bosom of his daughter. Miss McNaghten *was* dreadfully large. She was also dreadfully capable.

'Come along, Father. Time for home.'

McNaghten had a brief glimpse of his pocket watch before his daughter threw his Donegal over his shoulders. Three minutes past the half hour. 'Call the cab, Father.' McNaghten dumbly obeyed. He had long since ceased to think it odd that he who gave orders so unthinkingly in the line of duty should take them so unthinkingly in the line of domesticity. The constable wasn't in the corridor. Damn. He set off in search of him in the outer office.

In his absence, Miss McNaghten bustled round the desk, deftly produced a key identical to her father's and unlocked the desk drawer. A further deft movement and the ledger was under her pelisse and the drawer relocked.

McNaghten returned. 'Downstairs,' he said. 'Constable Dew will drive us home. Oh . . .' he remembered the ledger. It must go in to the safe. Miss McNaghten read his mind and blocked his way. Her tone and her logic belied the panic in her heart, thumping beneath pelisse, ledger and matronly bosom. 'The Commissioner, Father.'

'God,' mumbled McNaghten, as though they had axed his pension. 'It's tonight, isn't it?'

'Yes, and Cook has bouillabaisse.'

'Ah, I wondered why she walked like that.'

His daughter's gentle push nearly sent him reeling through the door. They clattered down the darkened corridor, lamps flickering on the institution green and cream. The ornate lift jarred and whirred its way to the ground floor. They stepped into the wet, chilly night. Constable Dew, never the same since he saw the corpse of Marie Kelly, held the door open for the McNaghtens. The police cab rocked as the Assistant Chief Constable's daughter entered. The hack recoiled several paces, bracing its back. While McNaghten Senior fastened the door, his daughter flicked the ledger out of the opposite window. A gloved hand caught it and the cab clashed its way out of the cobbled courtyard and along the Embankment, now green with the river's mist.

From the shadows, a figure emerged: Inspector Lestrade, in his damp Donegal, rain dripping from his Derby hat. He smiled down at the ledger and the little silver key. Moving to the nearest light, away from the drips, he opened the book. He flicked rapidly through the pages and pages of evidence, statements, depositions, theories. The letters met his gaze – *I am down on whores and I shan't quit ripping them till I do get buckled*. He knew all that. Nothing new, nothing different. It was the last page he wanted. There it was, the list of four names, stark in McNaghten's copperplate.

Lestrade smiled and his smile broke into a chuckle and his chuckle to a roar. He slammed the ledger shut. So Abberline took my advice, he thought to himself. And McNaghten. They listed all four of them. He was pleased. He knew his name appeared nowhere in the ledger. He knew he would not be remembered when they opened this file a century hence. But it didn't matter. It was enough for Lestrade to know that he had been right. It was that which time and again made his existence seem worthwhile. He did like being right.

'Sergeant,' Lestrade was inside the building again, the ledger under the flap of his Donegal.

The sergeant, who had been dozing, stood up at his desk.

'I'm going to Sir Melville's office – papers he wants me to check.' He made for the lift. 'Oh, at your relief go to Sir

Melville's. Give a message to Miss McNaghten – tradesmen's entrance. Tell her . . . tell her thanks and apologise to her. I shall be unable to join her this evening as planned. Pressure of duty.'

Lestrade felt the sergeant's eyebrows lower again behind his back and the smirk develop. 'Oh, and Sergeant,' Lestrade was still walking, still with his back to the man. He paused, turned round and smiled. 'Don't let me catch you asleep again.' The sergeant stiffened and tensed his shoulders. One good discretion, thought Lestrade, deserves another.

'Very good, sir,' mumbled the sergeant. 'Mind how you go.'

Lestrade was in the lift, raising his eyes heavenward at the inevitable cliché of that phrase. 'Goodnight, Dixon.'

When the good doctor alighted from the Southern Railway Company's train he was not in the best of moods. To begin with, his morning eggs had not been to his liking, and his mail had been late – three bills. Then the journey had been draughty and damp; the *Telegraph* full of misprints. But what had really irked him, as he took his hansom in the station forecourt, was the reason for his visit to the metropolis – to see his publisher. There had been no reply to his letters – it did not bode well.

He didn't notice the wet streets or the whipping wind. The jolting annoyed him from time to time, but they were soon there, outside Blackett's the publishers.

He was ready for the revolving doors, having caught his Gladstone in them last time. 'Do you know your bag is going round in the doors?' the doorman had asked him. 'He's a big bag now,' the doctor had answered through clenched teeth, 'he must go his own way.' It was a different doorman this time, for which the doctor was exceedingly grateful.

'Dr Conan Doyle . . . how nice . . . how nice.'

'Mr Blackett, you have not replied to my last four letters.'

'Dr Conan Doyle . . . it's . . .' Blackett was uncomfortable, shifting from leg to leg, wringing his handkerchief from hand to hand.

'You like *The White Company*?' Conan Doyle was relaxed, sure.

'Indeed, sir, indeed. A fine book – rich in historical detail. But . . .'

'But you don't like *The Refugees*?'

'It's not that I don't like it, Doctor . . .'

Conan Doyle sat motionless, cold eyes fixing his publisher.

'It's not . . . finished,' continued Blackett.

'It will be.'

'Of course. Of course. But the public likes new things. Crimes – suspense.'

'Like *The Sign of Four*?'

'Yes.' Blackett leaped at the memory, then was less sure. 'But . . . er . . . Mr Holmes of Baker Street?'

'What of him?'

'Well –' Mr Blackett was at his most obsequious – 'did he mind? I mean we do have the laws of libel.'

'Oh come, Mr Blackett. My stories of detection bear no relation whatever to the actual work of Mr Holmes. It would be more than my writing career or my medical practice is worth.'

'Well, as long as you're sure. That is the kind of thing the public wants. Plots, international intrigue.'

'Rubbish. Inconsequential bread-and-butter.'

Conan Doyle stood up purposefully.

'I would be grateful if you would return my manuscripts. I shall take my business elsewhere. It is obvious that the firm of Blackett has no concept of good literature. It wants twopenny trash that even the . . . *Strand Magazine* would turn its nose up at.'

Conan Doyle reached the door.

'By the way; that hand.' He pointed imperiously at Blackett. The publisher stared at his arm as though it had been severed. 'Come, come, man – the fingers.'

'Wh . . . what of them?' Blackett was startled.

'Unless I am mistaken – Grockle's disease. We get a lot of it in Southsea. Poor chap – probably a terminal case. Good Morning.'

Across the Solent from Southsea lies Roman Vectis, the Isle of Wight. There was no moaning at the bar when Lestrade put out to sea. Merely a stiff wind straining from the south-west. The steampacket bore him faithfully to Ryde and from the pier he took the train to Shanklin. He was nautically attired, as befitted the occasion, in pea jacket and peaked cap. But it was not a day for a jaunt. McNaghten had received the request. The grudging telegram for help. A body, it said. Found two days ago. Not a pleasant sight.

What bothered the Hampshire constabulary of course was the season. It was now late March; by the end of April, the tourists would be coming to the Island in vans and flies. Money, the Island's lifeblood. There must be no leakage, no panic. McNaghten had seen the point. He had seen what panic had done to the East End.

It surprised Lestrade therefore, in view of the need for secrecy, that the whole area of the Chine should be ringed, not only by constables, but by troopers of the Hampshire Yeomanry. He tackled his contact, a Sergeant Bush, about it as soon as he could.

'Ah well, sir,' was the sergeant's reply, 'it's Her Majesty, y'see. She's at Osborne for Easter – and we can't be too careful, can we?'

'Quite so,' replied Lestrade, but for the life of him he couldn't see how the presence of the Hampshire Carbs, complete with helmets and plumes, around the Chine could protect Her Majesty some miles away at Osborne. From what McNaghten had told him, this didn't sound like a Republican terrorist killing. But then McNaghten hadn't told him much. As Lestrade correctly surmised, McNaghten didn't know much.

He followed Bush and the two constables down the winding path that had been hacked in the Chine wall. The breeze from the sea caught them as they turned a corner. The sergeant ducked under a rope cordon and seemed to disappear through a cleft in the rock. The constables took up their sentinel position on the path.

'You'll need to watch your step,' the sergeant's voice echoed. Lestrade emerged in a world of total darkness. The smell was ghastly.

'Can we have a light, Sergeant?' he asked.

He felt a hand grip his arm.

'Inspector, this is not going to be pretty.' The sergeant was grim.

'I've been in the Force fifteen years, Sergeant. You get used to the sights.'

But Lestrade wasn't ready. Not for this one. Bush's arm swept up to strike the match and higher to show the 'sights'. A foot or so from Lestrade's face was the head. One eye had gone, the mouth gaped open, a gash in the livid skull. The hair stood on end, like a manic shrub blasted by the sea wind. The face flickered in the unreal sulphur glow. Lestrade swept Bush's arm down and the match went out. There was a silence. None of the three men in the chamber breathed. Lestrade turned for the entrance and breathed fresh air again. The helmets of the constables reassured him. Do I look as green as I feel? he asked himself. Come on, man, pull yourself together. You've been fifteen years in the Force. And these country bumpkins need your help.

Recovered, checked, in command, he faced Bush again. Now the sergeant *was* green. 'I'm sorry, sir,' he croaked, 'I can't get used to it. I've seen some "sights". Drownings, you know. Suicides in the Chine. Off of Culver Point. But this . . .' The sergeant's voice tailed away.

'Makes you glad of the sunshine,' commented Lestrade. 'Can we get to the beach down here?' He pointed ahead of him. Bush nodded. 'Be so good as to ask your man to stay here. Let's walk awhile.'

On the beach, drying now under the sun of the late morning and safe for an hour or two from the onslaught of the next tide, both men had a chance to clear their brains. At the back of each was a hideous head. Lestrade had not had time to view the rest.

'Tell me again,' said Lestrade.

'Well, sir. Workmen found it . . . er . . . him. Two days ago, it was. Let's see. Tuesday it would be. The Chine needed repairs. Erosion, you see. The land slips and we do get fierce winds in the winter. Well, the tourists will be here soon. Why, these sands are knee deep in donkey . . .'

'Spare me the holiday brochure, Sergeant.'

'Yes, sir. So, anyway, these blokes were chipping away at the cliff face in that particular area of the Chine when they found this crack.'

'Fissure.'

'Bless you, sir. Being of an inquisitive nature, these fellers cleared the rubble and went in. Well, at first they couldn't see nothing. Then, when they strikes their lucifers . . . well, there it were. They got hold of old Tom Moseley then and there – he's the local constable. Old Tom ain't very quick but he got the sense to rope off the place and inform me and I sent a telegram right away to Pompey. I don't think I expected them to send to Lunn'un though, sir. I mean, Scotland Yard itself – well!'

Lestrade sat on a breakwater, following the line of sandstone cliffs with his eyes. Above them a solitary gull wheeled and dipped, scanning the sea for movement.

'Pompey got the coroner over, but told him he was to leave . . . it . . . where it was.'

'Cause of death?' asked Lestrade, flicking the guano deftly from his cuff.

'Coroner didn't rightly know, sir. Said he'd been dead for a long time.'

Lestrade stood up. 'Get me a lantern, Sergeant. We must go back.'

This time Lestrade went in alone. He felt safer of his own emotions without Bush. The stench was still nauseating, but the steady light of the lantern gave the corpse a less hideous, less unreal aspect. This time Lestrade gave the task in hand his full concentration, his full professionalism. The body before him was male. Age – uncertain. He would guess about forty. The skin was the colour of old parchment, but here and there the bones of the skull were visible, a muddy, sickly white. One eyeball, or what was left of it, dangled from sinews on to the cheek. The other eye, sightless and pale, stared straight ahead. The clothes, muddied and drab, were those of a seaman perhaps – or a farm labourer. The dust of the sandstone had powdered them with grey and rivulets ran down the chest and arms where rainwater had seeped in. The bones protruded through. The hair caught his attention again – matted and long and grey – but, curiously, standing on end. He dropped to his knees and held the lantern at the floor. Gaiters. The man had been a farm labourer. What he saw next jarred him somewhat. The hands. Coarse, rough, almost devoid of flesh, but the nails were long – three or four inches long each one, curling out black and sharp. No working man grew his nails like that – he hadn't the leisure or time. For a moment, an image of mandarins came to mind. He had seen photographs of the Empress, and even a few of the Chinamen in his own city had nails like that. But the next moment he had dismissed it. What could be the connection? Opium? Secret Societies? He told himself to keep his mind open, not to be parochial. It wasn't every day a hideous corpse turned up in a beautiful valley in an English coastal resort.

Back to the matter in hand. Theories could come later. The body was propped up in a standing position, the legs turned in with the weight of the trunk, but it was clear that ankles, wrists and neck had once been tied. Strangulation? That was possible, but there was not enough of the neck left to tell. There was no more he could do. In the cramped space of the chamber it was too dark and airless for further work. He returned to the sunlight, older, wiser. He gave instructions for the body to be removed, and would supervise it himself. He must talk to the coroner, check the chamber measurements and look for clues. He must talk to the labourers who found it . . . him, to the Shanklin Chine Company.

But first Mrs Bush, rotund, homely, busy, was clattering around her kitchen. Lestrade sat in a withdrawn huddle seeing the dead face before him as Grace was said.

'Shepherd's pie, Inspector Lestrade?'

The labourers were unhelpful. They had been working under contract for the Chine Company for seventeen years, man and boy. The Chine had been closed earlier than usual the previous year because of a landslip. By early September, the ropes and chains had been strung up and the gates locked. Was it possible for anyone to enter? Yes, if they had a key. But in daylight, with a body? Unlikely. A night-time job, then? Certainly, but the path was treacherous and steep, with sharp turns and jutting ledges. It would have to be someone who knew the place

– and knew it well. One false step, carrying a full-grown man, and it would probably have been two bodies in the Chine.

It took Lestrade a week to interview all those who had regular contact with the area. At the end of it he was satisfied that no one knew anything. The inspector of works commented that there was evidence of rock-cutting and new mortar in the chamber, that the height had been altered and the body in effect bricked in.

'Are you familiar with the works of the late Mr Allan Poe?' he had asked Lestrade.

'Fleetingly, sir.' Lestrade had pondered the similarity already, as he faced the eighth consecutive shepherd's pie presented with glowing pride by Mrs Bush. But the connection didn't help him. Or did it? He had an uneasy feeling as he crossed to Portsmouth to the coroner's office; and it wasn't just the rolling and pitching of the steampacket.

'Dead for several months, I'd say.' The coroner was poring over a severed limb arranged tastefully on a slab. 'Yes,' adjusting his pince-nez, 'several months.'

'Cause of death?'

The coroner stopped his routine examination of the matter in hand and straightened. 'I'm not sure.' He twanged off his surgical gloves and rinsed his hands under a tap. 'Are you familiar with the works of Edgar Allan Poe?' Lestrade experienced an immediate *déjà-vu* – either that or the coroner was the inspector of works's brother. 'Fleetingly.' He really had had this conversation before.

'The short story called *The Black Cat*?'

'The cat is walled up in the cellar with the deceased?'

'Just so. No cat in the Chine chamber, eh?'

Lestrade shook his head. 'Are you telling me,' he asked, 'that the cause of death was . . .'

'Suffocation, I suppose,' was the coroner's verdict. 'That would have resulted before the other things – starvation, madness.'

'And the nails? The hair?'

The coroner wiped his hands on his waistcoat. He was uncomfortable. 'A ghastly thing. Shocking. Mind you, I can't account for it. Never seen anything like it myself, not in twelve years. Bizarre. That's the word. Bizarre.'

'What do you make of the man's occupation?'

'From his clothes, a labourer, I'd say. Smocking on the chest. Not from round here, though. Not the right pattern. Ah, but this was odd.' The coroner rummaged in a cluttered drawer. 'What do you make of this?' He handed Lestrade a piece of dirty material, metallic and torn.

'Military lace?'

'I am impressed, Inspector. Army, cavalry probably. But officer's certainly. How many officers of cavalry do you know who become farm labourers?'

'I take your point, sir.' Lestrade frowned, the plot deepening so fast as to make his head spin. But it was a clue, a tangible piece of evidence.

'And this is even more interesting.'

Lestrade saw, in the weave of the scarf, fragments that had been tucked under the collar of the corpse, the name 'Peter', embroidered in a coarse, childlike hand. 'What do you make of that?'

'As yet, sir, precisely nothing. But it's early days yet.'

The coroner showed Lestrade to the outer office. 'The lad will show you out. Spilsbury?'

A short-sighted urchin with acne lurched from an adjacent room. 'Look at him,' the coroner muttered. 'My cousin's boy from Leamington. He wants to be a coroner one day.' Under his breath to Lestrade, 'No hope, no hope at all. I think he's suicidal, you know.'

Not wishing to be a burden to Sergeant Bush any longer and totally unable to face his tenth supper of shepherd's pie, Inspector Lestrade moved in to Daish's Hotel. Daily he walked on the pier, breathed in the salt air. Daily he returned to the Chine, asked himself over and over – who? why? What, after all, did he have? A body. The body of a middle-aged man, walled up in an improvised cave at a popular holiday resort. The man was a labourer, named Peter, who may or may not have had contact with the army. It was thin, very thin.

But there was one last witness to see. A wild-eyed, melancholy old man with a massive barbed-wire beard mingling with the morning egg and pipe tobacco. Lestrade took a passing haywain by way of the worst roads he had ever travelled to the vast, overgrown country house at Farringford. Its owner, the Poet Laureate, was hobbling in the garden on his stick, examining with failing eyes the daffodils on the rolling lawns.

'Who is it?'

'Inspector Lestrade, sir, of Scotland Yard.'

'Lestrade of the Yard?' Tennyson would do anything for a rhyme.

'Very good, sir, very droll.'

'I don't usually see visitors, Inspector.'

'Quite so, My Lord.'

'Tea?'

Lestrade bowed. From nowhere, a butler brought the silver and the porcelain.

'Cream and sugar, sir?' The butler was pompous – he disliked policemen.

Lestrade felt uncomfortable in the presence of genius. He was not one himself and he was acutely aware that the Laureate did not tolerate visitors gladly. It was even rumoured that he leapt from rear windows and fled through orchards rather than face his butler's announcement of imminent guests. He had better get this over with. It would probably be of little value anyway.

'Forgive me for disturbing you, My Lord. I am told you are a frequent visitor to Shanklin Chine – out of season.'

'When I am at Farringford, I often wander there, yes.'

'You have a key?'

'No. My man calls on the gatekeeper when I wish to enter.'

'Have you been there recently?'

Tennyson's concentration began to wander. Lestrade busied himself searching in the delicate porcelain for a vestige of the tea. How he loathed the habit of filling only half the cup. He declined the butler's cream puff – for one thing the man had his thumb in it.

'Men may come and men may go,
But I go on for ever.'

Lestrade flickered a glance at the butler, who remained immobile, pompous.

'Er . . . quite.' Try a different tack, he thought. Eccentricity will out. 'On recent visits did you notice anything unusual?' He cursed himself for that vagueness. It opened the floodgates for senility.

'Break, break, break,
  On thy cold grey stones, O Sea!
And I would that my tongue could utter
The thoughts that arise in me.'

Amen to that, rejoined Lestrade silently.

'Did you notice any evidence of digging, My Lord?' He found himself talking loudly, as though to a deaf mute or a foreigner. 'Some new work on the Chine wall? A new cleft in the sandstone?' It was very hard work.

'But O for the touch of a vanish'd hand,
  And the sound of a voice that is still!'

That was more to the point. So Tennyson knew something. He was aware that there had been a murder. The papers had not yet released the story. The Noble Poet was hiding something.

'What makes you say that, My Lord.'

Tennyson stared unblinkingly under the over-shadowing brim of his Wide-awake. 'Forgive me, Inspector.' His tone was different. 'Sometimes I forget myself. Vain of me, isn't it, to quote my own work?'

Lestrade tried not to show he had not been following the drift of the last few minutes. 'Do you know anyone called Peter?' he asked.

Tennyson rose with the aid of stick and butler. Lestrade followed him towards the great house.

'Why are you asking me these things?'

'We have found evidence of foul play in the Chine, My

Lord. The body of a man whose name may have been Peter.'

Tennyson stopped and faced the inspector. He motioned the butler to go ahead.

'Inspector, I am not long for this world now. I have seen a great deal in my lifetime. Much sorrow . . . much sorrow. My mind is not so clear. If a body fell at my feet I doubt if I would notice it. The shadows are closing in. There are some days when I cannot tell if I am talking to men or ghosts.'

Lestrade, not usually a man of sympathy, patted the Laureate's arm. 'Thank you for the tea, My Lord,' seemed warm enough.

Tennyson was quoting again –

> 'If thou shouldst never see my face again,
> Pray for my soul. More things are wrought by prayer
> Than this world dreams of.'

He motioned the butler to him and hobbled on up the lawn. Lestrade waved his hat in token that he would find his own way out.

> 'Twilight and evening bell –' he heard the Poet declaim,
> 'And after that the dark!
> And may there be no sadness of farewell
> When I embark.'

Lestrade embarked on the steampacket later that afternoon. He had assured the authorities that there were further lines of inquiry to follow up and that the case was far from hopeless, but he was not very far forward. The local papers had been leaked the story – inevitably. And the name 'Peter', the labourer's smock and the notoriety for the Chine were all there. The editor had had the good taste to suppress the grisly details – or the coroner had been unusually tight-lipped.

No time for Lestrade to return to London. Instead he took the train, by easy stages, via Swindon and the wide gauge of the Great Western, to Haverfordwest. He was annoyed at having missed his connecting boat and had to spend a wet, cold night in the town with what appeared to be a single street. If there were further delays tomorrow, he ran the risk dreaded by all full-blooded Englishmen in a Welsh town – a dry Sunday. Methodist revivals and Mr Gladstone's Licensing laws had combined to kill Haverfordwest.

As it turned out, Lestrade would have preferred a dry Sunday to the wet Saturday he got. The ship lurched and rolled in the inhospitable Irish Sea. Lestrade, never a good sailor, found his stomach and his mind whirling together in speculation and nausea. Irish soil felt solid and safe. The cab clattered along Sackville Street and on into the suburbs. Dublin was still a lovely city, elegant, wealthy, English. And if there was an air of hostility, if the men and women did not look you squarely in the face, it wasn't to be wondered at. After all, wasn't that unprincipled maniac Gladstone playing with Home Rule? Playing right into the hands of the Fenians? And Salisbury couldn't last long – the Irish MPs at Westminster would see to that. At least, so *The Times* said and Lestrade had a great respect for that newspaper. Not that he was a political policeman, but he believed in keeping abreast of affairs.

Lestrade alighted at the barracks of the 13th Hussars to have his feet run over by their new maxim-gun detachment. Not wishing to appear unmanly before these fine fellows on manoeuvres, he buried his teeth into the rim of his bowler and drove his head a few times against the nearest wall.

'Did ya have a nice trip, sor?' chuckled the cabbie on his perch.

Lestrade flashed him a livid scowl and no tip and limped painfully into the regimental offices. The surgeon duly saw him, bandaged both feet and left him in the orderly room. It was some hours before the object of the inspector's visit arrived. Two burly privates appeared and lifted Lestrade between them down the corridor, across the courtyard and into the office of the colonel. The walls were hung with regimental trophies and photographs and the whole room had an aura of cigar-smoke and horse linament.

'Boys,' a sharp voice barked behind him. Lestrade leapt an inch or two and instantly regretted it, landing full on his bruised toes. Colonel Templeton-Smyth strode past him to his desk. He was a man of average height, brisk and straight-backed, with the inevitable military moustache, clipped somewhat thinner than Lestrade's own. He had the face of a hawk, clear blue eyes, firm chin and tanned, parchment skin – rather an odd hawk, really. He threw his forage cap on to the desk and unhooked the short, astrakhan trimmed patrol jacket before flinging himself into his chair.

'Boys,' he repeated, sliding a cigar box across to Lestrade. 'What do you think of 'em, Sergeant-Major?'

'Inspector, sir, Inspector of Police.'

'Ah, yes, of course. Sorry. Find these rank things confusin', what?'

'I think that boys have their place in the scheme of things, sir. They will at very least be boys.'

'Ah, yes, but you are a policeman. Right?'

Lestrade nodded.

'You must know some of these youngsters. You know, the ones old Barnardo doesn't get. I've got an idea . . .'

'Forgive me, sir' – Lestrade was trying to be formal, despite the throbbing in his toes – 'but I'm on important police business.'

'Ah, yes, 'course. Light?'

Somehow Lestrade leaned forward and puffed gratefully on the cheroot. The grandmother tolled the hour of four.

'Ah, tiffin.' The colonel rang a silent bell near his desk. 'But the prevention of crime, man. That Ripper chappie – he was a boy once. We can't wait until they grow up twisted and bitter. We've got to train them, make them into useful citizens. Now, my idea . . .'

'With respect, sir,' Lestrade cut in.

'Ah, yes, 'course. Fire away. Ha! Good that, what? Military joke, don't you know, fire away!' Templeton-Smyth saw that Lestrade was not amused. 'Well, to business.' His face straightened.

'I am making inquiries into a suspected murder which took place recently at Shanklin on the Isle of Wight, sir.'

'Ah, yes? How can I help?'

Lestrade fumbled in his wallet and threw the scrap of material on to the colonel's desk. 'What do you make of that, sir?'

Templeton-Smyth scrutinised it closely. He took it to the light of the window. Something in the square caught his eye and he threw open the sash.

'Not like that, Corporal,' he shouted. 'It'll never get better if you picquet!'

Back in the room, the colonel answered the inspector's question. 'Officer's lace. Thirteenth Hussars. Shoulder belt.' A pause, then – 'Could be Fourteenth Hussars, of course.'

'Thirteenth.' Lestrade was emphatic. 'This object was found in the lining of the clothes of the deceased, sir. I took the trouble of cleaning it. I also borrowed a copy of Her Majesty's Dress Regulations for Officers from Messrs Gieves & Company, Portsmouth branch. A brief consultation of that told me that the lace belongs, as you say, to a shoulder belt of either the Thirteenth or Fourteenth Hussars. If however you look again at the object' – the colonel did – 'you will notice that one edge of it is brighter, less tarnished than the rest.'

'I don't follow you, Inspector.'

'Your batman would, sir. Any man who has the job of cleaning regimental lace would know that where it is covered by a metal ornament, the lace is clean. The clean area on the scrap you have there corresponds in size and shape with a metal scroll on which a battle honour is blazoned. I need hardly tell you, sir, that the Thirteenth is the only cavalry regiment that wears its battle honours on its pouch belt.'

Templeton-Smyth's jaw fell slack. 'I admire you police chappies. First-class piece of deduction, Lieutenant.'

'That's Inspector, sir.'

'Ah, yes, 'course.' Templeton-Smyth returned the lace. The significance began to dawn on him. 'So this chappie, your . . . er . . . deceased. An officer of the Thirteenth?' His moustaches began to bristle with distaste.

'That is what I am here to find out, sir.'

'Now look here, Lestrade. This isn't on, you know. I mean, officers and gentlemen and all that. Bit unseemly, what? Chappie from one's own mess endin' up done to death.' But curiosity overcame the scandal. 'Tell me, how'd it happen? Sabre? Carbine? Maxim?'

Lestrade ignored these fanciful lunges into mid-air. The man had clearly no notion of the mechanics of murder. 'Have – or had you – among your officers, Colonel, one called Peter? The Christian name, I would surmise.'

Templeton-Smyth strode round the room. 'Peter, Peter,' he mused to himself, stroking the long lean chin. 'Well, I've been with the Thirteenth for fifteen years now since Cornet. There's only one Peter I've known among the officers.'

Lestrade straightened. Was this it? Had his gamble, his expensive, unrequisitioned trip to Dublin, paid off? Did he have a link with this fashionable cavalry regiment? What was Templeton-Smyth covering up?

'Peter Endercott. He's out there.' He pointed to the window.

Lestrade hauled himself upright, grimacing with pain. Those damned gun-limber wheels must have broken his toes. He reached the window. Below, a squadron of the 13th Hussars were going through their sword drill exercises, even though the afternoon was drawing in under a threatening sky. The clash of steel punctuated the harsh commands of the drill sergeants. Lestrade remembered his own days of such practice as a constable with the Mounted Division. He could see four officers standing casually around watching the men go through their paces.

'Which one is he, sir?'

Templeton-Smyth looked oddly at him and realisation dawned. 'Oh, no, my dear chap. Over there.' He pointed beneath a clump of elms, some distance from the parade ground. 'Third grave from the left. T.B., poor chap. Family insisted he be buried here. Full military honours, of course.'

'When?' Lestrade's optimism had already reached his bandages.

'Ooh, three – no, four years ago. June it was. Shame. He made up a good foursome.'

'Foursome?'

'Whist, Captain. Do you play?'

'Er . . . no, sir.'

'Pity. Now there's a good game for boys.'

The door opened and a tall angular woman in a frothy white dress appeared. 'My dear, I'm sorry tiffin is late today. Shall we take it in the ... oh, I'm sorry, I didn't know you had company.'

Lestrade staggered to his feet. 'Oh, no, please don't get up. Gout can be a frightful business, can't it?'

'This is Major Lestrade, my dear, of the Metropolitan Police,' offered Templeton-Smyth. 'Major, my sister.'

'Inspector, ma'am,' groaned Lestrade, as Miss Templeton-Smyth shook his hand heartily.

'We are discussing a delicate matter, my dear ...' said the colonel.

'Oh, Robert, my dear, can't it wait? This poor man deserves some tea.' She helped Lestrade to his bandages and steadied him on a wiry arm. 'Girls,' she said as they limped from the colonel's office. 'As a policeman, you must meet some of the wayward ones.'

Lestrade had been here before.

'Well, we have to train them, Inspector, to make something of them. I was talking it over with one of my brother's officers, Captain Baden-Powell, before he left for Malta. He rather ridiculed the whole thing.' The colonel fell into step behind his sister, 'We'll have some tea and I'll tell you of my idea ...'

So Lestrade had drawn another blank with the 13th Hussars, as he had with Tennyson. He had bruised his toes, been violently sick on the crossing back from Dublin and had been subjected to Templeton-Smyth's interminable ramblings about organising the youth of Britain into some ghastly regiment of paragons, helping old ladies across roads and hiking pointlessly around the countryside. What a fatuous idea – that Baden-Powell fellow had got it right. And how silly Colonel Templeton-Smyth would look in short trousers.

For the next eighteen days, a team of constables working from the War Office tracked down and interviewed the twenty-four Peters who were serving or had served in the ranks with the 13th Hussars. Lestrade was desk-bound while his toes subsided, but he was rather surprised that there were so many of them – Peters, that is, not toes. It was not after all so common a name. He was disappointed not to find anything tangible in the follow-ups. Eight of the Peters were dead, three of them were in jail. Two were abroad and likely to remain so and of the remaining eleven, no links could be established with Shanklin, the Isle of Wight or the disappearance of a middle-aged man in a labourer's smock. At least Lestrade now knew that the smock denoted Norfolk, but inquiries by telegram and telephone to the chief constable of that county achieved nothing – partly because the chief constable did not have a telephone. But there were no reports of a missing person answering to the description of what was once the man in the Chine. Several cats of course were listed and one rather nasty salamander, but no farm labourers, indeed no people at all.

Lestrade was about to conclude that an unidentified man, whose name may or may not have been Peter, who may or may not have had association with the 13th Hussars, had met his end by foul play by person or persons unknown, when a letter arrived by second delivery. It was a mourning letter, black-edged and the message was typed. Lestrade read it just once to realise its import –

Just look at him! There he stands,
With his nasty hair and hands.
See! his nails are never cut;
They are grim'd and black as soot;
And the sloven, I declare,
Never once has combed his hair.

The postmark was London and it was addressed to 'Inspector Lestrade, Scotland Yard.' The inspector looked again at the doggerel. Home-made? Yes, he surmised so. He wished he knew rather more about poetry but the crammer he had been to had not thought it necessary and most of his colleagues at the Yard – Gregson, Athelney Jones, even McNaghten – found poetry and poets faintly limp and unmanly. The typescript was odd – slightly uneven with a decided kick on the letter 'n' so that it stood a little below the line. He had always thought there must be a way of detecting a faulty typewriter, but he was damned if he could see how.

He remembered again the Ripper letters. Two of them he

knew were genuine. Nearly two hundred were from cranks, oddities who crawled from the woodwork whenever murder walked abroad. But these two had carried inside information. And so did this verse – the hair alone had been mentioned in the local papers and the case – for such it had become – did not reach all the dailies. Only the coroner's report, that of Sergeant Bush of the Hampshire Constabulary and Lestrade's own carried full information. There was the possibility of a leak, mused Lestrade, as he painfully took the lift to the ground floor. Perhaps someone in the coroner's office – that spotty lad Spilsbury, for instance – perhaps one of Bush's constables. But he didn't think so. In his heart of hearts he knew that this letter had been written, and the verse composed, by the murderer.

Well, so be it. This was 1891 and this was Scotland Yard – the foremost police headquarters in the world. This was Britain, the workshop of the world. Forensic science was at his disposal. Here, in the gloomy basement festooned with pipes of gas and water, here were the most brilliant men of science that Europe could boast. If they could not find clues in the letter no one could.

'Fingerprints?' repeated the boffin as he stared at the outstretched letter in Lestrade's carefully poised fingertips. 'What are they?'

A death in the morning

Lord Frederick Hurstmonceux lay on the billiard table in the gaming room. His normally immaculate hunting coat was thrown back in tatters, his shirt lacerated and congealed with blood, as were his hands and face. He had been dead for some six hours when Lestrade arrived, at McNaghten's personal request. The house, an extravagant Palladian monstrosity nestling in a curve of the Downs, was still and silent. After the shaking and rattling of the Daimler Wagonette horseless carriage, that silence was bliss. A grim butler met him at the door and showed him into the tiled entrance hall. His policeman's eye took in the aspidistrae, the elegant sweep of the staircase, the portraits of the Hurstmonceux, fathers and sons in their hunting pinks. A row of hushed frightened servants, stiff in their starched white aprons lined the passageway. They were unsure how to behave to Lestrade. They knew he was a police officer and why he was there, but many of them had never seen an officer from Scotland Yard, a man in plain clothes. Some of them curtsied, others followed him with their eyes.

The butler threw back the double doors. Lestrade blinked in the bright electric light which flooded the table. He looked down at the body. 'Ruined the baize,' he murmured.

'Will that be all, sir?'

'Yes. Would you ask Sir Henry to join me here?'

The butler vanished. Lestrade gave the body a cursory examination. Cause of death he assumed to be severe lacerations and shock. Or blood loss, he mused, as he turned the matted head to find the jugular ripped. Of his clothes only the mud-caked hunting boots remained unscathed. This was messy, a sticky end, even for a country squire of Hurstmonceux's reputation.

'McNaghten?'

The voice made him turn sharply.

'Oh, I expected Assistant Chief Constable McNaghten,' said the voice.

'Inspector Lestrade, sir.' 'At your service' sounded too deferential. 'Sir Henry Cattermole?'

The voice brushed past Lestrade and looked down at the corpse on the billiard table. 'Yes, I'm Cattermole.'

'Assistant Chief Constable McNaghten was unavoidably detained, sir. He asked me to give you his regards. I shall have to ask you a few questions, sir.'

Cattermole had not taken his eyes off the body. 'Come into the library,' he said, 'I can't look at him any more.' Lestrade followed him across the hall. Servants and butler had gone. The library was typical of these country houses, wall to wall with leather-covered books, which no one had read.

'Cognac?'

Lestrade accepted the proffered glass. 'In your own time, sir.'

Cattermole quaffed the brandy and refilled.

'Freddie Hurstmonceux was a bastard, Inspector. A professional bastard. Oh,not in the sense of lineage, you understand. They don't come with bluer blood.'

'I found it rather red, sir.' Lestrade could have kicked himself for the tastelessness of that remark.

'No, Freddie deserved this. Or at least, I'm not surprised by it.'

'Could you tell me what happened, sir?'

'He was out hunting. We all were. Freddie loved having open house and riding to hounds with his cronies. They all hated him, but he exuded a certain raffish charm. Anyway, we'd got a view and the hounds were off. This was in the Lower Meadow and Freddie, as ever, was off in hot pursuit. Whipping his hunter unmercifully.'

'He didn't treat horses well?'

'Horses, dogs, people. He didn't treat anything well. I've seen him whip a horse to death.'

'You didn't stop him?'

'Damn it, Lestrade. What business is it of yours?' Cattermole paused. Then, more calmly, 'You don't cross a man like Freddie.' A long pause. 'Well, he came through the thicket ahead of me, away to the left. Bertie Cairns and Rosebery were with him, but as he topped the rise he must have left them behind. Ploughed fields there of course, tough going. Freddie was a better rider than any of them. By the time I got to the rise, all hell had broken loose. The hounds set up the devil of a row beyond the wall, I thought they'd got the fox. They were tearing, limb from limb, howling and yelping. But Bertie and Rosebery were galloping down there, taking the wall and laying about them with their crops. It was obvious something was wrong. When I got there it was all over. The dogs were being hauled off and I could see it wasn't a fox. It was Freddie.'

Cattermole buried his face briefly in his hands. Lestrade returned to the subject of the body.

'Foxhounds did that?' he said incredulously.

Cattermole sat back in his chair. 'Impossible to believe? I saw it, Lestrade. They went for his throat. He had no chance at all.'

'Forgive me, sir, I don't mean to be in any way awkward. But this is accidental death. A quirk of nature in the breasts of vicious beasts.' He congratulated himself on having got that out in one breath. And then, perhaps a little pompously, 'I am from the C.I.D., sir, the Detective Branch.'

Cattermole stood up sharply. 'Inspector –' his face was dark – 'I could have called in the village bobby, but I didn't want huge feet trampling over the last vestiges of what was once a great family. That is why I contacted McNaghten. God knows I had no time for Freddie. He's dead and damned to all eternity. But there,' he pointed dramatically to the massive portrait over the empty fireplace, 'is the fourth Baron Hurstmonceux – and a better man never drew breath.' Henry Cattermole was of the old school, honest and loyal. 'Friendships forged at Eton and Quetta don't die, Inspector.' The inspector took his word for it. 'It's for his sake I sent for the Yard. No fuss, no scandal, you understand?'

'Perfectly, sir.'

'Poor Georgie. Freddie was his only son. The bastard killed him.'

'Would that be on our files, sir?'

'Oh, not literally, Lestrade. He didn't actually put a revolver to his head. But with his . . . ways . . . he might just as well have done.' Cattermole gazed long at the portrait. Then, 'Come with me, Inspector.'

The two men left the house by the vine-covered south wing and crossed the velvet lawns to the stables. Beyond the main buildings here, where the hunters and thoroughbreds steamed after their exercise, they came to the kennels. Lestrade was not taken with dogs. One or two of his superiors were keen on the use of bloodhounds, but they always seemed to urinate on him whenever he had been involved with them. He often wondered whether it was anything personal or whether it was somewhere he had been. In a yard, thirty or forty foxhounds, smart in black, tan and white, licked and snuffled. Lestrade was glad there was no growl, no howl. Not wishing to let Sir Henry believe he was afraid of these curs he extended a sure hand, praying that it didn't shake. A heavy jowled dog, perhaps older, certainly darker than the rest, buried its nose in his palm. Lestrade ruffled its ears. 'Good boy, good boy.'

'Do you notice anything about these dogs?' Cattermole asked him.

Lestrade hated being put on the spot in this way. Give him a burgled tenement, a done bank or even a forged fiver and he was on home ground. But hunting and shooting weekends and country houses were somebody else's patch. He checked the obvious – leg at each corner. None of the dogs had tried to pee on him yet.

'You mean . . .' Long years in the force had given him the slow amble, developed to the point which would give his questioner time to chip in.

'Apart from the blood.'

Lestrade whipped back his hand and hoped that the gesture hadn't been too sudden. He hadn't in fact seen the blood – until now. But there it was, dark and caked around many mouths. Human blood. Hurstmonceux blood.

'They're so docile,' Cattermole went on, 'you wouldn't think that six hours or so ago they tore a man apart, would you?'

Lestrade shuffled backwards as far as protocol would allow.

'That one by you,' Cattermole pointed at the dog which Lestrade had been patting, 'that's Tray, the lead hound. He would have gone for Freddie first. Rosebery said it had him by the throat.'

Lestrade was grateful for the fresh air. Across the courtyard, still in his hunting pinks strode Archibald Philip Primrose, 5th Earl of Rosebery. He was an anxious-looking forty-four.

'Ah, Rosebery. This is Inspector Lestrade – of Scotland Yard.'

'Oh, God.' Rosebery caught the proffered hand.

'My Lord,' Lestrade bowed stiffly. 'Can you shed any light on this unfortunate affair?'

Rosebery looked around him like a stag at bay, his large watery eyes flashing to every corner of the yard. He took Lestrade's arm and led him away down the lawns. Cattermole sensed his air of secrecy and suspicion and walked back towards the house. 'I'll see to your room, Lestrade,' he called.

'Thank you, Sir Henry.'

'Look, Balustrade, there's a Garter in the offing for me.'

'My Lord?' Lestrade would believe anything of the aristocracy, but Rosebery did not strike him as one of those.

'No scandal, y'see. I can't afford any scandal. Not now, I mean, Home Rule is one thing. And the gee gees, but this . . . God, poor Freddie.'

'What sort of man was he, sir?'

'Who?'

'Lord Hurstmonceux.'

'Oh, a bastard. An absolute bastard. He had his moments, mind.' Rosebery chuckled a brittle, distant laugh. 'No, I suppose Freddie wasn't what you would call a decent sort. Look here, er – Balcony – this won't become common knowledge, will it?'

Lestrade had met this kind of pressure before, but from a man like Rosebery, Gladstone's right-hand man, a foremost politician and Peer of the Realm, it was disconcerting. He wouldn't budge Lestrade himself, but an inspector's hands could easily be tied and he wasn't at all sure about McNaghten.

Influence and the old school tie were all they once had been, despite the extension of the franchise.

'You can't conceal the death of a member of the House of Lords, My Lord.'

'Death?' Rosebery's tone suggested that he had been misjudging Lestrade. Then, more calmly, 'Oh, quite so, quite so.'

But Lestrade had been quicker. He had read the signs. Rosebery was hiding something.

'Do you think it was something more, My Lord?'

'More?' Rosebery's effort to effect unconcern was pathetic.

'Murder, My Lord.' Lestrade turned to face the man so that their perambulations came to an abrupt end. Rosebery stared at him, his mouth sagging open.

'How?' was all that he could manage.

'That's exactly what's bothering me,' confessed Lestrade. 'I don't know. Yet.'

Rosebery blinked and walked on, following Lestrade's lead. The tone of the conversation had changed. The policeman was now in charge, leading the noble lord around with an invisible ring through his aristocratic nose.

'I take it Lord Hurstmonceux was an experienced huntsman?'

'Oh, yes, ridden with the Quorn, the Cattistock, the best of them.'

'Knew horses and dogs?'

'Like a native. That's what's so damned peculiar.' Rosebery was beginning to open up. 'I mean, he treated his animals badly, God knows. But dogs are faithful curs. They'll stand for a lot, y'know.'

'When foxhounds are on the scent, what do they go for?'

'Well, the fox, of course.'

'Because of the scent?'

'Yes. It's bred into them.'

'And what could make them turn on a man, especially when they are in full cry after the fox?'

Rosebery shook his head. 'I don't know,' he said. 'It's the damnedest thing.'

*

Dinner was surprisingly convivial. True, Rosebery was still nervous, but the wine flowed and the aristocracy found the presence of a Yard officer more novel than irritating. Lestrade deflected probes about the Ripper case as deftly as he could, but it was obviously still the talk of clubland. He coped remarkably well, for a man of his class, with the vast range of cutlery and silver which would have made Mrs Beeton's head spin. It was a curiously masculine evening. A 'stag weekend' was how Lord Hurstmonceux had termed these functions – by family tradition the last hunt of the season was a 'gentlemen only' affair. Over cigars and port, the third member of the house party, Sir Bertram Cairns, took Lestrade aside.

'They'll be talking Home Rule all night,' he motioned to Rosebery and Cattermole, heads together in earnest conversation by the roaring log fire. 'Bring your glass. There's something I want to show you.'

Lestrade followed Cairns through the house, past his own room and on through endless passages, twisting to right and left, until they came to a locked door, studded with brass. Cairns produced a key and unlocked it. It took a while for Lestrade to take in the contents. The room was obviously some sort of laboratory. Hanging from the ceiling were gruesome birds in the attitude of flight, casting large shadows on the walls. Pigeons disintegrating on the impact of hawks, and shrikes impaling insects on thorns. On the tables and benches was a vast array of glassware, bottles and flasks and tubing. In the centre of the room, the floor was bare, scarred with cuts and stained darkish brown. In jars on the shelves was every assortment of animal, floating in greenish liquid.

'Lord Hurstmonceux was a scientist?' said Lestrade.

'Not quite,' came the answer. Cairns pointed to an oblong box in one corner of the room. At one end of it was a series of black and white keys and the box was divided into compartments with piano wire strung across the base to the keys themselves. Lestrade felt it was legitimate to admit that he did not know what this was.

'The Cats' Piano,' said Cairns grimly.

'Er . . . the cats' . . . er . . .'

'The cats are placed into the compartments and locked in.

Then the . . . scientist . . . plays a tune on the keyboard, with the result that the wires spring up and lash the cats from below and the hammers hit their heads.'

'So this is not a laboratory,' said Lestrade, the light beginning to dawn.

'No, Inspector. This is a torture chamber.'

Lestrade noticed for the first time that the walls and door were heavily padded. Cairns caught his eye. 'Noise-proof,' he said. 'These animals around you in the jars. I'll wager any price you like that they were operated on while very much alive.'

Cairns crossed to a desk-drawer and produced a ledger. 'Here – a record of his "experiments".'

'Vivisection,' mused Lestrade.

'Oh, no, Inspector. The public might not like the idea, but true vivisection is at least for scientific purposes. But this – this is sheer sadism – torture for pleasure's sake. And Unnatural Acts,' he added cryptically.

Lestrade flicked through the ledger. Boiling hedgehogs, skewering thrushes on needles, snapping the front legs of foxes, castrating horses with dress-making scissors, blinding goats with hatpins. Hardly the usual pastime of a scholar and a gentleman. And what Lord Hurstmonceux attempted to do with the sheep on his estate was very definitely best left to the imagination.

'How does this help us, Sir Bertram?' asked Lestrade.

'I'm not sure,' answered Cairns. 'But we all know why you're here, Lestrade. This is not a simple death in the morning. It's murder.'

'By dog or dogs unknown?' added Lestrade.

'What do you mean?'

'Let me explain something about murder, Sir Bertram. When I am called in to investigate foul play, I usually have a victim and no murderer. The average killer does not stand over the corpse obligingly with a gun or knife in his hand until I arrive. I piece together the evidence – like the parts of a jigsaw puzzle – and I arrive at conclusions. Now, in this case, I have my murderer – or murderers should I say. Forty of them. But they are foxhounds, sir, and a foxhound cannot stand trial before one of Her Majesty's Justices. There is no precedent for it.'

'Good God, man, I'm not an idiot. Freddie Hurstmonceux was one of the most unpopular men in the country. There must be scores of people who would not have been sorry to see him dead.'

'Very possibly, sir. But unless you can tell me how they did it, I cannot proceed further.'

Lestrade slept little that night. In his room tucked away in the west wing he paced the floor. The oil-lamp cast a lurid glow on the heavy Chinese wallpaper. His bed was appallingly uncomfortable and the room cold. He had not come with the intention of staying but in view of the deceased's no longer wanting them, Sir Henry Cattermole had lent him a nightshirt and dressing gown of Lord Hurstmonceux's. They were a trifle large perhaps and decidedly ornate by Lestrade's rather drab standards, but they would do. He looked out from time to time across the lawns and caught the scurrying moon flickering on the waters of the lake. Occasionally the baying of a hound bore in on him the extent of his exasperation. But as dawn began to creep over the low trees below the house, a theory began to emerge. Well, after breakfast, Lestrade would see whether or not it paid off.

Cairns was all for it. Cattermole had his doubts, but would do a great deal for the good of the family name. Rosebery wished he wasn't there. Within an hour after breakfast, the pack was out with their handlers and the house guests, including Lestrade, mounted and ready to go. Standard police procedure, he had assured them – the reconstruction of a crime. He kept as far as he could from the hounds and each man carried a loaded revolver in case they ran amok again. Lestrade was a fair rider, but he wasn't used to rough country and five-barred gates. He hoped they would encounter neither.

It was a misty morning, raw-cold for early April and totally unlike the clear night. The ground was heavy with dew like tears as Cattermole sounded the horn and the pack moved off. A suicidal groom was riding far ahead with a dead fox over the cantle of his saddle, to draw the hounds the right way. It was an odd sight. A hunt, now rather out of season, if only by a day, with too few men, too few horses, no real quarry and an odd, gloomy silence. There was no jollity, no bantering and even Cattermole's horn sounded chilly and alone. They crossed the ploughed fields of the South Meadow, the horses sliding in the morning mud. Lestrade felt faintly ridiculous in Lord Hurstmonceux's spare pink and the ghastly uncomfortable hat bouncing around on his head. But the fields were a joy compared to the woods. Branches lashed at him as he doubled up to stay in the saddle. Splashed with mud and the dew from leaves he swung away from the path in an effort to find solid ground. His horse plunged and reared, snorting with annoyance at the increasingly less competent man on its back. Fleetingly, Lestrade saw Bertie Cairns across to his right, at the head of a scattered field. Fleetingly, because he saw him at a curious angle while somersaulting over the horse's head.

Lestrade landed squarely on his back, badly jarring his spine as he did so. He had the sense and training to cling to the reins as he fell, so was able to haul himself upright using the horse. There was no sign of the others. He hoped no one else had seen him. Two or three of the straggler hounds rushed past him, leaving him firmly alone. He remounted with difficulty and made for the light at the edge of the woods. Below him, he saw that the hounds had reached the spot where he presumed Lord Hurstmonceux had been killed. Beyond a low, dry-stone wall, unusual for the area, the dogs milled around, sniffing, yelping, obviously having lost the scent. The groom with the dead fox had done his job well and had effectively lost his pursuers. Cattermole, Cairns and Rosebery sat on their horses, looking around them for Lestrade.

The inspector urged his mount down the furrowed slope. The view in front of him bobbed and leaped. He dug his knees in hard and clung on as majestically as he could. The horizon dropped before him and he was down, wheeling his horse sharply in a circle to join the others.

'Bravo, Parapet,' called Rosebery. The name had lost all semblance of reality so that for a while Lestrade assumed he must be talking to somebody else. 'A yard or so to the left, however, and you would have caught that harrow.'

Lestrade just had time to catch sight of the implement, when it started. The hounds howled and snarled, springing up at Rosebery, jaws snapping as they turned in the air. Cairns and Cattermole drew their revolvers, firing wildly to left and right. Rosebery clung to the saddle for dear life, trying to extricate his plunging horse from the mêlée of dogs. Three or four grooms were hurrying down the slope towards the wall shouting harshly at the dogs. Lestrade drove his horse through the bedlam, caught Rosebery's rein with a deftness which surprised him and led him away over the furrows. By this time Rosebery had taken stock of himself and was controlling his horse. Lestrade swung back with his revolver cocked, but Cairns and Cattermole had done their business well and the hounds were recoiling, calmer now and stunned by the gunfire and the corpses by the wall.

The horsemen rode to higher ground as the grooms and handlers took charge of the pack. Rosebery, gashed and bleeding, slumped in his saddle in shock. 'It's the damnedest thing,' he said, staring blankly ahead.

'You're lucky to be alive,' said Cairns, handing Rosebery his hat.

'At least that lead-hound won't attack anybody else,' said Cattermole. 'I just shot him.'

'It wasn't the lead hound,' mused Lestrade, almost to himself.

'I saw it,' said Cattermole, 'exactly like poor Freddie.'

'Tell me, sir,' Lestrade turned in the saddle to face him, 'when you shot the dog, Tray, who killed him – you or the gun?'

'Eh?'

'I mean – the hounds killed Freddie Hurstmonceux. But who trained them to?'

'Trained?' snapped Rosebery. 'You can't train dogs to go for a man.'

'Yes, you can,' said Cairns, 'but they must have been trained to go for Rosebery, too.'

'No, sir, I don't think so. If my assumption is correct, then this morning's incident was merely an accidental repetition of the original. Lord Hurstmonceux must have been unhorsed. You were lucky, My Lord.'

'We've got to get you back to the house, Rosebery,' Cattermole urged. 'I don't know what you've achieved, Lestrade, except for nearly killing someone else.'

'Sir Henry, please bear with me. I believe I have the answer, but I must see the tenants first. Can that be arranged?'

'Good God, man, there are nearly two hundred of them. Can you spare that time from the Yard?'

It took Lestrade just over a week to interview all the Hurstmonceux tenants. With two or three sergeants to help him he might have halved this time, but Cattermole was insistent for the sake of the family honour that the incident must be hushed up. Lestrade knew all too well that whatever he uncovered here would never become public. Freddie Hurstmonceux had been notorious enough in his lifetime, but no one would be able to make matters worse after his death. The 'laboratory' would never see the light of day. Lestrade wasn't even sure if Cattermole knew about it.

Of the one hundred and eighty-three adults on the Hurstmonceux estate, one hundred and eighty-three had the motive and opportunity to kill their former master. Even some of the children looked murderous. But Lestrade only asked one question – at least he was only interested in the answer to one question: who placed the harrow against the wall in the Lower Meadow?

It transpired that none of them had. Lestrade prided himself on his judgement of men – and women. There were many tenants who would have split Lord Hurstmonceux's head with a hoe, blown it off with a shotgun or sliced it apart with a sickle, but who among them had the ability to kill him in this way? Trained policeman that he was, he noticed the tenants' reactions to the harrow question. They told him the truth. No one had moved it.

He then interrogated, with all the subtlety at his disposal, the handlers of the pack. It was a new pack to the hunt, they told him. Lestrade toyed with the question of whether the seal had been broken, but the gravity of the situation prevented it. Another gem, he mused, lost forever. Where had they been bought? At auction, of course. Lestrade broke the silence he had promised by sending a telegram to the Yard to check. As Lestrade guessed, the former owner could not be traced.

The inspector had one last card to play. Rosebery had gone, nursing his wounds, back to London to wait for his Garter. The funeral for Lord Hurstmonceux was due on the following day, in the family chapel a mile or so from Hurstmonceux Hall. Lestrade would not be there. His presence would not be welcome. The night before he left them, Lestrade crept from his room after dark. He crossed the moonless courtyard to the kennels. Once inside, his heart raced. Once or twice his nerve left him, but each time, he turned back. The dogs slept more or less soundly despite his entrance. But he knew, even in the dark, that one or two of them were awake, watching him. He levelled the revolver, a heavy Smith and Wesson, and prayed. His heart pounded in his ears. Flashing before his eyes he saw again the lacerated corpse of Freddie Hurstmonceux, the congealed blood on his throat and clothing, the dried trickle on the baize of the billiard table. He cocked the pistol – once, twice and somewhere from the depths of his throat came the whispered word – 'harrow'.

The kennels roared into life, hounds snarling and snapping. Lestrade threw himself back through the door, sliding the bolt and collapsing against the wall. He was right. He had proved it. But the house was coming to life, lights appearing in the servants' quarters. Voices and shouts in the yard. Lestrade saw no point in advertising himself. He put the gun away and crept via the shrubbery to the relevant wing. Up the stairway and into his room, before the house returned to an uneasy slumber. On the night before the funeral of the master, everyone was uneasy.

Lestrade travelled back to London by train. The newspapers had carried the headlines – 'terrible hunting accident'. Everything was neat, vague and unexceptional. Lord Hurstmonceux might simply have fallen from his horse. Only Lestrade knew *how*. Someone had placed the harrow by the wall in the Lower Meadow. They had then led the hunt that way, probably as Lestrade had done, getting a beater to carry a scent over his saddle. Hurstmonceux had leapt the wall, hit the harrow or narrowly missed it. What would have been his reaction?

'What's that bloody harrow doing there?' or something similar. Whoever had arranged this had already sold the pack to Freddie, and had taught them to react, viciously and blindly, to anyone who spoke the word 'harrow'.

Well, there it was. All the same, it was fantastic. It was astonishingly risky, uncertain. The murderer ran a risk in drawing on the hunt. He could easily have been seen. How did he arrange the sale? How could he be sure that Freddie would reach that wall first? And that he would use the essential word 'harrow'? That he was alone at the time was the good luck of others who rode in the hunt. Lestrade realised he should have talked to them. But by the time he had arrived, most of them had gone and they could probably have added nothing to the facts of the case. Still, there it was. Risky, uncertain, fantastic, yes. But it had worked.

So Lestrade knew how. What he did not know was who. He would put the evidence before McNaghten, who would brush his moustaches and straighten his cravat and consign the information to the bowels of his incomprehensible filing system. He could then compile a list as long as his arm of those who knew Freddie Hurstmonceux for the cad and bounder that he was. It didn't help him a great deal.

The letter was waiting for him when he got back. A mourning letter, lying square in the centre of his desk. Lestrade inquired why it was separate from the week's mail pile which stood to one side. The desk sergeant explained it had come this morning and looked personal, addressed to Lestrade himself. The inspector opened it. And then he placed it alongside the first. There was no doubt about it. They were written on different typewriters. But the doggerel sounded similar, if this time more informed:

Here is cruel Frederick, see!
A horrid, wicked boy was he;
He caught the flies, poor little things,
And then tore off their tiny wings,
He kill'd the birds, and broke the chairs,
And threw the kitten down the stairs;
The trough was full and faithful Tray

Came out to drink one sultry day;
He wagg'd his tail and wet his lip,
When cruel Fred snatch'd up a whip,
And whipp'd poor Tray till he was sore,
And kick'd and whipp'd him more and more:
At this, good Tray grew very red,
And growl'd and bit him till he bled;
Then you should only have been by,
To see how Fred did scream and cry!

The realisation was borne in on Lestrade. The mourning letters addressed to him at the Yard. No traceable clues in postmark or typeface. Two pieces of verse, each with definite knowledge of the murder under investigation. And, from the style of the verse, written by the same hand. Even Lestrade's unpoetical eye could see that. He placed the disturbing evidence before McNaghten.

The Head of the Criminal Investigation Department brushed his cravat and straightened his moustaches.

The vicar's daughter

It took Constable Dew nearly ten minutes to find it in the atlas.

'Here it is, sir,' he told Lestrade, 'Wildboarclough.'

'Ridiculous name,' grunted Lestrade.

'About six miles from Macclesfield, sir, as the crow flies.'

Lestrade did not fly. He caught a series of trains as far as Macclesfield and hired a pony and trap to get him on to the Pennines towards Wildboarclough. It was early May, but there was no sign of Spring up here. He was within a crow's flight of the Cat and Fiddle Inn, one of the highest in England. It was a hiker's paradise, but Lestrade saw no hikers today. As his pony climbed the narrow twisting roads, the snow lay crisp in the hollows. On the higher slopes above him, he saw the sheep, huddling together for shelter against the biting wind. He passed a lamb, dead by the roadside on the open moors. Its eyes had been pecked out by crows – one of those Dew was thinking of, no doubt, that flew from Macclesfield.

As Lestrade rattled into Wildboarclough, the moors were less visible. There were deep chasms here, haunting and dark, sheer cliffs of northern granite rearing up above the bare, still, winter trees. He passed the new post office, specially built for Her Majesty's visit to Lord Derby's estate, and the school. The vicarage was away to the left, above the small, grey church. All the houses were grey, tall and silent, stark against the evergreen clumps of rhododendron bushes.

A housekeeper-shaped woman answered the door as the gardener took charge of the pony and trap. Lestrade explained who he was and was shown into a drawing room. He peeled off his doeskin gloves and cupped his hands over a minimal fire. As he watched it, it went out, leaving a single spiral of smoke. Lestrade contented himself with blowing on to his fingers, trying to bury their tips into the thawing fronds of his moustaches. He stamped up and down trying to remember when he had last felt his feet. The books on the ceiling-high shelves were what he would have expected – theological tomes, discursive works on ecclesiastical history.

'Inspector Lestrade?'

The inspector turned to face a bull-necked, purple-faced man about twice his own width. 'Swallow.'

Was this an old Cheshire custom, wondered Lestrade. Or perhaps a cure for frostbite? He was in the act of complying with the command when realisation dawned – 'Inspector Swallow, Cheshire Constabulary.' Lestrade hoped his Adam's apple had not been too visible as he shook the inspector's hand.

'Bad business,' Swallow grunted.

'What happened?'

'I may as well be blunt,' Swallow announced grumpily. Looking at him, Lestrade wondered how he could be anything else. Swallow crossed to the window and looked out across the sweep of the lawn to the church. 'I advised 'em against it. I said we could handle it. I said we didn't need t'Yard.' Fearing he had been *too* blunt, he turned to Lestrade. 'Nothing personal, of course.'

Lestrade waved the insult aside. 'We all follow orders, Inspector,' he said. 'I'm afraid this thing may be bigger than both of us.'

'Meaning?' Swallow had missed the cliché.

'I can't be sure yet.'

Swallow thumped a framed photograph of a teenaged girl down on the mantelpiece near Lestrade's head. 'Harriet Elizabeth Wemyss. Aged seventeen. Burned to death.'

'So I gather.' Lestrade perused the photograph. A singularly plain girl, hair parted in the centre. Very old-fashioned. Probably the living spit of her mother. Dead spit now, he supposed. Better not pursue that. Rather unpleasant.

'I saw no damage as I came in,' chanced Lestrade.

'Nay, you wouldn't. This were no ordinary house fire. If it were, d'you think we'd send for t'Yard?'

'Your theory, then?'

Swallow was less sure of himself. 'Look, y'd better come and see for yoursen. The Reverend ain't home yet awhile. He won't mind.'

Lestrade was surprised to see Swallow apparently showing signs of sentiment or at least respect. He followed the burly policeman up the broad staircase, past the stained glass and *The Light of the World*. The body, what was left of it, lay on a bed in a room at the end of a passage. It was barely recognisable as a human form, much less the girl in the photograph.

'I 'ope you've a strong stomach, Lestrade,' grunted Swallow – 'they'll be taking her away t'Congleton later today. If y'want to examine the body y'd best do it now.'

'Who certified the death?'

'T'local doctor. Chap called Marsden.'

'Cause of death?'

Swallow looked askance at Lestrade. Is this t'Yard? he thought to himself. The man's some kind of cretin.

'Burning,' he answered.

Lestrade looked at the neck, or where the neck should have been. Strangulation would be impossible to detect. He looked at the rest of the body, charred and shrivelled. Perhaps a coroner could find something on that wreck, though he'd have to be a damned good one. But Lestrade couldn't. He must assume that burning it was.

'Tell me what happened,' he said.

'Can we go back t'drawing room?' Swallow looked surprisingly green. Lestrade followed him down the stairs. At the bottom the Reverend Wemyss met them on his way in through the front door. Within seconds he was knee deep in cats. Introductions were brief and to the point. The Vicar carried two of his favourite animals through into the drawing room. A third cat had twined itself round Lestrade's neck. Wemyss stopped in his tracks.

'Mrs Drum!' he barked.

The housekeeper bustled in amid the rustling of skirts. The

Vicar rounded on her as cats flew in all directions. 'You've had a fire in here!'

Mrs Drum dissolved into instant tears. 'I'm sorry, sir, I didn't think. We had guests . . .'

'Guests!' The Vicar was purple. Mrs Drum indicated Lestrade. 'I have forbidden any fires in this house, Mrs Drum. You will take your notice.'

The housekeeper exited among floods of tears. Wemyss visibly calmed himself down and instructed the officers of the law to sit.

'Please forgive me, gentlemen. As you can imagine, this is something of a trying time for us all.'

'Of course, Mr Wemyss,' said Lestrade. 'It is my painful duty, however, to ask you some questions.'

'Quite so, Inspector. But first, would you like some tea?'

'Thank you, sir.'

The Vicar pulled a bell cord, then settled back to fondle his cats. A maidservant swept in, curtsied and stood motionless. 'Tea, Hannah' – and then as an afterthought – 'no, wait. Of course, I have said no fires. We will have lemonade.'

Lemonade on top of a long cold journey was not Lestrade's idea of a good time. But, then, he was hardly here to enjoy himself.

'I have, of course, already made a statement to Inspector Swallow and his constable,' began Wemyss, 'but I understand it is police procedure to repeat oneself several times.'

'Occasionally, new points come to light, sir,' observed Lestrade. 'Pray continue.' And he could have kicked himself for that remark.

'I was attending a Temperance meeting in Macclesfield. This was, let me see, Thursday. The day before yesterday. I arrived home by trap, early evening. It was already dark. As I alighted and Beddoes was taking the pony, I heard the screams from within the house. I went in and found . . .' He paused, but seemed remarkably in control of himself. 'My wife and my daughter's governess, Miss Spink, were there ahead of me, both hysterical. The charred thing that was once my daughter was lying on the landing floor . . .' Another pause. 'Unrecognisable.'

Swallow slurped his lemonade at an unfortunate, poignant moment.

'I should explain,' Wemyss went on, 'that my wife and Miss Spink had themselves been absent, visiting the local elderly. They had arrived home moments before me.'

'And the servants?' asked Lestrade.

'Only Mrs Drum was in the house. The maid Hannah does not live in and it was her day off. Beddoes we share with the schoolmaster. He had been on the premises an hour or two only, before I arrived. I never allow him in the house.'

Charity, mused Lestrade to himself, did not begin at home in this establishment.

'Have you anything to add?' he asked.

Wemyss stood up, disarranging the cats as he did so.

'God moves in mysterious ways, Inspector. I long ago joined Brutus in his acceptance of death among his dear ones. It must happen one day and, knowing that, I can accept it.'

Lestrade and Swallow found themselves nodding in unison, like things on sticks at a fairground. They noticed each other and broke the rhythm.

'I'd like to show you something.' Wemyss selected a faded book from the shelf. 'The Annual Register for the year of Our Lord 1767. I have taken the trouble to mark the pages.' He read an extraordinary account. 'A lady was found burned to death in her bedroom in her London house. An old lady, certainly, but there was no source of fire. No candles, no grate, no tallow. Nothing particularly inflammable. She simply burned to death,' concluded Wemyss. 'A sort of . . . spontaneous combustion, I suppose you would call it.'

'You mean, like a 'orseless carriage, Vicar?' asked Swallow, quite perplexed. Wemyss and Lestrade both looked at him, and he sank back in his chair.

'Can that happen, Mr Wemyss?' asked Lestrade.

'According to the Annual Register, it did in 1767, Inspector Lestrade. But no, I think not. You see, I think my daughter was murdered.'

Lestrade looked at the older man. What sort of a murderer would kill a seventeen-year-old girl – the daughter of a vicar? It could have been a sexual crime, of course, but the state of the body made that hypothesis unprovable. It seemed a trifle inappropriate to ask the age-old question, but he did anyway.

'Did your daughter have any enemies, Mr Wemyss?'

'Inspector, my daughter was a shy little girl of seventeen. She had very few friends, poor lamb. We are rather remote up here, you know. But enemies . . . no, Inspector. She hadn't an enemy in the world.'

'Then why do you say she was murdered, sir? And why call in the Yard?'

'To answer your second question first. I have always insisted on the best for my family – the best food, the best clothes, the best education – which is not, mark you, your North London Collegiate School – and, without wishing to offend Swallow here, the best police.'

Lestrade bowed in acknowledgement of the compliment.

'To answer your first question. Because I don't believe in this' – pointing at the Register – 'I do not believe that a person can burn to death by themselves. There has to be a rational explanation. My daughter's body was found upstairs on the landing. There were no fires in the upstairs rooms. It was rather warm for May.'

Lestrade winced as he wondered what a cold May must be like.

'I shall examine the scene of death again a little later, sir,' he said, 'but first I would like to talk to your wife, Mr Wemyss.'

'I'm afraid that won't be possible, Inspector. You see, my wife is distraught. She is staying with her sister in Congleton. I must insist that she is not disturbed. Our doctor has warned that it would be unwise in her mental state.'

Lestrade glanced at Swallow for confirmation. The bluff Cheshire policeman nodded gravely. He had presumably seen Mrs Wemyss, Lestrade conjectured. Her testimony would be unhelpful.

'Then I must speak to Miss Spink.'

'Of course. I shall send her to you at once.'

But Wemyss had not reached the door when a silently weeping Mrs Drum appeared. 'I'm on my way, sir,' she managed between sobs, indicating a valise in her hand. 'Beddoes will send my trunk on. In the meantime . . .' At this point, coherent words failed her completely, and she merely indicated the entrance of visitors by a wave of her hand, clutching a copious white handkerchief.

'Very well.' Wemyss remained unaffected by the woman's distraught state. 'Do not look to me for a reference, Mrs Drum. Your action today obliterates your former unblemished record. My dear Watts.'

Wemyss shook the hand of the new arrival, a handsome man in his mid-fifties, Lestrade guessed, sharply dressed and distinguished. Behind him minced a small auburn-haired man with the narrowest, most sloping shoulders and largest head Lestrade had ever seen. With him, Wemyss was more reserved. 'Swinburne,' and a stiff nod of the head was all he received. The little man nodded in turn.

'My dear Hector, how positively dreadful. We came as soon as we heard. Swinburne hasn't been well. How is poor Dorothea taking it?'

'Badly, I'm afraid. You can imagine what a shock it must have been – finding poor Harriet like that. She's with her sister in Congleton.'

'Harriet?' asked the newcomer.

Everyone looked at him rather oddly.

'No, Dorothea.'

'Ah, of course.'

Introductions were perfunctory. 'Inspector Lestrade of Scotland Yard, Inspector Swallow of the Cheshire Constabulary, my dear friend, Watts-Dunton, the poet. And Mr Swinburne.'

Wemyss led his friend, the poet, to the door, the latter commiserating with him as he went. The door slammed shut and Mr Swinburne stood before it, rather spare and out of place. Lestrade took Swallow aside and asked him to find Miss Spink. He then tackled the little man.

'Algernon Charles Swinburne?'

The little man spun round as if he had been slapped. 'It's a lie, I wasn't there.' And then, more calmly, 'Oh, forgive me, Inspector. I forgot myself.'

'Algernon Charles Swinburne, the poet?'

'I have that honour, sir.'

'Do you recognise the style of this, sir?' Lestrade pulled from his pocket copies of the doggerel connected with the last two murders on his mind. He suspected that this one, bizarre and tragic, may be a third, but couldn't be sure yet.

'They're not mine,' said Swinburne. 'They're probably Browning's.'

Lestrade's professional ears pricked up. Swinburne knew something. 'Indeed?'

Swinburne relaxed a little now and sat on the settee. He reached in his pocket for a hip flask and uncorked it. 'Oh,' he paused, eyes pleading pathetically, 'you won't tell Watts-Dunton, will you? He thinks I've given it up.'

Lestrade waved aside the possibility.

'This Mr Browning. Would you happen to know where he is?'

'Westminster Abbey.'

'Poet's Corner?'

Swinburne nodded.

'You would assume that these verses were written recently?'

'Beats me!' said Swinburne, and chuckled to himself. 'Browning's been dead these two years.'

Another brick wall reared up at Lestrade, but Swinburne was already off on another tack.

'Tell me about police brutality,' he said.

'Sir?'

'Oh, come now, Inspector. When you have a man in custody – what is that quaint euphemism you chaps use – "helping the police with their inquiries" – isn't that it? What do you use? Truncheons? Whips? Thumbscrews?' His voice rose imperceptibly by degrees as he spoke, savouring each word. His knuckles were white as he gripped the arm of the settee. Lestrade narrowed his eyes as he began to see Mr Swinburne's problem.

'Rubber tubing,' he said.

Swinburne's mouth sagged open with pleasure and astonishment. Lestrade became confidential. 'It doesn't show, you see.'

Swinburne's voice was a rasping whisper. 'Where do you do it?'

'Cell Block A.'

'No, no, I mean where on the body? Buttocks, thighs?'

'No, thank you,' said Lestrade, 'I am trying to give them up.'

He left the room as Swinburne took refuge in his hip flask, and slowly began to tighten the knot of his tie so that his eyes bulged and his colour rose. 'Chastise me!' were the last words Lestrade heard as he made for the stairs.

In the study sat Miss Spink, a prim demure lady in her mid-thirties, hair strained back in the characteristic bun of the professional spinster. Swallow stood behind her like something out of a studio photograph.

'I would like to see you alone, Inspector,' she said to Lestrade. Swallow was about to object but Lestrade's gesture of the head sent him shambling to the door, grunting under his breath the while. 'Mr Swinburne is in the drawing room, Inspector,' Lestrade called after. 'See that he doesn't come to any harm, there's a good chap. And don't let him put your handcuffs on!'

'Inspector?'

'Ma'am.' Lestrade sat down in front of the governess. She was not conventionally attractive, perhaps, but there was a certain something about her. She gazed deeply into Lestrade's eyes. 'I could not bear to tell that oaf,' she motioned to the retreated figure of Swallow, 'but I feel there is something you should know.'

'I am all ears, ma'am.'

Miss Spink swept upright with a rustle of petticoats. She turned her back on Lestrade. 'This is very difficult for me, Inspector. You can't imagine what a shock all this has been.'

Lestrade sensed when a particular approach was needed with witnesses. He laid a reassuring hand on the governess's arm. She gasped and pulled back, but the expression on her face indicated that it had been precisely the right thing to do. She blushed and glanced at the ground. 'Harriet was seeing . . . a man,' she said.

'A man, ma'am?'

'All men are beasts, Inspector,' she suddenly shouted, then

realised the stupidity of the remark. 'Forgive me. Present company is of course excepted.'

'This man – who is he?'

'I don't know. Inspector, I have been guilty of neglect. I beg of you, don't tell the Reverend or Mrs Wemyss. I could not bear them to know the truth.'

'And what is the truth, ma'am?'

Miss Spink began to cry, decorously, of course, into a tiny lace handkerchief. Lestrade was the soul of consolation as she gradually pulled herself together.

'I regularly accompanied Harriet to Macclesfield. Beddoes drove us in the trap. We would visit the library, and the tea-rooms and on fine days walk in the park. Occasionally we would go further afield – to Buxton to the pump-rooms, for example, or Congleton.'

'Go on.'

'Well, about a month ago, Harriet went into Macclesfield alone – with Beddoes, of course, but the disgusting man finds a tavern and stays there until an agreed hour.'

'You were not present, ma'am?'

'No, I was . . . indisposed. When Harriet returned that day, she was excited, agitated. She danced and sang and chattered incessantly, to me, to her mama, to her papa. She would give no reason for this new elation – she was usually so quiet a child – except that her life had changed and that she would never be the same again.'

'From which you concluded . . .?'

'I could not believe it at first. A young lady of Harriet's refinement, the daughter of a clergyman, but I suspected – no more than that – that she had an admirer.'

Lestrade's headshaking and clicking of the tongue were taken at face value by the strait-laced Miss Spink.

'Pray continue, ma'am.'

'Harriet became a different girl. She went into Macclesfield two or three times a week and each time she returned she was ruder, more unbridled. She refused to attend to her studies and took to the vilest habits.'

'Habits, ma'am? Are you suggesting she was embracing the Catholic faith?'

'Why no, Inspector. She . . . smoked.'

'*Smoked?*'

'Here.' Miss Spink produced a tin of tobacco papers from a pocket in her voluminous skirt. 'Shameful, isn't it? A young lady of her refinement. The servants knew, of course, but we were at pains to keep it from her poor parents.'

'And how do you account for the acquisition of this habit, ma'am?'

'That man, that filthy beast whom she met in Macclesfield and whom she went on seeing in that clandestine way. It was he, I am sure, who introduced her to the habit . . . and the Lord knows what besides.'

'I repeat, ma'am. Who is the man?'

'I only saw him once. On one occasion I ignored Harriet's insistence that she go alone to Macclesfield. I went with her. As we neared the park, I saw her signal to a figure in the bushes. It was only a split second, of course, because the figure vanished. I asked Harriet who it was and she laughed and said a friend. I could extract nothing more from her.'

'Could you give me a description of the man?'

'That's very difficult, Mr Lestrade. He was large, big-built, wearing a long coat and a dark hat. I could not see his face. But I knew instinctively that he was a beast.'

'Of course,' Lestrade concurred, his tongue planted firmly in his cheek.

'And you never saw the man again?'

Miss Spink shook her head.

Swallow burst in. 'That Swinburne's a right . . .'

'Thank you, Mr Swallow.' Lestrade stood up sharply, gesturing to Miss Spink. Swallow coughed awkwardly.

'I am to join Mrs Wemyss in Congleton, Inspector. Please treat all that I have told you in the strictest confidence.'

'Of course, ma'am. Would you be so good as to ask Mr Beddoes to see me presently.'

Miss Spink floated out in a profusion of dignity. She tossed her head disdainfully at Swallow and glided across the hall beyond him.

'That one needs a bloody good . . .'

'Quite so, Inspector,' Lestrade interrupted him again.

'Ee, that Swinburne.' Swallow returned to his former topic. ''E's sittin' there, gettin' cats to sink their claws into his legs. Bloody weird, I call it.'

'Bloody weird most of us call it, Inspector. But it is hardly a police matter.'

Swallow shrugged.

Beddoes began by being far from helpful. Trouble at t'Vicarage was something he rather revelled in. A man of his class, he was no deferential tenant and it was clear that he had no time for the carriage folk whom he served. Yes, he had taken Miss Harriet on several occasions into Macclesfield. Yes, he had noticed a change in her mood, but it didn't surprise him. All carriage folk behaved badly to him. They upbraided him, looked down on him, ignored him. So the girl was going off the straight and narrow. Typical. Nothing about the gentry surprised him. A man? No, he knew nothing about a man. But then he had spent his time in Macclesfield at t'Rose and Crown, so he wouldn't a seen nowt, would 'e? But then, nothing about the gentry surprised Beddoes.

It took Lestrade some little time to elicit this slim information, as Beddoes was broad Cheshire and Lestrade wished at more than one point for an interpreter. But as Beddoes rose to go, he threw out a remark which he considered unimportant. To Lestrade it was vital.

'A pedlar?'

'Aye. On't morning of Miss Harriet's death, it were. Soom bloke comes round to sell brushes.'

'What did this man look like?'

'Oh, I didn't see him very close. I'd just come from t'school. Big bloke 'e were. 'Ad an 'at.'

'An 'at.'

'Aye.'

'Beddoes, where is Mrs Drum?'

'Vicar give 'er notice. She's off t'Macclesfield this hour since.'

'On foot?'

'Nay, I took her t'station at Rainow, seein' as 'ow I couldn't go mysen'

'Get your trap, man. We're going after her.'

'It's t'Vicar's trap.' Beddoes was suddenly astonishingly solicitous for his employer. 'Besides, y've got your own.'

'Inspector Swallow has borrowed my trap to pursue his own inquiries. I am commandeering the Vicar's in the name of the law.' Then, more forcibly, 'You wouldn't want to be accused of obstructing the police in the course of their investigations, would you, Beddoes?'

The odd-job man grumbled and muttered as he scuttled to the stables behind the house.

'Y'll not catch 'er now,' he shouted as the trap swung down the gravelled drive out on to the open road. 'T'train from Rainow leaves in ten minutes.'

'Use your whip, man. You're wasting time.'

They did catch Mrs Drum. So desolate had she been while waiting in the cold drizzle at Rainow station that the station-master had taken her into the shelter of his office and given her the proverbial cup of tea that did not really cheer. Consequently, while the garrulous Mrs Drum poured her heart out to him and he poured tea into her, she had missed her train. Lestrade had found her, still sipping tea, still in the stationmaster's office. She was not, however, terribly helpful. Lestrade's forthright questions brought her out of her mood of self-pity, but her description of the travelling salesman was vague. He was a big man, she said, but his face was partly hidden by a muffler and his voice distorted accordingly. She thought he had piercing blue eyes, but under the rim of the hat, it was difficult to tell. As to the death of Miss Harriet, Mrs Drum had been in the kitchen, it being the maid's day off, preparing dinner. It was about half past three. She remembered that because she heard the hall clock strike, but the hall clock was notoriously inaccurate. Safer to say it was between three and four. Mrs Drum had heard a roaring noise, and then the screaming started. By the time she reached the top of the stairs, it was too late. What was left of Harriet Wemyss lay blazing on the carpet. Shocked and sickened, Mrs Drum had thrown water on her and all the blankets she could drag from the beds. The smell, she said, was awful and the memory of it would remain with her always.

Lestrade gave the ex-housekeeper time to recover. It had been perhaps half an hour later that Mrs Wemyss and Miss Spink arrived, followed almost immediately by the vicar. Mrs Drum had sent Beddoes for the police, but they arrived later still.

'I can't understand how it happened, sir,' sobbed Mrs Drum, 'it's unbelievable.'

'The travelling salesman,' said Lestrade. 'What time did he arrive?'

'I suppose about half past twelve sir. I told 'im we didn't need brushes but 'e insisted on seeing the lady of the 'ouse. I told 'im Mrs Wemyss wasn't in, but Miss 'arriet came downstairs and took 'im into the drawing room.'

'What did you do?'

'I got on with my work, sir.'

'Did you not think it odd that Miss Harriet should deal with this pedlar herself? Was it not usually your duty?'

Mrs Drum had clearly not thought along those lines before, but she acknowledged that that was in fact the case.

'And what time did this pedlar leave?'

'I don't know, sir. I was in the kitchen most of the day and you can't see the front door from there. I suppose Miss 'arriet saw 'im out.'

'The pedlar used the front door. Was that not unusual?'

Again Mrs Drum had not thought of that. Again, she concluded that it was.

Lestrade thought now that he knew how the murder was accomplished. And he knew who – or at least he had a description of the man. But he needed to prove it, and to that end he took the protesting Mrs Drum along with the complaining Beddoes back to Wildboarclough Vicarage.

He was in time to see a cab leaving with Watts-Dunton and Swinburne and he thought he heard a superfluity of whip-cracking, but he couldn't be sure. The Reverend Wemyss was somewhat peeved to see the return of Mrs Drum, but Lestrade assured him it was necessary and she would not be there long.

It was nearly dark now and the housekeeper and the policeman ascended the stairs by the light of an oil-lamp, Lestrade once again insisting on overriding the Vicar's newfound aversion to naked flames. Harriet Wemyss's body had been removed to Congleton mortuary, accompanied by Swallow and one or two curious cats. Lestrade viewed the landing area where Mrs Drum had found the blazing girl. There were bad scorch marks on the carpet, through to the floorboards underneath. They formed a visible trail from a door down the corridor towards the dead girl's bedroom.

'What is that room?' asked Lestrade.

'The Chapel of Ease, sir,' replied Mrs Drum, showing signs of being overcome once again at standing on The Very Spot Where Poor Miss Harriet Died. Lestrade opened the door – a conventional middle-class lavatory, complete with blue-flowered porcelain bowl. Much to the distaste of Mrs Drum, he peered into the pan. There was a coloured film floating on the water, he noticed as he lowered his lamp towards it, and burn marks on the wooden seat.

'Has this lavatory been used since the accident?'

'Why, no, sir. Inspector Swallow told us not to touch or move anything. There is another on the other side of the house – as well as the privy in the yard.'

Lestrade was grateful that Swallow was enough of a policeman for that.

'Stand back, Mrs Drum, you are in for another shock.'

Lestrade poised himself, then flipped a lighted match into the pan. It exploded with a roar as a column of livid flame ripped upwards, illuminating the room, the landing and the terrified Mrs Drum.

Lestrade threw towels over the fire and it died, slowly, reluctantly.

'Is that the noise you heard, Mrs Drum, before the screaming started?'

Mrs Drum was standing back against the wall, visibly quivering, nodding silently the while.

'In the kitchen you would not have heard the cigarette – the furtive, clandestine cigarette that Miss Harriet was smoking – hit the water. But it wasn't water, Mrs Drum. Or at least the surface of it was not. It was petroleum spirit, instantly inflammable to a match or a lit cigarette. The poor creature must have gone up like a torch, and in her shock and agony, must have rushed headlong towards the sanctuary of her bedroom. But such was the power of the flames that she never got there. Not in this world.'

By now, the Reverend Wemyss, startled by the noise of the flames and the cry of terror from Mrs Drum, had joined the couple in the almost total darkness on the stairs.

'Come, sir,' Lestrade said to him. 'You and I must have a little talk.'

It did not unduly bother Lestrade that in telling Wemyss all he knew he was betraying an implied confidence to Miss Spink. His priorities were right, he felt sure. What was domestic tension compared with murder? The Vicar of Wildboarclough listened with an evertightening lip to the whole sorry bizarre story. He could shed no light. He knew of no man. He assumed that Harriet's increased visits to Macclesfield were due to an increasing interest in the newly extended lending library. It had never occurred to him that his daughter had become a libertine and that she had been seduced into the ways of the devil by an anonymous 'seducteur'. He would not tell his wife – the further shock would kill her. When she had overcome her immediate need for Miss Spink, he would dispense with the woman's services – Miss Spink's that was, not his wife's. Dorothea had after all been 'in his service', so to speak, for too long. Miss Spink had not been vigilant. She had known Harriet's secret and had said nothing. It was tantamount to murder. Even Lestrade fleetingly contemplated issuing a warrant as accessory, but he guessed that the governess's conscience was sentence enough.

The night at the Vicarage was cold and gloomy. A morbid stillness lay over the whole house. At one point Lestrade fumbled with a lucifer to light a cigar, but he had to admit that the sudden flare of flame in the house of death seemed unfitting, blasphemous almost. He blew it out and huddled beneath the blankets, chewing the tobacco instead. The cold water in the morning and the iced coffee and cold ham did nothing to cheer or warm him. He ate alone. Even the maid came nowhere near him. He could not find his grief-stricken host to say his farewells. He trod finally on one of the cats and left.

Dr Marsden was in mid-surgery when Lestrade found him.

'Breathe in.' The instruction was issued to an elderly gentleman stretched out corpse-like on a bed in his consulting room.

'I can't be of much help, Inspector.' The doctor blinked at his visitor through a screen of cigar smoke. Ash dropped sporadically on to the patient's stomach, causing him to wince somewhat. 'Shock or first-degree burns or both were the cause of death. Oh, it's all right,' he coughed through the fumes, noting Lestrade's concerned glance at the patient, 'he's deaf as a post. We're quite alone.'

'I was trying to draw your attention to his colour, Doctor. I believe he may have died.'

'Good God.' Marsden brought his hand down sharply on the chest of the recumbent form. 'Breathe out, man!'

Lestrade was relieved to hear the patient gasp and cough.

'Could I ask you a delicate question, Doctor? We are, after all, men of the world. In our professions we both see humanity in all its most naked forms.' He was rather proud of that line.

'Do.' Marsden forced the old man over so that his nose buried itself in his trousers. The look on the doctor's face evinced surprise that the patient could do this.

'Where would you say the worst burns were? Where was the point of impact of the flame?'

'Bum,' snapped the doctor.

'Doctor?' said the policeman in surprise.

'No, no. I've lost my cigar.' Both men peered into the hair of the old man and their eyes met above his head. 'Ah.' Marsden recovered it from the collar of his patient's shirt.

'It was the rectum that received the full force, I'd say. The burns on the upper torso, upper limbs and head were less severe. It must have been the inflammable material of her dress that proved her undoing.'

'The rectum then,' repeated Lestrade, making for the door.

'Bum!' roared Marsden.

'Thank you, Doctor, I am aware.'

'No, no, I've lost my cigar again.'

Lestrade was sitting in his office when the letter arrived. He had his feet in a bowl of hot water and a towel over his head. For three days he had lost all sense of taste and smell. For three nights he had not slept. Sir Melville McNaghten had told him to go home, but he was too busy. The ever-solicitous Miss McNaghten had sent him hot toddies and cordials. Lestrade responded with alternate shivers and fevers. In his bed at night he felt himself consumed by the flames which in seconds had engulfed Harriet Wemyss. In the day, he felt as dead and cold as the man in the Chine.

It was unquestionably another letter in the series, he realised as he laid the towel aside. A click of his fingers brought Constable Dew with the goose-grease. He looked at the grey slime in the cup, and sent Dew away. A mourning letter – the third such he had received. The same untraceable postmark, the same untraceable typewriter. The same untraceable verse.

It almost makes me cry to tell
What foolish Harriet befell.
Mama and nurse went out one day
And left her all alone at play . . .
And see! Oh! what a dreadful thing!
The fire has caught her apron-string;
Her apron burns, her arms, her hair;
She burns all over, everywhere . . .

Lestrade slammed his fist on the desk. He was being played with. This was a game of cat and mouse and he didn't care for it. He didn't care for it at all. Three murders – scattered over the country. Bizarre, vicious. What were the links? The common factors? Poetry of a sort – sent to the Yard. Sent to him. Lestrade had come to regard whoever was out there doing these things as a personal enemy. This was a duel of wits and so far Lestrade had come off second-best.

Three of spades

'I do think Dew will do, sir,' Lestrade was saying.

'That's easy for you to say, Lestrade,' McNaghten was answering, 'but this new chap is damned clever. His references are excellent. Dew is all right, but he'll never amount to anything. No finesse. No style.'

'But Eton, sir? A copper from Eton?'

'Oh, I know it's not the usual recruiting source, but you mustn't be an inverted snob, Lestrade. He may not have had the advantages of the Blackheath crammer, but you mustn't hold that against him.'

'I'll try not to hold anything against him,' said Lestrade reaching the door.

'Bandicoot?' repeated Lestrade.

'Yes, sir.'

'You can't be serious.'

'Sir?'

Lestrade paced the floor. He looked again at the young man before him. He stood, Lestrade guessed, at six-feet-four, broad, handsome even. His suit was crisp in grey check and his bowler perched neatly in the crook of his arm. Lestrade was temporarily lost for words. 'Your name is Bandicoot?'

Bandicoot began to take just a pinch of umbrage.

'Bandicoot is a well-established name in some parts of Somerset, Inspector. I, for example, have never met a Lestrade before.'

'Well, you have now.' Lestrade's morning was not going well.

Twice on his way in he had collided with the scaffolding still around New Scotland Yard which was in the final stages of being built. His tea resembled something one of the Reverend Wemyss's cats might have done. And now this – a novice constable from a public school. Lestrade sat at his desk and crossed his ankles on the polished, uncluttered top.

'How long have you been in the Force?'

'A little under one year, sir.'

Lestrade looked wide-eyed in the direction of McNaghten's glass-fronted door away down the corridor.

'Have you ever seen a body?'

'I'm not exactly a virgin, Inspector.' Bandicoot found himself, smirking, a little surprised by Lestrade's question.

'A *dead* body, idiot!' Lestrade shot upright, bringing his hand down on the desk.

'No, sir.' Bandicoot's smirk vanished and his eyes faced front.

'What made you join H Division, Bandicoot?' Lestrade's tone was now patience itself. 'No, don't answer that. Why did you join the police?'

'Well, sir, it's rather silly really.'

Lestrade somehow knew it would be.

'I joined the Officer Training Corps at Eton. A few chaps ragged me into believing it was the Police Officer Training Corps. It was three years before I found out otherwise and by then I'd rather set my heart on it. In the process I became something of a crack shot, a first-rate swordsman – and my military fortifications defy belief.'

'I'm sure they do, Bandicoot, but, you see, we don't have much call for a *beau sabreur* at Scotland Yard. Tell me, I always thought gentlemen wore top hats, especially Old Etonian gentlemen.'

'Oh, we do, sir, but never before luncheon.'

Lestrade stood corrected.

'Can you make tea?' he asked.

'Er . . . I think so. You use one of those kettle things, don't you?'

Lestrade applauded with a slow, staccato handclap. 'I've always found it helps. In my outer office you will find a constable. Ask him to show you how. And then, when you've made me a cup, I'll show you what a filing cabinet looks like and we'll start some *real* policework.'

Bandicoot was about to go, when Lestrade grabbed his arm. His stare down the corridor caused the younger man to freeze as well. An ample young woman in electric blue was bustling towards them. Lestrade flattened himself against the wall, then raced for the window and the fire escape.

'Bandicoot,' he hissed as he was departing, 'convince Miss McNaghten with that Etonian charm of yours that I am away on a case for a few days, and I'll make you the most famous detective in London.'

It was the beginning of the season and London was already full of weasel-eyed Mamas and blushing daughters; gauche, flat-footed youths and lecherous old men. After the severe winter that had passed, the fashionable areas of Belgravia and Mayfair came alive again in the endless round of balls and soirées. But this season was even more colourful than the last, for a new celebrity had arrived – the ex-slave Atlanta Washington. The press reported his every move. He had been made an honorary member of White's and Crockford's, had stayed at Sandringham with the Prince and Princess of Wales and was rumoured to be having an affair with all three of the Duchess of Blessington's daughters as well as the Duchess herself. He was not without his critics, however, for there were many who shared their white American contemporaries' views that an 'uppity nigger' had no place in polite white folks' company. Washington revelled in the limelight. He wrote equally offensive replies to the offensive letters in *The Times*, and when spat upon in the street, proceeded to horsewhip the culprits in full view of lookers-on and at least four Metropolitan policemen, apparently cowed by the prospect of a wealthy, educated coon. When they at last moved in, Washington accompanied them willingly enough – in fact led the way – to Cannon Row Police Station where he was bound over to keep the peace. Three men in particular hounded him – the three men whom Lestrade was called in to see in Battersea Park on a Wednesday morning early in June. The three men had two things in common – they were all dead and they were all covered from head to foot in black paint.

Their identity did not become apparent until the paint had been removed, and long before their cold corpses had been laid out for final examination by the Scotland Yard surgeon, their families were screaming out for revenge, or if that could not be arranged, justice. McNaghten was being pressurised from above. All three men came from eminently respectable families. Every effort must be made, no stone must be left unturned, etc. etc. Lestrade had heard it all before, but he needed no exhortations. He had received no letter as yet but he didn't need to wait. This was precisely the sort of bizarre behaviour he had come to expect. It was another in the series, all right, and the body count had now reached six.

'Asphyxiation was certainly the cause of death, Lestrade,' the surgeon told him. 'These men had the pores of their skin filled with paint and it was that which killed them. Lungs alone won't do it. The skin must breathe too.'

'How long would that take?'

'Hours, days possibly. You can see the marks on their ankles and wrists where they were tied. Ghastly way to go.'

'They weren't killed in Battersea Park, then?'

'Oh, no. They were placed there, but they died somewhere else.'

Once again Lestrade had his means. He lacked any notion of those other essentials of the detective's art – opportunity and motive. He looked at the names of his victims on his desk. Their families and friends would run into hundreds. It was time to despatch constables, but constables had notoriously flat feet and lacked finesse. He could give Dew and Bandicoot the basics, but the serious questioning must once again come from him.

Bandicoot peered over Lestrade's shoulder. 'Edward Coke-Hythe!' he shouted. Lestrade hurled the contents of his tea cup over his hand, and rushed to the rest-room, screaming as decorously as he could so as not to alert the whole of Scotland Yard to his accident. Bandicoot pursued him.

'A *little* more care,' hissed Lestrade, wincing as he ran his hand under the cold tap. The water suddenly stopped with a harsh, gurgling thump.

'Damn this new plumbing,' the inspector snapped. 'Bandicoot, get me some bicarbonate of soda and hurry, man. I'm about to lose the skin off my hand.'

When the excitement was over, Lestrade placed his bandaged hand carefully on the desk. Dew brought them tea this time and Lestrade made sure Bandicoot was in front of him as he drank it. 'Why,' he began, much calmer now, 'when reading over my shoulder, did you cry out the name of one of these victims.'

'I know him, sir. Or, rather, knew him. Edward Coke-Hythe. I was his fag at Eton. Capital sort of chap. Captain of Fives – and a Double First at Cambridge.'

'Popular?'

'Oh, rather, sir. Poor old Teddy. Dear, this will be a blow to his uncle.'

'Uncle?'

'Doctor John Watson.'

'Watson? As in Watson of Baker Street?'

'Yes. Do you know him?'

'I know him. I have been an acquaintance of his associate, Sherlock Holmes, for some years.'

'Ah, the Great Detective.' Bandicoot beamed.

'If you say so,' replied Lestrade. 'What about these others? William Spender and Arthur Fitz.'

'Fitz what?' asked Bandicoot jovially.

'I'll do the jokes, Constable,' murmured Lestrade.

'No, sir. Sorry. They're not Etonians, or at least, they must have been years my senior if they were.'

Lestrade shook his head. 'They were all in their twenties, healthy, strong, young men. All right, Bandicoot. Time you won your spurs. If you knew Coke-Hythe, get round to his family – they have a town house in Portman Square. Be circumspect, but find out the deceased's movements on or about last Tuesday. Contacts, friends, enemies. It'll probably mean some shoe-leather before this case is over. Oh, and Bandicoot –' the constable turned in the doorway – 'it's nearly luncheon. Don't forget your topper!'

*

Lestrade took the Underground to Baker Street Station and a brisk walk to 221B. Outside he saw a wizened old flower-seller, toothless, haggard, with iron-grey hair matted over an iron-grey face. 'Pretty posies, sir?' she squawked at him.

'Really, Mr Holmes, what would I be doing with posies?'

The flower-seller stood up to his full six feet and threw the matted hair savagely on to the pavement. 'Damn you, Lestrade, it took me nearly two hours to get that lot on.'

'Sorry, Mr Holmes. Is the good doctor in?'

'Who?'

'Watson.'

'I suppose so. Tell Mrs Hudson to put the kettle on, will you? I've sleuthed enough for one day.' He set to, sorting out his merchandise, while Lestrade went in search of his quarry. Mrs Hudson, the housekeeper, dutifully scuttled away to do her master's bidding. Watson was asleep over the newspaper in front of a roaring fire.

'Doctor Watson.' Lestrade cleared his throat. The doctor did not move. Again, 'Doctor Watson.' Louder still, 'Watson.' Then in a stage whisper, 'Your publishers are here.' Watson leapt to his feet, newspapers flying over the carpet.

'Damn you, Lestrade.' It began to sound like the refrain from a phonograph. 'That blighter Conan Doyle keeps publishing articles under my name and all you can do is make jokes at my expense. Can't the law touch him?'

'Whichever of you refers to me as "imbecile" and "ferret-faced" will discover what the law can do soon enough,' Lestrade felt it his duty to remind him. 'In the meantime I fear there is more pressing business.'

Watson replaced himself on the armchair and the papers on his lap. 'Ah, yes, my nephew. Dreadful, dreadful.'

'My condolences, of course. What do you have for me?'

'Not a great deal, Lestrade. We are not a close family. To tell you the truth, I hadn't seen Edward for some years – not since his fifteenth birthday in fact. Recently, of course, one has read various unfortunate things in the papers. This business with that black fellow, that slave johnnie. But I could have seen it coming.'

'Oh?'

'At Eton he was something of a hellion, I believe. His father threatened to cut him off, stop his allowance and so on, but incidents still occurred. There was some business with the tweenie and talk of a missing hundred pounds. I didn't pry too deeply.'

'Did your nephew have enemies, Doctor?'

'Dozens, I should think. My family have a knack of annoying people, Inspector.'

'You never spoke a truer word, Watson.' Holmes entered with armfuls of flowers, wigs, etc.

'Good God, Holmes, you look damn silly in that frock,' Watson chortled.

Mrs Hudson brought the tea. 'Here, Holmes,' Watson went on, 'you'd better be mother. Ha ha.' His laugh fell a little hollow in the face of Holmes's cheerless scowl.

'Look at this fire, Lestrade,' he said. 'Flaming June and Watson had a roaring fire.'

'I've been in India, Holmes. I feel the cold more than somewhat.'

'Who's that, Doctor?' asked Mrs Hudson, pausing at the door.

'Get out, woman!' shouted Holmes. 'To what do we owe the honour, Lestrade?'

'There's no such phrase, Holmes,' muttered Watson.

'You've clearly been in India too long, Watson,' snapped Holmes. 'You're beginning to confuse the Queen's English with pure Hindoostani.'

'Which brings me to my visit,' interrupted Lestrade, to calm the tension of the atmosphere more than anything else. 'The death of Doctor Watson's nephew, Edward Coke-Hythe.'

'Ah.' Holmes sat down, stuffing the voluminous skirts between his knees and reaching, without taking his eyes off Lestrade, for his meerschaum. 'I have a theory about that.'

Lestrade gritted his teeth. This wasn't why he had come, but Holmes had been useful in the past and for all his irritability and elitism and short temper, Lestrade had a grudging soft spot for him. Holmes lit the pipe and the flame lit his lean haunted features momentarily before they disappeared in a cloud of smoke.

'Revenge,' Holmes savoured the word. 'It's elementary, my dear Watson,' he said to the good doctor's quizzical look.

'I thought you never said that, Mr Holmes,' said Lestrade.

Holmes scowled. 'We all have our off-days, Lestrade. This black fellow – what's his name? Philadelphia?'

'Washington.'

'Bless you, Lestrade,' Watson chipped in.

'Yes. Well, Watson's nephew publicly humiliated Washington – or tried to. Washington resented it and retaliated brilliantly. He killed him and his two cronies in a perfect poetic murder. He not only turned them black – thereby forcing his deformity on them – but he killed them with blackness. His blackness.'

'Isn't that a bit obvious, Holmes?' Watson was speaking Lestrade's thoughts.

'No, no, Watson. You medical men, you're so black and white.'

'Oh, droll, Holmes, very droll,' chortled Watson.

Holmes ignored him.

'It's a double bluff, Lestrade. Precisely because it *would* be so obvious, Washington knew he would be safe. It's elementary, in fiction and life. Take my word for it, Inspector, Washington's your man.'

Lestrade looked at Watson. 'In the absence of another motive, gentlemen, I may as well start there.'

Holmes opened Watson's bag and pulled out a syringe. 'Join me, Lestrade?'

'No thanks, I don't,' the inspector answered.

Holmes disappeared into an adjoining room from which, shortly afterwards, emanated the most appalling noise of a bow on the strings of a violin.

'I'll see you out, Lestrade,' said Watson. 'Sorry I couldn't be of much help.'

'Not at all,' Lestrade said. 'Holmes has proved one thing to me.'

'What's that?'

'Atlanta Washington is an innocent man.'

'Oh, quite. He's not well, you know.'

'Washington?'

'No, Holmes. One day, that habit of his will kill him.'

'One day it will be against the law as well,' mused Lestrade as Mrs Hudson gave him his hat. 'It would be a sad thing, Doctor, if the Great Detective were to die in prison, an incurable addict.'

Lestrade reached the street. Above him a sash window flew up.

'Lestrade,' hissed a voice. Holmes peered out, violin gripped in his fist. 'I must apologise for Watson. He hasn't been well. He caught something in India. Never been the same since. You saw the symptoms. Giggling, sniping at me. He's supposed to be a professional man, for God's sake. Anyway, there it is. Sad, eh?'

'Very,' said Lestrade, tipped his hat and walked away.

He couldn't leave Coke-Hythe's family entirely to Bandicoot. Having given the young constable time to interview them, he took a cab to Portman Square, and in his most enigmatic, Scotland Yard manner, pursued his inquiries. Bandicoot had been surprisingly thorough. No doubt the Old School Tie had helped, but Lestrade went doggedly over the same ground, priding himself on his superior reading of facial expressions, casual gestures, but at the same time feeling that the metaphorical Blackheath Crammer Tie around his neck was decidedly inferior. Yes, Ned had been something of a lad. Never in trouble, Lestrade understood. No, he didn't care for black people, but that surely was understandable. After all, his cousin Rudolph had succumbed to a native assegai during the Zulu War when Ned was at a very impressionable age. And this slave chappie was flaunting himself somewhat. But really, Ned had grown a little apart from his family of recent years. He seemed to spend most of his time in Cambridge. And so pausing only to throw together a few necessaries in a Gladstone bag, Lestrade caught the evening train.

Most of the students had in fact gone down for the summer vac. The air was clear and cool as the inspector wandered through the town, down Silver Street and Sidney Street in his search for lodgings. He found a modest hotel near the college of his destination, Magdalene, and collapsed gratefully into bed.

He was up with the lark to hear cheery laughter in the punts below and the watery wobble of timber in rowlocks. 'Care for a dip?' a red-faced man in a boater and blazer called to him as Lestrade stuck his head out of the window ledge. The town came to life with the ringing of bicycle bells and the clatter and jingle of dray horses.

Lestrade downed his hearty breakfast of bacon, eggs, toast and coffee and emerged into the morning sunlight. He felt out of place in his black serge and bowler amidst the stripes and straw and on a whim he entered Fosdick's, the University outfitters and bought himself a blazer and a pair of flannels. He resisted the spats as being a little risqué for a man of his position and was not entitled, of course, to a college badge.

The Master of Magdalene greeted him on the steps of his college. He was a vast man, with flowing dundrearies which had gone out of fashion twenty years before and a mortarboard which hid, Lestrade suspected, a totally bald head. He was helpful after his fashion and between showing Lestrade the river walk, the chapel and the three Van Dykes so generously benefacted to the college, explained that he had never really known Edward Coke-Hythe or his friends and he had liked them even less. He might perhaps try the Albino Club in Jesus Lane.

'I am sorry, sir,' said the man on the door of that august institution, 'you are wearing a black tie. I cannot possibly allow entry to a man in a black tie.'

Lestrade flashed his identification. The doorman hesitated, then stepped aside. He showed Lestrade into a perfectly white interior – the walls, ceiling, even the furniture gleaming in ivory. Against the far wall was a piano, without ebony keys. One or two young men lounged about in white suits. Lestrade explained who he was and asked if any of them had known Edward Coke-Hythe. After a few in-suckings of breath, murmurings of 'Jolly bad form' and 'Chuck him out', the inspector was finally introduced to Hartington-White, the club's president, Fellow of Peterhouse and all stations west.

'Look here, Inspector, I mean arriving in a black tie is one thing, but asking personal questions about a member.'

Lestrade's mind turned for a moment on the exact meaning of the word 'member', but this was merely a club for eccentrics. He need look no further into an innocent and unconscious double-entendre, unless, of course, Hartington-White knew that Coke-Hythe's member was now lying black as the ace of spades along with the rest of him on a slab in Cannon Row Morgue.

'Edward Coke-Hythe is dead, Mr White. A police officer in the course of his inquiries is entitled to ask any questions, personal or otherwise. The fact that the deceased was a member of your club does not interest me one jot . . . Alternatively, it could be very illuminating.'

'Meaning? – and that's Hartington-White, by the way.'

Lestrade noticed the other man nodding in the direction of a few other club members.

'What is the aim of your club, Mr Hartington-White?'

'Aim? Why, recreation of course. Any member of the University is eligible.'

'And no one is black-balled?'

'That's not a term we care to use.'

'Don't you like the colour black, Mr Hartington-White?'

'I beg your pardon?'

'The decor, the black tie, even the piano keys. Isn't the purpose of this club to remove what you consider to be the black peril from white society?'

'Really, Inspector. Isn't this a little preposterous?' But Hartington-White was uneasy, his grin very fixed.

'Wasn't Edward Coke-Hythe running an errand for you? Isn't that why he was in London, in fact, since he kept his rooms in the north of town here? Wasn't he furthering the cause of white supremacy by attempting to humiliate the ex-slave Atlanta Washington?'

'That's insane, Inspector.' Hartington-White was on his feet, shouting. 'Now, I really must ask you to leave. Y . . . you do not have a white tie.'

'Neither do I have my answers,' Lestrade shouted in return. Then quieter, 'Nor blood on my conscience.'

Instinctively he heard the whirr as the billiard cue hissed through the air. He ducked and drove his shoulder into his opponent's groin. Grabbing the corner of the rug as he went down, Lestrade overturned a second attacker and kicked Hartington-White in the pit of his stomach. When he finally got up, Lestrade realised that his speed and his boot had eliminated only one permanently. The man with the billiard cue lay gripping his crotch with a distant look on his face. In front of Lestrade were four members and a footman, two of them armed with billiard cues. It had been some time since Lestrade had had to defend himself from such an attack – not since he was a sergeant at Wapping New Stairs in fact. The device he had used then, though hardly regulation police issue, was still in his pocket now. He was never without it. He deflected the sideways swipe of Hartington-White's cue, gripped the man's arm and jerked him forwards, twisting him round so that his arm locked under his jaw. Lestrade's left hand produced the Apache dagger, a needle-sharp stiletto with brass rings that went over his knuckles. The tip of the blade rested an inch away from Hartington-White's left eardrum.

'A step closer, gentlemen, and your revered President will be bleeding all over the carpet.'

They stopped, hesitated, looked at each other.

'For God's sake, do something,' screamed the President. 'The maniac will kill me.'

'The door, gentlemen,' hissed Lestrade, tilting his adversary's head further back. 'I want it shut with you on the other side of it.'

'Do as he says.' Hartington-White's voice was strained almost to inaudibility.

One by one, they dropped their guard and backed towards the door. One by one they left the room. Hartington-White was a big man and Lestrade knew now, if he had not known before, of his somewhat murderous tendencies. He was taking no chances. He spun round and drove knee and knuckleduster simultaneously into the pit of his stomach. The Club President went down, vomiting as he did so.

Lestrade knelt to one side of him to avoid the mess and

flicked his switch blade under his chin. 'Now, Mr Hartington-White, where were we? Ah, yes, you sent Coke-Hythe to London, yes?'

Hartington-White nodded, gulping for air.

'To bait Atlanta Washington?'

Another nod.

'To kill him?'

Hartington-White's head remained still. Lestrade's knife edged closer.

'If necessary,' the Club President whispered.

Lestrade put the weapon away, found his boater and looked around the littered room. Furniture lay in disarray. The member with the damaged member lay moaning in the corner. The President knelt, furious and shaking and in pain in the middle of the floor.

'Expect a visit from your local constabulary, Mr Hartington-White. The charge will be incitement to riot and attempted murder. By the time the police, the Church, the do-gooders and the press have done with you, there won't be much left of the Albino Club.' He glanced at the door. By now there would be reinforcements outside – a little army of racialists bent on preserving their anonymity behind the gleaming white walls of an eccentric gentlemen's club. Even an Apache knife wouldn't serve well against all of them.

'Don't bother to get up, I'll see myself out. 'And the inspector threw himself bodily through a plate-glass window.

When Lestrade came out of hospital three days later, events had moved apace. McNaghten was far from pleased at the ruckus at the Albino Club and one of the members had demanded a full apology. Lestrade refused and countered his principal's intervention by ordering the arrest of those present the day he had been attacked. All in all, it was unfortunate and had not got Lestrade much further. He assured McNaghten that he was on top of the case but could not promise him an imminent arrest.

There were still stitches in the inspector's face when he called in expert advice by visiting the studio at St John's Wood.

Studio it may have been, but to Lestrade it resembled a palace, vast and sprawling, each room hung with paintings, expensive tapestries and filled with lavish furniture. As luck would have it, Lestrade arrived in time to feel very out of place at a garden party in the grounds. A shifty-looking, rather neurotic man with furtive eyes and thinning hair pinched his sherry. Lestrade recognised him as Mr Burne-Jones, the Pre-Raphaelite. He and the name were all Lestrade remembered from a crash course in modern art five years ago when he was involved in the Frederick Leighton Fake Swindle. His quarry that day in St John's Wood he had never heard of, but a footman pointed him out.

'Mr Adma-Talema?' said the inspector.

The host of the party turned to the inquirer. He adjusted his pince-nez and responded, 'Something like that. No, don't tell me. You are a reporter from the *Daily Graphic*, an art critic and your last piece so provoked an artist that he smashed a canvas over your head?'

'Something like that,' replied Lestrade. 'Actually I am from Scotland Yard.'

'Really?' said Alma-Tadema 'I have never met a real detective before. Apart from . . . oh, but he doesn't count.'

'May we talk in private, sir?'

The artist took leave of the admiring circle around him, took two drinks from a passing tray and thrust one at Lestrade. They walked through a cloud of white peacocks on to a broad terrace and into the vast sunlit studio itself. An enormous canvas rested on three easels in the centre of the room. Partially draped, it was an ancient scene, classical and grand.

'Do you like it?' The artist asked, and grinned.

'Indeed,' said Lestrade, hoping he would not be lured into a conversation on the merits of gouache or the traps of chiaroscuro.

'So do I.' Alma-Tadema replenished his own and Lestrade's glasses with the finest claret cup Lestrade had ever tasted. 'Tell me something, I thought you police-chappies never drank on duty.'

'Most of us don't, sir. But if I may say so, most of us don't get offered claret of this vintage.'

'My dear . . . er . . . Inspector, is it? Not only have you a discerning eye for art, but you are also a connoisseur of the vine. A lucky day for me indeed.'

'I hope so, sir.' Lestrade produced a tin from his pocket. 'Be so good as to have a look at the contents of this.'

Alma-Tadema opened, sniffed, peered closely through the pince-nez, placed an exquisitely manicured finger in and licked it. 'Enamel,' he said. 'Black enamel. Aspinall's probably.'

'Is enamel paint unusual, Mr Ala-Tameda?'

'Indeed it is. It's not readily available yet and of course quite unsuitable for canvas. But the French are using it a lot on their blasted bits and pieces.'

'Don't you like the New Art, Mr Mala-Teda?'

'Oh, in its way, it's all right, but you can't build an Underground station that looks like a peacock. There isn't enough of the classical in art nowadays. Not like the Romans,' he said, waving in the direction of his canvas. 'You know where you are with Romans.'

'You said Aspinall's enamel?'

'Yes, that is the firm the produces it.' Alma-Tadema buried himself in a bureau. 'It's deuced expensive; even I only have . . .' He stopped. Lestrade crossed the room to him.

'Something the matter, sir?'

'They've gone. Six pots of Aspinall's black enamel. Gone.'

'When did you last see your enamel?'

Alma-Tadema chewed his thumb. 'Well, let's see, it must have been – Tuesday last, or Monday.'

'It may be crucial, sir.'

'Yes, yes of course, Inspector. Monday, week before last. I'm certain it was Monday because I had one of my sitters cancel at short notice. I was not too displeased. I hate painting portraits. Give me Romans every time.'

There was a pause.

'Inspector, may I ask why you came to me with this paint?'

'My chief recommended you, sir, as a prominent man in paint-consistency.'

The artist laughed. 'Well, I'm flattered. But what is this in connection with?'

'You don't read the newspapers, Mr Alma-Mater?'

'Only the art reviews, I'm afraid. Shockingly narrow of me, isn't it?'

'Had you read the headlines, sir, over the past ten days, you would know that three young men were found dead in Battersea Park. Each one had been painted black from head to foot. It was that very act of painting which killed them.'

'Good God!' Alma-Tadema sat down with astonishment. 'But that's incredible.'

'What is more incredible, sir, is that the paint seems to have come from your studio.'

Realisation began to dawn on the artist.

'I see,' he said, the smile leaving his face for the first time that day. 'So you came to me for expert technical advice and I end up as a suspect.'

'Not such a lucky day for you after all, then, Mr Alda-Tamer?'

'Indeed, no,' replied the artist.

'Who has access to this studio?'

'Oh, almost anyone. It's locked at night, of course and only the butler and I have keys, but during the day it's always open. Unless I have a finished canvas. The place is always full of people. You saw for yourself. It's open house. My hospitality is renowned, I blush to admit.'

Lestrade walked to the glass doors. 'I am sure you have no plans to leave town, sir, but please contact the Yard if you do.'

'Yes, of course, Inspector. I am only too anxious to clear this matter up.'

'May I suggest you take better precautions, sir? This little piece, now –' indicating the Roman canvas 'what might that be worth?'

'I have been offered eight thousand for that one.'

It was Lestrade's turn to be astonished. It was more money than he would make in a lifetime, if he continued straight.

'Pounds?'

Alma-Tadema guffawed heartily. 'Don't be unrealistic, Inspector . . . guineas.'

*

The family of Spender had aristocratic connections, but they themselves lived in a tawdry house in a tawdry suburb in Notting Hill. They were more anxious for blood than the Coke-Hythes had been and infinitely less polite. With his customary ease, Lestrade was able to defend himself and the Yard against the oft-heard cry from the deceased's grandfather in the corner: 'What are you fellows doing about it?' A combination of wheedling and bluff on Lestrade's part provided all he was ever likely to know about the late William Alphonse Spender. He was twenty-four, single, without a post ('job' was far too common a word for the Spenders), and kept unfortunate company. No one in the family seemed really upset to see him go; no one in the family seemed very surprised that he had met so 'sticky' an end. If only they hadn't sent him to Harrow in the first place, this would never have happened. Still, it was probably for the best. No, William had no real aversion to blacks, it was just that he enjoyed tormenting people. Coke-Hythe was obviously the instigator of the recent notoriety. But it was such a minor incident. Only the radical press would be so common as to blow it up out of all proportion. Enemies? Well, even the family conceded that William was an unlovely lad, but they could think of no one, no real individual, who stood out. Except of course for that ghastly black person. He had a motive. Why hadn't he been arrested?

Arthur Fitz had no immediate family. His parents had died in an avalanche some years before while visiting Switzerland and the boy had been bounced around various distant aunts who ended up cursing themselves for not being distant enough. It was this very distance which gave them an air of guilt. They had failed the boy. The least they could do now was to ensure that his murderer was brought to book. But Arthur spent most of his time in clubland, in disreputable company and his various aunts suspected that he was very horribly in debt.

Clubland proved chilly and unhelpful. Lestrade tackled some – Arts, Army and Navy, Crockford's. Bandicoot tackled others

– White's, Boodle's, Naval and Military. Dew held the horses. Their collective inquiries yielded almost nothing. A lot of shoe-leather worn, a lot of frosty silence, a lot of angry letters about police intrusion to McNaghten and the Commissioner. Lestrade's reputation began to sink in the mire of accusation and inefficiency. It was turning, slowly but surely, into a nightmare.

Lestrade was shown into the expensive suite of rooms occupied for the past four months by Atlanta Washington, the ex-slave. The inspector had not really known what to expect. Before him stood a handsome, dapper man about his own age, immaculately groomed with a rose in his button-hole. On each arm he wore an incredibly beautiful white girl, one of whom Lestrade thought he recognised as a former courtesan belonging to Lord Panmure.

'You sure took your time.' The Negro grinned, displaying a row of pearly white teeth. 'Honies, run along now, Atlanta wants to talk to de man.' He swung his body across the floor, as though to an imaginary tune, shooing the protesting girls out of the door in a flurry of feathers and furs.

'Well, now, Inspector honey, to what do I owe de pleasure?'

'I am pursuing a murder inquiry.'

'Right on. Why don't you siddown dere an' I'll have some mint julep sent right up, y'hear.'

Lestrade sat.

'I hope you won't take long. I's expectin' ma hominey grits in a liddle while an' I sure hates tuh be kept waitin'.'

'Atlanta Washington,' Lestrade stood up again, 'I arrest you in the name of the law. You are not obliged to say anything, but anything you do say will be taken down . . .'

'Now, hold it, man,' the Negro interrupted. He looked squarely at Lestrade for a moment. 'Aw, shit.' He pulled off his elaborate thick, curly hair to reveal a much less impressive balding pate underneath. Next, he unhooked his immaculate false teeth to reveal a few scattered brownish ones beneath.

'All right, Mr Lestrade, the show's over.' Even the phoney plantation accent had gone. 'What am I charged with?'

Lestrade sat down, triumphant. 'You're not,' he said. 'But I had to get through that barrier somehow.'

Washington grinned. 'You're smart and no mistake.'

'Why do you do it?' asked Lestrade.

'What – the lingo? The teeth? The rug?'

Lestrade nodded.

'It's a long story, Inspector.'

'Take your time, sir.'

'My father was Booker T. Washington, a slave. Maybe you read his book, *Up from Slavery*?'

Lestrade had not.

'Well, I was born a slave, like he was. Momma used to wash the Massa's clothes on the plantation – Georgia. Poppa was what they call in the States an "uppity nigger", but like all Negroes, he knew how to hide it. The lingo I was just using – and not fooling you with – is plantation jive. You see, the way to stay out of trouble and to stay alive is to act dumb, to play Sambo. Jig around a lot, roll your eyes and talk' – and he broke into it again – 'like de whities expec' a Sambo tuh talk. That way' – lapsing back – 'you don't get noticed. When the Lincoln soldiers came in '65 we were all told we were free. I was lucky. I went North with Poppa and learnt what freedom really meant. It meant the brothers living like pigs in Harlem while the white folks get the jobs and the handouts. You know how many black police there are in the great United States? How many black doctors, lawyers, judges, teachers? None, Inspector, none. Even the nigger minstrels on the stage are whities blacked up with burnt cork. That's the freedom Lincoln gave us. And they killed him for it. So I decided to hit back. Poppa wrote his book and got famous – and rich. So I became a celebrity – an educated nigger. Popular? No, I'm not. Whities hate me 'cos I'm black. But they're fascinated, too. They can't keep away because they're afraid of me. They're afraid that one day all my kind are going to be smart and sassie, and it scares the shit out of them. So, it's all a front, Inspector. The hair, the pearly teeth, the jive, it's what people expect. And who am I to let them down?' A pause: 'Tell me, do you think my secret is safe with you?'

'Did you kill those men?'

'Hell, no. I may be a coon, Inspector. I may be an ornery bastard. But I've never killed a man and I couldn't start now. Yes, I horse-whipped a couple a couple of weeks ago when the insults and the spittle came on a little too strong. But that's it, that's as far as it goes.'

'Do you know the studio of Lawrence Alma-Tadema?' Lestrade surprised himself in getting it right.

'If he's the photographer fella in Piccadilly, yeah.'

'What can you tell me about Aspinall's enamel?'

Washington looked blank. 'Nothing.'

Lestrade got up. He was impressed by the man's sincerity.

'Mr Washington, when are you leaving the country?'

The ex-slave put back his teeth and refitted his wig.

'Why, any day now, suh, fo' sure.'

Lestrade nodded his approval of that.

'What's gettin' you, man? Jus' 'cos some Massas in de cole, cole groun'.'

'I am wondering,' said Lestrade, 'how many more there are going to be.'

This time, the by now inevitable letter was a long time coming. Lestrade mechanically traced, as far as he was able, the last day in the lives of the three dead men. They knew a lot of people, were usually, though not always, in the public gaze and the contacts all drew blanks. The common factors in their lives, their tenuous friendship based on a love of limelight and of devilry, produced nothing that was concrete. No leads, no suspects. But, then, the letter came.

As he had often done before
The Woolly-headed black-a-moor
One nice fine summer's day went out
To see the shops and walk about.
Then Edward, little noisy wag,
Ran out and laugh'd and wav'd his flag;

And William came with jacket trim
And brought his wooden hoop with him;
And Arthur, too, snatch'd up his toys
And join'd the other naughty boys;
So one and all set up a roar
And laughed and hooted more and more
And kept on singing – only think –
'Oh, Blacky, you're as black as ink.'
He seizes Arthur, seizes Ned,
Takes William by his little head;
And they may scream and kick and call
Into the ink he dips them all;
Into the inkstand, one, two, three,
Till they are black as black can be.
They have been made as black as crows,
Quite black all over, eyes and nose,
And legs, and arms, and heads and toes,
And trousers, pinafores and toys –
The silly little inky boys!
Because they set up such a roar
And teased the harmless black-a-moor.

A longer verse than usual, mused Lestrade, and more of a story perhaps. No extra clues in letter-head or paper type or print, but there was something else – a signature.

'What do you know about Agrippa?' he threw at Bandicoot, who had just come in with an armful of written statements.

'Which one?'

'All of them,' answered the inspector, annoyed to find that his lieutenant seemed to have such knowledge at his fingertips.

'Well, there was Marcus Vipsanius Agrippa, the Roman General. If my Classics serve me correctly, he commanded Octavian's fleet at the Battle of Actium in 31 BC.'

'Did he like Negroes?'

Bandicoot thought hard. 'I think you must be confusing him with Scipio Africanus, sir. He was one.'

'Who are the other Agrippas?'

'Herods I and II – as in the New Testament. Puppet Kings of Judaea allowed to rule in name only by Roman order.'

Lestrade rubbed his eyes and lolled back in his chair. He was getting nowhere.

'Why do you ask, sir?'

Lestrade looked at him. No harm, he thought, in showing the letter to Bandicoot. Perhaps his literate brain, naïve and fumbling policeman though he was, might shed some light on the poetry.

'Oh, *that* Agrippa!' Bandicoot chuckled.

Lestrade sat bolt upright. 'What do you mean, "*that* Agrippa"?'

'Well, I didn't realise it was a joke, Inspector.'

'It's no joke, Bandicoot, I can assure you. Are you telling me you know this poem?'

'Yes, of course. Don't you?'

Lestrade looked like a man whose prayers had been answered. 'Dew!' he roared, 'fetch us a pot of tea. And toast. Bandicoot, have a cigar. You've earned that at least. We could be here for some time.'

The widow

'It comes from a series of, well, I suppose you'd call them cautionary tales for children, sir. As a boy Nanny was always reading them to me. I grew up with them. I thought everybody did.'

'We didn't all have your advantages, Bandicoot.' Lestrade felt himself sounding more like Mr Keir Hardie every time he opened his mouth.

'It's called *Struwwelpeter*, written by a doctor-chappie to amuse his little patients, I believe.'

'Strew what?' asked Lestrade.

'*Struwwelpeter*. I suppose . . . er . . . German wasn't really my strong point, but I seem to remember it was written as *Shock-headed Peter* in the English version.'

Lestrade's jaw dropped. 'The man in the Chine,' he murmured.

'Sir?'

Lestrade unlocked the confidential file in his bureau drawer. He threw the letters down on the table. 'I have received one of these after each murder. Do they all come from *Shock-headed Peter*?'

Bandicoot perused them. After a while – 'Yes, *Shock-headed Peter* all right, but they seem shorter. Bits must have been omitted.'

'Examples?'

'Oh, Inspector, I haven't read these for years, but, look, in this first one for example, the last line or so has gone. You've got –

And the sloven, I declare,
Never once has combed his hair;

'Then it goes something like this –

Anything to me is sweeter
Than to see Shock-headed Peter.'

Lestrade remembered the awful spectacle of the corpse in the Chine and wholeheartedly agreed with that sentiment.

'Anything else?'

Bandicoot thought again. He was getting into his stride now.

'Yes, this second one refers to a verse called "Cruel Frederick". He whips a Mary, sister, nurse, whatever she is and of course he doesn't actually die in the poem. I assume all these letters refer to murders.'

'Correct – to date six of them.'

'Well, I can see the picture now – the dog Tray ends up sitting at a table with a napkin on, eating Frederick's pies and puddings.'

Lestrade wandered around the room, swigging from the inelegant cup.

'With the Harriet story,' Bandicoot went on, 'I seem to remember great play about the girl's pet cats and nothing being left in her pile of ashes but her scarlet shoes. Presumably the murderer couldn't arrange it quite as neatly as that – to fit the rhymes exactly.'

'Well, he hasn't done a bad job so far. The Wemyss family were crawling with cats.'

'This last one is called "The story of the Inky Boys" – black-baiting. Agrippa is some sort of magician who champions the coons' cause and dips the baiters in a huge pot of ink.'

'Or Aspinall's black enamel,' chimed in Lestrade.

'It isn't clear from the poem whether they die or not of course. But the picture with it, I believe, indicates that they don't.'

Lestrade stopped pacing. He put his cup down and lowered himself on to his elbows on the desk next to Bandicoot.

'How many more cautionary tales are there?' he asked.

'Lord, I don't know, sir. A few. I don't know.'

Lestrade snapped into action, 'All right, Bandicoot, get to a booksellers, to the British Museum, wherever you have to, but get a copy of that book. It's a perfect text for the murders so far. Our friend isn't likely to deviate now. That's why he didn't include the lines about *Shock-headed Peter* after his first murder. It would have tipped me off too early. Chances are he doesn't think we've got him yet, but we have. I'm giving this to McNaghten, it might take the pressure off us all . . . Oh, and Bandicoot, before you go.'

'Sir?'

'Well done. We'll make a policeman of you yet.'

While Lestrade was briefing McNaghten about the advances he had made, making as little as possible of Bandicoot's role in it all and while Bandicoot himself was hunting purposefully through the Westminster bookshops, Albert Mauleverer lay dead in the well below Guy's Cliffe. A labourer found the body by chance and alerted the Warwickshire police. They had no clues, no evidence, no motive and no suspect. And it was only by chance some days later that Lestrade happened to see a tiny piece in the *Police Gazette*. 'Body found in well. Gunshot wounds.' By now he had the book in his possession, *Struwwelpeter by Dr Heinrich Hoffmann, Pretty Stories and Funny Pictures,* published 1845. Immediately he recognised the hallmarks of the 'Story of the Man that went out Shooting'. He read it again as he sped north on the morning train. In the poem, a hare did it. Having stolen the Man's spectacles and gun, while he is asleep, the hare shoots him when he has fallen into a well. Once again, the result in the poem is not murder, and there was various nonsense about the Man's wife drinking coffee nearby and the hare's child being splashed by it. But Lestrade knew only too well by now that none of this was nonsense. Some maniac was grimly acting out these cautionary tales, as meticulously as possible. But who? And why? There were just not enough answers. One thing and one thing only could be formulated about the murderer – he was damnably clever – and another thing – he was still, despite Lestrade's possession of the book, one step ahead.

Lestrade booked in first at the Clarendon Hotel at the top of the Parade. He had walked from the station, but felt the time well spent in that he had the opportunity to study the spa town of Leamington for the first time. Very like Cheltenham, he thought to himself, but when you've seen one spa, presumably you've seen them all. The wide streets, the leafy avenues, the opulent extravagance of shop fronts and offices, all bore testimony to the wealth and stability of the middle classes of the provinces. Lestrade was glad to change into his lightweight suit and he fancied the sun was strong enough for his Cambridge boater, a little battered around the brim though it was.

At the police station however, they were less than helpful. A portly sergeant eyed Lestrade from head to toe before offering him the use of a station cab. Lestrade took a constable with him and they drove to the morgue. This corpse was less bizarre than the last few, but no less grisly. The right side of the head was that of a man of middle age, greying hair and heavy features. The left side of the head was not there at all – merely a mass of dark congealed blood with pieces of whitish bone visible. Lestrade had seen such wounds before, but unfortunately, the young constable had not and he gracefully floated to the floor as the attendant lifted the blanket. Lestrade went on checking the body and asking the attendant mechanical questions, while the constable was carried out, his helmet resting on his chest.

'Three days ago, you say?'

'Yes, sir. He were brought in 'ere dead as mutton. I cleaned him up a bit but apart from that 'e 'aven't been touched, 'ere are his glasses.'

The attendant held up a shattered pair of spectacles. Lestrade noted the green Norfolk jacket, the crumpled bloodstained deerstalker and then he examined the shotgun. Standard twelve-bore, handsome piece. One barrel discharged.

'Is this the gun that killed him?'

'I don't know.' The attendant shrugged. 'That's your job.'

Impervious to Lestrade's scowl, he shuffled off, blowing hard on a pipe of vicious tobacco, his head wreathed in smoke. Lestrade looked at the wound again; point blank range, both barrels he'd say. He went out into the sunshine and found the pale constable leaning on the station cab. He attempted to stand to attention at the inspector's approach.

'All right, lad. Cigar?'

The constable declined with a pathetic faraway look on his face. Lestrade lit up, savouring the moment.

'Who found the body?'

The constable rummaged in his pockets for his notebook.

'Half a dozen eggs, two . . . Oh, sorry sir. The wife's shopping.'

Lestrade paused in mid-puff. 'Wife? How old are you, Constable?'

'I shall be twenty in the autumn, sir.'

Lestrade began to feel his age. It was the beginning of the end, of course, when policemen began to look younger than you did.

'Joseph Glover, sir. A labourer from Bubbenhall.'

'Where?'

'Bubbenhall, sir. It's a village' – the constable rummaged again and produced a map, which he laboriously unfolded on the rump of the horse – '. . . five miles from here.'

'Near Guy's Cliffe?'

'Oh no, sir.' The constable's concentration followed his finger again over the map. 'Eight miles from there, sir.'

Lestrade thought aloud. 'Now, what was a labourer doing eight miles from his village? What time of day was the body found?'

The constable referred to his notebook, 'Approximately half past seven in the evening, sir. Saturday, July the twenty-fourth.'

'This Glover – anything known? Try it without the notebook, Constable,' as the young man's head bent to the book again.

'Well, sir,' the mental effort was obviously crippling the constable, 'ploughing champion for the county three years running. One of the best hedgers I've seen. And he seems to eat a lot of other people's pheasants.'

'Right, Constable. That doesn't exactly constitute "form", but never mind. Give me the reins. I'm getting out of practice. And you keep your wits about you; I want to get home by tomorrow.'

They found Joseph Glover lashed to a ploughing team, two massive Clydesdales, huge and gentle, plodding through the furrows. Behind their tossing heads and the dust flying as they walked, could be seen a pair of gaitered legs and the odd flash of a switch.

'Ay up, Jewel, ay up, Dinkie.'

Lestrade crossed the furrows, the constable scrambling behind him.

'Joseph Glover?'

The little man growled under his breath and pulled the horses up short. He unhooked the reins from his neck.

'Who wants to know?' The truculent little labourer came up to Lestrade's tie-knot.

'Inspector Lestrade, Scotland Yard.'

'Scotland? You're a bit far from home.'

Lestrade bent over so that their noses were touching. 'Obstructing the police can get you five years, Glover. What would happen to your horses then?'

Glover flung himself back against the huge, glossy flank of one of them.

'Don't worry, Dinkie, I won't let him take you.'

'I'm from Scotland Yard, Glover, not the knacker's yard.'

Another gem wasted. Only one of the Clydesdales snorted in appreciation.

Glover hitched himself to the team again and switched them into action. 'I gotta get on,' he growled. 'Ploughin' contest next week at the Abbey.'

Lestrade looked to the constable for explanation.

'It's nearly harvest, sir. You don't plough at harvest time. You plough in the Spring.'

'Is he . . . er . . . all right?' Lestrade mouthed the words silently, nodding sideways at Glover, who chewed his grass with still more determination and annoyance, staring fixedly ahead.

'Oh, yes, sir.' The constable giggled. 'Each summer there's an agricultural fair at Stoneleigh Abbey, Lord Leigh's estate. It was his land the body was found on.'

'Why were you at Guy's Cliffe on Saturday last?' Lestrade asked Glover.

'Sparking.'

Lestrade turned to the constable for translation.

'Courting, sir.'

'What was the young lady's name?'

'Now look . . .' Glover broke off as he caught the look in Lestrade's eyes.

'Do you know what a treadmill is, Glover? Do you know what it feels like treading down on those rungs, fifteen minutes on, two minutes off, six hours a day?'

'Louisa Ellcock. Works for the folks in the big house at Guy's Cliffe.'

'The Mauleverers, sir.'

'Tell me,' said Lestrade.

'I was on me way to visit Louise. Promised we are. Well, I cuts across the fields from Old Milverton Church and there he was. I seen his gun first, sort of gleaming in the evening sun.'

'Never mind the poetry, go on.'

'I went over and saw him. Stuffed down the well 'e were. Dead.'

'Did you hear any shots?'

'On and off. But I'd walked near ten miles, there was lots of sportsmen about that weekend.'

'Did you see anyone about? Acting suspiciously?'

'That's a bloody daft question' – and then, softening the tone – 'beggin' your pardon, of course. But I had me mind on other things. I was 'oping to do some suspicious actin' meself in a minute. Know what I mean?' The jab from the elbow and the wry grin fell a little sourly on Lestrade. He wanted evidence, not rural erotica.

'This Louisa Ellcock. Where can we find her?'

'Now then, I don't want 'er bothered. Not in 'er condition.'

Lestrade stopped walking and raised a disapproving eyebrow.

'Chances are, Glover, that when your "suspicious actions" and 'er interesting condition produce something, the little bastard will have a dad rotting inside.' He dug Glover in the ribs with his elbow: 'Know what I mean?'

*

Guy's Cliffe House was tall and oddly foreboding. It was set back from the water, swirling and spraying over the weir. In the strong afternoon sun Lestrade and the constable crossed the rickety wooden bridge. Their occasional bursts of conversation were drowned by the noise of the rushing water and the rank, stagnant smell near the mill. The inspector inspected the well. If there had been blood, it had been washed off by rain or water from the well. The area around it was hopelessly trampled with countless footprints – Mauleverer's, Glover's, a dozen or so policemen's, newspapermen's and doubtless sightseers'. And somewhere, Lestrade pondered, somewhere in the Warwickshire dust, the footprints of the murderer. Lestrade's murderer. Lestrade's man.

Louise Ellcock was of little help. She was terrified that Lestrade would tell Mrs Mauleverer of her 'secret'. Lestrade told her her secret was safe with him, that he had other fish to fry. She showed him gratefully into the drawing room. Mrs Mauleverer joined the officers of the law there.

'Inspector Lestrade, ma'am, of Scotland Yard. This is Constable . . . er . . .'

The constable consulted his notebook.

'Prothero, ma'am.'

'Of the Warwickshire Constabulary,' Lestrade completed the sentence for him.

Mrs Mauleverer urged them to be seated.

'A distressing time, ma'am,' commented Lestrade.

'We can dispense with the solemn looks, Inspector Lestrade. I am naturally distressed at the sudden and ghastly death of a fellow human being. But the fact that that human being happened to be my husband is purely coincidental. Sherry?'

Lestrade glanced at Prothero. 'You needn't take this down, Constable. Wait with the horses.' The constable left.

'Mrs Mauleverer.'

'Inspector.' Mrs Mauleverer swept to her feet and poured some pale sherry for Lestrade. 'You must think me very unfeeling.'

'Not at all, ma'am. You have had a very trying time. May I ask you a few questions?'

'I cannot tell you more than I have told the local police, Inspector.'

'I have not yet consulted the local police, ma'am. The young constable is merely my guide around the neighbourhood.'

'You don't know Warwickshire then, Inspector?'

'No, ma'am.' Lestrade followed his hostess with his eyes. She walked away from him across the room. The sunlight fell on the dark green and gold of her velvet gown. It caught the lustrous black curls too, falling, no, cascading was the romantic word, over one shoulder. Mrs Mauleverer was a very beautiful woman, fine-boned, with dark, smouldering eyes that flashed in the pale, melancholy face.

'My husband and I were married for three years, Inspector. He was twenty years my senior and had spent most of his life in Africa. He was an engineer of sorts. I first met him in London five years ago. He was suave, debonair, travelled. I had just been presented at Court and Mama was anxious for me to make the perfect match. I was a fool, Inspector. I didn't have the courage to call a halt, to say no, this is not what I want. Women are slaves still. I felt it was my duty and I accepted when he proposed. It had not been easy for Mama. Papa had died some years before, and at least Albert offered us financial security. Oh dear, this all sounds so mercenary.'

'Not at all, ma'am.'

'It didn't last.' Mrs Mauleverer began to pace the room, wringing her hands. Occasionally her dark eyes fell on Lestrade and hurriedly looked away. 'Albert was attentive for a month, perhaps two and then he began spending more and more time away. Shooting weekends, card parties, always without me. Oh, I busied myself in the area. The poor are always with us, Inspector. I helped with charities and joined committees. I redecorated this house, this cheerless mausoleum Albert brought me to. It didn't help. It didn't fill the place of a husband.'

Lestrade sensed her sadness in the very shadows of the room.

'You were no doubt surprised, Inspector, when I did not appear to weep for my husband. You are no doubt surprised that I am not in mourning. But, you see, my husband died three years ago. I barely recognised the man they found in the well.'

There was a profound stillness between them. Lestrade mentally shook himself. He was thirty-eight years old, had been twenty years in the Force, fifteen of those with Scotland Yard. He'd known dozens, scores, possibly hundreds of bereft widows, yet none had affected him like this one. There was an honesty and a dignity about this woman that strangely touched him. In the silence his hard-bitten heart went out to her.

'The day of the murder.' He cleared his throat and blustered on. 'Tell me about that.'

'It was a day like any other.' A pause, 'No, not quite like any other.' She began again, 'It was the day someone murdered my husband. Tell me, Inspector. Is it wrong for me to want revenge – even revenge for the death of a man I did not love?'

'I am not a judge and jury, ma'am.'

'But you could be an executioner?'

'If I had to kill a man in the course of my duty, ma'am. On occasions we are issued with firearms.'

'I rose at half past eight. My husband had already gone out for the day. He had taken luncheon, in a knapsack, and his gun. He had apparently told Louisa, my maid, that he would not return before nightfall. I suppose it crossed my mind briefly that he had gone to Coventry to see . . . well, another woman. In the morning I busied myself with my correspondence. I heard distant shooting; it may have been Albert . . .' Mrs Mauleverer suddenly started: 'It may have been the shot that killed him. God. The well is only a few hundred yards away, Inspector, though we cannot see it from the house. In the afternoon I drove with Louisa into Leamington. I called at Warwick first and had tea with the Countess. It would have been about nine o'clock when the police called with the news. There had been an accident. Albert was dead.'

'You identified the body?'

'Yes, at Leamington that night.'

Their eyes met in the evening sunshine. The look spoke of all the emptiness in the heart of Mrs Mauleverer. And perhaps too in the heart of Inspector Lestrade.

'I can't tell you any more,' she said. 'My husband was a hard man, remote, silent. I have thought of who would wish him dead. I can think of no one who cared enough to pull the trigger. Isn't that a tragic thought?'

Lestrade rose and put the empty glass on the table.

'Thank you, ma'am. It cannot have been easy. I will take my leave of you.'

'My name is Constance, Inspector. It has not been easy. But you have been kind.'

'If I should need to contact you again . . .'

'I had planned to spend a while with my mother in Camberwell after the funeral.'

'If you would be so kind as to inform Scotland Yard of your London address . . .'

'Of course.'

'And Mrs Mauleverer . . . Constance . . . if I can one day be of help to you . . .' Lestrade took Mrs Mauleverer's hand and kissed it. She smiled.

As he crossed to the station cab and motioned to Prothero to move the horse on, the lines from *Struwwelpeter* came again into his mind –

The poor man's wife was drinking up
Her coffee in her coffee-cup;
The gun shot cup and saucer through;
'Oh dear!' she cried, 'what shall I do?'

'Watch what you're doing with those infernal pins.'

Lestrade entered the trophy room of Stoneleigh Abbey to the sight of Lord Leigh being fitted for a new uniform. He stood with left arm raised while a pair of tailors buzzed around him, putting the finishing touches to his tunic.

'This busby is ridiculous!' he roared. 'It's too tight and too high. If I break into a canter it'll fall off. Who the hell are you?'

'Inspector Lestrade, My Lord. Scotland Yard.'

'Oh.' Lord Leigh recovered quickly. 'Hamburger and Rogers, military tailors. Presumably you know who I am.'

'May I speak to you in private, sir?'

'Oh very well. Gentlemen, call again in a week – and make

sure this tunic sits better, will you? I shall be a laughing stock at the Review.'

The tailors dismantled the elaborate silver and blue uniform until His Lordship stood in his scarlet combinations. Lestrade thought how uncomfortable they must be in this hot weather.

'What is it, Lestrade?' A valet appeared from nowhere and helped His Lordship into a silk smoking jacket. 'I am a busy man.'

'Quite so, My Lord. A body was found on your property at Guy's Cliffe on Saturday last. Can you help me?'

'No.'

'Let me put it another way. I have come a long way at the taxpayers' expense to find out who killed a man. And perhaps to prevent that person from killing again.'

'Hmmm.' Lord Leigh poured himself a huge brandy. He did not offer one to Lestrade. 'I knew Mauleverer, of course. Even offered him a commission in the Yeomanry once. He couldn't have had a troop, of course. I mean he was an outsider. But a Lieutenancy. I could have got him that. Anyway,' Leigh swung onto a wooden frame on which a saddle rested, 'he refused. I never cared for him after that.'

'Did you kill him?'

Leigh sat bolt upright in the saddle. 'Damn you, Lestrade. I shall talk to your superiors. Anyway, if I had killed him, I should have used a sabre.' Leigh made a dramatic flourish with his right arm and returned gratefully to his brandy. 'I didn't dislike him enough to keep him off my land. The truth is he was a damned good shot – and a sportsman.' Leigh suddenly changed his tack. 'Anyway, what are you fellows doing about it? A murder takes place on a chap's land and you have the nerve to come round here accusing me. If this is the best old Jack Lamp can do . . .'

'Jack Lamp, My Lord?'

'County's Chief Constable. Blue Lamp they call him.'

'Original,' grunted Lestrade. 'No, My Lord, Chief Constable Lamp did not call me in. I have reason to believe that the murder of Albert Mauleverer is one of a series. It's not him, it's not your land. It's not even Warwickshire. It's just that it fits a pattern. That's all.'

'Do you Yard-wallahs always talk in riddles?'

'Forget it, My Lord. You saw nothing suspicious yourself?'

Leigh shook his head.

'And none of your people – servants or tenants – reported anything to you?'

'Not a thing. Look, Lestrade, I don't want to sound callous. Can I make a suggestion?'

Lestrade was grateful for the meagrest of straws.

'Mauleverer's wife. They didn't get on, you know. Common knowledge. I think she did it.'

Lestrade felt himself going white. Constance Mauleverer had flashed into his mind throughout a restless night. He could not forget the pale, haunted face. For a moment he thought of forcing the brandy, glass and all, down Leigh's throat. Then perhaps a quick backward flip over his saddle and frame. In the end he settled for a professional opinion.

'A shotgun, is not, in my experience, a woman's weapon, My Lord. Poison, yes; dagger, perhaps; pocket pistol, at a pinch. But shotgun, never. I'll see myself out.'

Lestrade stopped momentarily on his way to the door, which was miraculously opened by the vanishing valet. Leigh was prancing across the floor, posturing with a drawn sword.

'Mark my words, Lestrade, cherchez la femme.'

Lestrade hated the quarterly inspectors' meeting on the third floor. True, the new buildings had a polish and grandeur that Whitehall Place had lacked, but it was still the same in-fighting, the endless bitching about whose Division had managed the most arrests and endless exhortations from the Commissioner and McNaghten about greater care, more vigilance, good hard police procedure, with less money to do it with.

The first point on the agenda that dreary, drizzly August day was police pay.

'A strike?' McNaghten was gradually turning crimson from his cravat upwards.

'That's what they say,' Athelney Jones sat back in the leather armchair. Lestrade looked at him across the room. Jones was a round man, florid and moustachioed, his black-braided inspector's tunic straining across his paunch. He played with his thumbs, smug that he had efficiently landed the problem in McNaghten's lap. The Head of the Criminal Investigation Department threw it back. 'It's your problem, Jones. When I was constable we were glad of two guineas a week. Your men have pensions, free uniforms, sickness benefit, even jars of macassar. Tell them from me that I won't have the Metropolitan Police a laughing stock. Look at this – he slapped a copy of *Judy* down on the desk. It showed a policeman staring blankly at huge fingerprints on a wall. 'This kind of public scorn we can do without. Jones, if you hear the word "strike" again you have my permission to flog the bounder who uttered it.'

Jones growled under his whiskers something about McNaghten not being human. McNaghten heard it, but chose to ignore it. 'Well, Lestrade. Your case.'

Lestrade shifted the papers on his lap. He hated this. Especially now. Of course the others had unsolved or unsolvable cases. But this one he had already begun to take personally. It was an affront to his expertise, perhaps his whole career.

'Seven murders,' he said, leaping in at the deep end.

There were mumbles, the phrase repeated, the audible raising of eyebrows. McNaghten quietly tapped his pipe on the desk until the amount of tobacco cascading into his tea obliged him to stop. The noise abated of its own accord and Lestrade went on.

'All of them perpetrated within the last six months, scattered almost the length and breadth of the country. All of them by person or persons unknown.'

'Come on, Lestrade, you must have more than that.' It was Abberline, newly promoted, from the corner.

Lestrade protested. 'I feel this ought to be classified, sir. Remember the Ripper case.'

'I do,' snapped McNaghten, squirming at the memory of it. 'That was an entirely different business. Please don't bring it up again.'

'You were saying, Lestrade.' Abberline was persistent. The Superintendent was crisp in his light-blue suit and sniffed his gardenia ostentatiously. Lestrade's look should have withered it and him on the spot. He contented himself with the realisation that promotion to the river police was no promotion at all. He must spend his time chasing foreign sailors and stinking dockers up and down the Ratcliff Highway.

'What I have, gentlemen, is this.' He ignored Gregson's snort and went on: 'The murders conform closely to a children's book of cautionary tales called *Struwwelpeter*. If I had time I would itemise them.'

'Spare us the quotations.' Jones had regained his smugness.

'Murder one. *Struwwelpeter*, or *Shock-headed Peter* himself. A middle-aged male found walled up, possibly alive, in Shanklin Chine, Isle of Wight. Still unidentified. Cause of death – asphyxia. Suspects . . .' He dried.

'Well?' McNaghten prompted.

'Alfred, Lord Tennyson.' Howls of derisive laughter.

'I thought he was dead, Lestrade,' said Abberline.

'He is certainly not sufficiently mobile for my purposes. But at the time he had access to the Chine out of season, when it was normally kept securely locked. Once I'd met him I was able to eliminate him from my inquiries. Subsequent inquiries produced no individuals. All I can say is that the murderer was someone who knew the Chine, had access to it and was probably a dab hand at cementing, by candlelight.'

More assorted snorts.

'The more I dwell on the Chine murder, sir,' addressing McNaghten, 'the more I believe the similarity to the *Struwwelpeter* stories was pure coincidence. It was widely reported in the papers. Anyone could have got hold of the idea.'

Abberline broke in. 'This . . . er . . . *Struwwelpeter*. Who wrote it?'

'A German doctor. Heinrich Hoffmann.'

'Well, he's your man. I've never trusted these krauts. Not since Sedan.'

Abberline had blundered nicely into that one. 'I checked him, Superintendent. He really is dead – seventeen years ago.'

Abberline suddenly found something of great interest in the end of his pipe. Gregson was quietly sniggering.

'The second murder. Victim – Lord Hurstmonceaux.'

'I thought that was a hunting accident,' commented Jones.

'The press deferred to the aristocracy. Lord Rosebery was a witness. Family scandal and all that.'

'Are we in the business of hushing up murder?' It was Jones's question but the look on McNaghten's face told him and everyone else that it was not his day. Lestrade remembered the Ripper File and smiled to himself.

'I know the cause of death – and how the murder was committed. Other than that, I drew a blank.'

'As usual,' grunted Jones. McNaghten reprimanded him.

'Murder three,' Lestrade went on, his jaw flexing, 'a seventeen-year-old girl, Harriet Wemyss, burned to death at her father's home at Wildboarclough, Cheshire. She burnt her clothes and person with a cigarette end. Her murderer knew that she had a secret smoking habit.'

'Tut,' broke in Gregson, 'the youth of today.'

'I believe her murderer encouraged the habit for several weeks, having planned this all along. And for the first time we have an eye-witness description. That of a travelling salesman who came to the house on the day of the murder. The same travelling salesman who, I have reason to believe, was Harriet's lover. He was described as a big man with a dark hat and a muffler.'

'Hardly conclusive,' grunted Abberline.

'Murder four. Or should I say, four, five and six. Three upper-middle-class layabouts – Edward Coke-Hythe, William Spender and Arthur Fitz. You may have come across them in the *Gazette*; they were bound over by the magistrate for baiting the visiting celebrity Atlanta Washington. I came across them in Battersea Park, painted with black enamel from head to foot.'

'You questioned Washington, of course,' said Abberline.

'I did, sir, and decided he was in the clear.'

'Other suspects?'

Lestrade hesitated. 'I traced the paint to the studio of Mr Lawrence Alma-Tadema' (he'd got it right again) 'the artist.'

'Lawrie?' McNaghten broke in. 'You didn't tell me that.'

'He's hardly a suspect in the conventional sense, sir. He told me the stuff had been stolen from him.'

'Well, of course,' agreed Jones.

'Certainly not,' snapped McNaghten. 'Lawrence Alma-Tadema is a very great friend of mine. Why, at one time or another, he has painted all my family. It is only modesty which forbids me hanging his portrait of myself and my lady wife over that mantelpiece.'

Jones shifted awkwardly in his seat. Today he was very definitely under the weather.

'It was at this point that I saw the connection between the letters. After each murder, or set of murders, I had been receiving, here at the Yard, unsigned mourning letters in the form of verse, each verse relating to the specific murder committed. All of them from *Struwwelpeter*.'

There was a silence. 'You mean' – Abberline was first to break it – 'some maniac is going round the country, finding victims to order just to fit in with a kiddies' rhyme? Fantastic! Stuff and nonsense!'

'The facts speak for themselves,' was Lestrade's levelling answer. 'The final murder occurred three weeks ago. A certain Albert Mauleverer, a resident of Warwickshire, found shot with a twelve-bore down a well near Guy's Cliffe in that county.'

'Who does all the murders in the book?' asked Gregson.

'Not all of them result in death. What they have in common is that they are moral or cautionary tales – not to play with matches, not to bait blacks or be cruel to animals and so on. In most of them, the perpetrator survives. In the Inky Boys story, the victims are turned black by a tall magician named Agrippa.'

'No, I'm sorry,' persisted Abberline, 'I just can't accept it.'

'You can't ignore it either,' said McNaghten. 'The fact is that so far the murders have fitted the book like a glove. It's uncanny. Funny,' he mused, 'to think that stories I used to read to my children should be taken so literally, used in such a sinister way.'

'What concerns me, sir, is the future. We are all of us, in this room, concerned with the prevention as well as the detection of crime. If the murderer runs true to form, there are five more to come. How are we to prevent it?'

McNaghten rested back in his chair. 'That's quite simple, Lestrade. Catch yourself a murderer.'

Ball of lightning

The season was nearly at an end. Lestrade should have taken a holiday late in August, but he could not. He had asked McNaghten for more men. At all costs he must keep the lid on things before the national press began to see the connection which was now all too apparent to the Yard. McNaghten could spare him two constables and a young, impressive detective-sergeant, John Forbes. Lestrade had to admit the man was smart, eager and resourceful – a sort of Bandicoot with a brain. But he could not bring himself to like him. He was too arrogant, to opinionated. Five years on the Force and rapid promotion under Gregson had given him airs and graces. Lestrade preferred well-tired police methods, documents filed in shoe boxes, the banal joviality of Bandicoot and the doe-like loyalty of Dew.

'I think we're dealing with terrorists, sir. Take my word for it. Anarchy is at the heart of this.'

'How long have you been under Gregson?'

'That's a malicious rumour, I . . . Oh, I see.' Forbes grinned rather painfully. 'I have served in the Special Irish Branch for three years.'

'And do you see terrorists under *every* bed?'

'That's not fair, sir. And if Inspector Gregson were here . . .'

'I would show him the door,' Lestrade finished the sentence for him. 'Tobias Gregson was never this much of a pain in the arse when he was with A division. He's become obsessive.'

'With respect, sir,' Bandicoot raised his curly head from a mountain of paper, 'the sergeant may have a point.'

Lestrade glared at his newest recruit through slitted eyes. 'All right, Forbes, and make it convincing. It'll need to be to persuade me we're looking for Irishmen and Russian sympathisers, bent double under the weight of their bombs.'

He slowly lit a cigar, pointing to the kettle as Dew entered the room under yet another pile of paper.

'Motive – anarchy,' Forbes began. 'To embarrass the British police. To cause such uproar in the peace-keeping forces of the nation that the people would rise up and overthrow existing order. It's happening in Europe, as we speak.'

'Looking around me,' Lestrade commented, drawing slowly on the cigar, 'I believe I was the only senior officer present at Bloody Sunday in 1887. I didn't see any Anarchists, Forbes. I saw starving women and children, people in rags and dirt. Dockers who worked one day a month. Girls who had been selling their bodies from the time they were eight. Women who hadn't seen a bed in weeks. I also saw the truncheons of the police, Forbes, and the bayonets of the Grenadier Guards. Don't talk to me about Anarchists.'

'They're scum . . . sir.'

Lestrade leaned on his desk, pointing his cigar like a finger.

'I don't like you, Forbes. I don't like ambitious policemen who get where they're going by climbing over people. I've listened to your theory and it smells. Until you can show me evidence and a suspect based on the facts of the case, keep your opinions to yourself.' He flicked his ash down Forbes's waistcoat. The younger man leapt to his feet, brushing himself down. He made for the door. 'And if you want to put in for a transfer back to Special Branch, remember to fill in the forms in triplicate.'

Lestrade caught the broad grins on the faces of Dew and Bandicoot as Forbes disappeared.

'Gentlemen, to work.'

It was the night of the Police Ball. A starry night, pink with the glow of the fires of the metropolis. It was the end of September, cool after a week of rain. Lestrade was late. Lestrade disliked unpunctuality, but he disliked the annual Police Ball even more. This year the Commissioner had excelled himself. The venue was the elite Metropole, shimmering with its polished glass and candelabra, the four ballrooms heavy with opulence and dazzling with chandeliers. He had also excelled himself, in Lestrade's opinion, in stupidity, by insisting that this be a fancy dress occasion. Lestrade, therefore, felt particularly ridiculous in his Harlequin outfit, but nonetheless hurt when he counted three others in the foyer alone. He hoped that the mask would conceal his embarrassment and hopefully his identity as well, but in the latter, alas, he was mistaken.

'Good evening, sir.' It was Bandicoot, burnt cork from head to foot, with a grass skirt and assegae.

'Bit tasteless after the Inky Boys, isn't it?' Lestrade snatched a passing glass of champagne.

'Sorry, sir, I hadn't thought of that.'

'No matter, with the exception of McNaghten, you and I will be the only ones to grasp the significance. Who's here?'

'Well, sir, I've just met an old school chum of mine, Ferdy Rothschild.'

'I didn't ask for a Burke's Peerage,' Lestrade snapped. Oh dear, he thought to himself, he was taking this evening worse than he thought he would. 'From the Force, man.'

'Ah, well, Inspector Gregson of course – over there – I think he's supposed to be Charles the Second, but he really hasn't the presence for it.'

'No,' murmured Lestrade, 'more like Nell Gwynne.'

'But I do like Inspector Jones's Julius Caesar. He's already tripped over his toga twice tonight.'

'After a few more of those he'll fall over his shadow.'

'Evening, Lestrade. Good God, who's this?' Superintendent Abberline breathed champagne over the native gentleman.

'Good evening. This is Constable Bandicoot, my assistant.'

'Constable?' Abberline shepherded Lestrade away. 'Look here, old man, one doesn't want to pull rank at all, but a constable at the Ball. It isn't done. Have him wait with your horses.'

'I don't have any horses,' Lestrade replied. 'And, anyway, he is an Old Etonian.'

Abberline paused. His artfully painted clown's eyebrow disappeared under his orange hair. 'Ah well, I suppose . . .

Well, keep him out of the way. I hear we're expecting a Very Important Guest tonight.'

'Mrs Abberline?' Lestrade suggested archly, glancing in the direction of the ravishing young creature now in flirtatious conversation with Bandicoot. Abberline spluttered on his champagne. 'Where? Oh, I see, er . . . This is my . . . er . . . niece, Miss Hartlepool.'

'Ma'am.' Lestrade gave a stiff unHarlequin-like bow and Abberline whisked the girl away. 'Ha, ha, keep your wits about you, Bandicoot. Tonight could be more fun than I thought.'

Lestrade and Bandicoot began to work their way through the vast buffet supper, the inspector tending to follow the lead of the younger man in the hope that Bandicoot's breeding would enable him to make sense of the obscure French terms and to identify the multifarious delights on the table. Lestrade was happy enough with the cooked meats and roasts and even vaguely recognised escargots, but there were things there in aspic he'd only seen on mortuary slabs. Surprisingly, it was all beautifully edible.

He was just moving out of earshot of the Cannon Row and District Band when he noticed the McNaghten entourage enter by the far door. The redoubtable Miss McNaghten, eldest of his boss's crew, was with them and Lestrade felt the usual impulse to bolt for the terrace. But he had fled from her in Bandicoot's presence before – time to stand his ground. And, as a trombone slide whizzed past his ear, to face the music.

'Inspector Lestrade, isn't it?'

Lestrade recognised the public voice and the apparent distance.

'Ah, Miss McNaghten. I'm surprised you knew me in the mask.'

By now the daughter of the Head of the Criminal Investigation Department was close to him. 'Sholto, my dear, I'd know you anywhere. Oh, you poor darling, what happened to your face?'

'Oh, I walked into a plate-glass window in Cambridge.'

'Tut, tut. And what were you doing there, chasing the blue-stockings?'

'You know there is no one in my life but you, Arabella.'

For a moment, a hint of sadness flickered across Miss McNaghten's face, then the public face was visible again. 'You cad, Sholto. I don't believe a word of it.' She flipped him roundly with her fan. It would have broken the jaw of a weaker man. 'Shall we dance? I love the gallop.'

'Has no one ever told you, gentlemen are supposed to ask ladies to dance?'

'I haven't all night, Sholto dearest. It's nearly half past nine. Besides, I'm nearly twenty-eight. Mama tells all her friends I'm on the shelf. Time I rectified that. How do you like my Marie Antoinette?'

'Where am I supposed to be looking?'

'Oh, you naughty man. Keep your mind on the job. Which reminds me, what are you working on?'

'Arabella, you know I can't –' he was whisked away by a gawky girl he vaguely recognised as old Inspector Beck's youngest. She was having great difficulty galloping in her mermaid's tail and also in keeping her long wig plaits stuck to her breasts, covered in pink body-stocking though they were . . . '– divulge anything of that nature,' he called as Arabella swept past him in a glitter of sequins and lace. Lestrade had to admit that the redoubtable Arabella McNaghten did look surprisingly ravishing. Perhaps it was the white powdered wig, the low-cut bodice, the incandescence of the light. Or perhaps it was merely the champagne.

'Oh, come, Sholto, don't disappoint me. You know Papa doesn't tell me a thing. Is it a murder?'

'Arabella, I am not at liberty to . . .'

'Oh, Sholto, that's what I love most about you, your sense of duty. Not to mention that fetching little moustache.'

It was Lestrade's turn to tap Miss McNaghten's hand away before new partners swept them apart. The dance at last came to an end and Lestrade seized the opportunity to palm his boss's daughter off on Bandicoot. After all, they had met and Bandicoot was rather more Arabella's size. The lozenged inspector deftly extricated himself and rather furtively slid around a marble pillar and out of sight.

'I still think we're looking for international terrorists, sir.' Sergeant Forbes tried to look casual in the orange hair of an orangutang. 'Mind you, if their game is to embarrass the police, they need only to turn up here tonight and take a few photographs.'

'That's the Commissioner for you,' commented Lestrade. 'And you're still wrong. I'm thinking of working on a new tack now.'

'May I know?'

Lestrade checked that the coast was clear as though he were about to burgle a house.

'If you wanted to murder someone, Forbes, how would you do it?'

'Well, I'd . . . I haven't been long in homicide, sir. I'd need time to think.'

'Come on, man, this isn't a board examination. Try a method.'

'Poison,' said Forbes.

'Too easily traced. Where would you buy it? How much? What type?'

Forbes looked flustered.

'No, Forbes. Poison is risky. Long range, I'll grant you. Ah, good evening Doctor Cream,' Lestrade raised his glass to a medical acquaintance who was waltzing nearby. 'Where did he find *her*?' he muttered to Forbes, 'a Hyde Park girl if ever I've seen one.'

'Riff-raff,' was Forbes's stereotypical comment.

'It gives you an alibi,' Lestrade went on. 'Administer some poison in Winchester, you could be in Dundee before it worked. But it's too hit and miss. Too risky by far.'

'Gun, then. A shot through the head.'

'At point blank range, yes. Any further away and you might miss. But at point blank range, chances are you'd be covered in your victim's blood. And what about the noise? If you killed your man in a house, there would be other occupants, neighbours, itinerant pedlars with your luck. Always assuming you owned or had access to firearms, of course.'

'Well, I don't know,' Forbes snapped. He had the distinct impression he was being baited.

'Keep your fur on, Forbes. There is no safe way to murder. But there is a pattern. A poisoner always poisons. Goodnight,

Doctor Cream,' he called. 'Take William Palmer, the Rugeley poisoner in the '50s.'

'A little before my time,' said Forbes smugly.

'And mine, Forbes, and mine,' Lestrade was at pains to point out to him. 'But the *Struwwelpeter* murderer has killed several times and with the exception of three identical methods in the Inky Boys case, because the plot, as it were, called for it, we have death by asphyxia, walling up alive; death by burning; death by asphyxia, but by the totally different method of painting the skin; death by training a pack of hounds; and death by shotgun. Not necessarily in that order.'

'I am aware, sir. What is your point?'

'That chummy is damned clever, very versatile and . . . and this is where my thinking is really taking me – that our man is intent on killing *one* victim. Someone he wants dead, out of his way, for reasons or reason unknown. The others are red herrings, deliberately to put us off the scent.'

'Good God, Inspector.' Forbes swigged his drink. 'But if that is so, which is which?'

'That,' said Lestrade, exchanging his empty glass for a full one, 'is what we shall endeavour to find out. Tomorrow morning, you and I are going to start requestioning the next of kin of the victims. I shall start with Mrs Mauleverer.'

'Any reason?' asked Forbes archly.

Lestrade looked at him with disdain. 'She has better legs than Lawrence Alma-Tadema.' He'd got it right again. It must be the champagne.

In another corner of the ballroom, much later, Lestrade propped himself up against a handy rail. He had had just a little too much of the bubbly and Melville McNaghten's banal conversation was sending him gradually to sleep. Only the gold braid on the Commissioner's shoulder kept winking at him in the candlelight, keeping him awake.

'Arabella must be such a comfort to you, Lady McNaghten,' some faceless boot-licker was saying.

'Indeed she is,' crowed Mama, 'but she's a dutiful niece too. She's always visiting her aunts and uncles. It's one of the duties

– and blessings – of a large family. It's so nice to see you dancing together, you young things.'

A nudge in Lestrade's shoulder informed him that Lady McNaghten was talking to him.

'Enchanted, ma'am,' he said, raising his glass a little faintly, appalled to realise that Arabella's mother had seen them together, perhaps even, horror of horrors, 'linked their names romantically', as such mothers always do. Luckily for Lestrade, the band suddenly struck up the National Anthem.

'He's here,' the Commissioner was heard to cry, flinging his wife to a lackey and making a beeline for the main staircase. Those who were seated, rose and it dawned, with differing degrees of sobriety, on all of them who the surprise guest of honour was. In fact, there were eight of them, but the two at the head were the best known. The first was a balding, bearded man with poppy eyes, his immense girth somehow tucked into the elaborate mess dress of a colonel of the 10th Hussars. It was 'Bertie', the Prince of Wales. Behind him, younger, taller, slimmer, with a long neck and thin moustache, but the same uniform and poppy eyes, stood his son, Prince Albert Victor Christian Edward, the Duke of Clarence.

'Good God,' Lestrade hissed to himself, 'they've let him out.'

'No ceremony, no ceremony,' the Prince was saying. 'Sorry, gentlemen, to come unannounced. And indeed, out of costume. Another beastly regimental dinner. Couldn't turn up at the Mess in a Guy Fawkes suit, what?'

The assembly shook with laughter at the inane remark. Lestrade caught McNaghten's face as he watched the Duke of Clarence, every move registering itself. In that immense room, in that august gathering, only two men knew the significance. The name of Eddy, the heir presumptive to the throne, the Duke of Clarence, old 'Collars and Cuffs', was not just associated with homosexual brothels in Cleveland Street. His name should also have been on McNaghten's Ripper File. McNaghten knew it. Lestrade knew it. Eddy rarely appeared in public, but here he was in the middle of Scotland Yard's finest. There was a horrible irony.

Lestrade relaxed a little as Eddy was introduced to various

dignitaries. He appeared to be normal, polite, suave, if a little stupid. Lestrade chuckled as Eddy was introduced to McNaghten himself and he watched the Head of the Criminal Investigation Department straighten out the cravat, which, by virtue of his suit of armour, he wasn't wearing. His gauntlets rattled ridiculously on his beaver and he escaped into the refuge of the Dashing White Sergeant with the nearest woman.

'Remember, Eddy,' Lestrade heard the Prince say as he joined in the revels, alcohol having lightened his lead feet, 'the Tenth don't dance.'

'Quite so, Father.' Eddy sulked in a corner for the rest of the evening.

The storm arose when Lestrade had been out on the terrace for some minutes. The night air was cool and there was no rain at first. He puffed gratefully at his cigar and rubbed his nose where the mask had been chafing. Now and then, a flash of lightning lit the terrace and the shrubbery beyond. He caught the wandering forms of patrolling constables. All was well, all was calm. But he had a murderer on his hands. And so far, all efforts to catch him had failed.

'Oh, ho, Harlequin.' Lestrade spun round. A large bearded officer of the Hussars emerged into the lightning flash.

'Your Royal Highness.' Lestrade bowed.

'Glorious night,' said the Prince. 'Rain soon, I shouldn't wonder.'

'Quite so, sir.'

'Who are you?'

'Inspector Sholto Lestrade, Your Highness, Scotland Yard.'

'Ah, one of McNaghten's detectives, eh?'

'Yes, sir.'

'Good. Good. Got a light?'

'One thing Hussar uniforms and Harlequin costumes have in common, sir, is that they have no pockets. I got my cigar from a subordinate.'

'Quite right,' roared the Prince, 'that's where I got mine from too.'

'Would it be too presumptuous of me, sir?' Lestrade offered his cigar.

'No. Damned civil. I've been longing for a smoke for hours.' The Prince of Wales puffed heartily on his own cigar, pressed end to end with Lestrade's. He blew rings into the air with undying gratitude. 'Mama – that's the Queen you know – doesn't really approve of my smoking. Silly, isn't it, Inspector? I'm fifty years old and I still care what my mother thinks. Do you have a mother?'

'It happens to us all, sir.'

'Yes, yes, quite. Now tell me, I have a taste for the lurid. What case are you working on at the moment?'

'I'm sorry, sir, I cannot divulge, even to the heir to the throne . . .'

'Oh, balderdash, Lestrade. I know about Freddie Hurstmonceux, and a little bird tells me there were others in the series, as it were. It's not generally known that I am something of a sleuth myself. Perhaps I can help.'

Lestrade began to feel uneasy. The bushes below him were illuminated with lightning. 'May I ask the source of your information, sir?'

'Freddie Hurstmonceux from Rosebery. The business rattled him a great deal. He's sweating on Mama giving him a Garter, you know. He's prepared to do a lot of talking at the moment – in the right quarter, you understand.'

'And the others?'

'So there are others?'

Lestrade realised he had been caught out.

'Very clever, Your Royal Highness.'

The Prince chuckled. 'Yes, I thought so. No, actually, I wasn't, what's the phrase . . . fishing. You're not telling me anything new, merely confirming it. I'm afraid I can't tell you any more. It would be betraying a confidence.'

'Then you understand, sir, that I must be equally discreet.'

'Oh, you disappoint me, Inspector. A man without a mother must be a totally free agent.'

Before Lestrade could answer, they were joined on the terrace by a bevy of officers from the Tenth.

'I hope you are not checking up on me, gentlemen,' grumbled

the Prince. The company dutifully chuckled. 'Onslaught.' He summoned a young lieutenant to his side, 'Inspector Lestrade, this is Henry Onslow, my son's A.D.C. He has allowed my boy to escape him. The least he can do is to get you a drink. I have detained you long enough.'

Lestrade was grateful for the escape clause and returned with the lieutenant to the main ballroom. It seemed of little moment to the Prince that Eddy had given his watchdog the slip, but to Lestrade, it meant more. It meant more still when he saw his quarry in earnest conversation with a shapely raven-haired beauty at the far corner of the room. His arm was resting firmly against a pillar as if blocking her line of escape into the room. Two other things quickened Lestrade's step as he snatched a passing champagne glass and made for the couple. One was that the young lady was Constance Mauleverer, the other was that McNaghten had good reason to believe the man was Jack the Ripper. It was irrational, perhaps, of Lestrade to behave as he did, chivalrous to the point of folly. First he shoulder-barged the Duke of Clarence with something more than necessary force and then he poured champagne over his jacket with a scarcely concealed tip.

'Dolt!' The Duke was not pleased.

'My apologies, sir. Your gold lace blinded me.'

'Liar!' The volume was such that guests in their finery stopped waltzing to stare at the ugly scene developing.

'Mrs Mauleverer, isn't it?' Lestrade was attempting to change the subject. She smiled as the inspector kissed her hand. He was jerked upright by a strong right hand. For a split-second Lestrade glanced at the gloved fingers on his sleeve. If McNaghten were right, either of those hands had the power of life and death. The large eyes bulged and flashed. 'You have insulted me, Harlequin. Choose your weapons.'

'My dear Duke,' Mrs Mauleverer intervened, 'I'm sure that Inspector Lestrade meant no harm.'

Clarence checked himself a little. 'Inspector. So you're a policeman.'

'Most of us are, sir. This is a police ball.'

'And my father and I are guests of honour.'

'Well, your father is.'

'Damn you, Lestrade. You've insulted me again.'

By now three or four officers of the Tenth had joined them. 'I will have satisfaction.' This was delivered at such a pitch that the band began to waver. When Clarence's left hand snaked out and caught Lestrade across the face, it stopped altogether. 'My second will call on you.'

Lestrade recovered his composure although Mrs Mauleverer pressed his arm in a silent plea for restraint. 'If you are challenging me to a duel, sir, you are some decades too late. Duelling has been illegal in this country since Thornton and Ashford.'

Simultaneously, the silence was broken by two shouts, both harsh and guttural, both acutely embarrassed. One, from the Prince of Wales, 'Eddy!' The other, from McNaghten, 'Lestrade!' Both men reached the quarrelsome pair simultaneously. 'Lestrade, you will apologise to His Highness immediately.'

'I already have,' said Lestrade, unperturbed.

'Eddy, it is time we were away.' The Prince and his entourage bustled Clarence towards the door, Eddy scowling and muttering the while. The band struck up the National Anthem discordantly. McNaghten whisked Lestrade into an ante-chamber and proceeded to lecture him on the need for protocol and not upsetting Royalty.

One of many witnesses to the scene, Sergeant Forbes, was chuckling helplessly in a corner. Bandicoot was straight-faced and sober.

'Come on, Constable. Your inspector's had it. He's cooked his goose good and proper.'

'I don't care for your homespun smugness, Sergeant. The inspector always has his reasons.'

'Oh, good God, Bandicoot. I didn't think they made sycophantic policemen any more. If you want a *real* boss, go to Gregson, transfer to Special Branch.'

'I'm happy with Lestrade.'

'You'll never learn, will you. Waiter . . .' Forbes snapped his fingers and helped himself. As the ballroom returned to normal, Forbes spotted another target for his razor wit.

'Isn't that Sherlock Holmes?'

'I believe it is the Great Detective.'

Forbes looked heavenward.

'God, Bandicoot, there you go again. Toadying.'

'Steady, Sergeant. That's a little harsh.'

'Look at them. Holmes and Watson, like a bloody music-hall double act.'

'Excuse me, Sergeant Forbes, I think I'd prefer the conversation of the double act.' Bandicoot crossed the floor to Holmes, decked out like an Egyptian Pharoah. Watson had discarded the gorilla mask by this time as it was too difficult to get the champagne past the rubber lips.

'Hello, Banders, old boy. Didn't think you'd be here,' said Watson. 'Holmes, have you met Harry Bandicoot? Old Etonian, friend of my nephew, Edward.'

'Ah, yes.' Holmes suddenly came alive. 'The Atlanta Washington case. I read in what Fleet Street laughingly calls the newspapers that your Lord and Master, Lestrade, let him go.'

'I believe that was because he was innocent, Mr Holmes.'

Holmes shook his black wig tragically. 'What a pity. There seems to be no improvement in these Scotland Yard fellows. But then,' archly to Watson, 'he is a friend of *your* family.'

'I wanted to ask you, sir, if I may, about the . . .'

'Watson will answer any questions. I don't discuss my cases in public. God, Watson, why ever did I allow you to talk me into coming to this charade? I feel ridiculous.'

'Oh, I don't know, Holmes. It's difficult to tell you from Rameses himself.'

Holmes flicked up his flowing robes and swept majestically towards the ante-rooms. 'Bring your bag, Watson.'

The doctor's normally jovial moustaches drooped somewhat. He patted Bandicoot on the arm and followed the Great Detective. The constable saw Lestrade cross the hall in the opposite direction.

'You'll need a second, Inspector,' he said, intercepting him.

Lestrade looked at him hard. 'You don't imagine I'm going to fight that royal buffoon, do you?'

'If you were an Etonian, sir, you'd have no choice.'

'Where's Mrs Mauleverer?' asked Lestrade.

'I haven't seen her, sir. But Sergeant Forbes seems to be . . . er . . . looking after Miss McNaghten for you.'

Forbes was standing embarrassingly near the daughter of the Head of the Criminal Investigation Department. She seemed not to be displeased by it. 'Are you going to barge into him too?'

Lestrade flashed anger at Bandicoot. It had not been his night. 'Miss McNaghten can take care of herself.' And he moved to the door. A gloved hand caught his arm. 'Sholto.' It was Constance Mauleverer. Lestrade glanced behind him. Both Forbes and Arabella McNaghten had noticed. Bandicoot tactfully faded into the background.

'Sholto, what's happening? You can't fight the heir to the throne, especially over me. Why did you insult him?'

'I can't tell you, Constance.'

'You won't go through with it?'

'Of course not. Constance . . . I didn't think I'd see you again. Especially here.'

'I came with my uncle, John Watson.'

'Watson? Doctor Watson?'

'Yes, do you know him?'

Lestrade laughed. 'Indeed. Don't you read the rubbish that he and Conan Doyle cook up between them? One day I'll sue them both.'

'*You* are in Uncle John's short stories?'

'Some of them. Dear lady, I am cut to the quick. Not that my "appearances" are very flattering. Mr McNaghten is far from pleased that Scotland Yard detectives are held to ridicule and scorn.'

'Sholto.' Constance was suddenly serious. 'I hate to bring this up, but are you any nearer to finding my husband's murderer?'

Lestrade looked hard into the dark eyes of this woman who had captivated him. 'I didn't know John Watson was your uncle.'

'I don't understand.'

'You didn't know his nephew was murdered recently?'

'Edward Coke-Hythe. Of course, he was my cousin.'

'Why didn't you tell me?'

'I didn't think it necessary . . . You mean the two are connected?'

'I don't know, Constance. But I do know that most people have no connection with murder at all. You have a connection with two. You are a dangerous woman to know.'

'Am I accused, then?'

'Ma'am, I never arrest ladies at police balls.' Lestrade kissed her hand. He led her on to the steps of the hotel amid leaving guests. Suddenly, a deputation of Hussars stood before them. Onslow stepped forward.

'Inspector Lestrade, I am instructed by His Royal Highness the Duke of Clarence to offer you choice of time and place to settle this affair of honour.'

'Affair of . . . oh yes, of course.'

'Sholto.'

'No, Constance. This won't take long. Dawn, gentlemen. That gives us three hours or so. Time enough to get to the Headless Chicken at Highgate.'

Onslow saluted briskly. 'Very well, sir. His Highness chooses sabres.'

Lestrade thought of the débâcle of his constable days struggling through cutlass drill.

'Naturally,' he smiled.

Onslow and his party departed.

'Sholto.' Constance took the Harlequin's hand. 'He'll kill you.'

'Over my dead body, Constance,' smiled Lestrade.

Duels

True to the spirit of melodrama and Gothic novels, a chill mist swirled around the gravestones of Highgate cemetery. Two parties emerged through the wet greyness of the dawn, walking in parallel down the overhung greenness of Swain's Lane. To the left walked His Royal Highness, the Duke of Clarence, in the patrol jacket and forage cap of the 10th Hussars. Behind him, draped with cloaks and rattling with spurs and accoutrements, four of his brother-officers, grim-faced and moustachioed. To the right, arm in arm against the chill of the morning, Inspector Lestrade, wrapped in his Donegal, and Mrs Mauleverer in a velvet walking-out dress. Behind them, crisp in morning coat and non-regulation bowler, Harry Bandicoot, and, in his one and only suit, Walter Dew, constables of Scotland Yard. It made a faintly ludicrous and extremely unlikely picture. It was the morning of September 16th, 1891. It was the modern world. But one man was not going to walk away.

The officers of the law took their positions at the gates of the Egyptian Avenue. The Hussars tramped to the top. There was an awkward pause and then two of them came down to the centre.

'Sholto, do you read Sir Walter Scott?'

'Alas, no, Constance.'

'If you did, you would know that knights in the Courtly Age carried a lady's favour when they fought. Please, wear this for me now.' She tied her silk scarf around his neck. He held her hand briefly.

'I think they're waiting for us, sir,' said Bandicoot.

Lestrade turned to him. 'Bandicoot. Dew. Neither of you

should be here. You are officers of the law. You should both know better. Bad enough if I'm caught in this nonsense, but you two . . .'

'You need a second, sir,' Bandicoot broke in. 'Who will hold your coat?'

Lestrade allowed himself a smile for an instant. 'Very well, but Mrs Mauleverer should not be here. Dew, escort the lady back to the Headless Chicken. Inside the carriage, please.'

'I've come this far, Sholto. I'll stay with you a while longer. And besides' – in a stronger voice – 'you wouldn't order Constable Dew away at a time like this.'

'So be it.' Lestrade grinned. He threw his Donegal to Bandicoot and stripped to his shirtsleeves. The two men walked uphill to where Clarence and Onslow waited. To their surprise, it was Onslow who took off his cloak and jacket, rolling up his sleeves.

'Etiquette demands that I cannot fight you, Lestrade,' Clarence delivered haughtily. 'I am after all the heir to the throne. Besides' – he produced a handkerchief – 'I have a cold coming. I trust Lieutenant Onslow will do as my substitute?'

Lestrade bowed.

'Rather a sacrilegious choice, this place of yours, I must say,' the Duke remarked.

'It'll save the cost of burial,' quipped Lestrade, 'for one of us.'

Clarence drew a cloak from two cavalry sabres lying across his arm. Bandicoot, with his Etonian grasp of these matters, inspected both carefully and nodded. Lestrade took one and turned to take up his position. The sabre was a good foot longer than the cutlass he remembered and he had forgotten how damned heavy the thing was. He took his cue from Onslow, who bent his knees and assumed the 'en garde' position, having saluted Lestrade with his sword. On one side, Clarence drew his sabre and on the other Bandicoot held the points of all three blades together.

'What now?' Lestrade broke the silence, unable to take the while thing seriously. 'Do we all pirouette to the right?'

Clarence scythed his blade upward and Bandicoot sprang back. For a second which seemed to Constance an eternity, nobody moved, then Onslow swept forward, his blade licking in over Lestrade's guard to find his arm. The white sleeve darkened red and Constance started forward, checking herself before Dew had a chance to restrain her. Onslow straightened up, saluting.

'Sir,' he said to Clarence. Lestrade felt dizzy and not a little sick. There was a numbness in his left elbow.

'Again,' Clarence sneered.

Bandicoot cut in. 'By all the rules of duelling, sir, even among the less salubrious schlagers of German universities, first blood is sufficient.'

'I will decide what is sufficient. Onslow, again.'

Onslow saluted again and came to the ready. Yards away, Dew gripped Constance's arm. Silently her heart went out to Lestrade, left arm hanging useless, facing a professional swordsman again. Onslow's attack was slower this time and Lestrade banged it aside.

'You're not trying, Onslow. I want him taught a lesson.'

Onslow's pace increased. His feet slid forward, faster, faster, his blade circling Lestrade's, inches from the inspector's body. Lestrade was retreating, trying to keep in step as best he could. He could hear words of encouragement from Bandicoot on his right. Further away the shouts of the Hussars and the angry yells of Clarence. The family vaults in their granite silence swept by him, but all he could see was that flashing, probing blade and Onslow's sweating face behind it. Desperately he parried and cut, using two hands once when he felt his back against an Egyptian column. Onslow's sword crunched inches from Lestrade's face. He ducked under his arm and caught him high in the ribs, purpling the white shirt. He dropped to his knees, fighting for breath. Onslow staggered back against a vault.

'That's it,' Lestrade rasped to Clarence, 'no more. No more.'

'Damn you, Lestrade. You're not cutting up one of my officers and getting away with it. Onslow, can you stand?'

The lieutenant somehow came to attention.

'Then get on with it.'

Lestrade flinched as the sabre flashed past his face, slicing off the very tip of his nose. He lunged from the ground and grazed Onslow's thigh.

'You boys, stop that!' All eyes turned to the distant voice. At the top of the slope, beyond the knot of officers, silhouetted against the dawn sky stood a lone figure. The outline presented an immediate problem. It wore a Hussar busby and presented a generally military outline, but apparently wore a skirt as well, and was leaning against a bicycle.

'God, it's the Colonel,' whispered one of the officers.

For a fleeting second Clarence toyed with the notion of its being his formidable Grandmama in one of her unused Colonel-in-Chief's uniforms. But the preposterousness of the idea banished it from his mind. With astonishing presence of mind, Bandicoot threw Lestrade's Donegal over both sabre blades and the combatants, sweating and bloody, tried to look as nonchalant as possible, as though it were the most natural thing in the world for two men to be in Highgate Cemetery this early in the morning, bleeding from sabre wounds.

The intruder leapt on to the saddle of the bicycle and scattered the Hussar officers, who sprang back in amazement. The figure screeched to a halt in the centre of the duelling ground. All parties present stared in astonishment. Before them stood an elderly lady, with grotesque theatrical make-up, in the heavily braided fur-edged pelisse and tall busby, complete with lines and plume, of the 11th Prince Albert's Own Hussars.

'Ah, I know you, my boy.' She pointed an imperious finger at Clarence, 'You're Eddy aren't you? Oh, I haven't been allowed at court for years. Your grandmother never forgave James for marrying me. But I keep abreast of court gossip, you know. "Collars and Cuffs", eh? Yes, I see it. Besides, you've got your father's poppy eyes.'

'Madam, I don't know from which asylum you have escaped, but I strongly suggest . . .'

'Come, sir,' one of the Hussars intervened, 'shouldn't we be away?'

Reluctantly Clarence was led towards the main gates and the hill where the carriages awaited. As he left, Onslow shook hands with Lestrade.

'If you ever tire of the Force, sir, we'd be proud to have you in the Tenth Hussars.'

Constance wrapped the Donegal around Lestrade's shoulders, dabbing the blood from his mouth, and chin. Her eyes were wet and hot. 'Your colour, my lady.' Lestrade managed an uncharacteristic flamboyant flourish, removing the scarf.

'Come on, you need help,' announced the old Hussar lady. 'You, young man' – this to Bandicoot – 'take my bicycle and go on ahead. I've a private retreat nearby at the top of the hill. It's called Quorn. Tell them to prepare a room –' she glanced at Constance '– for two.'

There were silent protests all round, but between them the ladies helped Lestrade, dizzy from loss of blood, to the gate. Dew walked paces behind, anxiously peering through the lightening day for signs of coppers on their beat. To meet a constable in the pursuit of his duty would have been singularly unfortunate.

Lestrade fell into a fitful sleep. His head throbbed, his arm hurt, his nose was indescribable. But he had survived a duel and fell asleep holding the hand of a woman who had certainly become very important to him. It was not until he awoke that he began to take stock of the situation. The room in which he lay was pleasant enough, typically upper-middle-class, hung with mementoes of an earlier age. From somewhere he heard a clock strike – four. The blinds were drawn but it was daylight outside. Four in the afternoon. God, he was on duty in an hour. Time he roused himself.

'Sholto.' Constance swept noiselessly into the room. 'You shouldn't be getting up yet, dearest.' Lestrade realised the wisdom of her remark when he sat upright. His left arm was very stiff and his nose felt as if it reached the far wall.

'What time is it?' he asked.

'Just gone four. Shall I ring for tea? Lady Cardigan's staff are most obliging.'

'Cardigan? Oh, I see. That accounts for the uniform.'

'Yes, my dear. I've talked a great deal with her in the last two days. Ever since her husband, the seventh Earl, died, she has worn his uniform when in public. It somehow eases the pain of his going. Oh, he had a full life and she knew only too well that he was not exactly faithful, but they were fond in their own way. She took up bicycling a few years ago. She bicycles everywhere.' Constance chuckled. 'Even, it seems, around the colonnade in Highgate Cemetery.'

'Two days?' Lestrade stood up suddenly and immediately wished he hadn't. 'Good God, woman, have I been here for two days?'

'Calm yourself, Sholto. I am not used to being referred to as "woman", especially by a man I hardly know.' She was smiling tauntingly at him.

'I'm sorry, Constance. Good God, woman, here I am in my combinations at four o'clock in the afternoon and here you are, a recently widowed lady, in the house of a mad, old eccentric who . . .'

'That's less than kind, Sholto. Lady Cardigan is certainly eccentric, but she has placed her London home and its staff completely at our disposal. She has returned to Deene, her country home. She finds London a frightful bore now the season has ended. Anyway, I didn't know you were such a prude. This is 1891, you know. I have heard the new decade will be known as the "naughty nineties". Wouldn't you like to be just a little bit naughty with me?'

'Madam, you miss the point. I fought the duel on the morning of Saturday the sixteenth. What day is it today?'

'Tuesday the nineteenth.'

'Exactly. I have missed one turn of duty and am about to miss a second.'

'Bandicoot has reported you down with influenza, dearest. There's a lot of it about. No one will query your absence. Aren't you allowed to be ill in the Metropolitan Police?'

'In H Division, no.' Lestrade sat back heavily on the bed. He was beaten, he realised that. The thought of a cab or train ride to his lodgings and then to a pile of paperwork at the Yard did not appeal. Still less did applying his mind to the *Struwwelpeter* case. And before him, in the semi-darkness of the room sat the most beautiful woman he had ever seen. He looked at her smiling face, warm and soft. He reached out his good arm and ran his fingers round the smooth curve of her cheek. She pressed her head into the palm of his hand and kissed the fingers. Lestrade took her head with both hands and kissed her forehead lightly.

'I'm not going to break, Sholto,' she said, and their lips found each others in the darkness. It was not the most romantic love-making on record. Sholto Lestrade had never been a lady's man, until now. He was no novice, of course, but certainly a little rusty and most of his muscles had been put to the test too recently for this to be easy for him. Constance was of course no virgin, but despite her outward forwardness, she was still a woman of her times and the new decade was still too new to sweep away the time-honoured traditions of a lifetime.

The second time was better, however: both of them relaxed. It was nearly midnight before Constance lay curled up in Lestrade's arms, nuzzling her raven hair against his chest.

'Tell me about "Shock-headed Peter",' she whispered.

Lestrade shifted uneasily. 'At a time like this?' he asked.

'Sholto, you could have been killed two days ago. My husband and my cousin are dead already. This may not be the time. But it may be the only time. You will return to your beloved Yard tomorrow or the next day. I must go home to Warwickshire.'

He turned her head to him. 'What if I want you to stay?' he asked her.

She took his hand, squeezing it hard. 'You are a policeman, an Inspector of Detectives. I am a widowed lady with modest means and no future. We don't suit, Sholto. We wouldn't fit.'

'You once told me you didn't give a damn about convention,' Lestrade reminded her.

'I didn't think I did,' she answered. 'With another man, another time, I might not. But tell me, what would happen if your superiors found out that you were here and that I was here with you?'

Lestrade chuckled. 'I'd have another drubbing down from Sir Melville, then there would be a brief inquiry and I'd be kicked out of the Force. Your name would probably be dragged through the mud, though they wouldn't get it from me and they'd probably board this place up as a bawdy house and arrest Lady Cardigan as a brothel-keeper. The Commissioner's a stickler for the morals of his men.'

'Exactly. That's not a bright future for either of us, is it?'

He began to say something, but she stopped him with a kiss.

'How did you know about *Shock-headed Peter*?' he asked her afterwards.

'It was just something I overheard at the Ball. An orangutang was talking very confidentially to Marie Antoinette, I believe.'

'Oh, God, Arabella McNaghten wheedled it out of Forbes. I'll kill him.'

'Oh, Sholto, is it that secret? Isn't she the daughter of the Head of your . . . what do you call it, S.I.D.?'

'C.I.D. That doesn't matter. Regulations are very clear. All cases are classified information. They must not be divulged to any member of the public. Forbes knew that. I'll have that bastard . . . begging your pardon, my dear . . . I'll have that bastard back on the street for this.'

'Sholto,' she turned in the bed, pressing her naked thigh against his. 'You mean you aren't going to tell me anything about the case?'

She caressed Lestrade between the legs, her fingers sliding lightly at first, then harder as he rose to the occasion. 'Stop it, Constance,' he shouted hysterically, 'I'm too ticklish.'

For a while, as he travelled back to the Yard, Lestrade let his mind wander over the leave-taking. She said she was going. Back to Warwickshire. To sell the house. To move away. To begin again, without memories, without heartache. Change her name, perhaps. Go somewhere where no one knew about Albert Mauleverer, where Struwwelpeter with his sad cheeks was simply a child's fairy tale, not some sinister, ghastly reality. Lestrade had shaken his head as he held her hands. He had felt an iron lump in his throat. He was not a man of words. He was not a troubadour from one of Walter Scott's novels. He was not as silver-tongued as he wanted to be for Constance. 'I'll find you,' was all he had said. 'When this case is over, I'll find you.' Then it was her turn to shake her head. She did not cry. Her voice remained strong, her smile as dark and deep as ever. Lestrade had cried, inside, alone, but he was a hard-bitten copper and he betrayed no emotion at all. At least he hoped he hadn't.

Despite all this whirling in his brain, the atmosphere at the Yard was tangible. He noticed that in his brief absence, the scaffolding had been removed and that the new quarters gleamed in the afternoon sun that flashed on the river. But the place was like a morgue. A grim, silent desk-sergeant saluted him. He entered the lift with two ashen-faced detectives from Gregson's division.

'Sir Melville would like to see you, sir,' said Constable Dew as Lestrade reached his office. There was no cheery greeting, no cup of tea, no inquiry into the inspector's health. Lestrade knocked on the veneered door. A growl told him to go in.

McNaghten looked ten years older. Lestrade suddenly saw his whole career flash before him. Someone, Lady Cardigan perhaps, regretting her kindness, or Clarence, in a fit of pique, had shopped him. He even felt himself reaching into his pocket to hand over handcuffs and whistle.

'Forbes is dead,' McNaghten told him.

'Forbes?' Lestrade repeated.

'Dead. Gangland slaying. His body was found in an alley off The Minories this morning. I sent constables. Where the hell were you?'

'Er . . . recuperating.' No point in giving the game away now. There was nothing to be gained by it.

'I don't like it, Lestrade.' McNaghten was rubbing his moustaches repeatedly, smoothing the cravat every third or fourth rub. 'When a policeman is killed in the execution of his duty. I don't like it at all.'

'But what was he doing in The Minories, sir? He was supposed to be on the *Struwwelpeter* case. All my men are.'

'According to Bandicoot he'd had a tip-off. A nark, I suppose, told him to go to The Minories at midnight last night.'

'And he went alone?'

'Good God, Lestrade, you and I have done it dozens of times.' Lestrade laughed inwardly. He knew he had, but doubted it of his rather more feather-bed leader. He knew McNaghten had never walked a beat in his life. 'You don't take half the force with you for fear of scaring your tipster off. Come alone, the man says, and if you want what he's selling, you go alone.' The advice and the reasoning were sound enough.

'He must have been robbed. His watch had gone. We don't know if he was carrying money. Presumably, going to see a nark, he would have been. I want the man that did this, Lestrade. You are to drop the *Struwwelpeter* business and use all your available men on this. You can have dogs, back-up from Jones's division, anything you like. But these scum have got to learn.' He thumped the desk for effect. 'On my patch, no one kills a copper and gets away with it.'

Lestrade clattered down the corridor towards the mortuary. McNaghten must have been upset for he had not asked him to account for the bandage across his nose. He had worked out elaborate plans to explain an accident with the door of a hansom. He had also wrenched his arm, just for the record, should anyone ask, which would account for it hanging stiffly at his side. In the event he needn't have bothered. McNaghten's mind was elsewhere. It was largely in fact on the body of the man who now lay before Lestrade on the slab in the gleaming new white-tiled mortuary at Cannon Row. Forbes lay contorted, twisted slightly to one side, his body still stiff with *rigor mortis*, his face still wearing a slight look of surprise.

'Stabbed through the heart,' said the mortician cheerfully. 'Slim-bladed weapon. Might have been a hat-pin.'

'A hat-pin?' Lestrade was incredulous. 'They're breeding a new type of East End rough, aren't they?'

'I thought that. Mind you, I had a subject in the other day. Now where was it? Yes, that was it, washed up near Shadwell Stair, stark naked. Exactly similar stab wounds, but through the back.'

'I should have thought a common or garden chiv would have suited a sailor or a doxy.'

'You'll pardon me for saying this, Inspector. I mean, it's not strictly my job, I know, but I'm something of a student of the criminal classes. I've noticed that murders go in waves. A certain type of weapon catches on and hey presto, they're all at it.'

Lestrade looked at the cadaverous features of the mortician and the centre-parted, lank hair. All in all, he looked a lot worse than Forbes. Sensing that the inspector did not care particularly for his amateur sleuthing, the mortician shifted his ground.

'Of course, it could be a *lady's* hat-pin.'

If anything, that suited Lestrade less.

'Stabbing is not a female technique,' he said. 'Too physical, too messy. In twelve years of murder enquiries, I have never known a female knifer.' But at the back of his mind, and not entirely for reasons of pleasure, lurked the face and form of Constance Mauleverer. He dismissed the notion immediately. She had been with him at the time Forbes had been killed. All the same, he felt vaguely uncomfortable. Something about Forbes's death did not sit well.

'Of course, this is odd as well,' the mortician was saying and he pulled back the green sheet to expose the pale corpse. Lestrade visibly rocked backwards. Forbes's hands lay across his private parts. The mortician had forced them into that grotesque position as *rigor* was beginning to lessen, minutes before. Lestrade could not believe it. Both the thumbs had gone.

'Hacked off with a pair of scissors, I shouldn't wonder. Tough work, mind. The bone is very clean.'

But Lestrade had gone, nursing his arm as he leapt up the three flights of stairs to his office.

'No stomach for it, these brass hats,' muttered the mortician.

Feverishly Lestrade opened the book. There it was—

. . . The great tall tailor always comes
To little boys who suck their thumbs,
And ere they dream what he's about,
He takes his great sharp scissors out
And cuts their thumbs clean off – and then
You know, they never grow again.

'Dew, where's Bandicoot?'

'The Minories, sir. He said he ought to follow the trail while it was still warm.'

'You mean he's alone?'

'Yes.'

'Good God, man, you should have gone with him. What's an Old Etonian going to do in the East End? They'll have him for breakfast. Get a Maria and hurry.'

It was dusk before Lestrade and Dew found their quarry. Bandicoot was sitting in a corner in the dimly lit cellar bar of the White Elephant in Portsoken Street.

'I've been all over Aldgate and Houndsditch, sir. Nothing.'

Lestrade pointed at Bandicoot's beer. 'I hope that's not on expenses. Dew, your round.'

Dew disappeared into the jostling and the smoke.

'Who have you spoken to here?'

'No one, sir . . . yet. But I'm told an eye-witness comes in here every night about eight.'

'Who?'

Bandicoot reached for his notepad. 'A man named "Skins", sir.'

'Skins?' Lestrade leaned back in his chair, chuckling silently.

'Sir? Do you know this man?'

'The only one I know called Skins is one Albert Evans, a down-and-out. He'd tell you he'd stolen the Crown Jewels if you promised him a pint. Ah, thank you, Constable.' Dew arrived with the drinks.

'But what if he did see something?'

'All right, I'm prepared to wait. What else have you got?'

'Not a lot, I'm afraid. Sergeant Forbes received a note from a street urchin just before the end of his shift yesterday.'

'Did you see the boy?'

'No. The desk sergeant did. But that was the first place I asked. They hadn't seen the boy before and probably wouldn't know him if they saw him again.'

'That's what I like,' mused Lestrade, 'efficient, observant police work. What else?'

'I then thought to check the note – handwriting or something.'

'You're improving, Banders. And?'

'Sorry, sir. Sergeant Forbes must have taken it with him, but it wasn't on him when they found him.'

'Have you been to the scene of the crime?'

'Yes, sir. Two hundred yards from here in Gravel Lane. The constable who found the body was on a routine beat. He heard nothing, although he had passed the spot minutes before. Sergeant Forbes was due to meet his informer at midnight. His body was found round about half past two – the constable's watch was not accurate.'

'This constable, did he find any clues?'

'Nothing, sir. Which is odd. Sergeant Forbes was an experienced policeman and a well-built man. I would have expected him to put up something of a fight against the gang.'

'Gang?'

'The men who killed him, sir.'

Lestrade leaned forward again. 'Have either of you gentlemen seen the body?'

'No, sir,' the constables chorused.

'His thumbs are missing. We are not looking into a beating-up that went too far. We are looking for Agrippa.'

Dew and Bandicoot were astounded.

'So that's why Forbes didn't fight!'

'Whoever the murderer is, he took Forbes sufficiently by surprise.'

Bandicoot was thinking. Lestrade saw the strain showing on his face.

'If I recall rightly, sir, the next victim ought to have been little suck-a-thumb, named Conrad. Did Sergeant Forbes have that habit?'

'We needn't be too literal, Bandicoot. But you've got a point. I think Forbes was on to something. The murderer knew that and had to get rid of him. This is the first time we've rattled him. He's broken his pattern. Oh, the method is correct – the thumbs removed with scissors, but he's been so close to the text so far, I can't believe he wouldn't have had a Conrad in mind had he been given a little more leisure.'

'Wouldn't he have found it rather difficult to find a Conrad, sir?' asked Dew. 'There can't be many of them.'

'I'll grant you that,' Lestrade replied.

'Why not stay with the text, though?' asked Bandicoot. 'And bump off Sergeant Forbes anyway. Make it look like a gangland slaying, as we thought it was.'

'I don't understand Agrippa's motives, Bandicoot. If I did, we'd have him in custody, wouldn't we?'

'Excuse me, sir, isn't that Skins?'

Dew pointed to the door through which an ageing wreck of a man, toothless and grey, had shambled.

'Bandicoot, your round. Three beers and two gins. Dew, bring him over.'

The constables departed to their various tasks. For almost the first time Lestrade took in his surroundings. The cellar was filling up with people, beer fumes and smoke. Here and there carousers rolled drunkenly around a piano-accordion. A harlot was singing tipsily in a far corner. Three men had their hands up her skirt, but she appeared not to have noticed. The East End was crowded again after the recent return of the hop-pickers from the Kentish countryside. All human life lay before Lestrade as he watched Dew drag the struggling Skins across the sawdusted floor. Prostitutes, thieves, murderers, even the odd curate in silk top hat flashed before his gaze.

''Ere, wa's your game?' Skins was still squawking at the pressure of Dew's hand on his none-too-savoury collar. 'Oh, it's you, Mr Lestrade, sir.' Skins seemed to have gone even paler under the lurid lights when he saw Lestrade.

'Hello, Skins, how's the dead-lurking business? Set them down, Bandicoot. The gin is for Mr Evans, here.' Skins leapt for the glass, but Lestrade's hand slammed down over the top of it. He placed his bandaged nose an inch from the grey whiskery face of Skins. 'When he's told us what we want to know.'

'Look, guv'nor, you know me. I been in and out o' the Bridewell all me life, but there's some 'ard men around these parts now. 'onest, if I gets seed by one of them talking to the likes of you, why, then you'll find me floatin' and that's the Gospel truth.'

'"The likes of me," Albert. That's not very charitable.'

''Ave an 'eart, guv'nor.' Skins's eyes flashed round the room. The man was obviously terrified.

'Last night. Midnight. Gravel Lane. What did you see?'

'Nothin', guv.'

Lestrade sat up, staring long and hard at the other man. 'Albert Evans, dead-lurker, noisy racket man, snoozer, sawney-hunter, skinner . . .'

'Oh, no, sir.' Skins was indignant. 'Don't you know that's why they call me Skins? 'Cos I wouldn't do it. It's not natural.'

'You're missing my point, Albert. Do you know there are 20,883 men and women in prisons in this country? How would you like it to be 20,884? And I'm not talking about theft, Evans. Failure to report a murder will mean the crank and the treadmill.'

Skins fell back against his chair. He was steadied by Dew on one side and Bandicoot on the other. 'Think of it, Skins. Six hours a day, fifteen minutes on, two minutes off. You'll climb 8,640 feet a day. And of course for you we'll apply the brake to make it even more difficult.'

'Oh, no, sir. Not at my time of life. I couldn't take it, not again.'

'There again, murder carries the drop.' Lestrade quaffed his pint, artlessly. 'I was talking to James Berry the other day . . .'

'The public hangman?' Skins was pure white.

'That's him. He was telling me how he miscalculated the drop at Preston last week. Pulled the lever and the villain goes down, wham!' Lestrade brought his good fist down on the table. 'Unfortunately the rope was too short and his head came off. Blood all over the place . . .'

'All right, guv,' Skins sobbed. 'I get your meanin'. I'll tell you. Only I got to 'ave police protection.'

'We'll walk you to the door,' said Lestrade.

'Well, I was mindin' me own business . . .'

'Dead-lurking.'

'Shut up, Dew,' said Lestrade.

'An' I seen two men talking in Gravel Lane. It was a dark night last night so I couldn't see 'em clear, but they was both toffs. One of 'em had a topper and cloak. I thought, it's the bloody Ripper come back, I thought.'

'And?' Lestrade couldn't wait for asides.

'I couldn't hear what they was sayin'. They both whispered like. Then, and I was just about to turn into Gaydon Square, the gent in the topper ups and stabs the other one, thumps him in the chest, like.'

'Did you see the knife?'

'No, guvnor. I ran. Last thing I seed was the toff kneelin' down over the other 'un. And I said to meself, that's it, 'e's done for 'im.'

'Why didn't you report the incident?' asked Bandicoot. All three men around the table looked at him with utter scorn.

'The murderer,' Lestrade said, 'is there anything about him you can remember?'

'Like I said, guvnor. It was real dark. 'e was a big bloke. A bit taller than you.'

'As big as Bandicoot, here?' The constable obligingly stood up.

'No, I wouldn' say so. 'E walked funny.'

'Walked funny? What do you mean, man? Out with it.'

'Well, sort of . . . I don't know, sir, as if 'is feet was 'urting 'im. Can I have a drink now, guv'nor?'

Lestrade gestured to the glasses. Skins downed one gin, then the other, as if they were life savers.

'Hello, Skins.' An alien voice made them all look up. Four big men filled the space in front of the raised table. Their spokesman was a sailor by his coat and tattooes. Bandicoot was particularly aware of the smell. 'Talking to coppers again?'

As if at a signal, the music and drunken revelry died down. Beyond the four men, Lestrade saw all faces in the cellar turned towards them.

'We're not looking for trouble,' Lestrade told the sailor.

'Well, you've found it all the same.'

Bandicoot stood up, massive and immaculate. 'I should warn you that we are officers from Scotland Yard,' he said.

One of the men behind the sailor spat on the floor.

'Haven't you read the sign?' said Lestrade, pointing to the far wall, 'No hawkers. No spitters.'

''E's a big boy, ain't 'e?' said another man to his mate, eyeing Bandicoot.

Lestrade turned to his constable, 'Why don't you tell them you won a cap at Eton for boxing? That'll really frighten them.'

'Don't you think that's a little arrogant, sir?'

'Skins, you're a dead man,' the sailor snarled and aimed a burly right arm at him. Bandicoot caught it in mid-air and, spinning the man round, kicked him into the crowd. A roar went up as the fight started and tables and chairs were scattered as the crowd took up the best vantage points. The sailor got up, his pride more hurt than the rest of him. Skins had vanished in the smoke. Two other roughs in caps and monkey jackets sidled up to the raised table. Lestrade and Dew were now on their feet and the inspector began to walk steadily towards the centre of the room. A hundred miles away, or so it seemed, the staircase was bathed in a lurid green light. He saw the blow coming from his left but his left arm was too stiff and painful to deflect it. He spun round and his brass knuckles crunched head on with the wildly swung fist. The rough fell back, his hand broken. Lestrade staggered, too, his wrist aching. Only the knuckleduster had saved him from a similar fate. Two of them rushed at Dew and that valiant policeman was last seen by Lestrade disappearing under a tangle of arms and legs. Bandicoot was parrying blows with his shoulders and Lestrade saw him pick up one of the smaller roughs and throw him the length of the bar. More and more bystanders were knocked about as the mêlée spread.

When it became apparent that all three policemen were still essentially on their feet, and that three roughs lay unconscious on the floor, the mood turned nasty. There was an eerie pause, during which the cheering died down and then four knives flicked out, almost simultaneously, flashing in the sulphur light. Each of the policemen prepared for it in their own way. Lestrade flicked his own catchblade out, which certainly surprised Bandicoot and Dew, if not the clientele of the White Elephant. Bandicoot picked up a chair, like a rather unconvincing lion-tamer. Dew grabbed the nearest pewter mugs, two in each hand, and waited.

'Prepare ye for the Lord!' a harsh voice bellowed, shattering the stillness.

All eyes turned at once to the stairs. Half way down them, silhouetted against the gaslight green stood a white-haired, wild-bearded man in a military frock-coat. The light seemed to play around his head as if it were a halo. Around him, a number of burly, uniformed young men were gathering. He descended the stairs, his footsteps the only sound in the entire cellar.

'Repent, sinner,' he snarled at the nearest rough and brought his heavy Bible crashing down on the man's head. The rough collapsed among the overturned chairs.

'You likewise, brother,' and he smashed the brass clasps of the Bible into the teeth of a second. Before he reached the third, the area had cleared and some of the troublemakers had sloped towards the steps.

'No one leaves!' The terrible old man pointed towards the stairs and his henchmen formed a solid wall of blue. 'Time for a prayer meeting.'

To the constables' astonishment, the assembly – harlot, sneak-thief and drunk alike, all bowed their heads, as though they were in a church. Lestrade crossed the floor quietly.

'Something for your collection, General?' he produced a sovereign from his coat.

'And something for yours, Inspector.' The old man produced a book from his and pressed it into Lestrade's hand.

'Take your hat off, Dew,' Lestrade growled, 'you are in the presence of a great man.'

The assembly at the head of the stairs parted to let the policemen through.

In the alley above, it was Dew who first broke the silence. 'Was that . . .?'

'General William Booth of the Salvation Army, laddie. And thank his God he turned up when he did.'

From the cellar tap-room of the White Elephant, the strains of 'Abide With Me' and the incongruous rattle of a tambourine. Bandicoot glanced over Lestrade's shoulder at his book. *In Darkest England.*

'And is there a "way out", Inspector?'

'That's too clever for me, Bandicoot. Let's go.'

'One thing, sir. What did Skins mean when he said skinning

was unnatural? What is skinning, sir? I'm afraid I didn't understand any of that conversation.'

'Skinning, Bandicoot, as any novice bobby will tell you, is the crime of enticing children into alleyways and stealing their clothes.'

'No wonder he thought it unnatural,' said Bandicoot, distastefully. 'He obviously has a moral streak.'

Lestrade chuckled. 'No, no, Bandicoot. Skins thinks it unnatural because skinning is women's work. It would be a blow to his manhood. Dew, call me a cab in The Minories. We've got some bruises to look after.'

And Dew's voice echoed back as he disappeared into the darkness, 'You're a cab in The Minories.'

Seance on a cold Thursday evening

This time there were two mourning letters for Lestrade. They both came two days after the murder of Forbes. McNaghten had intensified the search for 'Agrippa', Agrippa the Elusive. Twenty-six constables and three sergeants had been found from somewhere, but house-to-house searches had revealed nothing.

The first letter Lestrade had been waiting for—

The door flew open, in he ran,
The great, long, red-legg'd scissor-man.
Oh! children, see! the tailor's come
And caught out little suck-a-thumb.
Snip! Snap! Snip! They go so fast,
That both his thumbs are off at last.

'Agrippa' had become the 'great, long, red-legg'd scissor man.' It was the same man, unruffled. So Forbes had found something, but what? He was on to someone, but who?

It was the second letter that took Lestrade by surprise. The scissors man had struck again, even before there was a body, even before the crime was reported. Somewhere, Augustus lay dead—

Augustus was a chubby lad;
Fat ruddy cheeks Augustus had;
And everybody saw with joy
The plump and hearty healthy boy . . .

Across the twilight river, the trees of October were dark and gaunt. A curlew called from the heathland. A knot of men wound their way up from the moored boat. Their lanterns swung as they walked, flinging shafts of light across the walls of the mill. Inspector Hovey of the Kent Constabulary looked at the huge, black building ahead of him. To one side the mill stream rushed and gushed, the overshot wheel groaning in the green darkness. A solitary light flickered in an upstairs room, high on the right.

'Somebody's in,' a constable muttered.

'Inspector.' Hovey held out his arm to the front door, by way of invitation to his guest. Lestrade took the bell pull. Far away, down an echoing hall, a distant answering ring.

'Old Prendergast's too mean to pay servants. And, as he's deaf, you'll wait for ever,' Hovey observed.

'This is your country, Hovey. It should be your boot in the door.'

'Vowles. You're the one with the shoulders. Open that door.'

Constable Vowles passed his lantern to a colleague and tried the door. It opened easily. 'It was nothing, sir,' he beamed. Hovey and Lestrade ignored the levity and in a confusion of courtesy, the inspectors collided abreast in the doorway.

It was Lestrade who finally led the way through the darkened house. There was no gas, not even any oil lamps that he could see. The lanterns threw long shadows across the faded wall-paper, peeling in the passageway. There was dust everywhere and cobwebs thick and white in the torchlight.

'Oh Jesus!' Vowles cried out. The others turned, constables' hands poised over their truncheons. 'Mice,' said Vowles, a little sheepishly.

'For God's sake get off that chair, man. You're a policeman.'

The party continued on its way, room by room. Empty, silent, dark.

'The light was at the top of the house. Furthest away from the wheel,' Lestrade observed.

'That would be through here.' Hovey now led the way, elbowing aside cobwebs as he reached the first landing. 'God, it's cold.'

The door at the end of the corridor was firmly locked. It took Vowles and the two other constables several attempts to force it open. The stench in the total darkness forced them back.

'Christ, what is it?' a constable asked.

'That's the smell of death,' Lestrade told him.

'I'm sure this was the room with the candle,' said Hovey.

Lestrade took a lantern. 'Opening the door probably blew it out,' he said. His feet crunched on broken glass. He glanced about him. A bed, a chair, a sideboard near the window. His feet hit something else. It rattled, clanked. It was a chain, heavy, long. He picked up the cold links and pulled them taut. There was something at the end of it. Holding the lantern up, he saw what it was. An old man, greyish-green, in tattered nightgown lay face up on the floor. Near his body the chain divided, one length attached to a bracelet on his wrist, the other on his ankle. Lestrade saw that the skin around these bracelets was cut and chafed. The man was skeletal, the eyes sunken, staring blindly at the ceiling. Lestrade looked up. Silhouetted against the dark blue of the night sky was a bowl of fruit. He could see by the lantern light that it was mouldy and shrivelled. He understood completely.

'Augustus,' he said.

'No. Isaac Prendergast,' Hovey corrected him, peering over his shoulder. 'God, the smell.'

Lestrade saw effluent all over the dead man's clothes and the floor. There was no sound now but Vowles quietly vomiting on the landing.

'Have your constables stand guard at the front door, Inspector,' Lestrade said. 'We can't do much until daylight.'

Daylight brought an unkind drizzle from the west. Lestrade had spent a cramped night sitting bolt upright in the settle of the snug of the Folded Arms. He was wakened by a tweeny raking out the fire with myriad apologies for disturbing 'the gennelman from Lunnon'. Breakfast was a cup of very mediocre tea and the journey, by trap and rowing boat back to the old mill, was equally wet and nasty. Vowles huddled against the doorframe, dripping wet and nearly as blue as his helmet. Lestrade threw off his Donegal and hung the soaking thing on another constable in the hall. Isaac Prendergast was even deader by daylight than he had appeared in the dark. The room was vile, floor and bed covered in excrement and the old man's body at the full stretch of the chains as though he had been reaching with his dying breath for the window.

'This is unbelievable,' Hovey was muttering. 'It looks as if some bastard chained him up so that he couldn't reach the fruit, leaving it there just out of reach. I've never seen anything like it in twenty years in the Force.'

'Nor will you again, Inspector,' said Lestrade. 'Are your men reliable?'

'They may not be the Yard, Inspector, but they are Kentish men. They know what they are about.'

'Good. Then have them go over this house with a fine toothcomb, especially this room.'

Hovey looked at the state of it. 'You're asking a lot . . .'

'Look, Hovey' – Lestrade's patience, after such a night, was wearing a little thin – 'why do you think I'm here, man?'

'I was wondering that?'

'Well, call it sixth sense. Let's say it fitted a certain pattern. Isaac Prendergast is not an isolated case. He is the ninth victim of the man I'm after. And I'll hang up my cuffs if he claims a tenth. So if you or any of your yokels are going to get squeamish on me, God help me, I'll see you drummed out of the Force.'

The silent response told him he had struck a chord. Hovey spun round and barked orders to his men. Lestrade went to find some fresh air. He watched the raindrops make ripples on the river, and the dark lines of the mill broke and shivered.

'He was a spiritualist, you know.' Hovey had joined him. 'I wonder if he'll come back.'

Lestrade turned to him with a rising feeling in his heart – the first he had had since the case began.

'Perhaps he will if we call him,' he said.

McNaghten's telegram was more encouraging than Lestrade had expected. *Go ahead,* it had read. *Have great faith in spiritualism. More Things in Heaven and Earth. Get some results.*

McNaghten. Lestrade was wondering how he could implement this decidedly odd piece of extra-curricular police work when the solution fell right into his lap. He was visited by a deputation of sinister-looking ladies and gentlemen from the Dymchurch Spiritualist Circle. It had been some time, they said, since Isaac Prendergast had joined them, but each member of the Circle had once promised to do his or her utmost to reach the others when he or she crossed to the Other Side and, by a fortuitous coincidence, the great Madame Slopesski had expressed a wish to attend a seance for this very purpose as part of her European and American tour. The time was Thursday at seven in the evening. The place was Carlton Hall, the old manor house beyond Dymchurch Level. The Circle had heard from Inspector Hovey of Lestrade's interest in the case (Lestrade hoped that his colleague had not given too much away) and invited both inspectors to the meeting.

In the event, Hovey had pleaded a previous engagement and Lestrade went alone. He crossed Dymchurch Level a little before seven. Far away he heard the rush of the sea, haunting, lonely. It was a clear night, starlit, cold. The turf was springy beneath his feet. He didn't quite know what to expect. He had played with table-rapping as a boy, when such things were more in vogue than they were now. But he had never attended a seance in his life. Those held by Mr Lees, the medium employed in the Ripper case, had been observed by a very small, select gathering, headed by McNaghten and Abberline. Lestrade had not been present. His directions for tonight had been very clear and by a quarter past seven his feet crunched on the gravel drive leading to Carlton Hall, an imposing mid-century house, turreted and bastioned. Very Gothic, Lestrade mused to himself. As a boy his favourite paper had been *Varney the Vampire*. He could almost hear the leathery wings flapping through the crypt.

A tall elegant Lascar took his hat and Donegal in the porchway. He was shown into the drawing room, heavy with velvet curtains, latticed screens and studded doorways. A huge fire roared and crackled in the grate.

'Not a night for smuggling.' A cheery voice welcomed Lestrade from an ante-room.

'If you say not,' he answered.

'No, too cold. Too clear. Hasdruble Carlton. Welcome to my home.' The squire extended a hand.

'Sholto Lestrade. Thank you.'

'Ah, yes, from Scotland Yard no less? Not much chance you being a smuggler, eh?' Carlton chuckled.

'I don't look too good in scarecrow's rags.'

'Ah, so you know our local legend – Dr Syn, the redoubtable Vicar of Dymchurch?'

'I get the impression that before the death of Isaac Prendergast, people in this part of the world talked of little else.'

'You may be right, Mr Lestrade, but please if I may be so bold, we of the spiritualist persuasion do not use the word "death", we don't acknowledge such a thing. We prefer "going over". Brandy?'

Lestrade accepted a glass gratefully and turned his backside to the welcoming fire. It looked as though they were in for another winter like the last, beginning in October and ending in May. Carlton was called away by the arrival of other guests. One or two of them Lestrade recognised as having been in the deputation who had called on him at the Folded Arms. Introductions over, the group was taken through into the ante-room from which Carlton had first emerged. The entire room was hung with black velvet and, under a single oil lamp in the centre, was a large oval table surrounded by nine chairs. Solemnly the guests took what seemed to be accustomed places. The Lascar showed Lestrade to a seat between two elderly ladies of the parish, lit a number of incense sticks and then retired, closing the double doors behind him.

'We have two surprises tonight, ladies and gentlemen,' Carlton said in a soft whisper. 'Apart, that is, from the welcome presence of Inspector Lestrade.'

Nods and beams all round in the direction of the inspector.

'One is that Madame Slopesski can be with us after all.' A ripple of applause. 'As some of you will know we thought yesterday she would be unable to be with us because of the pressure of her tour. I am delighted to report that I received a telegram but an hour ago and she will join us presently. The second surprise is that we have yet another guest, someone who is revered by you all and known I think to one or two of you, a founder member of the Society for Psychical Research, Mr Frank Podmore.'

Rapturous applause, somewhat at odds with the hushed tones which preceded and followed it, heralded the newcomer's arrival. Lestrade had heard of Podmore too, but in a rather different context. Gregson had mentioned him because the man was a Fabian Socialist and to Gregson, of course not terribly conversant with the finer points of politics, that smacked of anarchy. Athelney Jones was after him too, strongly suspecting that Mr Podmore was a secret cottage loaf who had other designs on a long string of paper boys and telegraph lads than merely cataloguing their supposedly paranormal experiences.

Podmore was tall, distinguished, with greying hair and side-whiskers, perhaps forty. His eyes were calm and kind and he showed a huge sense of occasion as he quietly took his seat. He made it clear that tonight's 'show', if such was the right term, belonged not to him but to Madame Slopesski.

It was some minutes before that Great Lady arrived. Carlton was the soul of courtesy and hostmanship, ushering the living legend to her place. Lestrade took her in at a glance. The light of the oil lamp shone mercilessly on her dull grey hair, wild and unruly by English standards. She was a woman of about sixty, he would judge, large, matronly with a chronic stoop and a pronounced limp. She bore a passing resemblance to the Queen, who also of course dabbled in such things, though hardly for a living. Her hands were strangely young with long, tapering fingers and when she spoke, it was in a deep, resonant middle-European boom. Gregson would no doubt have assumed her to be another anarchist, had he been here, Lestrade mused to himself.

For what seemed an hour, the Sensitive and her Circle sat in silence. The phonograph rasped out some anonymous music, somewhere behind Lestrade's head. Madame Slopesski spent most of this time with her eyes shut, breathing deeply ever sixth or seventh breath. The others sat with bowed heads, except Lestrade, who watched them all.

Then the Great Lady stretched out her arms. It was the

signal to commence. Carlton leapt to his feet with noiseless experience and turned off the phonograph. As he returned he dimmed the oil lamp and it went out. In the flickering firelight, Lestrade felt the hairs on his neck stand a little shamefacedly on end. He hoped he hadn't visibly jumped when he felt the two old ladies, one on each side of him, grab his hands, their bony fingers sliding into position until fingertips touched.'

'Is anybody there?' Madame Slopesski intoned.

Nothing.

Lestrade watched every face in the flickering light. They all had their eyes shut, except himself and Podmore, who was carefully watching the medium.

'Aaaggh,' Madame Slopesski cried out in a harsh guttural scream. Lestrade felt fingers tighten on his own. Madame Slopesski recovered her composure. 'Is it you, Isaac? Are you among us?'

Nothing.

A long silence followed. No one moved. Madame Slopesski occasionally murmured, sighed, arched her neck. Podmore gave nothing away. Lestrade was watching the others. Was it one of them? Was it Isaac Prendergast who was the real target? And had all the others been mere blinds? That was the theory he had put to Forbes the night of the Police Ball. The last time he had seen Forbes alive. Had Forbes followed up that line of inquiry? Had he been lucky where Lestrade had not? And was it that luck that had killed him?

'Isaac.'

A thump. Then another. The table shook and rattled. There were gasps from those present except Podmore and the medium.

'Knock once for yes, Isaac.' Madame Slopesski was swaying slowly from side to side. 'Twice for no. Are you near?'

A single thump. Lestrade tried to tune his ears to catch the direction of the sound. His detective's training had taught him to be suspicious of all this. It was trickery all right, but how was it done? He could not free his hands or break the circle and he could not see beyond the heads and shoulders of the members hunched around the table.

'Are you happy?'

A double thump and then several more, agitated, malevolent. The chandelier tinkled and rang, sending sparks of reflected light shooting over ceiling and walls.

'Have you a message?'

Yes, said the thump.

'Speak through me,' wailed Madame Slopesski, swaying now more violently.

Another long silence.

'Hypocrites!' It was Madame Slopesski's lips that were moving but it was not her voice. 'Isaac', whispered the old lady on Lestrade's left, 'that's Isaac's voice.'

'All of you, hypocrites. You left me. Deserted me. Where were you when I needed you?'

'Oh, Isaac,' sobbed another lady, 'we didn't like to disturb you. We know how you hated to be called upon.'

'Quiet, Esmerelda,' snapped Carlton, 'we'll lose him.'

Silence again.

'Mr Podmore.' Carlton turned to the *éminence grise* for advice. Madame Slopesski remained motionless, rigid in her chair. Podmore leaned forward without breaking the circle.

'Isaac,' he whispered. 'Is it warm, where you are?'

Nothing.

'Is it dry?'

Nothing.

'Are you cold?'

A thump.

'We've lost him,' hissed Carlton.

'Not yet,' Podmore answered. 'Isaac.'

Another silence.

'Is your murderer here?'

A single thump, followed by violent shaking of the table. The fire spat and crackled.

'Who is it?' It was Lestrade's voice, to his surprise as much as to everyone else's.

A deep guttural roar came from somewhere within Madame Slopesski. She stood up, hands outstretched. 'Beware,' she growled in Isaac's voice, pointing to Lestrade, 'beware, you will join us before long. Beware.'

She slumped back in her chair. Lestrade's eyes flashed from

side to side. Everyone was looking at him. Except Podmore, who was smiling to himself and looking at Madame Slopesski.

Hasdrubal Carlton re-lit the oil lamp and the Circle broke up.

'I believe this is all we shall have tonight,' he said.

Podmore took the limp wrist of the medium and checked the pulse. 'I think it would be unwise to ask Madame Slopesski for more,' was his verdict.

The Circle generally agreed that voice manifestation was enough for one evening. Madame Slopesski's speciality was ectoplasm, but all present, except Lestrade, knew that such physical manifestation was rare and that conditions had to be just so. The ladies in the Circle fussed around Madame Slopesski who began to revive. Some of the others began to make leaving noises. It was Lestrade who stopped them.

'May I remind you, ladies and gentlemen, that Madame Slopesski – or was it Isaac Prendergast? – told us that a murderer was present. I am afraid I must detain you for a while.'

'But you can't believe that one of us . . .' Carlton began.

'It is not a matter of what I believe,' Lestrade interrupted him. 'It is not my belief that is at stake here, but yours. If Madame Slopesski is wrong, then either she is a fake – or your whole spiritualist movement is.'

There were cries of indignation at this, but Lestrade had his suspects in a cleft stick. 'Mr Carlton, may I use your drawing room for the purpose of my interrogations?'

Grudgingly, mine host agreed. Lestrade began with Carlton himself, to give Madame Slopesski a chance to recover. He was aware of the danger of leaving the other members of the Circle together in an adjacent room, with a perfect opportunity to concoct and perfect a story. But without constables and without a telephone, he really had no choice.

'How long have you known the deceased?'

'We of the spiritualist persuasion . . .'

'. . . do not use the word "deceased". Yes, I know,' Lestrade chimed in. 'All the same, Mr Carlton, I am conducting a murder investigation and would be grateful for an answer.'

'About five years. I am not a Kentishman myself, Inspector.

I was until lately in Her Britannic Majesty's Civil Service in India.'

'Hence the servant – the Lascar?'

'Jat, actually. Jemadar Karim Khan. Late of the Viceroy's Bodyguard. A capital fellow, Lestrade.'

'These fellows have some interesting ways of dispatching their victims, I've been told.'

Carlton laughed. 'I see your reasoning, Inspector. I am supposed to have sent Karim Khan to do the evil deed, thereby giving myself a suitable alibi.'

'The thought had crossed my mind.'

'May I remind you, sir, that you are a guest in my house? The audacity of it!'

'Murder is an audacious enterprise, Mr Carlton. Although this particular murder wasn't. It can't have been difficult to overpower a weak old man.'

'Weak? Inspector, I don't know who you have been talking to, but Prendergast was far from that. I'll grant you, he must have been seventy, but he must also have weighed over twenty stone.'

Lestrade found it genuinely difficult to conceal his surprise. He had assumed that the emaciated corpse he had stumbled over at the mill was not appreciably lighter than the former living frame. Then *Struwwelpeter* came back ominously to his mind—

Augustus was a chubby lad;
Fat ruddy cheeks Augustus had;
And everybody saw with joy
The plump and hearty healthy boy . . .

'Yes, Inspector, your deceased was obese – and powerful with it. He would not have gone easily.'

'Did you like him?'

'God, no. No one did. I think it's probably true to say that the whole Circle hated him. He was an almost total recluse, especially of late. The only time he ventured out was to attend our meetings, and then grudgingly.'

'So why did he come?' probed Lestrade.

'He believed, Inspector.' To Carlton that was reason enough.

'When did you last see him?'

'It must have been three, no four, months ago.'

'And then he stopped coming.'

Carlton nodded.

'Why didn't you – one of you – check on him? After all, he was seventy.'

'I'm sixty-three myself, Inspector. Anyway, you don't bother a testy old gentleman like Isaac Prendergast. He hated callers. I've heard he put buckshot into the Vicar's breeches once. Vicar never admitted it, of course, but his progress to the pulpit each Sunday is painfully slow.'

'You attend church, Mr Carlton?'

'Why certainly, Inspector. And I am not, as you are probably thinking – what is the phrase – "Hedging my bets". I am simply a Christian spiritualist. There is no dichotomy here.'

Lestrade thought he had better change tack before the dialogue got beyond him.

'When Madame Slopesski – Isaac – whoever that was in there,' he said, 'told us that the murderer was present, whom did you have in mind?'

'Inspector, I have known all these good people for five years. I would stake my life on the fact that not one of them is capable of such a deed. When you share the shadows of the night with a fellow human being you get to know these things.'

Lestrade interrogated all of them and he had to admit that Hasdrubal Carlton was probably right. He spoke to six anxious people, deep believers all in what they were doing. He saw gullibility, sincerity, hope, but he didn't see a murderer. But he still had two to go, to his mind the most likely of all – Podmore and the medium. It was by now well past midnight. As the genial host, Carlton, had asked if those who had been questioned might be allowed to go home. Lestrade saw no reason why not. He asked the dark, silent Karim Khan, who understood but spoke no English, to show Madame Slopesski into the anteroom. In the event, it was Podmore who appeared and seeing Lestrade's annoyance at having his instructions misunderstood, said, 'I'm afraid she's gone, Inspector.'

'Gone?' Lestrade was furious.

'Yes, I didn't think you'd be pleased, but, I beg you, don't be hard on poor old Carlton. She is a very eminent lady in our field. If she pleaded tiredness due to her tour and the strain of tonight, how could he do other than to let her go?'

'Go where, exactly?'

'To her hotel. I believe she told me it was the Postgate, here in Dymchurch.'

Lestrade's eyes narrowed, 'I have been in this town for four days.' The clock struck one. 'Correction – five days', he went on, 'and I have not seen an hotel called the Postgate here. In fact I have not seen an hotel at all. Which is why I am staying at the pub. Did any of the Circle overhear this conversation?'

Podmore stretched out on the sofa in front of the dying fire, chuckling to himself. 'No, Inspector, they did not. And suddenly, it's all fallen into place.'

'What has?' Lestrade sensed that Podmore was playing games with him. He didn't like it.

'Have you attended a seance before, Inspector?'

'I have not.'

'Watch.'

Podmore sat bolt upright. 'Put your hands on the table between us,' he said. Lestrade did. Podmore turned out the oil lamps and resumed his seat opposite Lestrade. 'I'm going to place my fingertips against yours. Can you feel them?'

'Yes.'

'Right. Now be still. Absolutely still.'

Silence.

Podmore broke it first. 'Is anyone there?'

Silence.

Again, the repeated question.

Then, a thump, muffled, far off.

'Isaac, is that you?'

A louder thump.

Lestrade's heart was racing.

'Is your murderer here?'

A series of thumps, rocking the table.

'You did that with your knee,' Lestrade shouted.

'Yes, that wasn't very good, was it? Madame Slopesski was better.'

'She was a fake?'

'Please relight the lamps, Inspector. I haven't finished my exposé yet.' Lestrade did so and returned to his position. 'You noticed how the thumps were soft, then loud?'

Lestrade nodded. 'The soft thumps are done like this.' Podmore produced them again. 'I am merely pressing my toes against the soles of my boots. The harder knocks, as you guessed, are done with the knee. It is easier through skirts, of course' – Lestrade wondered in passing if Podmore ever wore them – 'and with the atmosphere so carefully created in the other room.'

'So Carlton was in on it?'

Podmore chuckled. 'What a marvellously quaint way you policemen have of putting things, Inspector. No, I don't think he was. Like all the other members of the Circle, he is a true adherent. Just like hundreds I have met all over the country. It's just part of the ritual which mediums insist on. The darkened room, the soft music. Oh yes, and the spitting fire.' Podmore threw a handful of something into the dying flames. They crackled into life. 'Salt,' he said to Lestrade's surprised look. 'Common table salt. Most mediums carry it in a purse attached to their wrists.'

'But the circle of fingers was unbroken,' said Lestrade.

'Indeed so.' Podmore smiled. 'As you see.'

Lestrade could not believe it. Podmore appeared to have three hands.

'This one is wax,' said the ghost-hunter. 'Most mediums are essentially conjurors. They cheat people as surely as your – what's the phrase – confidence tricksters do. Most of them in fact are just that – frauds who dupe innocents for money or the limelight. I am looking for the one who is not. For the one who is genuine.'

Lestrade was examining the wax hand.

'There is ample room in a lady's nether garments to hide one of these. I always carry a spare. It's sometimes fun to confuse the medium by slipping it in. Henry Sidgwick and I both did that once and the medium was exposed with five hands – two of her own and three wax ones.' Podmore laughed at the memory. 'In the darkness a dexterous medium can usually switch one of these for her own fingers. In the charged atmosphere of a seance, no one will notice when the light is turned off.'

'Why didn't you turn the light on?' Lestrade asked. 'I thought you ghost-hunters made your living by exposing frauds.'

'I don't know about a living, Inspector. Curious choice of words, really. But certainly I would normally have done that.'

'And tonight things were not normal?'

'No. To begin with, whoever that medium was tonight, she was not Madame Slopesski.'

Lestrade found his jaw behaving as it was frequently supposed to in the dubious literary concoctions of Doctors Watson and Conan Doyle, while Holmes suavely unmasked a villain. 'Not?' he repeated stupidly.

'Not.'

'How do you know?'

'My dear Inspector. I know Madame Slopesski. Oh, not well, I grant you. But I have been introduced to her on three or four occasions. Our impostor must have known that. She was visibly rattled when we met in the forecourt and blamed her surprise on the chill night air. Mind you, the disguise was good, very good. The stoop, the make-up, the hair, all excellent. Three things however gave the game away.'

'Oh?' Lestrade was beginning to wonder why Podmore had not followed a career on the Force.

'First, the tricks were not quite so slick. Madame Slopesski – the real one that is – is a genuine adept and, although she plays to the gallery, she does it better than our guest this evening. You must remember of course that she did not expect to find me here.'

'Second?'

'Second, her eyes. Madame Slopesski's are a dull grey. Our impostor's were a clear blue.'

'How observant of you.' Lestrade was exhibiting a tinge of pique.

'You policemen do not have a priority in these things, Inspector.'

'Thirdly?'

'Thirdly, the voice. It was a shade too deep. So much so in fact that . . .'

'Yes?'

'Inspector, I can't explain this, but I think our Madame Slopesski was a man.'

Silence as the two men looked at each other. Lestrade sank back in his chair.

'Could I be right?' asked Podmore. 'It's a sense I have – and it is what made me let her . . . him go. It was not a conventional fraud. Does that make sense to you?'

'Oh, yes, Mr Podmore,' said Lestrade. 'The murderer *was* in that room. He was Agrippa, the long, red-legged scissor-man. He was Madame Slopesski . . . and I missed him again.'

Madmen and fairies

It was nothing that Lestrade hadn't said to himself a thousand times as he rode in the train back to London. Even so, it came hard from McNaghten.

'It's out of my hands,' said the Head of the Criminal Investigation Department, folding down the cravat and sweeping up the ends of his neatly waxed moustaches. 'The Commissioner has asked that you be given a week's leave, Lestrade. Take it and be done.'

Lestrade looked at him sullenly. McNaghten felt even more acutely uncomfortable than usual. 'Look, Sholto,' the approach was softer, the tone more wheedling, 'you've had your share of bad luck in this case, I know. But God knows, man, you've made no headway.'

'And who will?' Lestrade asked. 'Who has my case when I'm thrown off it? Abberline? Gregson? Not Jones, surely to God?'

'No one, Lestrade.' Lestrade was pacing his office. 'Iaf04'm not taking this case off you, man. I'm merely saying, have a rest, come fresh to it in a few days' time.'

'By that time another three men may be dead. Remember the book – I've got Philip, Johnny and Robert to go. And I don't know where and when Agrippa will strike next.'

'That's exactly my point,' McNaghten railed on. 'With rest, you'll see things more clearly – connections, clues. This Agrippa – he isn't superhuman. He's made mistakes. Look, Sholto,' again the avuncular tone, 'you're tired, you're on edge. What do you do in your spare time? Fish?'

Lestrade grimaced.

'Well, whatever you do,' McNaghten blustered, annoyed at

revealing his lack of knowledge of his subordinates' lives, 'for the next seven days you are to do it. That is an order.'

In his own office, Lestrade packed a few things into a Gladstone bag. He saw little point in looking at the mourning letter lying on his desk, but Bandicoot and Dew hovered, waiting to see what he would do, how he would play it. No surprises, no clues. Typewritten, London postmark, the final verse—

Look at him, now the fourth day's come!
He scarcely weighs a sugar-plum;
He's like a little bit of thread,
And on the fifth day, he was – dead.

'Gentlemen, I am ordered to take a week's leave. During my absence you will do nothing, talk to no one. And if any senior officer asks, you know nothing. Understand?'

They understood. Lestrade had summed it all up perfectly. They did know nothing.

'What will you do, sir?' asked Bandicoot cheerfully. 'Go fishing?'

Lestrade looked at him. He smelt conspiracy for a moment, but dismissed it. Bandicoot wasn't good enough.

'I have friends to visit, Bandicoot. I think a turn by the sea will do me good.'

It didn't do Lestrade good. On the contrary, he staggered against the squalls and gusts which threw spray over the promenade at Southsea. Somewhere beyond the mist and the endless grey that was the Solent and the sky lay the Wight, where all this had begun, an eternity ago. He pulled up the collar of his Donegal and sank his hands gratefully into its pockets. Urchins ran by, shrieking and squealing in the fierce rush of the elements. It was Sunday, wet and dismal. Behind the white respectability of the houses he heard a church bell. Surely, he couldn't be much longer. He had been waiting half an hour already. A carriage hurtled from nowhere, smashing through the puddles and spraying Lestrade from the landward side. At least now he was wet all around. There was a sort of resigned comfort in that.

Then he was there. Respectable, prim, proper. Neat bowler, upturned collar. He wrestled manfully with his umbrella. Agrippa? The long-legged scissor man? Or a doctor-turned-author going to church of a Sunday morning? Lestrade followed him with the effortless casualness of fifteen years of such surveillance. He sat four rows behind him in church. His quarry seemed popular. People greeted him, laughed, joked. He was on his home ground, careless, off his guard perhaps. But this wasn't the time or the place. Lestrade had watched him for two days. It was time to make his move.

The afternoon brought the opportunity. Lestrade had followed his quarry to the Sally Lunn Tea Rooms. Odd that it should be open on a Sunday, out of season. But Lestrade was grateful enough for the roaring fire and the pot of tea that cheered. Apart from the waitress, a sour spinster with a head of hair the colour of barbed wire, they were alone.

'Lister,' said Lestrade extending his hand and approaching the other man.

'I beg your pardon?'

'My name is Lister. Er . . . may I join you? So hate to partake of tea alone.' Lestrade wasn't sure whether he could keep this plumminess up. Still, there were enough frauds and snobs in the world; a slip would betray his background, but not his occupation.

'Yes, do. Conan Doyle.'

Lestrade shook the offered hand. 'Not the writer chappie?'

'Why yes,' the doctor beamed, basking in the warmth of recognition. 'Have you read my work?'

'My dear chap, I am your most ardent reader. I never miss a copy of the *Strand* when I am up in town.'

Conan Doyle's face fell a little, 'Oh, I thought perhaps you meant *The Micah Clarke* – or *The White Company*?'

Lestrade looked confused, '. . . Er . . . oh, yes, yes of course, very good. Very good. But better than the . . . er . . . *White Micah,* I like your stories of detection – that fellow, what's his name, Burdock Holmes.'

'Sherlock,' said Conan Doyle, a little irritated. 'Sherlock Holmes. If you are in London regularly you must have heard of the man.'

'Oh, yes, in fact I'm only a visitor here, but I assume that your admirable works are not a statement of fact?'

Conan Doyle chuckled. 'No indeed. Mr Holmes is a celebrated amateur detective, but I fear he falls rather short of my hero. After all, my Holmes is superhuman.'

'I've often wondered, Mr Conan Doyle, this Doctor Watson, Holmes's friend and confidante – is he real?'

'Why, yes. He and I were at medical school together. At least, that's not quite true. He was attending a refresher course on comparative anatomy while I was a student. It was on his suggestion that I met Mr Holmes.' Conan Doyle sank his teeth into a Chelsea bun. Lestrade was glad to see that he was getting into his stride. 'It was Watson's idea to write a biography of Holmes, to do for him what Boswell did for Johnson.' Lestrade didn't know what that was, but he doubted whether it was legal. 'The snag was that poor old Watson isn't the world's best writer. So we agreed that I should write the thing – the old flair, you know, and he would feed me the information. Well, somewhere along the line, the serious biography went out of the window and the fiction started. Between you and me, Mr Lister, it has worked out very well. It appeals to Holmes's monstrous vanity, to Doctor Watson's need to idolise the man – and it pays my bills now that I've given up medicine, at least on a full-time basis – I too am visiting here as a change from town.'

'I've always thought,' said Lestrade, sipping his tea with a certain elegance, 'you and Watson are a little hard on the police force.'

Conan Doyle chuckled. 'Oh, Mr Lister, they do what they can, but you must realise, they are hampered by bureaucracy.'

Lestrade had realised this many, many times.

'And then of course, they are not among the brightest people in the world. Take Inspector Lestrade, for instance.' The inspector buried his slightly stiffening moustache in his tea cup. 'According to Watson, the man's a buffoon.'

Lestrade coughed, spraying the table with his tea.

'My dear chap,' consoled Conan Doyle, 'have a care.'

Lestrade was profuse in his apologies.

'Another cup?' the doctor asked.

They talked casually of this and that. Of the likelihood of Mr Gladstone's re-election now that Home Rule was the burning issue. Of the weather, threatening a repetition of last year's winter, of the return of the Ice Age. And as dusk threw long gloom across the silvered clutter of the tea-table, Lestrade edged the conversation around to spiritualism.

'I read somewhere,' he said, 'that you were convinced of the existence of another world hovering a little above our own?'

'A quaint way of putting it, Mr Lister, but yes, I am a spiritualist.'

'I attended a seance recently.' Lestrade was watching the good doctor's every reaction. 'The Sensitive was Madame Slopesski.'

'Good God!' Conan Doyle slammed the cup down. Guilt, thought Lestrade. He was visibly rattled, agitated, 'How marvellous! I've only read her *Mistress of Two Worlds* – magnificent. Do you know it, Lister?'

Lestrade did not. 'I would have thought that such an ardent follower would have at least seen his idol.'

'Alas, no. But great as Slopesski is, "my idol" as you put it is Daniel Dunglas Home – the levitationist.'

'I thought he was dead.'

'Please, Mr Lister, we of the persuasion do not use such a phrase.' Lestrade had been here before too.

'Do you know Albert Mauleverer?' he asked.

'Mauleverer. Mauleverer. No, I don't believe so. Is he a spiritualist? I don't recall the name in the SPR lists.'

'No, he isn't a spiritualist. What about Edward Coke-Hythe? Harriet Wemyss? Isaac Prendergast?'

A shake of the head to all these. Lestrade was fishing, but in very shallow waters. Either Dr Conan Doyle was as innocent as the day was long or he was an accomplished liar. But then, Agrippa was an accomplished everything. The red, long-legged scissor man was a master of the ancient art of murder. It was to murder that Lestrade now turned, introducing it via the vehicle of detective fiction.

'How would you kill a man, Mr Conan Doyle?'

The doctor was a little taken aback by the question, but answered anyway. 'Suffocation,' he said after a moment's deliberation.

'Why?'

'Oh, I don't know. It seems quiet, particularly while the victim is asleep. I'll let you into a little secret Mr Lister. I don't like blood. A poor admission from a doctor, eh? But it's a fact. No, I couldn't kill anyone if it meant a lot of blood.'

'Not a shotgun then,' prompted Lestrade, remembering Mauleverer's blasted head.

Conan Doyle shuddered.

'Nor a hat pin, followed by removal of the thumbs?'

Conan Doyle grimaced.

'Nor a hound pack to tear and rip the corpse?'

Conan Doyle fainted.

Lestrade had meant to wait until the all-too-good doctor recovered, to offer his apologies for offending him. It must have been the conversation on top of those rather sickly pastries. But somehow he couldn't face it. Conan Doyle would have wanted to know why he had been asking those bizarre questions. And at the back of his mind, Lestrade wanted to preserve his anonymity, at least for the moment. He had not broken Conan Doyle down and yet his reaction, if he were not guilty, was surely an odd one. A squeamish doctor? Who wrote murder stories for a living? It strained credulity. And his chosen method of murder when pressed by Lestrade – suffocation. The Man in the Chine, the Inky Boys – four of Agrippa's victims had died by a form of suffocation.

Lestrade left instructions with the waitresses of the Sally Lunn and then, collecting his baggage, caught the last and only evening train to town.

'Devil of a time to call,' snapped Watson, looking ludicrous in nightcap and shirt.

'I have no time for niceties, Doctor,' Lestrade answered him. He was tired, wet, dispirited. In the reflection of the carriage lights, rattling north on the brave curve below Arundel Castle he had seen the face of Constance Mauleverer. Distant. Smiling. Then it had vanished, and he saw only his own face, darkened by the darkness of murder. In that carriage, he had faced Death itself. He imagined as he stared beyond his own shadowed face, scarred by plate glass and sabre, Agrippa, sitting opposite him and a little behind. A big man, one moment in broad hat and muffler, as he had been when furtively meeting Harriet Wemyss months before in Macclesfield. The next, hunched, ancient, gnarled – Madame Slopesski with her bright blue eyes – the wrong colour – and the curse in her throat and the pointing finger. Again, the apparition became a series of night-marish scenes from *Struwwelpeter* – tall Agrippa, the long scissor-man, the hare with a shotgun and over all there danced that face with its sad cheeks – 'anything to me is sweeter, than to see Shock-headed Peter.'

No, Lestrade had no time for niceties. He had roused the sleeping cabbie at Waterloo and the hansom had creaked and clattered its way through the dark Sunday night, through the shining wet streets. There had been no lights burning at 221B Baker Street, though a ragged urchin was nodding off on the steps. Watson glanced down at him and tapped him with his foot. 'Go home, boy. Nothing for you tonight.' He showed Lestrade in. 'One of our Irregulars,' he said, gesturing in the lad's direction. 'They are all so loyal, you know.'

Lestrade followed the flickering oil lamp up to the parlour. 'Mrs Hudson sleeps so soundly. Sleep of the just I suppose.'

'Where is Mr Holmes?'

Watson stared at him. 'But isn't that why you've come?'

'I'm sorry, I don't follow.'

Watson straightened himself. 'Sherlock Holmes is dead.'

Lestrade felt his jaw drop. He recovered himself. 'Cocaine?'

Watson flashed him an angry stare. 'No, by God, Professor Moriarty.'

'Who?'

'The Napoleon of Crime, Holmes used to call him.'

'Perhaps I'd better come in again, Watson. I don't know what you are talking about.'

'Have a seat, man. And a drink. God knows I need one.'

Watson poured them both a voluminous brandy and sat by the fire's embers. 'Holmes had been aware of Moriarty's activities for some time. One of three appalling brothers, the man is a monster – a villain of international reputation. I wonder you haven't heard of him, Lestrade.'

'That's Gregson's department, Doctor – the Special Branch.'

'Anyway, Holmes was determined to face the man. He traced him to Switzerland. Master of disguise though he is, he daren't show his face here in England, not with Holmes after him.' Watson swigged heartily at his drink. 'I received this letter from Holmes and two telegrams. They all speak of optimism. He was to meet Moriarty at the Reichenbach Falls – a well-known tourist spot near Interlaken.'

'And?'

Watson produced a voluminous handkerchief and blew his nose loudly.

'I received another letter only this morning, by special messenger. Holmes did meet Moriarty apparently. They fought. Moriarty had a pistol. Holmes grappled with him and . . . they both fell over the edge.'

A chill silence descended. Watson hung his head, visibly sobbing. Lestrade felt uncomfortable. He had never liked Holmes, but the man had gone bravely. In the way he would have liked. He poured another drink for himself and Watson. He nudged Watson's shoulder with the glass and grunted to him.

'They found their bodies. Locked together on a ledge one hundred and fifty feet below. Their necks were broken.' Watson drained the glass.

Lestrade sat down heavily. He sat up almost immediately, pulling a fiddling-stick from beneath him, with a grimace.

'Oh, sorry, Lestrade,' mumbled Watson, 'his last bow.'

'Quite.' Lestrade allowed a certain interval. 'Is there nothing else you want to tell me, Doctor Watson?'

Watson looked up at the ferret-like features. They weren't ferret-like really. That was unkind. And the man was no buffoon either. He must write to Conan Doyle about that. But then, there was no point now, was there? The Great Detective was dead. There would be no more Sherlock Holmes stories.

'How did you know?' he asked.

Lestrade stood up. He thought his heart had stopped. 'I didn't at first.' He was wondering which of them, Watson or Conan Doyle, had played Madame Slopesski so convincingly and he was on the point of realising that neither of them had blue eyes, when Watson handed him a letter.

'You'd better read this,' he said. 'It's from the Minister Plenipotentiary in Geneva. Came this morning by special messenger.'

'Sir,' Lestrade read silently, 'I regret to inform you of the death yesterday of Mr Sherlock Holmes, late of 221B, Baker Street. As you know, Mr Holmes had been staying at the Travellers' Rest Hotel in Interlaken for the past three weeks. During that time he became increasingly unwell and took to wandering in the town and on the hills. He was warned about the dangerous slopes and precipices, but he persisted. At approximately ten o'clock on the morning of the fourteenth inst., Mr Holmes was seen to be walking near the Reichenbach Falls when he became extremely agitated, eye-witnesses testified. He began screaming loudly, "Damn you, Watson, will you never leave me alone," and leapt at a gentleman who happened to be standing nearby – a Professor Moriarty of Heidelberg University, who was on holiday with friends studying the rock strata in that part of Switzerland. The Professor and Mr Holmes were seen to disappear over the water's edge and their bodies were later found on a parapet one hundred and fifty feet below. Their necks had been broken. It grieves me, sir, to be the one to break this news to you. The hotel authorities took the liberty of searching through Mr Holmes's papers and your name came to light. In the absence of any other information, I would beg you to inform his next of kin and make arrangements for burial, Yours . . .

Lestrade dropped the letter to his side.

'How did you know,' Watson's voice was barely audible, 'about the cocaine, I mean? Did you know he'd always planned to kill me?'

'I guessed,' Lestrade lied. He wanted to stay on the offensive. Watson was vulnerable now and he might yet get a confession.

'Look.' Watson wearily dragged himself over to the wall. 'Had you asked about these bullet holes, Holmes would have told you they were target practice – neat in the Queen's cypher, eh? What he would not have told you was that every one of those shots was fired when I was only inches away. Yes, I know it defies belief. But eleven times Holmes pretended the gun went off "by accident". He never had the nerve, you see, to kill me. Until . . . five weeks ago we had a row. A blazing one. He accused me of treachery, deception, hiding his cocaine, pouring glue over his violin. Mrs Hudson left the room in sheer panic. I'd never seen him so incensed before, although, I suppose, I knew it was always coming. He packed his bags and left. He refused to say where he was going.'

'The letters? Telegrams?'

'I made them up. The only letter I have received is the one in your hand, telling me of his death. What hurts most is that in his deranged mind, he thought that poor old geologist was me. I suppose there may have been a passing resemblance.'

'And the Napoleon of Crime?'

'I made that up, too.'

Another long chill silence.

'Why did you come, Lestrade? At this hour of the night? If you didn't know about Holmes . . .'

'It will keep,' smiled Lestrade. He was getting soft. Or old. Or both. As he made for the door, he told himself it was because Watson was Constance's uncle.

'Lestrade.' Watson's voice was stronger now. He faced the inspector across the shadowed room. 'I'm not going to let Holmes die for nothing. I shall write to Conan Doyle tonight. Holmes will live again. He shall not die at the Reichenbach Falls – and a Professor of Geology at Heidelberg University shall achieve undying fame.' Watson was smiling. 'And you will never catch him, Lestrade, only Holmes will.'

As Lestrade reached the stairs, he heard the scratch of bow on violin. Rosin on catgut. He never went back.

On the day the papers carried the story of the return of Holmes's body to London for burial, the body of Philip Faye was being examined in the white-tiled laboratory at Scotland

Yard. Around the corpse stood Melville McNaghten, moustached and cravated, Dr Forecastle, the pathologist, Inspector Lestrade, back on duty, and Constable Bandicoot, attending his first autopsy.

'I'm not one to carp, Lestrade,' whispered McNaghten, 'but if you're right in the supposition that the name fits, then this is the ninth victim in this case of yours.'

'Tenth,' Lestrade corrected him calmly.

'It can't go on, Lestrade. We're being made to look fools. All of us. Have you seen the morning papers?'

'Burial of Sherlock Holmes?' asked Lestrade.

'Damn you, Lestrade. Burial of us all unless this man is caught. It's not just your career at stake now. The Commissioner is most alarmed. The public won't remain patient for ever, you know.'

'Cause of death?' Lestrade ignored McNaghten's blustering, addressing himself to Forecastle and the matter in hand.

'Suffocation.'

Lestrade swept from the room without further ado. He was Waterloo bound, for the Southsea train. Bandicoot hesitated in mid-corridor. McNaghten stopped him. 'Lestrade!'

'It's Conan Doyle,' the inspector answered. 'I wasn't sure at first. I thought it was a double act – he and John Watson of Baker Street.' Lestrade was thrusting a few essentials into a Gladstone bag. He always kept a spare shirt and collars at the Yard for just such a sudden departure.

'Conan Doyle?' echoed McNaghten. 'What on earth made you suspect him?'

Lestrade paused, searching the middle distance for an answer. 'Call it intuition,' was all he could muster. Then he had gone, Donegal flapping, into the chill, morning sun.

Bandicoot looked at McNaghten. 'Should I go with him, sir?'

'No need, Constable.' was the reply. 'Had the inspector bothered to wait for one moment, he would have discovered that I was to have lunch within the hour with Doctor Conan Doyle. He is in London for the funeral of Sherlock Holmes. I wonder Lestrade was not there himself.' McNaghten turned to go. 'On second thoughts, Bandicoot, you'd better get after him. Lestrade would never forgive me if I let him go all the way to wherever Conan Doyle lives on a fool's errand. Besides, he'll charge expenses to the Yard, and that would never do.'

And so it was nearly two before Lestrade and Bandicoot walked the Embankment. Leaves, crimson and yellow, were curling at their feet, gusting now and then across their faces. Lestrade was silent, nonplussed for the moment.

'Would it help to talk about it, sir?' Bandicoot was first to break the silence. 'I mean, I hope to be a senior officer one day and I'd like to understand something of the thought processes involved.'

Thought processes? Lestrade mused to himself. What the hell were they?

'It's funny, Bandicoot.' Lestrade reached a bench and sat down, tilting the bowler back on his head. 'I felt so sure this morning, but now . . . Listen to this. John Watson is related to two of Agrippa's victims – your school chum, Edward Coke-Hythe and Const . . . the wife of Albert Mauleverer. What if Agrippa intended, for reasons we don't yet know, to kill a certain victim – or indeed two certain victims? What if those victims are Coke-Hythe and Mauleverer?'

'Then why go on?' asked Bandicoot. 'Why is Philip Faye lying in the Yard mortuary?'

'Because Agrippa is a methodical murderer. Because he has used the *Struwwelpeter* stories and intends to follow them to the letter. Who can explain the workings of a mind like his?'

'And Dr Watson is the common factor?'

'At first I suspected Mrs Mauleverer. Two reasons told me I was wrong. First, these murders are not the work of a woman. They are too physical, too violent. Second, she has a perfect alibi for the murder of Forbes.'

'Perfect?'

Lestrade shifted a little uncomfortably and muttered, 'She was with me.'

'Ah, quite.' Bandicoot tried not to let the smirk show on his face. Lestrade tried not to let him know he had seen it.

'The only other common factor is Watson.'

'But could not Mrs Mauleverer have killed her husband and Edward Coke-Hythe?' Bandicoot persisted.

'Yes, she could, but that would mean that the murder of Forbes at least was the work of a copy-cat, someone who also knew the *Struwwelpeter* pattern. Remember, the press have not yet made that link. We are still the only ones who know the pattern. No, it strains credulity.'

'And Conan Doyle?'

'Co-author with Watson of *The Adventures of Sherlock Holmes* – you know, in the *Strand Magazine.*'

'I'm sorry, sir, I don't.'

'You're missing nothing,' Lestrade observed. 'In Kent I met Agrippa. Oh, I know, it's not in my report. I didn't tell McNaghten, you, anyone. But it was Agrippa all right; disguised yes, cleverly, very cleverly. But Agrippa nonetheless; I am sure of it. Through Watson I knew that Conan Doyle was an ardent spiritualist – and who better to play a leading medium than an ardent spiritualist?'

'So it was Watson and Conan Doyle?'

'Two murderers would be convenient,' Lestrade was talking to the middle distance again. 'Easier to accomplish the murders, provide alibis, leave a trail of red herrings, but . . .'

'But?'

'But, Bandicoot, it increases the risk enormously. Can one trust – *really* trust – the other? Remember his life depends on it. One slip, one wrong word – and the drop. No, that too strains credulity. Oh, I over-reacted this morning. Conan Doyle had chosen the method of suffocation when I asked him how he would kill a man. Suffocation, Bandicoot. The method of dispatch of one Philip Faye.'

'Then why don't you arrest Conan Doyle? Or at least interrogate him?'

Interrogate? thought Lestrade. Where did Bandicoot find these words? Had he perhaps swallowed a dictionary? Or perhaps his mother had been frightened by one? 'No, he's not our man. He's been in London for four days. And our revered Chief is lunching with him as we speak. Could we establish a link between the good doctor and our latest corpse, I wonder? I doubt it.'

Bandicoot looked confused.

'When you've been in this business as long as I have . . .' Lestrade checked himself; he'd always vowed he would never say that, but it was too late now, '. . . you learn to work on intuition – a feeling, vague, unsure, but there. Somewhere between your fob and your half hunter, Bandicoot. That something tells me Conan Doyle is not our man. We'll let him and Watson go on writing their detective rubbish. We can't hang them for that.'

Lestrade got to his feet. 'Come on, I'll buy you a Saveloy in the Coal Hole.'

Unsavoury was the word with which Bandicoot finally came up. The best word he could find in the circumstances to fit the late unlamented Philip Faye. Lestrade was cool, detached about the whole thing; he had after all seen it before, but it opened up a new world to Bandicoot. The radical press and the Evangelists called it White Slavery. Lestrade shrugged and called it a fact of life.

'Little girls,' Sergeant Dixon had repeated. 'Oh, yes, big market. Deflowering's the name of the game, Bandicoot. 'Course, it's not so common now as it was. When you've been in this business as long as I have . . .'

'So Philip Faye was a procurer of young girls?'

'So it says 'ere in records.' Course it wasn't illegal until Mr Labutcher's Bill.'

'I think that's Labouchere,' corrected Bandicoot.

'Right. Well, anyway. There's still money to be made. Big money. There's many a gentleman will pay well for a virgin. Don't say much for London, do it, that you've got to find 'em about twelve years old for 'em to be . . .'

'Virgo intacta?' asked Bandicoot.

'I don't see their birth sign has much to do with it,' commented Dixon sagely. 'They say they're all the same length lying down. Mind you, I'm a family man, me. If any pimp laid hands on my girls, I'd break his neck.'

'Or suffocate him?' Bandicoot was proud of that quip. It was worthy of Lestrade.

'I don't think immoral earnings was Mr Faye's only vice,'

said Lestrade, sweeping towards the lift. 'Come on, Bandicoot, we've got work.'

Faye had served a four-month sentence for procuring back in '86. Since then he appeared to have been clean – or lucky. But Lestrade had discovered, via his usual street sources, that the deceased had recently been moving in a rather different circle. He had gravitated, if that was the right word, from little girls to big boys.

'I always thought he had a hand in the Cleveland Street business in '87,' Jones grunted, picking his teeth with his gold pin. 'Mind you, there were too many big names involved in that. Half the Royal Horseguards, for a start.'

'For your benefit,' Lestrade turned to Bandicoot, 'a male brothel was uncovered in Cleveland Street. Some very prominent people, MPs, army officers and so on, were discovered to be using the place as a regular meeting point with errand boys.'

'Unfortunately most of them got off,' slurped Jones. 'Well, when you've been in the business as long as we have, Constable, you'll learn that the big fish usually get through the net.'

'And Philip Faye was a big fish?' asked Bandicoot.

'No,' said Lestrade levelly. 'And when you've been in the business as long as Inspector Jones has you'll learn that the little fish usually get through the net as well.'

The Cadogan Hotel was one of the most impressive in London. Like the Metropole it was one of the most fashionable among the Smart Set, in or out of season. It was mid-morning when Lestrade and Bandicoot arrived. They ordered coffee and brandy (Bandicoot was paying) and waited. Their targets were not long overdue. First, a large, scented man with a fur coat, thick, sensitive lips and a rather ridiculous Neronian haircut. With him, but always a little in his shadow, a slim, blond, young man with classical features.

'Mr Oscar Wilde?'

'I am he.'

'Inspector Lestrade, Scotland Yard. This is Constable Bandicoot.'

'Ah, how quaint. Part of the long arm of the law. You know who I am. May I present Lord Alfred Douglas?' The slim young man bowed. 'Bosie, be an angel and get us all a drink, will you? Unless of course you gentlemen are on duty and don't.'

'We are on duty and we do,' answered Lestrade.

'Now, gentlemen, pray be seated. To what do I owe the pleasure?'

'Pleasure, Mr Wilde?'

'Oh, Inspector,' Wilde tapped Lestrade's knee. 'You are a wag.'

'Philip Faye,' said Lestrade.

'Oh, dear me, yes. Poor Philip.' Wilde's face darkened and he rested his head in his hand in a flamboyant gesture. 'A tragedy. An absolute tragedy.'

'When did you last see him?' A waiter brought a tray of brandies to Lord Alfred Douglas.

'No, no,' he said, 'put them on Mr Wilde's bill.'

'Ah, let me see, Bosie, was it Monday last we saw poor Philip? At the Albemarle?'

'Possibly, Oscar. You know I always found him irritating.'

'Irritating, My Lord?' asked Lestrade.

'He had St Vitus's dance, Inspector.'

'Oh, come now, Bosie. He may have been a prey to nervous disorders. He always reminded me of a character in my *Canterville Ghost*. Have you read it, Inspector?'

'I only read the *Police Gazette*, Mr Wilde. Has it appeared there?'

'Oh, Inspector, I see I must watch out. You are within an ace of snatching my reputation.'

'Your reputation is quite safe with me, Mr Wilde.' Lestrade was emphatic. 'Have you any reason to wish Mr Faye dead?'

'Good heavens, Inspector, Philip was one of my dearest friends.'

'Did you know he had a criminal record?'

'You mean that phonograph thing old Tennyson did? Yes it was pretty awful, wasn't it?'

Lestrade brushed aside the attempt at levity. 'No, I mean procuring little girls and boys.'

Wilde licked his lips. 'He was just misunderstood.'

'Now he is dead.' Lestrade went on. 'Tell me, Mr Wilde, did you kill him?'

'Inspector, I have been patient.' Wilde's inane grin had vanished. 'But when you accuse me of the murder of a very dear friend . . .'

'I have accused you of nothing, Mr Wilde.'

'I must ask you to lower your voices, gentlemen,' snapped Douglas, 'Mr Wilde and I are regular patrons here.'

'So Faye's twitching annoyed you.' Lestrade now turned his attention to the young man.

'Eh?'

'You said he had St Vitus's dance. You said you found him irritating.'

'And that's not all I found him doing, eh Oscar?' Douglas smirked.

'You wicked boy,' scowled Wilde. 'Bosie, sometimes you can be so vulgar.'

'A lover's tiff?' Lestrade threw the challenge to the air.

Wilde and Douglas were both on their feet, protesting. Bandicoot thought he'd better get up too. He hadn't been happy about the way Douglas had been looking at him. Lestrade remained seated. 'He was a cottage loaf, My Lord – a homosexual under the meaning of the Act.'

'Act?' Douglas was furious.

'Say nothing, Bosie. Remember your father.'

'Do you know who he is?' Lestrade asked.

Douglas aimed a punch which Bandicoot caught and held easily in mid-air. Douglas scowled defiantly at Bandicoot's collar stud, on a level with his eyes. 'Doesn't say much for the Queensberry Rules, sir,' Bandicoot couldn't resist saying to Lestrade.

'You obnoxious bastards,' Douglas screamed at the policemen.

'Please, My Lord,' replied Lestrade, 'this *is* the Cadogan Hotel.'

Wilde stopped in mid-fume. 'What a superlative phrase, Inspector. I wish I had said that.'

And to a man, the clientele of the Cadogan Hotel turned and with one voice chanted, 'You will, Oscar, you will.'

The white lady

McNaghten had reached the end of his tether. Complaints from the family of Queensberry had been flooding in all week. Complaints too from a story writer named Wilde. The latter McNaghten could ignore – he had never heard of the man. But the Marquis of Queensberry, objectionable little man though he was, was of the 'fancy', the coterie of the P.O.W. himself. And that could not be ignored. One more instance of innuendo without fact, threats without proof and Inspector Lestrade would become Constable Lestrade, directing traffic in Piccadilly.

In the meantime, the inevitable mourning letter had arrived –

Where is Philip, where is he?
Fairly cover'd up, you see!
Cloth and all are lying on him;
He has pull'd down all upon him

Lestrade checked his copy of *Struwwelpeter*. Bandicoot had not remembered this story. It was too trivial, too ridiculous. And even Agrippa, it seemed, was finding it difficult to match a homosexual pimp with the innocuous boy who fidgeted at his papa's dining table. Lestrade was wondering who Johnny Head-in-Air might be and what might befall him, when Arabella McNaghten swept into his office.

'Sholto, you must come for Christmas. Papa is taking us all to Lynton. And I know you have three days' leave. Now, not a word. We shall expect you on the twenty-third.'

And she left.

Bandicoot buried his face in some suddenly absorbing papers. Dew was freezing quietly in the street some miles away, keeping a vigil near the house of Dr Conan Doyle, who had not yet gone south for the winter.

'Lynton,' Lestrade repeated mechanically.

'It's a rather quaint village, sir, situated above the mouth of the Lyn river, near Barnstaple.'

'Thank you, Bandicoot, we can dispense with the guide book. Is the woman mad?'

Was this another of Arabella's flights of fancy, he wondered to himself, continuing the rhetorical questions in the confines of his own mind. Or was it a clumsy attempt by McNaghten Senior to patch up the damage of a whole series of recent stormy exchanges in his office? Certainly Lestrade had not been invited before, although it was not unheard of for McNaghten to invite his staff, singly or in pairs, to his country house in the West Country. But he had no more time to ponder it at the moment. A tall young man with waxed moustache and centre parting appeared at the door.

'Mr McGillicuddy, sir,' a constable announced him.

'Oswald McGillicuddy,' the young man extended a hand. 'I expect you know my father, the balloonist?'

'No,' said Lestrade. He was not at his best at this hour of the day, especially as it was Saturday and he had just been rattled by the unrattlable Miss McNaghten.

'I've come to report what I think may be a murder.'

Lestrade felt even worse.

'Bandicoot, some tea for Mr . . . er . . .?'

'McGillicuddy. Oswald.'

'Tea for Mr McGillicuddy.'

Exit Bandicoot.

'I reported it at Bow Street yesterday,' the young man went on. 'They wrote it all down and then told me to see you. Er . . . you are Inspector Lestrade?'

'At the moment. What is your news?'

'Well, perhaps I should explain, if you are not aware' – McGillicuddy looked a little hurt – 'that I come from an aeronautical family.'

Lestrade attempted to look sage. 'Do you mean you are a trapeze artist?'

'No, no, Inspector. We are balloonists. It is a little-known fact that my great-great-grandfather gave Etienne Montgolfier his first lesson. Anyway, more recently, we have become interested in other forms of flight. My cousin Albert, you may remember' – Lestrade did not – 'leapt from the Eiffel Tower the year before last in an attempt to prove da Vinci's theory.'

'Which was?'

'Wrong.'

'Ah.'

'Well, we are a family used to sudden bereavement, Inspector. And to injury in the cause of aeronautical science. You'd never guess, would you, that this arm is not my own?'

'Good God,' marvelled Lestrade, 'whose is it?'

McGillicuddy waved a marvellously wrought limb. 'It's made of painted gutta-percha, you know. I can do almost anything with it, but I must take care when toasting crumpets.'

'A wise precaution.'

'It might melt, you see.'

Lestrade was becoming convinced he was in the presence of a madman when Bandicoot arrived with the tea. McGillicuddy deliberately used his left hand, curling the fingers by means of a switch wired beneath his coat lapel.

'Another of my family's interests,' he beamed.

Lestrade left that stone unturned. 'Your murder?' he said.

'Ah, yes. My cousin, John Torquil. He died when his Maxim steam-powered Bisley hit a tree at thirty-eight miles an hour.'

'You mean he was driving a horseless carriage?'

'No, no, Inspector. The Maxim Bisley is an aeroplane. A featherless bird. The tragedy was that Hiram Maxim was there at the time. I do hope he doesn't lose hope. It was not his machine that was at fault, you see.'

'Do I understand,' persisted Lestrade, 'that your cousin, the deceased, was actually flying?' He and Bandicoot felt their chins hitting their respective desks.

'Ah, there's the rub, Inspector. For flight to be called flight, an aviator must take his craft off the ground for a reasonable period of time. It cannot in other words be a fluke – a spring bounce or a freak gust of wind. John was, in my opinion, as a somewhat partial observer I admit, about to manage sustained flight, when the machine dipped and his superstructure disintegrated. Without wings, of course, he ploughed through a hedge, hit an oak and ended up in the lake. There was a resounding crash. We all ran to him, but it was too late. Poor fellow had broken his neck.'

'Forgive me, Mr McGillicuddy, but isn't what you're describing merely a regrettable accident?'

'Ah, no, Inspector. I thought you would say that, so I took the liberty of bringing along proof.'

McGillicuddy stepped into the corridor, operated his artificial arm and lifted in a piece of steel about four feet long, from which hung wires and wooden struts, dangling with canvas.

'Observe the end,' he said. 'Sawn through, gentlemen. Sawn through. When one is a scientific aviator, one is aware of stresses in metals. If steel sheers off, it does not do it like that. This machine was tampered with before John Torquil took to the air – if took he did.'

'And who had access to the machine prior to the . . . er . . . flight?'

'The mechanics who built it. Hiram Maxim who designed it. Myself and John Torquil. Oh, and possibly Armytage Monk.'

For a brief moment, Lestrade toyed with a Catholic inspired plot, then he rejected it.

'I have been in the Force long enough to know that I cannot exclude you, sir. Oh, please, do not take umbrage. I suspect that Bandicoot here is of the opinion that no sane murderer would walk voluntarily into two police stations and obligingly point a finger, albeit a false one, at himself.'

Bandicoot nodded. Lestrade felt a little pompous, rather like the late lamented Sherlock Holmes, but he was in his stride now and refused, mixed metaphor though it was, to back up.

'I, however, have known guilty parties do just that, in the mistaken belief that suspicion may be averted. Tell me, did the deceased leave a will?'

'I don't believe so. Both his parents are still living and he himself was unmarried. Presumably his worldly goods revert to his mater and pater.'

Lestrade faced the window. 'Where did this accident take place?'

'At Bisley, on the rifle ranges. Hence the machine's name. One needs the level ground, you see, for take-off.'

'Bandicoot, inform the desk sergeant. You and I are bound for Bisley.'

It was mid-afternoon when the three arrived. Raw. Cold. The sky promised snow, a return of the bitter weather of the previous winter. Lestrade inspected the mangled wreck of the Bisley, housed in an improvised shed McGillicuddy referred to as a hangar. Hiram Maxim, the inventor of the famous machine-gun whose carriage had once run over Lestrade's feet, was a large voluble American, though his accent broke through the interminable jargon of the scientifically obsessed only occasionally.

'The Bisley's wingspan is a hundred feet. The body is sixty-seven feet. The propeller is driven by a fifty-horse-power steam engine weighing three and a half tons. I think on my next attempt I'll use rails to help stabilise the thing.'

'You mean you're going to try this again?' said Lestrade.

'Of course,' Maxim and McGillicuddy chorused. 'The march of science,' Maxim went on alone.

'As I told you, Inspector,' McGillicuddy continued, 'the Bisley's prop was sawn through. This was no accident.'

There were only two mechanics who had worked on the Bisley on the days before the tragedy. Lestrade and Bandicoot interviewed them together and Lestrade was convinced at any rate they were honest as the day was long. Bandicoot was less certain; one of them, it came out in conversation, was a socialist.

Over brandy at the Commandant's house where the American inventor was a guest, Hiram Maxim that evening also convinced Lestrade of his innocence. Bore he may have been, murderer he was not. And as the snow flurries thickened across the silent ranges at Bisley, Lestrade became more convinced than ever that he had his eleventh victim. Agrippa had struck again. John Torquil was Johnny Head-In-Air.

'Tell me about Armytage Monk,' said Lestrade, rolling the brandy balloon between his hands.

'Not much to tell,' McGillicuddy answered. 'John brought him over to Bisley about a fortnight ago. I hadn't met the man before and I gathered John didn't know him well. It seems he was a keen aviator though and very anxious for John to fly the Bisley.'

'If he was such a keen aviator, why didn't he fly it himself?'

'Ah, he couldn't. He'd had an accident the year before himself, and had permanently damaged his neck.'

'His neck?'

'Yes, he couldn't speak properly, poor chap. Had a guttural, sort of rasping voice – and he always kept his throat muffled even indoors. There was one odd thing though.'

'Oh?'

'Well, this is going to sound ridiculous, but John and Armytage often seemed to be . . . well, giggling is about the size of it. Exchanging the odd glance as though they were enjoying some sort of private joke. Probably at our expense.'

'Is Monk a big man?'

'Yes, I'd say so. About six foot and broad.'

Lestrade leaned forward penetratingly. 'What was the colour of his eyes?'

'Good God, Inspector, I haven't the faintest idea.'

'They were blue, Inspector,' Maxim offered from the corner. 'Icy blue.'

'Why should you remember that, sir?' asked Lestrade.

'Why should you ask it?' Maxim countered.

'I have my reasons, sir.'

'I am a scientist, Inspector – a trained observer. I notice all sorts of things about all sorts of things – and people.'

'And what else did you notice about Armytage Monk?'

'I didn't like him, certainly. He had an air of falseness about him. And he didn't know a great deal about aeronautics for all that, as McGillicuddy says, he was so keen for Torquil to fly the Bisley.'

*

Lestrade tried to forget, at least for a while. It was Christmas, or nearly so. He caught the west-bound train to Swindon and cursed Mr Brunel anew for his wide gauge. One day they would change the damned thing and there would be no need to sojourn in Swindon again. By midday he was at Minehead and made the rest of his way by coach. This was a mistake and he regretted his momentary whim for the old-fashioned. Porlock Hill was still slippery with the morning frost where the sun had not penetrated through the thickly clumped trees. After a few horrendous slides and the whinnying terror of the horses, the driver gave up and demanded that the passengers get out and walk on up with their baggage. After an hour or so of whipping and yelling, the coach reached the top. Lestrade sat frozen on his Gladstone bag. The Christmas spirit, not surprisingly, had left him.

Consequently, it was nearly nightfall before the inspector arrived at The Tors. It was an immense house rather more like an hotel than anything, jutting out boldly from a dense covering of evergreens on the craggy outcrop below Countisbury Foreland. Lestrade looked out at the wintry sea curling under the ringed moon. What was he doing here? He looked at the opulent house and voiced silently his suspicion of a policeman with private means. Such things shouldn't exist. Then the house was alive with shouts, dogs barking and lights scurrying here and there in the driveway.

'Sholto!' It was Arabella, looming large and comfortable out of the dusk. She gave Lestrade a peck on his frozen cheek. 'You darling man, you're quite numb. Come in. Papa's expecting you.'

After hours in a draughty coach and on the road with silent or surly fellow travellers, Lestrade had about lost the use of his tongue, but a brandy and a crackling log fire soon revived him.

'I know it's Christmas, Lestrade,' McNaghten poured them both another drink, 'but I brought you here for a purpose. Tomorrow my other guests will be arriving. There'll be no time to talk to you then. Tonight, I want you to forget that I'm your superior. I want to talk to you man to man. The *Struwwelpeter* case. Do you have a suspect?'

'Several,' said Lestrade.

'Come on then, man. Let's have it.' Even in his dressing gown and smoking cap, McNaghten straightened the ever-present cravat.

'As you know, sir . . .' Lestrade began.

'Ah, no, Sholto. Man to man, remember. Sir *Melville* . . .'

Lestrade twitched his moustache at the unbridled generosity of that.

'At first I suspected Lawrence Alma-Tadema' – right again! – 'the artist.'

'Poppycock . . . Sholto.'

'As you implied . . . Sir Melville. You are of course quite right. I put some men on him.'

'Really, Lestrade, Lawrence is a family friend.'

'Even so, sir, I could not leave a stone unturned.'

'Very well.'

'He had a perfect alibi for the next two crimes. He is not Agrippa.'

'Quite.'

'But there is a connection. The black enamel that killed the Inky Boys did come from his studio, I'm sure of that.'

'How does it help?'

'I don't know . . . yet.'

'Go on.'

'Then it occurred to me that Agrippa might be killing red herrings. Multiple murders to disguise his *one* actual target.'

'Risky,' mused McNaghten, but both he and Lestrade knew it had been a prime suspicion in the Ripper case.

'But worth it. The question is, which is the real crime? My men and I have taken nearly two hundred depositions, Sir Melville. Perhaps somewhere in that two hundred is the man we are looking for.'

'Or perhaps not.'

'I then reasoned that Mrs Mauleverer was the murderer. She was related both to Albert Mauleverer and one of the Inky Boys, but that I rejected.'

'Why?'

'It's not a woman's crime, Sir Melville. Physical strength was required in almost all the murders. Constance Mauleverer is a small woman. It would have been beyond her.'

'What of Conan Doyle?'

'Ah, yes. I suspected him and Doctor John Watson of a double act. Their motives I could not guess at, but the fact that there were two of them explained Agrippa's rapid and effortless disappearance. One killed while the other kept watch and covered tracks.'

Again, unknown to each other, both men thought of the Ripper case.

'Again, I had them both watched. Their alibis are sound. And I know John Watson. Bad writer he may be, mediocre doctor he may be, but he is no murderer.'

'So where does that leave us?'

'The Tors, Sir Melville, Christmas 1891.'

'What? Oh, yes, I see. No more suspects?'

'Agrippa is elusive but he is not superhuman. We know some things about him. First, he is a big man, about six foot tall, heavy and powerful. He is a master of disguise, able to play a passionate lover as in the case of Harriet Wemyss, an aeronautical enthusiast in the case of John Torquil.' And Madame Slopesski in the case of Isaac Prendergast, Lestrade added silently to himself. He could not bring himself still to admit to his superior, now suddenly his 'equal', that he had once been in the same room with Agrippa. 'We know he has a warped sense of humour, using the children's verse, *Shock-headed Peter*, as a pattern for his crimes. And one other thing – Agrippa is a snob.'

'A snob, Sholto?'

'Look at his victims. Where is the costermonger, fishwife, cordwainer, flower-girl? Every one of his victims was well-to-do, genteel, rich.'

'What about Peter himself?'

'Ah yes. I'm coming to the conclusion that Peter, whoever he was, was not one of Agrippa's victims.'

'Not?'

'No. The story of the finding of the body in Shanklin Chine was widely covered by most papers. Anybody could have read it, been reminded irresistibly of *Struwwelpeter* and gone to his grisly work.'

McNaghten sat down by the fire. 'What happens,' he asked Lestrade, 'when the murders end? Isn't there one to go?'

Lestrade nodded. 'Flying Robert,' he said.

'Will we see an end then, Lestrade? Will we see an end?'

The Valley of the Rocks lies on the edge of Exmoor. Blackmore's Exmoor, the Exmoor of the wild Doones of Badgeworthy, who had terrorised the moor in the seventeenth century. It was also the Exmoor of The Chains, near Brendon Two Gates, where a man might drown in the clawing, sucking mud if he took one wrong step. The Valley was hardly the spot for a walk in winter, but Lestrade had agreed to accompany Arabella: he felt a little out of place as the massive McNaghten clan and friends began to arrive the next morning and Arabella had promised to break his arm if he refused. Even Lestrade felt the atmosphere. The sea was chiselled into steel-coloured ridges below him and it was unnerving to be higher than the gulls on those narrow ledges. Here and there sheep and goats clustered close to the rock for shelter. Lestrade kept as far as he was able in the lee of Miss McNaghten.

'Stand here, Sholto,' she called above the wind.

Lestrade stood opposite her in a whistling gap in the rocks.

'Look around you,' she said. 'We are standing in the White Lady.'

'Oh?'

'If you look at these rocks from the Valley road, this cleft is in the shape of a lady, outlined against the sky. Legend has it that if a girl stands with her lover in this spot, they shall be joined for ever.' Her hands reached out for his. He kept them firmly in his pockets. The silent pleading face turned to a smile as she turned out of the wind. 'Sholto, you've let me down. Again.'

'Arabella, there must be dozens of young men beating a path to your door. Why me? I can't rival all this – a house in the country, servants.'

'I don't want all this, Sholto.' She took his arm and pressed herself into his Donegal. 'Let's go home. Papa will be fretting.'

'Doesn't he trust me with his favourite daughter?'

'Oh, yes, Sholto. But he doesn't trust me with his favourite detective.'

*

Somehow Lestrade battled through the evening. Few people spoke to him. But in a way he was glad of that. He retired early and was in bed and asleep long before midnight. It must have been three or four and a raw, cold morning when he felt a body, a live one, sneak into his bed. He wasn't used to four-posters and completely misjudged the distance between it and the ground so that he fell heavily and hurt his shoulder.

'Sholto, don't be so ridiculous. You'll wake the whole house.'

'Arabella,' Lestrade hissed, 'what the devil are you doing here?'

'Get back into bed and I'll show you,' drooled the voice in the darkness.

'Good God, woman, have you no finer feelings? And in your mother's house.'

'Yes, and with my father's right-hand man.' She leaned over and tugged at his night shirt.

'It's nice of you to accord me that title, but I think you exaggerate. Anyway, you're missing my point.'

'Oh, I hope not.' And she heaved him into bed.

For once in his life, Sholto Lestrade laid his scruples aside. Arabella McNaghten was quite attractive in an odd sort of way. And it was dark. And it was Christmas. He put all thoughts of McNaghten Senior and of Constance Mauleverer out of his mind and rolled, a little coyly, into the arms of Arabella.

'Merry Christmas!' The noise boomed through the house. There were clashings and hurryings. Lestrade sat bolt upright as a scarlet- and white-clad Sir Melville swept into his bedroom. In a blind panic, Lestrade turned from right to left looking for Arabella. He thought in a split second of the feeblest of excuses – she had found the wrong room. The bed was so big he hadn't realised she was there. She had fainted, and he had taken . . . Oh, no, that sounded dreadful, but in the event, she wasn't there.

'Merry Christmas, Sholto.' Father McNaghten shoved a huge Havana into Lestrade's open mouth. 'Yes, I know it's a shock. And it's not something I'd care for you to relate at the Yard, but it's something of a family tradition here at The Tors.' And he scuttled off to distribute his other goodies to his other guests.

Lestrade somersaulted off the bed, landing on the same shoulder, of course, and peered beneath the gloom of the coverlet. An elegant chamber-pot, but no Arabella. Behind the curtains? No. The wardrobe? Only his one good suit.

There was a knock on the door to interrupt his search. It was the maid with his morning hot water and shaving tackle. In the corridor, Arabella swept past in a flurry of silk. 'Good morning, Inspector. Merry Christmas.'

It had been a long time since Lestrade had known a family Christmas. The glittering tree, the gaily wrapped presents, the chattering and squeals of children. Luncheon was splendid – goose, chicken, pheasant, dumplings, a light wine and seemingly endless claret. After the meal, during which Lestrade was bored to death by Arabella's deaf grandmama, who persisted with her reminiscences of her holidays in Hastings, charades was the order of the day. Lestrade grinned icily throughout the lame performances, but he had to admit secretly that he quite enjoyed himself. Arabella was busy with the children for most of the day and that night Lestrade locked his door and slept more soundly.

The feast of St Stephen was celebrated with rough shooting. McNaghten enlisted the aid of local beaters and Lestrade was given a twelve-bore. As he crooked it in his arm, he thought of Albert Mauleverer. And he was still thinking of him when the explosion ripped through his cap and collar. He felt the sting in his cheek and ear, which spun him round. He lay floundering awkwardly in a ditch. At first he thought he was dead, but the frozen bracken sticking in his ear convinced him otherwise. Next he thought his own gun had gone off and how stupid he would feel trying to explain that. Before he could realise anything else, he was being peered at by blue, anxious faces wreathed in icy breath. Hands lifted him out and on to a blanket. There were shouts, dogs barking and he passed out.

He awoke to the chime of the great-grandfather clock downstairs. He heard eight chimes, but he suspected it was later. He moved his right arm. Still there, still intact. And felt the crisp, clean bandage round his throat. He hauled himself upright. The room. The Tors. He was alive.

'My dear chap . . .' McNaghten swept in, brushing his wife and daughter back out of the room. 'How do you feel?'

'Would it be too much of a cliché, sir, to ask what happened?' He'd already answered his own cliché – 'Where am I?'

'Damnedest thing,' flustered McNaghten, 'my gun went off. I'd just loaded the thing and was bringing it up when I stumbled on a tussock and it went off. I could have killed you, Sholto.'

Lestrade mumbled that it didn't matter. All in a day's shoot, etc. etc.

'Doctor says you've a clean wound. Your hat and coat stopped most of it and you'll make up the loss of blood in no time. Feel up to some broth, old chap?'

Lestrade felt more up to some broth than the old chap routine. He felt even more embarrassed at being in this situation now that he was confined to bed. He stood it, the fussing of the McNaghtens, for one more day and then, despite their protestations, he struggled into his bloody Donegal and hailed a cab for the station.

As he trudg'd along to school,
It was always Johnny's rule,
To be looking at the sky
And the clouds that floated by;
But just what before him lay,
In his way,
Johnny never thought about;
So that everyone cried out –
'Look at little Johnny there,
Little Johnny Head-In-Air!

Lestrade read it – the mourning letter. Posted on Christmas Eve. London postmark.

'In the book, of course,' Bandicoot was musing intelligently (Lestrade surmised that Santa must have brought him a brain for Christmas), 'Johnny is nearly drowned. Falls into a river carrying a writing case. Agrippa must be slipping.'

'Agrippa's done a pretty good job so far,' answered Lestrade, settling into his chair as gently as he could without moving his head. 'He's entitled to a little lapse now and again.'

'May I venture an observation, sir?'

Lestrade nodded.

'I think you have quite a soft spot for Agrippa. Oh, it's grudging all right, but a soft spot nevertheless.'

'I do admire his planning, I'll admit. But it'll give me great satisfaction to see his neck stretched.'

'Tell me, sir, what happens when Flying Robert is dead? Will that be the end of Agrippa?'

Lestrade looked at him levelly.

'You have my word,' he said, 'that Flying Robert will not die, not unless Agrippa goes with him.'

Bandicoot chuckled awkwardly. 'Forgive me, sir, but how do you intend to protect all the Roberts in Britain?'

'I don't have to, Bandicoot. I only have to protect one.'

It was the first day of the New Year. 1892. The old Queen entered the fifty-sixth year of her reign. The constable entered the front door of the Yard to collide sharply with a grubby-faced street urchin on his way out.

'Now then, now then,' growled Dew, looking enormous above the lad, 'you're in a hurry, sonny.'

'I don' wanna be seen round 'ere, do I?' squawked the boy, trying to struggle free, 'I'd never live it down.'

'Why are you here, then?' asked Dew.

'Hold him, Constable.' Sergeant Dixon, crimson and sweating came tumbling along the corridor. 'This little bleeder was hanging round the front desk. I've been chasin' him all over the building.'

'No need, mister, I was only deliverin' a note.'

'Note?' asked Dew.

'Iss on the desk. I was puttin' it there when 'e come chargin' up.' The urchin jabbed a revolting thumb in Dixon's direction.

'Bring him along, Constable.' The sergeant picked up the note, sure enough where the boy said he had put it, and perused the contents. His eyes widened as he did so.

'Inspector Lestrade about?' he whispered to Dew.

'I don't know, Sarge. I've just come on duty.'

'Bring him!' The policemen and their struggling charge made for the lift.

Lestrade lolled back in his chair, feet crossed on the desk. He balanced his nose, tipless since the duel of last year, on his fingers. He suddenly found himself wondering what this street-Arab must think of his appearance. His face was seamed by myriad old cuts – the plate glass from the Albino Club in Cambridge; he had the crimson wrist from Bandicoot's careless tea-making on his first day and his neck still encased in bandages. He read the note again –

Come to Hengler's Circus, January 1st 1892

Agrippa.

It was typewritten, the paper and envelope edged in black. There was no stamp, no postmark.

'Who gave you this?'

'A bloke.'

'Bloke?' Bandicoot asked.

'Yer – a bloke. 'E's a bloody toff, ain''e?' observed the boy. Dixon cuffed him round the ear.

'What did this bloke look like?' asked Lestrade.

'I dunno.'

'Think!' Lestrade slammed his fist down on the desk.

The boy jumped. ''E was tall, wiv a titfer and muffler.'

Bandicoot looked perplexed. 'I'll explain it to you later,' said Lestrade. 'What did he say?'

'Nuffin. 'Cept give this note to them at the Cop Shop.'

'Which Cop Shop?' asked Dixon.

'*This* one, o'course.'

'How do you know?' asked Lestrade.

'Stands to reason, don' it? 'E was only 'cross the road and 'e pointed in 'ere.'

Bandicoot and Dew raced to the window, but of Agrippa there was no sign.

'Look, guv'nor,' the boy went on, 'I was only doin' a job. I didn't mean no 'arm.'

'How much did the bloke tip you?' asked Lestrade.

'A tanner.'

He felt in his pocket. 'Dew' – the constable fished out some coins from his pockets and handed them to Lestrade – 'here's a bob. Go on, get out.' Lestrade flipped him the coin. 'And sonny,' the boy stopped, 'tell your grandchildren you once spoke to the long-legged scissor man.'

The boy looked puzzled, bit his shilling piece and disappeared.

'I'll reimburse you, Constable.' Lestrade quieted the anxiety forming on Dew's brow.

'You're not going, sir?' Bandicoot asked.

Lestrade looked up at him. 'With your background, Bandicoot, you're not very good at working-class slang are you? Cockney patter?'

'No, sir.'

'What do they call policemen, Bandicoot?'

'Sir?'

'The great British public – what do they call us?'

'Er . . . Peelers, sir.'

'Sometimes . . .' Lestrade waited for more.

'Er . . . Bobbies?'

'Better. Why, Bandicoot?'

'Why, because the Metropolitan Police was founded by Sir Robert Peel, sir, then Home Secretary.'

'Quite so,' nodded Lestrade. 'You asked me a couple of days ago how I intended to protect all the Roberts in Britain. There is only one Robert at risk, Bandicoot – only one Bobby – and that's me.'

Finale

Melville McNaghten could not believe his eyes. There it was, on the front page of the *Evening Standard* that he had bought on his way into the Yard. 'Shocking series of murders,' it said. 'Eleven Dead – Whole Affair Based on Children's Rhymes – Scotland Yard Have Known For Months'. The editorial railed on about police incompetence and Sir Melville's name loomed larger than life, in thick black print. So did Lestrade's. McNaghten was still reading the fine print, his job becoming less secure every second when he overheard two women talking on the tram next to him. He didn't normally go by public transport, but he had returned from his Christmas vacation earlier than planned, leaving his vehicle at The Tors for the convenience of his family and guests. One woman said to the other, 'Really, my dear, these policemen. I just don't know what the world is coming to. And Scotland Yard, the paper says, Has Known for Months. Isn't it criminal?'

'Indeed, ma'am,' McNaghten butted in. 'Criminal's the word.'

The ladies huddled closer together, the furthest clutching her infant to her bosom.

'I don't believe we were addressing you, sir.' The nearest woman was arch.

'Forgive me, madam, I am not normally so discourteous, but you see, I am a policeman. Sir Melville McNaghten, Head of the Criminal Investigation Department.' He tipped his hat with unusual malevolence. 'And you are?'

The ladies hesitated. 'I am Miss August and this is Mrs Miller,' came the frosty answer. 'Don't tell me you're going to arrest us.'

'No, ma'am. I just feel that one good name deserves another. For your information, one of these victims was a policeman. And I've the best brains at my disposal tirelessly working around the clock to catch this man.'

The ladies were on their mettle. 'Huh!' it was Mrs Miller's turn to sneer. 'For all the success you've had my little Agatha could solve crimes more quickly than you.'

McNaghten snapped shut his paper and stood up. The ladies gasped, Mrs Miller burying little Agatha's face in her shawl, but they were witnessing not a defeat exactly, more a tactical withdrawal. Anyway, it was McNaghten's stop.

In his office, the Head of the Criminal Investigation Department twirled his moustache and smoothed down his cravat.

'Tea,' he bawled at Dew, 'and Lestrade. Not necessarily in that order.'

'I'm afraid the inspector is out, sir.'

'Out?' McNaghten was pacing the room. 'His duty doesn't end for . . .' he checked his half-hunter '. . . another hour. Where's he gone?'

'I don't know, sir.' Dew had his fingers crossed behind his back.

McNaghten fretted and fumed. Then he rang the offices of the *Evening Standard*. The line was dreadful, crackling and erratic, the incessant click of the presses and his own stirring of the tea didn't help. He ascertained from the editor that the reporter who had written the article was T.A. 'Scoop' Liesinsdad. 'Foreigner is he?' grunted McNaghten. 'Welsh,' was the reply. 'Thought so,' rejoined McNaghten. Liesinsdad, or at least his voice, appeared on the other end of the telephone. Yes, he had been given the story personally, over the telephone, by a man. Yes. Yes. With a husky voice. But it could have been the line. There's a lot of noise here, you know. McNaghten knew. Yes, it was true. Liesinsdad had no reason to doubt it. Could McNaghten comment? No, he could not. How had one man deluded the Yard for so long? And was it possible he was Jack the Ripper? McNaghten had had enough. 'Stay there,' he bellowed. 'I'm sending constables round. If you've heard Agrippa's voice, I want to talk to you face to face.'

As he hung up the receiver a thought occurred. Why not go himself? It could only be a matter of minutes before someone told the Commissioner that the press had the whole story. Tomorrow it would be in *The Times* and the Home Secretary would read it. Then the Prime Minister, then the Queen. Heads would roll, and the first to bounce in the gutter would be McNaghten's. But, if he could move fast enough, pick this reporter's brains for some minute but vital clue. If he could follow up this clue. Today . . . now . . . then he might just save himself. Damn the constables. He'd go himself.

Lestrade did not, despite what he told Bandicoot, go alone. He carried in the pocket of his Donegal the Apache knife and knuckleduster which he always carried when danger lurked. Besides, there were hundreds of people thronging through Argyle Street that crisp January evening. Upon the chatter and the laughter, the bright expectant faces of the children and the smell of roasting chestnuts, the stars looked down.

'How much?' inquired Lestrade of the ticket man at the Corinthian Bazaar.

'Yer pays yer money, guv'ner, yer takes yer choice. Move along now, there's lots wants to get in.'

Lestrade produced the coins and found a seat. The ring was lit with sulphur and electricity. Everywhere was the smell of greasepaint and elephants. In the centre was an artificial lake, with a real tree in the middle of it and armfuls of imitation shrubbery round the edge. The band of the Grenadier Guards no less had been hired to play for the evening and all the tunes of glory were trotted out. Lestrade had not been to a circus for years. The glitter and the dazzle made him forget, temporarily, why he was there. The clowns rolled about, spraying water over each other and throwing buckets of confetti at the crowd. Elephants danced and pirouetted, bespangled young men and women swanned through the air on their flying trapeze. Over it all were the roars and gasps of the crowd – as the foot slipped momentarily on the high wire, as the lion snarled and would not back away, as the dwarfs and giants and armless men and pig-faced ladies ambled in grotesque postures. There was even a touch of the Music Hall, the house roared along with the lyrics of a popular song, but it was a sudden memory, the music perhaps, that reminded Lestrade once more of *Struwwelpeter*. He knew the whole book off by heart, the whole stinking thing. And the last verse, the one yet to be acted out, he felt sure, on him –

Now look at him, silly fellow,
Up he flies
To the skies.
No one heard his screams and cries,
Through the clouds the rude wind bore him,
And his hat flew on before him . . .

'Sir.'

Lestrade spun to his left, jarring his neck. It was Bandicoot bending over him.

'Siddown,' yelled a man behind. A lady hit Bandicoot with her umbrella. He squatted awkwardly at Lestrade's knee.

'What in blazes are you doing here?' Lestrade hissed at him. 'I thought I gave instructions.'

'I'm sorry, sir, I couldn't stay away. If there's a chance to get Agrippa, I want to be there.'

'This is my collar, Bandicoot.' Lestrade didn't want this young man there. It was not something he'd dare admit, but he had a strange feeling that he would not come through tonight. He remembered the letter in his pocket. The one which served as a last will and testament. He had meant to post it outside the Corinthian, but the moment had gone.

'Now you're here, you can take this.'

'What is it, sir?'

'Even at Eton, Bandicoot, they must have told you what a letter looks like.'

'Yes, sir, of course. But it's addressed to the Commissioner.'

'Very good, Bandicoot. You're improving all the time.'

'Do you wish me to deliver it personally, sir?'

'Yes, but only in the event of my death.'

'That settles it! Bandicoot stuffed the envelope into his pocket and forced himself down on to the floor. 'I'm staying.'

'Bandicoot,' Lestrade's voice had changed, 'do you think I'd let a social misfit like you interfere tonight? I've spent ten months chasing Agrippa and this is the nearest I've come to catching him. The last thing I want is your great feet getting in the way. Now go home. That is an order. Ignore it and I'll have you off the Force so fast you won't be able to say "Dry Bobs"!'

Although he was amazed that Lestrade should know Eton terminology, Bandicoot was genuinely stung by the rebuke of his superior. He was, as Lestrade knew, a sensitive lump of a man at heart.

'Very well, sir, but at least take this. It belonged to my father.'

'The *Evening Standard*?'

'No, sir, what is wrapped in it. I'm not a particularly Godly man, Inspector Lestrade, but I hope He's with you tonight.'

'You and me both, laddie. On your way.'

'Siddown,' yelled the man in the row behind again, but Bandicoot had gone into the shadows before the same umbrella could descend.

Lestrade looked down. Gleaming in the newspaper was a revolver. A beautifully chased pearl-handled Smith and Wesson, .44 calibre. He had seen drawings of guns like this at the Yard, but never in the flesh. On the barrel, in the half light, he read the inscription: *To H.B. May you always have the last shot*. How Lestrade echoed those sentiments tonight.

Then Lestrade saw the headlines for the first time. Like Melville McNaghten, he couldn't believe it. He dashed for the door and read the story with the aid of the bright lights in the foyer.

'Are you feeling good-natured, dearie?' An ageing hag with rouge and bad breath fondled his arm.

'Not now, I'm not,' mused Lestrade, half to himself.

'Perhaps I can interest you in something juicy, dearie. My niece has just come up from the country. Thirteen, she is.'

Lestrade came to. 'Is that so, madam?' he rounded on her.

'Then you'd better send her back to the country, or I might start to remember Mr Labouchere's Bill concerning the use of young virgins for illicit purposes.'

The prostitute gave up, flounced her feather boa and swung her backside into the night. 'Suit yourself, dearie, she's no virgin anyway.'

Lestrade's brain was whirling. What he had dreaded for months had happened. Now it would be common knowledge. There would be panics, hysterics, witch-hunts. It would be the Ripper case all over again. He could just imagine it. Anyone who knew the *Struwwelpeter* rhyme would be under suspicion. Any tall tailor with scissors in his hand, any painter with a pot of black paint, any smoker with a box of lucifers. He and McNaghten could kiss goodbye to their jobs, of course. But then, he reflected, after tonight that wouldn't matter, would it?

He heard the finale beginning. Clowns dressed as policemen, grossly fat and crimson-faced were chasing sea-lions around the lake. Inevitably, with the perfect timing of circus clowns, one by one they slipped and fell into the water, the sea-lions applauding with the crowd as they clambered out, only to slip back again. The band struck up and out of the centre of the lake a tableau arose, mermaids and sirens dressed in dazzling colours, topped by Britannia, resplendent in helmet and shield. Fireworks shot starward through an aperture in the skylight. The crowd roared and roared again. Then the band fell silent. Only a drum roll carried on. The crowd were hushed. To one side of the ring a tall young man, glittering in spangles, climbed into a huge cannon. It was a new variation for a Hengler Circus, never seen in London before. All the handbills had carried the word 'Human Cannonball' and as soon as Lestrade saw it, he knew – 'Flying Robert'. Wherever Agrippa was, he planned to put Lestrade in there, and the last tale of *Struwwelpeter* would be acted out. The drum roll heightened. The fuse was lit. The ringmaster was shouting the numbers 'One – two – three – fire!' and simultaneously an explosion ripped through the hushed circus. The tall young man hurtled out, curled tight into a ball and splashed into the lake, inches short of the precariously balanced sea-creatures. There was silence. Even the sea-lions sensed the tension of the moment and then an astonishing roar of relief and delight as the young man straightened up out of the water and took his place beside Britannia. Lestrade's heart was in his mouth, as was the heart of every spectator there, but for different reasons.

Amid tumultuous applause, the parade of the animals began and the crowd, tired and happy, scattered for the exit. Lestrade sat there motionless, hands on his knees, the devastating newspaper on his lap. No one moved him on, no one approached him. Even when circus staff arrived to sweep the droppings and sprinkle fresh sawdust, they ignored him. Then he heard the main doors lock with a click and he was alone in the darkened circus. The moon and the stars lit the scene and what was colour and noise and life before was silver-black and silent and dead. Lestrade stood up. He left his end seat and stepped down towards the deserted ring. His footsteps echoed in the vast emptiness of the Corinthian. He thought of cocking the revolver, but he might blow his foot off. What bothered him most was that his neck was so stiff from the gunshot blast. He could not move suddenly and that put him at a disadvantage.

Then he heard it, that low, whispering guttural voice. 'Down here, Inspector, by the lake.' This was the voice that Harriet Wemyss had been wooed by, the voice that had coaxed old Isaac Prendergast, at least momentarily, out of his seclusion.

'Agrippa?' Lestrade faltered on the final step. He couldn't see anything. 'I presume the cannon is reserved for me?'

A chill, hollow laugh. 'Flying Robert,' the voice said.

Lestrade had pinpointed the voice. Its direction. Yes, there in the shadows. He was sure of it. A shaft of moonlight fell on to the buttons of a clown-policeman, grotesquely rotund in a hoop and braces. Lestrade stood in the open, with his legs apart, ready to roll either way if he had to. He levelled the Smith and Wesson and cocked it. Once . . . Twice. He saw the hand rise to twirl the moustaches and fall to straighten the non-existent cravat.

'Come into the open, Sir Melville, the game is over.'

'How did you know it was me?'

'I didn't. Not until The Tors. That morning you came in as Father Christmas. You were wearing built-up shoes, weren't you?'

'Very observant, Inspector.'

'The eye-witnesses who saw Agrippa all mention the bulk of the man. You are too small. But that disguise convinced me that you might be capable of others more convincing.'

'And the voice?'

No one had moved yet.

'Come out of the shadows.' Lestrade's palm began to sweat.

'And the voice? What about the voice?'

'It's good. Madame Slopesski, the travelling salesman, all very professional.'

'But did you know I could throw my voice, Sholto?'

'What?'

'You see, I'm not really here at all.'

The figure in the shadows raised something. It looked like a stick and it threw it at Lestrade. Instinctively the inspector moved sideways, jerking his neck and firing simultaneously. There was a crash of splintering glass and a heavy object caught Lestrade round the ear. He lay stunned in the sawdust and by the time his consciousness had focused on the gun lying some feet away, somebody else had picked it up.

'Then, of course,' the clown policeman bent over him, 'then there are the eyes. Did none of your witnesses mention them? It is one of my failings, Sholto. I cannot bear to have my eyes covered or drops put in. My sight is not all that it should be. Have you spent these *three years* working with a man and you don't know his eyes are grey? But mine, Sholto, are blue.'

The voice had changed. It was softer, warmer. The clown policeman swept off his helmet and let the long dark hair cascade on to his shoulder. Lestrade blinked up in disbelief.

'Arabella?'

She straightened and walked away from the recumbent form of the inspector.

'What I suspect you never discovered, Sholto, with your appalling working-class background, is that the original Agrippa was a German magician of the sixteenth century. I fancy I have produced more magic in these four years than he ever could.'

'Why?' Lestrade had struggled to his knees.

'Clever little trick this, isn't it?' She indicated the broken glass, 'it's all done by mirrors, you know. By standing behind you and throwing my voice – well, Papa's voice – I was able to steal quite a march on you, wasn't I?'

Lestrade rose to one knee.

'Stay where you are!' Arabella's voice was harsh, her meaning unmistakable. 'In all my murders, Sholto, I never gave my victims an even chance. After all, like Queen Elizabeth, I have only the body of a weak and feeble woman . . .'

Lestrade would have found some humour in that, had he not been staring down the muzzle of Bandicoot's .44. 'Pretty little gun,' mused Arabella, following his gaze, 'you didn't draw this with Father's permission, I'll be bound.'

Lestrade's one hope was to keep her talking, to play for time. 'You know as well as I do he doesn't know I'm here. The gun belongs to Constable Bandicoot.'

'Ah yes, sweet boy.' Arabella smiled. 'I toyed with making him one of my victims, to show you all how unsafe you were, how easy it was to strike into the very heart of the Yard itself, but Bandicoot was too endearing. Forbes took his place in my scheme of things.'

'Tell me about your scheme of things,' said Lestrade. He had hoped that someone would have heard the shot and the breaking glass. But it was as though Arabella could read his mind.

'You're playing for time, Sholto, you crafty old cove. Well, why not? You want a tedious run through all the *Struwwelpeter* victims?'

'It would be interesting.' Lestrade was collecting, as unobtrusively as he could, a handful of sawdust from behind him.

'Very well, but first, I think we'll tie your hands.'

Lestrade saw his chance, threw the sawdust in Arabella's face and deflected the gun. What he did not know, however, was that the iron bar she had lobbed at him minutes before was still in her other hand. She brought this cracking down on Lestrade's bandaged neck. He dropped as though poleaxed and was only barely conscious of her tying his wrists firmly behind his back. She hauled him with little effort into a sitting position, his back against the cannon.

'To begin with . . .' Arabella sat cross-legged in her enormous trousers opposite him. She produced a cigar from nowhere and lit it, passing it to Lestrade for one last smoke. She puffed rings into the air. 'The Man in the Chine had nothing to do with it. Had it not been for the description the local papers carried it would never have reminded me of *Struwwelpeter* in the first place. I don't know who killed your labourer, or fisherman or whatever he was, but the whole bizarre thing was perfect. The long hair, seemed an exact replica of Shock-headed Peter himself. And the name stitched into the smock – unbelievable.'

'And the regimental lace of the Thirteenth Hussars?'

Arabella laughed. 'God knows, but it was the first of many delightful red herrings. Papa, of course, kept me informed.'

'Of course. Which is why I thought he was our man.'

'Shame on you, Sholto Lestrade. To think such things of your superior.' Arabella clicked her tongue.

'Tell me about Freddie Hurstmonceux. How *did* you do it?'

'Ah yes, that was difficult. It's so useful, knowing so many people in so many walks of life. Papa has many contacts. One of them is . . . well, his name doesn't matter, after all he is an accessory to murder. He is Master of the Pytchley Hunt and knows more about dogs than you do about flat feet. Well, I bet him, to cut a long story short, a hundred pounds that he couldn't train a dog to go berserk at the mention of one word.'

Lestrade smiled to himself that his assumptions had been correct. 'The word being harrow?'

'Exactly. The old school of the Master of the Pytchley. We both laughed at that, but I already had my target – Lord Freddie, a thoroughly detestable pig of a man – and my means. I met Freddie through this intermediary and used all my wiles to make him buy a new hunting pack – the one with the lead hound Tray, who'd been taught to kill at the mention of a word. The rest of the pack would follow suit if he led. The most difficult thing was getting the harrow into position. It was all rather hit and miss of course: four earlier hunts had gone the wrong way. Even I can't control foxes, Sholto.'

'You amaze me,' said Lestrade. 'What about Harriet?'

'Yes, I didn't like doing that one. She was a very stupid girl, but I felt a certain sympathy for her. It was also riskier than Hurstmonceux. I had to be seen in public, as a man. Luckily, poor Harriet didn't know one end of a man from another. I played her along with secret rendezvous, flowers etc. and, of course, I taught her to smoke.' Arabella blew more rings skyward.

'Of course,' said Lestrade.

'It was simple to get into the house and pour petroleum spirit into the lavatory. Oh, sorry, Sholto, Chapel of Ease – I didn't mean to offend your sensibilities.'

Lestrade found himself smiling.

'It was beginning to get embarrassing. The silly little dolt talked of marriage. It was all rather sick. After all, Her Majesty has said that such unnatural acts do not go on between women.'

'What about the Inky Boys?' asked Lestrade.

'Ah well, the visit of Atlanta Washington had been planned for months. It fitted well, but the actual method of murder was tricky. I wasn't sure it would work. I spent hours poring over Papa's chemistry books and the Yard library. In the end I took a chance. I selected my trio of racists and invited them to a secret rendezvous in upper rooms in James Street. I drugged them, tied them up, painted them in black enamel . . .'

'Which you stole from Lawrence Alma-Tadema's studio?'

'Yes. I thought Papa would give the game away there, when he told you he knew the artist. I was the sitter who cancelled my appointment at the last moment so that I would have a chance to go to St John's Wood anyway and steal the paint. But you didn't get the point, dear Sholto, did you?'

'How did you get the bodies to the Park?'

'The same way I just overpowered you, Sholto. A combination of cunning and brute force. It was risky, of course – but there are many drivers and hauliers carrying bundles in the early hours. No one asked questions. The hire of the van was simple enough.'

'And Tall Agrippa appeared for the first time in a mourning letter. Tell me, Papa's typewriter?'

'At the Yard actually. I typed most of them together, feet away from your own office, Sholto.'

'Albert Mauleverer?'

'He was a non-event. The most difficult thing in the provincial murders, especially Macclesfield and Warwick, was getting away from the family for long enough. Luckily, we have dozens of distant aunts who do not contact us much. I was supposedly visiting them. I invariably used a male disguise at hotels so that there should be no awkward questions about a woman travelling alone. Of course, I didn't bargain for you falling for Mrs Mauleverer.'

'Did I?'

Arabella's tone changed. 'Oh, Sholto, I loved you. If you had shown the slightest interest . . . well, none of this would have happened.'

'Why Forbes?'

Arabella had nearly finished her cigar and Lestrade was anxious to keep her going.

'Conrad is the name in the *Struwwelpeter* rhymes. I couldn't find one. Anyway, I disliked Forbes intensely. He had an arrogance above his station. I got him, shall we say, interested in me at the Commissioner's Ball. Then I sent him that farcical note, as I did you; it never fails.'

'Was it a hat pin?'

'It was. Cutting the thumbs off was more difficult than you'd imagine. Ruined my dressmaking scissors.'

'And Augustus?'

'Ah yes, old Prendergast. I was staying – or rather wasn't – with another fictional aunt in Kent. As with Conrad it proved impossible to find an Augustus, so I selected this tyrannical old codger. Reprehensible, wasn't it, to tie him up out of reach of food like that? Even I had qualms. But then, I didn't have to find the corpse.'

'Why did you risk Madame Slopesski?'

'I don't know. Vanity, I suppose. I suggested to Papa he encourage the seance idea. I wanted to confront you, to be as close as we are now and to watch your reaction. I must admit, when I realised Frank Podmore was there, and I guessed he would know the real Slopesski, my heart sank. I think that was probably the most awkward moment of my life.'

'What about fidgety Philip?'

'Ah, yes, the unsavoury Mr Faye. I didn't like him at all. I'd met him through the Queensberrys. Friends of friends of friends, actually. He was physically very weak. I pretended to be enamoured of the ass, then pinned him down with my ample bosom and suffocated him with a sheet. John Torquil called for more ingenuity, but you know, Sholto, how I rise to a challenge. I played myself with him, risky but fun, but as he pointed out a woman aviator would be absurd, so again, male garb. I joined the aeronauts and awaited my chance. He would keep giggling to himself about the subterfuge. Pity really, I think Maxim's machine might actually have flown if it hadn't been for my tinkering.'

'Why did your father invite me to The Tors?'

'My idea.' Arabella threw the cigar butt into the sawdust. 'A woman is only a woman, Sholto, but a good cigar is a smoke. Come on.' She hauled him upright. 'I was determined to seduce you before . . . tonight.'

'What about the shotgun blast? I thought it was Sir Melville's deliberate attempt to kill me.'

Arabella chuckled. 'One of life's little accidents, Sholto. It would have been ironic, wouldn't it Sholto, if Papa had robbed me of "Flying Robert"? I'm sure you can manage the steps with your hands tied.'

'I'm not going in there, Arabella.'

She raised and cocked the revolver. 'Sholto, I have packed enough explosives into that breech to blow it and you apart. That way at least, death will be instantaneous. But there are five shots left in this revolver. That way, death can be very slow.'

Lestrade summed up his predicament in a second and reluctantly climbed inside the cannon's mouth. He slid down until his knees were against the circular wall. Above him, all he could see were the stars, crisp and twinkling through the glass night. The last verse of *Struwwelpeter* whirled through his brain –

Soon they got to such a height,
They were nearly out of sight!
And the hat went up so high
That it nearly touched the sky.
No one ever yet could tell
Where they stopped or where they fell;
Only this one thing was plain,
Bob was never seen again.

'How did you get the use of this place?' Lestrade's voice was echoing in its death chamber. Arabella was busy with the fuse.

'Charlie Hengler is a law-abiding soul,' she answered. 'And he doesn't know Papa. I came to see him yesterday claiming that I, Melville McNaghten, had an undercover job to do of the gravest importance. International espionage, no less. I needed to take part in the show as a clown and to have the theatre to myself at the end of the show. Oh, don't worry, Sholto, we shan't be disturbed.'

'One last thing.' Lestrade was still hopeful, the eternal optimist.

'What's that, Sholto?' Arabella struck her match.

'Why? Why?'

'Have you heard of Sigmund Freud, Sholto?'

'Is that a penny dreadful?'

'No, my dear.' She smiled acidly, looking up at the smooth-painted sides of the cannon. 'Mr Freud is a psychologist. His wife Martha and I were at school together. We keep in constant touch. His theory is that all little girls at some point want to be little boys. Penis envy, he calls it – oh there, I've shocked you again.' She clicked her tongue derisively. 'Willy envy, is that better? Well, I suppose I'm the classic case. Ever since I can remember I wanted to be a policeman, to join the Force, to be what Papa was. I couldn't do that, Sholto. Society wouldn't have it. But what I could do is to beat you all at your own game. All you men. With your cigars and your arrogance and your hypocrisy. I have killed ten people, Sholto, tonight will make it eleven. And you didn't have a clue. I left plenty, God knows, and the nearest you got was my father. And you're about the best of them, Sholto. Oh, by the way –' she applied her match, slow burning, to the fuse. It flashed and crackled. She stepped back. '– The Ripper File I stole for you, an eternity ago . . .'

'What about it?'

Lestrade could hear the fuse as well. His heart was thumping.

'There was one name missing from the last page, Sholto. The name of Arabella McNaghten.'

'You . . . you are Jack the Ripper?'

'An earlier, more amateur attempt, my dear boy. Rather ironic they should put Papa on the case at the end, wasn't it? Still, from tomorrow, Papa's job will be up for sale to the highest bidder. As will yours, but you won't be there to see it.' She lingered below the cannon for a few seconds. 'Goodbye, Sholto. I loved you once.'

Lestrade was still muttering in the echoing chamber. But Arabella was striding up the steps to the exit.

'Miss McNaghten.' A voice made her turn. A tall, square figure stood to her left in the next aisle. She drew the revolver and was levelling it when a shot rang out. Arabella McNaghten jerked back, eyes staring in disbelief, dark crimson spreading over the police tunic. She crashed heavily down the steps. The tall figure dashed from the pall of smoke his gun had left and scrabbled frantically for the fuse. It had an inch or a little less to go when he put it out.

'Bandicoot?' Lestrade's voice had a strange maniacal quality about it.

'Sir?'

'Bandicoot, Bandicoot, wherefore art thou, Bandicoot?'

'Are you all right, sir?' The blond, curly head appeared anxiously in the cannon's mouth.

'Yes, Bandicoot. It's just my appalling working-class background. Get me out of this.'

The constable helped the inspector out and untied his hands. 'Arabella?' asked Lestrade.

'I'm afraid I had to kill Miss McNaghten, sir.' Bandicoot looked decidedly shaken. 'I didn't tell you that my father had a brace of these things.' He brandished the other gold-chased revolver. He straightened. 'Sorry I disobeyed orders, sir . . . and came back.'

Lestrade looked at him. 'Tonight, Bandicoot, I looked death in the face. Thanks to you, I've got to do that all over again.'

They crossed to where the body lay, face down in the sawdust. Lestrade knelt and turned her over. He looked at the pale face, still streaked with make-up and looked at the blood on his fingers. 'You're wrong, Bandicoot.' He closed his eyes. 'You didn't kill her. Agrippa did.'

'Sir?'

'Give me a hand.'

Together they carried Arabella to the cannon and loaded her in. 'Now get back.' Bandicoot dashed for the tiers of seats as Lestrade relit the fuse. He had just time to reach the edge of the ring when the explosion ripped up and out, smashing the plate glass of the roof and sending debris in all directions, splashing into the lake and knocking over the tree.

Lestrade and Bandicoot were into the night air and away as the crackling flames behind them brought shouts and cries for water.

'I don't understand, sir,' said Bandicoot.

Lestrade stopped and faced him. 'You don't have to, Bandicoot. The world must know, Sir Melville must know, that Arabella McNaghten was the final victim of Agrippa, the long, red-legged scissor man. We never caught him, Bandicoot. He lives on, he walks the streets of London yet. Oh, people will panic for a while. There'll be demands for resignations.' They walked on. 'But you're safe, and perhaps I am too. In time people will forget. We'll make the right noises and pursue our inquiries, but you and I'll know it's all over.'

'Why, sir? Why did you put her in that thing?'

'Because . . . because I've got too much respect for a man to tell him his daughter is a monster. His favourite child an evil fiend without pity or remorse. Her death will finish him as it is, man. The least you and I can do is to leave him his memories.'

Lestrade was right. The story that Arabella had given the *Evening Standard* the day before appeared in *The Times* and all the other dailies the next morning. For a while, people panicked.

There was a cry for heads and Sir Melville McNaghten, a broken man at the news of his favourite daughter's death, offered his. He retired in the summer to The Tors, where he lived on for several years with his other children and his memories. Walter Dew became an inspector eventually and achieved undying fame as the man who arrested Dr Crippen – by long-distance wireless. Harry Bandicoot left the Metropolitan Police the following year, married a rich widow and they lived happily ever after. Constance Mauleverer vanished. No one saw her again.

And Sholto Lestrade himself? Ah well, that is another story.

Brigade: the further adventures of Inspector Lestrade

A day to remember

Alex Dunn took Edwin Cook's hard-boiled egg and peeled it carefully. He watched the pieces fall away beyond his stirrup leather and munched the egg gratefully. He'd had no breakfast, nor indeed any dinner the night before. His stomach was telling him loudly that his throat had been cut. Then, suddenly, there was a stir right front and he wished he hadn't made that mental analogy. A staff officer – Lewis Nolan, wasn't it? – galloped past the waiting lines to where Lucan sat his horse. He was the fourth galloper that morning, but Lewis Nolan usually meant business. Dunn finished his egg and turned in the saddle. Away to his left Roger Palmer was scribbling a note on the smooth surface of his sabretache.

Dear Father, Palmer's pencil was a stub and his hands were cold, *Just a hurried note* . . . His pencil snapped. He tucked the paper in his sabretache and followed Dunn's gaze along the line. Harrington Trevelyan was wrapping his sword knot around his wrist. Palmer did not approve of Trevelyan's forage cap. It was not regulation and Palmer was ever a man for regulations.

Henry Wilkin was delighted. He'd never really known why he'd become a surgeon. Up to the armpits in other people all day, what sort of life was that? A serving officer now, that was different. Mind you, if Yates hadn't reported sick, he wouldn't have been here this morning. If Nolan's gallop meant action he'd have to rely on his sword because his bullet pouch was full of laudanum – the legacy of a medical man. He really must quit the medical service. As if to take the first steps in that direction, he urged his horse forward to the front of F

Troop. Cook glared at him, snorting something about damned quacks, and Wilkin backed up a little. George Loy Smith was too old a hand to let a horse's arse in his face bother him. He was adjusting his stirrup leather when Wilkin attempted his backward manoeuvre. He straightened up and tilted his busby back into position, tucking the chain under his great auburn beard, and snarled at Bill Bentley to spit out his tobacco. No soldier of his troop was going into action with black spittle on his chin. Bentley hadn't really heard him, until he felt the sergeant-major's hand sting him smartly on the shoulder. He had been day-dreaming. Today was his Emma's birthday. She was eleven. And Bentley had been remembering the day of her baptism at Kilmainham. He had been a private soldier then, but proud in his regimentals carrying the baby to the font. She had been the most gorgeous baby in the world, snuggling into her dad's pelisse.

Seth Bond sat on the wing of C Troop. He was shivering from cholera and couldn't keep his horse still. He tried to keep his mind occupied by watching the altercation at the front. The staff officer was waving his hand behind him, scarlet in the face and defiant. Lord Look-On seemed bemused, uncomprehending. The staff officer wheeled away to join the 17th to the left. It was the first time Bond had seen the generals actually talking to each other – Look-On and the Noble Yachtsman. He couldn't catch more than a muffled conversation, what with the champ of bits and the muttering of the men behind him.

John Kilvert on his right was wondering why he had enlisted at all. He too had spent most of the night throwing up over his boots and was glad no one had offered him any breakfast. He wished he was back in Nottingham, selling wines and spirits. He wasn't likely to become mayor now, and the chance faded by the moment as he saw Cardigan walk his chestnut to the centre of the brigade.

It was not Cardigan's appearance that worried William Perkins, unless of course His Lordship were to place a beady blue eye down his trumpet that morning. He had traded some of his French photographs for Bentley's tobacco, but was dismayed to find that Bentley had used the photographs to fix a gap in his tent. He was even more dismayed to find that someone – he thought immediately of Jim Hodges – had wedged a plug into his mouthpiece. Still, Joseph Keates was trumpet-major for the 11th. If called upon to sound, he would have to hope Keates would cover for him. In the noise of an advance, no one could tell.

William Pennington was new to all this. Was the Mercantile Marine, he mused now as he sat his horse in B Troop, so awful that he should have left them? Perhaps it was the porter in Dublin that day in January, perhaps it was the glittering uniform of the Bringer, perhaps the bounty of £9, perhaps . . . but the moment for self-doubt had gone. John Parkinson nudged him in the elbow and nodded to the front. Cardigan nodded stiffly to John Douglas, tall and silent in the saddle in the centre of the 11th. They were going. Alex Dunn slid his sword upwards so that its extra three inches flashed in the sun breaking weakly on the tattered brigade below. Loy Smith barked as he saw that idiot Hope gallop into place to his right. The cripple was riding a troophorse of the Greys. Where the bloody hell had he been? Having a fit somewhere, he supposed. Well, he'd give him hell for it when this was over.

Stillness and sudden hushes don't really happen, Pennington was telling himself. But he was sitting in the middle of one anyway. Ahead stretched a long valley, parchment-coloured sand and rubble. On the hills to the right, a line of guns. Russian guns. On the left, more of the same. What was ahead? He couldn't see, but he felt panic grip his heart. Loy Smith turned in the saddle.

'All set, Mr Pennington?' and he gave a fatherly glance to Edwin Hughes, sixteen years old and less than regulation height. He'll outlive us all, the sergeant-major thought to himself.

'The Brigade will advance,' came Cardigan's hoarse, chesty bark; 'first squadron of the 17th Lancers direct.'

And the shrill notes of the trumpet drowned his words. For a second, three, perhaps four, the 11th, Prince Albert's Own Hussars sat motionless, each man a prisoner of his private thoughts and fears. Then they broke forward, shifting position as on the parade ground at Maidstone at Lucan's order for the

11th to fall back and the 17th to take the lead. The dark-coated lancers fronted the brigade, their pennons snapping in the wind that crossed the valley. It was the noise that Pennington remembered most, the snorting of horses and the jingle of bits and from time to time above the incessant sound of hoofs, the growling of Loy Smith to his men.

'Draw swords.' It was Colonel Douglas, freeing his own weapon as Cardigan increased the pace. He could see the leaders – Mayow and FitzMaxse – beyond the line of the 17th. The swords of the 11th shot clear.

'At the slope,' Loy Smith reminded his troop. Bentley cradled the blade against his shoulder and tightened his rein. They were at the trot now, rising and falling as a man. Still the lances were upright. Still Cardigan was leading. Like a church, thought Palmer. He moved neither to left, nor right, the sun flashing on the gold lace of his pelisse. He felt the line quicken, following the last of the Brudenells.

Loy Smith saw it first, as his wise old eyes saw any irregular movement in the line. The staff officer, the one who had brought the last order, was spurring ahead, out from the left wing of the 17th, chasing Cardigan, but cutting across to the right. He was waving his sword arm and yelling, but Loy Smith couldn't catch the words. The 17th began to waver. They were turning. Douglas checked his horse, Dunn began to pull his charger to the right. Was the Brigade turning? There was no trumpet call. Why wasn't there a trumpet call?

A whistle, moaning high above the wind. Louder. Louder. A crash and a burst of flame and smoke. The staff officer crumpled, hooked over like a crab in the saddle, but his right arm was still upright. The terrified horse swerved, wheeled round, reins hanging loose, and charged back through the lines. The 17th negotiated the mêlée and the line re-formed. One by one the serrefiles and troop sergeants and the centre men saw it and heard the unearthly scream. What was left of Lewis Nolan flashed past them all. His face was a livid white, his eyes sightless and his lungs and ribs visible where his gold-laced jacket had been.

'Look to your dressing,' Loy Smith reminded his troop, knowing the damage that sight could do to his callow boys.

The moment was past. Nolan had gone and the 13th saw him fall under their hoofs.

The trumpet sounded the gallop. Swords came up from the slope, ready and vertical in men's fists. The crash of artillery fire increased, drifting along the lines of horsemen. And those lines were less steady now. Dunn held his sword arm out to his side to correct the pace of the horsemen behind him. Was Cardigan mad? he found himself wondering. The enemy was visible now, despite the smoke – a row, perhaps a double row of reeking guns ahead, more on the hills on each side. It was a trap. A valley with a closed end. The 17th's lances came down, level, thrusting, twelve feet of ash and steel slicing through the air. The wind cut through the horsemen, each man now bracing himself for the impact. The roar of cantering horses moving into a gallop drowned the noise of the guns. But in the centre, where Pennington and Parkinson were riding knee to knee, the guns were evident. Charles Allured, on Parkinson's right, went down, his horse bucking and screaming. On Loy Smith's flank Joseph Bruton slumped over the neck of his troophorse. Isaac Middleton caught him momentarily, but lost his grip and the soldier fell.

'Mend your pace. Watch your dressing.' Loy Smith's calming words rang out above the slaughter. A shot smashed into a horse's head at Bond's elbow, and the blood spattered over his jacket and face. He could hear Robert Bubb to his left crying as his horse went down.

How long, thought Douglas, how long can we endure this? The 17th were closing ranks in front of him, as the murderous shot tore into them.

'Keep together, Eleventh!' he shouted, but knew as always it was his troop sergeants who were the steadying influence, the backbone. The roar of hoofs and cannon was unbearable. Horses were racing now, vying with the riderless mounts to get to the Russian guns and silence them. Cardigan had vanished into the smoke, the lances of the 17th jabbing the blackness ahead. Behind Bentley, Pennington's horse staggered, reeling to the left. Pennington struggled to keep him upright, but couldn't see where he was going. Men were standing in their stirrups, sword arms extended, yelling themselves hoarse in the confusion and noise. Loy Smith swore he heard Hope, that mad Welsh bastard, singing 'Men of Harlech', but it could have been Keates' trumpet notes, lost in the din. David Purcell was blown out of the saddle on his right, and he saw Tom Roberts fall back, clutching his leg.

Then, for Douglas at least, the smoke cleared. He was on the guns. To all sides, grey-coated Russians were scattering. There were horses and men heaped around the cannon, blackened and hot with rapidity of fire. The remaining 17th were leaping over them and Douglas leapt with them. A knot of the 11th, led by Loy Smith, were behind him. All semblance of order was lost, the lines so beloved of Maidstone and the Curragh gone in the frantic rush for the guns. Dunn was scything about him, hacking at the gunners. Palmer and Trevelyan rammed their spurs into their chargers' flecked flanks and leapt into the battery smoke. Flames and screams were all about them. Will Spring felt a searing pain in his shoulder and his horse dragged him for several yards before his foot fell free of the stirrup. Gregory Jowett tried to reach him, but was beaten back by the weight of numbers.

In the mill beyond the guns, Bond and Bentley found themselves together. Neither man could believe his eyes. Cavalry. Russian Cavalry. Perhaps four or five times their own number were advancing along the sand towards them. What was left of the 17th and 11th were fighting in tiny knots, steel flashing and ringing in the sun. There wasn't time for a word, or a glance, before the two sergeants were parrying for their lives. Bond wheeled his horse, hacking behind him in the most difficult cut of the 1796 Manual. Bentley did likewise, but his opponents were lancers. He felt a lance tip jab through his busby, parting his hair for a second time that morning. Another thudded into the saddle, an inch or so from his groin. He was turning in the air like a man possessed, snapping off one lance pole, then another. As he hacked, he prayed. But it wasn't Almighty God who cantered to his side, but Lieutenant Alexander Dunn, scything down one Russian, then two. He wheeled his charger across Bentley's.

'"Rear protect" never was a sensible guard.' He grinned and

batting aside another lance jab with his bridle arm drove his blade through the teeth of its owner.

Pennington's mare had fallen, sending her rider sprawling under the wheels of the guns. By the time he scrambled to his feet, the first line of the 8th Hussars swept past him. Pennington caught sight of the Old Woman leading his men in, clearing the guns with a thud and a spray of dust.

'Grab the rein, man,' the bark of a sergeant-major snapped him back to reality. He snatched the leather, somehow found the saddle and found himself charging the Russians with the 8th. The field was now a mass of individual duels. Gregory Jowett was laying about him alongside Roger Palmer. To his fury, his blade was bouncing off the Russian greatcoats around him and he cursed the Birmingham cutlers who had made such useless weapons. In the end he used the hilt like a knuckle-duster, aiming for the moustachioed faces under the fur caps. Lieutenant Palmer, swinging at his side, having given up the neat cuts of the Manual, was unaware of the Russian carbine aimed at his head. Jowett saw it and for a split second remembered that Palmer had upbraided him days before for being asleep at his post. The split second passed and Jowett's sword sliced down through neck and collarbone, the carbine shot flying wide. After all, he reasoned with himself, Palmer had not had him flogged. He owed him that at least.

Douglas, at the head of D Troop, had outflanked the guns on the left. His was the only unit marginally intact and he pointed his sword at the Russian squadrons advancing to meet him. 'Right Engage.' Stragglers of the 17th, bleeding, their lance caps gone, wheeled in behind him.

'Rally men!' Douglas shouted. 'Rally men of the Seventeenth.' But in the dust and smoke the majority of the lancers were not the 17th. Palmer saw it first.

'That's the enemy!' he said and swung in to the attack again. A rifle exploded near him, bringing down a soldier of the 4th Lights who had swept past the guns. For a moment he caught sight of Lord George Paget, a bedraggled cigar in his mouth, and then he turned to look for his own regiment.

Alex Dunn saw a remarkable sight he would remember for the rest of his days. Through the choking smoke he saw Cardigan, unhurt and upright, facing a mass of Russian lancers. The officer in their centre seemed to know Cardigan and the two men saluted each other with their swords. The general of Hussars wheeled away to another part of the field.

Paget had lost his own 4ths and was busy directing an aimless mass of the 11th. Loy Smith was doing the same thing beyond the furthermost guns. Instinctively, knots of survivors were breaking away, hurling tired insults at the hesitating Russians. Without cohesion or any real leadership, the enemy dithered at the end of the valley, allowing the British cavalry to pull back. Still the firing went on: Loy Smith's horse was now swinging a broken leg. The sergeant-major kicked himself free of the stirrups and ran as soon as his feet touched the ground. Bullets were kicking up the dust at his heels as he caught a riderless mount and clinging on for dear life, rode back up the valley. He saw Pennington running back too, but hadn't time to reach him before he fell, blood spurting from his leg. Undaunted, the soldier rolled upright, unbuckling his equipment to give him extra speed and hobbled onwards as Russian swordsmen swung at him. A soldier of the 8th lifted him awkwardly behind him and they galloped to cover.

To his right, Trevelyan saw the flashing sabres of the Chasseurs D'Afrique, briskly silencing the guns on the heights. The next moment, he felt a crippling pain as riderless horses, terrified by the noise and lack of weight, crowded in against his legs. Their staring eyes and foam-flecked nostrils were as painful to him as his legs, but he found himself using his sword to cut himself free of them.

Slowly, in ones and twos, the remnants of Cardigan's brigade limped back up the valley. They rode or stumbled over the debris of battle – horses with their intestines steaming on the ground – men with smashed limbs and unrecognisable faces. Here and there, a wounded man dragged between comrades. And as the bullets lessened and the shots died away, an eerie calm fell over the field.

Alex Dunn sheathed his sword, dark brown with the blood of Russians. He took his position at the head of D Troop and waited in the numbed silence as the stragglers came back through the smoke. Medical orderlies were everywhere and amid the cries for stretchers and the shots of farriers going about their grisly business, the solemn roll call was taken. In his own regiment the gaps were cruel – Lieutenants Cook and Houghton were unable to answer, Sergeants Jones and Jordan dead, Corporals France and Williams. And as the list increased, Dunn found himself counting the dead and felt the tears trickle down his cheeks.

Sergeant Bentley saw Dunn with his head in his hands and thought that this was not the moment to thank him for saving his life. Jim the Bear was cantering on his blown chestnut along the line, still as steady as a church. Bentley caught only part of it . . .

'It was a mad-brained trick, men, but it was no fault of mine.'

Behind him, the sergeant heard a voice. 'Never mind, My Lord, ready to go again.' Bentley prayed that Cardigan had not heard.

'No, no, you have done enough.' And he rode away from his old regiment.

In the silence of his tent that night John Douglas wrote to his wife. *My Dearest Rosa* . . . but he could not find the words. Of the 142 officers and men of the 11th Hussars on parade that morning, 25 were dead, 31 were wounded, 8 were missing and over half the regiment's horses lay rotting in the biting night wind out there in the valley. Alex Dunn walked the cavalry lines, cradling for a moment the head of his charger as he passed. He patted the animal's neck and pulling his cloak around him went into his tent. His orderly had laid out the writing case as he had asked. He forced his numbed fingers around the quill and began to write. *Darling Rosa* . . . and the lamplight flickered on the canvas walls . . .

It was October 25th, 1854. A day to remember.

The fire crackled as the logs fell. Joseph Lestrade straightened up and looked behind him.

'Time that boy was in bed, Martha.'

'Let's try him again before he goes, Joe, one last time.'

Lestrade looked at the woman kneeling on the hearthrug and the round, curly-headed boy on her lap.

'All right, Sholto. Come on, come on. Come to your dad.' The little boy gurgled and his eyes flashed, but he made no move. Joseph Lestrade knelt down, arms outstretched across the rug.

'Come on, lad. You can do it.' The boy's eyes caught sight of something flashing silver in the firelight. His father saw it too.

'What's that, Sholto? My coat? The numbers, isn't it? The numbers on the collar.' And the proud father spelt them out. 'PC one-six-five,' he whispered.

With a gabble of nonsense, Baby Lestrade struggled to his feet. For a moment he swayed back against the comforting breasts of his mother. She held him to her and then he was gone, staggering now to the left, now to the right. His eyes were flashing in the firelight as he advanced on his father and his father's coat.

'That's it. That's it. Good lad. Come and get it. Come on.'

And Baby Lestrade collapsed into his father's arms, his fingers grabbing at the buttons. 'He did it, Martha. How about that? Nine months old and his first step. How about that?'

But Martha's eyes were wet with tears. She whirled away to fetch her house-book and snatching up the quill wrote:

Little Sholto took his first step today, October 25th, 1854. A day to remember.

The new broom

Sholto Lestrade's walking had come on admirably. But then he was nearly forty years old. He found himself looking at his feet particularly hard that morning. That silly magazine *Punch* had been caricaturing Her Majesty's Metropolitan Police again, and inevitably most of the humour was of the street and at gutter level – tortuous jokes about 'A Policeman's Boot is not a Happy One.' Nothing outsize there, Lestrade thought to himself.

'Mornin', sir.' Dixon's hearty greeting brought his eyes up to the usual level.

'Sergeant,' acknowledged Lestrade. 'Anything for me today?'

''Is nibs,' Sergeant Dixon motioned heavenwards, 'would like to see you when you can spare a moment.'

''Is nibs?' queried Lestrade.

'Assistant Commissioner 'isself, sir. Proper gent 'e looks.'

Lestrade made for the stairs, then remembered the possible effect on his feet and took the lift instead. It whirred and clanked in the time-honoured tradition of a contraption less than three years old to the second floor, where Lestrade had his palatial office, wedged between a broom cupboard and a latrine. Constable Dew was waiting for him, mug of tea in hand.

'Not this morning, Dew, I've had the call.'

'What could it be, sir? Mrs Manchester's tart?'

But Lestrade had gone, leaving Walter Dew with one of those inevitable silences to which his humour usually entitled him.

The door, which Lestrade always thought of as McNaghten's, stood square and solid before him.

'Enter.'

It was not McNaghten. He had retired a month ago, lost and bewildered over the death of his daughter, and in his place stood one of the largest men Lestrade had ever seen. He weighed, Lestrade guessed, nearly nineteen stones and most of that lay somewhere between his chest and his knees. He had the look of a bulldog on heat, red-rimmed eyes and loose, quivering lips.

'Inspector Lestrade, sir. You wished to see me?'

'Yes.' The bulldog came snarling out from behind his desk. 'My name is Frost. Nimrod Frost.' The bulldog circled Lestrade, swinging his girth ahead of him like a coster-monger's cart in Covent Garden. 'Assistant Commissioner. The new Head of the Criminal Investigation Department.' Each word was delivered with precision and relish. Lestrade tried to place it. Dixon was wrong; wherever the bulldog came from, he was no gentleman. The voice was worked, moulded, hammered into shape by a man who had waited, watched, come up the hard way. There was no tougher policeman. 'You'll hear a lot of me in the days ahead.' The bulldog completed the circuit and regained his seat.

'Sholto Joseph Lestrade.' Frost's eyes narrowed over the stub that was his nose. 'Bachelor.' The word sounded like an accusation. Frost seemed to be waiting for some kind of admission. 'Born – Pimlico. January eighteen fifty-four. Father, Police Constable Joseph Lestrade, Metropolitan Police. Mother, Martha Jane Appleyard, laundress.' The bulldog waited again for some sort of statement. There was none. 'Eldest of three children, the others dying in infancy. Education . . .' Frost paused. 'Hmmm. School at Blackheath. Right, let's stop there.' The bulldog was padding round the room again. Occasionally he let his eyes wander to the window and the sun gilding the statuary of the Houses of Parliament. 'Lestrade,' he suddenly said; 'that's a foreign name, isn't it?'

'Huguenot French, sir. Or so I've always believed.'

'Frog?'

'Some time ago, sir. One of the things I picked up at Mr Coulson's Academy at Blackheath was that large numbers of Huguenot weavers came to this country in the late seventeenth century. My grandfather used to say the Lestrades came from La Rochelle and settled in Spitalfields where—'

'Thank you for the history lesson, Lestrade.' The bulldog appeared to have bitten off more than he could chew. 'Why did you become a policeman?' He turned again to the file on Lestrade.

'It seemed like a good idea at the time.'

'Quite. Regrets?'

'About the Force? No, sir. It's always with you.'

'Quite. McNaghten spoke highly of you. You've got some good collars.'

Lestrade was surprised momentarily by the compliment. 'I think smartness and efficiency go together, sir,' and as he said it, he realised Frost was referring to arrests, not his sartorial elegance.

'What I don't like in detective inspectors,' growled the bulldog, 'is a sense of humour. It doesn't become them.' A weighty pause, then a new tack. 'Are you familiar with the latest Home Office paper on the Metropolitan Police, Inspector?'

Blank.

'I thought not. Junior policemen, good, bad, or indifferent tend not to read such things. A pity. An awareness of the views of the hands that feed us is no bad thing.' Lestrade was vaguely aware of a mixed metaphor, but let it pass.

Frost produced a welter of official-looking documents, cleared his throat and read aloud: '"An inspector is looked upon as a guide, guardian and referee by those whose unpleasant business causes them to seek police aid. In contrast with bygone days an inspector must be a man of education' – the bulldog paused pregnantly – 'and capable judgement; the public must feel a firm reliance in him as such." Well, Lestrade, are *you* that man?' A dramatic finger stabbed the air inches from the inspector's face. 'Good God, man.' Frost was suddenly astounded. 'You've got no tip to your nose!'

'Some of it is probably still lying on a pavement in Cambridge, sir. In the line of duty. Still more of it is interred in Highgate Cemetery. That was a private matter.'

'Very cryptic,' scowled the bulldog, but Lestrade knew it wasn't a joke. 'This department,' Frost went on, 'is in for a shake-up. People haven't forgotten the Ripper.' Neither had Lestrade. 'Or the *Struwwelpeter* murders,' Nor had Lestrade. 'The magazine *Punch'* – it was as though Frost had been reading his mind on the way to the Yard – 'persists in calling us the Defective Force. It's not funny, Lestrade, not funny at all.' His voice fell from the crescendo he had been building to all morning. 'Sir Melville McNaghten spoke of you as his best man.'

'That's very flattering, sir.'

'Yes, isn't it? But I want to know if he's right. I don't want prima donnas on my Force, Lestrade. I want a team of dedicated, trustworthy officers.' He began his perambulations again, 'So I've got a little job for you. . . .'

To Sergeant Dixon the new Head of the Criminal Investigation Department quickly became, behind his back and always in hushed tones, 'His Nims', on account of his name. The new broom swept through the stuffy corridors of New Scotland Yard, kicked out the infestation of sergeants which had lurked for nearly three years in the basement, insisted that Inspector Athelney Jones replace the ill-fitting patrol jacket he had worn man and boy for sixteen years, and generally made his presence felt. If anything, communication within the great building was slowed down as the lifts, built to carry eight men, now carried five and Assistant Commissioner Frost. It did the other three good to run up and down stairs. After all, exercise was next to Godliness.

But Inspector Lestrade knew little of this. On the day after his first meeting with Nimrod Frost he was Swindon-bound. The last time he had taken this route he had had to change because of Brunel's blasted wide gauge. Now at last the railway companies had seen sense and demolished it. He still had to change at Swindon however because of track works, and the tea and sandwiches at the Great Western buffet were as nauseating as he remembered them. Mrs Manchester had begged him to take some of her pasties, but making for Cornwall as he was there was something of coals and Newcastle about the whole thing. He browsed through the periodicals on the shelves of the W.H.

Smith bookstall and he shuddered as his fingers alighted on a copy of the *Strand Magazine*. For a moment, he wondered if that idiot Watson was still feeding Conan Doyle those ludicrous stories about Sherlock Holmes, even though the man had been dead these eighteen months. He had no time to ponder as the whistle was blowing and he dashed through the steam to catch the twenty past two for Exeter.

He spent the night, warm for April, within the sound of the cathedral bells. Lestrade was not a romantic in the conventional sense, but the great grey stones and the solemn bell had a haunting quality all of their own. Supper was modest enough on the expenses Frost had been meagre enough to allow him and he dozed fitfully.

The following afternoon found Inspector Lestrade flanked by a sergeant and two constables of the Cornwall Constabulary overlooking the Helford River. Behind them was the huge, silent earthwork which surrounded the little church of Mawnan. Through the strange, stunted trees below them, the policemen could see the sea, shifting in its greyness, rolling in its quest for the coast. There was a stillness Lestrade found odd. He was still happiest in the clutter of the city, even if he hadn't actually been able to hear Bow Bells when he was born.

'You say it was sighted here?'

The sergeant nodded and, attempting to modify his broad Cornish for Lestrade's benefit, replied, 'Three times, sir. Once there, in the woods. Once on the banks behind us and the parson seen it in the crypt.'

'In the crypt?' Lestrade was incredulous.

''Ere's parson now.' The sergeant indicated an elderly gentleman striding manfully with the aid of a stick over the earthworks.

'Neolithic,' shouted the vicar.

'Lestrade,' the inspector answered.

'Ah yes. My name is Ashburton.' Lestrade must have misheard earlier. 'Yes, this earthwork,' the vicar went on; 'it's neolithic, you know. Where the church stands now was probably part of a Celtic fortress, of prodigious size, wouldn't you say?'

Lestrade would.

'If you've finished with the constables, Inspector, I can show you around. And then you're very welcome to partake of some supper. My good lady wife makes a marvellous Cornish pasty.'

Marvellous it was, but the Reverend Ashburton's brandy was better. In the mellow study of the parsonage that evening, Lestrade found himself becoming mellower with each moment. But he did have a job to do.

'Can we go over it again, sir?'

'Certainly, Inspector, but tell me, are you familiar with Gilbert White of Selborne?'

'Gilbert White the forger?'

The vicar chuckled. 'Well, he may have been, but he is best remembered as a naturalist. A long time before all this nonsense of Darwin's and Huxley's, the Reverend White collected specimens and made drawings of all the flora and fauna of his native Selborne. With far less skill, I have attempted to do much the same here in Mawnan. Around you, you see the fruits of these labours.'

Lestrade had thought the plethora of birds' eggs, stuffed newts and mounted butterflies a little zoological for an Anglican priest, but it took all sorts.

'I am familiar with all the animals native to Cornwall and Devon, Inspector, but I have never seen anything like the creature I saw in my churchyard last week.'

'Which was?'

'As I said, it was dusk. I had just finished bell practice. Are you a campanologist?'

'Politics aren't encouraged on the Force, sir.'

Ashburton gave Lestrade an odd look. 'Anyway, I was crossing the South Gateway – the entrance to the Old Fort, that is – when I hear this . . . well, unearthly scream. Fortified by the fact that the Lord was with me, I went to investigate. I was carrying a stout walking stick at the time. I heard noises in the shrubbery and saw a shape – huge.' The vicar swigged his brandy. 'It *was* a lion, Lestrade.'

'Have you had a travelling circus pass this way?'

'Er . . . I don't know. I don't follow such things. If there was a circus, I assume Exeter would be its likely venue. You think the beast escaped from a circus?'

'Unless you or Gilbert White know of Mawnan or Selborne lions, sir, I am forced to that conclusion. What I cannot understand is why I should be sent here.'

'Inspector,' the Reverend Ashburton refilled Lestrade's glass, 'although I would not wish you to repeat this to a living soul, I do not have the greatest respect for the County Constabulary. It was I who contacted Scotland Yard, although, I must admit, I did not think anyone would come. Over thirty sheep have been slaughtered, Inspector. Most of my parishioners are farmers. Their life blood is being drained away on the moors.'

A commotion in the hall brought the two men to their feet. Sergeant Winch of the Cornwall Constabulary almost fell in through the door.

'Sorry, sir, Mr Ashburton, to disturb you, sir. Inspector. You'd better come. The thing's attacked again, over at Constantine.'

Lestrade looked at the vicar. 'A village about four miles away. We can take my trap.'

'No need, sir. I've got the station wagon,' offered the sergeant.

The night had chilled. April was like that. Winch, Lestrade and the vicar found themselves bouncing off each other in the cheerless interior of the Maria. They jolted past midnight through the sleeping Cornish countryside, through the deserted main street of the curiously named Constantine, to the scene of the slaughter.

'I hope you've got a strong stomach, Inspector,' was Winch's parting shot as he jumped out of the Maria. With the aid of bull's-eyes, the little party stumbled and cursed – apologising to the vicar all the way.

'Over here!' a voice called in the darkness.

Lestrade and his party scrambled over the ling to a crouching figure.

'Good God,' the vicar crossed himself. Rather a Papist gesture, Lestrade thought.

Spreadeagled on the escarpment lay the body of a man. In the wavering light of the bull's-eyes it was obvious his throat had been torn out. There was blood everywhere, from the chin to the waist.

'I thought you told me lambs had been killed.' The sergeant

rounded on the crouching figure. 'You didn't say nothing 'bout a man.'

'No, no, you blitherin' idiot,' the other riposted. 'I told you Lamb was killed. William Lamb, my shepherd.'

'Who are you?' asked Lestrade, content to leave the body until later. William Lamb was going nowhere by himself.

'Who are you?' The other man was equally straightforward.

'Inspector Lestrade, Scotland Yard.'

'Oh,' the attitude changed, 'I'm John Pemberton. I own this farm. William Lamb, 'e works . . . worked for me.'

'What happened?'

'I was on my rounds. Lambin' time is always busy. Most of 'em have borned now, but it pays to watch, crows and foxes an' all. Well, I was just goin' home, when I heard this snarling and snapping, then a scream. My pony shied and by the time I got up here, William was lyin' like this.'

'Dead?'

'No. But 'e were goin'.'

'Did he say anything?'

'Well, it were difficult to hear . . . but . . .'

'But? Come on, man. Out with it.'

''E said one word, Inspector. Tiger.'

Lestrade looked at the assembled company one by one, as if for confirmation of what he had heard.

'"Tyger! Tyger! burning bright,"' the Reverend Ashburton was soliloquising,

'"In the forests of the night,
What immortal hand or eye
Could frame thy fearful symmetry?"'

'A tiger?' repeated Lestrade.

'It could have been,' the vicar answered.

Instinctively, the men on the hillside had huddled closer together. The bull's-eyes threw shafts of light over the ling and tufts of grass.

'Whatever it was, it's gone now.' Pemberton motioned to the ghostly grey shapes of sheep, munching, calm and oblivious in the distance.

'Even so, we'd better not risk spending a night in the open.' Lestrade longed for the claustrophobia of the city. 'Sergeant, get the blanket from the Maria. We'll take him back to your station. Mr Pemberton, we shall need a statement. And Sergeant—'

'Sir?'

'By morning I shall have a note for your chief constable. We'll need guns issued to your men.'

They laid William Lamb out, appropriately enough, on the slab in the local butcher's shop. The Sanitary Inspector was a rare enough visitor and as it was Sunday, no one was buying their viands that day. As the bell of Mawnan Church summoned the faithful to prayer, under the solemn auspices of the Reverend Ashburton, Lestrade stood alongside the deceased.

He was used to the sights. A hardened copper like him, he'd seen it all. Forget it's human, he told himself for the umpteenth time. It's a job. That's all. Do it. Have done. He laid his bowler down on the throat wound. It just fitted. Pretty massive jaws must have done that. Tiger? Perhaps. Lion? Perhaps. There were scratches, deep, parallel on the chest and face. There was something else. Hairs. Not Lamb's. Too coarse, too light in colour. Sort of tan. He held them up to the light. Tan colour with a hint of darker brown at one end. He put his nose to the corpse. A smell of wet grass, of sheep (the smell which had haunted Lestrade since he arrived) and something else. Was he sniffing tiger? Lion? Always the same vicious circle. The plain truth was the men of the Yard were not well equipped to deal with big cat spoors. Their training did not give them the edge against the call of the wild. Dead lurkers in Seven Dials. Gonophs in Whitechapel. All that was in a day's work, but tigers in Cornwall? No, that strained credulity. It just didn't fit.

He folded Lamb's arms, limp now after rigor mortis, across what was left of his chest. He looked briefly at his face. He was an old man. Small, weak. A curious scar ran across his forehead and dipped across his left eye. Not a recent wound. Not the mark of the beast. That was old. Years old.

There was no camera available at Mawnan police station. Lestrade doubted if there was room in the place to set up a tripod. He had sent for one from Falmouth. A photographer would chronicle the injuries later that day.

Lestrade had a mug of tea with Sergeant Winch before returning to the parsonage. He left word with the station to send a message to the Yard to tell Frost of the developments. His return would be delayed. On the way, the inspector met the faithful returning, shocked and gabbling, from church.

'Inspector,' Ashburton hailed him. 'Have you made any headway since last night?'

'A little sir.'

'May I introduce my brother, Percival?'

Lestrade found himself blinking in disbelief. The two men before him were virtually identical. Percival was a little taller, leaner, certainly more tanned.

'Sir.' Lestrade collected himself.

'Yes, it has that effect on most people. Percival is recently back from Australia. Sheep farming.'

Lestrade did not really have time for pleasantries.

'Did I see a microscope in your study, Mr Ashburton?'

'Yes, you did, Inspector. Do you wish to use it? Have you a clue?'

'We have those gadgets at the Yard, sir. Unfortunately I do not know quite how they operate . . .'

'That doesn't present a problem, Inspector. Be my guest. But do tell me. What have you found?'

Lestrade produced the tuft of hairs from the paper bag in his pocket.

'These.'

The brothers Ashburton peered closer. Percival broke away, a little sharply, Lestrade thought. 'Must be going, Thomas. Inspector,' and he tipped his hat.

'Oh, really? Well, don't forget tonight. Dinner after evensong. The inspector will be there, won't you, Inspector?'

'That's very kind of you, sir, but I could not impose—'

'Nonsense. Come on. Modern Science awaits,' and linking his arm with Lestrade's, the vicar led the way beyond the Neolithic earthwork, striding for the parsonage.

Over the vicar's brandy that night, Percival Ashburton became decidedly morose. Apparently, although there were a few sharp years of drought, endless attacks by dingoes had taken their toll. It took Lestrade a while to realise that the Alice Springs Ashburton had left behind was not an old flame. But the night was drawing on and the conversation was moving to the altar, how Cardinal Manning had gone too far, and the significance of the ivy in Holman Hunt's *The Light of the World*, all of which sailed sublimely over the inspector's head.

He made his excuses and decided to walk to the inn where he was staying. It was a chill night after a warm day, but the moon was bright and shone silver on the ribbon of road ahead of him. Dogs barked in the distance, answered as in a dream by the remote call of the curlews and the sibilance of the sea. Of these, Lestrade recognised only the dogs, and he didn't like dogs. The Reverend Ashburton's microscope had not proved very helpful. It showed what Lestrade had thought it would – a very large tuft of hairs. But he was absolutely no nearer tracing the animal from which it came, still less catching it. And what had possessed Nimrod Frost to send him on this wild goose chase? It couldn't *be* a wild goose, could it?

Lost in thought, it was a little while before Lestrade noticed him. It was only the moon that betrayed his presence, for he made no sound. A wizened little figure, small, like a monkey, was moving at a trot along the road towards him. As he neared, Lestrade saw that he wore no shoes. He also saw he had loose, straggly hair and a bone through his nose. Hardly a native of Cornwall, Lestrade mused and hailed him. The little man stopped and straightened up, his flat nose level with Lestrade's tie-knot. He grinned broadly, a row of yellow teeth appearing in the burnt umber of his face.

''Ello, boss.'

Lestrade had never heard an accent like it.

'Who are you?' he asked.

'Uku, boss. Mis' Ashburton's abo.'

'Abo?' Lestrade was lost.

'I 'is man, boss. 'Is slave.'

'Slave?'

'Yes, boss. I do work for Mis' Ashburton.'

The light of realisation began to dawn on Lestrade's knitted brow.

'You are an Aborigine? From Australia?'

'Australia. Yes, boss. I come back with Mis' Ashburton. I was hunter in bush.'

'Were you now?' Lestrade was interested. 'Can you track for me?'

'Track? Track what, boss?'

'I don't know,' Lestrade admitted.

'You crazy, boss?'

'Probably. Where are you going now?'

'Message for Mis' Ashburton, boss. I take to brother's house.'

'All right – er – Uku, is it? If you come here tomorrow early – at dawn, I want you to track for me – I will give you . . .' he fumbled in his pocket, 'a shilling.'

The abo snatched the coin, bit it and slipped it into his pocket.

'All right, boss. Sunarise. 'Ere. But you crazy, boss. No dingo 'ere,' and he padded off into the night as silently as he had come.

No dingo, eh? From the conversation earlier in the evening, it seemed as though the Australian wild dogs could easily bring down a sheep. And a man? Particularly an old man, slow, weak, a little deaf, maybe? Yes, it was possible. But first, he must get back to the parsonage. That library of the vicar's. There was some research he had to do. The vicar was bound to have a book on it.

'My dear Inspector, charity may begin at home but it is nearly' – the Reverend checked his half-hunter – 'two-thirty. Contrary to popular belief, I do work on other days than the Sabbath, you know.'

'Forgive me, sir. I have imposed on your hospitality too long,' Lestrade snapped shut the last of several tomes, 'but I think I have what I require.'

'A solution to the death of Lamb?'

'Perhaps.' Lestrade raised a solemn hand to the start from Ashburton. 'As you say, sir, it is late. And at the moment what I have is circumstantial and speculation. And even to say that at two-thirty in the morning is no mean achievement.'

It had been a long time since Lestrade had seen a country sunrise. He was tired and cold and the bed at the inn had been far from comfortable. The abo was waiting for him as he turned the corner, crouching, sniffing the wind.

''Ello, boss.' The same inane grin.

Lestrade found himself staring at the bone which ran through the elongated fleshy part of his nose between the nostrils. 'What we track?'

'What?' Lestrade came to. 'Ah, yes. Can you find me a dingo?'

The abo laughed, a short, sharp cackle, rather like the kookaburra Lestrade had been reading about in the vicar's library the night before.

'Dingo, boss. 'Ere? You crazy all right.'

'Look at this.' Lestrade produced the tuft of hair. 'Dingo, Uku?'

The abo looked, felt between his fingers, smelt the strands. He looked puzzled. 'No, boss, no dingo.' Then his face cracked into a wide grin. 'No dingo, boss. Tammanwool.'

'Tammanwool?' Lestrade was back to his usual repetition.

'You lucky, boss. I been Tamman. No abos there now. I seen tammanwool.'

The conversation had left Lestrade behind, which was exactly what the abo was about to do. 'Can you find the tammanwool for me?'

'Sure, boss. We go now,' and he took to his heels, moving off at a low run down the road, Lestrade staggering in his wake. Probably, thought Lestrade, the wake of the long white cloud. Or was that somewhere else? The sun began to climb as the abo took to the moors, padding silently through the yellow fields of mustard around the village and up on to the greyness of the hills, splashed here and there with the white of the heather and the yellow and green of the gorse. Lestrade prided himself on being a fit man, but his temples and lungs felt as if they were going to burst. Always, the retreating figure of the abo ahead was like a needle in his flesh, forcing him on. God, thought Lestrade, the black bastard's going all the way to Constantine.

Four miles. God, he thought again, perhaps he's going all the way to Australia? His shirt was hanging out in an undignified flapping at his waist. He had long since lost his bowler and his collar stood out at an angle from his neck. He hoped to God he didn't meet anyone who knew he was an inspector of detectives from Scotland Yard, as his image would never recover.

Then he realised the abo had stopped. He was crouching, like a coiled spring, in the low, twisted trunks below Mawnan Church, where the vicar had seen his lion weeks earlier. The bastard wasn't even out of breath and Lestrade was on his hands and knees, fighting to keep the pain out of his tortured lungs.

'There, boss. Tammanwool hole.' The abo pointed ahead, to an overgrown outcrop of Neolithic earthwork. Lestrade saw nothing but an overgrown outcrop of Neolithic earthwork, but the abo was adamant, and Lestrade followed him through the undergrowth to a concealed opening. Even the nostrils of a city copper, unused to the country airs, and wide now with the exertion of the run, could not fail to notice the stench. Lestrade pulled back, almost gagging. The abo chuckled, seemingly revelling in it. 'Tammanwool,' he said triumphantly.

'Well, where is it?'

'Not 'ere now, boss. Gone away. We find 'im,' and he sprang to his feet. Lestrade caught the dark, sinewy arm.

'Will it come back, the tammanwool?'

'Oh, yes, boss. Tonight, late. 'E come back 'ere.'

'Then we'll wait.' Lestrade was emphatic. 'You go home now, Uku. Don't tell anyone about our hunt this morning. Do you understand? Anyone.' It couldn't have sounded very authoritative, even though Lestrade was recovering his composure. A wreck of a man sprawled in the undergrowth hardly inspired confidence. But the abo had gone.

Lestrade had gone alone. Ordinarily, he would have taken constables with him. Sergeant Winch would have been at his elbow. But the whole thing was too bizarre. Too untried. He was aware always of Nimrod Frost – 'People haven't forgotten the Ripper. Or the *Struwwelpeter* murders.' Lestrade was McNaghten's best man and somehow his whole career was on the line, hunting dingoes in the outback of Cornwall.

So he was alone. The moon wasn't there to help him tonight. Or at least, the clouds were hiding it, scudding, conspirator-like across the sky. Lestrade didn't like dogs. Big ones, little ones, it didn't matter. And here he was crouching in the thickets below Mawnan Church, waiting to catch one. True to the speed of the Cornwall Constabulary, the chief constable had not yet responded to the urgent appeal for firearms sent by Lestrade. Fortunately, the inspector had been able to borrow a 12-bore from Farmer Pemberton and it was crooked in his arm now. Lestrade was never *very* happy with a gun this size. He had seen the result of too many careless loadings and he even carried the scars of a rogue shot on his own shoulder. He fumbled with the cartridges. One. Two. Click up the barrels. Now to wait.

Behind him reared the blackness of the Mawnan earth-work, silent as the graves that lay beyond it. William Lamb was to be buried the next day. If Lestrade was lucky tonight, his killer might be buried before him. The owls were flying, hooting as they swooped over field and forest. Lestrade had seen one at dusk, an eerie white in a ghostly silence, winging its way over the heather in search of prey.

Policemen – those who become detective inspectors anyway – have a sixth sense. Not that Lestrade felt at one with Nature. Yet it was *something* which made him turn, gun levelled. There had been no noise, no warning. But there it was. Above him on the earthwork, an animal he had never seen before, and never would again. In the split second before he fired, he saw its teeth gleaming, its tongue hanging out, its eyes small and piggy in the fox-like head. His fingers squeezed on both triggers and the roar lit up the bushes. He fell backwards, unprepared for the recoil and rolled through the trees before struggling upright. Had he hit it? Was it coming for him? Could he outrun it? After this morning, out of the question. Could it climb trees? Could he? But the panic within him subsided. There was no movement, no sound. He fumbled in the leaves for the gun and reloaded. He must have killed it. Both barrels, at almost point-blank range. He must have killed it.

He hadn't.

There was nothing on the crest of the earthwork but leaves and grass. Damn. Lestrade whirled round, now in this direction, now in that. Nothing. For a long time, nothing. Then a crack. A twig snapping? Over there, down in the trees. The inspector crawled forward, his fingers sweating now on the trigger. Please don't let me blow my foot off, he thought. The awful smell came to him again, and for the first time a snuffling whine, then a snarl. There was a hiss above his head, then another. He crouched lower, trying to focus his sights on something ahead. But it was so dark. He couldn't see anything.

'Tammanwool, boss.' A voice sounded behind him. It was the abo, grinning as ever. Even Lestrade's twin barrels pointing at him didn't seem to lessen the grin. Lestrade momentarily flopped back, his heart descending from his mouth. He'd nearly shot the man.

'Dis way, boss,' the abo was calling from beyond the earthwork. On the far side of the parapet lay the body of an animal. It was about five feet long, with the head of a wolf and a cunning, cruel mouth. Its fur was tawny, with broad, dark stripes across its back and less obvious ones on its tail. Two barbed arrows lay embedded in its flanks. The stench was strong.

The abo retrieved his arrows and slung the animal over his shoulders.

'We'll *walk* back.' Lestrade was insistent.

Percival Ashburton was not pleased to be brought from his bed at that hour. In fact, he was about to summon pen and paper to dash off an angry letter to Lestrade's superiors when the abo dropped the dead animal on his feet.

'Yours?' asked Lestrade.

'What the bloody hell do you mean?'

'Your abo calls it a tammanwool. What do you call it?'

'Is this some sort of joke, copper?'

The colloquialism when ascribed to an officer of Lestrade's rank sounded a little odd, but perhaps it was an Australian commonplace, the inspector mused.

'I'll tell you what *I* call it, Mr Ashburton. I call it murder,' he said.

'Murder?' Ashburton kicked the animal off his slippered feet and strode for a brandy. 'You'll forgive me if, under the circumstances, I don't offer you one?'

'You brought this . . . thing . . . back with you, didn't you? A souvenir of the Antipodes. But it got out, didn't it? What I don't understand is how your abo here didn't know about it.'

'Well, he'll be looking for another job come the morning,' Ashburton snapped and roared something at the little brown man, who scuttled out of the room.

'What did you say to him?' asked Lestrade.

Ashburton slammed the stopper onto his decanter. 'If you must know, I threatened to point a bone at him.'

Lestrade looked bemused.

'The abos are a superstitious people, Lestrade. Backward. He believes bones can kill.'

'And I believe these things can too,' said Lestrade, crouching to peel back the animal's lips to reveal a row of razor teeth. 'All right when it was a few sheep, wasn't it? Some stray dog, no problem with that. But a man. When Shepherd Lamb died, that was different. That was why you were offhand when we met. It wasn't just your outback taciturnness. You were afraid.'

'I've faced mad abos, dingoes, drought, swollen rivers and plagues of everything from boils to rabbits. There's nothing I'm afraid of.'

'Except imprisonment for life.'

'What?' Ashburton's knuckles whitened round the glass.

'Unless you trained that thing to kill Lamb—'

'That's not possible.' Ashburton's assertion was too quick.

'– In which case you'd get the drop. As it is, you are an accessory to the fact of murder.' Lestrade circled his man, watching him closely, but painfully aware of the corpse, grotesque and evil-smelling at his feet. 'Take Pentonville,' he went on; 'five hundred and twenty cells. Each one is seven feet square. You will wear a brown cloth mask. No one will recognise you. You will recognise no one. Once a day, you will walk in a circle with a hundred or so others of your kind, the sweepings of society.' Lestrade was becoming lyrical. 'You will eat ten ounces of bread and three-quarters of a pint of cocoa for breakfast. For dinner you will have half a pint of soup, five ounces of bread and one pound of potatoes—'

'For God's sake!' Ashburton broke in.

'You will be a number, working on a treadmill all day, every day, climbing eight thousand, six hundred and forty feet into nothing. And you know the worst thing, Mr Ashburton,' he leaned close to his ear, 'me ol' cobber, you'll never see the sky again.'

Lestrade walked to the door. 'Now let's see if your brother can identify this,' pointing to the corpse.

'All right,' Ashburton sat heavily down in the nearest chair, 'All right, Lestrade.' He sat with his head in his hand for a moment, then looked at the animal. 'It's a thylacine, better known as a Tasmanian wolf or Tasmanian' tiger. As my brother would tell you, it's actually neither. It's a marsupial, Lestrade. Do you know what that is?'

Lestrade did not.

'A pouched animal, like the kangaroo. It carries its young in a pouch on its belly. This one is a female, a species, I can tell you, more deadly than the male. The Tasmanian wolf is very rare, Lestrade. There may be a handful in the wild. Nobody knows. I went out on a hunting trip there recently and caught it. A miracle. A bloody miracle, it was.'

Ashburton prowled his study, an odd figure, his face tanned and furrowed under the ridiculous nightcap. He chuckled. 'It was supposed to be a present for Thomas. I'd thought he might appreciate it. But before I could tell him about it, the flaming thing escaped. They're unpredictable, Lestrade. It was used to killing to survive. Sheep went. One here, a couple there. Then people began to see it. Thomas saw it. He thought it was a lion.'

'Why didn't you tell him?'

'Oh, I was going to. On several occasions, I was going to. I don't know why. I went out myself, a number of times, with a gun. No luck.'

'I used your abo to track it. Why didn't you?'

'The same reason I didn't tell him I'd brought it over. I told you, Inspector, abos are superstitious people. I thought if he knew I'd brought the Tasmanian wolf he'd go berserk. They can, you know. They've got a sixth sense when it comes to animals. They're part of them, almost. When Lamb was killed, I guessed what had happened. He was probably tending a ewe at lambing time. A new-born lamb and its mother are easy meat. Lamb must have got in the way, somehow. I never thought it would kill a man. God.' He buried his face in his hands again. 'Then there's rabies,' he suddenly remembered.

'What?'

Ashburton was pacing again. 'I don't know if it's likely, Lestrade. Dogs get it. So do other animals.'

'I do know the word, sir. One day they'll muzzle all dogs. Not to mention Tasmanian wolves.'

'What happens now?'

Lestrade looked into Ashburton's eyes. 'Now, I go to bed,' he said.

'What about . . . Pentonville?'

Lestrade allowed himself to smile. 'Don't worry, Mr Ashburton, we're not going to take away your sky. The wide-open spaces are important to you, aren't they?'

Ashburton nodded.

'Being in the Outback as long as you have has dulled your sense of British law, sir. I shall, of course, report my findings to my superiors and the Cornwall Constabulary will require a statement from you. I should think the most you'll get is a fine for not declaring a wolf at customs.'

'But there's a man dead,' said Ashburton.

'Such is life,' said Lestrade – and vaguely wished he hadn't.

Inspector Lestrade climbed the parapet again where the abo had killed the Tasmanian wolf. It was raining as the little funeral cortège wound its way through the trees below him. He took off his hat and nodded to John Pemberton. He noticed the coffin was of the finest oak, resplendent with gleaming brass fittings, by courtesy of Mr Percival Ashburton. Momentarily, the vicar stopped as the party went on to the place.

'He's a good man, Lestrade,' he said, motioning towards his

brother, 'but the Outback has coarsened him. We've all learned a lesson.'

'Amen to that,' said Lestrade and he walked away. As he crossed the churchyard, graves leaning aslant in the drizzle, he heard the vicar's voice. 'William Lamb, late of Her Majesty's . . . –' and the wind in the trees drowned the rest. As he reached the road and the waiting trap, he saw a lone figure on the parapet. A little brown man stood, almost silhouetted against the skyline. He waved his bow and arrows at Lestrade and then was gone.

'Gooday,' Lestrade found himself saying softly. 'Good hunting,' and he cleared his throat and straightened up as he noticed the cabman was looking at him strangely. It was, of course, entirely the cabman's fault therefore that as Lestrade climbed into the trap he caught his hand in the door and broke his little finger. He didn't remember much about the journey home. Except that his hand was about a foot across and every image in his brain was curiously finger-shaped and throbbing.

Beastie

Benjamin Beeson, ex-sergeant of the Metropolitan Police, sat in Lestrade's office with his massive fist around the inevitable mug of tea. Walter Dew, constable of the Metropolitan Police, lounged on Lestrade's desk in front of him, until the inspector swept in, whereon the aforesaid Dew swept away to busy himself with filing. Beeson stood to attention as his old guv'nor came in.

'Hello, Beastie,' grinned Lestrade. 'I'd shake your hand, only . . .' and he held up his bandaged finger.

'Oh, dear,' growled Beeson in the familiar old way. 'Nothing trivial I hope, sir?'

Lestrade had forgotten, momentarily, the sense of humour. He motioned to Dew to pour him some tea and offered Beeson a cigar.

'No, thank you, sir. I don't any more . . .'

Lestrade sensed the man's discomfort and noticed the frayed cuffs and shabby shoes. The pension didn't go far, he mused to himself and stuffed two cigars into Beeson's top pocket.

'Well,' he said, negotiating the steaming mug with his moustache. Shaving wasn't what it had been before he'd broken his finger. And all in all, he'd thought he'd better decline Mrs Manchester's offer of help with the cut-throat razor. 'Well, how is it, Ben?'

'Not good, sir.'

Lestrade's grin faded. 'The pension?'

'Love you, no, sir. I can get by on that. No, it's my old mate Joe Towers. He's dead.'

'I'm sorry to hear that, Ben. What was it? Accident?'

'No, sir. I think it was murder.'

Lestrade leaned forward in his chair. 'So this isn't exactly a social call?'

'No, sir, not exactly. I don't like coming to you, sir, but I thought perhaps twenty-six years on the Force counts for something.'

Lestrade nodded. He had been here before. 'Dew, get more tea for the sergeant. You'd better tell me about it, Beastie.'

Had Beastie Beeson been an ordinary member of the public, it might have been different. Had his description of the corpse and the manner of death been more unusual. Had Joe Towers not been sixty-two years old. If all this had been so, or not been so, Lestrade would have applied for an exhumation order in the usual way. Triplicate. Forms. Hours bashing away on the upright Remington on the first floor.

As it was, Lestrade trusted to Beastie's sixth sense. To the 'nose' he knew this old sergeant possessed. After all, the man was right – twenty-six years on the Force must count for something. And he laid his career on the line.

Kensal Green had never been Lestrade's favourite part of London. Especially at night. Amazing, isn't it, he thought to himself as the wrought-iron gates chinked and shook under the heavy pincers he carried, amazing how sounds carry at night. Breaking and entering. He swung the gate back. He could get ten years for that before a pious beak, out to prove that the law was harsher on bent coppers than on bent civilians. His breath wisped out before him and wreathed back around his face.

'This way, sir.' Beeson crunched with all the weight of his twenty-six years' service on the gravel. Without the aid of lights, the going was hard. The two men stumbled through the undergrowth and tangle of rhododendron bushes, making for the grave they wanted. Around them, in rows neat and clipped, the tombs of deceased Londoners bore silent witness to their intrusion. Tailors from Pimlico rubbed dusty shoulders with bank clerks from Norwood and the odd retired admiral, aptly enough from Gravesend. Beeson collided with a weeping angel, but only his hat brim was dented. In the flitting moon, the smooth white of the draped urns and the grooved columns, broken to the sky, threw shadows across the grass, crisp in the frost of the early hours.

'Here.' Lestrade dropped to his knees beside the fresh grave Beeson indicated. A single wreath on the wet, brown earth. Lestrade checked his watch. In the moonlight, he caught glimpses of the hands. Nearly quarter to two. They set to work, each man with his spade, slicing through the earth. Beeson, for all his strength, was past his best. A man retired for three years is not in peak condition. Lestrade's contribution was also limited, digging as he was with hand and elbow, to minimise the pain in his finger. Beeson was concerned, in fact something of a mother hen, as, with every other stroke, he apologised again to Lestrade for putting him through this. For a thousand reasons, Lestrade breathed a sigh of relief as his spade struck wood. Getting the coffin to the surface, even with the ropes Beeson had brought, was no mean feat and both men were cursing and panting as Joe Towers flopped limply into the waiting canvas and Beeson trussed him up.

'Sorry, Joe,' he muttered, 'but it's for the best. You know, Inspector, I feel like old Ben Crouch, the Resurrection Man.'

'Before my time,' hissed Lestrade, lowering the coffin as best he could. 'Let's cover this up.'

A casual observer, at dead of night, would have noticed little difference in the appearance of the grave now that the wreath and temporary marker were back in place. Lestrade wondered if the same lack of critical observation was likely to apply to an astute grave-digger in the broad daylight of the following morning. But it was too late to worry about that now. That same morning was showing signs of breaking through to the east, lending an eerie light to the hoar frost on tomb and vault. Between them they carried their tragic bundle down the hill, quickening their pace as they reached the gate. They steadied Towers against a pillar, where he rested his sack-covered head on Beeson's shoulder, while Lestrade deftly replaced the snapped chain with another from his pocket. He clicked the padlock into place, flattering himself on the skills he had learned from dozens of bettys, now mouldering no doubt as surely as Joe Towers, but in the living graves of Pentonville or the Scrubs.

'Remember, Dew,' Lestrade called to the hooded figure sitting atop the Maria, 'you've seen nothing. Heard nothing.'

'I shall be as silent as the grave, sir.' Lestrade and Beeson looked at the constable, now feeling rather silly and small on his high perch. At a signal from Lestrade, he slapped the reins and the wagon lurched forward, Croydon-bound.

It was nearly dawn as Joe Towers lay on the kitchen table at 20 Sanderstead Road. The gaslight flickered green on the walls.

'I never got on with post-mortems,' Beeson was saying, 'but there's something don't sit right with old Joe.'

'Tell me again,' said Lestrade, as he undid the linen shroud. 'From the beginning.'

Beeson sat back in the chair and lit his pipe.

'Like I said, sir. Me and Joe was mates, from way back. Went through the army together, India. Then I was transferred to the Twelfth Lancers and he stayed with the old mob. We lost touch for a while, and I joined the Force. That would be in' – he paused to count his fingers – 'early 'sixty-seven. Well, I was a copper on the beat for years, and one day – I'll tell you when it was, it was the day old Dizzy died in 'eighty-one – one day I was patrolling along the Ratcliffe Highway.' (Lestrade was grateful the sergeant had not used the immortal 'Proceeding in an easterly direction in the execution of my duty'.) 'And I saw Joe Towers, me ol' mate. Well, we had a jar aplenty that night, I can tell you – after my duty hours, of course, sir.'

Lestrade smiled mechanically, loosening the funeral tie of Joseph Towers and unfastening the collar stub. There was a mild smell of putrefaction. Not bad. Lestrade had smelt worse, but he must remember to tell Beeson to open his kitchen window once this was over.

'Joe was working in the Royal Albert. Stevedore, he was. Well, we saw a lot of each other after that. 'Is missus was a good sort and she gave us breakfast many a time after a session. He did like 'is pongolo, did Joe.'

''Is missus still with us?' asked Lestrade, checking the blackened, numb fingers for signs of a struggle.

'No, guv'nor. She went of the diptheria four years back. Salt of the earth, she was.'

'How did Joe die?'

Beeson began to prowl the length of his meagre kitchen, glancing sadly every now and again at the yellow-black face of 'is 'ol mate, staring sightlessly up from the kitchen table at the bowl of the gas light.

''E was the fittest man of 's age I knew. 'E'd work all the hours God and Ben Tillet sent. Never missed a day.'

'Ben Tillet?' As he opened the striped shirt, Lestrade's nostrils quivered. There was something else.

'Joe was 'is right-hand man in the Dock strike. "Tanner" Towers, they used to call him. Course, that was a bit awkward. You know how we used to be called out then, truncheons, cutlasses an' all.' Lestrade knew.

'I found 'im, in 'is parlour. Sittin' in 'is armchair, 'e was. I thought 'e was 'aving me on, at first, you know. Then I realised. 'E was dead.'

'How long do you think it had been, Ben?'

'Well, 'e was as rigid as a board,' offered the sergeant.

'Rigor mortis,' mused Lestrade, quietly enjoying the role of coroner as he lifted Towers' eyelids. 'About twelve hours, then.'

'If you say so, sir. I was never very good at that scientific sort of thing – leave that to the jacks. Oh, beggin' your pardon, sir – the detectives.'

Lestrade looked at Beeson under his eyebrows. 'Come here, Ben.' The sergeant dumbly obeyed. 'What do you smell?'

'Death, sir,' came the answer.

'Yes, that's what I smelt too, at first. But sniff deeper. Here, under the shirt especially. Something else.'

Beeson virtually buried his nose in 'is 'ol mate's chest. 'No, sir. Nothing.'

'Bitter almonds, Beastie. Can't you smell it?'

Beeson shook his head.

'And I'll lay you five to one the coroner couldn't, either. Nor the doctor who signed the death certificate.' Lestrade paused. 'Was there one?'

'Oh, yes, sir. Poor Law doctor, name of . . . I can't remember.'

'It doesn't matter.' Lestrade plunged his hands into the water bowl on the draining board. The water was freezing to the touch.

'You were right, Beastie. You didn't know why, did you? What was it you said? "Something didn't sit right." Well, it's paid off. Joe Towers was murdered, Ben. Cyanide.'

'Straight up?' exclaimed Ben.

'I don't know how it was administered,' answered Lestrade. 'When you found him, did you notice any foam or spittle around his mouth?'

Beeson hadn't.

'Signs of a struggle? Convulsions?'

No.

Lestrade realised after the first flush of triumph that he had saturated the bandage on his finger. It would take hours to dry.

'What happens now, sir?'

'Now, we put him back, Beastie. It'll have to be tonight. And Beastie . . .'

'Sir?'

'We'll get him. Make no mistake about that. But because of the . . . er . . . unorthodox way we lifted old Joe, there'll be too many questions asked. I've got a new guv'nor myself now, one Nimrod Frost. He's very much a man who does things by the book. We'll have to tread softly, softly.'

That night, with the same ease as before, Lestrade and Beeson reburied 'Tanner' Towers. It was so smooth, so simple, that Lestrade felt vaguely uncomfortable. Perhaps he'd joined the wrong side after all.

So Lestrade trod softly, softly. And before he could tread at all, he had a visit from one John Watson MD, of Baker Street.

'But it's here in black and white, Lestrade. In *The London Charivari* for April eighth – "The Adventures of Picklock Holes". *And* they've the nerve to make a pun on Conan Doyle's name – Cunnin Toil! Pathetic!'

'So what has you miffed, Doctor, is that they haven't mentioned you?'

'Nonsense! In fact, they have.' Watson drew himself up to his full height. 'I am referred to as "Potson". Puerile nonsense!'

'Your Sherlock Holmes stories?'

'No. The *Charivari*'s plagiarism. Damn you, Lestrade, you are deliberately goading me.'

The inspector chuckled. 'No, no, my dear Watson. Dew. Tea,' he shouted through to the corridor, waving his bandaged hand by way of explanation of his own inactivity. 'Tell me, do I appear in this plagiarism?'

'No,' Watson snorted, as he subsided into Lestrade's other chair.

'Well, that's a relief,' said Lestrade. 'At least I won't have to charge the editors of *Punch* with libel.'

'What do you mean?'

'For the past two years, you and Dr Conan Doyle have been taking my name in vain. You have done your best to undermine the confidence of the people in Scotland Yard. And in particular, me.'

Watson blustered, sweeping his grey whiskers from side to side in embarrassment. 'But it's all done in the best possible taste, Lestrade. Holmes and I . . .'

'Sherlock Holmes is dead, Dr Watson. As I recall, he hurtled over the Reichenbach Falls eighteen months ago, struggling with an innocent bystander whom he mistook for you.'

'Ssssshh!' Watson spun round in all directions in case of Ears.

'It's all right. Dew is deaf and dumb. Isn't that so, constable?'

Dew placed the tea on Lestrade's desk and went about his business as though he hadn't heard. 'See what I mean?'

'Good God, Lestrade. It's terrible that a man so depleted as that in natural functions should be allowed in the Metropolitan Police!'

Lestrade's resigned look would have withered a brighter man.

'Lestrade. Sholto. You promised . . .'

Lestrade waved aside the doctor's mute protestations.

'In all seriousness though, Dr Watson. I cannot take any action against *Punch*. They have their little jibes at the Yard, too, you know. In any case, there are more pressing matters.'

'Oh?' Watson examined his tea carefully before taking his first sip.

'Are you living now in Baker Street?'

'Yes,' said Watson. '221B. I . . . I've tried somehow to keep Holmes' spirit alive. I'm afraid Mycroft was no help.'

'Mycroft?'

'The Great Detective's brother, at the Foreign Office.'

Lestrade winced at the description of the dead addict.

'And Mrs Hudson?'

'It's all lies, I tell you.' Watson realised he had been a little too vehement. He checked his pulse, momentarily. Lestrade sensed the raw nerve and took a different tack.

'You have a surgery in Butcher Row, off Ratcliffe Highway?'

'I have.' Watson began to feel uneasy.

'You are what is known as a Poor Law doctor?'

'I believe it is my Christian duty to—'

'Quite. Quite. And did you attend a death at eighteen Havering Court on March the seventeenth last?'

'March the seventeenth? Er . . .'

'A docker named Joseph Towers.'

'Oh, yes, now I remember. Natural causes.'

'Cyanide poisoning.'

'What?' Watson was on his feet again.

'Can you smell almonds, Doctor?'

Watson looked around him, sniffing manically.

'Not at the moment,' said Lestrade, 'In the natural course of things.'

'Almonds? Of course.'

'But you can't smell them on a corpse, evidently. What about the pupils?'

'Whose pupils?'

'The deceased's pupils.'

'Er . . . God, Lestrade. You're talking about three weeks ago.'

'I'm talking about murder, Doctor. Were the pupils dilated?'

'No.' Watson was as emphatic as he could be, bearing in mind he hadn't the faintest recollection. 'But how do you know it's murder?'

Lestrade wasn't going to compromise his career before the good doctor, so he resorted to all the subtlety at his command. 'We'll ask the questions, sir.' Lestrade began to wander the confines of his office. He had time again to glimpse the grandeur of Norman Shaw's architectural style as the view of the blank wall from his window met him. If he craned his neck a little and stood on Dew's shoulders and then stooped, he could catch a flash of the water in the morning sun on the river. But he had seen the river before and it wasn't really worth the contortions.

'So there was nothing about the case that led you to suspect foul play?'

'I'm afraid not.' Watson was doubting not only his many years as a medical practitioner, but his many years in association with the Great Detective.

Lestrade decided to let the matter drop. Watson sensed it and pursued a new tack.

'I read about your West Country adventure, Inspector. How you found the . . . er . . .'

'Tasmanian wolf.'

'Yes.' Watson thumped his knee and strode to the door. 'Er . . . I hesitate to mention it, Lestrade. Especially in view of the *Charivari*, but . . . well, I've been' – another glance round to see that Dew was still deaf – 'I've been thinking that I might resurrect Holmes, give him a new case. How about . . . "The Wolf of the Ashburtons"?'

'You're going to give Holmes *my* case?' snarled Lestrade, even his bandaged knuckle turning white.

'Well, no, not exactly. But . . .' Watson was edging through the door, 'how about "The Beast of the Aborigines"?' and he dodged out as Lestrade threw his bowler at him. The inspector called out as the doctor fled the building, 'You may as well call it the Hound of the Baskervilles.'

Ben Tillet sat as though in a studio portrait, in his waistcoat, sleeves rolled up, flanked by two heavies from the Dock, Wharf, Riverside and General Workers' Union, who Lestrade thought he recognised from innumerable editions of the *Police Gazette*. Either of them, Lestrade surmised, could have cracked walnuts with his elbows.

'I'd lost touch with him, Mr Lestrade,' Tillet was saying,

never a man to acknowledge titles. 'The last time I saw Joe Towers was – oh – three years ago.'

'You've moved on to higher things?' ventured Lestrade.

'I don't consider being an alderman of the City of London, a member of the Parliamentary Committee of the Trades Union Congress and a prospective Member of Parliament "higher things". No, I'm still a man of the people, as I was in 'eighty-nine. Aren't I, boys?'

'Yes, Mr Tillet,' chorused the heavies, as though he had pressed the switches on two automata.

'And what of your work with the Independent Labour Party?' Lestrade thought he might as well get in a bit of fishing while he was there.

'Forgive me, Mr Lestrade. I thought you were enquiring into the death of Joe Towers, not my political affinities. If I am wrong, then of course I must have my lawyer present.'

'Towers, then.' Lestrade returned to the point. 'The man worked closely with you. How well did you know him? Did he have any enemies?'

'We all had enemies in 'eighty-nine, Mr Lestrade – the pillars of society, the wealthy, the bourgeoisie in their smug middle-class houses – not to mention, of course, the boys in blue.' Lestrade ignored the jibe. 'But we had friends too – thousands of dockers in the Port of London, engineers like Tommy Mann and John Burns. We even got thirty thousand pounds for our cause from our brothers in Australia. Now that's working class solidarity, Mr Lestrade. Something I'm proud of, Joe Towers was part of all that. I remember the first time I met him in the main yard at the West India. He was a casual, Mr Lestrade, one of those countless numbers who drifted to work each day until 'eighty-nine, hoping for a ship to unload. He told me he hadn't worked for four days and hadn't eaten for three. It's funny, but Joe Towers, as much as anybody, is why I called the Dock Strike. It was for men like him we fought for the "Tanner". I can see him now, standing in the Committee Room alongside Cardinal Manning, his face a picture of rapt attention to the great man speaking on our behalf.'

'But he didn't have any specific enemies?'

'No, he was a mild man. Everybody liked Joe.'

Lestrade felt Tillet could help him no longer and rose to go.

'Of course,' the Alderman went on, 'we are all mild men and there are thousands of us. There is a Union of Clerks and Teachers, of Shop Assistants, a Miners' Federation with two hundred thousand members this year. Altogether we number over one and a half million. How many Metropolitan Policemen are there, Inspector Lestrade?'

'Enough, Mr Tillett.'

'Of course,' the alderman began again, 'if you can't beat us, you could join us. Think of it, a Police Federation. Full pension rights, sick benefits, funeral expenses, strike pay. It's got to come.'

But Lestrade was already on the stairs whence he had come, out into the warm sunlight, where the air was fresh.

Walter Dew was a copper of very average ability. There was nothing disparaging in that. Wasn't it a fact, regularly voiced by the *Charivari* itself, that the vast bulk of the Metropolitan Police were of average ability? But on the subject of vast bulk, Nimrod Frost, the Head of the Criminal Investigation Department, was anxious to weed out the weak ones in his department. So it was that Constable Dew, hair macassared to perfection, moustaches combed just so, stood in Frost's office that day at the end of April, unusually for a plainclothesman, bedecked in his full uniform, helmet glittering in the crook of his arm. Perhaps crook wasn't the right term and he shifted it as the thought struck him. Lestrade had told him to box clever, to be circumspect (something which Dew thought only happened to Jews) in that the evidence pointing to foul play in connection with the death of Joe Towers *without* Lestrade's unofficial post-mortem findings was thin indeed. Even so, Frost was as impressed with Beeson's suspicions, based on long service within the arm of the law, as Lestrade had been, and so sanctioned Dew's depositions taken from all and sundry who had known Joe Towers and who were among the last to see him alive.

'All right, Dew, let's have the last of them.' Frost rested his podgy hands on the enormous velvet area of his waistcoat.

Dew flipped the page of his notepad and began, 'On the twenty-fourth instant I had reason to attend a public house—'

'A public house, Dew?' Frost interrupted him.

'In the pursuance of my duty, sir.' Dew was quick to reassure him. 'A public house called, appropriately, the Pig and Helmet—'

'Appropriately, Dew?'

Dew cleared his throat to cover his failure at levity and went on: '. . . where at twelve-thirty p.m. I met one Abel Seaman—'

'Abel Seaman, Dew? Are you trying to be funny?'

Dew noted that Nimrod Frost's face was slowly turning the purple of his waistcoat.

'I'm sorry, sir, that was the man's name – or so he claimed.' Frost's eyebrows disappeared under what was left of his hairline, but he said nothing. '– Who told me that he had seen the deceased Joseph Towers at approximately three-thirty on the day of his death and accompanied him some little distance towards his destination, viz and to wit—'

'To wit, Dew?' repeated Frost, doing a passable impression of a barn owl.

'Er . . . Mr Lestrade told me to put that in, sir.'

'Go on.'

'This Abel Seaman is known to us, sir. He was a one-time cash carrier, known to be a bug hunter and cly faker, who—'

'Dew!' Frost rose with all the speed and majesty his paunch would permit. 'Could we have this in English, please? It is, after all, the language of the Queen.'

Dew looked a little shamefaced. 'Of course, sir. He was a one-time prostitutes' manager, who has done a little bit of pickpocketing and stealing from drunks.'

'Not a man whose word is reliable?' Frost took a pinch of snuff from the elaborate silver box on his desk. Dew could read, upside down (in fact, rather better than the right way up), the inscription 'From the grateful people of Grantham' before Frost snapped shut the lid and proceeded to inhale violently the orange-coloured powder from the back of his hand.

'I rather think in this instance, yes, sir.'

Frost waited for him to go on.

'Seaman talked with Towers about this and that and Towers had told him that he was expecting someone that afternoon and declined his offer of a gatter . . . er . . . beer. Seaman was on his way to the penny gaff . . . er . . . Punch and Judy Show, and spent perhaps five minutes in Towers' company.'

'A grown man attending a Punch and Judy Show, Dew?' Frost was incredulous.

'Well, if you ask me, sir, it was probably an Under and Over,' and as Frost spun round with the speed of a laden sloth, Dew corrected himself, 'a fairground swindling game, sir.'

'Did Seaman learn more of Towers' visitor?'

'No, sir, except that he was Trasseno.'

'An Italian?' Frost felt he was learning the lingo quite well.

'No, sir, a bad person.'

Frost humphed his indignation at being wrong and continued to strut round his office.

'So it is likely that Seaman – if we can accept his word at all – was the last person to see Towers alive and that the . . . er . . . Trasseno was the murderer – if indeed he was murdered at all, and of course we only have ex-Sergeant Beeson's sixth sense on that.'

Dew felt the ground shifting beneath him. Box clever, Lestrade had said, box clever.

'Yes, sir,' was the height of Dew's wit and repartee.

Frost took Dew's notepad and thumbed through the pages. The man was barely literate, he thought. The lines could be the work of a deranged chimpanzee.

'Tell me, Dew, what do you want to be when you grow up?'

'Sir?' Dew frowned at the unusual levity from the Head of the Criminal Investigation Department.

'What are your ambitions, Dew?' he said by way of an explanation for the feeble-minded.

'Well, sir,' Dew was grinning at the prospect, 'I'd like to be a chief inspector one day, sir . . . and . . .'

There was an 'and' Frost realised. As if the first hope wasn't forlorn enough.

'And?' He leaned over towards Dew's right ear.

'And I want to write a book, sir, a biographical account of

my greatest case. It will be called "I Caught . . ." and then the name of the arch-criminal.'

Frost sat silently down in the folds of his leather armchair, whence he only ever rose with difficulty.

'That will be all, Dew,' he said, and as the ambitious young constable turned to go, he said, with all the sympathy and encouragement at his disposal, 'I think you'd have difficulty catching a cold.'

To the lighthouse

Joseph Towers had been dead for exactly one month. He had been buried for three weeks. And reburied for nearly two. Lestrade reflected again, as he had so often in the past, how difficult it was to reconstruct the last hours of a man's life. Particularly an old man, a man with few real friends. And in a way, Joe Towers had been lucky. He had a good friend in Ben Beeson, whose nose had smelt a rat, if not bitter almonds. How many more old men, and young ones too, and women, mouldered in paupers' graves or the elegance of Abney Park, apparently dead of natural causes, precisely because they did not have Ben Beeson for a friend?

And had one such case now landed on Lestrade's desk, in the form of a plea from the Norfolk Constabulary? It was Sergeant Edgar Bradstreet who brought it to Lestrade's attention – Gregson's blue-eyed boy.

'The inspector thinks it's anarchists, sir,' Bradstreet was saying. 'He suspects the Russians, perhaps using Irish *agents provocateurs*.'

'Inspector Gregson always suspects Russians, Sergeant, and he usually throws in an Irishman or two, for good measure. After all, he does help run the Special Irish Branch. What would we do without Irishmen, eh?'

'Do I detect a note of cynicism, sir?'

Well, thought Lestrade, Gregson had chosen a bright one this time.

'Realism is, I think, a better word, Bradstreet. Do I understand I am to have the pleasure of your company on this little visit?'

'I have been seconded to your division, sir.'

'Not enough anarchy in London at the moment, hmm? Well, never mind. If you're right, we'll smoke a few out in the fleshpots and opium hells of Cromer, eh?'

Lestrade was suffering from a superfluity of sergeants. In addition to Bradstreet, a new boy was thrust upon him – one Hector Charlo, by special recommendation of His Nims. 'He has friends in high places,' Frost had said. 'He looks to be a good boy, Lestrade. I think you can rely on him in a crisis.'

In the event, Lestrade couldn't. Sergeant Charlo stood before the inspector in the angle of the Yard's plumbing system that passed as Lestrade's office, a cherry nose swathed in a muffler, and eyes swimming with all the signs of terminal pneumonia.

'I'b sorry, sir,' he mumbled. 'Not good forb, I know, and by first assignbent with you, but I'b afraid I . . . I . . .,' and his whole body shook with the violence of his sneezing.

'You don't fancy the Norfolk air then, Charlo?' Lestrade proffered.

'With respect, Inspector, the odly place I fancy dow is by bed.'

'All right,' sighed Lestrade, never impressed by physical illness. 'Get your head under a towel and dose yourself up. You'd have thought they could have cured the common cold by now.'

'There's nothing common about by cold, sir,' said Charlo, with a brave stab at some dignity. 'It's probably turning to bronchitis as we speak.'

'We should be back in a day or two,' Lestrade went on. 'Report bright and early Monday morning.'

Bradstreet hoped that Lestrade had been joking about the flesh-pots and opium hells, but he had never been to Norfolk before and he didn't know *quite* what a hell-hole Cromer was. The representatives of Her Majesty's Detective Force caught the train from Liverpool Street, Lestrade having made some quip about Bradstreet's railway guide, which fell on professionally deaf ears, and they journeyed without incident to Norwich.

Thence by another train to Cromer, where they found, with surprising difficulty for two men trained to know their way around, the Police Station.

The chief constable, no less, informed them that the body was still *in situ*. Lestrade allowed a whimsy to enter his mind that had Dew been with him he would have been searching his gazetteer of Norfolk to find the village of Situ. He was grateful that Bradstreet seemed to have a smattering of Latin, or perhaps it was just that he did his naïvety better than Dew. The deceased was one William Bentley, lighthouse keeper, and the cause of death was natural. The only reason that the Yard had been called in was one of mere formality since one of Her Majesty's lighthouses constituted an area of strategic importance. Should a French or even a German fleet appear in the Wash, Cromer Lighthouse could be instrumental in their landing. As such, and as a matter of course, an officer of the rank of inspector or above from the Metropolitan Police was duty-bound to carry out the aforesaid formalities. In view of the threat from possible espionage, that some dastardly foreign power was eliminating lighthouse keepers one by one, presumably before starting on the garrisons of the Martello Towers and Palmerston's Follies around the south coast, it was natural that the Special Irish Branch and its most noted bloodhound, Tobias Gregson, should be involved. Gregson however had larger problems. It was rumoured that William F Cody was staging another British visit at the closing phase of his Continental tour and if there was a nation other than the Russians whom Gregson suspected, it was the Americans. So Bradstreet had been sent instead. Lestrade wondered why he too had been sent. The reason that appealed most was that he hoped Nimrod Frost shared his suspicion of the Special Branch and daren't let Bradstreet out alone.

The little party of policemen picked their way across the cliffs that evening. The dying sun lent a magical glow to the small town clustered below them, gilding the great grey tower of St Peter and St Paul. Below to their right stretched the sand and shingle of Foulness, nearly dry now at low tide. The light flashed with its inevitable regularity above the whitewashed building. No one spoke. They were greeted at the door by the head keeper, Nathaniel Blogg, whose family, the Yard were told, had for years been rescuing sailors and fishermen from the jaws of the sea. The skin of his weathered face was the colour of the crab shells which littered the rocks. There was no trace of humour, no trace of warmth. It was the face, thought Lestrade, of a man who had looked too often on death. It was like looking into a mirror. Shifting the metaphor mentally, it was the face that saved a thousand ships.

Blogg led the way, with a series of grunts and rustic growls, to one of the upper rooms. On a makeshift bunk inside lay the body of William Bentley, dead these four days. The sea air through the window had removed the smell of death. Lestrade looked at the body, checked the eyes, having removed Blogg's pennies first. Something. What?

'Bradstreet,' he motioned to the sergeant. 'Your views?'

The sergeant looked carefully. He was not used to whole bodies. Most of the corpses he saw in his current line of duty had been eviscerated by explosives. Cause of death seemed a little academic after that.

'Age about seventy, sir. Height, five feet eight inches or so. Colour of eyes, hazel. Not much hair. I would have to remove his clothes for distinguishing marks. Dead about four days.'

'Hmm.' Lestrade looked at the chief constable for confirmation. He nodded. 'Cause of death?'

'Natural, sir. Old age?'

'Mr Blogg, you found the body?'

'Ar.'

'What?'

'Ar,' said Blogg louder, assuming the moustachioed Londoner with his distinctly inland pea-jacket to be deaf.

'Who else has been in this room?'

'Er – until today only me, young Emma and 'er fella and Jem.'

'Who are these people?'

'Jeremiah Rook is the local constable who Mr Blogg sensibly summoned,' offered the chief constable. 'Emma Hopkins, *née* Bentley, is the daughter of the deceased. She arrived from York yesterday with her husband. Is any of this relevant, Inspector?'

'Yes, sir, it is. You see, my sergeant's description of the corpse is admirable, but he did get one thing wrong.'

'Oh?' Bradstreet thought it best to straighten himself so that he was a full inch taller than Lestrade.

'Your lighthouse keeper was murdered.'

'Murdered?' The word was echoed round the octagonal room, chorused by all but Lestrade and the corpse.

'Who has examined the body?'

'Er . . . only me and Jem,' Blogg answered, as the one-most-likely-to-be-in-possession-of-that-information.

'No doctor? No death certificate?'

The chief constable blustered. 'A matter of security, Lestrade. You know as well as I do that lighthouses are of strategic importance.'

Yes, Lestrade knew that.

'Look here.' Lestrade lifted Bentley's eyelids, first the left, then the right. 'You see these tiny specks of blood? Mr Bentley was suffocated. Oh, expertly, certainly. One of the neatest I've seen. Normally you'd expect blood at the lips and nose and more discolouration of the face.'

Lestrade mechanically sniffed the various cups and glasses in the room. 'He was probably drugged first. Quite a painless way to go, actually; if you must go at all, that is.'

'I want to go at sea,' Blogg informed the company, 'with a good nor' easter blowin'.'

The chief constable looked at him curiously. 'Well, each according to his taste, I suppose.'

'You and Bentley took turns about on duty here?' Lestrade put the question to Blogg, still gazing into the middle-distance of his vision of a viking's funeral.

'Ar.' He recollected himself.

'So you wouldn't know if he had any visitors, say, within the last five days?'

'No, I . . . Although . . .'

'Yes?' The word was chorused by the policemen assembled. They all looked at each other a little sheepishly.

'Well, it's probably nothin' really.'

'We'll be the judges of that, Mr Blogg,' said Lestrade.

'Well, I did see a ship moored 'ere. Must of been last Sunday.'

'The day before Bentley died,' Bradstreet said aloud.

Lestrade ignored him. 'Was that usual, Mr Blogg?'

'No, not really. Oh, boats come alongside now and then. Nosey parkers from Lunnun, mostly.' He scrutinised the present company.

'Was it a supply boat?' Bradstreet was getting above himself.

'Of course not,' Blogg said flatly. 'What do we need with a supply boat when you can walk to the bloody lighthouse?'

The chief constable and Lestrade turned to Bradstreet with an I-told-you-so expression on their faces. The sergeant had an inclination to follow this up by asking Blogg if the craft had been a submersible, for it had been rumoured for some months at the Yard that such an infernal machine was being manufactured for a forthcoming invasion. In view of his superiors' faces, he decided against it.

'Did you see anyone in the boat?' the chief constable asked, desperate to prove that the weight of silver braid had not diminished the incisiveness of his enquiry-making.

'No,' said Blogg.

'What sort of craft was it?' Lestrade asked.

'A ketch.'

'Did you see a name?'

'Ar.'

The company waited.

'Well, out with it, man. What was it?' Lestrade's patience only extended so far.

'Furrin.'

'Furrin?' the inspector repeated.

'Ar. You won't find it registered in an English port, I'll wager.'

'So,' mused Bradstreet, 'Gregson and I were right. It *is* a foreign power, bent on eroding British manpower gradually, here and there, whittling away the watchful eyes on the coast, ready for the great onslaught when there were no watchers left. Diabolically cunning.'

'Bradstreet.' Lestrade's voice snapped the sergeant back to reality. 'Mr Blogg is about to tell us the name of the boat, aren't you, Mr Blogg?'

'No,' said Blogg, being as obtuse as possible, 'but I'll tell you the name of the ship. As near as I can, anyhow. It was somewhat like . . . like . . . "Ora Rosa".'

'Spanish,' said Lestrade.

'Italian,' said Bradstreet.

They had spoken simultaneously.

'Bradstreet,' said Lestrade. 'Wear out some leather along the coast here. Check all the boats,' he glanced at Blogg, '– and ships – in harbour.'

'You won't find it 'ere. I never seen it roun' before or since.'

'We shall need to talk further, Mr Blogg,' said Lestrade.

And so it was with Nathaniel Blogg that Lestrade and Bradstreet began their enquiries. Unfortunately for them both, Blogg was only a part-time lighthouse keeper. The rest of the time he was a fisherman, when he wasn't manning the lifeboat, that was, saving souls from the deep. And Bradstreet in particular, looking every inch the city gent in his bowler and Donegal, kept hearing that word 'deep' each time the boat took a plunge into the grey of the North Sea. Looking back at the land was worse. The line of cliffs at Cromer yawed up and down like a demented seesaw, the spire of the church leaning at a rakish angle. It wasn't long before Bradstreet had turned the colour of the sail creaking tautly overhead – the colour of old parchment.

True, Lestrade was more suitably attired. Whenever his job took him to maritime areas, he tried to dress the part, but the jaunty black sailor's peaked cap and the matching pea-jacket could not disguise the landlubber's inability to roll with the ship. Most of the time, in fact, he rolled against it, barking his shins on lobster creels and smearing his sleeve with tar and foul-smelling bait. The smack bellied and plunged on the roaring surf, making interrogation of a crucial witness well nigh impossible.

Bradstreet's task was to commit the vital deposition of Blogg the fisherman to his notebook, but when he looked at the page of jottings, he realised that it would do justice to Mr Isaac Pitman, except that it wasn't shorthand. When Lestrade saw it later, in the relatively tranquil surroundings of the Fisherman's Arms, he pronounced it unintelligible. As well, then, that Lestrade's memory served to record the conversation. William Bentley, it transpired, was a native of Yorkshire, had served some time in the Army, and had been a lighthouse keeper for eight years. He was past retiring age really, but nobody else wanted the job. It didn't pay well and most of the younger men were either fishing or moving into the new profitable tourist trade that was becoming the vogue along the coast. Folk from Lunnun mostly and it was the railway that brought 'em there. Blogg spat volubly and contemptuously into the hurtling waters in scorn of both institutions. The act alone was enough to send Bradstreet over the edge, not literally, but metaphorically, and he vomited copiously over the side.

Friends? Only one really – a royal coachman from Sandringham, the Prince of Wales' estate, who came over once a month to play chess with Bentley. Enemies? Well, there was the Tuddenhams. Tough bunch they were. Bentley had fell foul of 'em almost as soon as he arrived. Blogg didn't rightly know why. The Tuddenhams, it transpired, were a family of fishermen from nearby Mundsley whose names were well known to the local constabulary as trouble makers, drunkards and shifters. Jem Rook had had his nose broken by one of them only last year, simply because the constable had smiled at him funny one morning. Yes, the Tuddenhams were the boys. If anybody had murderous inclinations in the area and bore Bill Bentley a grudge, it was them.

The conversation ended there, as nets were cast and hands dashed here and there, flinging ropes, hauling weights. Bradstreet was quietly wishing he was dead. Even Lestrade felt a little green round the gills, much like the wet, flapping mackerel that flopped down on the slippery deck. There were shouts and laughter and it was well into the afternoon before Bradstreet's prayers were answered and Blogg turned his smack for home.

Another magic evening, the sun casting long shadows across the shingle. Lestrade's legs had returned to his body and leaving Bradstreet flat on his back in his room at the Fisherman's, the inspector walked the beach with Bill Bentley's daughter. Emma Hopkins, as she now was, was a middle-aged woman who still retained much of the striking good looks of her youth. She spoke fondly of her father, but was not surprised that he had enemies.

'Always in trouble, that was Dad,' was saying with her soft-spoken Yorkshire accent. 'If there was a family like that here that didn't like him, you can bet – mind you, 'e weren't a betting man – but you can bet 'e'd put up a fight.'

'Liked a scrap, did he, your dad?' Lestrade asked.

'Aye, 'e did.' Emma Hopkins chuckled. 'Eeh, there were times Ma didn't know what to do wi' 'im, but 'is heart was in't right place. Y'know, I've seen that man take on't bare-knuckle champion of Bradford just to buy me a dolly I'd seen in Mr Althorpe's toy shop. He damn near won, too. I can see 'im now, Mr Lestrade, smilin' as 'e give me the doll, 'is knuckles all red and raw and 'is face a mass of cuts. I loved 'im, Inspector. 'E was a darling old man,' and she brushed a single tear from her cheek. 'No', she breathed in the sea air sharply to recover herself, 'I'm not surprised 'e died the way 'e did, though I'll wager – not that I do wager, y'understand – they didn't give 'im a fighting chance.'

Lestrade ignored the fact that Mrs Hopkins was contradicting herself. It was one of the more controlled manifestations of grief. He'd seen it before, countless times. Why was it, he mused to himself, that even before the season began, they exercised donkeys on these beaches? And he shook his trouser leg with the resignation of a man who did always look where he was going.

'I 'adn't seen 'im in, oh, five or six years,' Mrs Hopkins was going on. 'Well, you know 'ow it is when you've a family. My own children are nearly full grown now and there's John, my 'usband. Have you a family, Inspector?'

Lestrade hadn't.

The couple turned for the cheap hotel in the wrong part of town where the Hopkinses were staying. Lestrade watched the darkness settle over the sea before he began his journey back.

'Can we take 'im 'ome, soon, Inspector? The old man, to York. 'E'd want that. We'll bury 'im in 'is native peat. 'E'd like that,' Lestrade heard Emma Hopkins say again, in his mind.

'Yes, you can take him back,' Lestrade found himself saying aloud, hoping suddenly that there was no one nearby. He picked himself up from the sand of the cliff walk and made his way back to the town, the great perpendicular tower of the church black and silent now in the gathering gloom. Beyond that, the sibilance of the sea, a band of mauve-grey under a purpling sky. But Lestrade, as ever, had other things on his mind.

Blogg had told him that the Tuddenham tribe could usually be found in Cromer of a Friday night, in the tap room of the Cuttlefish, a far less salubrious hostelry than the one in which Bradstreet still lay, trying, no doubt, to make the bed lie still under him. It was one of the last refuges of the old Cromer, local Cromer, the Cromer that was the fishing village before the well-to-do began to spend their summers there. The place was crowded enough, with brawny good-natured fishermen and labourers, the smell of the salt and the brackish beaches lost in the all-consuming ether of Norfolk beer – a pint of which Lestrade ordered and took to one of the quieter corners, with his crab supper.

The girl who served him didn't seem too anxious to help him by pointing out the Tuddenhams, but in a few minutes it became obvious that Lestrade had found his quarry. He recognised the signs, the hurried glances in his direction, the lips moving silently behind cupped hands, the emptying of the bar and the tables around. And the final signal, the abrupt end of the fiddle music in the corner. Lestrade summed up the situation. His back was to the wall, a crackling log fire to his right. He had one good hand, but the other would not serve him well in a fight.

He transferred the pewter mug to his left hand and noiselessly slipped his right into the pocket of his Donegal draped over the settle behind him. He felt warm brass and waited. Four men, rough seafaring types, stood before him, all bearing a vague resemblance to one another, watching him in silence.

'Mr Tuddenham?' Lestrade ventured.

'Yes,' the four chorused.

'Who wants to know?' The eldest of them edged forward, elbowing aside the rest.

'Inspector Lestrade, Scotland Yard.'

'Where?'

A growl and a ripple of laughter. The fiddler flashed his

bow suddenly across his instrument, as though to punctuate the joke.

'I would like to ask you a few questions,' Lestrade went on, as the merriment subsided.

'Oh, ar? What about?' The older man hurled his tobacco plug around his mouth and spat it with unerring accuracy into a spittoon some yards away.

'The death of William Bentley.'

A murmur and a rumble this time. If Lestrade had been asked to swear on oath what had been said, he would have been bound to say it sounded like 'rhubarb'.

'What be that to do wi' us?' one of the younger Tuddenhams asked.

'Stow it,' snapped Tuddenham the Elder; then, fixing his beady eye on Lestrade, 'What be that to do wi' us?'

'Mr Bentley was murdered.'

Another ripple of rhubarb.

'Ay, we'd heard that. So?'

'So, how did you kill him?' Lestrade always tried the direct approach with the lower orders. It wasted less time, and there was less chance of a charge of wrongful arrest.

The murmur ran to positive allotments of rhubarb.

'What be you accusing us of?' another Tuddenham asked.

'Murder,' said Lestrade.

'And how are we supposed to have done it?' the eldest Tuddenham enquired.

'You tell me,' goaded Lestrade.

'Better yet,' snarled the biggest Tuddenham, 'I'll show you.' And he lunged at Lestrade with both massive hands outstretched.

It was one of those pieces of pure poetry of which inspectors of Scotland Yard are occasionally capable in moments of stress and which would be talked about in Cromer for years to come. Lestrade brought up both forearms simultaneously, spreadeagling his opponent's arms so that Tuddenham's chin crunched down on the table, narrowly missing the shell of Lestrade's crab. As he landed, Lestrade brought both his fists together on Tuddenham's temples, which would have been painful enough had they been fists, but in his left hand Lestrade still held the pewter mug and in his right the brass knuckle-duster without which he never ventured far. The assaulted Tuddenham knelt on the flagstones with his tousled head in Lestrade's supper, groaning. Apart from that, the tap room was silent and Lestrade had not left his seat.

After what seemed like an eternity, the two other Tuddenham children broke forward, but Papa restrained them, forcing them back with his scarred, burly arms.

The tension was broken.

'That's Matthew,' he said, pointing to the prostrate Tuddenham, 'this be Luke, this be Mark,' to the other sons; 'I be John.'

'I thought you might be,' said Lestrade. 'Landlord.' A figure answering that description appeared from behind the bar. 'A pint of your best ale for the Messrs Tuddenham – and some butter for the head of this one.'

Lestrade proffered a chair to John Tuddenham and as he took it, slowly, uncertainly, the whole tap room unfroze and returned to life. The fiddle struck up, even the fire crackled anew. The Tuddenham boys carried off their fallen brother like some tragic hero in a play.

'Did 'im good, that,' mused Tuddenham Senior over his pint, 'I'ope 'e didn't spoil your supper, sir.'

Lestrade shook his head. The new-found submission he could do without. 'Now,' he said, 'about Bill Bentley.'

'I'm not sorry 'e's gone. I won't say that I am. Whatever else I am, I bain't be no 'ypocrit.'

'I've heard of your feud. That's what brought me to you. What caused it?'

'That's no secret,' Tuddenham gazed obviously into the abyss of his tankard and continued only when Lestrade had signalled mine host to refill it. 'When 'e first come 'ere – upstart 'e were. From Yorkshire. What did 'e know of the sea? Landlubber, 'e were. We don't cotton to strangers here. Saving your pardon. We don't mix wi' them Lunnuners wi' their airs and graces.'

'The feud,' Lestrade reminded him.

'Oh, ar. Well, 'e accused us Tuddenhams o' wrecking. I be a fisherman, Inspector. All me life. Man and boy. And my father before me. Why, there's been no wrecking on this coast for years. Not since I . . . not for years.'

'So you hated each other.'

'We did.' Tuddenham Senior quaffed off his second half pint. Lestrade signalled for a third. He promised himself it would be the last. He didn't yet know Nimrod Frost reacted to 'expenses'.

'Mind you, we didn't kill 'im. Matthew there, 'e's always been a bit hasty, but in a way 'e was right. If we wanted to do in old Bill Bentley, I'd 'ave gone round there and wrung his neck like a chicken.'

Looking at Tuddenham's fist around his mug, Lestrade was in no doubt that that was so, but he wasn't letting the old fisherman off the hook just yet.

'So it was you who broke his neck?'

'It was not.' Tuddenham was adamant. 'Is that how he died, then?'

Lestrade finished his drink.

'No, Mr Tuddenham, it wasn't. Can you account for your movements on the twentieth inst?' And as he said it he realised the futility of his breath and changed tack. 'Where were you last Monday?'

'At sea, with me 'ol' family, and that's gospel.'

And from a man named John, with sons called Matthew, Mark and Luke, that seemed fair enough.

Lestrade ate a hearty breakfast – of crab – while Bradstreet resolutely looked the other way and sipped his water. As Blogg had surmised, Bradstreet had come up with nothing in connection with the foreign-sounding ship moored off the lighthouse. He had of course come up with much else, but it was not material to the case. Then out into the cold grey of the first morning of May, 1893. Over the cobbles the policemen trudged, wrapping their Donegals around them. Constable Rook dragged their valises and loaded them onto the station wagon. Much to the chagrin of Bradstreet's stomach, it lurched forward to the driver's whip, and they were gone, rattling out of Cromer across the pastureland of Norfolk.

'God, it's flat,' was really the only comment Bradstreet could muster.

'I smell something,' said Lestrade, trying to doze under his tilted bowler.

'I'm sorry, sir. I thought I'd sponged my waistcoat.'

'Not you, Bradstreet. I was being metaphorical.' He hoped that was the right word. 'I smell conspiracy.'

'Anarchists?' Bradstreet had woken up.

Lestrade opened a weary eye from under the rim of his hat. The question was not worthy of comment, but Bradstreet would not leave it alone. 'So that's why we're going to Sandringham. I knew it wasn't just the coachman you were after. It's the Royal Family, isn't it? They're in danger.'

'For all I know, Bradstreet, a madman with a Maxim has killed them all and they're lying on Sandringham's lawns as we speak, but that's not my case. I'm concerned with Bill Bentley, lighthouse keeper of Cromer. Your views?'

'An old man.' Bradstreet was marshalling his powers of detection. 'Suffocated. That would be easy. He died – let me see – latish on Monday afternoon, probably. Perhaps he was taking a nap.'

'Motive?'

'Not robbery. Nothing had been taken – Blogg told us that. Didn't he? I wasn't really concentrating on his boat.'

'Not robbery,' Lestrade agreed. 'Anarchy?'

Bradstreet took Lestrade's point. The obsession of Inspector Gregson loomed less large in a station wagon lurching through the dawn of a sleepy Norfolk.

Even so, the mysterious ship could not be ignored.

'We can't ignore the mysterious ship, sir.'

'No, we can't,' said Lestrade. 'But you Special Branch see *agents provocateurs* everywhere. A foreign-sounding name that only one witness remembers, but not well enough. I don't think it's anarchy,' Bradstreet.'

'Not anarchy,' echoed Bradstreet.

'Well then. Old scores?' Lestrade offered.

'Vengeance. The Tuddenhams. But they have an alibi. They were at sea.'

'It's not watertight, if you'll excuse the pun, but every sense

I've got tells me they're clean. Oh, they're up to their row-locks in smuggling and even a bit of wrecking if the chance comes their way, but that troupe of aboriginals didn't kill Bill Bentley.'

'Family then? His daughter? His son-in-law? What was he worth?'

'I like the deviousness of your mind, Bradstreet, but he was worth pretty well what he stood up in. No stashed cash, no annuities, no private means.'

'So, where are we then, sir?'

Lestrade glanced out of the window.

'Fakenham,' said Lestrade.

No need to be offensive, thought Bradstreet, but he did not dare say so to the little ferret-faced man beside him. After all, he'd seen the size of Matthew Tuddenham, probably still spark out on a table in a back room of the Cuttlefish, and was just a little awe of his guv'nor now.

It was Lestrade who told the constable to pull off the road and to wait with the wagon, sheltered under the trees. He and Bradstreet walked to the main gates, huge, elaborate, wrought iron, a masterpiece of royal heraldry. A liveried lackey opened them after establishing who was who. The detectives discussed tactics as they followed the widening driveway under the elms and cedars. They would not go to the main house. Protocol and all that. If the coachman who played chess with Bentley was their man, his royal master would hear of it soon enough. Bradstreet made his way direct to the stables, Lestrade by a more circuitous route to the woodworking school, where Close the coachman also had duties.

But before he could get there the inspector took a wrong turn and found himself in the confines of a sheltered garden edged with privet. A fountain played in the centre and although it was far from warm, a solitary figure sat taking tea on the matchless lawn. The figure had his back to Lestrade and was wearing a foreign-looking tunic, sky blue, laced in gold. Lestrade turned to go, but was stopped in his tracks by a gruff command, 'Halt!' Lestrade did. The figure rose from his seat, still carrying the delicate porcelain cup and saucer and approached him.

'Who are you?' The accent was clipped, foreign. Kraut, Lestrade hazarded.

'Inspector Lestrade, sir, Scotland Yard.'

Scotland . . . ach, zo.' The figure transferred his cup and saucer to his left hand rather awkwardly and saluted stiffly, his heels clicking together in what Lestrade knew was a Prussian tradition. With sudden realisation, it dawned upon him. The character before him with the fierce grey eyes, the hearty manner and the ludicrous upturned moustache was the King of Germany. Lestrade returned the bow.

'I am always impressed,' the Kaiser was saying, leading Lestrade to his table, 'by the efficiency of ze British police. Even zo I am travelling incognito, you fellows are neffer ferry far away, eh?'

'I am here on a case, sir,' pointed out Lestrade. The Kaiser looked at Lestrade's posture as he took the proffered chair, wondering perhaps whether it was an English custom for policemen to sit on suitcases. But then, he had noticed no hand luggage. Neither did Lestrade seem to be sitting uncomfortably. He decided to let the moment pass.

'You are from ze . . . now, vat did Bertie call it? . . . ze Special Irish Trunk, yah?'

'Special Irish Branch. No, sir, I am from H division, sir. We specialise in murder.'

'Murder?' The Kaiser poured Lestrade a cup of tea. 'Tell me, hev you read ze *Handbuch für Untersuchungsrichter*? Ve Germans are, of course, ahead of the world when it comes to the science of forensics.'

No, Lestrade had not read it.

'For instance, how would you tell if someone had been strangled?'

'Discolouration of the skin, bulging eyes and tongue, perhaps broken neck, bruising certainly on the throat—'

'Yes, yes,' said the Kaiser rather patronisingly, 'but be specific.'

Lestrade failed to see how much more specific he could be, but before he had time to try again, the Kaiser had grabbed his hand and placed it on his own neck. 'Now,' he said, 'ze fingers are positioned zo. Vat marks vould zis leave?'

Lestrade felt quite decidedly uncomfortable with the Kaiser's throat and life in his hands, but before he could move or answer, the hedges were alive with uniformed men who leapt upon him. The Kaiser sprang back as the table, tea, chairs and inspector sprawled across the grass.

'Don't worry, sir, we've got him,' Lestrade heard a burly sergeant say as he felt the cuffs click on his wrists, wrenched painfully behind his back.

'Damned anarchists!' A booming voice behind the struggling company caused them all to turn. 'Lestrade!'

'Gregson.' Lestrade was peering round from the kneeling position into which the half-dozen constables had forced him. 'Would you mind calling off your monkeys before one of them gets hurt?'

'Ach, I see,' roared the Kaiser, 'zis is a test, yah? To keep your staff on zeir toes. Yes, ferry good, yah.'

It was not Lestrade's toes that worried him at that moment. At least, he would not have given them priority over his neck and wrists, aching dully under the edge of a couple of truncheons.

'What the hell are you doing here, Lestrade? Muscling in on my patch?'

'Gregson, I wouldn't willingly enter your patch if you paid me. Now get these bloody handcuffs off me!'

A constable complied and the blood began to flow back into Lestrade's fingers.

'I'm following a line of enquiry, with your Sergeant Bradstreet.'

'Line of enquiry?' Tobias Gregson was suspicious. 'You're up to something, Lestrade. Your pardon, Your Imperial Majesty,' and he bowed almost double to the Kaiser, who was obviously amused by the whole thing and then whisked Lestrade into the bushes. 'Look, Lestrade. These bloody foreigners come over here at the drop of a hat. I had a call yesterday – a telegram – to say he was staying at Sandringham as a guest of His Royal Highness. I expect His Royal Highness is as browned off with Villy as I am. But I had to be here. Frost sent me packing on the first train. And as if this isn't difficult enough – he goes where he likes, when he likes, refuses a bodyguard – you have to turn up like a bad penny, trying to strangle the man.'

'I'm pursuing a murder enquiry, Gregson,' Lestrade spat back at him (all this in vicious whispers, Gregson occasionally smiling and waving at the Kaiser while the constables righted his table and salvaged what was left of his currant buns). 'And you can play bloody nursemaid to that,' he pointed contemptuously, 'all you like. But get in my way again, and I'll get you back on the beat.'

'How is he involved in murder?' Gregson demanded to know.

'Not him, somebody else.'

'Who?'

'That's my business.'

'If you're interrogating a Head of State of a major European power, it becomes my business.'

'I'm not interrogating *him*. How many more times?'

'Lestrade, you are evading my questions. If I didn't know better, I'd say . . . God, you're not a Communist, are you?'

'If I were, Gregson, I'm sure you'd be among the first to know.'

'Well, I never was very sure about some of McNaghten's appointments. Wait a minute, you were there on Bloody Sunday, weren't you?'

'That was six years ago, Gregson. Talk about the long memory of the law.'

'We have our uses.'

'Gregson, you can look under every bed in Sandringham for Communists, anarchists, shopping lists, whatever you like. All you'll catch is your own tail. Me, I've got a murderer to catch,' and Lestrade broke away from the bitchy conversation under the privet, and, barely acknowledging the Kaiser, who was now busy instructing the constables in truncheon drill, made for the stables and Bradstreet.

'I warn you, Lestrade,' Gregson shouted after him; 'this will go further.'

Hell broth

Jacob sat in the attic room, cold and alone. The sun didn't seem to enter the cobwebbed windows, but the wind shivered the yellowed nets and rattled the door behind him. He took up the pen again and wrote.

Sir, I must warn you that . . . and again the muse failed him. He threw the crumpled paper to join the others littering the floor. He must have been here an hour, perhaps two, and had got no further in his letter than the first line. At least he had addressed the envelope, *To Whom It May Concern, New Scotland Yard, London.*

The whole thing was too preposterous, too outrageous – who would believe him? He must go in person. And yet. What of them? Each rattle of the latch saw him turning, paralysed for a moment with fear. Then finer emotions took him. What of him? It was a matter of honour, really. A family affair. Across the wilderness of rooftops he heard a church clock striking. Six. He could stay no longer. He would write to the Yard again later, when he could. Now, he had to go north.

They stood before Nimrod Frost in his office. Tobias Gregson, thick set, squat, fuming. Sholto Lestrade, taller, thinner, calmer. The pattern Frost was prepared for, the pattern that so angered Gregson.

'So, that's it, is it?' Frost was glowering at Lestrade, but talking to Gregson.

'I wouldn't belittle it, sir. If need be, I can go to the Home Secretary himself.'

Frost turned an odd sort of white. 'Don't you threaten me with the Home Secretary, laddie. I'm not at all sure you're necessary on this Force, Gregson. In fact, once this Home Rule nonsense is over, I'm considering scrapping Special Branch once and for all.'

Gregson was speechless. He stood there with his mouth open.

'No need for you to smirk, Lestrade. You tread with your great feet,' again the unfair jibe, 'all over Norfolk, harassing European royalty. Who the hell do you think you are?'

Lestrade opened his mouth, but in the event got no further than Gregson. Frost wallowed to his feet. 'Consider yourself under suspension, Lestrade. Half pay. Go home. Cool off.'

Now it was Lestrade's turn to be speechless. Gregson was smirking triumphantly while Frost rumbled out a tirade against inspectors who could not operate efficiently, about what the yard was coming to, blah, blah, blah.

'Now, get out, both of you.'

Gregson turned for the door, smarting under Frost's attack, but pleased and justified as well.

'Lestrade, before you go.'

Frost slumped into his chair and fixed the inspector with his sharp little eyes.

'I know what you're thinking, Lestrade. Twenty years on the Force. All for nothing. What will you do now?'

'Grow geraniums, like other retired coppers.' Lestrade shrugged.

'Do that if you like but first I've got a little assignment for you.'

Lestrade looked at his chief. That couldn't be a smile playing around Frost's blubbery lips, could it? No, a trick of the light.

'I thought I was suspended – indefinitely,' he said.

'So you are.' Frost struggled to his feet. 'Show me your hands.' Lestrade held them out. 'You'll have to take that bandage off. And toughen them up. Get yourself some rags. Don't shave from today. Eat as little as you can.'

'Sir?' Lestrade already knew Frost too well to believe the man had cracked, yet certainly he couldn't follow his train of thought.

'Can you do a Lancashire accent?'

'No.'

'Cockney up your own, then. Bow Bells stuff, yes?'

'Yes, if I must.'

'You must. How will Mrs Manchester take it?'

'Sir?'

'Don't hedge, Lestrade. You have a housekeeper named Mrs Manchester, haven't you? Sarah Manchester? Aged sixty-one?'

Lestrade smirked. 'Is that a crime?'

'On the contrary. I'm glad to see my inspectors improving their social position. It gives them the air of authority they ought to have. But you'll have to tell her you'll be away for a while – one month, two, who knows?'

'I have a feeling you do, sir.'

Frost chuckled mirthlessly. 'Quite right, I do. You spoke of a conspiracy, Lestrade. Well, Gregson might not accept that, but I think you may have something. Three old men in as many months, dead from poisoning or suffocation – all made to look like the ravages of time. It's a coincidence, Lestrade.'

Lestrade was hearing his own words bounce back at him.

'Well, I've got a fourth for you, I think.'

Lestrade was all ears – especially now the tip of his nose had gone.

'An inmate of Manchester Workhouse, Lestrade. Another old man. Nothing odd in that, you might think. Old men die in workhouses every day. Except that this one was poisoned, like the others. But this one was obvious – strychnine. Very messy.'

'One murderer for them all?' Lestrade was thinking out loud.

'That's for you to find out,' Frost answered. 'Give yourself a week to roughen up. Then go to Manchester and get yourself committed.'

'Sir?'

'Special request from Superintendent Olds. Jack and I were at school together back in . . . back in the old days. His men are too well known for undercover work. But yours is a new face, Lestrade. We must think of a new name for you, a new identity. Get into that workhouse and find out how that old man died.'

'Why undercover, sir? Why not make enquiries in the usual way?'

'As I said, Lestrade. Conspiracy. You know the worst thing about conspiracies? You never know who's involved. It could be Jack Olds. The entire Manchester Board of Guardians of the Poor. It could be me . . .' A pause. 'For all I know, Lestrade, it could even be you. But we'll have to chance that, won't we?'

'And the suspension?'

'As far as the rest of the Force knows, Lestrade, you are out, at least for a while. Only you and I will know different. You can use Charlo as a go-between. Don't come to the Yard yourself. How's he shaping up, by the way?'

'I wish I knew, sir. All I've seen of him is a red nose and he didn't exactly say a lot between sneezes. He should be in my office now.'

Frost extended a chubby, powerful hand, and as Lestrade caught it he said, 'Keep your wits about you, lad. It's a rough world north of Hampstead. Think of it as a challenge.'

Lestrade smiled.

'And Inspector . . . Don't go annoying any more Visiting European Nobs. Or your suspension might be real.'

Sergeant Hector Charlo was not in Lestrade's office. He had attempted to rise, said the note that *was* there, from his bed of pain, but his doctor had advised him to stay where he was. As he feared, the cold was bronchitis and the doctor had warned of pneumonia if he left his boudoir. There was even a doctor's note confirming it, pinned to Charlo's spidery, handwritten missive. The inspector was to rest assured, the sergeant would be back on duty just as soon as the swellings had gone down. Mind you, his back wasn't what it was . . .

Manchester. The city. Not the housekeeper. It had a tart and a school named after it. Lestrade had never been before, but Frost had told him before he left the metropolis that it would be raining. It was. Grey rain was driving across a grey city. Its buildings were uninspiring and when Lestrade walked through it he found himself jostling with labourers on the last stages of cutting the Ship Canal which was to link the cottonopolis with the Mersey. He spent the day, with the rain soaking to his skin, acquainting himself with the place. He didn't like it. After this, the workhouse would come as a relief.

It was night before he found it – a long, low building in the shape of a cross, no doubt the pride and joy of some civic do-gooder under the shadow of the great Chadwick. He was admitted through a side door by an overseer with a hacking cough, to whom Lestrade gave his chit. By the guttering light of a solitary candle, the overseer read it: *James Lister, labourer*. It was an alias Lestrade had used before. The overseer peered at him through a greasy pince-nez. He saw the usual run-of-the-workhouse vagrant, unkempt, dishevelled, not perhaps as bowed of back or world weary as they usually were, but a month or two in this place, he knew, would alter that.

'Last known address?' The overseer, at this time of night, was forced to do his own paperwork. He perched on the upright desk that Mr Dickens had probably written on about fifty years before. Or if not him, then certainly Mr Disraeli.

'Last known address?' he repeated, quill poised.

'Ratcliffe Highway,' Lestrade lied.

'Where?'

'London.' Had the man heard of it, Lestrade wondered?

He scratched something incomprehensible on the ledger.

'Right, turn out your pockets.'

Lestrade complied. One pocket knife, handle broken, a length of string, one apple. 'Stolen?' asked the overseer. No comment. Lestrade would play it dumb with the authorities. He knew a chirpy workhouse inmate was as unpopular as a chirpy prisoner. And, looking about him, this was very little different from stir. 'Tuppence ha'penny.' The overseer slipped the change into his pocket and, as if to anticipate Lestrade's protest, said, 'which will go towards your keep.'

The overseer spat copiously in a corner and slammed shut the ledger. He beckoned Lestrade to a door in a grey wall, on which he knocked. A grill slid back and a face appeared.

'Male, age unknown, former labourer. Bath, bed and oakum.'

Lestrade shuffled down endless corridors, dark and dank.

Overhead in the lanterns' flicker he caught the elaborate gilt hypocrisy of the Manchester Board of Guardians, 'God is Love, God is Faith, God is Trust, God is Good,' and he was forced into the conclusion that God was probably Somewhere Else. He shambled more convincingly now, aware of his warders at his elbows, though they barely noticed him. He stooped, tilted his head to one side. Perhaps deafness might be worth a try. After all, he was physically fit enough for labouring work. His presentation at the House of Industry had to be – and to remain – legitimate.

'Strip.'

He did, standing naked in the dark of a circular room, in the centre of which he could see by the lantern's light, was a bath. Had they heard of the Poplar Reform Movement this far north? he wondered. And his question was answered as they pushed him roughly into the icy water.

'One hot bath,' said the warder and he was thrown a grubby towel to dry himself. His rags were bundled together and tied with string. 'For your release,' the warder told him and he was given a thick, drab fustian jacket and trousers. This place, he mused to himself, makes Cold Bath Fields look like the Strand Palace.

He was shunted into the East Wing, for adult males between sixteen and sixty. His bed was a trough: rough, splintered wood worn smooth by countless derelicts collapsing into it. The mattress was thin, straw-stuffed and the sheet a single layer of cotton. It was past May 1st and the blankets had been withdrawn.

'No beer. No spirits. No tobacco. No spilling your seed on the ground,' and the warders left. Lestrade let his eyes attune to the darkness. A long, dank room, stone floor, with high barred windows the length of it. The noise was of snoring, coughing, and the occasional breaking of wind – not unlike the sergeants' room at the Yard. But the smell was different. It was the smell of poverty, of despair, of death.

He didn't sleep at all, but the morning bell rang as punctually as ever. Five o'clock. Cold water, what passed for a meal of bread and black pudding, which Lestrade had never seen before and didn't really want to see again and then out to the labour yards to pick oakum. He studied the faces around him, grey, lifeless, identical. It wasn't easy to tell a man's age in here, much less his former calling. A pile of evil-smelling hemp was thrown at him. Like the others, he adopted the position of back against the wall of his stall, cross-legged, and proceeded to do as they did, hammering the rope with a broken mallet, teasing out the greasy, sharp threads until his hands were a mass of blood. At the end of the first day, he had spoken to no one, no one had spoken to him. He had failed to reach his quota of three and one half pounds of oakum. He was given a day to rectify that or it would be loss of privileges – no meals for two days.

He endured the night of hacking coughs, the tuberculous hours, yet again, wondering why exactly Nimrod Frost had chosen him for this, and the morning bell clanged the Unfaithful to work again. After hell broth on the fifth day, his hands red raw but his quota achieved, Lestrade made his first contact – a knot of men of varying ages, their skins the colour of the workhouse walls. Yes, they had known Richard Brown. How old was he? God knew, they didn't. Everybody looked the same age in here. All they knew was that he had worked on the canal side and when his rheumatics got too much, he came in here. Nice enough bloke. Honest. Mind you, he died funny.

'Oh?' Lestrade was all ears.

'Where did the say that knew 'im from?'

'In the docks.' Lestrade hedged.

'Liverpool?'

'Yes. How do you mean, he died funny?'

'Well,' another inmate chimed in, ''e were all reet one mornin', then be night time, 'e were gone.'

'And 'is face,' whispered another.

'What about it?' asked Lestrade.

'Grinnin''e were, like the devil 'isself.'

Lestrade felt the hairs rise on the back of his neck, where the short crop given by the warder three days ago was still smarting from the nicks of the razor.

'I seen plenty of dead men. They die every day in 'ere – and t'womenfolk, and t'kids,' another went on, 'but nothing like 'im. He was smiling with 'is eyes bright and 'is teeth bared. Like a rabid dog, 'e were.'

'I saw 'im die. I were wi'im.' All eyes turned to the Little Fly in the corner.

'Tha never said,' another chided him. 'I thought 'e were alone in bed.'

'Nay, I were going to ask 'im for some snout when 'e went rigid. He screamed out – you all must've 'eard it.' They hadn't. ''E arched 'is back a couple of times, like 'avin' a fit, like, and 'e died. It were all over very quick.'

So was the conversation. A warder rang a bell deep in the bowels of the workhouse and the inmates scattered, like the zombies of a Gothic novel – the undead going about their business. Silence, but for the coughs, reigned.

It had been confirmed. Lestrade's ravaged fingers curled painfully round the mallet again. The classic symptoms of strychnine poisoning. But this time Lestrade had to go further. He had to see the doctor who pronounced Richard Brown dead – and there was only one way to do that. He waited until the moment was right, heart pounding with the concentration, sweat breaking out on his forehead, then crushed his thumb with a mallet. He rolled sideways, crying out in agony. A warder was at his side, prodding him with his truncheon, 'You there, Lister. What's t' matter wi' ye?'

Lestrade held up the blackening digit.

'Malingering bastard,' was the warder's only comment, and he went away. Lestrade knelt there in pain and surprise until he passed out. The rest was easy.

When he awoke he was in a different room. Not the dormitory of the East Wing, but in a hospital room.

'Oh, so you're awake are you?' A burly woman with a starched but grubby apron stood before him, sleeves rolled to reveal muscles not out of place on a circus strongman, hair strained back in a silver bun. 'Malingering bastard,' she grumbled, tucked Lestrade in bed even harder and stalked off, bellowing orders to other unfortunate inmates, whose terminal tuberculosis or tertiary syphilis had brought them to their last days in the infirmary of the Manchester House of Industry, Openshaw district.

It was the best part of a day before his quarry arrived, a sallow-faced man in his mid-forties, shabby frock coat and faded silk vest. He handled Lestrade's thumb with something less than a charming bedside manner, but was alarmed when the inspector yanked him down to pillow level with his good hand. 'I am Inspector Lestrade of Scotland Yard. I must speak with you on an urgent matter of the gravest importance.'

The doctor pulled away, shaken. He recovered himself. 'See him over there.' He pointed to an old man staring at the ceiling, his fingers endlessly fiddling with his sheets. 'He thinks he's Nero. And I of course am Florence Nightingale. This one can chop wood with his right hand. There's obviously nothing wrong with that. Only his mind and his thumb need attention. Wood chopping tomorrow!' he barked at an accompanying warder. 'Let him sleep here tonight,' and he swept away. Lestrade's silent protestations as he craned out of bed were met with a swift tap from the burly woman, who had miraculously reappeared at his bedside. 'No broth for you tonight, me lad. Grabbin' the doctor like that, indeed! Who do you think you are?'

'Napoleon Bonaparte,' said Lestrade and sank down in discomfort and despair into his bed.

Most of the night was spent fighting off the advances of an old cottage loaf who would not take no for an answer. In the end, Lestrade brought his knee up rather sharply into the old man's groin, which cooled his ardour more than somewhat – and probably made him sing in a rather higher key. Nero in the meantime was composing odes of indescribable nonsense and the night would have been funny had it not been so unutterably sad. An inspector of Scotland Yard, Lestrade kept telling himself, had seen it all before. Remember that, keep your identity and this madhouse won't get you. An inspector of Scotland Yard. Remember. . . . Or was it Napoleon Bonaparte?

The dawn saw Lestrade standing with the others, huddled against the driving rain. God, did it never stop raining in Manchester? Beyond the limits of the city, mused Lestrade, in the airy uplands of Failsworth and Stalybridge (he had studied the whole area on a map) the sun shone out in splendour, but the smoke of the cottonopolis and the gleam of the cotton masters' brass conspired to reflect it back and keep it out of inner Manchester. Or perhaps even the yards of the House of Industry. Perhaps even beyond those high, grey walls, the world was turning still.

A whistle signalled a break in work. The woodcutters stopped. But this was no rest period. Even without his half-hunter, Lestrade kept his sense of time. The bells never missed. It was not rest period for an hour or more. The gates of the yard opened to admit a Visiting Pair of Dignitaries. A good-looking lady, perhaps thirty or so, swept in in a flourish of velvets and silks. The sweetness of her perfume flooded the air of sweat and sawdust. From nowhere, little workhouse children, the friendless boys and girls, scampered to her. She bent to them, kissing them, distributing sweets and liquorice.

'That's Mrs Lawrenson,' came the whispered answer to Lestrade's query. 'She comes twice a year to give us baccy and the kids sweets. She brings pins and combs for the women-folk.'

'That's charitable of her,' Lestrade commented.

'You don't often get that. I was in the workhouse at Kensington a year or two back.' Lestrade thought he recognised the south-London drawl. 'Bloody Miss Louisa Twinning stoppin' our porter. Bloody do-gooder. This un's all right, though. Knows how to treat a man proper, she does.'

'Aye,' whispered another. 'I wouldn't mind changing my place with that Dandy Jack of hers. I bet she's a real hot'un between the sheets.'

'Just remember,' the Londoner broke into verse:

'The paupers is meek and lowly,
With their "Thankee kindly, mum"s;
So long as they fill their stomachs,
What matter it whence it comes?'

'Is that Mr Lawrenson?' Lestrade asked, though he couldn't see the gentleman with her very clearly.

'Dunno,' said the Londoner. 'Fancy done up though, ain't 'e?'

'Nay,' the Mancunian spat a gob into the sawdust. 'I seen 'im when they came last Christmas. Introduced to us, 'e was. 'E's 'er intended. Name of Bandicoot.'

Lestrade dropped his axe, clanging loudly on the cobbles of the yard.

'Watch out, you clumsy ba . . .' and the Mancunian broke off as Mrs Lawrenson made her way towards the clump of woodchoppers.

'Good morning, gentlemen,' she beamed. 'Not a fine one, I fear.'

'Your radiance is sun enough for us, ma'am,' the poetic Londoner replied.

Mrs Lawrenson curtsied graciously and began to distribute largesse in the form of tobacco. 'Harry, help me here.'

'Of course, dearest,' and the tall, good-looking fiancé lent a hand. As he came to Lestrade, he stared in astonishment, his jaw hanging open. 'Good God,' was all he could say. All eyes turned to Lestrade.

'What is it, Heart?' Mrs Lawrenson asked.

Lestrade burned his eyes fiercely into the fiancé's. He could tell that it wasn't doing the trick. 'James Lister, sir, from the Ratcliffe Highway, labourer.'

'Has it come to this?' Bandicoot persisted. What an idiot, Lestrade fumed inwardly. Still the same copper of very little brain he used to be two years ago. What though he owed his life to the man, this was no way to treat him now, breaking his cover on an assignment.

'Do you know this man?' Mrs Lawrenson asked.

'No, ma'am,' Lestrade broke in. 'Begging your pardon, sir,' and then with vehemence, 'You must be confusing me with someone else.' He felt his stage Cockney fooling no one, but Mrs Lawrenson, accepting the statement at face value, gently pulled the uncomprehending Bandicoot away.

The others still looked a little oddly at Lestrade, not least the warders, whose truncheons were not in evidence this morning. Mrs Lawrenson swept away, with soothing words of comfort, surrounded by workhouse children, gobbling and sucking gratefully on their sweets. As the whistle signalled the men back to work, two warders strolled past Lestrade's group.

'She's 'ere a lot these days. Only, what were it, two weeks back? Three?'

'Nay, it weren't that recent,' said his mate.

'Aye, it were. Don't you remember? She visited Brown on t' day 'e died. No wonder t' old bastard died wi' a smile on his lips.'

Lestrade's ears pricked up. Was that it? Was that how strychnine was administered in this hell-hole? By the unsuspected hand of a social worker? A sister of mercy? Of course. It must be. Why else had Mrs Lawrenson visited Richard Brown? Had she visited him alone? Had she visited others? Had those other visits merely been to disguise her real purpose? Had she given anything to Richard Brown? What about a plug of snout? Strychnine on the tobacco. Yes, it was too easy. But she was Bandicoot's lady. His intended. Had that muddle-headed ex-constable from the right side of the tracks, old Etonian and friend of kings, taken a viper to his bosom? And while the inmates nearest the gates were secretly admiring Mrs Lawrenson's bosom, Lestrade hatched a plan.

He had to wait more than a month before he could make any move. Then, armed with a chit signed by a Guardian of the poor, he trudged out of the Openshaw Workhouse in search of work. Three others with him went straight to the nearest tap room, in the hopes of cadging or stealing the price of a pint. One, perhaps with greater resolve than they, set out for the diggings at the canal. But then it was easier for him; he *was* teetotal. Lestrade was choosier in his search for employment. He passed the rows of bleak, mean streets, silhouetted against the glower of the Manchester sky. Why were so many of them called Coronation Street, he wondered? He passed the gaunt, monolithic cotton mills, rows and rows of windows, repaired and buttressed against the escape of valuable steam. He passed the queues of women waiting their turn, with the resignation of the poor, at the standpipes. He avoided signs saying 'Cotton operatives wanted' and the pairs of uniformed policemen of the Manchester Constabulary. He was looking for one place of employment only – at the home of Mrs Lawrenson.

He had covered many miles in his workhouse hobnails before he found it, a large town house surrounded by acacias and planes. Dogs barked at his entry and the door was opened by a pompous butler of the old school, Scots and sandy-haired.

'Who is it, Dudson?' a voice called from the hall.

'A vagrant, ma'am. A person of no consequence. Shall I give a shilling, ma'am?' 'And may I keep the change?' he muttered under his breath.

Mrs Lawrenson appeared, gorgeous in a swirl of crimson satin – the afternoon dress of the rich. 'No, poor fellow. Come in, come in,' and she extended a hand and helped Lestrade over the threshold. Dudson, though used to this sight a hundredfold, showed with every movement of his body that he had never approved. What, he wondered for the umpteenth time, was a good Lowland Liberal like himself doing in the employ of a Socialist? And he was careful to keep upwind of Lestrade.

'Tea, Dudson. In the drawing room.'

The butler bowed to the inevitable and vanished, clapping hands to attract unseen maids.

'Pray, be seated.' Mrs Lawrenson extended a hand to the sofa.

'I'm dirty, ma'am.' For the moment Lestrade kept up his Cockney idiot.

'Nothing that can't be cleaned. Dirt, like poverty, is only skin deep. Are you in search of work?'

Lestrade decided to drop the guise and go for the kill.

'If I don't complete this case, I may be.'

Mrs Lawrenson looked a little taken aback at the brightness of the answer, the loss of accent. She peered for the first time under the grime, the blackened hands and the blue shaven head and caught the flash of eyes, purposeful, sure, even haunting.

'Who are you?' she found herself saying.

'Inspector Sholto Lestrade, ma'am, Scotland Yard.' He rose and bowed stiffly but watched her every reaction. She broke into a merry, musical laugh. 'Lestrade. Why, Harry has spoken of you so often. But why . . .?' Then it dawned. 'Wait, you were in Openshaw Workhouse, last month. *That* was why Harry was so odd. He recognised you.'

'He did indeed. It was all I could do to shut him up.'

'Oh, he is a silly boy, isn't he? Hasn't the brains he was born with.' A sudden seriousness. 'So, you are on a case, incognito?'

Lestrade was about to say 'No. In the workhouse,' when the timely entry of Dudson with the tea saved him unawares from social embarrassment.

'I though I'd better bring the tea myself, ma'am,' explained Dudson in his impeccable Lowland-Liberal delivery, 'bearing in mind the present company.' Had there been a clothes peg handy, Lestrade felt sure it would have been clamped firmly on the butler's nose.

'Vagrant be damned!' cried Harry Bandicoot as he rushed into the room seconds behind Dudson. 'This is Inspector Lestrade of Scotland Yard. You mind your p's and q's, Dudson, or he'll feel your collar.'

The very thought of Lestrade's grimy hand coming anywhere near Dudson's collar made the butler pale. He had read that the police were badly paid, but could it be as bad as this?

'What do I call you?' Bandicoot extended his hand. '"Sir", it always was. And yet now . . .'

'The least I can do for a man who saved my life is to let him call me Sholto, Harry,' and the two men shook hands warmly.

'You've met Letitia?' said Bandicoot, indicating Mrs Lawrenson.

'Bless you,' said Lestrade. 'Oh, I see. Yes, indeed.'

'Sit down, sir . . . er . . . Sholto. Please. Tell us why the disguise.'

'Undercover,' said Lestrade, and flashed a glance at the butler eavesdropping splendidly near the door.

'That will be all, Dudson.' Bandicoot flicked him away like a fly in summer.

Letitia poured the tea, and handed round the Madeira cake.

'It's rather difficult,' Lestrade began. 'You're a member of the public now, Harry. And it's I who should be calling you "sir".'

'We only worked on one case, Sholto, but I would hope we may be friends. I will never forget Hengler's Circus that night.'

'No more will I. It was nearly my last.'

'Well, then.' Bandicoot's mood lifted. 'You must have come here for a purpose. You're not a man who makes social calls. I remember that much.'

'May I speak to you alone?'

'Sholto,' began Bandicoot, a trifle outraged.

'No, no, dearest heart, the inspector has his reasons. Besides I have letters to write. Mr Morris will be in Manchester next month and I have not arranged the details with him. I shall be in the study . . . should you need me,' and she looked meaningfully at Lestrade. The men rose as she left the room.

'Look, Sholto,' Harry Bandicoot's new-found independence had increased his self-confidence; 'you may have been my guv'nor once, but that doesn't give you the right to pull rank now. Letitia and I are to be married in four months. In fact,' and he paced the room, 'in fact, she wrote you an invitation only last week. It's probably sitting on your desk at the Yard.'

Lestrade walked to the window, then turned back to the ex-constable.

'What do you know of Letitia?' he was bound to ask.

'Know? That I love her, of course. And that she loves me. And that's all I need to know.' Indignation was followed by a realisation. 'Why are you asking all these questions?'

'I've only asked you one.'

'All right.' Bandicoot was more reasonable, remembering his police training. 'Let me ask you one. What has Letitia to do with the case you're working on?'

Lestrade answered with another question. 'Who is Mr Morris?'

'William Morris, of the Kelmscott Press.'

'The Socialist?' He sounded like Gregson.

'Yes, he's a Socialist. He's also an artist, a writer, a thinker and a Great Man.'

'Like Sherlock Holmes was a Great Detective?'

'No, not like Holmes!' Bandicoot was thundering in a way Lestrade had not seen before. Then calmer, 'Sholto, as a vagrant you were welcome here. As a policeman, I'm not so sure. Unless you tell me what this is all about, I must ask you to leave.'

Lestrade looked at Bandicoot. He was half a head taller,

considerably broader, and eleven years his junior. Furthermore, he had not lived on hell broth and beef tea for the past five weeks and his hair, unlike Lestrade's, was not falling out. Anyway, physical attributes apart, this man was Harry Bandicoot, the curly-headed, good-natured young constable who had shot and killed one of the most accomplished murderers of the century to save Lestrade's life. He couldn't let it come to blows. Besides, he hadn't got his knuckle-duster.

'All right, but you must promise to answer some questions first – for old times' sake.' He didn't want to say for auld lang syne in case Dudson was listening at the door. Bandicoot sat down, rational, reasonable again.

'How often does Letitia visit Openshaw Workhouse?'

'A few times a year, I believe. Christmas and the spring, certainly. Other times if she has the opportunity.'

'Why?'

'Why?' Bandicoot appeared genuinely taken aback. 'She believes in her fellow man, Sholto. You and I may have seen the dregs of humanity on whom any amount of sympathy would be wasted. But Letitia believes man can change his base nature.'

'What about Richard Brown's base nature?'

'Who?'

'The name means nothing to you?'

'No.'

'What about Bill Bentley?'

Nothing.

'Joe Towers?'

Still nothing. Bandicoot was as blank as ever he was.

'Richard Brown was visited by your lady love some seven weeks ago,' Lestrade offered by way of explanation. 'Is she in the habit of visiting individuals in the workhouse?'

'Not usually, no, but it has been known. Sholto, what exactly are you accusing her of?'

Lestrade let out a long sigh. 'Probably nothing,' he said; 'possibly murder. Would you ask her to join us?'

Lestrade knew he was breaking all the rules in the book, letting Bandicoot fetch a suspect himself, with all the emotional ties he had with her. But Lestrade was having a private bet with himself that Bandicoot was still too much of a policeman to permit anything untoward. A bolt for the backdoor? A rush to the stable? A concocted story at the very least? But no, a few seconds and Letitia Lawrenson stood before him, her intended bridegroom at her side.

'Did you know Richard Brown?' Lestrade was standing facing her, eyes and voice as cold as the workhouse hot bath.

Mrs Lawrenson visibly sank. 'So you know?' She waved aside Bandicoot's outstretched arm. 'No, Harry. It's time I . . . what is it you policemen say? . . . came clean?'

'Letitia, don't—'

'Letitia Lawrenson,' Lestrade broke in, 'you are not obliged to say anything, but I must caution you—'

'No, Inspector,' Letitia cut him short, 'this is not a confession to you. It is a confession to Harry.'

And all three of them sat down to hear it.

'George, my husband, died six years ago; he was killed in a mountaineering expedition, Inspector – the Matterhorn. When he died I was twenty-two, scarcely a woman at all. Some women might have broken down, withdrawn behind the weeds of widowhood as the Queen did, I have read. I found a cause, Inspector. The people. Good, honest people, like your friends in Openshaw. I buried my love for my husband in them.' Bandicoot held her hand, tenderly, for a fist so large.

'But, my dearest, I know all this,' he said.

'What you don't know,' and she pulled herself away from him to the window, 'is that I had an admirer. I never told you about him because . . . because, well, it was all over nearly a year ago.'

'Well then . . .' Bandicoot offered acceptance, but Letitia spun round; 'he was sixty-three years old, Harry. Old enough to be my father.'

The policemen, past and present, looked at each other.

'Richard Brown?' asked Lestrade.

Letitia took her eyes with difficulty away from Harry Bandicoot. 'No, Inspector. Richard Brown knew this man in the Army. He worked on his estate for a while, but drifted away in later years. I came to know him for a time before he left. His rheumatism had got worse very quickly. When I first saw him in Openshaw I could scarcely believe it was the same man. I visited him when I could. I learned later he died on the day of my last visit.'

So now we are getting somewhere, Lestrade hoped.

'Did you give him anything?' he asked.

'Some tobacco. And some words of comfort.'

'Tobacco,' repeated Lestrade, almost hoping now he was wrong.

'Yes, as I gave you and the rest some on my most recent visit. As a matter of fact, I had neglected to bring any on the day I visited old Richard. The surgeon gave me some.'

'The surgeon?' repeated Lestrade. 'Do you know how Richard Brown died?' he asked.

'A convulsion, the surgeon told me,' Letitia answered. 'He would say no more.'

'The surgeon?' Lestrade was beginning to sound like a wax cylinder.

'Yes, Dr Foster.'

He couldn't be from Gloucester, could he? thought Lestrade. But this was hardly the time to be flippant. 'This Foster. Was he the man who gave you the tobacco?'

'No. Dr Foster joined the infirmary a day or so after Richard Brown's death, I believe.'

'So who gave you the tobacco, Mrs Lawrenson?' Lestrade was persistent.

'Well, presumably Dr Foster's predecessor. I didn't have much to do with the medical team. I believe his name was Corfield.'

'Corfield. Corfield.' Lestrade had heard that name somewhere, but he couldn't remember where.

'And you didn't poison Richard Brown?' Lestrade was to the point.

Bandicoot and Letitia looked at him speechless. It was she who found her tongue first.

'Inspector, I told you my confession was for Harry. I was . . . close . . . to a man nearly forty years my senior, and that within the last year. I could not believe . . . cannot believe Harry could still love me once he knew that. But dear God, can either of you think me guilty of murdering that dear, sweet old man?'

Lestrade collected together his rags. 'No, Mrs Lawrenson.

We can't. I am very sorry to have bothered you. I will take my leave. But first, I must know the name of this man, on whose estate Richard Brown worked.'

'Inspector, I cannot tell you that.'

'Old ghosts,' said Bandicoot. 'Better let them lie.' And he took Letitia's hand firmly in his.

'I hope you will both be very happy,' said Lestrade and made for the door. As he turned, they were locked in each other's arms, oblivious to his going.

In the hall the pompous Mr Dudson approached him. 'Er . . . Inspector . . . I could not help overhearing. The man you seek is Major General Edward Harnett. I . . . er . . . hope I have been . . . helpful to you.' The Scotsman was actually rubbing his hands together in anticipation. 'Is there a reward?'

'Oh, yes,' smiled Lestrade. 'There's always a reward for people who listen at keyholes,' and he jabbed two grimy fingers into the butler's eyeballs. Dudson fell back, screaming in pain and Lestrade was on the steps before Bandicoot caught up with him.

'Sholto. Don't go. You see, I knew Letitia wasn't your man. Please, stay to dinner. A bath? A soft bed? Letitia insists.'

'Tempting indeed, Harry. But I'd better not. How will I face the hell broth tomorrow after a fine meal tonight? Besides,' he began scratching, 'there are too many of us.'

'Will we see you at the wedding?'

'You might, Banders old thing, you might. Oh, and by the way,' he pointed to the doubled-up sobbing form of Dudson, 'I recommend you get yourself some new staff,' and he turned into the rain.

Daisy, Daisy

It was appreciably easier getting in than getting out; Lestrade's overhasty grasping of the workhouse doctor's lapels had earned him something of a reputation. God knows to how many people the good doctor had repeated Lestrade's bizarre claim to be an inspector from Scotland Yard. Perhaps for that reason, perhaps for others, Lestrade found himself watched more closely than before. He had returned to Openshaw that evening without employ – not unusual in the Manchester of the nineties. Times were hard and despite the 'Hands Wanted' signs, workhouse Hands were not required. At least Lestrade had eliminated Mrs Lawrenson from his enquiries, but before he could follow up Dudson's tip, he had to see the good doctor again.

Days followed days slower than Lestrade had known. And in the course of them he noticed a shadow; a slim young fellow who watched him more closely than the warders. In a rest period late on the Wednesday, he engaged Lestrade in conversation, though the inspector's mind was elsewhere. He was what Madge of *Truth* referred to as a comtemptible cur. Educated at Charterhouse, he had fallen on hard times and his family, of *nouveau riche* stock from Altrincham, had deserted him. A few indiscreet card games, a torrid affair with the daughter of a Stalybridge banker and he found himself in here, in coat crawling with company and his once immaculate hands ragged with oakum. He could leave tomorrow. They all could. Couldn't they? Lestrade looked at him. He wasn't at all sure *he* could.

'A bounder. That's what her father called me,' said the young man, looking up from his knees drawn tight under his chin. 'Just before he had me horse-whipped. Want to see?'

Lestrade declined the offer. He had decided the Bounder was harmless enough. He wasn't a threat, a plant by the authorities. The very improbability of his story ruled that out. He was just lonely, feeling sorry for himself. Lestrade nodded, shook his head, said 'Yes' and 'No' a few times, more or less, he hoped, in the right places. He was waiting for night, for the sound barrage of hawking and spitting. The lights flickered out at ten as they always did. He did not have long.

Time was of the essence. Noiselessly he slipped out of his trough and between the rows of snoring men. A faint light shone from the bull's-eye, swinging in the wind of the labour yards. Beneath the oakum, when he wasn't being watched, Lestrade had been hammering into shape the iron wedge he had wrenched from the rotten wood of his bed. It had taken him a week, but it was ready. He slipped it between the door and the jamb. Damn. Too tight. He bent it against the door and it clicked into position. No danger in the cacophony of coughs behind him of the door being heard. He swung it open and was about to close it when he felt fingers grip his arm. He swung round, ready to slam the door on whoever it was and in the dim light recognised the Bounder.

'Take me with you,' he rasped.

'What do you mean?'

'You're going over the wall.'

There was really nowhere else Lestrade could have been going. The latrine was at the far end of the room. Midnight raids on the pantry belonged to the days of Charterhouse and if this was sleepwalking, Lestrade was a very determined example of it.

'And you can go through the door tomorrow. Go back to bed, man.'

'I can't stand another night in . . . there.' The Bounder was quaking.

'They'll be after you by morning.'

'What for – breaking and exiting?'

Lestrade did not appreciate the light relief.

'All right, but keep low, keep quiet and do everything I tell you.'

They ran across the yard, the inspector and his shadow,

scattering rats to left and right. Lestrade flattened himself against the wall, ramming the Bounder into a corner. A whistling warder lurched across the steps on the way to the outer gate. He paused, looked briefly around and then fumbled with his trouser buttons. The Bounder raised his nose helplessly in anticipation of a sneeze and Lestrade clapped his good hand over his face. The sensation in the Bounder's nose went away as the warder adjusted his clothing and growled, 'Who's there?'

Lestrade pressed his conveniently flat-tipped nose further into the stone.

'Oh, it's you, Doctor. Just off home?'

'That's right. I've got my keys. You needn't bother,' pre-empting the warder's attempt in the darkness to find the relevant key.

'Good night to you, then, sir,' and he went on his way.

Couldn't be better, mused Lestrade and springing back from the wall rolled under the doctor's feet, bringing him down in the straw with a crunch. Before he could cry out, Lestrade had straddled him, a hand over his mouth and a forearm at his throat.

'One sound and you're a dead man,' he hissed in his ear.

The Bounder sat in the shadows, amazed.

Something in the glint of Lestrade's eyes told the doctor he meant business. And something in the doctor's eyes told Lestrade he could relax his grip. He hauled the man upright.

'To resume our conversation of a couple of weeks ago. I am Inspector Lestrade of Scotland Yard. Were I not attired in the sartorial elegance of Openshaw District Workhouse, I would be able to prove it. As it stands, you must take my word for it, Doctor Foster, and I am not a patient man.'

If this man is insane, thought Foster, he's extraordinarily single-minded. But then, wasn't that a symptom of one kind of clinical madness? He wished he'd been to that lecture.

'You signed the death papers on Richard Brown?'

'I did.' The lunatic was well informed.

'Cause of death?'

Silence.

'Doctor, you are familiar with all sorts of deaths in establishments like these. What was the cause of his?'

Foster relaxed with a shrug. 'Actually, I'm not very experienced in establishments like these, as you put it. My practice was not . . . well, let's just say things were not working out. I became a Poor Law doctor. Openshaw is my first workhouse.'

'How long have you been here?' The soggy, rat-soiled floor of a workhouse labour yard was not the ideal place for a prolonged interview. Lestrade was trying to hurry things up.

'A few weeks. Look,' the doctor's tone changed, 'are you who you say you are?'

'On my word as an English gentleman,' was the least fatuous thing Lestrade could think of.

'All right. I'll trust you. I'll have to. It was I who contacted the Manchester Police. I managed to obtain an interview with Chief Superintendent Olds. I couldn't make much of it. After all, I didn't know – don't know – if the authorities are involved.'

'Authorities?'

'Richard Brown died of strychnine poisoning, Inspector. Risus sardonicus. Heard of it?'

'Strychnine, yes.' Lestrade rested back on his heels. 'What's the other? A monkey?'

'The smile of death, Inspector. The poison causes the muscles of the face to contract, baring the teeth in a maniacal grin. It's not something I'll forget. Ever.'

'What's your point about the authorities?' Lestrade persisted.

'You've been in here, Lestrade. How many inmates do you know who have access to strychnine?'

'It wasn't Mrs Lawrenson, who visited him on the day he died. Although unwittingly she may have given him tainted tobacco.'

'Tobacco,' Foster shouted, until Lestrade's hand silenced him. 'Of course,' he went on in a whisper, 'that's it.'

'No, it's not. We want the man who gave the tobacco to the lady.'

'So our murderer is a tobacconist?'

'Not necessarily, Doctor.'

'Have you asked her?'

'Of course. She obtained the tobacco from your predecessor.'

'Prior?'

'Prior to what?'

'No, no. Dr Prior. That was the name of my predecessor.'

Lestrade didn't follow. 'Not Corfield?' he said.

'Corfield? No. Wait a minute. I believe the name does appear in the day book.'

'What's that?'

'As surgeon and practitioner to Openshaw, I have to sign daily in the day book, as evidence of my attendance on duty; otherwise they don't pay me.'

'And you say Corfield's name is in it?'

'Yes. He was probably a *locum tenens* for Prior.'

'A what?' This man was speaking a different language.

'That means he filled in for Dr Prior if the man was off sick or otherwise unable to attend the infirmary.'

'Do you remember when Corfield's name appears last? Think, man. This could be vital.'

'Er . . .' Foster's face screwed up with the effort. 'I think it was May the tenth. Good God!'

'What?'

'That was the day that Richard Brown died.'

'This Corfield,' Lestrade went on, 'have you ever seen him?'

'Never. But I don't understand. Why wasn't I told you were here, incognito?'

Lestrade knew the meaning of that one now. He wouldn't show ignorance again.

'You wouldn't have been the first murderer to report his suspicions of the crime to the police.'

'You mean . . . you mean I was a suspect?' Foster was outraged.

Lestrade straightened. 'When exactly did you take up your present post?'

'May the seventeenth. A week to the day after Brown died.'

Lestrade turned to the Bounder. 'Laddie, you've heard a few things tonight it would be better you forgot.'

'Inspector . . .' and he started to say something, then fell back into the shadows. 'What things are they?' He grinned uneasily.

Lestrade patted him condescendingly on the cheek. Foster

unlocked the outer gate and the three of them slipped into the night:

'One last question,' whispered Lestrade. 'Do you in fact come from Gloucester?'

'No, actually I . . .' and the doctor's face hardened into the resolution of ages as he caught Lestrade's smirk.

With one Bounder, Lestrade was free.

Letitia Lawrenson was of little more use to Lestrade than Foster had been as to the physical description of Doctor Corfield. Greying, she thought, quite distinguished. But other than that, she could not help. And she begged Lestrade to believe, in Bandicoot's absence, that she did not habitually find older men attractive. That was one reason why she had not particularly noticed Corfield. It was one reason indeed, though not paramount, why she was marrying Harry . . .

They sat beneath the sheltering arms of a Cedar of Lebanon. The Prince and his lady. Below them, in rolling ground falling away from the great house, stretched Derwentwater in Derwent Dale and away to their left the hills of Stanage Edge and High Neb. The incredible summer of 1893 really began then, in the shimmering heat of July's end, and for them it began at Ladybower, overlooking the Derwent.

It was into this idyllic scene, the *fin de siècle* sun throwing long, deep shadows across the lawns, there walked a man in a shabby duster coat, worn among the *nouveaux* and *anciens riches* for driving their horseless carriages. His hair was cropped short, in the manner of the working classes, and he didn't appear to have eaten well for some time. His skin had the jaundiced look of old parchment and he seemed unused to the fresh air. But his step was jaunty enough and he threw the Gladstone bag to the ground as the station wagon lurched to a halt beside him.

'You take a devil of a lot of finding, Inspector.' The asthmatic wheeze behind the muffler was vaguely familiar.

'Charlo?' Lestrade peered into the gloom of the cab.

'The same, Inspector. As you see, much recovered,' and he fell into a paroxysm of coughing.

'How did you find me?'

'It wasn't easy, sir. But duty called. May I ask, sir, what we are working on?'

Isn't 'we' a little presumptuous? thought Lestrade, but the man had obviously been suffering.

'Get rid of this wagon and walk with me,' he said. 'I'll explain as we go.'

The constable snapped the whip and rattled away down the drive. In the dust and gnats of the summer evening, the policemen strolled down the drive.

'How can you bear that scarf in all this?' Lestrade gestured to the heat of the day.

'Oh, I have to be careful, sir. I've never been strong, you see. Even as a child—'

'Yes, let's leave that stone unturned, shall we, Charlo? I'm going to use you as a brick wall to bounce a few ideas off. Ready?' And Lestrade told Charlo all he knew.

'Which leaves me,' said Lestrade as they crossed the Palladian bridge, 'two niggling questions. If I can answer them, I'm close to my man.'

'Sir?'

'How is your grasp of languages? What do you make of Blogg's "Ora Rosa"?'

'That being . . .?'

'Come on, Charlo, concentrate. That's the name Blogg thinks he remembers on the boat – er, ship – moored at Cromer Lighthouse.'

'It's all a bit vague really, isn't it?' Charlo was adjusting his eye shade to avoid the glare of the setting sun. 'I'm not sure Blogg knows anything.'

'I should have though an up-and-coming pillar of the Yard like you would have had a command of languages, Charlo,' Lestrade persisted. 'I thought it was Spanish. Bradstreet thought Italian. What's your reading of it?'

'Perhaps it was neither, sir. What if Blogg's "Rosa" was really someone's name? How far away was he when he saw it?'

Lestrade hadn't checked that.

'It's true, I do have a certain natural linguistic talent.' Lestrade had obviously touched his sergeant's vanity. 'If I'm right, it means "scent of roses". But that doesn't make much sense, does it?'

'About as much as this case does at the moment. What about the name Corfield? The *locum tenant* doctor at Open-shaw? Does that sound familiar to you?'

Charlo searched his memory. He'd known lots of doctors in his time, but he couldn't help his governor on this one.

'Excuse me,' Lestrade called to the couple sitting under the tree. 'It's a devil of a way from the gate. Am I right for the house?'

'Over the rise,' the Prince called back. 'You can't miss it. Thirty-two bedrooms, Palladian style, copper cupola. Usual thing.'

'Are you house guests?' the lady asked, gliding over the lawn towards them.

By now, recognition had dawned on the dusty traveller. 'Not exactly, ma'am. Your Royal Highness,' and he nodded in a stiff bow.

'Good God,' the Prince chuckled, waddling behind the lady to the drive. 'You've been taking lessons from my nephew. That reminds me, Daisy, the damned whippersnapper is bringing the *Meteor* to Cowes this year. He's bound to win the Cup, damn his eyes.'

'Ssshh, Bertie.' Daisy motioned towards the traveller. 'I'm not sure these gentlemen are Edward's guests. . . .'

'Allow me to introduce myself, sir. Inspector Sholto Lestrade, Scotland Yard. This is Sergeant Charlo.'

'Good God,' said the Prince again. 'Your husband?' He turned to Daisy, nudging her with a well-padded elbow.

'Bertie!' She rapped his chest with her fan.

'Wait a minute . . . that name is familiar,' said the Prince. 'Haven't we met?'

'I am flattered Your Highness remembers me. It was the Commissioner's Ball, eighteen ninety-one. You and the late Duke were guests of honour.'

'Aha!' the Prince roared again. 'Harlequin!'

'Correct, sire.'

'Would you believe it, Daisy, this man was got up as Harlequin. One of old McNaghten's best men.' Then, more confidential, 'I seem to remember you made a fool of my son.'

'My apologies, sir.'

'Don't wish to speak ill of the dead, eh? No, Lestrade, don't let it bother you. Eddie had his fling. We none of us are masters of our fates, eh? Anyway, if my memory serves me correctly, he was being his usual boorish self, annoying a lady; cracking creature, dark eyes, dark hair . . .' and he cleared his throat forcefully, having caught Daisy's eye catching his. A new tack, 'So who's this new chappie . . . er . . . Orion Snow?'

'Nimrod Frost, sir.'

'Yes, of course. Sorting out the sheep from the goats, eh? Well, new shepherds will. And your case, Lestrade? What brings you to Ladybower?'

'As ever, sir, I fear I cannot divulge . . .'

'Oh, quite, quite. But come, Lestrade, your professional advice at least. I've heard that some chappie has written some nonsense about tracing cracksmen and the like by the pattern on the end of a man's fingers. That can't be true, surely?'

'There are those who say it is, sir.'

'What about you, man? Commit yourself.'

To a workhouse, thought Lestrade, no, never again. 'Let's just say I shall keep an open mind, sir.'

The Prince roared again. 'Well, let's see what old Harnett's been up to, the dog. I assume you have come to see the master of the house?'

'We have, sir.'

'Right, we'll walk with you. Oh, Lestrade, now that Mr Gladstone had at last persuaded Mama – that's the Queen, by the way, I think I mentioned her when we last met – to let me see Cabinet papers, I'm a pretty busy chappie. I must be away before dinner on pressing affairs of State. I take it I *can* leave? I mean, I'm not part of your enquiries?'

'No, sir.'

'Good, then you must squire Lady Warwick here this evening.'

Lestrade was a little non-plussed. 'Your Highness, I . . .'

Daisy Warwick took the detective's arm. 'You're not refusing a royal command?' she mocked, wide-eyed.

'Ma'am, I'm hardly dressed for . . .'

'Oh, Eddie Harnett will have something for you and your chappie here. The truth is, Lestrade, I don't trust the other old lechers here this weekend. I know Daisy's safe in the arms of the law. Metaphorically speaking, of course.'

And they walked, Lady Warwick arm in arm with the Prince and the inspector, towards the house. Charlo tagged behind.

Major-General Edward Harnett, Master of Ladybower, sat on the edge of a leather sofa with outstretched arm. He was dressed in his scarlet uniform, dripping with gold, a plumed cocked hat on his head. The only incongruity, apart from the fact that his charger was mere horse-hair, was the glass of Cognac in his rein hand. In front of him, agonising over every stroke and flourish, crouched an artist of the Bohemian set, swathed in smock and beret.

'I don't think I can help you, Lestrade,' the general was saying. 'I'm sorry old Brown has gone, but I can't see why this is a police matter – and Scotland Yard at that. Oh, do hurry, Mr Sickert, my arm is killing me. This damned Mameluke is heavy,' and he twirled the sword wearily.

'Richard Brown was murdered, sir.'

Sickert's brush slid inexorably over the canvas, driving scarlet across the general's moustaches. 'Is something amiss, Mr Sickert?'

'Er . . . no, no.' The artist fumbled with his turpentine substitute, 'Murders. Violence. Such things bother me.' He visibly paled.

'You know where the latrine is, man,' the general motioned and the artist sped for the door. 'Sickert by name and Sickert by nature.' He yawned. 'Still, it gives me a chance to "dismount", what? Drink, Lestrade? Charlo?'

'Not when we're on duty, sir – but that's not for an hour or two. Brandy, please.'

'A glass of water, please,' said Charlo, and as if to avoid the glances, 'It's my stomach, you see.'

'Brown was murdered?' Harnett took the weight off his boots. 'How?'

'Strychnine.'

'Poisoning. Good God,' and Harnett swigged his glass. 'Why?'

'I hoped you might tell me, sir. When did you see him last?'

'God knows. He left me . . . ooh . . . nearly three years ago now. I never really knew why. He seemed happy enough. Perhaps the call of the city. Manchester claimed him.'

'Did he have any enemies here?'

'Here? No, I don't think so. In fact, he was a popular man. Scrupulously honest. He always was, right from way back, in the Crimea.'

'The Crimea?'

'Yes, he was my orderly for a time. But then, he was Lord Cardigan's orderly too – and Colonel Douglas'. A very orderly man, you might say.'

'His regiment then, sir?' Lestrade pursued.

'The Eleventh Hussars, Prince Albert's Own,' and Harnett raised his glass in a toast. 'God love 'em. Tell me, Lestrade, why the death, albeit murder, of a lonely old labourer commands the attention of Scotland Yard? I thought you chaps guarded the Crown Jewels, that sort of thing.'

'It's a long story, sir. And I fear I am not at liberty to tell you.'

'Ah, quite, quite. Anyway, it's almost dinner time and I must see His Royal Highness to the station. See my man, Burroughs, he'll kit you both out. I insist you stay for breakfast too; Mrs Carpenter's kedgeree is legendary.'

One couldn't say fairer than that.

Dinner was superb. After weeks on hell broth and only a day of London fare before catching a train north again, Lestrade wasn't sure he was up to it – twelve courses, eyes dazzled by the crested silver, brain seething with the champagne. Charlo declined most of it, devouring what seemed to be large quantities of Carter's Little Liver Pills. Half the county seemed to be there; ladies in their pearls and diamonds, gentlemen of the Hunt in their elegant black and white. But Sholto Lestrade found himself looking increasingly at his beautiful escort, Daisy, Countess of Warwick. A hostile observer would have found the mouth too hard, the eyebrows too dark, but Lestrade, mellowed by wine and the sparkling conversation, was far from hostile. He forgot, in the course of things, that the tails lent to him by the general were rather too roomy, that his neck swam in the collar like Gladstone's, an old tortoise reaching for a cabbage leaf, and that the jacket shoulders drooped off his own. It had been a long time since he had found himself in such company.

He tolerated the exclusion of the ladies after the coffee with a marked reluctance, but Daisy Warwick's hand lingered longer than was strictly necessary in his. She blew him a kiss with her eyes.

He lit his cigar from the candelabra and made himself as much a part of the conversation as he could. Harnett was reliving the Ashanti War in one corner, surrounded by crimson-faced cronies of the old school. Elsewhere, the old chestnut of Home Rule was being trotted out, if one did trot out chestnuts. Charlo rotated around the room in the opposite direction from Lestrade, avoiding the smoke and keeping, as his guv'nor had suggested, his ear to the ground. And horses dominated the field in other corners. Those buffoons in the Quorn. Who was tipped at Epsom this year? And Goodwood? And in the Prince's absence, Persimmon was a Shetland pony fit only for the knacker's yard. Or perhaps a police horse. Lestrade, incognito again, refused to bridle at that.

'Now Bertie's gone, we could play baccarat,' suggested a guest.

'Damned bad form,' growled another and flopped back into the champagne fug of his corner.

'Let's look at the garden,' a soft voice whispered in Lestrade's ear and Daisy, as bored with female company in the next room as he was by male, swept him out on to the balcony.

It was a glorious evening, that one in late July, over the Derwent at Ladybower. And they walked hand in hand over the sun-gilded lawns, the Detective and the lady.

'Do I shock you, Sholto?'

'Ma'am?'

'Oh, come.' She shook his hand teasingly. 'You can call me Daisy.'

'If I may say so, ma'am, we are from different stations, you and I.'

'Bow Street and Clerkenwell?' she quipped.

Lestrade stifled his smile.

'Ah, I saw it, Sholto. You almost cracked, then. Seriously, Inspector Lestrade of Scotland Yard, you won't compromise your position – or derelict your duty – by calling me Daisy. Just this once.'

She turned and took both his hands in hers, gazing into his eyes. What's behind them? she wondered. What makes this man? What kind of man becomes an inspector of detectives? What sights have those eyes looked on?

'Very well. Just this once,' he said, 'Daisy.'

She laughed, a bright, tinkling sound that danced with the rose trees down the lawns. 'You know, dear Bertie thinks the world of you, Sholto. He likes you.' And then suddenly serious, 'Isn't it nice to be liked, Sholto?'

He nodded, unsure of himself, missing the familiarity of danger, the boredom of routine. Walter Dew with his inane grin, his cup of tea at the ready. Sergeant Dixon with his 'Mind how you go.' Nimrod Frost with his ferret eyes and his wobbling girth. It all seemed an eternity ago. And here he was, a suspended policeman, gazing into the dark, hypnotic eyes of a Countess of the Realm, on the lawns of Ladybower, eighteen hundred and ninety-three.

'You knew Eddie?' she went on.

'Let's just say we met.' He remained cryptic.

'Tell me, this lady Eddie was annoying at the commissioner's ball. How did Bertie describe her? Dark hair? Dark eyes? Mrs Lestrade?'

'No.' Lestrade straightened. 'No, there is no Mrs Lestrade.'

Daisy smiled to herself in the dusk.

'Who was she, Sholto?'

'Someone,' he said, fighting down the memory.

'Someone?' Her voice was a whisper, her mouth closing towards his chest.

'Her name was Constance. Constance Mauleverer.'

Daisy stepped back. 'And you loved her?'

Lestrade nodded.

'You love her still?'

He did not nod this time, but walked on. 'I met an old friend of mine recently, Daisy – a young constable I knew when I knew Constance. He said something I shan't forget. He said "Old ghosts. Better let them lie."'

'I wonder if Constance feels that way.'

There was something in the way Daisy said that that made Lestrade catch his breath. He stopped and looked at her. 'Yes, Sholto. I know Constance Mauleverer. Have you forgotten that my husband is now Earl of Warwick? The Mauleverers lived at Guy's Cliffe, didn't they? I remember when Albert Mauleverer was killed. Were you on that case?' Realisation dawned.

Lestrade nodded. 'For a time, I thought I'd go back to Guy's Cliffe.' he said. 'Find her. When we parted, it was like losing a part of myself.'

Daisy sat on the cool grass under the Cedar of Lebanon and spread her gown.

'She's gone, Sholto. Gone for ever.'

'Do you know where?' Lestrade sat beside her.

She looked at him hard. 'Yes,' she said slowly, and placed her fingers on his lips to stop the next question. 'And I'm not going to tell you. Your friend was right, Sholto. Let old ghosts lie.' And she curled her hand round his neck, drawing him to her.

Their lips met under the boughs of the cedar. From somewhere in the woods a peacock called, echoing across the lawns. Daisy Warwick was an expert at seduction of this type. Her mouth was warm and yielding, her fingers running tantalisingly through the fuzzy crop of hair.

'For one night, Sholto,' she whispered, gazing into his eyes, 'forget Constance.'

'As you will forget Bertie?' he asked.

She smiled. 'I have always thought,' she said, 'there are degrees of love. My husband and I are . . . comfortable together,' and she kissed him again. 'Conventionally so. Bertie is like . . . a rich old uncle. We don't . . . well, I'll leave that to your imagination. He's a darling, he feels like an old glove, warm, moulded to your hand.' Her tongue found his in the French manner, to which Lestrade was unused. 'And there is the degree of a summer night, Sholto, when a man and a woman are thrown together by chance, to enjoy the moment, to enjoy each other. No regrets, no second thoughts, just the moment . . .' and she sprawled beneath him on the grass, wild with the cool scent of clover and honeysuckle, opening her bodice to his searching fingers.

Mrs Carpenter's kedgeree was as magnificent as Harnett had predicted. Lestrade tucked in with a will and maidservants came and went with clashing tureens. If anyone had seen the figures writhing under the cedars the previous night, they were not letting on. Such servants were used to such sights. Harnett chose them for their discretion. Charlo toyed with a water biscuit.

'What did you get last night?' Lestrade asked him.

'Rather less than you, sir, I should imagine.'

Two gentlemen joined them whom they had not noticed at dinner. They were both middle-aged, heavily built, one with a centre parting and a walrus moustache which put Lestrade's in the shade. They grunted good morning to the policemen, simultaneously stuffed napkins into their cravats and waited in silence while coffee was poured.

'What's this?' one of them grunted to the other, fingering his breakfast.

'It's a croissant, you peasant. The circular thing it is resting on is called a plate.'

'Bumroll,' and the two men looked up and around in case someone should take umbrage at their conversation.

'Croissant? That's French isn't it? What the hell is it doing at an Englishman's table?'

'The word "chauvinist" is French as well, Sullivan, but it fits you like a glove. How can you be such a philistine?'

Lestrade listened with half an ear, but his thoughts still whirled with the events of the night before and his back ached. Sullivan glanced around again, then rapped his spoon savagely on the back of his companion's hand. Lestrade looked up as the companion jack-knifed in pain, banging his head sharply on the table.

'Oh, careless, William, careless. You'll do yourself an injury, dear friend.'

William stared maniacally at his companion, then caught Lestrade looking bemusedly at him, and attempted a chuckle. 'Yes, silly of me. I . . . er . . . tripped. Allow me to introduce myself, William Gilbert.'

'The playwright?' asked Lestrade.

Gilbert bowed.

'William *Schwenck* Gilbert,' bubbled his companion, and collapsed in fits of mocking laughter.

'And you, sir?' asked Lestrade.

'*Sir* Arthur Sullivan, at your service.'

'You sycophantic crawler,' hissed Gilbert. 'Why Her Majesty did you the honour of . . .'

'I am honoured, gentlemen.' Lestrade finished his coffee.

'And who might you be, sir?' Sullivan asked.

'Sholto Lestrade, of Scotland Yard.' He saw no reason to hide the fact. 'This is Sergeant Charlo.'

The playwright and the musician advanced on them, napkins still dangling and sat on either side. '*The* Scotland Yard?' Gilbert asked him.

'Well,' said Lestrade, unsure whether their interest was criminal or architectural, '*New* Scotland Yard.'

'Have you seen, dear Lestrade, our *Pirates of Penzance*?' Sullivan asked him.

'Don't you mean "my" *Pirates*?' Gilbert corrected him.

'Bitch,' hissed Sullivan.

'I believe I have,' Lestrade answered, becoming increasingly edgy in the presence of these two maniacs.

'Good,' said Gilbert. 'Now then. The portrayal of the policemen. Was it fair? Is a policeman's lot not a happy one? Eh, Charlo? Eh?'

'Tarantara,' broke in Sullivan and launched into a stanza, fingers pounding dramatically on the tablecloth. Gilbert looked coldly at him.

'I believe your sub-title for the piece was "The Slave of Duty",' said Charlo.

'Ah, a fan,' beamed Gilbert, clasping his hands together poetically.

'Now that fits a policeman very well,' said Lestrade.

'Have you heard my *Haddon Hall*?' Sullivan asked.

'Nobody has,' snapped Gilbert. 'Let's face it, Arthur dear, without me you're a flop.'

Sullivan leapt to his feet. 'Flop, am I? You conceited imbecile. You have the talent of that scrambled egg.'

'Kedgeree,' said Lestrade and mentally withered as he realised he had entered the colleagues' quarrel. He had no place there and was about to rise and make his excuses when Edward Harnett entered the room, pale and stern-faced. The bickering ceased as Gilbert and Sullivan noticed the deathly appearance of their host.

'Lestrade,' said Harnett. 'You'd better come with me.'

The inspector whipped the napkin from his collar and he and Charlo followed the general through the marbled hall. Lady Warwick reached the bottom of the stairs as they passed. She took Lestrade's arm.

'Not now, Daisy,' barked Harnett. 'A man is dead,' and her hand fell away as the inspector walked into the sunlight.

He lay on a handcart, head lolling back, grey hair sweeping the ground. He wore the leather gaiters of a labourer, a shabby waistcoat and rolled sleeves.

'The others found him this morning.' Harnett motioned to a knot of grim-faced labourers nearby.

'Where?' Lestrade asked.

'Out by the Lower Meadow, sir,' one of them answered. 'Hedging we were.'

'Is there somewhere I can examine the body?' Lestrade asked Harnett.

'Yes, of course. You men, take old Jim to the outhouse.' Charlo wrapped his muffler around his face, presumably against the raw cold of the July morning and followed the bier and the pall bearers. 'Lestrade.' Harnett took the inspector aside. 'It's his heart, surely? Nothing suspicious, is there?'

'Then why did you call me?'

'All right, I must admit, it's damned odd. If you'd have asked me last night to pick out the fittest man on my estate, I'd have said Jim Hodges, without a doubt. And yet this morning . . . It's damned odd.'

'How old was he?'

'I don't know. Sixty or so. Best damned hedger I had. The men used to joke about it – Hodges the Hedger, they called him. What will I do for a decent hedger now?'

'I shall need your help, General.'

'Of course, dear chap. Anything.'

'I shall need to speak to your guests and to your staff. All of them. Can you arrange that?'

'Er . . . I suppose so. But look, you can't hold up my guests for long. Most of them will be going today. Some already have.'

'Ask them to assemble in the drawing room, would you? And inform the local police force. I shall need constables.'

Lestrade's difficulty, apart from the scale of the investigation, was that technically, as far as anyone other than Nimrod Frost knew, he was under suspension. As such, he had no actual right to be making enquiries at all. If this was a routine sudden death, he decided, he would turn the whole thing over to a local sergeant and make a discreet exit. Charlo was chancing his arm too to be working with a suspended man. It was high time Nimrod Frost made up his mind about that. But Lestrade feared that this death would be far from routine. It fitted all too well the familiar pattern of those with which he had been involved over the past weeks.

He locked the outhouse door and examined the body. When forced to, Lestrade relied on coroners' verdicts for this work, but they operated too late in many cases, when valuable clues had gone. Besides, they didn't know a great deal more than he did. Some of them a damned sight less. His attention was drawn to the cuts on Hodges' left forearm, over a much older scar. There was a small amount of fresh blood on the arm, trickling down towards the wrist. On an impulse and checking first to see no one was around, he first sniffed the arm, then licked the scratches. He spat viciously, the taste bitter and acrid. No blood of his own ever tasted like that and, he suspected, neither did anyone else's. He must get to a chemist's as soon as possible. It was poison, he was sure. But what?

As to its administration, that was easy, but ingenious.

Lestrade went with the hedgers to the spot where they had found the body. The inspector checked the hedge – brambles, sharp ones with thick, purplish stems. He ran his fingers over their points and sniffed and licked while the labourers looked on in amazement. He spat again – the same bitter taste. He quizzed the labourers on the make-up of the hedge. They confirmed his townie's verdict – bramble, with a threat of blackthorn. He had them hack off a few pieces for testing, although he knew he couldn't take it back to the Yard. He would have to find a competent chemist in Manchester.

Lestrade had not spoken to Charlo throughout. He had noticed him swaying a little as he watched his guv'nor examine the body. Now, in the sun, as the labourers returned to their work and their gossiping he took him by the arm.

'Are you alright, Charlo?'

'I'm not quite myself, sir. I've never really been one for the sights. It's blood, you know. Brings me out in a rash.'

'Yes, quite.' Lestrade found himself wondering what Frost's idea of a good boy was. Still, he'd tracked the inspector down to this neck of the woods; he must have some merit in him. 'I shall need help in interrogation. Are you up to that?'

'Oh, yes, sir. Yes,' and he gulped in the country air. 'Now I'm away from . . . the deceased . . . I feel much stronger.'

Lestrade and Charlo stayed at Ladybower for four days. On the first they and two local sergeants interviewed the thirteen guests that remained. Gilbert and Sullivan were as bitchy to each other and about each other as ever, each of them sure that the other was Lestrade's man. Gilbert in particular said he felt sure the cause of death was listening to Sullivan's music. Lestrade ruled them out as serious suspects. Bearing in mind that the guests were now prisoners at Ladybower, they held up remarkably well under questioning. Lestrade deliberately left Daisy Warwick until last.

'I have kept you waiting, Lady Warwick. I am sorry.'

Daisy noticed the new frostiness in Lestrade, but chose to ignore it.

'That's all right, Sholto. If I can help in any way in this dreadful business. That poor man. . . .'

'Do you feel for the labouring poor, ma'am?'

'As a matter of fact, I do.' Daisy was as arch as the inspector. 'Although I'm not really sure I understand the question.'

'Did you know the deceased?'

'No. I didn't.'

'Are you familiar with poisons and their administration?'

'Good Lord, no.'

'The Prince of Wales left in a great hurry the other night, didn't he?'

'Sholto, you can't possibly think that Bertie or I had anything to do with that poor man's death?'

Lestrade relented. 'No,' he said, 'but you must appreciate I must have my suspicions, even about the heir to the throne. About the other night . . .'

Daisy rose and held her fingers to her lips. 'Old ghosts,' she said and swept, as gorgeous as ever, from the room.

The subsequent days saw Lestrade and Charlo doggedly questioning every tenant on Harnett's estate. Jim Hodges had been popular, a practical joker, yes; but no one bore him a grudge. It was good, honest fun – like the time he had plugged the general's hunting horn with tobacco and the time he'd tied the bootlaces of the visiting Bishop of Durham together as he dozed after tea. Well, yes, the old boy had lost three teeth when he stood up, but unless Lestrade was suggesting His Grace had vengeful, murderous tendencies, it was best left alone. Lestrade decided it was. Hodges had worked on the estate the best part of thirty years. His wife had died years ago. The marriage was without issue. Charlo coughed his way through dozens of cottages, declining tea and lemonade, staying in the shade whenever he could. The result of his meticulous and painful enquiries? Nothing.

But what was of greatest interest to Lestrade, and he learned this when he checked the old man's personal effects in his cottage, was that the link was established, at least between two of them. Wrapped in crimson cloth in a corner of a cupboard in Hodges' cottage was a medal. It had a faded blue and yellow ribbon and a single clasp, ornate, like the label on a sherry bottle, which read 'Balaclava'.

The old ghosts had come home to roost.

Soldier old, soldier new

It had been a long time since Nimrod Frost had ridden on an omnibus. He regarded the stairs to the upper deck as a challenge and in the shimmering sun of the last day of July he slumped heavily into the seat. Summer in the city was no joke to someone of his girth. His shirt and necessaries clung to him as if he had been wading through an Amazonian swamp. The buildings wobbled in the heat-haze as the horses, lathered and fidgety, swung left beyond the Old Lady of Threadneedle Street and on to the wider concourse of Cornhill.

The scruffy man in the tropical-weight duster sat behind him, tilted the bowler back on his head and lit a cigar.

'No shortage of cash then, Lestrade,' murmured Frost out of the corner of his mouth. The men sat back to back, like bookends of Jack Spratt and his wife.

'I could get used to suspension on half pay, sir,' the inspector answered.

'I was about to square it with Gregson,' said Frost, 'and reinstate you.'

'I'm flattered, sir, of course, but frankly on this particular case, I can probably do more as a free agent.'

'Less clutter from the Yard, eh?'

'Well, sir, triplicate does have its disadvantages.'

'Quite. Charlo's been filling me in. He's not a well man, you know. I wanted to assign him to other duties, a desk job. But he wouldn't hear of it. That's devotion, Lestrade. I like a man like that.'

And despite the fact that Lestrade had only spent a few days in Charlo's company, so did he. It was Frost's turn to light up. 'Damnably hot, isn't it?' For a while Lestrade thought he must mean the cigar and found the remark rather odd, but then the oppression of the city heat bore in on him too and he understood.

The two men spoke in stifled monosyllables, blowing rings of smoke into the air at the approach of a fellow traveller. The bookends gave nothing away. At Knightsbridge, Lestrade deftly palmed the roll of notes passed to him by Frost and got off the 'bus. The huge placard bearing the legend 'Nestlés' lurched away, topped by the lugubrious features of the Head of the Criminal Investigation Department.

Once again, Lestrade had had only time to meet his chief, collect a change or two of clothes (his salary would permit no more), leave a garbled note for Mrs Manchester and board yet another train. Why was it, he wondered as he sped north, that country air always made him sneeze? For all the heat, he loved the firmness of those city pavements, the sharp shadows of the Tower, the stench from Billingsgate, the endless suburbia of Norwood and Camberwell. It really was inconsiderate of the murderer to kill in the provinces. What were the criminal classes coming to?

He passed the high, wild hedges of Deene and the little church, lost in the wilderness of spurge and rough cocksfoot. Not that Lestrade knew these terms. A blade of grass was a blade of grass to him. So, Jim Hodges had died of aconite poisoning. He chewed again on the information he had, teasing it, worrying it until it made some sense. The aconite, mixed, the chemist in Manchester had told him, from a compound of wolfsbane, must have been smeared on the section of hedge where Hodges had been working. Who then knew where he was working? Any one of a dozen or more of his fellow workers. But Lestrade had interviewed them. And he prided himself on knowing a dishonest man when he saw one. None of these salts of the earth was a murderer. How many labourers had access to wolfsbane? And how many of them had the knowledge to prepare it? There again, there were strange things in country lore. Stranger than he knew. He longed for the pavements again, and sneezed uncontrollably.

Aconite. Aconite. Wolfsbane. The words ricochetted around Lestrade's brain. Was the chemist right? It was a rare poison, he had said. It could be absorbed through the skin. Death could result in as little as eight minutes. But anybody could have been scratched by those brambles. It was a chancy killing – dicey, uncertain. And the chemist was more interested by the printing errors in the *Guardian* that morning than he was in Lestrade's withered brambles. Still, this was 1893. The march of science in all its magnificence was at Lestrade's disposal. The trap halted suddenly and the lathered horse broke wind, depositing its load with symbolic grandeur before the front door.

Deene Park was a superb Jacobean building, a mellow grey in the heat of this first day of August. Her Ladyship, Lestrade was informed, was taking tea on the terrace. Would the gentleman care to join her? Lestrade had met Adeline Brudenell before – two years ago under rather odder circumstances. And so he was prepared for the sight that met him. A mature lady, still slim, still agile, wearing too much make-up, and a waistcoat of crimson laced with gold. On her head, at a rakish angle, a forage cap of the pill-box type. She offered tea to Lestrade.

'Young man, we've met before,' she began once the servant had bustled off about his duties. 'I never forget a face. And I believe I was there when you lost the tip of your nose.'

'Indeed you were, ma'am.' Lestrade took the proffered chair.

'Glorious weather, is it not? You know I sold my house in Highgate last year and I find Portman Square so depressing.'

'Are you not in town for the Season, ma'am?'

'Tsk, you naughty boy. I am heart-broken, of course, that you don't remember, but I am disappointed that my notoriety does not seem to have filtered through to Scotland Yard. Who am I?'

'You are Lady Cardigan,' Lestrade replied. 'A gracious lady indeed.'

'Twaddle!' Adeline rang her handbell. 'Yes, yes, I know, the relict of the Seventh Earl, the hero of Balaclava and I keep his memory alive by wearing his old uniforms. But in my day. Ah, Inspector, when Cardigan brought Adeline Horsey de Horsey to town, everyone knew it. God, how the heads turned.' She alarmed Lestrade a little by lighting up a Havana and puffing viciously at it. 'I remember the carriages, the glitter, the rides in Rotten Row and the Steyne.' Then she laughed. 'The Queen, God rot her, didn't like me. Actually, it was Albert, the sanctimonious old Prussian. I was not considered – am not considered – polite society, Inspector. Time-honoured phrases like "No better than she should be" et cetera, et cetera. Do you know, he actually resigned the colonelcy of my husband's regiment rather than be a party to me? And Her Majesty, she of the poppy eyes and elephantine girth, had herself painted out of a portrait of James explaining Balaclava to His Royal Highness! Small wonder I didn't get an invitation to the wedding.'

'Wedding ma'am?'

'Come, Inspector. Where have you been?'

'Manchester, ma'am.'

'Ah, I see, that explains it. George and May – a charming couple. I wasn't sorry to see Clarence go. I never liked him. Fancy not fighting his own duels! I never forgave him for that. Still, George will never be king. Victoria will outlive us all. I doubt if Bertie will get a chance.' She sighed. 'It's a terrible thing, longevity.'

A servant arrived, wheeling a bicycle.

'We have a guest, Meldrum,' she pointed out and the servant scurried off in search of another machine. 'You do ride?' she asked.

'Let us say I am safer in the saddle of one of these than a horse, ma'am.'

'Good. A pity though one can't ride to hounds on a Waverley. It's the five-barred gates that are the problem, you see. I never miss my morning ride, so you'll have to come with me.'

Meldrum brought a sturdy, black-painted Raleigh and Lestrade, stripping to his waistcoat at Her Ladyship's insistence, straddled it manfully and away they sped. He hadn't expected Adeline to take the steps down the terrace, but down she went, like a church. It was a physical fact, however, which Lady Cardigan may have forgotten, that for a gentleman to ride a bicycle down steps requires a great deal more courage and agility than Lestrade could, at that short notice, muster.

There were twelve steps. Lestrade counted every one of them, inwardly and with feeling. Had Adeline cared to glance behind her she would have seen an altogether older and paler man.

She pedalled furiously along the lawn, dust flying out behind her, skirts billowing in the breeze and the sun flashing on the lace of her forage cap. From the hedgerows, here and there, as they crossed into the fields around Deene, labourers popped up, saluting briskly at the sound of Her Ladyship's bell. Was it the country air, Lestrade wondered? His cramped journey in the trap? His recent near-emasculation on the steps? Whatever it was, he found it very difficult to keep up with Adeline and she seemed to be increasing her pace the whole time.

It was to his intense relief then that having crossed the lake (he was pleased to see she did it via the bridge rather than by skimming the lilies) Adeline screeched to a badly oiled halt by the summer house. She waited for Lestrade to catch up.

'It was here he used to bring his maidservants,' she said. 'He used to take an evening constitutional on the terrace and wander in this direction. Minutes later you would see a woman in white, his chosen companion for the evening, scurrying across the lawn.' She became distant, with a smile on the faded lips, etched in deepest crimson. 'But,' she regained the present, 'you did not come here to reminisce.'

'As a matter of fact, Lady Cardigan, I did.'

And the inspector and the dowager sat in the shaded bower of the summer house, while Lestrade attempted to jog old memories.

'I understand that one of your late husband's orderlies in the Crimea was one James Hodges of the Eleventh Hussars. Did your husband ever speak of him?'

'My husband spoke of many people, Inspector. Most of it was malicious and disparaging. But that, I fear, was the sort of man he was. Oh, brave as a lion – and vain – but not gracious. He did not suffer fools gladly. Hodges. Hodges. Yes, of course. I remember now. Hodges was his favourite orderly. Something of a practical joker I was given to understand. But James hadn't seen him since the Crimea. That would have been eighteen fifty-four, shortly after Balaclava. His Lordship was bronchitic, you see. He had to come home. But why these questions, Inspector? I would have thought Hodges would have been dead by now.'

'Indeed he is, ma'am. And by the hand of another.'

'Murder?' Lady Cardigan was incredulous.

Lestrade nodded.

'Inspector, my husband has been dead for twenty-five years. Do you assume he has reached out from his grave to kill this Hodges? Or do you think I had a hand in it?'

'Neither, ma'am. But we of the Yard leave no stone unturned.'

Lady Cardigan was already on another tack. 'If my memory serves me correctly, Hodges was also orderly for a time to John Douglas. He was colonel of the Eleventh at the time of Balaclava.'

'Do you know where I might find him?' Lestrade asked.

'Aldershot,' Lady Cardigan answered and again her lightning mind was up and away. She took Lestrade's hand in hers and gazed into his steady eyes. 'My family are afraid I will re-marry,' she said. 'That would scotch their inheritance plans. It would also solve my present insolvency. These old houses cost a small fortune to run, Inspector.'

'Is that a proposal, ma'am?' Lestrade asked.

'Why not? It may not be a leap year, but I *am* the notorious Adeline Cardigan. People expect it of me.'

Lestrade patted her hand and rose.

'I couldn't afford you, ma-am,' he smiled and turned to the Raleigh. The sight of the saddle unnerved him and he kissed Her Ladyship's hand, bade her goodbye and walked, a little shakily, to the waiting trap.

Lady Cardigan was not being quite level with Lestrade. Yes, John Douglas, colonel of the 11th Hussars was to be found in the vast complex of camps at Aldershot, but he was mouldering in a stone vault, having passed away in 1871. Literally a dead end, thought Lestrade. Even so, for the record, he would dig a little deeper, in the metaphorical sense, to see what those at

Aldershot could tell him about John Douglas or his orderly, Jim Hodges.

'You're talking about forty years ago,' he heard as though on a phonograph countless times during the day. By nightfall he was about to retire to the cell-like visitor's room in the sergeants' quarters (the AQMG obviously didn't feel that an inspector of police merited the more salubrious apartments in the officers' block) when he bumped quite literally into an elderly gent who teetered gingerly along the curb, trying valiantly to walk in a straight line and treading through the horse manure in the gutter.

'Ah, thank you, dear boy.' The elderly officer tipped his cap and regained the pavement. 'I wunna if you'd be sho kind . . ., and he aimed his swagger-stick vaguely at the door in the nearest wall. He stumbled violently and only Lestrade's presence saved him from smashing his head against the door frame. He spun round, on one leg, the other pirouetting like a skater in mid-turn, glaring accusingly at the ground. He bent nearly double, pointing threateningly at the grass.

'I've been crossing thish threshold for nigh on fifty yearsh,' he mumbled. 'I've never notished that there before.' He started upright, remembering that Lestrade was with him. 'Ah, dear boy, you're back. You have been sho kind. Would you like to join me for some liquid refes . . . liquid ref . . . a drink?'

'Tell me, sir,' said Lestrade, 'did you know Colonel Douglas, late of the Eleventh Hussars?'

The old man swung up a leg extraordinarily high to reveal the crimson trousers of the 11th, before his balance got the better of him and he toppled gracefully back into the shrubbery. Lestrade lifted him out and helped him into his quarters. He fumbled for a lucifer and lit the lamp. The room was a little austere, but cluttered here and there with papers.

'In the umbrella shtand,' the gent called out as he gracefully collapsed across the bed. Lestrade found the bottle of Dewar's and poured them both a glass.

'Your very good health,' slurred the old man, still prone, but his hand rock steady around the glass and his arm erect and firm, 'Mr . . . er . . . Mr . . .?'

'Lestrade, Sholto Lestrade.'

'Solto?' the old man asked.

'Sholto,' Lestrade repeated, moving a mountain of screwed-up papers in order to find a seat. 'And you are?'

'Drunk as a lord,' the gent answered and by a feat of astonishing agility, poured the contents of the glass from where it was into his mouth.

He sat up.

'Allow me to introduce myself. The Reverend Wilberforshe Battye, late chaplain to the Eleventh, Prinsh Albert'sh Own Hussarsh. At leasht,' he rose uncertainly to his feet, 'that'sh what is saysh on this dinner invitation,' and he waved his glass vaguely at a card pinned to the wall, 'doeshn't it?'

'So you knew Colonel Douglas?' Lestrade asked.

'Who? Oh, yesh. I knew John. Funny thing,' he poured himself another Scotch, 'he had the shame name as you, y'know. Solto. Not related, are you?'

'I don't think so,' said Lestrade.

'Matter of fact,' he peered under the rim of Lestrade's bowler, 'you don't look unlike him, y'know. He was taller. I'd shay. And of courshe, he had a noshe.'

'A noshe?'

'Yesh,' and the chaplain waved an inebriated finger somewhere between his eyes.

'Did you also know his olderly, James Hodges?'

'Never heard of him.'

Lestrade drew another Scotch, to drown his sorrows. It had been a long shot, of course. He had no right to be disappointed, really. The chances of this old wreck having anything to help his case were pretty remote. The old man fell back on to his bed again. Lestrade took off Battye's peaked forage cap, folded his arms across his chest and crept towards the door.

'Mind you,' the chaplain suddenly came to life, 'I've always sushpected him of killing Alex Dunn, you know.' His arms flopped down again and he began snoring, loudly, erratically.

Lestrade closed the door and silently began knocking his head against the wall. Who was Alex Dunn? John Douglas a murderer? Why should he bring up murder? Lestrade had not told Chaplain Battye that he was a policeman. He ransacked the rooms to find tea, coffee, anything to sober the old fool up.

His hand found a bottle of Vino Sacro, and a voice behind him said, 'That'll do nishely,' and the chaplain, eyes still closed, held out his glass for a drop. He drank it down, then sat up, demanding another. It followed the first.

It's a funny thing,' he said. 'The only thing that bringsh me round ish Vino Shacro. The waysh of the Lord are shtrange. Cheers. God Bless,' and he downed a third, shaking his head, blinking to clear his vision. 'Now, what did you want to know?'

'You mentioned something about John Douglas having murdered Alex Dunn.'

'Did I?' The chaplain was trying hard to recollect. The Communion wine had obviously sharpened him more than somewhat, because he suddenly said, 'Now, why should that be of interest to you?'

'Because I am from Shcot . . . Scotland Yard,' said Lestrade, 'and murder is my business.'

'Ah, well,' the chaplain cleared his throat, 'it'sh a long shtory.'

'I have all night,' said Lestrade and settled himself down.

'Alex Dunn was the mosht brilliant officer in the Eleventh in thoshe daysh.' He downed a fourth which clarified his sibilance instantaneously. 'Tall, handsome, debonair. I had only been with the regiment a few months. My first commission. Dunn took me under his wing, as he did with all new boys. I can see him now, laughing at the head of his troop, six foot two, he stood. Shoulders like lecterns. One helluva . . . oh, pardon me . . . one devil of a swordsman. Born to horses of course, they all were in those days. Not like these whippersnappers of today. Public school johnnies. Wet behind the ears, most of them. They don't know one end of a horse from another.'

'Dunn?' Lestrade reminded him.

'Well, yes, some of them are. But the Eleventh ride chestnuts mostly. Anyway, to get back to Alex Dunn. I'm not one for gossip, you understand, but that's why Douglas didn't like him. He always fancied himself as a bit of a *beau sabreur*, but he wasn't in Dunn's class. And then, when he took up with Rosa . . .'

'Rosa?' Lestrade repeated. That was the name of the ship moored at Cromer Lighthouse at the time of Bentley's death.

The chaplain reached across for a fifth Vino Sacro, but Lestrade clamped his hand firmly over the glass. Battye continued to pour it over his fingers and was surprised to find nothing trickling down his throat as he knocked the glass back.

'Douglas' wife. She fell for Alex Dunn hook, line, and sinker. Talk of the regiment, it was. She left Douglas eventually and went to live in Canada with Dunn.'

'When did Dunn die, and how?'

'Eighteen sixty-eight, I think it was.' The same year as Cardigan, thought Lestrade, if Lady Cardigan's mental calculation had been correct. Coincidence? Perhaps. 'A hunting accident, apparently. Shotgun. Very nasty. Of course, he was with the Thirty-third by then. God knows where they are stationed now.'

'The Thirty-third?' asked Lestrade.

'Oh, what's this new-fangled name for it? The Duke of Wellington's Regiment, is it? I don't know.'

'And you think Douglas pulled the trigger?'

'That was the rumour at the time. But I'm a charitable man, Solto. I prefer to think it was an accident. Of course, Rosa could tell you.'

'Rosa Douglas is still alive?'

'Yes, I think so. The last I heard she lived Warwickshire way. A village called Tysoe. But tell me, Solto, why are you chaps looking into all this now? It's been years.'

'The machinery of justice grinds slow,' said Lestrade, proud of that piece of philosophy. 'And you're sure you didn't know the name James Hodges?'

'Solto.' Chaplain Battye staggered to his feet. 'There are times when I'm not quite sure of my own,' and he fell back, snoring rapturously, on the bed.

It was a noise Lestrade had not often heard before. And never at five o'clock. It fitted in well with his dreams. A voluptuous woman was kneeling naked at the foot of his bed, breasts full and rising with desire, legs opening as he watched. When suddenly, for no reason that he could fathom, she brought two brass cymbals clanging on both sides of his head. He was standing upright, his forehead having collided with the ceiling, and his erection having crunched against the wall, when he woke up fully. Cymbals and siren were gone and in their stead the realisation that it was a bugle he was hearing. He ripped aside the curtain to see a soldier, sickeningly smart in scarlet, blasting the reveille for all he was worth across the expanses of Laffan's Plain.

Why? mused Lestrade as he subsided in his nightshirt, why at five o'clock? And why outside *his* window?

Breakfast consisted of toast and black coffee, the milk train having failed to arrive as it was too early for the milk train. Lestrade endeavoured to stay awake. Was this not the man who had hunted the Tammanwool? Who had ridden to hounds with a murderous pack in the *Struwwelpeter* case? Who had flown almost single-handed in a balloon over the Pennines in search of his quarry in the Adair Affair? No, he thought, as he dropped coffee on his tie, probably not.

That morning he would make for Warwickshire again and perhaps revisit Lady Cardigan in the process. The plot, for such the novelists called it, was beginning to thicken, for such was the cliché they used. What would John Watson make of this? And Conan Doyle? Probably rather more money than he would by attempting to solve it.

First, he must drag his weary carcass to the station. The logistics of reaching Tysoe were complicated. He even began to toy with hiring a bicycle, but that was too hearty. Better stick to the safety of train and trap.

'Inspector Lestrade.' A voice behind him made him turn.

'Yes.' He was grateful to drop the Gladstone bag, feeling he could not impose on some woebegotten recruit to carry it for him. He saw a slim young man, perhaps twenty, standing before him in the uniform of an officer cadet from the Military College at nearby Sandhurst. The young man clicked his heels and saluted briskly, 'My name is Churchill, sir. Winston Churchill. Would you accept a lift?' And the cadet extended a hand to a waiting trap nearby.

Any port in a storm, thought Lestrade, mixing metaphors and Forces just a little. But as he suspected, there was an ulterior motive. As they lurched off across Laffan's Plain, it became clear.

'Actually, our meeting like this isn't exactly chance.'

Here we go, thought Lestrade.

'You see, I shall be twenty next birthday and I haven't done anything with my life yet. The truth is, I can't decide whether to become a field marshal or Home Secretary. Either way, I shall have to get a medal pretty soon or there'll be no point at all. Some of the chaps around here were saying that you're interested in Colonel Douglas and the Eleventh Hussars.'

'That's right,' said Lestrade.

'Well, look, if I'm going to become Home Secretary, I shall be giving orders to chaps like you, won't I?'

'In theory,' Lestrade agreed.

'So I thought I might tag along with you, sort of find out what you chappies do for a living. All right?'

'No, Mr Churchill, I'm afraid it isn't,' and Lestrade pulled the horse up. 'You see, I am engaged in a murder enquiry. And such things are always confidential.'

'At least, let me buy you a drink. My local is only a few miles up the road. It won't take long.'

'I really ought . . .'

'Nonsense,' and the cadet cracked the whip and sent the horse cantering along the road to Sandhurst. They alighted at the White Swan a little before eleven and Churchill led the way to the tap room. After the merciless heat of Laffan's Plain, the coolness of the deserted inn was joy itself. There was silence apart from the ticking of the grandfather clock and Lestrade took advantage of Churchill's temporary absence to stretch his legs before the gaping darkness of the empty fireplace. Young Churchill's driving was not as immaculate as it might have been and various parts of Lestrade were decidedly numb. The cadet returned with a ruddy-faced man in a white apron, carrying a tray with three pewter mugs, filled to the brim with local ale.

'That'll be eightpence ha'penny, please.' The barman held out his hand to Lestrade.

'I'm sorry, Inspector,' said Churchill. 'My allowance hasn't arrived yet this month. Father is none too well at the moment.'

Reluctantly, Lestrade ferreted in his pocket for the cash. He found ninepence and said magnanimously, 'Keep the change.'

The barman's face registered his undying gratitude, but to Lestrade's slight surprise he sat down and made it obvious who the third jar was for.

'Allow me to introduce Mine Host,' beamed Churchill. 'Mr David Grantham, Inspector Lestrade of Scotland Yard.'

Mine Host mumbled something in his beer.

'Show him your leg, Grantham,' said Churchill.

Lestrade wondered what sort of young man they were taking at Sandhurst nowadays. The publican rolled up his trouser leg to reveal a livid white scar across his shin and ankle. He thought he had detected a limp as he had entered the room.

'Now the wrist.' A similar scar appeared.

'Very nice,' said Lestrade, on whom these obviously very ancient injuries were lost.

'What made those, Grantham?' asked Churchill, as though putting a forward child through its paces, a party-piece for doting grandparents.

'A sabre, sir.'

'And where did you get those scars, Grantham?'

'At Balaclava, sir, a-serving of Her Majesty the Queen.'

'And which regiment were you with, Grantham?' Churchill noted with triumph Lestrade's growing interest.

'The Eleventh Prince Albert's Own Hussars, sir.'

Churchill rested back in his chair, his victory complete. Lestrade flashed him a glance. 'Remind me to have a word with the Queen,' he said, 'about your promotion to Home Secretary. Now, Mr Grantham, how about another drink?'

The story unfolded, haltingly, between beers, while 'the girl' to whom old Grantham constantly referred, manfully served the steady stream of off-duty soldiery in the other bar. Churchill, with what Lestrade soon realised was customary savvy, had placed a makeshift notice on the door saying 'Closed'.

David Grantham had enlisted in the 11th Hussars in 1850.

He had served in F Troop for the first three years, biting the tan with the rest of them, and more than once had felt the lash for slipshod appearance, at Hounslow and Brighton. One particular bastard he remembered, Sergeant-Major Loy Smith, a hard man who picked on people for no reason. Grantham had never been more grateful than when he had been transferred to C Troop, out of Loy Smith's clutches. Then he heard the bastard sergeant-major had begun using a Welshman named Hope as his whipping boy. Grantham was circumspect about Dunn. He too remembered Dunn as a handsome man, casual, careless even, but all right for an officer. Of Colonel Douglas he remembered little – fair, courteous, not a hard man by the standard of the times. It was rumoured they didn't get on. But that was of little interest to the common soldier. And it was forty years ago.

'The girl', a pretty slip of a thing who made eyes at young Churchill, brought them the umpteenth beer as Grantham switched his reminiscences to the surgeons of the regiment.

'A right lot they were. Wilkins, Crosse, the others. Did a proper job on my leg. Why, that's why I still limp today. Sabre wounds should have healed better than that. Doctors! They're all the same.'

Lestrade could learn no more. Yes, Grantham had known Jim Hodges, but not well. He had had a reputation of being a joker and ex-private Grantham had no sense of humour whatever. He wasn't sure he'd keep his present job for long. His customers found him morose, he said, taciturn even. He'd probably end his days in the workhouse.

'I'm heartily sorry for you,' said Lestrade with feeling.

It was on his way out that one of those ludicrous accidents that seemed only to happen to Sholto Lestrade happened. As he reached the door of the White Swan, a passing sergeant dropped his swagger-stick. It rolled under Lestrade's feet and for a moment the inspector teetered on it like an acrobat at the circus. Then he collapsed backwards, jarring his back as he did so, spilling the contents of a spittoon over his jacket. Churchill, suppressing a fit of the giggles as best he could, helped him to his feet.

'Are you all right, Inspector?'

'Thank you, Mr Churchill. By the way, if when you retire at a grand old age from the post of Home Secretary or general or whatever it is you are going to be and you write your memoirs, publish one word about me ending up "head first in a spittoon" and I swear I'll rise up from my grave and haunt you.'

Young Churchill accompanied Lestrade as far as Oxford, whence he alighted among the dreaming spires to make his way home to Blenheim. The conversation had turned on many things. On the possibility that Lord Randolph's debilitating illness was caused by poisoning. And how it would be possible to prove that the murderers – or intended murderers – were a conspiracy of Her Majesty, Mr Gladstone and Lord Salisbury. Or there again, it might be Churchill's old nanny, Mrs Everest. The possibilities were endless. Lestrade remained unmoved. Bearing in mind the stories he had heard about Lord Randolph's liking for the ladies, the debilitating illness of the noble lord had but one source as far as he was concerned – Cupid's measles. But he was not going to let the young man down so heavily.

What of Lizzie Borden? Churchill had also wanted to know. The American case that had recently filled the papers. His mother was American, did Lestrade know that? What was Lestrade's professional opinion? Had she hacked her father and mother to death? Lestrade was non-committal in his answer. After all, no one had committed Lizzie Borden, either.

It was evening before Lestrade sat in the parlour of a neat little house in the village of Tysoe. Thatch, new and clipped, topped the old cottage nestling on the side of the hill as the shadows lengthened. For the second time that day he was alone with a ticking clock, a grandmother made in Coventry. He took in the contents of the room – small windows which let in a little light, two oil lamps steadily burning. A table covered with a cloth of purple velvet and on the sideboard a cluster of faded photographs. Two in particular caught Lestrade's eye. Two rather similar men, one with magnificent flowing dundrearies, popular in the fifties, in the Review Order of the 11th Hussars; the other, taller, younger, neater, a more handsome face, in the uniform of an infantry regiment. The two sides of the triangle, thought Lestrade. And the third side, perhaps the vital clue to all the deaths so far, swept noiselessly into his presence.

'It is not often I am visited by an officer from Scotland Yard, Inspector. Won't you sit down?'

Lestrade eased himself into a tapestry chair, his back, from the day's fall, still causing a certain stiffness. He dared not relax a single muscle – he knew from experience of many such accidents the pain this would cause. At times like these the children of passers-by had been known to comment, 'Mama, there is a man with a coat-hanger still inside his coat.' He carefully laid the metaphorical hook against the antimacassar.

'I will come to the point, ma'am,' Lestrade began as Mrs Douglas rang a tiny silver bell to summon tea. 'The death of your late husband.' Beneath her veil, the widow made no outward sign. She sat, reserved and demure in her black bombazine, a delicate woman of uncertain years. She had once been very beautiful, even the veil and the gathering dusk could not deny her that.

'It has been twenty-two years, Inspector. What possible interest could it be now to Scotland Yard?'

'Ma'am, I appreciate it must be painful for you, even after all this time, but I fear I must persist. What can you tell me about Colonel Douglas?'

'"And darest thou then to beard the lion in his den, The Douglas in his hall?"'

'Ma'am?'

'Sir Walter Scott, Inspector. His poem, *Marmion*. My husband was descended from the Douglases who waged war on the Marches those long centuries ago. They were ever a fighting family. You have heard of the Black Douglas?'

'Would that be the African branch of the family, ma'am?'

'Oh, Inspector,' chuckled Mrs Douglas. 'You're teasing me.'

Lestrade was about to protest that he wasn't when a maid brought tea, curtsied and left the room.

'John Douglas was a fine man, Inspector. A fine man. Where can I start to tell you about him? His Army career? Well, Hart's List will tell you all that.'

'I do not have a copy with me, ma'am.'

'No, of course not. Sugar?'

Lestrade nodded, but declined the Madeira cake.

'He enlisted as ensign in the Sixty-first Foot in eighteen twenty-nine – my, an eternity ago now, isn't it? Then, let me see, he joined the Seventy-ninth Highlanders. I never really understood why he exchanged into the cavalry. After all, the Highlanders were his own clansmen. It must have been his awful legs. Forgive me, Inspector, but at my age, I am allowed to transcend etiquette. "Lower limbs" are for the young. I call them legs.'

'Quite so, ma'am.'

'Yes, he looked quite dreadful in kilts. When I first received his attentions in a serious way, he was a captain in the Eleventh Light Dragoons. We married after a whirlwind romance – well, three years was a whirlwind in those days. He was tall, handsome, dashing, kind, considerate, everything a girl could wish for. By June eighteen fifty-four he was lieutenant-colonel commanding the regiment. There was only one cloud on the horizon.'

Lestrade braced himself to hear it.

'Lord Cardigan, colonel of the regiment. Ever since that foul old man had been lieutenant-colonel of the Eleventh in the thirties he had regarded it as his pet. Ten thousand pounds a year he spent out of his own pocket to equip his men,' she chuckled. 'I remember a ditty going the rounds in those days – *The London Charivari* coined it – concerning the tightness of the trousers of the Eleventh. It went, let me see, it went,

"Oh pantaloons of cherry,
Oh redder than the berry.
For men to fight in things so tight,
It must be trying, very."'

Lestrade tittered too.

'None of which, of course, had the remotest thing to do with soldiering. God, how John hated that man. Cardigan was a perfect swine to his officers, Inspector. Upbraiding them in public, accusing them of drinking porter at his table. Small wonder there are now Socialists in the world when men with the arrogance of Cardigan strut upon it. The last years were quieter. John became colonel in eighteen fifty-seven and assistant adjutant-general of cavalry after that. He was commanding the Cavalry Brigade at Aldershot when he died. Doubtless you have seen his memorial there, in the garrison church?'

'How did your husband die, Mrs Douglas?'

'In his bed, Inspector.'

'With respect, ma'am, I asked how, not where.'

'What do old men die of, Inspector? My husband was fifteen years my senior.'

'Hence Lieutenant Dunn?' Lestrade rose with difficulty and handled the photograph of the officer in infantry uniform. Mrs Douglas recovered the slight slip in her composure and poured them both another cup of tea.

'Alex Dunn,' she said with a sigh and gazed into the leafy middle distance of her youth. 'Would you like me to tell you about him, too?'

Lestrade nodded.

'Alex was younger than I, Inspector. Does that shock you? Well, it shocked a good many at the time. He was Canadian by birth. Perhaps it was that initially which made John dislike him. Inspector, the portrait I am painting of my husband is not a flattering one, I fear. He will seem to you petulant, anti-social. He wasn't really. Not really. At least Alex went to Harrow. John and I had been married ten years when Alex joined the Eleventh. He was a young cornet, a dandy, broad shouldered, good looking. I was the colonel's lady. I remember the night he first danced with me. Forgive my memories, Inspector. They cannot be of interest to you.'

'On the contrary, ma'am. Go on.'

'He had booked me for one waltz. And ended up dancing with me all night. Every head in the room turned. You could see all the ladies, the wives of the regiment, fluttering their fans and gossiping. Oh, how I loved it. John was furious.'

'And you became . . . friends?'

'We used the term "lovers" in those days, Inspector. Has it gone out of fashion now?'

'No, ma'am,' smiled Lestrade.

'For two years we met in secret. God, I hated the lies, the

deceit. But I was the colonel's lady, Inspector. And it would have broken John's heart. I have all of Alex's letters still. I keep them in the same hat-box I hid them in all those years ago. Then came the Crimea. Alex was awarded the Victoria Cross for valour. He saved the lives of two of his men at Balaclava. Sergeant Bentley I think was one; the other I forget.'

Bill Bentley, thought Lestrade. Somebody saves him from Russian lances so that somebody else can put a pillow over his face. But here at last was a tangible link.

'Alex came home in 'fifty-five,' Mrs Douglas went on. 'I don't know why; perhaps because he had come so close to death out there, so far from home. His attitude had changed. He was not prepared now to steal the secret moment, to brush my hand as though by accident. He had it out with John. They had a terrible row. I thought they would come to blows. When it was over, I could not stay with John any more. When Alex went to his estates in Toronto, I went with him.'

'And then?'

Mrs Douglas let out a long sigh. 'I knew Alex's army days weren't over. We were blissfully happy, Inspector, for the rest of his life. He became colonel of the Thirty-third Foot in 'sixty-four. We travelled first to Poona, then to Abyssinia, his last posting. He died in a hunting accident on the twenty-fifth of January eighteen sixty-eight.'

The same year as Cardigan, Lestrade reminded himself. 'How did it happen, Mrs Douglas?' he asked.

'A party of officers were hunting buck on the plains near Senafe. They say his rifle jammed and he was checking it when . . . when it blew up. It's funny, I still have the clothes he wore that day.'

'May I see them, ma'am?'

Mrs Douglas looked a little taken aback, but nodded and rang the bell.

'Fetch Colonel Dunn's things.' She sent the maid scurrying into the bowels of the cottage.

'And after Colonel Dunn's death?' Lestrade persisted.

'Afterwards, I came home. To John. Oh, I know it was feeble. My own family did not want to know me. His still less. But we effected a reconciliation – of a sort. I somehow continued the dutiful wife at Aldershot. I still retained some affection for him, Inspector. Perhaps I even loved him a little.'

She paced the darkening room.

'Was I wrong, Inspector? To run away with a younger man, a subaltern in my husband's regiment? Oh, it's the stuff dreams are made of for silly girls at school, their heads full of poetic nonsense. But in eighteen sixty-eight, I was forty-four years old. And romance had been shattered that day at Senafe.'

The maid brought in, with difficulty, a tin trunk. Lestrade helped her with it and immediately wished he hadn't, because the ladies then had to help him upright. Mrs Douglas took out with loving care the shirt, trousers and duster coat with long white scarf and laid them on the table.

'You had these cleaned of course, Mrs Douglas?'

'Cleaned? No, Inspector, I did not. It is common knowledge that Her Majesty has her late husband's evening clothes laid out on the bed each night at Osborne, as though he were there to wear them. Alex and I lived as man and wife for nearly thirteen years. No, Inspector. I wanted to remember him, his strength, his very smell. Does that seem strange to you?'

Lestrade picked up the coat and shirt.

'You say the rifle jammed and exploded?'

'Yes, Inspector.'

'Then how do you account, ma'am, for this?' and Lestrade placed a finger into the single bullet hole through the back of the coat, caked with the faded dark brown stain of Alex Dunn's blood.

Mrs Douglas lit an oil lamp silently and raised her veil to let the light shine eerily from below, highlighting her once fine features, wrinkled now with age and the breaking of her heart.

'Very well, Inspector.' Her voice was still strong. 'I have loved two men in my life – John Douglas, my husband, and Alex Dunn, my lover. How could I know the one would kill the other?'

'How long have you known this, ma'am?'

'For twenty-two years, Inspector. The night my husband died, he told me. He had been ill a short time only. Days, in fact. That last night, he held my hand and said, "Rosa, I cannot go with a lie on my lips. I shot Alex Dunn at Senafe. I killed him to get you back and I would do it again." I just looked at him. "Don't hate me," he said, "I couldn't bear that. My dearest Rosa," and he slipped away.'

Lestrade folded the clothes neatly on the table.

'So you have me at last, Inspector. I didn't realise the holes in his clothes were not consistent with the kind of accident reported. I suppose Alex's friends covered up out of loyalty to me. They didn't want me hurt further. Tell me, will I go to prison?'

'Technically, ma'am, you are an accessory after the fact of murder. But since the murderer is dead, I don't suppose . . . And anyway, I have other fish to fry. You mentioned Sergeant Bentley earlier – the man Alex Dunn saved at Balaclava. What about Jim Hodges? Richard Brown? Do these names mean anything to you?'

'I believe there was a Brown in my . . . in Alex's troop in the Eleventh, Inspector. But it is a common enough name.'

'Indeed, ma'am.' Lestrade's face fell.

'But let me give you two more names, Inspector. Men who can help you more than I – Seth Bond and "Poppy" Vansittart. And now . . . leave me alone with my memories.'

'Of course, ma'am. One last thing. Do you own a ship – or a boat – called *Ora Rosa*? Or do you know anyone who does?'

Mrs Douglas shook her head. And Lestrade closed the door.

Fatima's

The black reaper clanked and rattled its way across the hill, moving inexorably from left to right, over the field of gold. There were shouts from the men, black dots in the distance, walking alongside the horses, checking strap and chain. And the dogs wheeled and yapped around the huge machine, driving obliquely against the jut of the hill.

Nearly a mile away, resting on the five-barred gate in the early morning sun, sat Inspector Sholto Lestrade. He was already in his shirt sleeves, for the day promised to be long and hot. He watched the reapers for a while, but every so often would check the road, left and right, for something more important.

Something More Important arrived after a few minutes, in a phaeton, drawn by two lathered horses.

'Bandicoot.' Lestrade took the driver's hand and helped him down. 'Thank you for coming. What news?'

'Well, Letitia is having problems with her dress apparently. And we haven't had all the replies yet.'

'Banders, delighted though I am that your nuptials are drawing on apace, I do have more pressing business.'

'Of course, Sholto, sorry. You asked me to find these two. Seth Bond and Poppy Vansittart. Well it wasn't easy. I don't understand why you can't use the resources of the Yard for this.'

'Let's just say I am rather "persona non regatta" at the moment. I'm on my own, Harry. My sergeant has gone down with something again. So I have to use rather unorthodox measures.'

Rather hurt to be considered an unorthodox measure, Bandicoot quickly recovered nevertheless his sangfroid.

'Seth Bond is no problem. He lives in a village called Southam, not far from here. Retired labourer was all I could glean. Oh, that's rather good, isn't it? Glean?'

Lestrade ignored the levity. 'And Vansittart?'

'Ah, yes, that's more difficult. He's dead.'

'When?'

Bandicoot, Lestrade was intrigued to notice, was using his old pocket book for the storage of information. Old habits die hard, even to a policeman of Bandicoot's limitations.

'Er . . . fourteenth of April, eighteen eighty-six. In Paris.'

'Paris?' Lestrade threw up his hands in exasperation. 'All right. Bond it is. I'll start with him. Look, Bandicoot, I need hardly say how grateful I am for this information. Especially from a man about to tie the knot. I appreciate it.'

'How will you get to Southam?' asked Bandicoot.

'I'll hitch a ride, I suppose.'

'Nonsense, Sholto. I'm not tying the knot as you put it for ten days yet. Climb up.'

'I thought you'd never offer,' and the phaeton whirred away down the road.

'What have you got?' Bandicoot asked. 'Isn't that how we used to do it? Sound each other out. You, Forbes, Dew, myself.'

Lestrade chuckled. 'What made you leave the Force, Harry? Given time, you'd have made an average copper.'

'Nice of you to say so, Sholto.' The blond man grinned. 'I don't know really. I think it was the *Struwwelpeter* business. When you've killed someone . . . Anyway, I met Letitia and I realised there was more to life than pounding the beat.'

'So they tell me,' said Lestrade.

'Then there's London. I mean, it's marvellous to come up to town for the theatre and so on, but working there day in, day out . . . And in this heat! How do you stand it?'

'At least you're never alone in the Strand,' commented Lestrade. Bandicoot could not argue with that and accepted the inspector's cigar.

'Talking of which – is Dr Watson still writing about you in that journal?'

'Currently, no. But I fear it will only be a matter of time. You asked me what we've got. Well, chew on this.'

Bandicoot removed the cigar from his mouth, expecting Lestrade to place something between his lips. He realised his error without appearing too much of an idiot and took up the reins again.

'Four murders. All the victims elderly men. Cause of death in three cases, poisoning. Poisons various. Cause of death in the fourth case, suffocation. Two of them formerly soldiers of the Eleventh Hussars; rode in the Charge of the Light Brigade.'

'Gosh,' Bandicoot was impressed.

'No definite enemies. No obvious motive. All I have is the means. There is no geographical pattern. These corpses have turned up all over the place. But the murderer knows his poisons. That much we do know.'

'Why the suffocation in one case?' asked Bandicoot.

Lestrade shrugged. 'Even your Great Detective would be baffled by that one, I suspect.'

Bandicoot snorted. 'I must admit I was impressed by the late Mr Holmes.'

But as Lestrade knew, it didn't take much to impress Bandicoot.

'I've been given no end of leads,' Lestrade went on. 'I've been passed from pillar to post. And so far, nowhere.'

'Except that you've been suspended.'

'How did you know that?' Lestrade was incredulous.

'No, Sholto. I'd like to claim it was a flash of the old Bandicoot inspiration.'

Lestrade racked his brain to think of an earlier instance of this supposed phenomenon. He could not. 'But in fact, I read it in *The Times* this morning.'

Bandicoot fished about in the boot at his feet and produced a crumpled newspaper. Lestrade found it at the bottom of column three, the sixth page.

'Yard Man Suspended. Suspected Attack on Royal Personage,' he read aloud, and ploughed on silently through the rest.

'It says here I attacked the Kaiser. *Inspector Sholto Lefade* – I don't know whether to be outraged or relieved they got my name wrong – *was apprehended with his hands around the throat of His Imperial Majesty at Sandringham on the* . . . This is libel, Bandicoot. Not only libel, but sheer bloody nonsense.'

'One thing is certain, Sholto,' said Bandicoot, optimistically. 'Somebody up there doesn't like you. Doesn't it say you're supposed to answer charges?'

'Yes, next month. Why didn't Frost get a message to me? He knows where I am. And what is the matter with Charlo, with all his devotion to duty?'

'I never understood the workings of the Yard, Sholto. Even the plumbing mystified me.'

And the phaeton wheeled into Southam.

They found Seth Bond in the Churchyard, dozing against a buttress, his scythe beside him. A stocky man, with white wispy whiskers, battered derby hat and the traditional leggings of the agricultural labourer. His pipe had slipped from his mouth and lay quietly burning a hole in his waistcoat as he snored. Lestrade kicked him with just enough force to impress upon him the need for urgency in stamping out the minor conflagration growing on his chest.

'Thank'ee, sir. Everything's so tinder dry, it is. We'll have some bad fires this year, I shouldn't wonder.'

'Inspector Athelney Jones of Scotland Yard,' Lestrade said by way of introduction and stamped hard on Bandicoot's foot as the younger man called out in surprise at the lie he had just heard. 'This is Constable Bandicoot.'

Bond looked up at the golden-headed man blotting out the sun. 'You're a fair cop, guv,' he said and allowed the policemen to help him to his feet. 'You don't mind if I carry on? The vicar wants this churchyard cleared by night. Says yer can't see the stones proper. Besides, I shall be lyin' 'ere meself one of these days. I 'ope as 'ow somebody'll be doin' this for me. 'Ow can I 'elp you gentlemen?'

'Cast your mind back,' said Lestrade, 'to your days with the Eleventh Hussars.'

'Ah, great days, they was,' beamed Bond, 'if yer didn't mind the cholera and the flies,' and he swung with extraordinary gusto for a man of his age into the yellowed churchyard grass.

Lestrade sneezed several times in quick succession. Townie, thought Bond, and carried on swinging.

'When did you join the regiment?' managed Lestrade.

'Oh, it must have been . . . yes, eighteen-forty. The year the old Queen married.'

'Which troop?'

'F Troop. 'Til I was promoted sergeant-major of C Troop.' He straightened himself with the pride of it. 'That was after the Charge, of course.'

'Balaclava?' Lestrade checked.

'That's right, sir. Now there was a battle! I remember old Bill Lamb . . .'

'Who?' Lestrade snapped.

'Bill Lamb,' Bond repeated, somewhat taken aback. 'Funny, 'e were a shepherd before 'e enlisted. And became one again, I believe. I thought 'e'd lost 'is eyes in the Valley of Death, to be sure.'

Lestrade held the scythe arm. 'His eyes?'

Bond nodded.

'Did your Bill Lamb have a cut across his forehead, narrowly missing both eyes?'

''E did, sir. A damned Roosian did that for him. So much blood on 'is face, yer couldn't see. Neither could Bill. 'E was stumblin' around the field, calling out "Englishman, Englishman." Must have been a bit light-headed.'

Lestrade let the scythe arm go, and looked at Bandicoot. He spun to Bond again. 'What about these names – Joseph Towers?'

Bond grinned. 'Yes, 'e were with us. I remember old Joe.'

'Bill Bentley?'

'Sergeant, 'e were. Family man. Always talkin' about his wife and kid.'

'Richard Brown?'

'Oh, yes, A do-gooder 'e was. Always lickin' around the officers. 'E were the colonel's orderly. I never liked 'im.'

'Jim Hodges?'

'Hodges? Oh, ar, I remember now. Wild man 'e was. Always given to jokes and that. 'E once crep' into the tent of one of the officers an' spent all night sewing the legs of his overalls together. 'Course, 'e was put on a charge for that.'

'The Charge of the Light Brigade?' chimed in Bandicoot. Bond and Lestrade looked at him.

'Mr Bond, you have made my day.' Lestrade shook the labourer's hand. 'Take care of yourself. Come on, Bandicoot,' and the ex-constable dashed after the pending ex-inspector.

'It's falling into place, Bandicoot,' Lestrade said as they reached the lychgate. 'There's the common pattern. Not *two* former members of the Eleventh, but all five of them.'

'A sort of red-trousered league?' mused Bandicoot. Lestrade ignored him.

'The question is, why? And why did Nimrod Frost send me to Mawnan to find the corpse of Bill Lamb? Come on, Bandicoot. You can go to the theatre and I'm going home. It's time Assistant Commissioner Frost came a little cleaner than he is at the moment.'

Hot town. Summer in the city. Lestrade and Bandicoot got off the train at Paddington and made their way to the Yard. While Bandicoot waited in the hansom, the inspector entered the building by the back stairs under the shadow of the gateway.

'I'm sorry, Inspector.' Sergeant Dixon was firmer than Lestrade had ever known him. 'Mr Frost won't see you, sir. I 'ave my orders. Now, you're not goin' to make a try for the lift are you, sir?' You see, in this 'eat, I'd 'ate to 'ave to give chase. Cruel, ain't it. And as for that bleedin' river! I remember the Great Stink of 'fifty-eight but it couldn't 'old a candle to this. Them archaeologists blokes keep findin' bits of old iron in the mud at low tide and doin' their nuts about 'em. Reckon they're from the Bronze Age, or something. . . .'

'You're changing the subject, Dixon. I have to see His Nims *now*.'

'Inspector Lestrade. Look at it from my position, sir. I'm a married man, four kids, two years orf me pension. I shouldn't even be talking to you, sir. Not at the moment. You know 'ow it is.'

Lestrade stood back from the desk. 'Yes, Sergeant, I know how it is,' and he strode to the door.

'Thank you, sir. And mind 'ow you go.'

Bandicoot had bought a morning paper from a street vendor and was eagerly perusing the shares and city news page when Lestrade returned.

'No joy?' he asked. Lestrade shook his head. He was about to climb into the hansom when the headline caught his eye. *Goron In London. Head of Sûreté On Flying Visit.*

'Bandicoot. It's a long shot, but it could pay off. Where do you stay when you're in town?'

'The Grand, of course.'

'Of course. Well, get me a room too. Don't worry, I'll charge it to expenses. And use the name Athelney Jones. I'd like to see his face when Frost queries *that* bill! I'll join you there later. There's another question I have for Sergeant Dixon.'

As he rounded the corner, a hoarse whisper crackled in his ear. It was Hector Charlo in the shadows, beckoning to Lestrade to join him.

'I'm extraordinarily glad to see you, Sergeant.' Lestrade shook his hand. Charlo whisked him behind a plane tree. 'What the hell's going on? When I saw Frost a few days ago he was all for reinstating me. Now I find I cannot even get to see him. And that fanatical nonsense of Gregson's is all over the papers.'

'I don't know, sir.' Charlo scanned the upper storey windows of the Yard for signs of life. 'All I know is, I've been ordered off the case. I've been told,' he edged carefully round the tree, 'that if I have any dealings with you whatsoever, I'll lose my job.'

Lestrade fumed. 'You got this from Frost?'

'Himself,' nodded Charlo.

'Well, that's it,' shrugged Lestrade. 'Good luck, Sergeant. I'll see you around perhaps, one day.'

'Inspector,' Charlo stopped him, 'if I can get over this damned pleurisy, I'll stay in touch. Where can I reach you?'

'Sergeant, you are putting your head on the block. You realise that?'

'I've been called a chip off the old block before, sir.' It was the first time Lestrade had seen Charlo smile. Lestrade slapped his arm in gratitude, a little too heartily as it transpired, for Charlo winced with pain.

'The Grand Hotel. Under the name of one Athelney Jones, Inspector of River Police.'

Charlo positively beamed.

'Listen. I understand that Monsieur Goron, Head of the Sûreté is visiting the Yard. Any idea of his movements?'

'It's common knowledge where he goes of an evening, sir. Fatima's.'

'Does he now?'

'Why do you want him?' Charlo was puzzled.

'I'm not really sure, Charlo. Take care of yourself.' And he vanished again.

The lamplighter was doing his rounds in the Haymarket when Lestrade and Bandicoot found their quarry. A squat, iron-grey man with untypical pince-nez bustled through the doorway and the knot of evening strollers.

'Well, well, well.' Lestrade clicked his tongue.

'What is it, Sholto?'

'You never did find your way round town, did you? In a professional way, I mean. That establishment is Fatima Charrington's, the best-known bordello in London.'

'Fatima's?' Bandicoot was impressed.

'The logical successor to Kate Hamilton's,' said Lestrade.

'But what would a man of Goron's reputation be doing in there?'

Lestrade looked with faint surprise at his ex-and-acting-constable. 'Bandicoot, before you and Letitia go through with your ceremony, remind me to have a word with you,' and he dashed away across the street.

Bandicoot had not seen the inside of a bordello before, but on the surface it was no different from the hundred or so music halls that littered the West End. Waiters scuttled here and there with trays of champagne. Customers lounged around, laughing and eating grapes proffered by attractive young ladies. On the stage, garishly lit with sulphur, a painted woman sang 'The First Shove is the Sweetest', to a rather discordant accompaniment by a female quartet. Here and there, heavies stood in key positions; one near the bar, another at the door, two more by the stage. The air was thick with smoke and the fumes of alcohol, all of it very expensive.

'Can I help you, gentlemen?' An enormous lady with a blonde wig piled high and cascading over one bare shoulder about the width of Bandicoot's chest barred the way.

'Miss Charrington, I presume?' ventured Lestrade.

Fatima curtseyed, her breasts wobbling like so much whale meat.

'Athelney Jones, Scotland Yard. This is Constable Bandicoot.' And as if to forestall her complaint, 'Don't worry. This is not an official visit. We are here at the request of Monsieur Goron. May we see him?'

'In person or through the spy hole, dearie?' Fatima asked.

Lestrade chuckled. 'In person, please.'

'This way. Now, dearie, what can we interest you in? A chambermaid, is it? Vicar's daughter? Perhaps – yes, I see it. An Amazon?' She was fondling Bandicoot's arm, gazing into his rather crossed blue eyes and running her toad-like tongue over her thick lips.

'Madame, please. I think you have misunderstood . . .'

'Oh, I see,' and she dropped her fatal charm. 'You want Bertram's across the road. Errand boys. Barnardo brats. More cottage loaves in there than a bakery.'

Bandicoot's mouth opened in silent protest.

'Monsieur Goron,' Lestrade reminded Fatima, and she took them up the velvet stairway to an upstairs room, past chandeliers tinkling and dazzling in their myriad brilliance. 'Keep your hand on your wallet, Bandicoot – and leave the talking to me.'

Monsieur Goron sat in an elegant parlour, reclining on a chaise longue of immense proportions. He looked vaguely comical in his pink underwear and top hat, which he now tipped to the newcomers and raised a glass of vintage champagne. The Sûreté certainly do themselves proud, thought Lestrade.

'Who are zees gentlemen?' he asked Fatima. 'I distinctly ordered two *ladies*. And besides, zees two are both white.'

'I fear there will be a slight delay, Monsieur,' she fawned, in what Lestrade would have sworn was a telephone voice had she had such a piece of apparatus in her hand. 'Celeste and Angeline are not yet ready. They are making themselves *extra* beautiful for you. In the meantime, these gentlemen would like to join you.'

'Oh, I see. You wish to see 'ow 'an expert operates, uh? Well, I 'ad no idea zat ma reputation 'ad spread so far.'

'It has, Monsieur Goron, but it is not your prowess in the boudoir we wish to assess.'

'Non? Perhaps eet ees a matter of length?'

'Good God!' Bandicoot was beside himself with indignation.

'No, this is professional business,' insisted Lestrade. 'My name is Athelney Jones, Inspector of Scotland Yard. This is Constable Bandicoot.'

'*Ah, Inspecteur. Enchanté. Enchanté*. You know I am studying La Yarde Ecosse for a few days. You are in charge of the River Police, non?'

'Er, yes,' lied Lestrade.

'Bon. And do you find ze Londres underworld ees particularly prone to ply the river?'

'Er, no more I am sure than their counterparts in Paris ply the Loire.'

'Seine,' said Bandicoot.

Lestrade wondered momentarily whether this was Bandicoot's summation of Goron's state of mental health. It was not particularly helpful or relevant.

'Whenever I come to Londres, I like to spend my first night at Fatima's,' and he kissed the chubby, bejewelled hand of the lady as she swept past in search of Celeste and Angeline. 'I particularly like two girls at once.' Bandicoot was surprised he had the stamina. 'One white, ze other black. It adds to ze zest of the thing, don't you think?'

Lestrade did.

'Uh, Bain-de-Coute, what ees your preference? Non, don't tell me. Beeg, uh? Blonde, like yourself? Probably ze older woman? I know, eet ees ze thighs you go for, locked around your back, uh? I can tell you are a leg man.'

Lestrade sensed the 'constable' tensing at his side. He realised that Goron's description fitted Letitia Lawrenson exactly, although he couldn't really speak for the thighs. His cry of 'Not this one, Bandicoot,' was drowned as the young man snapped at the supposed insult to his lady's honour and, snarling, flung himself at the prone Goron. Lestrade need not have worried, at least not about the little Head of Sûreté. The Frenchman deftly rolled off the chaise longue and brought his shin up smartly into Bandicoot's groin. Another second and Goron was upright, the twin barrels of a vest pocket pistol nudging Bandicoot's ear. It had appeared so fast Lestrade had no inkling where it had come from.

'Ees thees 'ow you London bobbies treat visiting dignitaries from abroad?' snapped Goron.

'Er . . . a test,' Lestrade was suddenly inspired; 'we have of course heard of your legendary command of self-defence.'

'Ah, oui, the *Système Goron*.'

'Quite so, and Assistant Commissioner Frost has given orders that various constables should learn all they can from you.'

'The hard way,' Bandicoot mumbled into the silk of the chaise longue.

'Personally, I would like to know more of your Cookshop.'

'What?' Bandicoot struggled upright as Goron uncocked the hammers of his pistol and equally skilfully secreted it God-knows-where about his person.

'Quiet, Bandicoot. The grown-ups are talking,' said Lestrade.

'Goron's Cookshop, young man. A suite of rooms at the Sûreté where I interrogate prisoners. Of course, in this sophisticated age, this *fin de siècle*, such things should not be necessary. But you know, both of you, what scum stalks ze earth. I can do things with a leather thong that would make your eyes water – literally.'

'There is one case you can help me with, sir,' said Lestrade. 'Poppy Vansittart.'

'Ah,' said Goron, adjusting himself on the sofa once more and pouring more champagne. 'An Englishman in Paris.'

'You knew him?' Lestrade asked.

'Oh, yes, quite well. Aahh,' and he rose as Fatima returned with an ingratiating smile. 'Celeste and Angeline.' Fatima beckoned with a pudgy finger. He whispered as he passed Lestrade's ear, 'Actually, their names are Gertrude and May and they are both from Glasgow, but Monsieur, the grip . . . Shall we talk as I perform?'

'Thank you, no, Monsieur,' Lestrade declined. 'That is not quite the British way. We will wait for you here.'

Goron shrugged and left the room, unbuttoning his flies. 'Bon appetit,' Lestrade called after him.

What a tasteless remark, thought Bandicoot, but he was still recovering from the kick in the groin and thought he would let it pass.

For a while, they waited, helping themselves to Goron's champagne, then Lestrade slowly leaned forward and put his glass on the table.

'Bandicoot,' he murmured, 'I want you to say nothing. Anything you do say may well be taken down and conceivably used against you. You see, we are about to be raided by the police.' Even as they made for the door, the whole building shook with crashing glass and the scream of police whistles. Truncheons rained through the air as blue helmets appeared at every window. Naked girls ran everywhere, screaming and crying. Equally naked gentlemen, tugging on recalcitrant combinations and grabbing somebody else's hats, canes and scarves, hurtled along the corridors and tumbled down the stairs. In an instant, the place was in uproar.

'What will Letitia say if this gets out?' Bandicoot wailed.

''Not half as much as if *we* don't get out. Come on. Remind me you were an Eton boxing champion,' and he dashed off along the corridor.

''Ere, I want a word with you,' called a uniformed constable. Bandicoot planted a straight left on his nose and the constable crumpled. A second sprang at him, truncheon raised. Bandicoot ducked aside, threw the constable against a wall and tripped up a third.

'That's the way,' shouted Lestrade. 'Not bad for a beginner,' and began to check the rooms one by one while Bandicoot, like a latter-day Horatius, kept the landing so well. The first two rooms were empty, but the third caught the attention of the hastening Lestrade for longer than he intended. A tall, distinguished-looking gentleman was sitting, fully clothed, talking on the telephone. It was obvious he was wearing a false beard and his conversation was not of the ordinary.

'And then what would you do, Fifi?' His voice was strained

and his eyes bulging. Lestrade noted that the wires ran through a hole in the wall, presumably to an adjacent room.

'Fifi, what then? I am desperate.'

A semi-naked girl wearing headphones rushed past Lestrade.

'I believe your telephonist has gone,' said Lestrade. The tall man dropped the apparatus and leapt to his feet. In doing so, his beard fell off at his feet.

'Why, Mr Chamberlain,' smiled Lestrade, 'I didn't recognise you without your monocle,' and the tall man swept past him into the battle-ground below.

'Hurry, Lestrade. Er . . . I mean Inspector Jones. Er . . . I mean . . . oh, God?' Bandicoot was valiantly fending off punch, kick and club alike. He could not hold out for ever. One of his wrists was handcuffed already. At the end of the passage, the lights had gone out, but Lestrade recognised the accent in the eighth room he tried.

'Ah, chéries. Vous êtes merveilleuse. Merci, mes petites. A bientôt,' and the Head of the Sûreté backed into Lestrade. In a flash, the pistol was against the inspector's nose, or what was left of it.

'Oh, Jones. Eet ees you. Not your idea of un petit joke this, uh?'

'Certainly not,' said Lestrade. 'If my memory serves me correctly, there is a fire escape here somewhere. I would like to talk further with you, Monsieur Goron. Will you wait in the street below while I bail out our friend?'

Goron tugged on his evening jacket and with an agility astonishing in a man his age, and bearing in mind his activities for the last few minutes, leapt out of the fire escape. Celeste and Angeline emerged, staggering uncertainly from the darkened room.

'Eh, hinnie, he's one hell of a goer, that one.'

'Aye, chuck. You can say that again. They're a' the same, these bloody coppers!'

Lestrade realised the odds at the end of the corridor were lengthening, so he searched around frantically for assistance. If only he hadn't left his trusty knuckle-duster and switch-blade in his room at the Grand. He ought to have known better, going to Fatima's of a Saturday night. What came to hand, however, was every bit as useful – a chamberpot. He threw the contents at the first constable and clanged a second across the head with it.

'Come on, Bandicoot. Anybody would think you were enjoying yourself. Get out of it, lad,' and he kicked another attacker in the pit of the stomach. For a split second, he recognised the plain-clothes figure making up the stairs through the jostling mass of bodies – Edgar Bradstreet, Gregson's man. What was he doing in a routine raid by the Metropolitan Police? Bradstreet had time too to recognise Lestrade as the inspector flung the chamberpot, pretty with pink flowers, and followed Bandicoot into the darkness of the fire escape and the night.

Lestrade's superlative knowledge of the streets enabled the three respectable fugitives to dodge the crowds of ladies of ill repute, shame-faced clients busily waving bundles of notes at policemen and the scattering Saturday-night crowds, drawn like flies to a corpse to the noise and scandal of the Haymarket. The name of Fatima would resound in many a magistrates' court on Monday morning and would meet the furious gaze of many a wife across the breakfast table from a nervous, sweating husband. It was the way of the world. It was what made the nineties naughty. As dawn broke, pearly and hot as ever over the sleeping city, three policemen, one foreign, one suspended, one retired, sat in the rooms of the Grand Hotel, sipping champagne. It had been Goron's first request as he arrived with the exhausted Bandicoot and Lestrade at their rooms. Now, as they recovered, the Frenchman once again produced his pocket pistol and held it generally at Lestrade's head.

'Now all ze shouting is over,' he said, 'why don't you tell me who you *really* are?'

Lestrade held up a calming hand to prevent Bandicoot repeating his calamitous attempt of earlier in the evening.

'I told you,' Lestrade stuck to his story, 'I am Inspector Athelney Jones of Scotland Yard.'

'You are not, M'sieur, unless of course you have lost five or six stones and had your face radically altered – since yesterday.'

Lestrade and Bandicoot exchanged glances.

'You see, I met Athelney Jones yesterday. Indeed, I met all Nimrod Frost's inspecteurs – expect one. And now I believe I have met him too.'

'Has Nimrod Frost offered you a job at the Yard yet?' Lestrade asked, bemused. 'I think we have need of you.'

'Ha, ha.' Goron once again put up his pistol, this time in the more conventional holster of his waistcoat pocket. 'You would not approve of my methods. Mind you, having seen you in action wiz a chambre pot as I left Fatima's last night, there is 'ope for you British bobbies yet. Now, Inspecteur Le Strade, as one Frenchman to annuzzer, what do you wish to know about Puppy?'

'Puppy?' repeated Bandicoot, wondering if they were talking about a missing pet.

'Coleraine Robert Vansittart; Puppy to his friends.'

'A curious nickname,' commented Lestrade.

'Not if you 'ad seem 'im, Le Strade. He was long and thin wiz a red-gold beard. 'E was a crack shot, a founder member of the *Tir au Pigeon*. 'E was greatly respected in Parisian society. A personal friend of Prince Achille Murat and,' he leaned closer, confidential, 'Napoléon III.'

'His death?'

'Natural causes. He died in bed, in his rooms in La Rue Vernet. Spacious, comfort. It comes to us all, mon vieux.'

'But to some of us earlier than others,' was Lestrade's comment.

'Puppy 'ad a full life. Funny 'e never married.'

'You mean . . .?'

'*Un pédéraste*? *Non*, there was nothing odd about Vansittart. But . . .'

'Yes?'

'There was something strange about 'im. I 'ad a feeling 'e was on ze – how do you say it – fringe of something.'

'Something?' echoed Lestrade.

'Ah, non, Inspecteur. You and I are too old hands to deal in speculation. Let's just say 'e was a . . . uh . . . deep one.'

'Do you know anything of his early life? In the British Army?'

'I believe 'e 'ad been a lieutenant in the Elevent' Huzzards.

His country seat was in le département . . . er . . . county of Berkshire, but I believe 'e 'ad no family of which to speak.'

Lestrade slumped in the chair.

'A wall of bricks, Inspecteur?'

Lestrade nodded.

'Je regrets. But now, you can do something for me. Jews. Do you have a problem wiz zem 'ere?'

'Not unduly,' said Lestrade. 'There were those who thought Jack the Ripper was a Jew – a slaughterman.'

'Ah, oui. The apron of leather.'

'You are remarkably well informed,' said Lestrade. 'That case was five years ago.'

'Ah, but what a case. I also know a great deal about your Adelaide Bartlett . . .'

Don't you mean *your* Adelaide Bartlett? thought Lestrade.

'And your Charles Hurrah.'

Lestrade frowned for a moment. Bandicoot was completely out of his depth. 'I think that's Bravo,' the inspector corrected him.

'Oh, no, it is nothing really,' Goron swaggered. 'But we 'ave ze serious Jewish problem. Ze army, in particular. There id one little Yeed I am after. An insignificant captain of artillerie named Dreyfus. What about scientists? Do you trust zem?'

'Well, I . . .'

'Oh, don't misunderstand me. Some of the best gadgets in my Cookshop have been invented by scientists. Madame Guillotine, of course, so preferable to your English drop. And the father of forensic science is a Frenchman, Bertillon. But there are others I do not trust. Anarchists. Socialists. . . .'

Lestrade had heard this somewhere else.

'I 'ave my eyes on les frères Curie of the Sorbonne. Now, there is a 'otbed of anarchie if ever there was one. Do you 'ave a similar place?'

'The House of Commons,' said Lestrade, and finished his champagne.

Lestrade was entirely grateful that Goron had announced that he would be collecting the bill for breakfast. It, both bill and breakfast in fact, was immense and the policemen, British and foreign, spent over an hour regaling each other with celebrated cases and the problems of the modern police force. There were times when Bandicoot might as well have been the aspidistra in the corner for all he was able to add to the conversation. When it came to the food, however, it was Lestrade's turn to take a back seat. He felt sure that Arthur Sullivan would not have approved of the range of *haute cuisine* before him, little of which Lestrade had seen before, and none of which he could pronounce. The more cosmopolitan Bandicoot sampled with relish – Gentleman's, of course. The only thing Lestrade felt safe with was the coffee and he confined himself to that.

The dining-room clock at the Grand had just struck ten when it happened. Goron's face seemed to turn the colour of the rainbow in the space of seconds. He choked, tugging at his starched collar, and pitched forward, his nose burying itself in the confiture. The buzz of conversation around the room stopped and as Lestrade reached out to help him, Bandicoot slumped sideways from his chair, dragging the tablecloth and most of its clutter to the floor.

'Get an ambulance!' Lestrade roared, desperately lying both men on their backs and loosening their clothing. Ladies were hurried from the room. The *maître d'hôtel* shepherded them to the swing doors and did his best to form a human screen between them and the collapsed men.

'What is it, Inspector Jones?' He scuttled back to the scene.

'Looks like beriberi to me,' a red-faced man pronounced.

'Are you a doctor?' Lestrade snapped at him.

'Well . . . no, but I've spent years in the tropics. I know beri—'

'Thank you, sir. I will wait for an informed opinion.'

Under the snapping fingers of the *maître d'hôtel*, waitresses and waiters swarmed everywhere, beginning to clear the debris. 'Leave it!' commanded Lestrade. 'Nothing is to be touched.'

'Sir,' began the *maître d'hôtel*, 'I hope you don't think . . . That is, the food . . .'

'Gangway! Gangway! Let me through there. I'm a doctor.' A rubicund gentleman, clearly staying at the Grand by virtue of his still being in pyjamas and dressing gown, threw down his professional bag at Bandicoot's side and looked at the casualties. 'Dead?' he asked Lestrade.

'No, but that was the intention, I think.'

The doctor checked pulses and eyeballs. 'Are these gentlemen guests at the hotel?'

Lestrade nodded.

'We must get them to their beds. You men, lend a hand.'

While the doctor supervised with the *maître d'hôtel* the removal of Goron and Bandicoot to Bandicoot's rooms, Lestrade had the remains of the breakfast collected for him and placed in the kitchens. He bombarded the entire staff with questions for nearly twenty minutes, despite the entreaties of the *maître d'hôtel* to allow his people to continue their duties. Luncheon after all was not long away.

'If either of those men dies,' Lestrade rounded on him, 'this hotel will not be serving luncheon or any other meal again. That much I can guarantee.'

Lestrade had just come to the conclusion that nothing else could be wheedled out of the array of cooks and bottle washers, when one of them mentioned a new man. A temporary he was. Filling in for Smithers who had the flutters. I know a policeman with that problem, thought Lestrade. No. He wasn't still there. He had gone. Odd that. Not particularly, thought Lestrade. What had been his duties? Preparing the preserves and confitures.

Lestrade fled the kitchen as if his tail was on fire. Into the ante-room where the breakfast remains still lay. He dipped a tentative finger into the nearest preserve. No taste other than cherries. He tried a second. Then a third. He stopped at the third. The smell of almonds.

'What sort of jam is this?' he asked the *maître d'hôtel.*

'No sort of jam at all, sir.' The *maître d'hôtel* was desperately attempting to regain something of his dignity after the bewildering events of the morning. 'It is apricot preserve.'

'And do you put almonds in your apricot preserve?'

The *maître d'hôtel* looked puzzled and whispered to the chef beside him. The little white-hatted man shook his head. 'No.' The *maître d'hôtel* was authoritative.

'Just apricots and cyanide?'

'Precisely,' and the *maître d'hôtel*'s mouth fell slack at the realisation of his admission. 'Er . . . that is . . . I . . .'

'Don't worry,' said Lestrade. 'Your secret is safe with me.'

He was there when Bandicoot came round, a little before Goron. Both men were a little pale, a little weak, a little prone to making staggering visits to the bathroom to rid themselves of what was left of their breakfast and the doctor's emetic.

'I can only apologise, gentlemen,' said the inspector. 'Your discomfort was caused by cyanide jam. And it was almost certainly intended for me.'

'Scientists. You see what I mean?' Goron reminded him.

'You may be right, Monsieur Goron, but we have a game in England called Hunt the Thimble. One child hides the thimble. The others look for it. When a child approaches the hidden object, the hider calls out "You're getting warm". And that is what this morning proves. I'm getting warm.'

The back of beyond

This time Jacob wrote his letter. Family affair or not, the matter was now beyond his control. He wrote it down, all of it. All he knew. The whole black, bloody mess. And he knew this time exactly where the letter must go. He addressed it to Inspector Sholto Lestrade, New Scotland Yard. He would do something now. Now he had the facts, Lestrade would act.

The inspector had been in the back of beyond before. This time it was called Bishop's Castle, in the country of Salop and, having left the comparative civilisation of the Shrewsbury-bound train, he had to resort to pony and trap for the last leg of his journey. Through the flies and cow dung of the late summer hurtled Lestrade. He made enquiries in the town with its steep cobbled streets and taking a chance that the Shropshire Constabulary would not be familiar with the pattern of suspensions at the Yard, used his own name. A family called Hope, he was told, had a farm out Cefn-Einion way, on the lower slopes of Offa's Dyke. Lestrade had to ask for several repetitions of this, because the constable seemed to have a peg jammed on his nose and to talk as though his cheeks were full of cotton-wool – that is when he had finally abandoned his native Welsh for something that Lestrade vaguely understood. Lestrade in turn found himself shouting monosyllables at the constable as though he were the village idiot. It didn't help. And wasn't it just his luck that the Hope farm should be on the Welsh, and not the English side of this border county?

The first glimpse of a Hope that he caught was a switch flying erratically into the air behind a small herd of Friesians winding their way homeward o'er the lea. Not that they were Friesians to Lestrade. In fact, they closely resembled black and white cows. The one at the front, with the rolling pink eye didn't look at all friendly, however. And it wasn't until Lestrade took in the bulk of the beast, its stamping hoof and tossing head in the fierce afternoon sun that he became aware of its sex. Surprisingly for a man who had seen it all and been everywhere, it was not until the animal had shouldered aside his flimsy trap that Lestrade was aware of its masculinity, sweeping nearly to the ground. By that time, he was wrestling manfully with the reins as his pony bucked and shied, unaware in its blinkers of the size of the problem.

'You silly ut!' screamed a voice. The switch emerged from the rear of the milling cattle to reveal at its other end a short square woman, in drab blouse and apron, hair strained back in a bun. She swung back a chubby fist and hit the bull firmly on its ringed nose. The animal snorted and waddled off a little sheepishly.

'Sorry about that.' The cowherd shielded her eyes from the sun. She waited for Lestrade, dusty and sweating in his suit and bowler, to calm the horse.

'I'm looking for the farm of Mr Hope,' said Lestrade.

'Oh, English you are, is it? I'm Mrs Hope. It's Will you've come to see, is it?'

Lestrade looked blank.

'My husband, Will,' Mrs Hope prompted him.

'No, actually, I was looking for Henry Hope,' he answered.

Mrs Hope's face fell. 'Duw, I'm afraid you might be too late. Gransha's at death's door. That's why I'm out yer with the animals. Will's with his Tâd. What do you want Gransha for? 'E'aven't done nothin' wrong, 'ave he?'

'No, Mrs Hope. My name is Lestrade; Inspector Lestrade, Scotland Yard.'

'Well, I never!' Mrs Hope climbed up beside him, leaving him to ponder all the way down the hill what it was she never did.

They reached, in the fullness of time, behind the plodding cows, a little thatched cottage. The sun dazzled on its white-washed walls and the hollyhocks completed the picture of rustic idyll. Only the flagstone floors betrayed its dampness and the only sound within it was the rattle of a dying man.

'Gransha,' Mrs Hope called loudly to the bearded old gentleman propped up on his pillows. 'There's a gentleman to see you – a policeman.'

Two younger men, in leather gaiters and bowler hats, sleeves rolled up for the harvest, stepped aside at the word 'policeman', rather than at Lestrade's entrance.

'I am sorry to intrude,' he said to them all, 'but I must ask Mr Hope some questions. It may be a matter of life or death.'

'Aye, his,' one of the men mumbled.

'This is Will,' Mrs Hope said, as though by way of an apology. 'Don't mind him. Ask away. Oh, he's gone again,' and she leaned over, tenderly slapping the old man's cheeks as he lay, pale and silent. 'He goes like this now and again,' she explained; 'the falling sickness, see. 'E've always had it. Aven't he, Will?'

'Aye.' Will was clearly a master of wit and repartee.

'Can we help, Mr Lestrade?' she asked.

But with that, the old man stirred.

'Oh, 'e's back with us,' and she shook him gently, motioning Lestrade forward as she did so.

'This is Inspector Lestrade, Gransha, from Scotland Yard. London, you know. 'E wants to ask you something.'

The old man muttered something incomprehensible, probably in the nasal Welsh dialect of the district which had so thrown Lestrade before.

'I understand you were once in the Eleventh Hussars,' said Lestrade. No response. He repeated himself, talking more loudly.

'No need to shout, I'm not bloody deaf, mun,' growled the elder Hope. 'Yes, I was in the Eleventh Hussars. And I rode the Charge of the Light Brigade.' He struggled upright in his bed at the remembrance of it. 'And the Heavy Brigade too.'

Lestrade looked for confirmation at Mrs Hope.

'Oh, yes, he rode in both Charges, all right. The only one to do it, mind.'

'I was in the guardhouse, see,' Henry Hope wheezed, 'on the mornin' of Balaclava. Well, seein' all the activity goin' on, and no guards about, I just walked out of the hut and grabbed the nearest 'orse. I felt a silly bugger, mind, the only Hussar in all them Heavies – and on a trooper of the Greys, isn't it? But I galloped with them into the Russians. Too late to turn back, see, by then. Of course, when I got back, my boys were formed up for the ride and old Loy Smith would 'ave 'ad my guts if I 'adn't been there. Afterwards, Lord Cardigan 'isself let me off my charge – I was asleep on duty – well, it was the fits, see,' and he collapsed in a paroxysm of coughing. His family clucked round him and Lestrade recognised in the greyness of the face all the tell-tale signs. With less than his usual respect for death, he persisted.

'Think back to the old days, Henry. To the Crimea.'

'Leave 'im alone, mun!' bellowed Will, reaching the heights of articulacy.

'Don't call Will on your father!' barked the old man, with one of those magnificent pieces of Welsh rhetoric utterly lost on Lestrade. 'I pawned my bloody medal years ago,' old Henry moaned.

'Do you remember Jim Hodges?' Lestrade knelt beside the old man, his bowler awry, his hand gripping the old man's.

'Aye.'

'What about Richard Brown? Joe Towers? Bill Bentley?'

Nothing.

'Think, Henry, think,' hissed Lestrade. And, with the desperation of a drowning man, 'There's not much time.'

Henry Hope looked up at Lestrade. His eyes widened in realisation of what the younger man meant.

'Aye, I remember them all. All F Troop.'

'They're dead, Henry. Murdered. All of them. So's Bill Lamb. Do you remember him?'

'Murdered?' The old man tried to sit up. Lestrade cradled his head.

'Why, Henry, why? Why should all your old messmates die?'

'Ask Miss Nightingale,' he said. 'The Lady of the Lamp we called her. She can tell you . . .' He fell back.

'Henry . . .' Lestrade called to him.

'Can't you see he's dying, mun?' Will snarled.

Lestrade ignored him. 'Henry, why? Why Miss Nightingale?'

'Surgeon . . .' gasped Henry.

''E wants a doctor. Where is the old bugger?' Will snapped, whirling to the tiny window and back.

Henry shook his head. 'Kill . . . Cro . . . Kill . . .' and he faded away.

Lestrade let the cold hand fall and laid it gently across the old man's chest.

Will and the other man loomed over him, threatening, bewildered at his intrusion and their sense of loss. It was Mrs Hope who intervened. 'What's done is done, Will,' she said. 'Twm. Find the doctor. Make yourself useful,' and slowly the other man shambled out. She saw Lestrade to the waiting trap.

'My condolences, ma'am,' said the inspector. There was really nothing else he could say.

'Was it any help, Inspector – what Gransha said?'

'I don't know, Mrs Hope. Perhaps only time will tell us that,' and he drove away from the whitewalled cottage, over the edge of Offa's Dyke and away to the north east.

They met as arranged before the altar in the north west transept. Two gentlemen, enjoying the sun of September and the cold stone of their mediaeval heritage in the double cruciform pile of Canterbury.

'They found Becket's bones in the crypt five years ago,' Charlo informed Lestrade, as though a local antiquary was exhibiting his knowledge for a visiting tourist.

'Foul play, I understand?' Lestrade could not resist treading on professional ground, even when pretending to passers-by to be an innocent abroad.

Shop again, thought Charlo, but to be fair that was exactly why he had come to Canterbury.

'I got the preserve you left with Bandicoot,' Charlo whispered out of the corner of his mouth as they moved towards the crypt.

'I would love to see the Huguenot Chapel,' Lestrade said, for consumption of the passing public. 'And?' His voice fell to a whisper.

'You were right. I had it analysed by a chemist friend of mine. Cyanide.'

'It's high time the Yard had laboratories of its own,' was Lestrade's comment. 'What news of the Establishment?'

'We've been ordered to take you in for questioning, sir, if you don't attend your hearing today.'

'You've got no nearer to Frost, then?'

'You must remember, sir, I'm only a sergeant. I'm afraid the assistant commissioner doesn't take me into his confidence.'

'Point taken. What about Gregson?'

'The gossip is he's still convinced you tried to kill the Kaiser. Do you think he's sane?'

'Gregson or the Kaiser?'

'Take your pick,' said Charlo, as they descended into the crypt. It was dark here and colder than the nave.

'How is Bandicoot?' Lestrade asked.

'Well, when I saw him.'

'And Goron?'

'Gone home. He didn't appear to bear any grudge.'

'Do you know if he said anything to Frost – about me, I mean?'

Charlo shrugged. 'Why did you want me to meet you here, sir?' The sergeant was positively shivering.

'Well, I might have His Grace the Archbishop on my list of suspects, but in fact we have to look up some records. Coming?'

The short-sighted young officer yawned and shook himself. He looked at the date on the calendar – September 26th. He crossed to the litter bin, stumbling over something, and began to sharpen pencils. The something he had tripped over, a floor-coloured Irish wolfhound, growled resignedly.

'Come in.' There was nothing wrong with the officer's hearing and there had definitely been a knock at the door.

'Inspector Athelney Jones, Scotland Yard, to see you, sir.' The corporal saluted briskly. The officer adjusted his thick-lensed glasses and peered around the door, tripping over the dog again on his return to the desk. 'Sorry, Paddy,' he had the courtesy to apologise.

Lestrade entered. 'I was looking for the adjutant of the Eleventh Hussars,' he said.

'You've found him.' The officer extended a hand, missing Lestrade's by several inches. 'Charles Davenport . . . the Honourable.'

'Athelney Jones, the Quite Ordinary. This is Sergeant Charlo.' Lestrade caught the searching hand. Davenport waved vaguely at the wall somewhere in front of which he assumed the sergeant was standing.

'I'm afraid you've missed the others,' he said. 'They're all out.'

'Out?'

'Yes, in India, in fact. We have a skeleton staff here and I'm it. How can I help you?' Davenport squinted through gritted teeth. Lestrade realised he'd have no problem with his subterfuge here. Athelney Jones could have been Davenport's Siamese twin and he wouldn't have recognised him.

'I am making certain enquiries into the deaths of five men who were all formerly members of your regiment. I wonder if I might see your roster books from the eighteen-fifties?'

'The fifties?' The adjutant stroked his chin. He rang a number of items on his desk, first a paperweight, then a bronze statuette and finally a bell. The orderly reappeared.

'Corporal, get me Ledger E5/21a, could you?'

'Er . . .' the corporal began.

'Oh, God, it's green with gold letters, eighteenth from the end, top shelf.'

The corporal left.

'Why they give me secretarial staff who can't read, I'll never know. Cigar?' and Davenport offered Lestrade a pencil.

'No, thanks, I find the lead doesn't agree with me.'

The corporal returned, miraculously, with the relevant book, and the adjutant began flicking through the pages. Perhaps it's in Braille, thought Lestrade.

'Yes, this is the one. May eighteen-fifty to January eighteen-sixty. You should find what you want in there.'

And Lestrade did. John Douglas, Lieutenant-Colonel, Lieutenant Alexander Dunn, with a pencilled VC alongside. But what really interested him was F Troop – Lamb, Bentley, Towers, Brown, Hope, they were all there. So were others, many others. He scribbled down the other names on a notepad.

'Did all these serve in the Crimea?' That, he reasoned, must be the link.

'Those with a "C" by their name,' said Davenport.

That cut down the field a little.

'Do you have any way of knowing whether these are still alive?' asked Lestrade.

'God, no,' replied the adjutant. 'Some of them would have been getting a pension. You'd have to go to the War Office for that.'

And the War Office meant London, where Lestrade would be recognised, checks made, verification in triplicate, and so on. Here in Canterbury a man on the run could still be reasonably safe. He needed the resources of the Yard, above all, its miles of shoe leather for this. And that was precisely where Charlo came in. A sudden thought occurred to him.

'Will you be offended if I make an observation?' he asked.

'My dear fellow . . .' said Davenport, obviously inviting him to feel free.

'I couldn't help noticing you were a little . . . er . . . short-sighted.'

Davenport bridled slightly. 'I wouldn't have said so,' he said, petulantly.

'Well, anyway, I was wondering if you had a spare pair of spectacles. I need them for another case I'm working on.'

'A spectacle case?' – the adjutant wished he hadn't said it – 'Well, yes, I have actually. For close work, you understand. But how could a pair of specs possibly help?'

'I'm afraid I'm not at liberty to tell you that, sir.' It was the sort of phrase Athelney Jones might use, but Lestrade wondered how long he might be at liberty at all.

'Very well,' said Davenport. 'But I will get them back, won't I? Could you sign here for them?'

Lestrade signed the bus ticket Davenport nudged towards him.

'And here?'

And he likewise signed the serviette.

'And finally here.'

The space on the desk between the blotter and ink stand accordingly received Jones's signature. Davenport handed Lestrade a pair of spectacles the inspector assumed had been made from the bottoms of bottles.

'Let me see you to the door,' said Davenport.

'No thanks, I can manage,' said Lestrade and tripped headlong over the wolfhound, which merely raised its head.

'Perhaps you ought to put those on, old chap!' chuckled Davenport. Lestrade smiled weakly and left, Charlo coughing again in his wake.

Lestrade sent a telegram to Mrs Manchester that day from Canterbury. *Stay with friends. Stop. Police watching house. Stop. Trust me. Stop. Sholto. Stop.* Then he shaved off his beloved moustache, combed his hair in the centre and travelled to London. Money was running out. So was time. It was September 26th, the date, Charlo had told him, of his hearing, but he would not be there. He was alarmed to find his face staring back at him from the front page of the *Police Gazette*. But it wasn't a very good likeness and with the changes he had wrought and particularly wearing Davenport's glasses, he ought to be all right. Just keep away from police stations and don't accept sweets from strangers.

He and Charlo parted company at Waterloo. It was not fair to the sergeant to be in Lestrade's company in London. After all, he had been expressly ordered to break with the man. His very career was at stake.

'I can't order you to do this, Hector,' said Lestrade. 'I can't really even ask it . . .'

'Don't worry, sir. I won't be far away,' and the sergeant wrapped his muffler against the September winds and was lost in the crowd.

*

'Inspector Jones?' asked the old lady in the wheelchair.

'Miss Nightingale.' Lestrade shook the limp, outstretched hand.

'I don't get many visits from Scotland Yard. How can I help you?'

'The Crimea, ma'am.'

'Ah, yes,' she smiled. 'Always the Crimea. Sometimes, Inspector, I can see it still. Even after all these years, the hospital at Scutari. The dirt. The smell. You know, we found a dead horse blocking the drains! And the men, boys, many of them. I still see their faces, too. That's the worst of it.'

'In particular, I wanted to know if you remembered any names. Joe Towers?'

Nothing.

And nothing for the others who had died.

'What about Henry Hope?' Lestrade ventured, since it was he who had mentioned Miss Nightingale in the first place.

'Oh, yes, now I *do* remember him. A simple, passionate Welshman. He had *petit mal*, I believe. He was with us for two months or so, that would have been the spring of 'fifty-five.'

'When he was under your care, particularly when he was delirious, did he say anything . . . odd?'

'When men are delirious, Inspector, they often say odd things. I . . . can't recall anything particular about Hope.'

'What about the regimental surgeons, ma'am, of the Eleventh Hussars, I mean?'

'Regimental surgeons were our greatest obstacle in the Crimea, Inspector Jones. I don't hold with the new feminism of today, but by Jove we needed it in the fifties. What could I, a mere woman, they used to say, know about medicine? How could I help when they could not? It was war and war was bloody. There was no changing that. The Eleventh, no, I don't suppose they were any better or worse than the others. Most regimental surgeons stayed with their regiments. One or two of them crossed to Scutari.'

'The regiment's records do not appear to show all their names,' said Lestrade.

'Ah, Inspector. Something else I learned about men, army

men that is, is that then, medical men, chaplains, veterinary officers, all were regarded as inferior. I do remember one surgeon of the Eleventh come to mention it, Henry Wilkin. He was a good doctor, but he longed to be a fighting officer. Regiments didn't even give their surgeon a horse, or a military burial. I have always found that sad. That a man who made passing as easy as he could for a soldier should be denied full membership, as it were, when his turn came.'

'Do you remember other surgeons, ma'am? Perhaps one whose name begins with the letters C-r-o?'

'C-r-o? Why, yes, I believe you must be referring to John Crosse. And he's not far from us here. For several years now he has been the medical officer at the Royal Military Asylum, Chelsea.'

The Rabbi Izzlebit took rooms in Sussex Gardens. He shuffled as he walked, head bent down, as though to peer over the thick-lensed glasses that he wore. He was visiting London from York, or so he told the landlord and anyone else who cared to ask. His black coat was shabby in the extreme and his greasy black ringlets hung sparsely over his hunched shoulders. On the first full day of his stay, he took an omnibus and train to Croydon, to Sanderstead Road, where he knocked vigorously on the door of Number 20.

The burly ex-policeman was not pleased to see him.

'Look, I don't want to be unpleasant,' he said, 'but I don't give money away to charities, least of all yours.'

'But charity begins at home, Beastie, my dear,' lisped the rabbi.

'Who are you?' Beastie demanded.

'Sholto Lestrade, you idiot. Let me in, for the love of Allah. Or am I mixing my religions?'

Safe inside the portals of Number 20, Lestrade took off the broad-brimmed hat and ringlet wig and peeled off the false beard and moustache. Over a steaming and welcome plate of tripe and onions, Lestrade told Beeson all – or nearly all – that had occurred since Joe Towers had lain on the very table off which they now ate.

'I heard you was on the run, sir. I couldn't believe it. What's going on?'

'I wish I knew,' said Lestrade. 'Gregson's always been a fanatic, but I can't understand Frost backing him this way. I'd got him down for a shrewder man.'

'What happens now?' Beeson asked.

'We work our way through the list. All the members of F Troop. I want to know everything about them. Right down to their inside legs.'

'I don't know, sir. It's been forty years.'

'Why didn't you tell me you were with this outfit in the first place?' Lestrade asked him.

'I told you I'd known Joe Towers in the army. I didn't think it was relevant beyond that. Anyway, sir, how did you think I got the name Beastie?'

'Your surname, I always supposed.'

'Nah,' the ex-sergeant of police drawled. 'I transferred to the Twelfth Lancers after the Crimea. Did a spell in India. "Bhisti" is the Hindoo name for a water-carrier. God knows why it stuck to me, but it did.'

'All right. This is what we've got. The officers . . .'

'I didn't know them all, sir. You just didn't talk to officers in them days. I don't suppose you do now.'

'I've got a sergeant named Charlo from the Yard still willing to speak to me. He got access to the War Office. He waited until lunch-hour, nobody much about, then claimed to be anxious to trace a missing relative. It worked a charm, really. God knows what secrets he might be able to uncover just for the asking. Makes you realise why Gregson is so insane. National security, and all that. Anyway, he came up with a few deaths. There's no way of telling now whether they were natural or odd. Here goes,' Lestrade read off the list, crossing out the deceased as he went, 'Captain Edwin Adolphus Cook, died eighteen seventy-two. Lieutenant Alexander Dunn. Yes, well, I know about him. Died eighteen sixty-eight. Lieutenant Edward Harnett. I didn't know he was in F Troop. Still alive. He's helped on the case already. Lieutenant Roger Palmer. Remember him?'

'Yes, Jowett saved his life in the Charge. Fair man, if I

remember right, but you must remember I was only in F Troop for a few weeks.'

'At the time of the Charge?'

'No, I was in D Troop then. What's the importance of F Troop?'

'If I knew that, Beastie, I'd have our man. Palmer is a lieutenant-general now apparently. He's got more property than you've made arrests – Ireland, Wales, Berkshire. I'd need time and the Yard behind me even to track him down. Lieutenant Harrington Trevelyan. Retired. Now residing in Fresno, California.'

'Where's that, sir?'

'West of Pimlico, I think you'll find, sergeant. Ah, now that's interesting.'

'Pimlico?'

'No. "Poppy" isn't here. No mention of Vansittart, so either he wasn't with F Troop or he didn't ride the Charge.'

'That's right, sir.'

'Which?'

'Both. He was in my troop and if I remember, he was at Scutari at the time.'

'Scutari?' Links were forging themselves in Lestrade's addled brain.

'The hospital base, sir. On the Black Sea.'

'Yes, yes. I know. A little east of Pimlico. Was Miss Nightingale there then?'

'I believe so, sir, towards the end of Lieutenant Vansittart's time. He retired soon after, I believe.'

'Funny she didn't mention him. Still, I didn't ask her directly.'

'Funny he never married.'

Lestrade had heard that statement somewhere before.

'Ah, now, two surgeons with F Troop. Henry Wilkin. He rode the Charge.'

'Yes, sir, he did. He left the medical service the year after Balaclava. Always wanted to be a serving soldier.'

'He died two years ago.'

'Brave man. Should have got a VC in Hindia.'

'Do you remember John Crosse?'

'Not really, sir; except he runs the fund now.'

'Fund?'

'Yes, sir, for the survivors of the Light Brigade.'

'Beastie, what a mine of information you are. How much is this fund? Who puts up the money?'

'Well, I don't rightly know, sir, except that Dr Crosse administers it.'

'Have you ever had cause to claim, Beastie?'

Lestrade had touched the old man's pride. 'Love you no, sir. I'd crawl in the gutter first. I've never taken charity in my life. Too old to start now.'

Lestrade was racing ahead. 'Don't you see, Beastie? Money. Money gives us a motive. The first one I've got, anyway. Surgeon Crosse merits a visit. Let's go on. Sergeant-Major George Loy Smith.'

'Bastard, he was. Tough old soldier. Joe went in mortal fear of him, I remember.'

'From what I've heard, you all did. He died in Bart's, what . . . five years ago.'

'Serves him right. I've never liked beefeaters.'

'Is that what he became?'

'Yers.' Beeson spat his tobacco quid in the grate. 'I seen him once at the Tower when I were on duty. Told me to push off or he'd knock my helmet off with his halberd. He never forgave or forgot anything; his sort never do.'

And so they worked on through the list of the dead, wringing Beeson's memory for all it was worth on the living. It was dark when they had finished.

'What do you think then, sir?'

'We've got somebody who knows poisons. That points to a surgeon. If it's somebody in F Troop, my money is on Crosse. He also holds sums of money, perhaps considerable sums. How he gains financially from the murders, I don't know – yet. We've got somebody who can travel easily around the country, apparently at will. That points to someone with private means or at least no regular employment. But the fact that this somebody can get close to Mrs Lawrenson, slip her poisoned tobacco. Can also get unnoticed into a lighthouse from a foreign ship. Can wander around a country estate and smear poison on bramble hedges. We might just have a—'

'A master of disguise,' Beeson broke in. 'I remember reading a story in the *Strand Magazine* about this man—'

'Professor Moriarty?'

'That's right!' Beeson was amazed. 'How did you know, sir? Have you read the story too?'

'No, I haven't,' sighed Lestrade. 'Just a lucky guess. I don't think we need to stoop to the mythology of the late Mr Holmes.'

'But he could be an actor, sir, couldn't he?'

'Why do you say that?' Lestrade thought he saw a spark of connection flashing round Beeson's head.

'One of the names on your list, sir. William Pennington.'

'What about him?'

'He's an actor now, sir. I have heard him described as Mr Gladstone's favourite tragedian.'

'*That* William Pennington.' Recognition dawned on Lestrade too. 'Now, that is interesting, Beastie. Good man.'

'There's something else, sir. You mentioned a while ago that as he died, Henry Hope said "C-r-o". Well, all right, that's Crosse, obviously. But he also said "Kill". Am I right?'

Lestrade nodded.

'What did you take that to mean, sir?'

'Well, that Crosse, if that's who it is, had something to do with these deaths.' Lestrade couldn't accept that Beeson had slowed up *that* much.

'Right. That's what I took it to mean too. But what if it doesn't? Your list has the name of Corporal John Kilvert. What if Hope was trying to say Kilvert?'

Lestrade sat in silence. Then he grabbed the list. 'He's still alive all right. The Mayor of Wednesbury.'

'Where, sir?'

'That's north of Pimlico, Beastie.'

'We've got three men, sir – Crosse, Kilvert and Pennington. Placing any bets?'

'There are shorter odds on me staying free until the morning. Beastie, I want you to do something for me. Send a telegram, will you? I'll write it down. I should have gone to the wedding of a friend of mine recently, but what with the way things are . . .'

'I'm sure he'll understand, sir. Oh, by the way. You'll laugh at this.'

There wasn't much Lestrade felt like laughing at.

'I've agreed to sit for Lady Butler, the artist who does the military paintings. She's doing one – "Waterloo Roll-call" – and heard I was an ex-soldier. She knows Pennington too.'

'Does she now?' Lestrade was more professionally interested than amused at the prospect of Beastie in theatrical uniform seated on a wooden horse.

'Oh, yes. He was the central figure in her Charge picture. Funny how people suddenly want to know all about the Light Brigade. But there's somebody killing us. Even those who are already dying in workhouses are targets.'

'When do you go for your sitting?'

Beastie consulted the letter. 'Next Thursday, at ten.'

'I'll come with you if I can,' and he slipped on his beard and moustache, glancing at Lady B's address.

'Where will you be in the meantime, sir? Er . . . in case anybody asks, like.'

Lestrade chuckled. 'Wednesbury. It's time I met Mayor Kilvert.'

'You'll meet him soon anyway, if you want to.'

Lestrade frowned.

'The one place you'll find us all together. I don't know why I didn't think of it before – the Annual Reunion Dinner.'

Lestrade dropped his ringlets.

'Beastie, you never cease to amaze me. When is this?'

'The twenty-fifth of October, sir, of course. Balaclava Day. That was a day to remember.'

They made tubes in Wednesbury. And boilers. And iron plates. Lestrade guessed they very probably wouldn't have a very large Jewish community so a rabbi, particularly one who habitually bumped into things, might attract too much attention. On the other hand, the papers now carried the information that Lestrade was posing as Inspector Athelney Jones, so he would be unwise to use that one. He decided instead to go one better. He arrived in Wednesbury as Chief Inspector Abberline, the man who made his name, about the only one who did, in the Ripper case of '88. Sergeant Charlo sent in to the Yard to say he was sick and caught the train with him. Lestrade was impressed by the man's loyalty and the chances he took.

But they had arrived nearly too late.

A manservant told them that the Kilvert family were at church, attending a funeral. Mrs Kilvert had died the previous week. Lestrade and Charlo joined the mourners by the graveside at St Bartholomew's Church. 'Earth to earth, ashes to ashes . . .' How often had Lestrade heard those words? He assessed the mourners. Solid, respectable, middle-class men and women. Dignitaries from the environs. All the brass of the Potteries. Staffordshire's finest. As soon as was decent, Lestrade buttonholed the man with the mayoral chain, John Ashley Kilvert, formerly 11th Hussars.

'Chief Inspector,' the mayor shook his hand. 'I'd no idea the Yard was to be called in.'

Lestrade did not know what he was talking about.

'Oh, yes,' he said.

'Have you any news, then?'

'No.' Lestrade tried to sound vague at moments like these.

'Shall we talk in my carriage? I've said my goodbyes to my wife already. She'll not miss me for a moment.' The mayor and the inspector strolled towards the black-draped brougham. 'You know, I still can't quite believe it. I can trace my family back to the Conqueror. Nine hundred years. And it all comes down to this in the end.'

Lestrade nodded in sympathy, desperately hoping for a clue from Kilvert.

'I always wanted to be Mayor of Nottingham, you know. I'll have to settle for Wednesbury now, I suppose. It's a shame Alfreda won't be here to share it with me.'

'Alfreda?'

'My wife, Chief Inspector. Surely the chief constable has filled you in?'

'Not exactly.' Here was Lestrade's opening.

'Oh, I see. Well, painful as this is, I suppose it has to be done.

It was a week ago yesterday. Alfreda had a restless night. She doesn't . . . didn't sleep too well. Back trouble, you see. Well, it was all those crates of spirits she used to carry. We ran a pub in the old days. I worked for a wine and spirit merchant. Anyway, that day she was up and helped Emily – our maid – with the breakfast. I was about to sit down and eat, when a deputation from the Tube Makers' Union arrived. I am a man of affairs, Chief Inspector – oh, that's municipal, not extra-marital, by the way. Anyway, by the time I returned, Alfreda was complaining of stomach pains. As the morning progressed, they grew worse. She died at lunch-time, as the clock struck twelve.' Kilvert steadied himself against a tree.

'She was poisoned.' Lestrade was after confirmation.

'Nicotine, the coroner said. Her end was very painful.'

And prolonged, thought Lestrade. He knew that nicotine usually worked very quickly.

'Her face swelled up . . .' Kilvert's voice drained away.

'Mr Kilvert, I have called at a dreadful time for you, but circumstances dictate that I must be quick. Am I right in assuming that you served in F Troop, Eleventh Hussars in the Crimea?'

'Well, yes, but—'

'You knew men like Joe Towers, Bill Bentley, Richard Brown, Jim Hodges, Bill Lamb . . .?'

'Yes, I did, but—'

'Did you know Henry Hope?'

'Very well. Inspector, what has all this to do with the death of my wife?'

'For the moment, sir, I will ask the questions, if you don't mind.' In his haste, Lestrade was descending to cliché.

'You say your wife and the maid prepared breakfast?'

'Yes, that's right.'

'What was it?'

'Er . . . coffee, eggs, scrambled, I think, on toast.'

'Is that your usual breakfast?'

'It varies . . .'

'Could the coroner say in what part of the breakfast the poison was contained?'

'No, he could not. You must have read the report?'

'Just double checking,' Lestrade lied. 'This maid, Emily, how long has she been with you?'

'Nearly twelve years.'

'Is she trustworthy?'

'Totally. At any rate, she doesn't go around poisoning her employer.'

'Have there been any strangers at your home recently, say, within the last month?'

'Good God, man, I don't know. As I told you, I am a man of affairs. A municipality of this size doesn't run itself, you know.'

'I'm sure not.'

'Chief Inspector, what has all this about the Eleventh to do with my wife's death?'

Lestrade scanned the cemetery. There was no sign of a uniform. And no one he would immediately place in a plain-clothed category either, except Charlo, trying to look like a mourner and keep abreast of his guv'nor's conversation.

'Your wife's death was an accident, Mr Kilvert. Or at least it was by the way.'

'By the way? How dare you, sir!'

'Don't misunderstand me. *You* were the murderer's target, not your wife. Were it not for the timely arrival of the Tube Makers' Union, they would be laying you to rest today as well.'

Kilvert looked astounded. 'Well, I know I have enemies on the Council, But this . . .'

'I don't think this is municipal murder, Mayor. You – or your wife rather, by accident – are but one link in a chain. A chain that runs right back to the Eleventh Hussars and the Crimea. The names I mentioned earlier – Towers, Bentley and the rest. All of them have died violently in the past months. What is the link? You were all in F Troop. You all rode in the Charge of the Light Brigade. Who wants to see you dead? Think!'

Lestrade relaxed his grip on Kilvert's velvet lapel. The mayor was frowning, racking his brain. Then his frown vanished. He straightened. His face turned the colour of the ashes to which the vicar had referred. His eyes assumed a faraway, sightless look. 'The golden dawn,' he whispered. Lestrade searched the sky. It was mid-afternoon. It was drizzling.

'What?'

The mayor turned away, like a man possessed.

'What did you say, Kilvert?' Lestrade now doubted his ears.

'Nothing,' the mayor answered, dumbly. 'Leave me, Chief Inspector Abberline, to mourn my wife.'

Charlo was at Lestrade's side. 'What is it, Inspector?'

'I don't know, Charlo. He said "the golden dawn". What does that mean to you?'

Charlo sought carefully for the right words. 'Nothing,' he said.

The bearskin did nothing for Ben Beeson. He sat on the arm of a sofa, head tilted to one side, hands resting on the rim of an aspidistra pot.

'I know you were a cavalryman,' Lady Butler was saying, 'but I do hope you don't mind posing as a guardsman for this one. Rabbi, do you like it?'

Lestrade had come as a rather unlikely friend of Beeson's and a connoisseur of art. And he was now heartily regretting the whole thing. He pressed his nose against the canvas, the thick glasses delineating only the vaguest of outlines.

'Delightful, delightful.' Lestrade was lisping, hoping Her Ladyship had not had much regular conversation with Jews. Especially art-loving rabbis.

'It's to be called "The Dawn of Waterloo",' Lady Butler glowed, smearing the contents of the yellow ochre the length of her smock. 'Or is this one "Steady the Drums and Fifes"?'

'Foggy, was it?' Lestrade continued, 'the morning of Waterloo?'

'Foggy?' Lady B's tone was a little too brittle to allow Lestrade to think he was still on the straight and narrow. 'Oh, I see. My dear man, no, these are but the preliminary sketches. I shan't use this canvas at all.'

'How long will this take, mum?' Beeson began to feel himself distinctly uncomfortable under the bearskin.

'About three years,' she said confidently. Beeson's eyes crossed and he resigned himself to a long wait.

'When did you begin to paint soldiers, my lady?' Lestrade

ingratiated, stopping short of actually rubbing his hands together.

'Oh, let me see.' She flicked charcoal effortlessly over the canvas. 'It must have been eighteen seventy-two. Yes, that was it. I was watching some manoeuvres. General Butler's influence, you see. I do so love the way soldiers move, don't you?'

Lestrade looked over his glasses at Beeson, a particularly unprepossessing sack of potatoes galloping to nowhere on a sofa.

'Quite,' he said.

'Since then I've never really looked back. Don't move!' she suddenly snapped at Beastie, who froze in terror, though his right buttock was totally numb.

'I particularly like your Balaclava paintings,' Lestrade was worming his way to the matter-in-hand.

'Ah, "After the Charge"? Yes, one of my favourites too.'

'Did Beastie – did Benjamin sit for that too?'

'No, no. But a number of the Light Brigade did. Mr Beeson, could you refrain from doing that? Lestrade turned too late to see what it was. 'Mr Pennington, the actor, for instance. He was a lovely sitter.'

'Anyone else?'

'Yes, Poppy Vansittart. I asked if he'd mind appearing as a private soldier rather than an officer. Dear old Poppy. He understood.'

'But he didn't ride the Charge, mum,' Beeson commented.

'Neither were you at Waterloo,' glared Lady Butler, rapidly losing patience with her latest sitter. Then, acidly, 'Were you?'

'Vansittart?' Lestrade brought her back to the subject other than Beastie.

'Yes, that was rather odd, actually.'

'Odd?' Lestrade asked.

'Yes. You see, I also used photographs of survivors of the Charge. When Poppy saw one of them, he tore it up. When I asked him why, he said, "He was never there. He never rode the Charge. You cannot use him. Let's just say it would have been better had he never existed!" Odd.'

'But our mutual friend has just said that Vansittart never rode the Charge either.'

'Quite. And really, it didn't matter that much. I wonder who he was, the man in the photograph he tore up?'

'He was a murderer, ma'am,' said Lestrade, without the accent. And left the room, leaving Beastie to sort that one out.

He opened the letter with Lestrade's paper knife and began to chuckle at the contents. Yes, it was all there.

My dear Inspector Lestrade,

It has been some weeks since I wrote to you concerning my brother. I have received no reply and must urge upon you again the need for immediate action. You cannot know how grave is the danger.

The tale was spelt out, as far as the writer knew it. It was signed 'Jacob'.

His mood darkened for a moment, then he tore up the letter, throwing the pieces carelessly into the nearest waste basket.

'Oh, I'm sorry, sir, I didn't expect to see you in here. Anything for me today?'

He chuckled. 'No, Dew. Nothing today.'

Mad houses

Conspiracies, thought Lestrade. Everywhere he went. Conspiracies. As Rabbi Izzlebit he wore more make-up than the witches on stage. The thunder roared through the crowded theatre, howling winds screamed round the proscenium. In the savage green-yellow of the limelights, the weird sisters cavorted and twirled. A drum, a drum. Henry Irving doth come. The audience broke the dramatic impact of the blasted heath by applauding rapturously at the princely appearance of the man. He stood centre-stage, tall and imposing, dragging his leg as he always did on stage, sweeping his cloak around him. He spoke slowly, deliberately, in that strange, weak voice of his. This was the last night of the run. He had delayed his American tour just to appear before his beloved admirers. It was they who packed the house to overflowing and one of them had been reluctant to give up his seat to the culture-hungry rabbi from York, who just had to watch Irving's last night. It had cost him three pounds, leaving a vast hole in Lestrade's pitifully limited funds.

It was not of course Irving that Lestrade had come to see at all. He wondered why people looked at him oddly when, to appear at one with the adulators, he had whistled and stamped and cried 'Author! Author!' Obviously he was overdoing it. That was not how rabbis behaved. He was more restrained during the rest of the play, largely because he was asleep. He remained awake, however, long enough to catch sight of his quarry – King Duncan. It wasn't only the Macbeths who were after him. Lestrade wanted a brief word too. The old king was suitably regal and suitably trusting as he all-unwittingly entered

Macbeth's castle. Was the man under the disguise, William Henry Pennington, as naïve as the character he portrayed? Time would tell.

Perhaps it was Lestrade's seventeen years on the Force. Perhaps it was a gut reaction born of instinct and that indefinable sixth sense which makes a great policeman. Perhaps it was the accidental prod in the vitals from the umbrella of the old lady beside him. Whatever it was, something woke him in time to witness Shakespeare's characterisation of murderers. He found his interest growing in spite of himself. They were professionals, paid killers. But they bungled it. Crime never pays, Lestrade reminded himself. Ah, if only that were true. This Shakespeare fellow knew nothing about the criminal classes. As for this witchcraft rubbish. . . .

Lestrade toyed with going backstage as soon as it was apparent that Duncan was dead. Another killing offstage. What were the public paying their money for? But he thought better of it.

Hats and gloves shot into the air and the atmosphere was electric with applause as Macduff rounded off the play. All this and a happy ending too, thought Lestrade. But he still preferred *Mother Goose*. The cast assembled before the velvet curtains in reverse order of importance. Pennington had solid applause, but the most deafening rapture was, of course, reserved for Irving. He stood in the limelight, where he always wanted to be, proud, lonely and self-centred. A ham of hams.

Backstage, the Lyceum was a maze of corridors, doors and fire escapes. A wonderland of tinselled costumes, wooden props and painted backdrops. Lestrade walked into or tripped over most of them in his hurried search for two things. First, a room in which to change his rabbi suit and second, the dressing room of William Pennington. The place was crawling with admirers, dashing hither and thither with autograph books. Stage-hands and theatre attendants were everywhere. Lestrade kept one hand firmly on his wallet, deep in the long pockets of his long coat. The other he clamped permanently on his right temple as the heat of the sulphur lamps and the hot air spouted by Irving had conspired to unhinge his false beard.

Intent as he was on all this, he did not notice the large woman with the huge, ostrich-feathered hat, although probably the man sitting behind her all night had. She and the rabbi collapsed in an undignified heap on the floor.

'Letitia, are you all right?'

Lestrade fumbled for his thick-lensed spectacles immediately, but was too late. 'Sholto!'

Well, the name sounds Jewish enough, Lestrade hoped. For the second time in a few months he was denying any knowledge of Mr Bandicoot.

'Oh come, Sholto. You can't wriggle out of it this time.'

After what seemed an eternity of Lestrade contorting his face and flapping his hands in incomprehensible gestures, Bandicoot lowered his voice. 'What are you doing here?' he hissed. 'And disguised as a Jehovah's Witness?'

'May I remind you,' Lestrade fumed through clenched teeth, 'that I am still under suspension. And, indeed, a wanted man.'

'Wanted?' Mr and Mrs Bandicoot chorused.

Lestrade flattened himself against a stack of halberds, which instantly crashed noisily to the floor, thereby attracting far more attention than the Bandicoots' simultaneous outcry.

'From where I'm standing,' hissed Lestrade, 'everybody in London seems to know I'm a wanted man. Where have you been, Bandicoot?'

'The south of France,' Bandicoot answered. 'On our honeymoon, Sholto,' and he pulled the former Mrs Lawrenson closer to him.

Lestrade felt suitably embarrassed. 'I'm sorry,' he said. 'Mrs Bandicoot, please forgive me.'

'There is nothing to forgive, Sholto. We understand. And we were sorry not to see you at the wedding.'

'Under the circumstances, ma'am, I felt it best to stay away. Can you imagine the scene? You and Harry poised before the altar and me being carried away by four burly coppers? It would have hardly made your day. Are you recovered, Harry?'

'That's rather indelicate, Sholto,' Bandicoot answered.

'From the cyanide, man!'

Letitia reached out and kissed Lestrade tenderly on the cheek, her lips smeared now with his running make-up.

'How can we help?' asked Bandicoot.

'You have the knack of turning up at theatres and circuses and such,' grinned Lestrade, remembering the New Year of 1892 at Hengler's. 'Don't tell me you've brought your trusty brace of pistols.'

''Fraid not, Sholto.' Bandicoot actually looked apologetic. 'We were breaking our honeymoon to see Henry before his American tour. Wasn't he marvellous?'

'Er . . .'

'Letitia's known him for years. Haven't you, Letitia?'

'We were going to see him now. That's when we . . . ran into you, so to speak,' the new Mrs Bandicoot added.

'I'm looking for Pennington.'

'Yes, he was good, wasn't he?' beamed Bandicoot.

'Somehow, Harry, I don't think the inspector wants to offer Mr Pennington his congratulations. They'll all be together, Sholto,' said Letitia. 'There are usually parties after a run. Come with us,' and she led the way.

'We could use her on the Force,' Lestrade told Bandicoot as Letitia unerringly found the right door. The actors were still in costume and the air was thick with the roar of the greasepaint and the smell of the crowd. A cigar looked incongruous protruding from the bloody lips of Banquo and the witches were busy downing liquid of a clear, sparkling consistency, far different from the gruel, thick and slab, they had been concocting all night.

'Lettie, darling,' Lady Macbeth hugged Mrs Bandicoot and when introduced to Harry hugged him as well. She declined to follow suit with the unsavoury-looking Jewish gentleman with them, particularly as his beard was peeling off at one side.

'Er . . . this is . . .' Letitia was lost for words.

'Rabbi Izzlebit.' Lestrade nodded and bobbed as he assumed rabbis did when they were introduced to people, but it didn't matter; he couldn't make himself heard above the noise, anyway.

'Lettie, darling.' A moustachioed man in evening suit hugged

Mrs Bandicoot too, and shook hands heartily with Harry. He was content to nod to the rabbi.

'May I introduce Bram Stoker?' Letitia said. 'Henry's manager and a very dear friend.'

'Lettie, darling.' Macbeth whirled cloak and arm in a magnificent theatrical gesture. He bowed low, kissed her hand and pulled her to him as though to break into a gallop.

'Mr Henry Irving, my husband, Harry.'

Irving stamped his feet, pirouetted once and took Bandicoot's hand between both of his. 'My dear boy. You are a lucky man. A lucky man.' His voice was as odd and camp offstage as it was on. 'Ah, if only I were fifteen years younger . . .'

'Twenty-five' corrected Stoker, sipping his champagne with the deadliness of a viper.

'My dear fellow.' Irving tripped across to Lestrade, ignoring his manager entirely. 'Where are you running?'

'I'm sorry . . .' Lestrade lisped, not following the Great Man at all.

'Don't apologise, dear boy. Rushed over here still in make-up to see me. Entirely understandable. Entirely. What did you think? Come now. Candidly. How marvellous was I?'

Lestrade stood there, momentarily lost for words.

'He is momentarily lost for words,' said Letitia. 'Henry, you are off to America tomorrow. We just had to see your last night. A triumph. An utter triumph.'

'Please, my dear. You know how I hate fuss. A simple "incredible" would have done. Not as good as *Becket* though?'

'Better,' said Stoker, without feeling, diving again into his champagne.

'Well, perhaps, perhaps.'

'Speech,' muttered Stoker, and the cry was taken up.

Irving passed a mirror on the way to a table and checked his appearance before mounting the rostrum.

'Friends . . .' He held up his hands in self adoration.

'. . . Romans, countrymen . . .' mumbled Stoker behind him.

'This is so unexpected.'

'Stoker blew bubbles in his glass.

'What I . . . what we have accomplished tonight is little short of . . .'

'Average,' said Stoker.

'. . . magnificent,' Irving went on. 'You heard them out there tonight. I . . . we never faltered. The Bard . . .'

'. . . must be turning in his grave,' said Stoker.

'. . . could not have wished for better.'

While the Lyceum's lion roared his prowess to the howls and delight of his second audience that night, Lestrade edged as close as he could to the late king.

'Mr Pennington?' he lisped.

Without taking his eyes off Irving, the old actor answered, 'If it's elocution lessons you want, I'm fully booked until the end of the year.'

'Not exactly.' Lestrade tried to stay in character.

Undeterred, Pennington soldiered on. 'Well if it's a repeat of my "Little Nell" may I remind you people, chosen though you may be, that I haven't been paid for the last time yet.'

Lestrade could see he'd have difficulty in removing Pennington from the crowd scene. Perhaps a threat of force? He pressed the rim of his spectacles, still in his pocket, into Pennington's regal robes, as close as he could to the small of his back.

'Can you feel that?'

'Yes,' said Pennington.

'Then I suggest you come with me now, quietly and without fuss into an ante-room. Or I'll use it.'

'Very well,' replied Pennington, unruffled. 'But I'd be intrigued to see in what way you would use a pair of spectacles.' And he opened a door behind them.

Suddenly, he paused. 'They're not loaded, are they?'

Both men were pushed into the room. They spun round to see Bram Stoker, pistol in hand, staring hard at Lestrade.

'I think we'd better let this gentleman do the jokes, William. Rabbis with false beards who don't know Shakespeare from their elbow must have a few good one-liners up their sleeves.'

The suave man with the soft Irish brogue was no fool. Gregson would have a field day with him. Obviously, he was Parnell's successor, intent on blowing up the Houses of Parliament and strangling the Queen, while eating his breakfast.

'All right.' Lestrade broke cover, snatching off the hat and wig.

'Hurts like hell, doesn't it?' Pennington sympathised as he tore off what was left of the facial hair.

'I am not Rabbi Izzlebit.'

'Lawks a mussy!' drawled Stoker, feigning shock and horror. He was still pointing the gun.

'I am Chief Inspector Abberline of Scotland Yard.'

'This is better than a play,' chortled Pennington.

'Is it usual for theatrical managers to carry guns, Mr Stoker?'

'Is it usual for chief inspectors to pass themselves off as rabbis, Mr Abberline?' and he holstered his weapon in his coat.

'Point taken. Believe me, I have my reasons. This is a delicate matter, Mr Stoker, and it is between Mr Pennington and myself.'

'Anything which concerns the Lyceum and its staff concerns me too, Chief Inspector. I'm staying.'

Lestrade shrugged and the three men sat down.

'Mr Pennington, how long have you been an actor?'

'It's kind of you to accord me that title, sir.' Pennington smiled. 'Let me see. I first appeared at the New Royalty in 'sixty-two. Good Lord, more than thirty years.'

'And before that?'

'Well, I was a soldier. The Eleventh Hussars. And before that—'

'And you rode in the celebrated Charge of the Light Brigade?'

'One of the proudest moments in my life. Mind you, I was not so brave that day. When my horse was killed under me, I thought, This is it, Penners old boy. You've bought it. It was George Loy Smith who pulled me through. He was a hard man, too hard, but he knew soldiering. A cooler man under fire I've never known. Why the interest in the Light Brigade, Chief Inspector?'

'Perhaps you've been fiddling your pension all these years, William,' said Stoker. The theatricals chuckled.

'Not all the Light Brigade,' said Lestrade, watching Pennington's every reaction carefully. 'Just the Eleventh Hussars. Just F Troop.'

'F Troop?' said Pennington. 'Why? Most of them must be dead.'

Was this a confession? Lestrade wondered.

'At least four of them have been murdered.'

Pennington and Stoker exchanged glances. 'By whom?' the actor asked.

'By you, Mr Pennington.' Lestrade pushed as far as he could.

Pennington was on his feet in an instant. 'You're mad, sir. I couldn't kill a man. I don't think I killed anybody in the Crimea. I certainly couldn't start now. What's my motive?'

'Calm down, William. I've a feeling the chief inspector is trying you out. Isn't that so, Mr Abberline?'

'Perhaps.' He handed Pennington a piece of paper. 'Here are the names of the dead men. Do you recognise any of them?'

Pennington did. What Lestrade had not divulged was that he had written down the wrong names, including Kilvert's. Again, he watched intently for a reaction, a flicker. There was nothing. Remember, he told himself; this man is an actor. And he was no judge of how good he was. But in the world of murder – and getting away with it – plausibility was everything.

'Well, well,' said Pennington. 'Old Ben Beeson dead. He was a nice fellow. . . . Wait, I thought you said F Troop.'

'That's right,' said Lestrade.

'If my memory serves me correctly, Beeson was in D Troop, at least, while I was with the Brigade.'

'I think the chief inspector is still trying you out,' commented Stoker.

'Come, Chief Inspector. No more games. These men were friends of mine. They shall be missed at the Dinner this year. How can I help you? You have my word as a private and a gentleman that I did not kill them.'

'I know that,' said Lestrade.

'Then why . . .?' Pennington began.

'I checked at the box office before the show . . . er . . . performance started. Being up there on stage before hundreds of people each night is quite an alibi, Mr Pennington. And I doubt if even you are actor enough to be in two places at once.'

'Well,' sighed Pennington. 'That's a relief!'

'The fact remains,' Lestrade went on, 'that somebody killed those men. If it wasn't you, I must find out who it was.'

Pennington was stumped.

'Does the phrase "golden dawn" mean anything to you?' He clutched at meaningless straws.

Pennington thought for a moment, then shrugged.

'I'm afraid not,' he said. A series of cheers from the adjoining room brought him back to the present. 'Chief Inspector, Henry is leaving for an American tour tomorrow, attempting to take some culture to those woefully callow people. I really must bid him bon voyage.'

'Of course,' Lestrade was no further forward.

'Chief Inspector. Might I have a word?' Stoker closed the door as Pennington left. The manager crossed the floor to the oil lamp. 'I pride myself on being an intelligent man,' he said. 'I have a Master of Arts degree from Trinity College, Dublin. I am Sometime Registrar of Petty Sessions at Dublin Castle. I could forge a soup tureen from my silver medals for History. And I write. Oh, nothing you've read, I don't suppose. *The Snakes' Pass*?'

Lestrade shook his head.

'No, I didn't think so. Well, we writers keep irons in the fire, Chief Inspector. I'm working on various things now. But there is one work, one work of a lifetime which every writer hopes to complete. I have that work in mind now.'

'An historical romance?' Lestrade was proud of that conclusion.

'Not exactly. Are you familiar with Styria?'

'I don't go to the theatre much, Mr Stoker,' Lestrade confessed.

'Styria isn't a play, Chief Inspector,' said Stoker patiently; 'it's a place. Transylvania? Central Europe? Well, I've been there. And I know strange and terrible things.'

Lestrade felt the hairs on the back of his neck crawl. If Stoker wrote as he spoke there would be no doubt of the best-selling qualities of his book.

'No doubt you found Shakespeare's witches tonight a little false. Funny even?'

'Well, I wouldn't have wanted to be the one to say so,' said Lestrade.

'When Shakespeare wrote that he wrote in deadly earnest.

Witches were real to him. The powers of darkness were real.'

'But wasn't that . . . some time ago?' Lestrade was hazy on these matters.

'Do you think, Mr Abberline, because we live in the age of the electric light and the horseless carriage – in the age of the train – that those powers are no more? Go to Styria, Chief Inspector. Ask them about Vlad Sepêc, the Impaler. I tell you, Chief Inspector, if we put Macbeth on in Budapest, the people would riot.'

Having seen Irving, I'm surprised they didn't here, thought Lestrade, though it may have been out of place to say so.

'Forgive me, Mr Stoker, but I don't see what this has to do with the murders of members of the Light Brigade.'

Stoker faced Lestrade over the oil lamp, his smooth features suddenly dark, haunted.

'You mentioned "golden dawn" earlier. Why was that?'

'It was a phrase I heard. From another ex-Hussar. Do you know it?'

Stoker hesitated. 'I know of it.'

'What is it?' Lestrade could not bear the silence.

'It is evil, Chief Inspector. Evil incarnate.'

'But . . .'

'Don't press me further.' Stoker's hand shot out. 'I don't know details, man. But this much I do know. If it's the golden dawn you're after, look to yourself.'

The Royal Hospital at Chelsea was one of those buildings with which Lestrade had grown up. Founded in Good King Charles' golden days, the long sweep of its red brick buildings was a familiar sight to all – the office clerks going about their daily business, the Bohemian artists wandering in varying degrees of inspiration up and down the King's Road. Lestrade entered its portals as Chief Inspector Abberline, praying that the real one was not known to the gatekeeper, or anyone else with whom he might come in contact that morning. On his way up the labyrinthine stairs, he passed a number of proud old soldiers, doddering around in their blue winter uniforms. The morning was crisp, with one of the first frosts after the long summer. Even indoors the standards hung stiff and starched, weighty with their battle honours on the old canvas.

The attendant hurried on into the bowels of the building, turning now left, now right. At an ominously padded door he stopped, tapped sharply three times. A grille high in the studded woodwork slid back with a grating sound reminiscent of the portals of Hell. Or at least, the Openshaw Workhouse, Manchester.

'Visitor for Dr Crosse.'

The door swung back and the next attendant took Lestrade into an ante-room. He was asked to wait. He was not alone. Three men sat at points around the room, all of them dressed in disreputable nightshirts. One stared ahead, unblinking. Another rocked backwards and forwards. A third was mumbling to himself.

'What are you here for?' the mumbler suddenly asked Lestrade.

'To see Dr Crosse,' he answered.

The man's eyes widened in terror. 'Him?' he gibbered. The rocker turned in his chair, attempting to climb the wall, sobbing quietly and burying his head in his arms. The starer stared on. He had not moved, not blinked.

'You see how they love me?' A voice brought Lestrade back to reality. In the doorway stood an elderly man in a white coat, for all his years still erect and fit-looking. He motioned Lestrade to enter his office, then quietly shut the door.

'John Burton St Croix Crosse,' he said, extending a hand. On the telephone you said you had to see me urgently.'

'That is correct, Doctor.' Lestrade sat down. 'When I heard you were medical officer of the Royal Military Asylum, I assumed that—'

'That I patched up abrasions and prescribed for gout? No, Chief Inspector, I deal with wounds of the mind. Look at this.'

Crosse dragged a large glass jar into the centre of his desk. Floating in its semi-opaque contents was a human brain.

'You know what this is?'

'I've seen a few in my time. Or what was left of them,' said Lestrade.

'This particular one is rather special. It belonged to the poisoner, Dr Neil Cream.'

Lestrade was interested. Why should Dr Crosse find a poisoner's brain interesting?

'I knew him,' said Lestrade

Crosse looked at him. 'Alas, poor Yorrick, eh?'

Lestrade didn't follow that.

'Then you will know better than I,' Crosse said, 'that this man was hanged in November last for the murder by strychnine of several prostitutes. Nux vomica, gelatine capsules and some bottles of strychnine were found at his home. Not very careful, was he? I look at this sometimes,' he said, indicating the brain, 'wondering what it is about the brain that makes a man a murderer. There is a theory, of course, that physical deformity deranges men. Oh, I know phrenology is old hat now, but to an old stager like me, it still has its appeal. You will know that some of the most murderous monsters in history have been deformed. Genghis Khan. Richard III. Cream of course was cross-eyed. His optician swore this was the cause of his crimes.'

'Interested in poisons, are you, Doctor?' Lestrade fished.

'No more than the next man.' Cross shrugged and slid the brain to one side. 'But I digress. What can I do for you?'

'You were once a surgeon with the Eleventh Hussars,' Lestrade asserted.

Crosse chuckled. 'In my dim and distant past,' he said. 'I was born in the year of Waterloo, Chief Inspector. And my memory goes back a long way. Don't tell me someone has stolen the regimental plate?'

'No, sir, someone is killing survivors of the regiment. Or of F Troop to be more exact. Joseph Towers, Bill Bentley, Richard Brown, Jim Hodges. And I have reason to believe that others may yet be targets. I have to work fast to stop this maniac – oh, begging your pardon, Doctor.'

'How did they die?' Crosse asked. 'They must all have been old men.'

'They were,' answered Lestrade; 'but not by natural causes. One was suffocated, the others poisoned.'

Crosse looked at the swimming brain. 'Ah, perhaps it's Cream reaching from the grave?'

'What do you know of aconite, Doctor?'

'Aconite,' Crosse repeated. 'Never heard of it.'

'But you are familiar with strychnine?'

'Of course. Is aconite a poison too?'

Lestrade sensed he could fence all day with this man. Old as he was, his mind was as sharp as a razor, honed no doubt in countless battles of wits with half-wits, whom Lestrade had learned over the years never to underestimate.

'I understand there is a fund for survivors of the Light Brigade,' Lestrade changed tack.

'Indeed there is. I have the honour to be in charge of it.'

'How much money are we talking about?'

'I don't believe I have to tell you that, Chief Inspector.'

'No, sir, you don't. But please believe me when I say it may be fundamental to my enquiries. That only with that information may I prevent more deaths.'

Crosse ruminated for a while, then crossed to a safe tucked in a corner. He pulled out a sheaf of papers and riffled through them.

'At the last count, two hundred and sixteen pounds, sixteen shillings and fourpence,' he said. Hardly a fortune, thought Lestrade. Another wall reared up as he realised financial gain as a motive fluttered out of the window. Surgeon Crosse's pension alone would be worth more than that. Still, he had better leave no stone unturned.

'And where does the money come from?' he asked.

'Oh, various sources. Bequests. Donations from various individuals, ex-officers, mostly. It doesn't go far, I'm afraid. Perhaps one day a philanthropist will come along and really provide for these men. I feel sorry for them. However,' he grew stern, 'there are people who are prepared to go to extraordinary lengths to be deemed eligible for a share.'

'Indeed?' said Lestrade, sniffing a suspect.

'Unprofessional though it is, I shall name names. Robert Davies, formerly sergeant, Eleventh Hussars, now honorary lieutenant-colonel, has had the bare-faced effrontery to ask for a share. I ask you, lieutenant-colonel! The man of course was promoted officer without purchase – no tone at all!'

'Do you remember a soldier in the Eleventh named Hope?'

'Why, yes I do. Epileptic. Interesting condition. Always falling asleep all over the place. Why?'

'He remembers you,' answered Lestrade.

'That's nice.'

'Have you heard the phrase "golden dawn"?' Lestrade tried another new tack.

Crosse looked levelly at Lestrade. 'Yes, Chief Inspector, I have.'

'What does it mean?' Lestrade sensed the electricity in the air.

'I'm not sure,' Crosse said. 'A former patient of mine was obsessed with it.'

'Go on,' said Lestrade.

'Come with me,' said Crosse and led the inspector out of the double windows into a quiet courtyard overhung with ivy and privet. The dew was still on the grass and as they walked beneath an archway, they emerged into a small graveyard. Crosse pointed out a grave, complete with gleaming marble headstone. It read 'In loving memory of Donald Crowley, Surgeon, 11th Hussars 1820–1893'.

'This was the patient to whom I was referring,' said Crosse.

'Did he serve in the Crimea?' asked Lestrade.

'Oh yes. There were five of us. And Gloag, the vet.'

'May I have the names of the others?' Lestrade whipped out his trusty notepad.

'Er . . . oh, God . . . Wilkin. Henry Wilkin.' Lestrade knew he was dead. 'Malcolm Ancell. He died at Kadiköy in 'fifty-five.'

Lestrade wrote the name anyway.

'Ormsby Miller. Funnily enough, I read about him only the other day. He's high sheriff for Galway now.'

Crosse tapped with his rattan cane on the headstone.

'And poor old Crowley here.'

'You said he was a patient of yours. . . .'

'Yes, on and off for nearly twenty years. More or less since I've been here.'

'Did he . . . er . . . live in?'

'Towards the end, yes. He was . . . not fit to be by himself.'

'And the golden dawn?'

'It was some sort of organisation, I think. He always spoke of it in awe, but never in detail. I don't hold with this hypnosis nonsense, Chief Inspector. My patients only tell me what they want to tell me.'

'An organisation,' mused Lestrade. He had sensed conspiracy all along. Every since he had been rattling across Norfolk with Bradstreet after the Bentley investigation. The pieces of the jigsaw were starting to fit.

'The odd thing about Crowley,' Crosse went on, 'was that he rode the Charge of the Light Brigade. So did Wilkin, mind. But *he* longed for action. Wrong temperament for a doctor, really. I never took Crowley for that type, but still. He was captured by the Russians. We thought he was dead. Then, oh, years later, he turned up in England. That would be about eighteen-seventy. He'd lost his memory. With care and the love of a good woman we nursed him back to health.'

'Why is he buried here?'

'This was the nearest he had to a home recently. His wife died some years ago.'

'We were speaking of Henry Hope earlier,' said Lestrade. 'He died last month. I was with him. He said two things I couldn't understand. "Kill" and "Cro . . ." I took "Kill" to mean John Kilvert, also of the Eleventh. And "Cro . . ." I took to be you, but what if I was wrong? What if Hope was referring to Crowley? And why should he want to kill him?'

Crosse's mood changed suddenly. 'Chief Inspector, I have given you all the help I can. As you saw earlier, I have patients to treat. Go through that door. It will take you to the street. Goodbye.'

'One more thing.' Lestrade stopped him. 'The names you mentioned, your fellow surgeons of the Eleventh. I recognised all those names. Except one. Why should someone have removed Crowley's name from the muster-roll?'

'I really couldn't say, Chief Inspector,' and he vanished through the archway.

Lestrade looked down at the grave. He crouched, sifting the marble chippings with his hand. For a while he ruminated on the transient nature of man. Then he opened the door and walked into the street.

Except that it wasn't the street. Instead, he found himself standing in a long dark corridor. After the sun in the courtyard, the darkness was total. He must have taken the wrong door. He turned, but the door was shut tight. He rattled the lock. It did not give. He heard something behind him. A rasping sigh. He was not alone. He turned to face the darkness, feeling the lock in the small of his back. As his eyes accustomed themselves to the dark, he made out figures, rising up from benches on both sides of the corridor. He heard the rattle and slither of chains.

'Who's there?' he called.

A mocking laugh answered him. Then another.

'Nobody here,' a hollow voice said. 'Nobody at all.' He felt hard steel jam into his throat and a powerful force spun him round and down. He was on his knees facing the door, a steel chain round his neck.

A ragged figure with mad, staring eyes appeared before him, giggling hysterically. In the darkness, Lestrade saw his predicament. There were five figures, perhaps six, with enough chain between them to armour all the ironclads in the Navy. The pressure on Lestrade's throat grew greater and in a moment of inspiration – or was it panic? – he fought his way upright and gasped out the opening words of a ditty which might have some effect on these lunatics.

'We're the soldiers of the Queen, my lads . . .'

And one by one, they took up the chorus. A mumble at first, but Lestrade stood to attention, his hands pinned to his sides, unable to reach for his trusty brass knuckles, singing for all he was worth. It wasn't exactly Marie Lloyd; after all, Lestrade's voice had never been trained and he did have iron links wrapped around his throat. The mumble rose to a crescendo and one by one the sad ex-soldiers, stirred by their memories, came to attention and the grip relaxed on his neck.

They were still singing and he was by no means sure how many verses there were to go before they became bored and returned to their previous amusement. As it was, he was already at the 'la, la, la' stage. So he bolted forward, the chain bruising his neck as he lunged and threw himself bodily at the door. It gave under his weight and he rolled into the sunshine. Behind him he was aware of a whip cracking and cries of 'Get back'. By the time he had knelt upright, the door was back in place and all trace of his would-be attackers was gone. Suddenly, he was aware of a pair of blue uniform trousers inches from his head, above a pair of large, black hobnailed boots. He didn't really have to look up to know he was in the presence of a constable of the Metropolitan Police. The voice confirmed it.

Balaclava revisited

They detained Lestrade for an hour or two at Bow Street where he gave his name as Chief Inspector Abberline. 'I'm sorry, sir,' the constable had said, as though it were quite permissible for chief inspectors of the Yard to be found, bruised and with a dislocated shoulder, on Chelsea pavements. 'I didn't recognise you.'

I'm not surprised, thought Lestrade; but thank God for the lack of observation of the copper on his beat. He had spent a further couple of hours being generally made to feel a lot less comfortable by a doctor and nurses at St Thomas's Hospital. The doctor, it is true, found Lestrade's injuries a trifle inconsistent with being run over by a dray, which was the injured man's story. But then Lestrade reasoned, he had to keep his stories to police and medical authorities the same or awkward questions might be asked. In any case, who would have believed him had he said he had narrowly escaped a beating in a dark corridor full of homicidal lunatics and had damaged himself in a bid to escape? No, the runaway dray it had to be.

'Good God, sir, you look terrible,' was Ben Beeson's comment as Lestrade walked stiffly over his portal. 'How's the other fella?'

'Chained to a wall in Chelsea,' Lestrade croaked, edging to a chair. 'How I got to Croydon, I shall never know.'

'What happened?'

And the whole story came out.

Beeson sat motionless, with his hands clasped around a mug of steaming tea. Lestrade's hands did likewise around his.

'So you've got him,' said Beeson. 'You've avenged Joe Towers.'

'Not yet,' said Lestrade. 'Surgeon Crosse is still at large. Anyway, I don't think it's quite as simple as that.'

'I don't follow you, sir.'

'Whatever the golden dawn is, Beastie, it's made up of more than one man. John Kilvert, Bram Stoker, John Crosse, they all spoke of it as being something evil. Something. Not someone. Actually, John Kilvert didn't talk about it at all, but he *was* a frightened man. The golden dawn isn't just Crowley. Besides, when Joe died, Crowley had been in his grave a week. I checked. What do you remember about him, this Crowley?'

'Not much. He joined the regiment late. We were already at Balaclava, I seem to remember. He kept to hisself, mostly. Then he rode the Charge and didn't answer the roll-call.'

'Crosse thought it odd that he should have ridden in the Charge at all. Why?'

'Well, medical men usually keep to the rear in action, sir, waiting to pick up the pieces afterwards, so to speak. But Surgeon Wilkin rode the Charge. No reason why Crowley shouldn't. Good God!'

'What's the matter?' asked Lestrade.

'Oh, it's nothing probably. Only I've just remembered it. You bringing up Crowley again after all these years. It was the morning of the Charge. I was sitting my horse with old John Buckton. He was in F Troop, come to think of it. Strange you didn't mention him on your list.'

'Somebody got to that list, Beastie. Crowley's name wasn't on it either.'

'Well, anyway, John was going to tell me somethin' about Crowley. Somethin' I'd never have believed, 'e said.'

'What?' Lestrade threatened to dislocate his shoulder all over again.

'I dunno.'

Lestrade flopped back in the chair.

'That's when the galloper came with the orders and we all had to shift.'

'This Buckton. Is he still alive?'

'I dunno. I last saw him at the Annual Dinner three years ago.'

'Will he be at this one, do you think?'

'It's possible. I haven't been since 'ninety.'

'You said you could get me in,' said Lestrade.

The ex-sergeant's face fell. 'I may have been a little hasty there, sir. The dinner is for members of the Light Brigade only.'

Lestrade fell silent. Painfully, he got to his feet and paced the kitchen. The sight of his arm in its sling in the kitchen mirror made him turn.

'Beastie, do you think I resemble, in the remotest sense, Joe Towers?'

Beeson got up and walked over to him. Lestrade saw the old copper's disbelieving face in the mirror.

'Not even in the remotest sense, sir,' he said.

'Come on, Beastie. In a bad light, old men's eyes. Most of them won't have seen him for years, will they?'

'No, I suppose not,' Beeson said. 'In fact, Joe hadn't been to a Dinner since the first, back in 'seventy-five. But you're . . .'

'Yes, I know. Thirty years younger! But with some of this,' he held up a greasy stick, 'I might just get away with it.'

'What's that, sir?'

'A spot of five and nine, Beastie. Theatrical make-up. I used it as Rabbi Izzlebit. And when I was at the Lyceum recently, I liberated a little more. A man never knows when a little discreet make-up is going to come in handy.'

Beeson took the inspector's word for it.

'What's the date?' Lestrade asked.

'Er . . . the twenty-third, I think.'

'That gives us two days before the dinner.'

'That's right, sir. It's the day after tomorrow.'

'Right, Beastie, I've got to get there. To get in amongst your old mess mates of the Light Brigade. To talk to John Buckton, if he's there. The answer's there somewhere, damn it. Mind if I get my head down until then, for old times' sake?'

'Lord love you, sir. You only got into all this on my account. I owe you that at least.'

Lestrade settled into the chair again, nursing his aching arm.

'Beastie, have a butcher's out of that window, will you? I've had the strangest feeling since I left the Lyceum that I've been followed.'

'Perhaps they want their make-up back,' grunted the ex-copper, flicking aside the nets. 'Wait a minute.' Lestrade struggled upright. 'There is somebody there. Youngish bloke, dark hair, wearing a grey overcoat. . . .'

By the time Lestrade got to the window the figure had vanished.

'Shall I go after him, sir?'

'No, Beastie. Let him go. Whoever it was, I daresay we'll see him again.'

'You're going to the dinner, sir?' Charlo's consumptive croak was worse than ever. 'Is that wise?'

'Good God, man.' Lestrade was past all that. 'There comes a time when wisdom follows other things. Like survival. There's a maniac trying to kill what's left of F Troop, Sergeant.'

'And he's trying to kill you, sir. The breakfast at the Grand? The Chelsea incident? I've got to admit, sir. I wish you'd give it up.'

'But we're so close, Hector. After all these months, we're nearly there. Would you have me stop now?'

Charlo leaned back in his chair. 'I can't help any more, Inspector. My doctor says I must rest. Have a long break. I've seen Frost. He's given me a month's leave.' He extended a hand.

Lestrade rose painfully and took it.

'Hector,' he said. 'You've risked a lot for me. I want you to know – whatever happens – I appreciate it.'

October 25th, a Wednesday, dawned hard and cold.

'What were you doing thirty-nine years ago this morning, Beastie?' Lestrade asked.

Beeson fell silent for a moment, doing some mental arithmetic. Only his frown, his silently moving lips and his wildly twitching fingers bore witness to the exertion it was causing.

He smiled at the end of his calculations. 'Shivering,' he said. 'We'd stood to since five o'clock. Saddled and waiting. My fingers were so numb I could barely work the leather. I remember we had no breakfast. Some of the officers had boiled eggs. We didn't even get our rum ration that day. Wait a minute,' and he dashed into another room. Back he came with an old uniform of the 11th Hussars, the colours still bright, the yellow cord still intact on the jacket and the brass buttons shining.

'I gave mine up when I transferred to the lancers,' he said. 'This was Joe's. I don't think he'd mind if you wore it tonight. Not if it helps get his killer, anyhow.'

'Thanks, Ben.' Lestrade smiled.

'Chances are you'll get into it. Oh, and this,' and he pulled out a small box. 'Joe always kept it polished. As I have kept mine,' and he flicked the lid to show a silver medal with a pale blue ribbon and on it the clasps for Sebastopol, Inkerman and Balaclava.

So Lestrade began another subterfuge. In the past weeks he had been Athelney Jones, Chief Inspector Abberline, the Rabbi Izzlebit. He was fast forgetting his real name. And now he was Joseph Towers, deceased, former private, 11th Prince Albert's Own Hussars.

The two men walked slowly into St James's Restaurant a little after seven o'clock. Beeson looked as smart as his police pension would allow in formal grey suit and bowler hat, his Crimean medal sported proudly on his lapel. Lestrade was wearing the braided jacket and crimson overalls of Joe Towers. They were just a *little* snug. His hair, beneath the crimson forage cap, had been clipped short on top and greyed with powder and greasepaint. Lestrade had etched in wrinkles and lines where he could, ignoring Beeson's constant clicks of the tongue and shakings of the head. He would have to do.

The foyer was already full of old men getting plastered. What was still a sacred trust to many of them was also an excuse for a knees-up, although it was very debatable how far up any of these knees would come. Lestrade counted twenty-five, including Beeson. He was one of five in uniform, although he couldn't help noticing that the others had been let out considerably here and there to accommodate advancing years and advancing girths. And patched here and there with the passage of time. Only medals and eyes were bright. And hearts were great.

He was relieved there was nobody else in the 11th uniform. If his limited knowledge served him correctly, one was from the 17th Lancers, two more from the 4th Light Dragoons as they then were and one from the 8th Hussars. It suddenly dawned on him, however, that had any of his co-banqueteers been in his 'old' regimentals Lestrade would have been able to avoid them so as to avert any awkward questions about his miraculous change in appearance. As it was, any one of the bowler- or top-hatted gentlemen might suddenly say 'Who the hell are you?'

'Who the hell are you?' The bombshell burst behind him. He opened his mouth to attempt an answer.

'Ben Beeson, Eleventh Hussars,' his companion answered.

'Of course,' beamed the other man. 'I didn't recognise you. You've put on some weight. Job Allwood, Thirteenth Lights.'

'How are you?' Beeson returned the handshake. 'Er . . . you remember Joe Towers?'

'Yes, of course,' beamed Allwood. 'Good to see you again, Joe. My God, can you still get into your old uniform? The years have been kind.'

Let's hope they go on being so, thought Lestrade.

'Well, well.' Beeson moved on like a shield before the doubly vulnerable Lestrade. 'Jim Glanister. How are you Jim?'

'Not bad,' slurped the other, the left corner of his lip dragging to reveal a row of brown, uneven teeth. 'I can't complain.'

'Remember Joe Towers, F Troop?'

'Oh, yes.' Glanister was having serious salivary problems as he shook Lestrade's hand. 'That's funny, I remembered you being taller.'

'I haven't been well,' ventured Lestrade.

'You don't look well, either,' another man chipped in.

Lestrade turned to face John Kilvert, socially superior as always in his astrakhan collar. Kilvert's smile vanished.

'Haven't we met recently . . .?' he said. Lestrade glanced at Beeson for support. None was forthcoming.

'Not since the Crimea,' said Lestrade, hoping he had said the right thing.

'Oh,' was Kilvert's limp and dissatisfied rejoinder. And the gong sounded to summon them to dinner. It was a fine spread. Roast goose with all the trimmings. Unfortunately, Lestrade found himself next to Glanister and spent most of the meal watching items of food miss the old man's mouth altogether, slithering down his left arm.

'Pistol ball at point-blank range,' Beeson whispered in Lestrade's other ear, as though to explain Glanister's problems.

'Time heals all wounds,' Glanister said at some point during the conversation. Not very well, thought Lestrade, flicking cream off his sleeve.

'Gentlemen, pray silence for the regimental tunes,' a major-domo barked from a corner. The good-natured banter stopped as one by one the regiments' marches played. As the band struck up, knots of men stood here and there at the sound of their own regiment's calls. Beeson tugged Lestrade to his feet at the commencement of 'Coburg', the slow march of the 11th. Lestrade hoped his delayed reaction was explained by his age and his recent fall.

Across the room from them, away from the 11th men, a figure stood alone while Coburg played. He had arrived late and was not in time to take his place alongside his old messmates.

'John Buckton,' hissed Beeson from the corner of his mouth, nodding in his direction. Something fell from Glanister's mouth too, but Lestrade didn't care to notice what.

When the Tunes of Glory were done and the handkerchieves put away for another year, the major-domo rose again.

'Gentlemen, pray silence for His Excellency the Quartermaster-General, Sir Evelyn Wood, VC, GCB.'

'And bar!' shouted Sir Evelyn, one of the halest men there, though as old as any of them. 'Which way is it?' The veterans broke into cheers and applause. 'Gentlemen, I will not keep you long. I am here tonight as your guest of honour. Some of you may think me a fraud.' Cries of 'No,' 'Shame,' and 'Resign.'

Wood held up his hand. 'But I am here for two reasons. I had the distinction many years ago of sharing quarters in the Sepoy Mutiny with a fine and gallant gentleman, now, alas, deceased, Colonel Morris of the Seventeenth Lancers.' Cheers from the men of the 17th. 'And I am proud to say that I was greatly honoured to serve with him and some of you in that fine regiment. Shortly after the Crimea, I joined the Thirteenth Light Dragoons' – the veterans of that regiment whistled and stamped – 'and no more loyal and impressive body of men could be found anywhere.' Applause.

Get on with it, thought Lestrade. If we are going to have Sir Evelyn's life story, I'll never get across to Buckton.

'Some thirty-nine years ago tonight, gentlemen, I was a midshipman in the Royal Navy. And on my ship I heard of what was described as "a short, sharp, cavalry action".' Guffaws and poundings on the table. Beeson was working things out on his fingers again. 'I think in all my years of service I have never heard of an engagement described with such woeful inadequacy.' More poundings. 'Gentlemen, I can only misquote the late Poet Laureate, Lord Alfred Tennyson, and say to you, men of the Light Brigade, "When can your glory fade?"'

The rapturous applause from so small a group of men promised to bring the chandeliers down. Even Lestrade found himself joining in in full measure, physically painful though it was to him. Toasts to Her Majesty, to Sir Evelyn, to the commanders of the various regiments at Balaclava, all now dead, followed.

Then the major-domo announced 'Coffee and brandy, gentlemen, by courtesy of Sir Evelyn Wood.' Poundings on the tables greeted this not altogether unexpected privilege. Cigars appeared from leather cases. Kilvert, not for the first time that evening, studied Lestrade closely through wreaths of smoke. Lestrade himself was about to make a move to contact Buckton, when there was a resounding crash in the passageway leading to the banqueting room. A white-coated waiter burst in, rushing in Buckton's direction. 'Don't drink the coffee!' he screamed as the man had the cup poised at his lips. Even as he reached Buckton, a shot rang out and a scarlet gash appeared in the centre of the waiter's back. In the seconds of panic that followed, a figure stood in the shadows, aiming his pistol first at Buckton, who ducked under the table, then at the knot of 11th men around Lestrade. The first bullet whistled past Beeson's head. A second shattered the coffee cup between Lestrade and Glanister. The latter crumpled, though unhit, clutching his jaw and moaning, 'Not again!'

Lestrade wasn't waiting for the next shot. Needs must when the devil drives and he stood up, hurling over the table. He and Beeson clambered over it as the others crouched, bewildered and confused, in the smoke.

'Our friend isn't much of a shot, thank God,' said Lestrade. He reached the fallen waiter and turned him over. 'Good God,' he said, recognising under the slicked-down hair the mournful, haunted face of the Bounder, with whom he had absconded from Openshaw Workhouse, an eternity ago. 'He's still alive, Beeson. Look after him.'

'I'm coming with you, sir.' All pretence at his being Joe Towers had gone.

'No, no. This one's mine,' and Lestrade dashed for the door. 'Sir Evelyn, I wonder if I might use your sword for a moment?'

The general, who had not moved from his seat during all the shooting now stood up and drew the ivory-hilted weapon from its scabbard. 'My dear fellow, be my guest,' and called after him, 'Remember the "Rear Protect", private,' as Lestrade disappeared down the darkened corridor.

'Was it the Russians?' asked Glanister, emerging from the tablecloth. Someone patted him calmingly on the head.

Lestrade dashed, as fast as his bruises would permit, past the milling waiters and servants, through the kitchen swarming with hysterical cooks.

'That way,' somebody shouted at him, pointing to the open back door.

'Who was it?' he yelled.

'One of the waiters,' came the reply. You can't get decent staff these days, thought Lestrade. But that was what he wanted to know. He had not seen the figure who fired the shots at all closely. Now he knew his target wore a white jacket and shouldn't be difficult to see in the dark. He edged into the yard. Empty, save for a couple of dogs tethered and barking. Behind him, the noise and lights died away. He was aware of men coming out of the doors and windows being opened overhead. But no one followed him.

He took stock, as he moved, of his situation. He was carrying a general officer's mameluke sabre. A beautiful, ornate weapon, but it gave no protection for the hand. In a fight, he would have reach, but his adversary, whoever he was, had a gun. All right, he was no great shot, but he could get luckier. And Lestrade couldn't move as he usually could. He turned into an alleyway. Ahead, a brick wall, the intangible counterpart of which had risen before him so often in this case. He stood still, panting with the effort of having run this far. No other sound, except somewhere a distant train whistle and the snort of a hackney horse.

He slithered round the corner into a second yard. It had been raining and the cobbles glistened wet in the green gaslight. A white jacket lay at his feet. The would-be murderer's disguise had gone, but it didn't matter. Lestrade knew where to find his man, if he had left the yard. He advanced slowly, sword arm extended. To each side were piles of timber and sacking. Good hiding places for a desperate man. His lips were dry. He licked them, tugging open the Hussar jacket for a bit more air, a bit more freedom of movement. His breath was visible on the air before him. And then he heard it. A tapping on the cobbles. Footsteps. He threw himself against the wall, trying to melt into the shadows.

A thick-set man in a Donegal and bowler stood squarely in the light from the gaslamp. He had a revolver gripped firmly in his right hand, raised at shoulder height.

'I know you're there, Lestrade,' the killer spoke. 'Come out, come out, wherever you are.'

Silence.

'I'm not a patient man.'

Lestrade lurched forward from the wall, some yards away from the man with the gun.

'Hello, Gregson,' he said.

The Head of the Special Irish Branch brought his pistol hand down on his left wrist to steady the gun for the recoil.

'So, it was you all along?' said Lestrade.

'Me? You mean that bungled shooting tonight? You're upsetting me, Sholto. You know I wouldn't miss.'

'The murders, then. The poisonings.'

'My God, you really haven't a clue, have you? I took you for a better policeman than that.'

He clicked back the hammer. Once. Twice.

'I tried to make it easy for you. That trumped-up charge of mine about attacking the Kaiser. But you went on, didn't you? Worrying it. Teasing it. You wouldn't leave it alone. Well, you've only yourself to blame, Lestrade. For what follows. Only yourself to blame.'

For a long second, Lestrade stood there, expecting Bandicoot's cased pistols to blast out or the Abo's silent arrows to hiss through the air. In the event, all he heard was the roar of Gregson's revolver. Too far away to reach his man, he spun round, attempting God Knows What. Perhaps just to be spared the bullet in his face. Perhaps it mattered how you died. As he turned, the sword came up behind his right shoulder, roughly in the position of 'Rear Protect' and the bullet clanged off the blade and ricochetted across the cobbles.

Lestrade continued his turn as Gregson recocked the weapon, cursing his luck, and threw the general's sword for all he was worth. The tip sliced deep into Gregson's stomach and the second shot went wide. In disbelief, Tobias Gregson staggered backwards, the gun gone from his grasp, Wood's blade gleaming from his stomach in the lamplight, blood trickling over his fingers. He looked uncomprehendingly at Lestrade, reached out as if to drag him to Hell with him and pitched forward, driving the blade right through his body, so that the crimson tip protruded steaming through the folds of his Donegal. Lestrade eased himself down on one knee, and checked his pulse. Weakening. Gone. Police whistles were sounding from nowhere. He kicked Gregson's body over and wrenched out the sword, wiping the blade clean on his coat. Then he stumbled back to the restaurant.

*

Beeson was cradling the fallen waiter in his arms. As Lestrade arrived, he looked up and shook his head. Lestrade took the Bounder's face in his hands. 'Can you hear me?' he asked.

The Bounder opened his eyes and flickered into liveliness. 'Did you . . . get him?'

'Who?' asked Lestrade.

'Oliver.'

'No, I got Tobias Gregson.' Beeson's eyes nearly popped out of his head. Had Lestrade gone mad?

'Oliver . . . Oliver's the one you want. You must get him,' and he began to cough up blood.

'I will. I think I know where he is. Listen, you haven't got long.' There was no time for niceties. 'Who are you?'

'Jacob Crowley,' the Bounder/waiter answered. 'I wrote to you. Twice. Three times. I can't remember. Why didn't you answer my letters or at least *do* something?'

'I received no letters. Beastie, get these men away from here.' Lestrade waved an arm in the direction of the stunned bystanders.

'Come along now.' Beeson the old copper was in charge again. 'There's nothin' to see. Move along, now. Move along.'

'And Donald Crowley . . .?' Lestrade turned to the Bounder again.

'My father. Oliver is my brother. They're both mad, Inspector. Quite mad,' and he coughed again.

'Beeson, water,' snapped Lestrade.

The Bounder waved it aside. 'I've got to tell you. Got to explain,' he mumbled.

'Why the murders?' Lestrade tried to simplify things for the dying man. 'The men of F Troop. Why?'

'My father joined a religious sect called the Order of the Golden Dawn when he was a . . . young man.' His speech was slurring now. Lestrade knew he would lose him soon. 'They are Satanists, Inspector. They worship the Devil,' and the pain took him again. He writhed, then lay still. Lestrade mopped his sweating forehead until he recovered. 'The night before Balaclava, F Troop were on patrol. A few of them got separated from the rest and in the hills above Kadiköy they found my father carrying out his rites.'

'Rites?' Lestrade checked he had not misheard.

'Sacrifice, Inspector. Human sacrifice. My father was a neophyte then. He . . . had to attain a higher level within the Order. The only way was to . . . kill and devour a human being.'

Lestrade sat upright. In all his seventeen years on the Force he had heard of nothing like that.

'He was . . . in the act of eating a Turkish boy when some of F Troop found him. He did his best to get himself killed. The . . . next day . . . he rode the Charge . . . expecting a bullet or a cannon ball to end it all. He reached the guns. He was taken prisoner by the Russians. . . . His life for the next sixteen years is a closed book to me. What he did in Russia, how he lived, I cannot imagine. But . . . the Golden Dawn is an international sect, Inspector. The Russian Golden Dawn may have found him, rescued him from the threat of suicide.'

'So, that's why he rode the Charge,' Lestrade said.

The Bounder nodded. 'When he came back to England, and I never knew why he came back, he feigned . . . loss of memory. But my brother Oliver was brought up in the foul traditions of the Golden Dawn. And he is as mad as Father.'

'Go on, if you can,' said Lestrade.

It was becoming increasingly difficult. 'Who can understand a madman?' the Bounder asked. 'Father had remembered the names and faces of those men who had seen him that dreadful night before Balaclava. Perhaps he knew he was dying. Perhaps the Golden Dawn demanded it. Anyway, he killed the first one. William Lamb.'

'Lamb?' Lestrade broke in. 'But he was killed by an animal. A Tasmanian wolf.'

The Bounder managed a chuckle. 'Yes, I read the newspaper reports at the time,' he said. 'I'm sorry, Inspector. That poor dumb beast may have killed sheep, but it did not kill a man. Father was carrying out his murder in the old ritualistic way.'

'He was trying to eat Lamb?' Lestrade asked, incredulous.

The Bounder nodded. 'And then he died. Merciful heaven released him.'

Lestrade thought quickly. The hairs from the thylacine which he found on the body must have got there *after* Lamb died. The smell of blood would certainly have attracted it.

'And the poisonings?'

'Oliver. He too trained as a doctor. For some years he served with the Army Medical Corps. He knew a great deal about poisons . . . .'

'And had access to them,' Lestrade added.

The Bounder coughed his agreement.

'And when we met at Openshaw?' prompted Lestrade.

'I was trying to stop him. All along, I've been . . . one step behind Oliver, one step ahead of you. He was the medical officer who was the locum before you arrived. He used the name . . . Corfield, Inspector. A pun. A taunting, arrogant pun. The Latin for the crow family is *corvus*. And another name for ley is field. Corfield and Crowley were one and the same. He gave the poisoned tobacco to Mrs Lawrenson.'

'And it's you who has been following me since the Lyceum?'

'And before. I should . . . have confided in you earlier, Inspector, but . . . I was trying to save Oliver from himself. From his insane desire to carry out Father's wishes; and all the time I thought you had received my letters telling you all this.' He tensed, and tremors shook his whole body. 'Lestrade,' he clutched convulsively at the policeman's sleeve, 'stop him. And look after cousin Aleister. I'm afraid he's going the same way.'

'I will, and we'll watch out for cousin Aleister.'

And the Bounder died in Lestrade's arms.

'Beastie.' Lestrade folded the man's arms across his chest and closed his lids. 'The police will be here any minute. Inspector Gregson's body is a few yards from here. Tell them what you know. And tell them that I shall be calling in to the Yard as soon as I can. General, thank you for your sword.'

And he handed it back.

'Glad it was of service, Private . . . er . . . Inspector,' said Wood.

'Sir,' Beeson joined Lestrade, 'I wish you'd let me come with you.'

'No, Beastie. There's only room for one in that corridor.'

'I thought you might say that, sir, so,' and he produced an obsolete pistol, Lancer pattern, 1842. 'This belonged to George Loy Smith,' he said. 'The old bastard was hard enough on F Troop while he was alive. Let him strike a blow for them now he's dead.'

Lestrade took the weapon.

'And remember,' said Beeson, 'that's cap and ball. You've got one shot in the breech already. Miss with that and you're a dead man.'

'This is a devil of a time to call, Bradstreet.' Nimrod Frost was less than chipper. 'God, man, it's the early hours.' He looked like Wee Willie Winkie, well, Willie Winkie anyway, standing in his hall in nightshirt and cap, holding aloft a candle. 'Go to bed, Richards. It's only one of my officers with a bad sense of timing. You're out of breath, man,' he rounded on Bradstreet, 'and you know I don't like calls at home at any time. Go to bed, Wilhelmina,' he roared to the apparition on the stairs. 'There's nothing wrong.' He ushered Bradstreet into the study. 'Or is there?'

'It's Inspector Gregson, sir. He's dead.'

'Good God.' Frost sat down heavily on the chesterfield.

'But that's not the worse of it. Lestrade killed him.'

'Lestrade?' Frost was on his feet again.

'I knew the man was suspended from duty, sir, but frankly . . .'

'Yes?'

'Well, I worked with him, sir. Frankly, I thought Inspector Gregson was overhasty. . . . It's not my place to say, sir.'

Frost whirled round the furniture, brain and fingers fidgeting wildly. He stopped before Bradstreet's tie-knot.

'What's your view of conspiracies, Bradstreet?'

'Life is one big conspiracy in the Special Branch, sir.'

'Yes.' Frost scrutinised him closely. 'Yes, I suppose it is. You were Gregson's right-hand man, weren't you?'

'I worked with him, sir, yes.' Bradstreet was beginning to smell a rat. It was not every day that inspectors of the Yard tried to kill each other.

'Well, get back to the scene of the crime, Bradstreet. I'm

going to the Yard. I'll want a full report tomorrow. Er . . . later this morning.'

Bradstreet departed. Frost saw him to the door and summoned a figure from the shadows.

'Follow him, Constable. I want to know exactly where he goes.'

Lestrade took a hansom in the street, dodging the coppers running to the scene of Gregson's death and swarming into St James's Restaurant. He'd given the cabbie strict instructions and with cries of 'I'll lose me licence for sure,' he hurtled through the makeshift cordon of policemen who, as Lestrade knew they would, broke at the last minute to avoid impact.

The Royal Hospital was in darkness and silent. The inmates were in their beds now. Except one. Lestrade crossed the frontage, past the Chilianwalla Memorial, past the silent cannon, mouths gaping to the night sky. His hand rested on the pistol butt, jutting awkwardly from his barrelsash. The front door was locked. Never mind, always worth a try. He circled the main block, trying first one door, then another. At last one gave under his weight and he was inside. A faint light flickered on the wall at the far side of a large hall. He recognised this. He had been taken this way on his last visit. For a man in cavalry boots, he moved like a cat. But when he began to count his lives, he decided to leave that analogy alone.

Up the twisting staircase, past the dormitories of snoring soldiers. The sky, blue against the blackness of the window-frames, lit his movements. Now and then the moon scudded into view, to vanish again in her shyness. Perhaps there were lovers out there somewhere, arm in arm and heart in heart, Lestrade thought. Then, reaching for the studded door, he remembered, and dashed back to the window. It wasn't a *full* moon, was it?

The padded door opened noiselessly. There was no one at this time of night to work the grille. Across another moonlit hall, below the silent standards. Past Crosse's door.

Lestrade stopped. There was a light in his office. Faint. An oil lamp, he guessed, trying to remember whether there was one on the desk or not. He cocked the pistol. Well, Sergeant-Major Loy Smith, let's hope you kept your gun in good order. And let's hope Beastie has since. And Lestrade crashed through the door, flinging it wide on its hinges. Crosse leapt upright behind the desk, rattan cane poised in his hand.

'Put it down, Doctor.' Lestrade's voice was firm, the pistol aimed at the old man's head. 'Or I'll kill you where you stand.'

'Abberline.' Crosse threw the cane onto the desk. 'I hoped it might be you.'

'Not Abberline, Doctor. Lestrade. Inspector Sholto Lestrade.' He tugged off the forage cap. He had all but forgotten it was still on his head.

'I . . . don't understand,' said Crosse.

'Never mind that. Where is he?'

'Who?'

'Doctor, I was nearly beaten to death by your maniacs, almost given poisoned coffee to drink, and shot at, all in the space of three days. I am not at my best at the moment. Now, once again and for the last time, where is Oliver Crowley?'

'Upstairs. Second door on the left. Lestrade, he's armed. . . .'

'And dangerous. Yes, I know that, Doctor.'

'Lestrade.' Crosse crumpled into his chair. 'Let me explain. I owe you that much at least. Don't worry, he's not going anywhere. He's waiting for you. Up there.'

'Quick then, man.'

'I panicked the other day. I have been working in this living hell for twenty years, Inspector. Twenty years of trying to give men back their sanity while somehow hanging onto mine. In that time, in all that lonely time, I made one mistake. I let a man escape. A dangerous man. Oliver Crowley. He was my patient too, like his father. I didn't tell you that. As a boy he seemed normal; oh, a little quiet, perhaps, a little solitary; not like Jacob, the younger brother. Oliver was born shortly after Donald had sailed for the Crimea. He wanted to go in for medicine and to join the army, just like his father. Well, why not? Perfectly laudable profession. But he began to take after his father in other ways. He joined the Golden Dawn – and as God is my judge I know no more about that. He became moody, unpredictable. The same curse that fell on his father also fell on him. I tried to persuade his mother, while she was alive, to talk him into coming here, as an in-patient. He wouldn't do that, but he did visit his father now and again, sometimes staying for days at a time. Occasionally, he would talk to me. It was working; we were getting somewhere. And then . . .'

'Then?'

'His father died. He became inconsolable. Irrational. He had to be admitted as an in-patient after all. But he said he had things to do. His father's work, he said. One night, he overpowered his orderly and fled.'

'And you did nothing?'

'If you mean did I report it? No. I paid the orderly to keep his mouth shut. Crowley had a private room. Few people saw him anyway. It was easy.'

'And the killings? Did you know about them?'

'No.' Crosse buried his head in his hands. 'God in heaven, no. But I couldn't find him. He had vanished without trace. I knew Jacob was looking, but it seemed hopeless. When you came, three days ago, pressing me about the Golden Dawn, I knew it was all over. Unless . . . unless I could silence you somehow. I didn't mean those inmates to kill you. Just rough you up a little. Frighten you. . . .' A pause. 'What happens now?'

'Now I'm going upstairs. Whether I come down or not remains to be seen. Either way, Doctor, you can reckon on a well-earned retirement. Where you spend it depends on me, doesn't it?'

Crosse slumped head down on the desk, a broken man, as Lestrade turned for the stairs. The second door, Crosse had said, on the left. Lestrade steadied the pistol in his hand. He had no idea what lay behind that door, but he knew that if the room was in darkness, he would present a perfect target silhouetted against the faint light in the hallway. He could of course wait for daylight, but by that time Crowley could be down the drainpipe and away.

He dithered for an instant, then threw his less painful shoulder at the door. It swung open, crashed back, the noise simultaneous with two pistol shots. Plaster rained down on his head. The room was in darkness as he kicked the door shut again. Crowley's eyes were more acclimatised to the total blackness than his, but unless the man were totally blind, the angle of the shots which had hit the plaster meant he was on the floor. That was where Lestrade was too, face down behind a sofa. He still held the horse pistol, still cherished his single shot. He had to make it a good one.

'Hello, Inspector.' The voice was hollow, mocking, unreal. 'I wondered when it would come to this.'

'Give yourself up, Oliver. You haven't a chance.'

'Oh, but you're wrong, Inspector. You see, I haven't finished my holy mission yet. John Kilvert. John Buckton. When they're dead, all those my father cursed will be gone. The prophesy of the Golden Dawn will be fulfilled.'

'You know I can't let you do that, Oliver.' Lestrade was working his way on knees and elbows to the right of the sofa. Two more flashes and crashes. The wood from the sofa splintered in Lestrade's cheek. Either that was luck, or Crowley's aim was improving.

'I know exactly where you are, Inspector,' the mocking voice went on, 'and don't bother to count the shots. I have an arsenal with me here. And you have one bullet.'

The Devil, thought Lestrade. How did he know that?

'You have violated the Golden Dawn, Inspector.' Crowley's voice was rising. 'For that you must die.'

'Gregson's dead.' Lestrade tried to rattle Crowley, distract him just for long enough to squeeze off a shot.

'He knew the risks. As we all do. But the Power, Lestrade. It is worth daring all for the Power.'

Lestrade bobbed up, trying to bring his right arm with him. Crowley blasted again, once, and the bullet hit the wall an inch or so above the inspector's head.

'Gregson kept me informed about your enquiries and unwittingly poor Jacob did too, in stumbling so ineptly about all over the country. But the best informant of course was . . . Hector Charlo.' The voice was transformed at the mention of the name into an asthmatic rattle. There was a livid flash of light as Crowley lit a torch above his head. Lestrade fired wildly, the ball lodging somewhere in the ceiling.

'Charlo,' the inspector repeated dumbly. Before him in the

flickering flame light was the sergeant of the same name, sitting cross-legged on the floor, dangling with magician's robes and wearing the horns of a goat.

'Crowley,' the magician roared in reply. 'And you didn't have a clue, Lestrade, did you? As feeble, loyal Charlo tramped around with you, following when you thought he was flat on his back. You fed all the information I needed. You poor bastard.' Crowley's pistol was pointing at Lestrade's head.

The inspector tried desperately to keep the conversation going.

'So it was your ship at Cromer lighthouse?'

'Yes. That fisherman nearly did for me, there. Only he didn't get the name quite right. *Aurora Aurosus* – Latin for the Golden Dawn. If he'd remembered it correctly and if you'd checked it, you'd have solved this months ago.'

'Or you'd have killed me months ago?' Lestrade was scanning the room, trying to find something to use as a weapon. He still held Loy Smith's empty pistol in his hand, but knew he couldn't throw it faster than Crowley's bullet. Nor would he be as lucky again as he had been with Gregson.

'And that's why you wore the muffler at Ladybower? In case those labourers recognised you?'

'I'd been there the day before. But you know what these clods are, Lestrade. They wouldn't have recognised me again if I'd been wearing these robes in broad daylight. Yes, it was risky to smear those hedges. But I'd watched Hodges for days. It was likely he'd scratch himself on them at some point. It's a wonder no one else did.'

'What if someone else had?'

'Do you suppose the Golden Dawn cares for human life, Lestrade? Any life? Yours will come as cheap as the rest.' The flames crackled and spat on the pole gripped in Crowley's right hand.

'Clever of you to get into the workhouse like that.' Lestrade tried, the old ploy of flattery, as he slowly uncoiled himself into a position to try something at least. 'But you made one mistake.'

'Not the disguise. Letitia Lawrenson was as unnoticing as the rest.'

'No, not the disguise. The name. Oh, Corfield is a clever enough pun. But you'd already used it, hadn't you? You see, I'd heard it before. I told you I had. Only I couldn't remember where. Now I do. When we first met, when you were unable to go with me to Cromer – unable because you had sailed there ahead of me and didn't want to risk being recognised – you sent me a doctor's note. It was forged, of course. Written by yourself, as a doctor. And you signed it Corfield.'

Crowley's eyes blazed. He laughed, deep, booming. 'Yes, that was stupid. But it doesn't really matter now, does it?'

Lestrade saw him cock the pistol.

'But to kill your own brother . . .' Lestrade blurted.

'Yes, poor Jacob. The silly meddling boy kept writing you letters. I, of course, as the devoted, efficient Charlo, kept intercepting them. It was all too easy. You see, poor Jacob did not know about my other existence at the Yard. And there are higher loyalties, Lestrade. I have many brothers in the Golden Dawn. But you got one thing wrong, Inspector, when you suspected way back that the solution might lie with the Dunn-Douglas ménage. You were wrong about the shape. It wasn't a triangle, Inspector, eternal or otherwise. It was . . . a pentangle.'

Crowley plunged the torch downwards to reveal for a split second a five-pointed star marked on the floor with black powder. The star exploded into a sheet of livid flame, and in its centre Crowley rose up like a great beast, arms outstretched. The flames engulfed him, shattering the windows with the blast and Lestrade was somersaulted to the door. Desperately, he tried to reach Crowley, but the magician had gone, disintegrating in the terrible heat and dense acrid smoke.

Lestrade somehow found the door handle and fell out into the corridor. He reached the stairs as he heard the alarm bells ring and a terrible, half-human, half-beast – 'Ipsissimus.' Nothing more.

End game

There were odder sights on that sunny October morning than an 11th Hussar in obsolete uniform, jacket open, overalls torn, face and hair scorched and blackened with fire, walking purposefully towards Scotland Yard, but one would have been hard put to it to find one.

But something nearly as odd was walking towards Lestrade as he neared the river.

'Lestrade – Good God, not another commissioner's fancy dress ball?'

Lestrade's heart sank. Of all the people to meet on one's way to twenty years in Pentonville – Dr John Watson, sometime of Baker Street.

'Good morning, Doctor. I really can't stop.'

'One moment, one moment, I must tell you this. I met a young chap called Friese-Greene the other day.'

'A refrigerator manufacturer?' asked Lestrade.

'No, no, a film maker. He's just taken out a patent on what he calls stereoscopic cinematography. It's rather like the wheel of wonder, only better.'

'Fascinating.' Lestrade passed on.

'But the best part is,' Watson continued, 'he says he can make moving pictures of one of my books . . . well, mine and Conan Doyle's. Can you imagine it? – Moving pictures of the great Sherlock Holmes himself!'

'Who in their right minds would pay money to witness such a spectacle?' sighed Lestrade. 'Or do you pay them?'

'Why, anyone would be delighted, delighted.'

By now quite a crowd had gathered around the oddly

scorched soldier and the gesticulating general practitioner. 'And actors will be queueing up for the honour and privilege of portraying him on the cinematograph. Pennington. Irving, even.'

'Madam.' Lestrade buttonholed a curious lady with husband and child. 'May I ask, how old is your lovely boy?'

'He's thirteen months,' she answered in a clipped, unusual accent.

'My family and I are here on holiday,' said the father, 'from Johannesburg.'

'Here you are then, Watson. Someone with just the right mental skills to play the Great Detective.'

'That child?' said Watson disparagingly.

'Basil is a very bright baby.' His mother was on the defensive.

'Oh, er . . . of course. I had no intention of giving offence, Mrs . . . er . . .'

'Rathbone.'

Watson tipped his hat.

'You see, Lestrade . . .' but Lestrade had gone.

There was to be no pussy-footing around this time. No sneaking in the back way. Straight up the steps and into the front door of the Yard marched Lestrade.

'Morning, sir,' Sergeant Dixon greeted him, as though it were perfectly natural for a suspended inspector, wanted for the murder of another inspector, and for attacking a Foreign Important Dignitary, to saunter in to work done up like a nigger minstrel.

'Got you . . . sir,' said Dew, leaping forward with one hand on Lestrade's collar, the other on his wrist.

'Not now, constable,' Nimrod Frost bellowed from the cloakroom door. 'Got it at last, have you, Dew, your great collar? Yes, I can see the book title now – *I Caught Lestrade*. Except he hasn't done anything. Now be a good chap and put the inspector down, there's a good lad.'

'Sorry, Walter,' grinned Lestrade. 'Better luck next time, eh?'

'Yes, sir . . . er . . . no hard feelings, sir?'

'A cup of tea, Dew. I'll be down for it later.'

'Yes, sir,' and the crestfallen constable scuttled off to do what he did best.

'I'm glad you've lost some weight, Lestrade,' said Frost 'or I doubt we'd both get in this lift.'

They travelled in silence to the first floor.

'There's some sorting out to be done, Inspector. But first, there are two gentlemen who'd like a word with you.'

Frost kicked open his office door to reveal a tall, dandyfied gentleman with a gardenia in his buttonhole.

'Chief Inspector Abberline.' Lestrade grinned through gritted teeth. The man with him, shorter, stouter, wearing the black patrol jacket of the River Police.

'Athelney Jones,' said Lestrade.

'You've been taking our names in vain, Lestrade.' Abberline pompously rocked on his heels, then broke into a broad grin. 'But I suppose it was in a good cause,' and he nodded to Frost as he bade him good day.

'Good to have you back, Lestrade.' Jones slapped him heartily on the shoulder as he left the office.

'Now then, you'd better sit down and tell me all about it,' said Frost.

'It's difficult to know where to begin, sir.'

'How about with the Golden Dawn?'

'Ah, Beeson told you about that?'

'Beeson? Good God, no. I don't listen to retired coppers, Lestrade. They can get you into all sorts of trouble. No, I've known about the Golden Dawn all along. We grocers' kids from Grantham are nobody's fools, you know.'

Well, thought Lestrade, I've arrived. He'll be offering me a cigar next.

'Have a cigar, Lestrade.'

'You've known about the Golden Dawn all along?'

'Yes, why do you think I sent you to Mawnan all those months ago? We got a tip-off. Anonymous, of course. Aren't they all? It simply said that a shepherd was going to be killed. When you found that hyena thing, I assumed that was it, but the killings went on.'

'I suspect your tip-off was from a hapless young man named

Jacob Crowley. I assumed William Lamb had no connection with the other deaths. Why was a warrant put out for my arrest?'

'To trap Gregson. I'd had my suspicions about him from the start. Too fanatical. Too suspicious. Of everything. Everybody. That sort of man has something to hide. That's why I sent you undercover to Manchester. Official enquiries, great feet, anything like that would have frightened him off. I wanted him to dig himself in deep. He was a neophyte, a novice if you like, in the Order of Golden Dawn.'

'Are you seriously expecting me to believe, sir, that Tobias Gregson worshipped the Devil?'

'No, Lestrade, he worshipped the pound note. Or to be more precise, lots of them. As far as we know, the Golden Dawn is a society of cranks, like the Flat Earth Society. Only occasionally, along comes a maniacal family like the Crowleys and all hell breaks loose. For most of the Golden Dawn, it is a matter of power, politics, big business. Things you and I don't understand, Lestrade.'

'So you knew about the Crowleys too?'

'No, not in detail. Until I had a visit not an hour ago from a Doctor Crosse. I believe you've met him?'

'And who paid Gregson?'

'Ah, there you have me. Whoever paid him wanted you out of the way. Off the case entirely. Hence this trumped-up nonsense about the Kaiser and hence my need to play along with it. Mind you, you kept out of my constables' way fairly effectively. Calling yourself Abberline at Bow Street took some nerve.'

'So the Golden Dawn still exists?'

'Yes, it does. We only found the tip of the iceberg here, Lestrade. Most of it is in the murky depths somewhere, but we do what we can.'

'And in those depths you didn't suspect Charlo?'

'Charlo?' Frost's composure was rattled. 'What has he to do with this?'

'You will find his charred body in whatever's left of the wing at Chelsea Hospital, sir.'

Frost blinked as realisation dawned. 'You mean, he and Crowley . . .?'

'. . . were the same man. Yes, sir.'

Frost's lower lip threatened to disappear below his cravat for a moment. 'I must confess, Lestrade, I never gave him a thought. Oh, I found his chronic absences suspect and I began to doubt my judgement. But I just assumed he was work-shy, a hypochondriac. Charlo, a neophyte of the Golden Dawn! No wonder he didn't look well. To be candid, Lestrade, I had my doubts about Bradstreet, but this . . . And I gave him to you as your go-between with me. My dear chap, I could have been the death of you.'

Lestrade was just about magnanimous enough to wave that aside. 'What does Ipsissimus mean?'

'Ah, Ipsissimus. As I said, I don't know much about the Dawn, but Ipsissimus is the Top Dog, the leader of the whole stinking lot. They aren't all madmen, they aren't all Satanists, but they play a dirty game and they are probably everywhere.'

'Sort of Freemasons?' ventured Lestrade.

'If I'm right, the members of the Golden Dawn would make the Masons look like choirboys. Which reminds me, when is my next Lodge meeting?' Frost consulted his diary. 'You know the definition of Ipsissimus, Lestrade? Evil beyond all comprehension. That frightens me, Lestrade. That frightens me.'

'I've an idea you know who Ipsissimus is, sir,' said the inspector.

'I was talking to the commissioner the other day. He had been talking to the Home Secretary—'

'Mr Churchill?' interjected Lestrade.

Frost ignored him. 'Let's just say I have a few ideas.'

'May I hear them, sir? After all, I have been through rather a lot on this case. You see, there is one thing I don't understand. Donald Crowley came back to England in eighteen-seventy, but it was twenty-three years before he began to kill, before Lamb's death. Why the delay? Why did he wait to carry out "the prophesy of the Golden Dawn"?'

Frost looked at him hard. He opened the door and checked the corridor outside. 'Let's just say this, Lestrade. You breathe one word of this to a living soul and I'll have you off the Force, I swear it. All I have is conjecture. Circumstance. Absolutely nothing that would stand up in a court of law. Ipsissimus is not one man, Lestrade. At least, he is a man who changes with another post, simultaneously held by the incumbent. I am not going to tell you what that post is, Inspector. Suffice to say that the residence that goes with it is Number Ten in a certain street by the river.'

'You mean . . .'

'As that office changes, so does Ipsissimus. It has been so since the days of Walpole.'

'I still don't see, sir.'

'Only one man in that post has refused to assume the title and role of Ipsissimus, Lestrade. The man who currently holds it. Educated at Eton and Oxford, one of the ablest lieutenants of the late Mr Peel; he has a perfectly hideous wife and spends a great deal of his time chopping down trees.'

'The GOM' said the inspector.

'Lestrade!' Frost clapped an hysterical hand over his subordinate's mouth, eyes swivelling manically round the room. Then, in a whisper, 'He's on his way out, Lestrade. The man who has held the position by the river four times this century. He probably knows as much about the Dawn as any of its members and you know what a confounded Christian he is? Well, it's my belief that before he goes – and he has said he will not stand again – it's my belief he'll speak out. Denounce the Dawn and all its members.'

'Then he is in danger?'

'Yes. Don't worry. I'm working on that one.'

'And Ipsissimus?'

'Take your pick. The title must have been transferred. I'm sure your knowledge of the current political situation is as good as mine. They'll bring the' – again the whisper – 'GOM down soon. Ireland. The Naval Estimates. It won't matter what. They're preparing for that day, Lestrade. Whoever the new Ipsissimus is, he's a new broom, sweeping clean. Donald Crowley represented a cobweb. There were men alive – the men of F Troop – who had knowledge which could, in the right hands, draw attention to the Dawn and all its machinations. These men had to be silenced. And madmen like the Crowleys were the very ones to do it.'

'The irony was,' said Lestrade, 'F Troop had forgotten. The

Charge on the following day had pushed what they had seen at Kadiköy out of their minds. And what did they see? On patrol in a hostile land? Far from home? And at night? None of these deaths need have happened at all.'

'Lestrade,' said Frost, 'I have said more than enough. You've been playing chief inspectors for too long. Now go and get your tea.'

Lestrade turned to go.

'Oh, and Sholto,' said Frost softly; 'apart from the GOM, you are the first, as far as I know, to break the Dawn's defences. We may both be marked men, you and I. Mind how you go.'

'Oh, Sholto, all I heard from you was "Stay with relatives. Stop. Away for some time. Stop." I wasn't there when you needed me.'

Lestrade reached over to the lovely warm body of the woman beside him.

'You are now, Sarah. That's the important thing. And God, I need you now.'

He kissed her cascading blonde hair where it tumbled over her bare shoulders and full breasts.

'Mrs Manchester, I think it's time I made an honest woman of you.'

'What, Inspector Lestrade, you mean you're going to pay me the back rent you owe me?'

'Sshh!' whispered Lestrade. 'You're supposed to be my housekeeper, not my landlady. The shame of it.'

'Sholto.' She was suddenly serious. 'You won't . . . won't go away again, will you?'

'No, Sarah, I won't go away again.' Do you hear that, Constance? Do you hear that, Daisy? He vowed to the night, I won't go away again.

'You know the funniest part of all this?' Lestrade turned to the voluptuous Mrs Manchester again. 'Nimrod Frost thinks you're sixty-one.'

And they laughed together in the darkness . . . .

Lestrade and the hallowed house

A scandal in Belgravia

The Great Queen was dead. All the years of tribulation – and the trials – over at last. The century had barely begun before the great heart had given up the ghost. And peace came. So much for Oscar Wilde.

Within three months, at Osborne in the Isle of Wight, Victoria, Queen Empress by the Grace of God, also shuffled off the mortal coil. Her passing went more noticed than Oscar's. After all, she had not outraged society during one of its periodic bouts of morality. Neither had she called the Marquis of Queensberry a libeller. And she remained strangely unmoved by errand boys. All in all, most people said, a very pointful life. Under her auspices, Britain had become truly great. And the Empire had been created on which the Sun Never Set. It was a gilded age of cliché and pomposity. But most people, while looking back with more than a hint of *fin de siècle*, looked forward too. A king again after sixty-four years! Only the feminist coterie around Mrs Pankhurst failed to stand and cheer for that. It was a brave new world, a new century. And if the tiresome Boers insisted on dragging their petty problems into that century, well, rest assured that Bobs and this new fellow – what was his name? – Kitchener? They would soon put that right.

Walter Dew stood in the changing room in the basement of Scotland Yard. He carefully macassared his hair for the second time that morning and admired again the metaphorical stripes on his sleeve. Not bad, he thought to himself. Fifteen years in the Force and a sergeant at last. He was just burnishing the new tiepin in the spotted green of the mirror when a face appeared over his shoulder.

'Very nice, Dew. Very nice.'

'Oh, good morning sir.' Dew snapped to attention as the Donegal and bowler hat hit him in the chest.

'Vanity,' the newcomer clicked his tongue, 'all is vanity.'

'Well sir, it's just . . . my new position sir.'

The newcomer wondered if it was the translation of that naughty Indian book by Sir Richard Burton which was currently doing the rounds at the Yard that prompted the new sergeant's remark, but he dismissed it. Dew didn't have the intellect.

'Tell me, Sergeant, between polishing your stripes and your hair, have you had a chance to read the Orders of the Day?'

Dew racked his newly promoted brain. 'Quantity of ping-pong balls stolen, sir. And the Egyptian Ambassador has reported people calling him a damned fuzzy-wuzzy again.'

'Forgive me, Dew,' the newcomer checked his half-hunter, 'I was under the impression this was H Division. I'm sure Superintendent Abberline can handle serious crime of the ping-pong variety. As for the Egyptian gentleman, I don't think we need trouble Special Branch, do you? Especially since the last person I heard refer to His Potentateness as that was the Commissioner of the Metropolitan Police!' He tried again, 'Anything for me?'

'Ah, yes sir. His Nims would like to see you, sir. Matter of the utmost urgency, he said.'

The newcomer nodded with a tired look on the narrow, parchment-coloured face. He checked his moustaches in the mirror momentarily, careful not to let the sergeant see, and made for the stairs. Dew reached for the telephone on the wall. It clicked and vibrated and a whistle answered.

'Mr Frost sir, this is Sergeant Dew.'

A silence ensued.

'Sergeant Walter Dew, sir. H Division.'

'Well?' an unreasoning crackle snapped back at him.

'Inspector Lestrade is on his way up, sir.'

'Well, you'd better hand up his hat and coat, hadn't you?'

And the whistle sounded in his ear. He was still standing there, open-mouthed, wondering how Nimrod Frost knew he was holding Lestrade's accoutrements, when the inspector reached the lift.

He missed old Dixon on the front desk. There was a blue-eyed boy there now – whose, he wasn't sure. But certainly it was true what they said. When policemen started looking younger than you, it was time to hang up your truncheon.

'Come!' the voice bellowed through the ornate glass-fronted door. Why was it, Lestrade wondered, that Heads of the Criminal Investigation Department never said 'in' at the end of that sentence?

'Good morning, sir.' The inspector beamed.

'Lestrade, you look terrible. Have a cigar.' Frost shoved a cheroot into the inspector's lips. He rang a bell, which summoned a demure, middle-aged lady with iron-grey locks and a face to match.

'Miss Featherstonehaugh, tea, please.'

'Lemon?' she asked.

'No. Cream and sugar.'

'It's not good for you, Mr Frost. Your arteries.'

'My arteries,' Frost heaved himself upright to his full five foot six and his complete nineteen stone, 'are the least of my problems this morning. Inspector Lestrade always looks worse than I do.'

Miss Featherstonehaugh smiled coyly at the inspector, then reached up and tweaked his cheek, chuckling as she did so. 'Never,' she sighed, her matronly bosom heaving with lust or the discomfort of her stays, 'you gorgeous boy,' and she swept from the room. Lestrade wished again that the ground had opened up for him.

'She'll have to go,' grunted Frost, accepting Lestrade's proffered Lucifer. 'You wouldn't think a woman of her age and marital status would harbour such indecent thoughts, would you?'

'I prefer not to think about it, sir. I'm a funny age myself.'

'How old now, Lestrade? Not long to retirement, eh?' The Head of the Criminal Investigation Department blew smoke rings to the ceiling.

'Forty-eight, sir. I have given it some thought.'

Frost grinned. 'I can't see you growing petunias in Peckham, Lestrade. Not for a while yet at least. Which is just as well.' His face darkened. To business thought Lestrade. 'What do you know about Ralph Childers?'

'Nothing, sir.'

Frost was checked, momentarily. 'Come, come, Lestrade. You are a man of affairs . . .'

For a second, Lestrade's heart skipped a beat. Who had been talking?

'I happen to know you read the *Sun*. News, man. Parliament. You know, that collection of misfits and pederasts who presume to run the country.'

A little strong, Lestrade thought, for the Head of the Criminal Investigation Department, but it wasn't his place to say so.

'Ah,' he volunteered, 'Ralph Childers the MP.'

'Ex-MP.' Frost corrected him.

'XMP, sir?' Clearly the *Sun* had let Lestrade down. He hadn't met those initials before.

'His body was found early this morning, Lestrade. At his home in Belgravia.'

'And you suspect—'

'Everyone.' Frost nodded.

Miss Featherstonehaugh scuttled in, fussing round Lestrade with the cream and sugar and leaving Frost to help himself.

'When you've finished,' bellowed Frost, more loudly than he intended, 'helping the inspector, Miss Featherstonehaugh,' mellower now, 'perhaps you could leave us?'

She snorted indignantly and drew up her skirts, sweeping noiselessly from the room.

'You'll find the local boys on hand of course,' Frost went on, applying his blubbery lips to the porcelain. Lestrade enjoyed the luxury of a cup with a handle. So superior to the mugs in his own office on the floor below. Frost leaned forward. 'But this is a delicate one, Lestrade. There are rumours . . .'

'Rumours, sir?'

Frost looked around him, checking particularly that the horizon was free of Featherstonehaughs.

'Let's just say,' he whispered, 'that the late Mr Childers'

favourite reading, apart from Private Members' Bills, was the Marquis de Sade.'

Lestrade was sure there was a joke there somewhere about the bills of private members, but he let it go. What did Frost mean? Was there a French connection?

'Any leads, sir?'

Frost slurped his second cup, having doled in his usual three sugars.

'None. Apparently, the body hasn't been moved. The coroner will take over when you've finished.'

Frost looked up. Lestrade knew the interview was at an end. He left what remained of his tea and took his leave. 'Oh, and Lestrade,' Frost stopped him, 'let's be careful, shall we? It's a jungle out there.'

Lestrade collected his accoutrements from his sergeant. For a moment, he toyed with taking Dew with him. He could see the mental anguish on the man's face as he screwed his courage to the sticking place and sharpened a pencil prior to tackling the morning's paperwork. But no, Frost had implied the matter was delicate. And Dew would be no use in this case. He could barely read English, let alone French. The inspector caught a hansom and hurried west.

He alighted within the hour – the new Underground *would* have been quicker, he now realised – and looked up at the Corinthian columns of 102 Eaton Square, an imposing edifice, Georgian and opulent. Lestrade didn't like it. Wealth on this scale both annoyed and unnerved him. Two burly constables saluted as he leapt up the steps between them and turned not a hair as the inspector somersaulted gracefully over the top step and caught himself a sharp one on the brass jaws of the lion knocker. Another constable opened the door, by which time Lestrade had recovered his composure and wiped the tears from his eyes.

'Who are you?' a voice from the aspidistra grove in the far corner demanded.

'Inspector Lestrade, Scotland Yard,' he answered.

'Oh, I'm Smellie.' A man appeared from the foliage.

Probably, thought Lestrade.

'Pimlico.'

'Inspector?' asked Lestrade.

'Nine years tomorrow.'

'Doesn't time fly?'

Lestrade had worked with bobbies outside the Yard before. To a man they resented him. The Yard. The very Force itself. No point in being polite to them. As you walked away, you felt the knife between your shoulder blades.

'He's in here.' The uniformed inspector led the way into a vast library, wall to wall in red leather. Chairs, lamps, books by the hundred. It was a veritable British Museum. But there was no body. In answer to Lestrade's silent enquiry, Smellie pressed the spine of a rather out of place Mrs Beeton and the entire wall swung away to reveal a passage, dark and bare.

'After you, Inspector.'

And although that sounded uncomfortably like a sentiment of Miss Featherstonehaugh's, Lestrade complied.

For a man with Lestrade's problem, to lead the way in a darkened space, especially a confined one, was not the safest of moves. Still, he wasn't about to embarrass himself in the presence of this lesser mortal from the Metropolitan Police. Lestrade had his pride. It was the Smellies of this world who brought it out. Even so, he was grateful for the glow of light as he turned the corner.

'We're going west under the servants' quarters, now,' Smellie informed him. Lestrade turned in the gloom to look for the compass. There wasn't one. Perhaps Inspector Smellie had a naval background.

The glow was coming from a single oil lamp which threw long shadows on the red walls of another room, smaller than the one upstairs and almost directly under it. The passage must have wound back on itself in a tight angle. But there were no books. Lestrade saw a second lamp, a third, a fourth, until he realised he was surrounded by mirrors and it was the same lamp. Even on the ceiling, though the ascending smoke there had darkened the glass and spoiled the effect. The blood red around the mirrors burned back from every side, plush and sickening.

A study in scarlet, mused Lestrade until something more prosaic caught his attention. Smellie moved to turn up the lamp.

'Gloves, man.' Lestrade checked him.

Smellie complied, cursing himself that the Yard man had caught him out in an elementary slip.

The full light rose on the late Mr Ralph Childers. Or what was left of him. He was hanging upside down from a chain pulled taut from the centre of the ceiling. He was naked, his hands manacled together and wrenched behind his back. From them the chain ran back to his ankles and joined the single links from the beams. His back and buttocks were scarred. Old ones, new ones. Some still sticky with blood. Others livid white in the flickering lamplight. Lestrade pulled Smellie's arm closer. There was no sound but the quiet click of the chains as the former Member of Parliament swung gently in the draught. The odour in the room was sweet – a sickly combination of sandalwood and cedarwood – and lurking there, in the experienced nostrils of Lestrade, the familiar smell of death.

As Lestrade urged Smellie's arm lower, the local man paused, 'It's not a pretty sight down . . . there.'

Lestrade glanced at the deceased's private parts. Not the prettiest he'd seen, but he felt Smellie was over-reacting. Then he realised it was the head to which his colleague referred. The hair swept the ground. It had been grey; now it was matted with blood and the head above it was split open, like the water melons Lestrade had seen at the Albert Dock when he'd been a Bluebottle in the days of his youth, catching villains at Wapping and wading up to his armpits in cold, brackish water at Shadwell Stair. One bulging eye, sightless and dull, gleamed white as the body twirled. Carefully, Lestrade parted the unkempt beard to reveal the iron collar with its spike driven deep into the throat.

'Is he dead?' Smellie asked.

Lestrade straightened. 'I thought you'd checked all this,' he said.

'No, I only just came on duty. My constables told me it was a messy one. I've never seen anything like this.'

Lestrade noticed how the colour had drained from Smellie's face. 'Come on,' he said, 'let's get some fresh air. Then I want more light down here. And no one,' he paused and took Smellie's sleeve, 'no one gets in here until I say so.'

'There is a coroner upstairs.'

'Let him wait. The last thing we want is his great feet sloshing about down here. Who found the body?'

The policemen reached ground level. 'Beales. His man.'

'How many other servants?'

'Eight. The others are at the weekend retreat in Berkshire. A house called "Draughts".'

Lestrade gave explicit instructions to Smellie, who vanished with his constables to carry them out. At least, thought Lestrade, the man isn't going to be obstructive. Whatever private thoughts he harbours about the arrogance of the Yard, he's keeping them to himself.

It was nearly lunchtime before the inspector sat down at Mr Childers' magnificent desk in the library. He had gone back to the weirdly scented little room below. This time he had gone alone. Years of 'the sights' had taught Lestrade that he operated best on his own. He was surer of his emotions – and his stomach – that way. He flicked open the notepad to make sure he hadn't overlooked anything. Cause of death? A blunt instrument to the back and top of the head, he would guess. Or perhaps the collar had been snapped shut first so that the iron spike had penetrated windpipe and spinal cord. So was he dead when he was hauled upside down so cruelly near the floor? And what about the whipmarks on the body? Or was 'whipmark' too much of an assumption? Lestrade had learned a long time ago to keep an open mind, almost as open, he mused in one of his more grisly moments, as that of the late lamented who had been twirling below stairs. Childers had been taken away through the tradesmens' entrance, of course, but even there a crowd of fascinated sightseers had slowed his undignified journey to the waiting Maria. Lestrade had watched from an upstairs window. Errand boys and shop lads nattering like fishwives over the handlebars of their Raleighs; the servants of neighbours who 'happened-to-be-passing', and as Lestrade's eyes shot up to the nearest windows on his own level, the neighbours themselves, curious behind the shivering nets. Smellie's constables elbowed the gathering crowd aside and Lestrade heard the familiar cry, 'Move along there, move along.' He noticed one or two young men scrabble nearer than the rest, prying under the grey, regulation blankets and then break away, scattering in different directions, ahead of the more idly curious. He recognised the gait and the lean and hungry look – newshounds from Fleet Street. So much for Nimrod Frost's 'delicate one'. It would be all over London by nightfall – the *Standard* would see to that.

'You found the body?' Lestrade looked up from his notepad.

Beales, the gentleman's gentleman, nodded. Lestrade looked at him hard. Every gesture, every move was ordered and precise. He mentally crossed the man off his list of suspects. Here was a man who did not like to soil his hands or spoil his routine. A little Goddards for the silver cleaning, the odd funeral of a maiden aunt in Cheltenham, but not a waistcoat drenched in his master's blood and not the appalling physical and emotional wrench of smashing in a skull. Where was the economy of word and manner in that? But Lestrade was leaping howitzers. He had already envisaged a frenzied attack – the work of a deranged maniac. As for the bloodsoaked waistcoat, the murderer had been as naked as his victim . . . But all this was surmise. Facts, he told himself. What of the facts? And this careful, calm, studied man before him. He at least knew something of his former master's habits. Lestrade slowly produced a cigar and it shook him a little as Beales leapt upright to light it for him. The gentleman's gentleman's nostrils quivered disapprovingly as he inhaled the smoke. He found himself looking Lestrade up and down. A man of middle years – forty-five, forty-six. Five foot nine or ten. Appalling dress sense. No one wore Donegals any more. He looked like a coachman.

'You found the body?' Lestrade's question ended the valet's rambling assessment of his interrogator.

'Yes sir.' Beales thought perhaps a vocal answer would satisfy the man. A nod clearly hadn't worked.

'Tell me about it.' Lestrade began to circle the room, glancing occasionally at Beales, occasionally fingering a book on a shelf. To Beales' domestic brain, it appeared as though the inspector was looking for dust.

'It was six thir—' Beales was unnerved by the whirling policeman. He turned one way, then the other, trying to fix him with his eyes. All his training had taught him to look a man in the eyes, except of course when receiving a gratuity or when one's master, believing himself to be alone, began to pick his nose.

'You are very precise,' Lestrade cut in.

'I am a gentleman's gentleman, sir. Precision is my trade.'

Lestrade stopped. 'Go on.'

'My late master was also a creature of habit. I had strict instructions to wake him at six thirty each morning. He invariably bathed and took a ride along the Row before lunching at his club or going to the House.'

'His club?'

'The Diogenes.'

'The House?'

Beales looked up, his look of amazement turning to contempt. 'Of Commons, sir,' he said acidly.

'Just checking,' said Lestrade. 'Go on.'

'Mr Childers was not in his room. I brought the tea here, thinking he might be working on some papers. He was not.'

'So you went downstairs?'

'Not immediately. I checked the dining room and the breakfast room, although I knew his breakfast was only then being prepared. I was about to try the stables in the mews. Sometimes Mr Childers could not sleep and had been known to saddle his horse himself.'

God, thought Lestrade, the versatility of the landed classes.

'I don't know what made me go to the Cell.'

'The Cell?' repeated Lestrade.

'The room in the basement, Inspector. Where your constables found the . . . Mr Childers.'

'You said Cell. Do you mean cellar?'

'No sir . . . Perhaps I had better explain. After all,' Beales began to twitch his fingers a little, the first sign of a slipping composure, 'I am anxious to help all I can. It's just that a gentleman's gentleman must be loyal. And discreet.'

Lestrade played the moment as it came. He supposed, at that moment, that Beales was everything he appeared to be. The inspector placed an avuncular hand on his shoulder. 'It's a little bit late to be loyal, Mr Beales. And discretion isn't going to help me catch his murderer, now, is it?'

Beales breathed in tortuously and nodded. 'Have you heard of the Hell Fire Club, Inspector?'

'Is that the little one in Cleveland Street?'

Again, amazement swept briefly over Beales' face. This time it was not followed by contempt.

'No sir. It was organised by Sir Francis Dashwood a hundred and fifty years ago. It was composed of gentlemen – bloods or rakes I suppose they would have been called – who were known as the Monks of Medmenham. They practised every vice known to man. Not to mention woman.'

'Women?'

'Please,' Beales started in the seat, 'I asked you not to mention women. Mr Childers was a bachelor, sir. He never officially entertained ladies. Nor was he seen in their company. Without wishing to be unkind to my staff, he chose the plainest of females for his household. His misogyny was well known.'

Lestrade had no answer to that, but his straying hand came fortuitously across a dictionary and he riffled through its pages. After what seemed to both men an eternity, Lestrade snapped shut the book triumphantly.

'So he didn't like women?'

'No, sir.' Contempt had returned to the gentleman's gentleman. 'However, when the fit was on him, sir, he . . .' Beales was uncomfortable, 'he occasionally gave way to . . . excesses.'

'You interest me strangely,' said Lestrade, stubbing the cigar on an ashtray as he alighted again in Childers' chair.

'He would put rough clothes on and slip out at night.'

'And?'

'He would find an unfortunate, a lady of the streets, and bring her back here. There is a door your men will not have found, Inspector. It leads directly to the Cell. There, Mr Childers would don his monk's robes and indulge in . . .'

Lestrade remembered the whips and thongs that lined the scarlet walls below. And the iron shackles. And the chains. And the mirrors for a better view.

'Hunnish practices?' he asked.

'The English Vice,' nodded Beales, as though it were a loyal toast.

'Tell me, was Mr Childers the only member of this reincarnated club?'

'No sir. On high days, the Cell was a hive of activity.'

'Beales,' Lestrade was perambulating again, 'I pride myself on being abreast of current affairs.' He hoped Frost couldn't hear him. 'How is it that I have never heard a whisper in what Fleet Street have been known to call their "newspapers" of Mr Childers' habits?'

'I clean them myself sir. Oh . . .' And for once it was the gentleman's gentleman's turn to misunderstand. 'There are laws of libel as I am sure you are aware, Inspector Lestrade. In any case, Mr Childers was the soul of discretion. The Cell is carefully padded so that no sound escapes. That is why I would have heard nothing of this dreadful deed in the night. Only I – until today – knew of the room's existence. No one else – not the staff, not the master's colleagues – knew that he . . . er . . . entertained. He used to say . . .' Beales stopped.

'Yes?' Lestrade chipped in.

'He used to say that when his back and buttocks hurt him after a debauch, he would find the seats in the House very uncomfortable. And at those moments, he swore that the Grand Old Man was watching him.'

'You mean Gladstone?' Lestrade asked.

'When the old gentleman was alive.' Beales assented.

'Didn't the late Prime Minister have similar habits?' the inspector ventured.

'I'm sure I don't know, sir. But you must remember, Mr Gladstone was a Liberal.' To Beales that explained it all.

'When you said earlier,' Lestrade flicked aside the nets to look at the mews in the watery afternoon sun, 'that no one but you knew of the Cell, you were not, of course, including the other members.'

'Members?'

'Of the Hell Fire Club, man,' beamed Lestrade. 'Those latter-day bloods and rakes who joined your dear departed master in his interesting habits.'

'They of course knew of the room, sir.'

'Tell me, was 102 Eaton Square the headquarters of the club?'

'As far as I am aware, sir.'

Lestrade dropped the joviality. 'I want their names.'

Beales leapt to his feet. 'Sir, I am a gentleman's gentleman. Loyalty and discretion are my watchwords. Nothing will drag that information from me.'

'Beales,' Lestrade leaned towards him, 'I am an Inspector of the Metropolitan Police. I don't have any watchwords at all. And I can get you fifteen years for obstructing a police officer in the pursuance of his duty. I think Pentonville will drag any information out of you.'

For a moment, the two men looked at each other. Then Beales summoned what dignity he could. 'If you go to Mr Childers' country house in Berkshire,' he said, 'you will find a red leather box in the centre drawer of his study desk. This,' he produced it deftly from his pocket, 'is the key to that box. I think its contents will give you the answers you need.'

'And why should you have a key to such a Pandora's delight?' It was the only bit of mythology that had stayed with Lestrade since Blackheath crammer days.

'I was to destroy the box, sir. In the event of Mr Childers losing an election. But now that he has lost his life . . .'

Lestrade took the key. 'What will you do now, Beales?' he asked.

The gentleman's gentleman shook himself from the new realisation of his master's death. 'Mr Joseph Chamberlain has often hinted to me that I would be most welcome in his service, sir.'

'Well, then.' Lestrade patted the valet's shoulder.

'Oh, no, sir,' Beales looked horrified, 'Mr Chamberlain *was* a Liberal!'

And that again seemed to say it all.

On his way through the hall, Lestrade met Smellie.

'I'll leave the other servants to you,' he said, 'they may be able to add something. Send your report to the Yard, will you? Oh, and Smellie . . .'

The inspector looked up.

'With your compass-like sense of geography, where is Berkshire?'

Smellie thought hard. 'On the map, it's the bit on the left-hand side. Turn right out of the door.'

*

Lestrade took the train to Hungerford and a carrier's cart to Ogbourne Maizey. Smellie's geography may not have been what it once was, but he had elicited the name of the village of which the great house of 'Draughts' was the manor. It was sunset when the cart crunched on the gravel outside the mellow, yellow entrance porch. The dying sun threw long shadows of the twisted chimneys across the lawns. Lestrade tipped the carrier, making a mental note to charge it to expenses and pulled the doorbell. He heard the answering ring down the hall and waited as the bolts slid back. A sour-faced housekeeper appeared. She had heard the news from Mr Beales via the telephone. Yes, the house had all the modern conveniences. There was a shower, if the gentleman cared to use it. Lestrade wondered if his armpits had betrayed him; but he stoically declined the offer and was shown into the study.

It was scarlet again, a copy, if the inspector's memory served him aright, of the one in Eaton Square. Around the walls hung a number of framed Spy cartoons, characters of today and yesterday, colleagues of the former back-bencher. There was even one of Nimrod Frost, looking stones lighter than he actually was. Was one of them, Lestrade wondered, the murderer of Ralph Childers? He'd always thought the Archbishop of Canterbury looked a bit shifty, but the man was eighty if he was a day. How many octogenarians were capable of hoisting a dead weight of twelve or thirteen stone off the floor with chains? No, Cantuar could sleep easy in his bed. Lestrade unlocked the drawer and placed the walnut burred box on the desk. It was inlaid with the initials of the late lamented, and a series of incomprehensible hieroglyphics. The inspector inserted the key and the lid flipped open. Nothing. The box was perfectly empty. So Beales had sent him here on a wild goose chase. Lestrade fumed at the waste of his time. He fumed still further at being taken for such an idiot. In an uncharacteristic gesture he slammed the box down hard on the red leather of the desk only to see a drawer at its base slide open. 'Ah,' he smiled, 'the old secret-drawer ploy.'

In it lay a book, in plain black leather and its pages were filled with notes in Childers' handwriting. Lestrade had seen examples of it at Eaton Square. The book appeared to be a diary and the inspector read until darkness drew over the house. The sour-faced housekeeper solemnly lit the lamps around Lestrade.

'Mrs . . . er . . .' The inspector stopped her.

'Smith,' said the housekeeper.

A likely story, thought Lestrade. 'Tell me, does – did – Mr Childers entertain?'

'Now and again, sir. But he didn't come here often. Most of his friends were Members of Parliament, sir, like himself. He didn't bring many of them here.'

'And has he had any condolences?'

'The vicar, sir. Nobody else. His colleagues would use his London address.'

'Mrs Smith, is there lodging in the village?'

'There's an inn, sir, but it's not the best. I had instructions from Mr Beales to accommodate you here. There's plenty of room now the master's gone.'

And so it was that Lestrade spent the night at 'Draughts'. He couldn't sleep. It was probably the pork and pickles of the melancholy Mrs Smith. Or the changeable weather of the early spring. He'd seen no other servants, only a couple of gardeners pruning the privet, glimpsed from the study window. There was no life in this house. It was obvious that Childers used it infrequently. Everywhere druggets were pulled over the furniture, giving each room a ghostly appearance in the gloom of the April evening.

A little before midnight, showers beat on the leaded panes of Lestrade's window. He disliked four posters. They made him feel claustrophobic. And he'd never really recovered from being seduced in one. So he sat in the deep recess below the window, and ploughed on through the diary he had found. What was it Beales had said? The contents of the box would give him the answers he needed. But most of it was cryptic nonsense. A series of jumbled letters, spaces and dots. Perhaps the cypher department at the Yard could make something of it. Certainly Lestrade could not.

The inspector wandered with his oil lamp through the upper reaches of the house. The modern conveniences of which

Mrs Smith had spoken did not extend to electricity and by the morning Lestrade had hammer toes to prove it, where he had tripped over the wainscotting in the long, dark shadows.

Breakfast was as unadventurous as his supper of the night before and he was glad to be aboard the Western Region again, rattling towards the City, with his book and his problem. He turned to his own face in the window. Who would kill a Member of Parliament? Six hundred odd other Members of Parliament? But no, this was not political. It was sexual. Whatever torrid events went on in the Cell at Eaton Square, there was one person who was sure to know. And it was on her door that Lestrade was knocking by mid-morning.

The grille in the little door in Greek Street slid back. A heavy black face shone through. 'Yes?' it asked. Lestrade fanned the air with a roll in the time-honoured manner.

'Miss Labedoyere.' He made a brave stab at the French.

The shining pink eyes in the shining black face didn't blink. 'Who sent you?'

Lestrade gambled on the inhabitants of Greek Street bordellos not reading newspapers. 'Ralph Childers,' he answered.

The grille slammed shut. Had he said the wrong thing? Given the wrong password? Perhaps if he'd said, 'The boy I love sits up in the gallery'? Still, it was too late now. He heard the bolts jar and clank. The way was opened by a huge negro, in loud check suit and silk shirt. The black man snatched Lestrade's money and locked the door behind him.

'Miss Labedoyere don't really receive guests at this hour.'

Lestrade tried to place the accent. Caribbean with a hint of Seven Dials.

'I'm sure in my case she'll make an exception.'

'Wait here.'

Lestrade was shown into an anteroom, hung with plush velvet and heavy flock wallpaper. Everywhere was the smell of cedarwood and sandalwood. It was the Cell at Eaton Square. He sensed he was on the right track. The beaded curtain swished and rattled behind him and a powerful woman strode into the room wearing a basque bodice bedecked with bows, and a vast plume of ostrich feathers in her hair.

'Mr . . . er . . .?'

'Lister.' Lestrade used his favourite alias.

'I am Fifi Labedoyere.'

No, mused Lestrade.

'What can I do for you, for' – she riffled the notes in her hand – 'five pounds?' She swirled around Lestrade, studying him carefully. 'A bit of brown?' She laughed. 'No, silly of me. A handsome, full-blooded man like you,' she swept off his bowler hat, 'will want a bit of red.' She pushed him back onto a *chaise-longue* with a tap which could break a swan's wing. 'Now . . .' She tickled his moustache with her tapering, pointed finger nails.

You're a man of the world, Lestrade told himself. Don't sneeze.

'There is Charlotte. Fresh from the country. A virgin, Mr Lister. Only fourteen years old.'

Yes, Lestrade could imagine. A raddled bag of forty done up in ringlets and rouge.

'Ah, but no. I have Celeste. A nymph of the Orient. With skin like a ripe peach. She has ways of driving a man mad.'

Some dragon from Chinatown, without a tooth in her head, Lestrade imagined.

'I . . . er . . . was hoping for something a little . . . stricter,' he ventured.

'Ah,' Fifi's eyes lit up, 'you require Tamara. She is Bavarian. I have seen her reduce men to putty under her tawse.'

'Miss Labedoyere, forgive me,' smiled Lestrade, 'but I was hoping for your own exquisite services.'

Fifi laughed so that her bosoms, threatening and wide, wobbled above their whale-bone cages. 'For five pounds, dearie? I'm not that good natured.'

'A pity,' Lestrade was trying to keep the madam's fingers away from his groin. 'Ralph Childers highly recommended you. What was it he said? "The iron of a gauntlet and the velvet of a glove."' Lestrade flattered himself on that one. Look to your laurels, Alfred Austin!

'And how is dear Ralph?' Fifi had expertly undone three of Lestrade's buttons and was whisking aside his shirt flaps.

'Dead.' Lestrade stood up, hastily adjusting his dress.

Fifi was alongside him. 'Dead?' she repeated. And realisation dawned. 'I smell copper.' The soft French had become harsh Bermondsey.

'Very astute, ma'am,' answered Lestrade.

'Bert!' the madam bawled and the Caribbean gentleman blocked the doorway. 'It's the Bill,' she snarled in a confusion of Christian names, 'he's leaving.'

Lestrade had to think fast. The bouncer was four or five stone heavier than he was and if the inspector had stood behind him, he wouldn't have been visible at all. And he appeared to have muscles like a steam hammer. Lestrade fumbled in his pocket for the brass knuckles he kept there but when he pulled his hand free, he was only holding a pair of spectacles. They helped with the mild disguise. Men called Lister always wore glasses. The negro paused momentarily, one hand on Lestrade's lapel, the other in mid-air, lining up the copper's jaw with all the science of an ex-prize fighter.

'You wouldn't hit a man with glasses?' Lestrade whined, gripping the useless rims in both hands.

'No, I'd use my bloody fist,' the negro snarled.

But Lestrade was faster. For years, the bouncer had been used to cringing middle-aged men and had learned to take his time. This time, the pause was nearly fatal. Lestrade jabbed upwards with both hands, the spectacle arms ramming painfully into the bigger man's nostrils. As the black buckled, clutching a bleeding nose, Lestrade's knee came up. Simultaneously he found the knuckles in his other pocket and brought them down with both hands on the bouncer's skull. There was a dull thud and a gurgle and the building shook as he hit the floor.

'Now then, Miss Labedoyere.' Lestrade turned to the madam. Fifi spat contemptuously, although she was a little nonplussed at seeing the unstoppable Bert lying in such an ungainly heap. She backed away, uncoiling a whip which Lestrade had not noticed dangling from her wrist.

'Nice of you to offer,' said Lestrade, 'but I'm afraid I told you a teensy fib. Mr Childers did not recommend you. His tastes and mine scarcely coincide at all.'

'You flatfoot bastard!' Fifi shrieked, her breasts slapping from side to side as she let fly with the rawhide thong. It ripped across Lestrade's nose and cheeks, drawing a crimson line the width of his face. He spun round, bouncing off the wall and stumbling over the prostrate Bert. Can't win them all, he mused as his tear-filled eyes attempted to focus on Miss Labedoyere. The lady in question was snaking back her arm for another lash, when Lestrade rolled backwards, tugging hard on the beaded curtain. It ripped away from the wall, a shower of beads clattering and bouncing on the floor. Lestrade was already down and within seconds, Miss Labedoyere had joined him, floored by the rolling beads. She cursed and swore until Lestrade wrapped the whip around her neck and sat back against the wall with the quivering heap trussed in his lap.

'Here's a new position for you, Gertie,' he hissed, trying to catch his breath. A man on the brink of his fifties shouldn't be doing this. Time to leave it to the younger coppers.

'Who?' Fifi snapped.

'Gertie Clinker,' said Lestrade, 'late of Wapping and all points east. You know, you and I are getting a bit old for this sort of game, aren't we?'

'You speak for yourself, copper!' she bellowed.

'Shame on you, Gertie. You didn't know me, did you? And me the only boy in blue who ever gave you the time of day.'

'Blimey,' she muttered, 'Sergeant Lestrade!'

'Well, that dates you, dearie,' Lestrade said. 'I've been an inspector for sixteen years.'

Gertie giggled, despite the ligature around her neck, 'Course you'ad a nose then. Where d'you get all them cuts?'

'Well, at least one of them I got from a madam of a bordello in Greek Street.'

Gertie giggled again, 'Sorry, lover. Me eyes ain't what they used to be.'

'Are you sitting comfortably? Or shall I go on talking to the back of your head?'

'I won't give you no more trouble, Mr Lestrade. 'Onest. I'll come quiet. Make a change for me.' And she giggled again. Lestrade uncrossed his hands. He was glad because Gertie was a big girl and his knuckles had long ago turned white.

'Without wishing to offend, Gertie,' he said, uncrumpling his Donegal and skating warily to the corridor, 'it's not you I'm after.' He mechanically checked the bouncer. Broken jaw, he guessed. 'You will, however, need a new fancy man.'

'Well, after today's performance, I should think I do,' agreed Gertie.

'Ralph Childers,' Lestrade came back to the point.

'Oh yeah, you said.' Gertie poured them both a sizeable slug of gin. 'Here's mud in your eye, Mr Lestrade.' And she downed hers in one.

'You know I can't drink on duty.' The inspector toasted the madam and sipped the clear liquid. It affected his focus again.

'Come on dearie. Let me put something on that face.' And she ferreted in a cupboard and began dabbing away the blood. Between Lestrade's jerking and inward gasps, Miss Clinker took up his line of enquiry.

'Did I hear you say Mr Childers was dead?'

'As a doornail, Gertie.'

'Well, I'm not surprised. Did'e overdo it a bit?'

'It?'

''E took and gave, 'e did. A right one. My arm would ache for days after one of his visits.'

'Could he have overdone to death, Gertie?'

She looked at him, pausing from her ministrations. 'In all my years in the business, Mr Lestrade, I've never known it. Everybody has a point when enough is enough. Course if 'is ticker was dicky—'

'I don't think it was his heart that took the punishment, Gertie. When did you see him last?'

'Oohh, three, maybe four months ago. 'Ere, you ain't suggestin' . . .?'

'Did you ever pay Mr Childers a house call?'

'I don't do house calls, Mr Lestrade. Mr Childers may have had floozies at his place, but for a professional service, 'e always came here.'

'Did he have any friends with him on any occasion? Or was anyone introduced to you by him? Someone with similar tastes, perhaps?'

Gertie racked what passed for a brain.

'There was one bloke. In politics 'e was, like Mr Childers.

Name of . . . cor, luv a duck. What was it now? Cor, brain like a sieve, Mr Lestrade, I always 'ad.'

Lestrade reached wearily into his pocket and produced another handful of notes. 'This is the second roll, Gertie, and the last.' He placed it in her hand. She smiled triumphantly, squeezing the money into the infinitesimal space that formed the edge of one breast and the beginning of another.

'Holmes,' she said. 'Tall bloke. Thin face. Smoked a pipe.'

Lestrade was halfway down the corridor before the bewildered Gertie called him.

'One roll deserves another, dearie,' she said, standing with legs apart and hands on hips, 'for old times' sake.'

Lestrade glanced back as he reached the door.

'Gertie, I couldn't afford you,' he said.

The blue carb uncle

They had found him in the morning, when the grass was still wet from the night and the woods were dripping in their dampness. He lay on his back, legs outstretched, hands gripping with all the iron of rigor mortis the shaft of the bamboo lance jutting upright from his chest.

His friends and his beaters had carried him back on a barn door and they had laid him out on his bed. The woman of the estate, who knew about these things, had stripped off the bloodied hunting pinks and had washed him. The lance was removed and wiped clean. They had to break his arms to relax his grip. And it was over sixteen hours before the local constabulary were contacted. The Chief Constable was a thinking man. He had the sense to call in the Yard. And no faith in his own clodhoppers. Lestrade had just finished typing up his reports – in triplicate, of course – when the urgent summons came. 'Major Deering dead. Stop. Suspect foul play. Stop. Send your best man. Stop. Or failing that, Lestrade. Stop.'

Immune to the insult, eyes bleary with the concentration of typing and the bruising of Gertie's whiplash, the inspector dug out his faded Gladstone, threw in a shirt, a spare collar and his cut-throat and made for King's Cross. He had had no time to check the coroner's report on the late Childers. No time to deposit the diary with the Yard's code breakers. No time to brief the two new men that Frost had sent him. They, like all else on the first floor, would have to wait.

They met him at the station in a landau draped in black. Introductions were made briefly, sombrely, in the twilight and the vehicle rattled through the gathering dark.

'So you are the deceased's brother?' Lestrade asked the man facing him under the silk of a top hat.

'I am,' he asserted.

'I have no information, sir. Could you tell me what happened?.'

'We have no idea, Inspector. There was a hunt yesterday. The Hall was packed. Loving cups and hounds all over the place. Uncle was in fine fettle in the morning, eager for the fray, as always.'

Lestrade turned to the older man on George Deering's left. 'You would be the deceased's uncle, Mr Sheraton?'

Mr Sheraton looked a little surprised as his monocle slipped from his eye.

'No, sir. I was a brother officer.' And both men looked to an imagined altar in the middle distance.

'Forgive me,' said Lestrade, sensing he was about to be crushed by the falling branches of the family tree, 'then who is your uncle?'

'John,' they both chorused.

Lestrade looked uncomprehending.

'Major Deering,' Sheraton went on, as Lestrade saw the lights of Deering Hall shining through the evergreens, 'was known as "Uncle" to all the officers of the regiment.'

'Regiment.' Lestrade was blankly registering the deceased's rank.

'The Carabiniers, man,' Deering explained a little testily, 'the Sixth Dragoon Guards. We are all – were all – officers of that great and distinguished company.'

It had been some time since Lestrade had been in the company of army men. He had forgotten their lack of chin, their narrow vision, the extent of their snobbery and the flash of the spoons they carried with such hauteur in their mouths.

The landau jolted to a halt and Lestrade was shown into Deering Hall. He felt as though he was being frogmarched to his own execution, the riding boots of his fellows clanking on the polished wood and marble of the floors. He was shown into a room lit with candles. The walls were hung with banners and portraits of flinty-eyed colonels, proud in their scarlet and gold. On a gun-limber in the middle of the room lay Major John

Deering, late of His Majesty's Sixth Dragoon Guards. Lestrade looked at the corpse. Peaceful. Content. He lay with his arms crossed over his chest, resplendent in the dark blue and white of the Carbs, the candlelight flashing on the gold lace at his throat and his cuffs. They had buckled his sword around him and on the velvet cushion by his head lay his gauntlets, his spurs and the tall, white-plumed helmet. It reminded Lestrade of the tomb of the Black Prince he had seen at Canterbury. Even the major's sweeping moustaches were reminiscent.

'Who certified the death?' he asked.

'I did,' said Sheraton. 'I am the regimental surgeon.'

'We don't hold that against him,' the younger Deering proffered as a matter of fact rather than an attempt at humour.

'And?' the inspector was waiting.

'The aorta was severed by the head of a cavalry lance.'

'A cavalry lance?' Lestrade looked up incredulously.

Deering crossed to a corner and returned with the weapon, handing it to Lestrade, who hesitated, then with a certain resignation, took it. 'It's been wiped, I suppose?'

'Of course,' said Deering. 'People have been coming all day to pay their respects to Uncle. There'll be more in the morning. One couldn't just leave that lying around covered in Uncle's blood, could one?'

'The wound, doctor?' Lestrade turned to Sheraton.

'Captain,' insisted the doctor.

'How was it made?'

'A single thrust, I would say, from the front, probably when Uncle was on the ground.'

'Is it customary to hunt foxes with lances?' Lestrade put the point to his not-so-genial hosts.

'We are a heavy cavalry regiment, Lestrade,' snapped Deering, we don't use lances at all. I believe the Scots Greys employ the lance for their front ranks, but . . . well, the Greys . . .' He and Sheraton snorted in joint contempt.

'Then whose is this?' Lestrade asked.

'I've no idea,' said Deering. 'It doesn't belong in the house. It has to be the murderer's.'

Lestrade held the weapon horizontally for a moment, then swung it upright.

'Show me how it was done, Captain,' he said to Sheraton, 'in your opinion.'

The good captain took the shaft, curled the leather thong around his wrist and tucked it under his right arm.

'A lancer would use it like this. Elandslaagte, Omdurman, all lancer actions involve the weapon this way. I would say for the depth of the wound, it was used thus,' he gripped the lance in two hands, like a spear, 'and delivered from a standing position.'

'There were no other wounds on the body?'

'None.'

'I suppose it would be superfluous of me to ask whether the major was a good horseman?'

Sheraton looked at Deering.

'The best,' George Deering affirmed.

'Gentlemen, I was unable to bring a constable with me. Perhaps I might use your telephone, Mr Deering?'

'Captain,' insisted Deering.

'To ring the local constabulary?'

'Can't you manage by yourself, Inspector? After all, we don't really want the local bobbies trampling all over the place. Our Chief Constable expressly asked for you, I understand?'

'In a way,' mused Lestrade. 'Cheer up, gentlemen,' he said, making for the door. 'We at least know that Major Deering's murderer is unlikely to be a lancer. Such a one would surely have killed from the saddle. And he would not have left his weapon behind. That must eliminate two or three thousand men.'

Lestrade's cheery optimism was not shared by his hosts. For the remaining hours before the clock in the hallway struck twelve, they continued their story of the previous day. The hunt had got off to a flying start and they expected a good day's sport. Uncle was mounted on a new gelding, a bay, and was soon ahead of the field. There had been some confusion at the water and the pack had separated, Sheraton and George Deering taking the high ground towards the moor. Uncle and a few others had cut through the gorse bushes after the other hounds, trusting to luck in the tangle of undergrowth. When the two groups met up again, there was a terrible to-do because

Lady Brandling's horse had thrown her and there was some suggestion on her part that as she lay dazed in the Lower Moorgate, she had been interfered with. Certainly, she said, she had felt a man's hand on her knee. Anyway, it was some time before it was realised that Uncle was not among those solicitous for her full recovery. But he was a good horseman, George Deering was at pains to remind Lestrade, and he knew the estate and the neighbouring woods like the back of his hand. He would return in his own good time and with a brush to boot. But evening had come and the bay had been found in the gorse, wandering alone, its saddle ominously empty. Deering, Sheraton, the others and the beaters had gone out again to look for him. Perhaps he had hit a tree. The bay was relatively untried. Who knew what might have happened. Perhaps he had seen the bounder who had accosted Lady Brandling and had taken off after him. But the beaters found nothing and he did not answer the calling of his name. At nightfall, they called off the search, to resume again at first light. And it was then that one of the gamekeepers on the estate found him.

'Why a lance?' Lestrade was talking to himself really.

'India,' mused Sheraton, fitting his monocle as he poured himself another brandy.

Lestrade looked at the reflection of the flames in the monocle.

'India?' he repeated.

'When I first joined the regiment,' Sheraton explained, 'we were stationed in India. Meerut. Our favourite sports there were horse-racing and pig-sticking.'

'Pig-sticking?'

'Boar hunting, to be precise,' Deering explained. 'Tricky beggar, your boar. Nasty. Turns on you in a tight corner. And those tusks are no joke.'

Sheraton concurred.

'So our man may be someone who knew Major Deering in India? Did he have enemies?' asked Lestrade.

'What man doesn't have enemies?' Deering replied. 'John was an enormously popular man, Inspector. Everyone in the mess called him "Uncle". But couldn't that very popularity have made him the envy of one?'

'Any one in particular?' Lestrade asked.

Deering shrugged. Time for Lestrade to try a bit of pig-sticking of his own.

'One who stood to inherit his elder brother's estate, perhaps?'

George Deering leapt to his feet. 'That's a foul and offensive remark, Lestrade. You will withdraw it immediately.'

Lestrade looked at Sheraton, also on his feet by now. 'One who, as a surgeon in a fashionable cavalry regiment, is regarded as the lowest of the low, and who was insanely jealous of the most popular officer in that regiment?'

'Lestrade, you go beyond the bounds of decency!' roared Sheraton.

'Frequently,' said Lestrade, rising now to their level, 'but only because murder takes me there. Sit down gentlemen. If I have given offence, I am sorry. But I need to start eliminating suspects. I have just eliminated two.'

'How so?' Deering demanded.

'Captains, I have been in the murder game for a long time,' he stared wistfully into the crackling fire, 'a very long time, I sometimes think. And I get to know a lie when I hear it. And a murderer when I see him. Oh, not every time, of course. But there is usually something. And in your case, I can't see it. And I can't hear it.'

'As well as the fact of course,' Deering went on, 'that we have witnesses who will swear we were with them all day.'

'You give me ten men who all see the same thing at the same instant and I'll give you ten different versions of that thing,' said Lestrade. 'Your friends will swear you were there because they are your friends. Because they would have expected you to be there. Because they saw a horse similar to yours. Because someone mentioned they had seen you. Even so,' Lestrade quaffed the last of his brandy, 'I would like a list of those who rode with you and especially those you remember riding with Major Deering when the pack parted. If you'll excuse me, gentlemen, I'll to my bed. I will have to intrude on the solemnities tomorrow in order to ask your mourners a few questions.'

And he left.

George Deering blew out the lamp and turned to Sheraton still standing by the fire.

'I think our flatfoot friend has presumed too far, Arthur, don't you?'

'Suggestions, George?'

'If our dear Chief Constable has the measure of this man,' Deering was making for the door, 'he's the no-stone-unturned type. When he's finished annoying our friends with his ghastly bourgeois questions, he'll probably go to Brighton.'

'To the regiment?' Sheraton was aghast. 'The disgusting boundah!'

'Quite. I think we can manage something for him there, don't you?'

They came and went all the next day, depositing their cards in the morning, returning in the afternoon. The drive looked like Hyde Park on a sunny Sunday, choked with carriages and cabriolets. Lestrade ensconced himself, with Captain Deering's grudging permission, in the late major's study. He had got his reinforcements after all – a sergeant and three constables to take notes and otherwise do the bidding of the man from the Yard. Deering and Sheraton kept out of his way, but could not fail to notice the sour looks of those whom Lestrade had questioned. Of those who had ridden to hounds two days earlier and whose names appeared on Deering's list as having ridden with the deceased when the pack broke up, Lestrade interviewed eight. Their stories were substantially the same and of little help. They had all lost sight of the major at the watercourse. One of them said he seemed to be having trouble with the bay. Another mentioned a figure on a grey horse he did not know, riding near to Deering and a little to his right, but there were several faces in the hunt he did not know and he could not place much significance in that particular one.

Then, Lestrade interviewed Lady Brandling. She was a large woman, probably the wrong side of forty, but then, who wasn't these days? She wore purple as a token of mourning and her golden hair hung in tresses – a style a trifle passé – over her shoulders. Her eyes sparkled with a sapphire intensity however and she insisted Lestrade walk with her in the garden and without the constable in attendance if the inspector didn't mind, as the matter they were to discuss was a delicate one.

'You are here about . . . the incident?' Lady Brandling asked him as they passed beneath the apple blossom.

'Indeed, ma'am,' he replied.

'There is little I can tell you.' She sighed.

Lestrade had heard all this before.

'Whatever crumb you may have, ma'am, is of the utmost importance.'

She looked at him. 'Of course,' she said, 'I had been riding for nearly an hour. There had been no sign of a fox in that time, but the hounds clearly had a scent. I had just heard the "View Halloo" when I realised I had ridden too high into the woods. I was alone, although I saw various people below me, through the trees. I must have hit a branch, because when I awoke, I was lying on the ground, and my head hurt.'

Lestrade noted the small bruise.

'There was . . . a man . . . bending over me. He . . . had his hand on my knee and was pushing up my riding gown. Then he tried . . . to kiss me . . . Inspector, is all this necessary?'

'No, ma'am, it is not. I am making enquiries into the death of Major John Deering. I fear you and I are talking at cross purposes, Lady Brandling.'

She broke away with a start, then turned back to him. 'No, Inspector, I do not believe we are. You see the man in question *was* Major John Deering.'

Lestrade narrowed his eyes and took the lady's elbow gently. 'Are you saying the deceased attempted to rape you?'

Lady Brandling blushed. 'He had been . . . amorous, shall we say, for some time. Making advances . . . suggestions.' She heaved her more than adequate bosom. 'I of course resisted.'

'Of course.' Lestrade was solicitous.

'He was a fine horseman, Inspector Lestrade. He would never have allowed an animal to throw him. He had obviously been following me. Waiting for his chance.'

'What happened then?'

'As soon as I realised what was going on, I fought him off.'

Highly probable, thought Lestrade, having sensed Lady Brandling's biceps beneath the velvet.

'He must have felt ashamed, because he helped me up and rode away. That was the last time I saw him until . . . this afternoon.'

'Who else knows of this?' Lestrade asked.

'No one. And that is how I would like it to stay. Uncle was a fine man in many ways. The regiment loved him. The county loved him. Here and there you might find a lady – or a downstairs maid – who did not choose to love him. He had this fatal weakness you see. A weakness for women.'

'Fatal, indeed, ma'am,' echoed Lestrade. 'Tell me, my lady, do you yourself come of a military family?'

'Why yes, Inspector. My father was a colonel in the Dorsetshires and my grandfather fought in the Crimea, in the Royal Horse Artillery.'

'So your home . . . er . . . forgive me . . .'

'Brandling Hall.'

'Brandling Hall, is hung with trophies of a military kind?'

'Why, yes.'

'Cavalry lances?'

'Yes, I believe . . .' Lady Brandling was suddenly on her guard. 'Inspector, what are you implying?'

'You are a woman outraged, Lady Brandling,' Lestrade reminded her. 'What is more natural than that you should want revenge?'

'And how was I to achieve this revenge?' her ladyship asked. 'Did I secrete a lance in my skirts with which to skewer Uncle Deering? Or did I ostentatiously carry it as lancers do, in a lance shoe fitted to my stirrup? No, wait. Perhaps I hid it privily in the woods, persuaded the fox to run that way and waited there until Uncle pounced on me. Then I ran him through with it.'

Lestrade burst out laughing in spite of himself. And after a moment or two, Lady Brandling joined in.

'Forgive me, my lady. My job is to leave no stone unturned. You have reminded me of the little matter of logic, however. And you have admirably acquitted yourself in the process.'

'Inspector,' she said, when the laughter had subsided, 'it is not proper that we should be so merry on a day like this. I trust that the incident to which I referred earlier will go no further?'

Lestrade looked gravely at her. 'I see no reason, ma'am,' he said, 'why it should. One last thing,' he led her towards the house, huge and impressive in its Palladian red brick, 'did you see a rider on a grey horse?'

'Three or four, Inspector. Is it important?'

'Probably not.' And they went indoors.

Lestrade had not visited this part of Norman Shaw's noble pile in eight years. Not since he'd been working on the Baskett case and that was in very different circumstances. It was somewhere in the bowels of the earth. In fact, he fancied if you kept very still you could hear Old Father Thames, gurgling and growling only feet away.

'Not much headway yet, Inspector,' the boffin said, scrutinising Lestrade over his pince-nez. 'It does appear to be a diary, but the system is a complex one. Do you know anything about codes?'

'Not much.' Lestrade shrugged.

'Well, there are numerical and alphabetical, syllable and word, stencil and blackline. On the other hand, there is the miscellaneous range – angle writing, thread writing, the puncture system, the foot rule cypher and so on.'

'Which is this one?'

'I don't know. But I think I've ruled out puncture, stencil and foot rule.' He riffled through a forest of papers, 'That's progress. The simplest of all is the five element code – Francis Bacon's – for example "fly" is written "aabab". But it could be written "ababa" or even "babba" – do you see?'

'No,' said Lestrade. It was no more than the truth. Give him a corpse, a bloodstain, a fingerprint even and he was on firm ground. But this man was talking nonsense.

'The Paris International Telegraph Conference issued an Official Vocabulary of some two hundred thousand words in eighteen ninety. That was for commercial codes really, but it has its application in other spheres of course.'

'Of course,' concurred the bewildered Lestrade.

'The New Official Vocabulary has extended this to one million words. That was supposed to reduce the risk of faulty transmission, but I don't personally think it's very successful.'

'Er . . . no, I suppose not,' Lestrade observed.

'Of course, if this diary – if that's what it is – uses artificial words, then we're sunk.'

'Without trace.' The inspector was forced to agree.

'I've even tried tilting the book through three hundred and sixty degrees, to find a cryptographic disc. No luck. What I'm working on now is . . .' But he was talking to himself. Lestrade had gone to the upper reaches of the Yard, where men spoke a language he understood.

Three such men stood before his desk in the office on the first floor. One of them was Walter Dew, newly promoted sergeant of H Division, Scotland Yard. The other two were recruits – Constables Dickens and Jones – bright eyed and bushy tailed in their Cheapside suits.

'Dickens,' said Lestrade, surveying the paperwork before him. 'Christian names Charles Boothby.' He looked up as the young man advanced. 'Charles Dickens?' Lestrade scowled. 'Any relation?'

'To whom, sir?' the constable asked intently.

'No relation,' sighed Lestrade. 'How many years in the Force?'

'Three, sir – next September.'

'Two and a half,' Lestrade observed mechanically. He scanned the papers again and his attention fixed on something. 'You were the arresting officer in the Terris case?'

'Yes, sir. It was my first night on the beat. On my own that is.'

'It took some bottle to face that maniac, Constable.' Lestrade was not a man easily impressed.

'No, sir, I didn't use a bottle. I relied on my truncheon.'

Thank God, thought Lestrade to himself, you didn't use your brain. 'Why did you put in for the Yard, Dickens?' he contented himself with asking.

'Scotland Yard are the finest body of detectives in the world, sir. I wanted to be part of that body.'

Lestrade refrained from mentioning which part of the body

he felt Dickens was most likely to resemble and turned to the second constable.

'Jones,' he said. The aforementioned stepped up smartly and saluted. 'No,' said Lestrade dejectedly, 'we don't do that in plainclothes. It sort of gives the game away, you know. There you are, working undercover in a gin palace, about to break a ring of opium smugglers or white slavers. I walk in, looking for all the world like a punter and you salute! So you see, thanks, but no thanks.'

Now it was Jones' turn to look dejected.

'Christian names, John Thomas . . .' Lestrade looked at him and saw the smirk vanish from the faces of Dew and Dickens. He checked the record sheet, 'So you're Athelney Jones' little boy?' he clicked his tongue.

'Not so little, sir. I shall be nineteen next month. One year in the Force.'

'How's your old Dad? Enjoying his retirement?'

'Thank you, sir. He sends his regards.'

'Bearing in mind he and I barely exchanged the time of day, Constable, that must represent quite an effort on his part. So you've spent most of the last year walking up and down the Mile End Road. Any action?'

'A few trassenos . . . er . . . villains, sir.'

'Good. A man who can patter East End. That's useful. Why the Yard? Daddy's footsteps?'

'Yes, sir.' Jones was making no apology for the fact.

'Fair enough.' Lestrade lolled back in his chair. They stood before him like peas in a pod, like Tweedledee and Tweedledum. What a trio – Dee, Dum and Dew. Why did he always seem to get the rookies? And simple rookies at that? It didn't seem all that long since he had sat in this chair and looked at the granite bulk of young Harry Bandicoot. But Harry, with all his faults and his Old Etonian sense of honour and fair play, had been a useful man to have at your back. Lestrade could always rely on Dew. But what of these two? What if Tweedledee and Tweedledum should happen on a battle? And what, if any, routines of police procedure could he expect them to follow? They had less – appreciably less – than four years' experience between them. Anyway, no time like the present.

'Dickens.'

'Sir?'

'What do you know of the Sixth Dragoon Guards?'

Dickens looked blank for a moment then launched himself.

'The Sixth Dragoon Guards. His Majesty's Sixth Regiment of Heavy Cavalry of the Line. Raised in sixteen eighty-five. Originally called "The Queen Dowager's". Later "The Carabiniers" because of the short musket they carried into action. Due to be converted to Light Cavalry in India forty years ago. They were ordered to change their uniform from blue to scarlet. The conversion never took place, and they are now the only Heavy Cavalry Regiment to wear blue tunics. Battle honours include—'

'Thank you, Constable!' Lestrade's amazement had been growing for a while. 'You know all this and you don't know anything of your namesake?'

'Who might that be, Inspector?'

'Never mind.' Lestrade managed, when he found the ability to close his mouth. 'Where are the Carbs stationed now?'

'Carbs, sir?'

'Carabiniers, man. The regiment we – you – have just been talking about.'

'Oh, Brighton, sir.'

'All right.' The inspector reached with trembling fingers for a cigar. Dickens' Lucifer was waiting for him before it reached his lips. Lestrade blew smoke through his nose, living up to the grim picture which Dew had enjoyed painting of him for the new lads.

'Jones.' Lestrade turned his guns on Tweedledum.

'Sir?'

'What do you know about cavalry lances?'

'Cavalry lances, sir?' Jones checked that he had heard right.

Lestrade nodded, waiting for the 'Nothing' or the silence. Instead he got a lecture.

'The lance as a weapon of war disappeared from the battlefield during the seventeenth century as it was found to be unwieldy and no match for firearms. It returned into the British service in eighteen sixteen as a result of the impressive use of the said weapon by Napoleon's Polish levies, especially the Lancers of the Vistula, under Marshal Poniatowski. British lance regiments at first carried a sixteen-foot shaft weighing four pounds and made of ash wood but recent experience in India has led to the development of a shorter weapon, made of bamboo and weighing—'

'Thank you, Constable.' Lestrade had let his cigar go out in amazement at the display of erudition. 'Sergeant Dew,' he said, 'I'll wager you still make a better cup of tea than either of these walking encyclopedias. Hot, and lots of it. I'm not feeling well.'

Lestrade could have sent Walter Dew. He could not yet trust Dickens or Jones. But he had a grudging respect for them in an odd sort of way. Though how two men from such humdrum backgrounds – and one of them the son of the biggest idiot ever to put on a Metropolitan uniform – could possess such knowledge, Lestrade was at a loss to explain. No wonder Nimrod Frost had said he thought Lestrade would like these two. But he had liked constables before. Two had been killed serving under him. One had been crippled. One had resigned to marry a rich widow. Constables had a habit of not staying around. Except Dew, but even he was a sergeant now. Best not to get too fond of them. Lestrade caught the noon train to Brighton by himself.

He knew the town vaguely. In the short time he and Sarah had had together, they had occasionally come down, by this very train, if he remembered rightly. Still this was no time to be maudlin. He'd promised her he wouldn't be. And he had a murderer to catch.

Lieutenant-Colonel Gilmartin, officer commanding His Majesty's Sixth Dragoon Guards, the Carabiniers, was a martyr to gout. Lestrade found him growling behind a pair of huge white dundrearies at least forty years out of date, lying on a *chaise-longue* in his quarters at the camp. A subaltern taking down the colonel's memoirs in longhand was ushered out of the room and Lestrade took his place on the stool.

'Pour me a brandy,' grunted Gilmartin, 'before my good lady

wife returns from her blasted temperance meeting. Are you married, Inspector?'

'A widower, sir.'

'Oh,' the colonel grunted. 'Don't mean to be offensive, old boy, but you're a lucky man.'

Lestrade smiled.

'Now . . . agghh,' and he grimaced as he tried to settle his heavily bandaged foot on the cushion, 'how can I help you on poor old Uncle?'

'What kind of man was he?' asked Lestrade.

'Marvellous fellow. Marvellous. Competent soldier. Thoroughly good egg of course. A demon at baccarat . . . er . . . have they legalised that yet?'

'I'm looking for a murderer, Colonel Gilmartin, not a card-sharp.'

'Quite, quite.' The colonel swept his moustaches into the brandy. 'Something of a ladies' man, I understand.'

'I understand that too,' said Lestrade. 'Did he leave a string of loves scorned? Jealous husbands?'

'God knows. I had the misfortune to marry the only filly I ever paid my devoirs to. Completely misunderstood the term filly. By the time I realised, it was too late. I don't see what men see in women. Give me a horse and a brandy any time.'

Each to his own, thought Lestrade, that must be what gout does to a man.

'He was popular in the regiment?'

'God, yes. People here in Brighton call us Uncle's Own, y'know. Good for morale, was old Uncle. We'll miss him. Here's to you, Uncle Deering, wherever you are!' And he downed the brandy and hurled the glass at the grate. Lestrade drank the toast, but refrained from following suit. The cut glass would cost him two months' salary.

'I don't know what I can tell you, Inspector.' The colonel was rearranging his feet as painlessly as possible. 'Uncle had been with us for nearly twelve years. His father was with the regiment, and his father before him. But we'd have missed Uncle anyway.'

'I don't think I follow, sir,' said Lestrade.

'He was leaving us, Inspector. Didn't his brother tell you?

Perhaps George didn't know. How odd. Yes, he was going to resign his commission. Going into politics, I believe. Now, there's a rum life for a man. Can't abide it myself. Not done in the mess, y'understand? No religion. No politics. Yes, we'd have missed him.'

'Politics,' repeated Lestrade, and faint warning bells began to ring in his head. The itch he couldn't scratch was starting up. He thanked the colonel for his time and his brandy and an orderly showed him out. On the way, he tipped his bowler to a lady he presumed to be the colonel's good lady wife. He knew her by her resemblance to a filly, swathed in the ribbons of the Rechabites, piety and starchiness etched into every line of her face.

He found himself in a lane, cobbled and twisting, with high brick walls. This was not the way he had come and he was temporarily lost. As he rounded a corner, he was faced by two burly troopers of the Carbs, the afternoon sun shining behind them, silhouetting their stable dress and forage caps. There was something in their walk, something in the clubs they carried that told Lestrade they were not out for a stroll. Discretion, ever a policeman's ally on these occasions, came to the rescue of valour and Lestrade turned back the way he had come. There stood two more Carbs, bigger and uglier than the first. They advanced at a measured tread, cradling their wooden sticks in their arms. Lestrade knew the damage those things could do. They looked uncomfortably like the batons of the Mounted Police. He had swung one himself in his time. He felt for his brass knuckles, raising his other hand in a token or surrender. He saw for the first time the black arm bands above their left elbows. Mourning for their Uncle. He twisted round, this way and that, watching for the first blow. What he said was pointless, but he said it anyway.

'I am Inspector Lestrade of Scotland Yard. Striking a police officer is a serious—' And the first cudgel hissed towards him before he'd finished the sentence. He caught it expertly and wrenched its wielder forward, slamming him into his second attacker. The second club was faster, or Lestrade slower and it caught him square in the back. He hit the wall, the rough bricks grazing his already scarred face. He swung round, crouching low, and heard two more clubs crunch uselessly against the wall. His boot jabbed into the knee of one of the four and the man stumbled. Lestrade's brass fist came up for the first time and bloodied the man's nose. For a second he heard the cursing and grunting of the others, then dull aches on both arms, a sickening crack on his head and the cobbles hurtled up to meet him. The rest was silence.

Boscombe's odd place

Lestrade awoke to a resplendent evening, more typical of July than April. There wasn't a cloud in the sky and the sun dazzled through the boughs of the elm towering over him. At first, his head felt detached from his body, as though when he struggled upright, anything above his neck was still lying on the grass beside him. Only slowly did his vision focus on the clump of bushes to his right and the sweep of the downs beyond. He felt the rough bark of the trunk at his back and was about to attempt to rise when a shattering scream ricocheted around the empty echoing space which had been his head. For an instant his eyes took in a bevy of young ladies in frothy blouses and straw boaters. He registered that it was they who screamed. He knelt up with difficult and reached out as though to calm them, when he realised the full horror of his situation. Beneath the voluminous Donegal, he was stark naked.

He leapt for the shelter of the nearest bush, but landed badly and found out the hard way, as most non-countrymen do, that it was gorse. As decorously as possible, he wrapped the coat around the portion he assumed had given offence, but by that time the bevy of ladies were scurrying out of the little hollow and making for high ground.

Lestrade had little time to consider his situation further, for as he emerged, battered but unbowed from the tangle of the bush, he caught the full impact of a hockey stick across his nose. Eyes swimming with tears, he ducked and stumbled backwards, so that the coat flapped open again to reveal his all.

'You disgusting beast!' his assailant roared in a falsetto shriek, covering her face with her left hand, while holding back with the hockey stick in her right the hastily returning bevy of young ladies. 'Don't look, girls!' she bellowed. 'Keep behind me!' And she swung to the attack again, brandishing her stick with all the zeal of a whirling dervish. Even her hairstyle bore similarities.

'Madam, I—' But Lestrade had to duck before he finished his sentence and thought it best to take to his heels. He found himself in a broad field, angling down to the sea and heard, rather than dared look at, the pack of furious females at his back. The air was alive with the hissing of a hockey stick and he actually heard at least one 'View Halloo' before he leapt the barbed wire fence and rolled headlong through the long yellow grass into a steep ravine.

It may have been muddy, wet and rank at the bottom, but it was preferable to the harpies who had driven him to its brink. He crouched in the sheltering bushes until the pack gave up the chase at the boundary fence and went away.

Now, the problem was to get back to the road. This time he buttoned his Donegal and picked his way gingerly through the ravine into which he had fallen. The sea sparkled away to his right and the winds from it began to rise as the purple shadows lengthened. He had just picked his way over the agonies of ling, unable to decide whether it was his head or his feet which bothered him most, when he heard a distant voice shout, 'Fire!' Turning to find the pall of black smoke that cry had led him to expect, his eyes caught instead a long figure silhouetted on a curve of the downs. In an instant, he realised that the figure was not alone, but that a row of heads bobbed up along a ridge to his left. The shout was followed by a noise he had heard before, though not often and a sharp whipping wind which came from nowhere and ripped the flap of his Donegal. Instinctively, he followed the path of the wind and saw a hole appear in a black and white painted post between him and the sea.

'Good God!' he heard the watcher cry. 'Cease fire!'

It was only then that Lestrade understood the ambiguity of the word and flung himself headlong on the grass. He was lying, he now realised, on a rifle range and was inches from the targets. He saw the heads emerge as men, running towards him through the gathering dusk.

'I told you we should have finished before this, Gigger!' he heard one say. 'You can't see a damned thing in this light.'

'I can't see much, anyway,' Gigger replied and then to Lestrade, 'My dear chap, let me help you up.'

Two or three of the men began to brush Lestrade down until they noticed his bare legs below the Donegal, and one by one they drew back, looking with varying degrees of puzzlement and distaste according to their predilections and their view of the world.

'Didn't you see the sign?' one of them snapped. 'It says quite clearly "Keep out".'

'No,' said Lestrade, 'as a matter of fact I was being pursued by a rather irate group of young ladies.'

'I'm not surprised,' said another, 'dressed like that.'

'Obviously a pervert, Gigger. What'll we do?'

'Call the police,' another offered. 'This is private property. I don't care what a man does in his spare time, but this is the Rottingdean Rifle Club. He can't do it here.'

'No, no, wait a minute,' Gigger answered. 'I'm sure there's a reasonable explanation Mr . . . er . . .?'

'Lestrade, Inspector Lestrade – of Scotland Yard.'

'Good God,' murmured Gigger, 'undercover work, eh?'

'You might say so,' Lestrade replied.

'Come on,' said Gigger, grinning through his pebble glasses, 'you look as though you could do with a pair of trousers. I've a Lanchester at the club house.'

Lestrade had not heard of that make of nether garment before, but if it kept the Downs winds from racing up his Donegal, he was all for it. Amid mutters of abuse from the rest, Lestrade and his shooting companion strode for the club house.

'I fear I have upset your friends,' said Lestrade.

'Ah, flannelled fools at the wicket,' grunted Gigger. 'Besides, it's too dark for any more practice tonight. I'm Rudyard Kipling.' And he heartily shook Lestrade's hand.

The Lanchester to which Kipling referred was not a pair of trousers at all but a horseless carriage. It didn't help Lestrade that his new-found acquaintance kept referring to the machine as Amelia. At least, Lestrade assumed that, as he couldn't believe that Kipling would be so tasteless as to imply that a lady known to him was a bitch to start of a frosty morning. On second thoughts, Lestrade had known women like that.

They drove through the dusk of the April countryside, Lestrade cold and dispirited, aching and annoyed, while Gigger was roaring above the rattle and growl of Amelia sonorous comments on Sussex by the sea which Lestrade supposed must be poetry. It was not the inspector's first ride in such a contraption, but by the time they reached the looming granite of Kipling's house, he was heartily hoping it would be his last.

'So how did you come to be trouserless on the downs, Lestrade?' asked Kipling over an especially cheering glass of port.

'I'm afraid I am not at liberty to divulge . . .' began Lestrade in the jargon which constabularies the country over had made their own, but Kipling was persistent.

'Come on, man. Here you are drinking my port, warming yourself by my fire. You've ridden in my Lanchester and now you're wearing my clothes. Don't you think I deserve a little confidence?'

Lestrade looked at the man. He was the colour of mahogany, his Indian complexion tanned further by the sun of the veld. A firm imperial chin jutted below a walrus moustache of total blackness and over the spectacles which gave him the nickname of Gigger – 'Giglamps' – the eyebrows met with a fierce friendship. Lestrade's old granny used to say that those whose eyebrows did that were destined to hand. He told the poet the gist of his clash with the Carbs, but was at a loss to explain his arrival on the downs near Rottingdean wearing only his overcoat.

'Well, one thing's for sure,' Kipling mused, 'the Misses Lawrence will be out for your blood.'

'Misses Lawrence?' Lestrade repeated.

'Almost certainly the matron who set about you with her hockey stick was a Miss Lawrence. Oh, she's a formidable dragon. And you exposing yourself to her young ladies, well . . .'

'It was a girls' school then?'

'Roedean. Founded some years ago by three dreadful sisters. The eldest of them was called Medusa . . .'

The classical quip was lost on Lestrade, whose antiquarian knowledge all began and ended with Pandora. But Kipling had moved from the fire now and he picked up a framed photograph of a little girl. His mood suddenly changed. 'I might have sent her there,' he murmured.

'Mr Kipling?'

'Have you ever lost anyone dear to you, Lestrade?' His eyes were sad in the firelight.

'I have,' the inspector answered.

Kipling nodded, then he blew his nose with a deafening report and poured them both another drink.

'What will you do about those chappies in the Carbs?' he asked. 'If I may retain your clothes, sir, until I can get to the nearest tailors—'

'My dear fellow, the nearest tailor is an ass. I saw better stitching in Zulu Kraals when I was in South Africa. Besides, my time is my own for a while. I'm not on semaphore duty at the club again for a week. And I'm intrigued by you police chappies. The lure of the bizarre, I suppose. I saw some of it in India. Oh, inferior, I'm sure, to your *métier*.'

Lestrade was equally sure, although he didn't know what that was.

'I could be your driver,' Gigger volunteered.

Lestrade hesitated. 'Well—'

'Good!' shouted Kipling. 'So it's agreed. Now, let's eat. Mrs Kipling makes exceedingly good cakes.'

Lestrade had a memory for faces, especially those belonging to men who had beaten him up. While Kipling adopted curious poses on the road, his head and body hidden under Amelia, in the nicest possible way, the inspector in poet's clothing waited near the barracks gate. Shortly after eleven, his target emerged, in walking-out dress, and began the journey into town. He caught an omnibus on the corner and alighted near the shore where the old Daddy Longlegs used to run (when it did run, so prone was it to break down). He was crossing the sands already strewn with early holiday-makers with their parasols and deckchairs in the warm April winds when Lestrade caught up with him.

'A word in your ear,' hissed the inspector, spinning his man round and pushing him backwards so that his head jarred against a great girder of the place pier. The trooper cried out, but Lestrade was faster and slapped him round the cheeks a few times.

'You bastard,' the soldier roared and lunged at Lestrade. He was younger and bigger than his opponent, but it had to be said that he had not Lestrade's experience in tight corners. The inspector merely stepped aside and with the grace of a music-hall turn, caught the man's ankle with his own and sent him sprawling in the sand. He landed with a crunch on the sandcastle of an indignant infant who bawled with such vigour that his mamma hurried over to accost the men.

'Disgusting!' she snorted, snatching the wailing child away. 'Drunken brawls in broad daylight,' and she turned to see Kipling dashing towards the group. 'You there! Call the police!'

'Inspector!' obliged Kipling.

'Yes, sir,' Lestrade played along for the lady's benefit, 'what seems to be the trouble?'

'Disgusting!' the woman said again, 'I'm going to call a *real* policeman!' and she hastened away in a flurry of sand, dragging the sobbing urchin in her wake.

Lestrade had not time to ruminate on the philosophy of her remark – whether or not he was a *real* policeman – because he was too busy sitting on the recumbent Carabinier.

'Blast. I missed all the fun,' moaned Kipling. 'That crank shaft of Amelia's has got to go.'

'There may be more fun yet,' said Lestrade, tugging up the trooper's head by his hair, 'if our friend here is going to be uncooperative. I am Inspector Lestrade of Scotland Yard. Who are you?'

'Williams, Ezekiah, Private three-four-one-eight-two, Sixth Dragoon Guards.' The reply was to the point and, as far as Lestrade could judge, honest. He was after all half throttling the man by virtue of the angle at which he held his head.

'Why did you and your messmates set about me the other day?'

'Orders.'

'Whose?'

A hesitation. Until Lestrade reminded the soldier of the vulnerability of his windpipe.

'Captain Deering's.'

'Would you care to elaborate?'

Kipling sat cross-legged in the sand, evidently enjoying Lestrade's bedside manner.

'He just told us to – rough you up a bit, that's all. He didn't say why.'

'What did he pay you?'

'Five shillings,' the trooper rasped.

Lestrade stepped off him and pulled the man up by his hair.

'Think yourself lucky, Williams, that I've got bigger fish to fry. Or you'd be serving of His Majesty the King behind prison bars by tonight. And they haven't banned flogging in military prisons yet, have they?'

Williams shook himself and stumbled off up the beach, cursing under his breath.

'You let that bounder get off lightly,' observed Kipling. 'Fancy a crack at the rifles on the pier? I'll buy you a hot potato.'

And that was an offer Lestrade could not refuse.

By evening, the inspector was back in his native city again, where he felt at home. And back too in his own suit. He was still shaking from his ride to Brighton station in Kipling's Lanchester and he reminded himself that he must return the poet's clothes by the morning post. As it was, he took advantage of a break in duty and caught a hansom to the Yard. It was raining as he crossed the courtyard, shining in the lamplight that flickered with the rustling trees. Strange how chill it was after the glory of the Downs and the baked potatoes with Kipling on Palace Pier.

He had not reached the side door which led to his office when the bright young face of Jones appeared in the half-light.

'Ah, I was on my way to your chambers, sir.'

'Chambers?' Lestrade didn't live in the Inner Temple.

'Telegram, sir. Just arrived.'

Lestrade pushed the constable back into the doorway. He scanned the telegram's contents. 'Where's Dickens?' he asked.

'Off duty, sir – an hour ago.'

'Dew?'

'I believe he's looking for that stolen cache of ping-pong balls, sir.'

'Where? Chinatown?'

'Sir?'

Lestrade looked at Jones. As he thought, the same lack of humour his old man had.

'Can you drive a Maria, Jones?'

'Yes, sir.'

'Then what are we standing here for, like the weather man and woman? Get one. I'll handle the paperwork later.'

The telegram was from one John Watson MD and it spoke of dark doings at the Diogenes Club.

'Diogenes, Jones,' said Lestrade as he gripped the seat rail on top of the Maria lurching towards the Mall. 'What can you tell me?'

'Would that be Diogenes of Apollonia, Diogenes of Babylon, Diogenes Laertius or Diogenes the Cynic, sir?'

'If there are four of them, Jones, I haven't got time to listen to the answer. Did any of them have a club?'

'Not as far as I am aware, sir.'

'All right. Just drive.'

They rattled through the advancing night, Lestrade increasingly aware that Jones was an infinitely worse driver than Kipling. At least the lurches of the Maria were comfortable ones, however, and the horse did not growl and cough like a tuberculous tin can. They found a uniformed man on the door of the Diogenes and a number of faces peering through the upper windows of the Carlton down the road. The bobby saluted Lestrade who took one look at the clubland portico and ordered Jones to stay outside.

In the entrance hall, with its double stairway and its marble pillars, a crimson-faced gentleman, the years catching up with him, hurried across to Lestrade. For a silly moment, the inspector stood rooted to the spot, his hand extended inches from that of the gentleman, until he realised his coat tails were caught in the door. Why did he always have trouble with his entrances?

'Lestrade. Thank you for coming so promptly.'

'Sssshhhh!' The sibilance echoed down the corridor although there was no one about.

'He's in here,' he went on in a whisper.

'Are you a member of this club, Doctor Watson?' Lestrade said.

'Be quiet!' a disembodied voice snapped. Lestrade could still see no one.

Watson led him down a short flight of carpeted stairs to a niche, heavy with flock wallpaper and lit by a small lamp. A member of the Diogenes lay dozing in his chair, *The Times* folded over his face. Watson pulled away the paper and Lestrade saw that the member was not dozing. He was dead.

Mechanically, the inspector checked the pulse, placed his ear against the immobile chest.

'Your story, Doctor?' Lestrade had dropped his voice to a whisper now.

'We can't talk here, Lestrade,' Watson's eyes swivelled nervously from side to side. 'This club is not like the others.'

A black-velveted flunkey appeared from nowhere, carrying a silver tray with brandies. He began to place one at the dead man's table.

'I don't think he'll need that,' said Lestrade.

'Sir?'

'The gentleman is dead,' the inspector informed him.

'Oh dear,' said the flunkey and stood with his head bowed for a moment.

'Who is in charge here?' Lestrade asked.

'Well, Mr Mycroft Holmes is a founder member – I believe he is the only such present this evening.'

'Where will I find him?'

The flunkey bowed and vanished through a forest of aspidistrae.

'One moment,' Lestrade raised his voice.

'Bad show!' someone grunted.

'Resign,' growled someone else.

'No, no, Lestrade. It's a club rule in here. No one, not even the staff, may speak more than three times or they are dismissed or black balled,' Watson told him.

Lestrade looked nonplussed.

'Diogenes,' said Watson, by the way of explanation.

Lestrade looked blanker than ever.

'Diogenes the Cynic,' went on Watson, 'one of the most anti-social men in classical antiquity. This is a club for the anti-social.'

'Shut up!' a voice bellowed.

'Get out!' roared another.

Lestrade strode for the door.

'Constable,' to the man on the steps, 'has anyone left by this way since you arrived?'

'No, sir.'

'How long have you been here?'

'Since that gentleman,' pointing to Watson, 'hailed me in the street over an hour ago.'

'Is there another way out?' Lestrade asked Watson.

'Yes, a back way, I believe,' the good doctor answered.

'Damn! Jones, find it and stay there until relieved.' The young constable sprang down from the Maria's high seat. 'And, by the way, it's Diogenes the Cynic.'

'Ah,' said Jones, scurrying off in search of the back door, 'Diogenes the Cynic. Circa four hundred to three hundred and twenty-five BC. Born at Sinope on the Euxine. Pupil of Antisthenes . . .' But Lestrade had gone, urging on the other constable the need to let no one pass.

'There must be somewhere in this mausoleum where we can talk at more than a whisper, Doctor Watson.'

'Yes, the visitors' room. This way.'

As the door of that room closed, Watson raised his voice to its usual level.

'My dear Lestrade. How are you? It's been a little while.'

'It has indeed, Doctor, but I fear we must dispense with the pleasantries. A man has been murdered.'

'How do you know it was murder, Lestrade?'

'Come now, Doctor Watson. I'm not playing one of your detective games. I've still got blood on my ear from the hole in the deceased's chest. And a hole in the chest is not a natural cause. Not in my book. Why else did you send for me?'

'Talking of books, I've nearly finished my latest – *The Hound of the Baskervilles*. Like the sound of it?'

Lestrade raised the Eyebrow of Exasperation.

'Well, er . . . where shall I start, Inspector?'

'A good story writer like you should know the answer to that one, Doctor – I'm sure Conan Doyle would. At the beginning of course.'

And he did.

But he hadn't finished when the door was opened by the monosyllabic flunkey, who ushered in a large man in evening suit. He was not unlike Nimrod Frost viewed in a funny fairground mirror and he shook hands as though with the flipper of a circus seal. There was something else in the steel grey of the eyes that was vaguely familiar and when Watson introduced him, Lestrade knew what it was.

'May I present Mr Mycroft Holmes, founder of the Diogenes Club. This is—'

'No!' Holmes held up his flipper, 'Let me guess. You are a policeman, sir, a detective of Scotland Yard. With the rank of . . . let me see . . . inspector?'

Holmes began to perambulate around Lestrade. 'You lost the tip of your nose in a duel with swords and have recently been on the receiving end of several blunt instruments – wooden clubs, I would deduce. You are married . . . no, a widower. Without children.' Holmes beamed. 'How am I doing so far, Inspector Lestrade?'

'Better than your late brother, Mr Holmes,' the inspector answered.

'Have a care, Lestrade,' the loyal Watson felt bound to interject.

'Yes, Sherlock always said I was,' grinned Holmes. 'Actually I cheated. I've seen you before – in the *Police Gazette* wasn't it? Weren't you wanted for attempting to murder the Kaiser?'

'You have a remarkable memory, Mr Holmes,' smiled Lestrade. 'All that was, of course, a misunderstanding.'

'Of course,' Holmes smiled in return. 'Boscombe,' he turned

to the flunkey, 'brandies. Large ones. And would you ask Mr Aumerle Holmes to join us?'

The flunkey vanished.

'Should have succeeded – the bounder!' growled Watson.

'Aumerle?' Holmes challenged him.

'No – the Kaiser. Lestrade should have succeeded in killing him. Damned upstart. I've never forgiven him for the Kruger telegram, you know.'

'Gentlemen,' Lestrade broke in, 'as much as I would like to reminisce on assassination attempts past, I fear we have one which is with us in the present and was very much successful. Mr Holmes, I wonder if you'd mind accounting for your movements since . . . say . . . five o'clock this evening.'

'I'll make myself scarce, Mycroft—' Watson began.

'I'd like you to stay, Doctor,' Lestrade stopped him.

'Oh, very well.' And the good doctor sat down.

'I was in my office in Whitehall at five, Inspector.' Holmes made himself comfortable. 'It had been a devil of a long day – I'd been there since three—'

'Your office, sir?' Lestrade checked him.

'The Foreign Office, Inspector.'

'What is the nature of your work there, sir?'

'My dear fellow, I am not at liberty to divulge that. National security, you know.'

All this reminded Lestrade of his deranged colleagues in the Special Branch, but he dismissed the idea and Holmes went on, 'At six precisely, I crossed to my rooms, washed and changed and came here to the club.'

'What time did you arrive?'

'Oh, it must have been nearly seven. For once, I broke my habit.'

'Habit?' Lestrade wondered what nauseating little confession was to follow.

'I invariably arrive at a quarter to five and leave promptly at twenty to eight. As I said, it had been a devil of a day and of course I would have left almost an hour ago had it not been for poor old Waldo.'

'How well did you know the deceased?'

'Know him? Watson, have you told the inspector nothing?

This is the Diogenes Club, Mr Lestrade, and I am a founder member. We are the most anti-social and unclubbable men in London. We don't *know* each other. We merely come here for the certainty of peace and quiet. Many of us lead very exacting lives. It is a rule of the club that we ignore each other as far as possible.'

'Even to the point of murder, Mr Holmes?'

'Ah, yes, unfortunate. But if I may shift your meaning, my dear Lestrade,' Holmes patronised very well, 'there is in my experience always a point to murder.'

'And in this case? You've seen the body?' Lestrade too was capable of semantics when pressed.

'Ah yes. 'The "point" in this case, I would say, was that of a stiletto. Clean, precise. Straight through the heart.'

'You disturbed the body?'

'Dear me no, Inspector. I leave that sort of bungling to the police – excepting present company, of course.'

'You are more than kind,' Lestrade bowed in his chair. 'What happened when you arrived at the club?' he asked.

'Let me see. I had a sherry wine and ordered dinner. Doctor Watson joined me as my guest a little after seven. He wished to discuss his latest masterpiece with me.'

'Masterpiece?' Lestrade was glad to see that Holmes was finding it difficult to stifle a guffaw, too.

'What's it called, Watson? *The Dog of the Barsetshires*?'

'*The Hound of the Baskervilles*, as well you know, Holmes.' Watson bristled and he attempted to shift the blame, 'Actually it was Lestrade who gave me the idea.'

'Oh?' Lestrade raised an eyebrow.

'That thing you caught in Cornwall a few years back.'

'Food poisoning?' Holmes asked in all innocence.

'A Tasmanian wolf.' Lestrade put him right.

'Yes, that's the chappie. Well, I talked to Conan Doyle about it and that's what we came up with. I think it's pretty good. I think Sherlock would have approved.'

'Anyway, we'd just sat down for a chat and Boscombe told me Aumerle had arrived.'

'O'Merle?'

'My cousin, Inspector. Aumerle Holmes. He joined us here

in the Strangers' Room – it's the only place where conversation is allowed.'

'And then?'

'Then we ate a hearty dinner. Capital pig, Watson.'

'I beg your pardon?' The doctor flushed behind his off-white whiskers. 'Oh, I see. Yes, it was. Capital.'

'And after the meal?'

'Boscombe came over to me and told me that Waldo didn't look well. I left my guests and went to his alcove. He was dead. Recently, I'd say. Perhaps half an hour. There was no sign of rigor mortis.'

'He's as stiff as a board, now,' Watson informed them, almost gleefully.

'What happened then?' Lestrade continued to press his man.

'Watson here suggested we contact you. So you see, my deductive reasoning when we met was not so impressive.'

'Impressive enough,' grunted Watson. 'Er . . . mind telling me how you did it, Holmes?'

'May I indulge him, Inspector?'

Lestrade nodded.

'Without wishing to be unkind to Mr Lestrade, no one but a policeman wears a Donegal these days. Or a coachman. And his hands weren't rough enough. I'd just shaken one of them.'

'What about the rank?'

'Yes, I cheated there. Remember the *Police Gazette*?'

'The nose?' Watson pursued, mentally making notes for his next outpouring with Conan Doyle.

'Straight cut. Clean. The blow must have been delivered by a single-edged weapon and with some force. It was either a sword or a meat cleaver. I opted for the former. Call it a lucky guess. The widower is easy. The inspector wears a wedding ring on the relevant finger, but his clothes and general air are of a man without the fussing attention of a woman. An inspector cannot afford divorce. So I surmised that Mrs Lestrade must be deceased. My condolences, Lestrade.'

The inspector smiled fleetingly.

'Which reminds me, Watson. How is Mrs Hudson these days?'

'Anything you may have heard . . .' Watson blustered, and then relented, 'oh . . . well, well.'

'Unlike the deceased in his alcove.' Lestrade brought them back.

'Ah, yes . . .'

The door opened and a tall young man came in. He was stones lighter than Mycroft and he carried a white stick.

'Ah, Aumerle.' Mycroft led the man to the inspector.

O'Merle? mused Lestrade. Was this the Irish branch of the family?

'I'd like you to meet Inspector Lestrade of Scotland Yard. My cousin, Aumerle.'

'Not *the* Inspector Lestrade?' Aumerle clumsily transferred his stick and grasped for the policeman's hand.

'None other,' grunted Watson.

'When cousin Sherlock was alive he spoke highly of you.'

'Highly?' Lestrade repeated quizzically, staring at the sightless eyes gazing at the ceiling.

Aumerle broke into a short, brittle laugh. 'All right then, not so highly. But Watson has been kinder.'

'Gentlemen.' Lestrade aided Aumerle Holmes to his seat and turned to the others. Boscombe brought the brandies and left with Holmes and Watson as Lestrade's gesture had indicated he should.

'Why did you do that, Mr Lestrade?' Aumerle asked.

'What, Mr Holmes?'

'You have cleared the room, have you not?'

'You are very perceptive, Mr Holmes. May I ask, how long . . . er—'

'How long have I been blind? For nearly two years, Inspector. An unfortunate accident, but I am learning to cope. These things take time. For instance . . .' And his hand snaked out to the brandy balloon on the table. He took it unerringly to his lips. 'My sense of smell has come on apace.'

And he laughed with Lestrade.

'What happened this evening?' the inspector asked.

'Let me see. Ah,' he smiled, 'strange how these meaningless

phrases come to mean so much. I took a hansom to the Diogenes. My rooms are in Jermyn Street – one day I'll walk it. The clock was striking the half hour in the lobby. That must have been half past seven, I suppose. Mycroft met me and escorted me here. Watson had already arrived. We went into dinner. Excellent fare. And then Mycroft was called away. One of the club members taken ill. I remember hoping it wasn't the pork.' He chuckled. 'When Mycroft returned, he told us the man was dead. He couldn't say more in the dining room. He'd used up his three conversations to us in passing the cruet. Watson took me into the Snug. The poor man gave me a copy of *The Times*. In the excitement, he'd forgotten I couldn't read it. The dear man was quite upset, but I told him not to trouble himself. He'll get his reward in heaven.'

'Won't we all,' murmured Lestrade.

'That's all I know. Until Boscombe fetched me, I'd heard nothing. What has happened, Inspector?'

'A man has been murdered, Mr Holmes. You chose a bad night to dine out.'

Lestrade left the blind man where he was, making successful inroads into the brandy and rejoined the corpse in the alcove. 'Poor old Waldo' was a man in his early sixties, he surmised; thinning grey hair, a monocle dangling now on his bloodied chest. Lestrade checked the position of the body. Never leave to a coroner what you can do better yourself. It lay back on the velvet, hard now with dried blood. The newspaper lay in a discarded heap on the table, together with an empty glass. Lestrade fished out his Apache knife cum knuckle duster and scooped the glass up on the blade. He sniffed. Port. He wasn't gentleman enough to tell how good, bad or indifferent it was. A club member walked past, studiously avoiding the sniffing policeman and the stiffened corpse. What did it take, Lestrade wondered, for anyone to take notice in the place? He checked the carpet under the deceased's feet. Unmarked. No sign of a struggle. He looked with the aid of an oil lamp at the wound itself. Mycroft Holmes had been right – a slim, narrow blade through the centre of the heart. Lestrade felt gingerly along the shoulder blade and realised Holmes had been wrong. No stiletto could have gone straight through. The blade had been longer –

a rapier, perhaps. And of course everybody carried rapiers in twentieth-century London.

'Well, that's it then,' a voice behind him whispered. Lestrade straightened. 'That's another damned by-election.'

It was Mycroft.

'By-election?' Lestrade echoed.

'Of course. I may not have known Hamilcar Waldo, Inspector, but I do know what he did for a living. He was a Member of Parliament.'

The adventure of Roedean School

'Right, gentlemen!' Sergeant Walter Dew of the Criminal Investigation Department was getting into his stride nicely. He had held this august position for nearly three months by now and not a day had gone by without a reminder of the fact. Even Mrs Dew and the eight little Dews had to call him 'Sergeant'.

Tweedledum and Tweedledee, alias Constables Dickens and Jones, newly assigned to H Division, stood staring at the blackboard, on which were scrawled in the joined-up writing at which Dew was improving all the time, the facts of the case of Major Deering, late Carabiniers.

'Mr Lestrade has much to occupy his time. Two other murders on his desk. So he has given me the honour of solving this one. And while other officers are out . . . er . . . following leads – that's the phrase we use here, you know – I intend to teach you lads a bit about policing. So, Jones. What have we got?'

'Sergeant?'

'What are the facts as presented in this case?' Dew was being as patient as he knew how.

'Well, Sarge—'

'Sergeant.'

'Well, Sergeant. We have a corpse. Major John Deering, age forty-one. Late Sixth Dragoon Guards.'

'Modus of opera?'

Constable Jones looked oddly at him.

'Death was due to shock as a result of being skewered by a cavalry lance.'

'And how do we know that?' Dew paced the floor, his hands

locked behind him, contorting his lips much after the manner of a ruminating cow.

'The coroner's report, sir.'

'And what do we know about coroner's reports, lad?'

'Sergeant?'

'You remember the old rhyme, surely – "Five per cent wit, ninety per cent shit" – all right?'

'Sergeant?' Dickens interrupted.

'What is it, lad?' Dew was polishing the frosted glass of Lestrade's door.

'What happened to the other five per cent?'

'What?'

But Dew was saved any mathematical embarrassment by a knock at the door he was polishing. Indeed, the knocker's knuckles bounced dangerously near his nose.

'Yes?' he opened it to reveal the desk sergeant. 'Hello, Tom. How's the missus?'

'Same as ever,' grunted the other, 'suicidal. You owe me two bob from last Friday. That horse had three legs—'

'Thank you, Sergeant.' Dew stiffened as the Donegal and bowler swept along the corridor. 'I'll be sure to give Inspector Lestrade the telegram. Ah, there you are, sir.'

Lestrade snatched the missive the sergeant had brought with the air of a man in a hurry. 'Dickens, tea,' he ordered, and threw himself into the worn old chair. The blackboard caught his eye, but it only caused minor bruising. And when he'd recovered, he read Dew's jottings.

'I see you've been playing at being a policeman again, Walter.'

The sergeant blushed a little, needled by the attitude of his superior officer in front of the constables.

'No, seriously, Sergeant. You can forget all that. I have a sneaky feeling that we are not talking about three murderers but one. Gentlemen, what do Ralph Childers, John Deering and Hamilcar Waldo have in common?'

'They're dead, sir,' Jones announced proudly.

Lestrade's look would have calcified a brighter man.

'Think again,' he said.

There was silence.

'Were they all single, sir?'

'No, Dickens. Waldo was married, though not closely: Do your homework.'

'Wasn't there mention of a certain club, sir?' Dew hazarded.

'The Hell Fire, yes. But as far as I know so far, only Childers was a member of that. Unless there's more to the Diogenes than meets the eye. Childers was a member of that, too. You're getting warm, Dew.'

'Give up, sir,' said Jones cheerily.

'Well, that runs in the family,' Lestrade observed. 'Politics, gentlemen. Ralph Childers and Hamilcar Waldo were both Members of Parliament. John Deering had intended to resign his commission and go into politics. No one but his commanding officer seems to have known that, probably because politics isn't discussed in cavalry messes.'

'So it's a job for Special Branch?' Dew was excelling himself.

'You're excelling yourself, Dew.' Lestrade had noticed too. 'But I'll rot in Hell before I hand this one over to that bunch of maniacs.'

'Would that be Inspector Bradstreet, sir?' Dickens asked.

'It would. When I knew him he was a sergeant. Amazing how promotion goes to people's heads.' For an unkind second, Lestrade flashed a glance at Dew. 'He's not a bad copper. But for the moment, we'll keep it to ourselves. Ah,' he took the steaming mug, 'the cup that cheers.'

As he sipped, contemplating Dew's puerile scribblings on the board, he opened the telegram. His face darkened as he read it. He snatched up the battered Gladstone.

'Dickens. Jones. How would you like some sea air?'

'Sir?' they chorused.

'Get your things. We're off to Rottingdean.'

'Rottingdean?' Dew repeated.

'Rottingdean,' Dickens answered. 'A small resort on the south east coast between Brighton and Newhaven. The beach is rocky and the houses are built of the same flinty—'

'Thank you, Constable,' Lestrade swigged the last of his tea.

'Sergeant, tell His Nims where we've gone. Attempted murder of a celebrity, national figure etc. He'll like that. We'll be back Thursday.'

'Right, sir.' Dew made for the door, bellowing for a constable as he reached it, 'Macnee! Get in here!'

'Walter,' Lestrade extended an avuncular arm around his sergeant's shoulders, 'you want to get on, don't you? Be somebody in the CID?'

'Oh, yes, sir.' Dew squared his shoulders.

'Well then, remember,' Lestrade was whispering, 'a sergeant may shout, but an inspector calls.'

Carrie Kipling hadn't expected three officers of Scotland Yard by the afternoon train, but three they were, Donegalled and bowlered despite the mellow warmth of May.

'He isn't here, Inspector. Rudyard is at the school, helping the police with their enquiries.'

'The school, ma'am?'

'Roedean, Inspector. Where it all happened.'

'You'd better tell me the full story, Mrs Kipling. Jones, your pad.'

At Mrs Kipling's behest, the policemen sat in the drawing room and listened to the extent of the problem.

'It all began over a year ago, at least, that's when Rudyard first told me about it. He didn't think much of it at first. A horseless carriage backfiring. A narrow miss with a tram. A stampeding herd of cattle – we were in Calgary at the time,' she offered by way of explanation when she saw Lestrade's incomprehension. 'Rudyard put it all down to coincidence, accident. But yesterday. There could be no mistaking yesterday. I rang the police at once. He hesitated and then sent you a telegram.'

'What happened yesterday, Mrs Kipling?'

'I am still reeling from the shock, Inspector.' Carrie Kipling looked remarkably solid to Lestrade.

'Excuse me, sir,' Jones butted in, 'how do you spell Calgary, Mrs Kipling?'

Lestrade flashed an inspectorial glance in the constable's direction and he withered on the spot.

'Please go on,' he said.

'Well, Rudyard was invited to a Founders' Day celebration at Roedean. He's such a silly when it comes to girls. I think it's because we lost our favourite, you see.' She smiled and Lestrade noticed her eyes shining at the portrait Mr Kipling had been holding when he was last there. 'There were several dignitaries – oh, no one quite of dear Rudyard's stature, of course—'

'Your husband is a big man, Mrs Kipling?' Dickens interjected.

'I'll ask the questions, thank you, Constable,' said Lestrade, 'you stand by with your trusty penknife should Jones' pencil give out.' Dickens folded in on himself like a pack of cards.

'Rudyard had just risen to make his speech. He'd read it to me the night before. It was marvellous. When, suddenly, while the applause was still ringing out, a maniac stepped forward and fired at my husband . . .'

A superbly timed handkerchief fluttered into view and Carrie Kipling blew her nose with a resonance not quite becoming the wife of a possible future Poet Laureate. They waited for her to recover.

'The bullet was wide of the mark, thank the Lord, but the assassin escaped in the confusion.'

'Did Mr Kipling – did anyone – get a good look at this man?'

'I fear not, Inspector. My husband's eyesight is not of the best. At school, they called him Giglamps, you know, because of his spectacles.'

'Indeed so, ma'am.'

Mrs Kipling could help them no further. With various reassurances they left her, although Lestrade left Dickens at the front door in case some maniac should try again, assuming the master of the house to be at home. The inspector and his remaining constable caught a cab to the school.

Roedean School for Ladies of Good Family was a new building on the broad sweep of the Downs above the sea where Lestrade had stumbled, naked but for his trusty Donegal weeks earlier. Now, despite the fact that the young ladies of those good families lived in, the playing fields were deserted and the place had a general air of fear and stealth. Two police vehicles, stamped with the crest of the Sussex Constabulary, tried to look inconspicuous under a clump of elms. Here and there, pairs of policemen patrolled, in the time-honoured tradition, bull's-eyes and truncheons swinging at their waists.

Lestrade announced his presence to the constable on the door and entered the main hall. Why was it, he wondered, that all schools, even this one for young ladies, smelt like that? Only the liniment and linseed oil for the cane was missing from this one. It had not been from his own. The officers from Scotland Yard entered a large hall, with high oriel windows and a platform at the far end. Lestrade took in the neat rows of wooden chairs, the music stands now derelict and behind him as he turned a minstrel's gallery with winding stairs.

'That's him!' a voice shrieked from nowhere. 'That nasty little man in the Donegal. I'd know that ferret face anywhere.'

The hall was suddenly alive with uniformed men, who variously laid hands on Lestrade. Jones too was leapt upon, his head forced to the ground and a knee jammed into the small of his back while his hands were wrenched behind him and the cuffs put on.

'Are you sure, ma'am?' A burly grey-haired figure led the way, but he was dwarfed by a giant apparition in frothy blouse who lurched forward to identify the culprit.

'I am positive, Inspector. Arrest him at once!'

Lestrade was prevented from commenting on any of this by the firmness with which a constable's hand covered his mouth.

'I arrest you in the name of the law. You are charged with the attempted murder of Mr Rudyard Kipling on the—'

'Imbecile!' roared the iron matron. 'This is not the man. He's a foot too short!'

The local inspector looked perplexed.

'Then why—'

'This is the sickening monster who exposed himself to me and my girls last month. Lurking in the bushes, he was, and unless I am mistaken, wearing that same Donegal.' She bridled. 'He was certainly wearing the same leer.'

Lestrade attempted a defence, but a gurgle was all he managed.

'I've heard that criminals always return to the scene of their crimes. You bestial swine!' And she walloped Lestrade around the head with a sheaf of papers.

'Lestrade!' a voice called from overhead. Everybody looked up to where Gigger Kipling was peering myopically over the gallery rail. 'You've got the wrong man!'

He scuttled down the stairs to the tableau in the hall.

'Inspector, you are about to arrest a fellow officer.'

'What?' the iron matron roared. 'This Peeping Tom is a policeman? Disgusting!'

The constables relaxed their grip on Lestrade and Jones.

'It's what I've come to expect now that the old Queen has gone. It's a world gone mad,' she went on.

'Who are you?' the inspector asked the inspector.

'I might ask you the same thing,' Lestrade retorted.

'I asked first.' The conversation was already degenerating.

'Inspector Sholto Lestrade, Scotland Yard.'

'Oh.' The local man's face fell and his constables stood sheepishly by, vaguely wishing the ground would swallow them. 'Inspector Daniel Clutterbuck, Sussex Constabulary. Er . . . I'm sorry, Mr Lestrade. I appear to have been a little over-zealous.'

Lestrade brushed himself down, 'No real harm done, Mr Clutterbuck. Jones?'

'I'm all right, sir.' The constable was trying to bend his neck back into position.

'When you have finished being polite to each other,' the grey lady stormed. 'This man, from Scotland Yard or not, is a pervert, Inspector. I demand that you take some action.'

Clutterbuck looked agonised. God knew, he wasn't fond of the Yard, but to arrest his equal, nay, his superior, on the insistence of a madwoman was risking all. In the event, it was Lestrade who took charge.

'Who might you be, madam?'

'I might be Lord Salisbury!' she replied.

No, thought Lestrade, the beard isn't full enough.

'In point of fact, I am Miss Lawrence, Headmistress of Roedean School.'

'Then, Miss Lawrence, I would like to talk to you in your study. Clutterbuck, whatever you've done so far, I want a detailed account of it. And post some constables at Mr Kipling's house in Rottingdean. You'll find one of my men there. Constable Jones here will take notes. He's getting quite good at it.'

'I will not be alone with this man.' Miss Lawrence was obdurate.

'May I act as chaperone, Miss Lawrence?' Kipling suggested.

She reflected for a moment. A man who wrote such stirring poetry and such beautiful stories for children was surely a man to trust. 'Very well,' she assented.

Kipling winked at Lestrade and they followed her through cheerless corridors to a panelled door. Here a willowy child in school uniform stood, curtseying as the headmistress approached.

'Oh, not again, Annabelle. I've told you before about those second helpings of mince, have I not? Go and find Nurse – and quickly!' The pale child vanished. Miss Lawrence suddenly lunged sideways and crashed through another door.

'Remember the ablative absolute!' she bellowed.

'Yes, Miss Lawrence,' a dozen voices trilled.

Lestrade and Kipling looked at each other, each according to his level of understanding and his upbringing, rather surprised by the meaninglessness of the remark.

'Gentleman,' Miss Lawrence ushered them into her study, 'and Inspector Lestrade.'

'May we clear up one thing?' Lestrade ventured.

Miss Lawrence raised a matriarchal eyebrow.

'I am entirely innocent of the crime of which you accuse me. The truth is I was set upon by paid ruffians in Brighton and deposited senseless in your playing fields. My clothes, with the exception of the Donegal, had been stolen.'

The headmistress looked unsure.

'It's true, Miss Lawrence,' Gigger confirmed. Thank God, thought Lestrade, for one sane voice in all this.

'If you say so, Mr Kipling, then it must, perforce, be so.' She gave him a saccharine smile which sent Lestrade's scalp crawling with unease. He preferred the Medusa scowl any day. 'But,' and it duly appeared, 'on no account will you interview any of my young ladies unless I am present throughout. Is that understood? It's high time there were women on constabulary forces, revolting though I find the idea.'

If they were all like you, Lestrade mused, the rest of us could go home.

'Now, madam, to the events of yesterday.'

But the redoubtable Miss Lawrence had barely embarked on her tale when the door opened and two ladies, larger and more terrible than she, swept in.

'Violet, my dear. We came as quickly as we could,' said the first, hugging and patting the headmistress.

'Petronella, how kind. Agatha, my dearest.' And the claspings to matronly bosoms were only disturbed by a discreet clearing of the throat from Lestrade.

'Oh.' The headmistress remembered the presence of the men. 'These gentlemen are involved in their differing ways in the horrors of yesterday. Oh, I don't know what the bishop must have thought. This is Mr Kipling, the poet and author. My sisters, founders with me of this school – Petronella and Agatha.'

'Charmed, ladies,' Kipling bowed ceremoniously.

'Ah, Mr Kipling. I particularly liked your Departmental Ditties. May I ask what you are working on now?'

'A tale of the Raj has just been published, ma'am. It is called *Kim*.'

'How marvellous!' Petronella clapped her hands excitedly.

'Ladies, may we return to the matter in hand?'

The withering look of all three Miss Lawrences was directed at Lestrade.

'This is a policeman,' the headmistress informed her sisters.

'From Scotland Yard.' Lestrade felt he ought to establish some sort of level. 'Ladies, may I ask you to retire until I have spoken with your sister?'

'We *have* retired, young man,' Petronella informed him.

'Anything Violet has to say concerning this school concerns us.' Agatha was defiant.

'Very well,' Lestrade bowed to the inevitable, 'but first, would you tell me why two out of the three founders of Roedean were not present on Founders' Day?'

Agatha blushed the colour of her sister's curtains.

Petronella blustered, 'Personal reasons. Absolutely nothing to do with you. Violet sent us a telegram last evening. We came as quickly as we could. Poor dear.' And the sisters began again the handkerchief-waving routine they had just finished.

'Miss Lawrence.' Lestrade's patience was wearing a little thin.

'Yes,' they all chorused.

'Your story, ma'am.' He tried to be gentler.

'Well, Inspector, the day was progressing well. There had been that nasty moment when the Bishop of Bath and Wells had fallen down the stairs, but I am a great believer in splints. Mr Kipling was about to speak – *such* a speaker –' she gushed in Gigger's direction, 'when suddenly, there was a scuffle at the back of the hall, under the minstrels' gallery. I thought at once it was Angelique—'

Again the Lawrence sisters chorused in assent.

'Angelique?' Lestrade repeated.

'Angelique D'Umfraville. Our French girl. Not quite the ticket. Given to odd bursts of nervous energy.'

'She is deranged, young man.' Petronella was more direct.

'A trifle strong, Petra, old thing. A trifle strong—'

'It was not Angelique,' Lestrade broke in. Anything, he thought, to prevent them from going off at a tandem.

'Indeed no. The cut of the deerstalker was all wrong for her.'

'Deerstalker?' said Lestrade.

'That is what I said, Inspector. One of those shooting caps that disgusting man Keir Hardie wears. This man stepped forward, as though dressed for a coach journey and aimed a gun at Mr Kipling.'

Miss Lawrence wavered, but was saved from total collapse by a bottle of smelling salts thrust under her nose by Agatha.

'And then?' Lestrade pressed, once Violet's eyeballs had ceased to swivel.

'We all just stood there, rooted to the spot. There was a report—'

'The chairman of the governors' report, dear?' Petronella asked for clarification.

'A gunshot, dear lady.' It was Kipling who translated for her.

'I don't remember much else. The bishop fell over again,

I do remember that, because the poor man broke his other arm.'

'He must look rather like a windmill,' Agatha ruminated.

'There was screaming and panic. But, I must say, the gels behaved admirably. Two or three of them took after the fiend, I understand, with hockey sticks.'

'Did you recognise the man?' Lestrade asked.

'No. He was tall.'

'I thought of medium height,' said Kipling.

'Would you know him again?'

'Most assuredly,' asserted the headmistress.

'Possibly,' hedged the poet.

'Mr Kipling, may I talk with you? Misses Lawrence, thank you for your patience. I shall need to talk with all those who were present yesterday, especially those at the back of the hall.'

'My gels have been subjected to enough, Inspector.' Violet was on her feet, lowering down at Lestrade. 'Shot at, bullied by policemen from Sussex, and now threatened again by policemen from London. The Lord knows what the newspapers will do with all this. I shan't have a gel left. Roedean must close.'

Petronella and Agatha supported the wilting Violet as Lestrade bowed three times and took his exit with Gigger.

'What do you make of the weird sisters?' Kipling asked Lestrade as they reached the gravel drive.

'I don't know what our education system is coming to,' observed Lestrade. 'Tell me, this man who is trying to kill you. Why didn't you mention him when we last met?'

'The whole thing wasn't apparent – until yesterday. You must understand, dear Lestrade, that a man in my position makes enemies. If you support the things I do, you must expect to encounter opposition. True, that opposition usually appears in the form of literary critiques or angry letters to *The Times*. But after yesterday, any vague sense of unease has now crystallised. What I took to be a series of unrelated incidents are now obviously attempts at murder – mine.'

'And yesterday? The man with the deerstalker?'

'I was probably the last to see him. These poor old eyes of mine,' he rubbed them behind the thick lenses, 'years of close work by candlelight. By the time I'd focused he was firing.'

'Did you see the gun?'

'I think it was a carbine. Too short for a Lee-Metford, though. Perhaps a Martini-Henry.'

'Your poor old eyes couldn't make out the man, but you could tell the make of a gun, whose narrow end was towards you, what,' Lestrade glanced back at the hall behind them, 'sixty, seventy feet away.'

'Ah, but I know my guns, Inspector. I did establish a rifle club down the road.'

'Am I right in assuming that a carbine is a weapon used by cavalry?'

'And mounted infantry.' Kipling had recently returned from the theatre of war.

'A pity we couldn't make some headway there,' Lestrade mused.

'But we can, Inspector. Don't you have coroner chappies who dig bullets out of people?'

'Er . . . yes,' said Lestrade, not following Kipling's drift.

'Well, then. Have a rummage around in poor old Arthur L'Estrange. You must come up with something. Isn't it called ballistics?'

'Arthur L'Estrange?' Lestrade had stopped walking.

'Yes.' Kipling began to realise something was amiss. 'My dear fellow, has no one told you? The bullet that was meant for me went wide as Miss Lawrence told you, but it hit another guest of Founders' Day, standing feet from me. When I think how close I came—'

'Where is he now?'

'L'Estrange? In the morgue, I suppose. Isn't that where you chappies put people? Better ask Clutterbuck.'

'I will. Now, to your description of the man under the deerstalker . . .'

The poet and the policeman strolled along the downs for an hour or more, Lestrade learning all he could of the various attempted murders. In the end, for all the informant's powers of observation as a storyteller of distinction, it was vague and inconclusive. A man of medium height, middle build, clean shaven, though possibly with a moustache; hair – so-so; eyes – indeterminate; no other distinguishing features. Only the deerstalker and the Ulster and a short gun. The last at least made sense. The gun would need to be short to fit under the Ulster and not attract attention. People didn't go to speech days armed openly with Martini-Henrys. Not even at Roedean.

For a day and a half, Lestrade, Jones and Dickens went over the ground traversed with enormous feet by the Sussex Constabulary. Dickens got the gels – forty-three of them who all swore they were standing right next to the assassin. It was interesting that when Inspector Clutterbuck had asked for such eyewitnesses, he had got one, an odd, manic young lady named Angelique something or other. When young, blue-eyed Dickens asked, the queue went round the chapel. Jones got the staff, except the redoubtable Miss Lawrence, who now refused to speak to any policeman below the rank of Chief Superintendent. Lestrade telegraphed Nimrod Frost whose answer was to the point, monosyllabic and rather Anglo-Saxon. Lestrade himself interviewed the guests – septuagenarian governors and Friends of the School, variously cobwebbed and mildewed – all screaming to the best of their abilities that the country was going to the dogs and why weren't the Labour Party behind bars? Lestrade coped as best he could and spent the day he had promised to return to London knee deep in depositions in Clutterbuck's office, drabber and more tawdry than his own, in the less salubrious part of Brighton. The only thing which kept him going, apart from endless cups of tea, was the fact that Jones had unearthed a carrier, delivering to the school on that day, who had come from Goodwood. Said carrier knew the Lawrence sisters well and had seen them that morning. Lestrade now knew that the personal reason intimated by Petronella Lawrence to explain their absence from Founders' Day, was that Diamond Jubilee was running in the two-thirty and they were having a flutter.

The corpse of Arthur L'Estrange told him one thing only – and that he knew already – namely that the man had been shot. After interminable queries as to whether the inspector and the deceased were related on account of the similarity of their names, the coroner showed Lestrade the entry wound, high above the heart. The bullet must have hit the shoulder blade and deflected to smash the aorta. Death occurred within minutes. The bullet? The coroner showed it to Lestrade. It had probably come from a Martini-Henry. That narrowed the field down to a few thousand.

Lestrade was dozing by the oil lamp in Clutterbuck's back room late that night, when his eyes fell fleetingly on a folded copy of the Brighton *Argus*. The banner headlines read, 'Brighton Mourns MP'. Lestrade's stupor gave way to amazement as he read the rest. A lavish funeral was planned for the following Wednesday. No expense was to be spared. It was hoped the Bishop of Bath and Wells could be winched in to conduct the service. A glowing obituary followed. Yes, Brighton would miss the man who had served it faithfully and well for nigh on seven years. It would miss the Right Honourable Arthur L'Estrange.

It was with a mixture of emotions that Lestrade broke the news to Rudyard Kipling the following morning. In Lestrade's view, and it was still a guess, though one borne of years of experience, the maniac in the deerstalker had not been an erratic shot. The fatal bullet was not at all wide of the mark. On the contrary, it had found its home.

The fine Oloroso problem

That was the summer that Nimrod Frost died. Rumour had it that he had been ill for years, a shadow of his former self. Those in the know claimed it was the strain of the job that killed him. No one in the City Force was in the least surprised. Faced with a rabble like the Metropolitan Police, the man had obviously found it all too much and had taken his own life. Miss Featherstonehaugh knew better. It was the endless sugar and cream that finally got him, that and the exertion of pressing the button in the lift each morning. She had warned him and reminded everyone of the fact at every conceivable opportunity. A man couldn't go on carrying that weight around indefinitely. There were those, of course, and at times Lestrade was one of them, who reasoned that Frost's arteries had hardened in order to escape further contact with Miss Featherstonehaugh – but perhaps that was unkind.

It was an impressive funeral for a grocer's son from Grantham. The commissioner was there, of course. Sir Frederick Ponsonby represented the King. Chief Superintendent Abberline was chief mourner and most of the other superintendents came. Because of the deceased's nineteen stone, it took six bobbies rather than the customary four, to carry the coffin, draped in purple velvet and surmounted by Frost's cap and ceremonial sword. The stream of policemen, uniformed and plainclothes, stretched for nearly a mile. Frost would have liked that. Even a few of the underworld came to pay their grudging respects, standing like shadows along High Holborn, their caps in their hands. Frost would have liked that even more.

It was a curious choice of cemetery, the graveyard of

St Sepulchre's. Mrs Frost, erect and dignified throughout, explained through the vicar that dear Nimrod had expressed a wish to be buried near to Newgate, to keep an eye as it were, on the reprobates he and his men had put there. She had not, apparently, realised that they had pulled Newgate down and as the procession reached the church, the workmen on the roof of the criminal court in the Bailey tugged off their caps.

Lestrade looked up at the gilded figure they were winching into position. Justice, sworded and balanced. He mused again, as he had countless times before, on the ambiguities of her blindness. He read the inscription on the great bronze bell: 'And when St Sepulchre's bell in the morning tolls, the Lord have mercy on your souls.' But it tolled for executions no longer. As he took his seat, with Bradstreet and the other inspectors of the Yard, he noticed the fresh cement at the entrance to the tunnel which had led to Newgate's condemned cell. It was a tunnel he knew all too well. More than once, he'd walked that way himself, with men bound for the gallows. Now, they were even considering the removal of the black flag to show the crowd that justice had been done. What was the world coming to? The smugness of Miss Featherstonehaugh at last gave way and she sobbed quietly into Dew's handkerchief as the Scotland Yard Glee Club broke into 'Nearer My God to Thee'.

It was nearly three weeks before Nimrod Frost was replaced. In that time, Lestrade absented himself again and with Sergeant Dew at his elbow, returned once more to Brighton. At the height of June, this was clearly a mistake. The sun burned fiercely through the serge which a sergeant's pay allowed him to buy. Had Dew's spelling been better, he might have made a whimsical connection between his rank and the material of his suit. As it was, he contented himself with sweating. And envying the cooler attire of his guv'nor, nattily turned out in white waistcoat and boater. There were children everywhere, scampering between the two men as they strolled the promenade. More than once, Dew 'accidentally' tripped a sailor-suited darling and offered the most hollow of apologies to it and its adjacent parents.

Lestrade waded through the dollops of dropped ice-cream and made for the Grand Hotel, magnificent in the ivory of its classical lines. He flicked open the register, despite the protestations of the clerk and found what he wanted, staying in room 15. The officers of the Yard took the stairs and waited for the occupant to answer the knock.

'Good morning, Captain Deering. So glad I found you.'

'Who the devil are you?'

'Tut, tut.' Lestrade pushed past the good captain, still in smoking jacket and carpet slippers, 'Lestrade of the Yard. This is Sergeant Dew. And you have a very short memory.'

'Oh, yes,' Deering was calmer. 'Well, what do you want? I haven't finished my breakfast.'

'I am continuing my enquiries into your brother's death, sir.' Lestrade trailed round the room, observing in a desultory way, calculated to irritate the officer of Carabiniers. Dew stood like a door stop to prevent any escape. Lestrade had not discussed tactics with him, but he knew his guv'nor too well not to be ready for any eventuality. He stood with one hand poised over his notebook and the other near his cuffs, ready to leap into action with either or both.

'I believe your brother's murder to be one of a number.' Lestrade looked levelly at Deering. 'The common factor in all of them is politics.'

'Politics?' Deering looked blank.

'Your brother was about to leave the regiment. To resign his commission and enter politics.'

Deering stood with his mouth open, the buttered toast drooping limply in his hand.

'Rubbish. Preposterous nonsense!' he finally managed.

'I must ask you, sir, as perhaps the man closest to your brother. What party was he about to join?'

'Damn your impudence, Lestrade!' Deering slammed down the wilted toast. 'A man's politics is his own business. We do have the ballot, you know! I mightn't agree with it totally, but I'll be damned if I discuss my brother's convictions with a common policeman.'

Dew shifted uncomfortably. He'd never really thought of the

inspector as a common policeman, but then he hadn't realised the late John Deering had any convictions, either. He wondered momentarily what they were for.

'Ezekiah Williams,' Lestrade said quietly.

'Who?'

'One of your troop, isn't he?'

'Williams, you say?'

'You are trying my patience, Captain Deering!' Lestrade stepped forward. 'Shall we pay a call on Colonel Gilmartin this morning?'

Deering's composure temporarily failed him. 'All right, Lestrade. What do you want?

'We'll overlook the fact that you or Captain Sheraton or both hired four regimental thugs to beat the living daylights out of me. If I chose to push matters, you'd go to jail for four years for that.'

Lestrade perambulated again. 'We'll also overlook the Army Remount business—'

Deering was back on the attack again, 'You haven't a shred of proof. I . . .' and he fell silent.

Well, thought Lestrade smugly, amazing what targets shots in the dark can find.

'As far as I am aware, Inspector, my brother always voted for the Conservative and Unionist Party. But as God is my judge, I had no inkling he planned to leave the regiment. Er . . . about the . . . other business . . .'

'All I lost was my consciousness and a bit of pride, Captain,' Lestrade answered, 'but take care our paths don't cross again, or I'll call it attempted murder.'

The policemen made for the sunlight.

'Army Remount Service, sir?' Dew was the first to break silence.

'You read about it, surely, Dew? The papers were full of it. I was fishing.'

'And what did you catch, sir?' Dew was proud of himself for taking up the metaphor.

'The quarter past twelve train to Victoria, Dew. If we hurry.'

*

Mr Edward Henry was the umpteenth occupant of the Assistant Commissioner's office on the first floor of Scotland Yard. Rowbottom, Anderson, McNaghten, Frost, they had come and gone. And now Lestrade stood on the timeworn carpet, the one Rowbottom had brought from Egypt, facing the Coming Man. Rumours had been flying around the Yard for weeks. He was from India, some said. A Jat. Others claimed he was from South Africa. Black as your hat. Still others reckoned he was a Boer spy. Inspector Bradstreet of the Special Branch would have to watch him.

'What's this?' the small, balding, dark-skinned little man said to Lestrade.

'It's your finger, sir.' Lestrade was convinced this was some sort of initiative test.

'No, no, man, on the end of my finger.'

'A nail, sir?' Lestrade was doing his best.

'Are you deliberately being obtuse, Inspector?'

Lestrade cleared his throat. In effect, he refused to answer on the grounds that it might incriminate him.

'We've met before, you know,' Henry went on, 'the Belper Committee, in 'ninety-nine.'

Realisation dawned. 'Forgive me, sir. Of course. Finger-prints.'

'Fingerprints,' beamed Henry, 'you've read my book?'

'Er . . . no, sir.'

Henry's face fell, the walrus moustache obscuring his chin completely.

'But I have been taking fingerprints from known criminals for about six years, sir.'

'Yes, I remember your testimony before the Belper people. I was impressed, Lestrade. Now, I want your help. I want to set up a Fingerprint Department, here at the Yard. Chief Superintendent Abberline suggests a sergeant named Collins. Your views?'

'Stockley Collins is a good man,' Lestrade concurred, though it stuck in his throat to have to agree with anything Abberline suggested.

'What would the chaps think of such a venture, Lestrade? You must have your ear pretty close to the ground. How would they view it?'

'Would you like the political answer, sir? Or the truth?'

'When you come to know me better, Lestrade, you'll know that I will settle for nothing but the truth.'

So help me, God, mused Lestrade to himself. 'Most of my brother officers are still taking the inside leg measurement of known criminals, sir. Some of them wouldn't know a finger-print if it upped and bit them.'

'That's what Abberline said.' Henry nodded.

Damn, thought Lestrade, twice in one day.

'Now, to your caseload, Lestrade. You'd better sit down.'

God, thought Lestrade, is it as large as that?

'You smell conspiracy?'

'The coincidence seems extraordinary if not, sir.'

'Coincidence?' Henry pursued his man with the ferocity of a miffed ferret.

'The fact that all the deceased had a parliamentary connection.'

'So do I, Lestrade. My cab passes Parliament Square every morning. So, I imagine, does yours.'

'I walk in the summer, sir.'

'What about this one?' Henry consulted the typed papers on his desk. 'John Deering. He was a soldier.'

'But one with political leanings, sir. As the report says—'

'I've read the report, Lestrade. And up to this point, I buy your story. But either Major Deering is a different case altogether, or your whole theory falls flat. Consider the methods of murder. What do we have? One man tortured to death, another impaled on a lance, a third shot. What sort of murderer employs that range of methods?'

'Are you familiar with the Struwwelpeter case, sir?'

'I've read those reports too, Lestrade. But you didn't catch your man there, did you?'

Lestrade was stung by the rebuke. It was untrue. He had caught his man, but for old reasons, for personal reasons, he had not committed the fact to paper.

'Are you saying this is the work of the Struwwelpeter maniac?'

'No, sir.'

'So positive?'

Lestrade smiled. 'Let's just say I have a sixth sense.'

'I'm not sure how much sense you have, Lestrade. It will take me time to learn that. In the meantime,' Henry rang a little silver bell on the desk, 'I think we'll play it my way.'

There was a knock and two men entered, both known to Lestrade and both calculated to get right under his skin.

'Lestrade, you know Inspectors Gregory and Bradstreet?'

'Intimately, sir.'

'Let's assume for a moment that your conspiracy theory is correct – that someone is killing off Members of Parliament. If that is a fair assumption, it is a job for the Special Branch. The Commissioner has graciously allowed us the time and talents of Bradstreet, here.'

'Sholto.' The aforementioned grinned icily.

'Edgar,' Lestrade replied with the affability of a corpse.

'Bradstreet, your views,' Henry gestured to the newcomer to sit.

'Well, sir, at first sight it looks like the Irish.'

Lestrade's eyebrows disappeared under his hairline, which gave them a fair distance to travel. How often had he heard this rubbish? From a man of Bradstreet's intelligence, he'd hoped for better.

'Why?' Henry badgered him.

'Ralph Childers, Arthur L'Estrange and Hamilcar Waldo were all Conservatives – and Unionists. Natural targets of the Fenians.'

'We haven't seen a Fenian in the last twelve years,' Lestrade replied.

'Allow me to correct you –' Bradstreet began.

'Gentlemen, gentlemen,' Henry refereed, 'it seems to me there is room in this enquiry for Inspector Bradstreet to pursue the Irish track and for Inspector Gregory to follow other lines.'

'Gregory?' Lestrade was unaware of the man's involvement in the case.

'Gregory will be working with Dew and your men during your leave, Lestrade.'

'My leave?' Lestrade was on his feet.

'Yes. I intend to give all my officers a period of leave as soon as possible. It will have to be staggered, of course. I'm giving you a week – next week to be precise. I know what overwork can do. It makes you stale, careless.'

'With respect, Mr Henry, I don't—'

'I'll brook no arguments, Lestrade. You will take your leave. Gregory will keep you posted on your return. Well, gentlemen, I think that must suffice for now. I have a meeting with His Majesty.'

The inspectors filed out, Lestrade smarting from this first encounter more than somewhat.

'Sorry, Sholto,' said Bradstreet, 'it really wasn't my idea.'

'When we worked together last, Edgar, you were a sergeant. As far as seniority goes, I still outrank you.' It was beneath Lestrade's dignity, unworthy of him, perhaps. But he was miffed. He turned to Gregory, acknowledged by all and sundry as the Most Boring Man at the Yard, a title he had held, behind his back, for four consecutive years.

'Tom, don't tread on my feet, there's an old love.' Lestrade patted his shoulder.

'Do my best, old chap. I say, have you fellows heard the one about the bishop and the chorus-girl?'

'Yes,' echoed Lestrade and Bradstreet in unison and left their colleague telling the tale to a hat stand before he realised they had gone. At the end of the corridor, the inspectors went their separate ways.

It had been three years, since Lestrade had seen her. Three long years of aching feet, of clicking typewriters, of stewed, cold tea and wet socks. He kept telling himself, give it up man, give it up. Put in for retirement. But what would he do? The pension went nowhere. He had no yen, like Dew the Semi-Literate, to write his memoirs. He didn't like petunias and the thought of growing them for the rest of his life filled him with foreboding. What, then? Nightwatchman? Jailer? Tinker? Tailor? Soldier? He was too old, too stubborn, too proud and too ham-fisted for any of these. Harry Bandicoot of course, years before, had found himself a rich widow . . . There was still, perhaps, even now, that possibility. And it was to Harry's he caught the train. To see her again. Three years. How had she changed? Would she know him now? What would he say to her?

These thoughts and a jumble of others rolled around the grey area he called a brain. Even as he reached the door and rang the bell, nothing was resolved. He renewed his acquaintance with the butler and was shown into the grounds, where the family were taking tea.

'Sholto.' It was Harry who saw him first. Three years hadn't changed him. He must be in his late thirties by now, but apart from the air of affluence and tranquillity, he hadn't changed a jot since Lestrade first knew him, a young copper, lettuce-green. The huge, amiable Old Etonian heartily shook the hand of the raddled old Yard man. Bandicoot saw an older man before him, rather more perhaps of the ferret face attributed to him by the dubious Dr Watson and the collaborating Conan Doyle.

'Sholto, what a surprise.' Harry's wife, Letitia, ravishing as ever in the frothy lace of the first Edwardian summer, crushed him to her ample bosom.

'I should have written,' he said.

'Nonsense,' Letitia kissed his cheek, 'you're always welcome. You know that. Children!' she called down the lawn.

From the twisted old trees of the orchard, three baby Bandicoots scampered, laughing and tumbling. 'Say hello to Uncle Sholto,' Letitia said. The two boys hit him first, the time apart forgotten in a second as they climbed onto his lap.

'Rupert. Ivo. Don't hurt your Uncle,' Letitia scolded them.

'Now then, now then,' Lestrade did the bobby-on-the-beat impression he had done since the boys were in their cradles, seven years ago, 'you'd better come along with me, if you please,' and he buried a hand in a battered Gladstone. The boys fell silent and tried to peer into his bag, their eyes shining with excitement. Lestrade made a great play of lifting something heavy and then, in a move which astonished all present, handcuffed the boys together. They laughed and cackled, falling over each other on the floor in their attempt to get free.

'The cuffs are a present for you,' Lestrade said to them. 'And the key,' he handed it to Letitia, 'a present for your mother.' They all laughed.

Emma was slower, shyer than the boys. She came forward, nestling a little against Harry's legs. She wore a cream dress like Letitia's but it was not Letitia's eyes that looked up at her Uncle Sholto from beneath the bonnet. It was Sarah Lestrade's. Lestrade pulled from his Gladstone a doll, with a pale, smiling, china face. The little girl held out her hands and hugged Lestrade and the doll. The Inspector of Police pressed her gently to him, suddenly aware of his rough hands and the coarseness of his waistcoat. Little Emma pulled back and looked up at his face, drawing her fingers over the scars that crossed it, wondering in her own childish way where the top of his nose had gone. Sholto Lestrade had come home.

He stayed for three days, though he had intended not to stay at all. It was like another world, the Bandicoots' summer retreat. Warm and sunlit, noisy with the rough and tumble of the children and hot with the breath of dogs. That was the only thing that jarred a little. Lestrade had never been able to bring himself to like dogs. But Squires, Harry's gamekeeper, had them well trained and only the St Bernard, its nose constantly nudging Lestrade's groin, caused him any real worries.

On his last evening, Letitia had retired after a magnificent dinner, leaving Harry and Lestrade to their brandy and cigars. They discussed Kruger and the de Dion Harry had his eye on, Lestrade expressing his doubts whether the horse would ever be replaced by a lump of iron you had to pump up each morning. As a small boy, of course, he remembered the red flag.

'About Emma, Sholto.' Bandicoot suddenly changed tack.

'What about her?' Lestrade asked.

Bandicoot poured him another brandy. 'Letitia and I have been talking,' he said. 'We were wondering—'

'Is she a burden?' Lestrade asked.

'My dear fellow, absolutely not. When you asked us to take her in after . . . Sarah died, we were delighted to be able to help. And we'll go on helping. For as long as you need us to. But . . .'

'But?' Lestrade blew smoke rings to the ceiling – the one thing he and Conan Doyle shared, a love of good shag.

'Damn it, Sholto, she is your daughter. You've seen her these past few days. She's a lovely girl. She ought to be with her father.'

'You haven't told her –' Lestrade sat upright.

'No, of course not. As far as Emma is concerned, Letitia and I are her parents and Rupert and Ivo are her brothers.'

'And that's how it must stay, Harry. For her sake.' Lestrade strolled to the window where the last glimmer of day was disappearing. 'Seven years ago, when Emma was born and Sarah died, I couldn't provide a home, not a real home for a little girl. I still can't, Harry. The only difference is that I'm older. Slower. I'm still living in rooms – and I don't exactly mean the Grand, either. Most of my life is in that Gladstone bag upstairs. Some nights, I don't go home. And one day, one night, who knows? Perhaps I won't come home again.'

He caught Bandicoot's look in the oil lamp's flicker. 'That sounds like self-pity, doesn't it? It isn't meant to. I've made my bed and I'm quite content to lie in it. But it's a single bed, Harry, and I can't take Emma back to it.'

He stubbed out the cigar. 'Better for her to know me as Uncle Sholto, and to see me now and then, if that's all right with you.'

'My dear fellow.' Bandicoot rose and placed a hand on his shoulder.

'It's late,' said Lestrade.

'It is,' Bandicoot agreed. 'And tomorrow you're going?'

Lestrade nodded.

'Yard can't do without you, eh?'

'It never could, Banders old thing. Only it hasn't realised that yet.'

'When does your leave end?'

'Wednesday.'

'Good. Then, tomorrow, you and I are going to an auction.'

'An auction?' Lestrade echoed.

'You've drunk me out of house and home the past three days,' Bandicoot was mock-indignant, 'I've got to replenish my stock of sherry!'

*

Lestrade read the catalogue again. 'For sale by auction, by Messrs Christie, Manson & Woods, at their Great Rooms, 8 King Street, 5000 dozen bottles of fine old sherry, all laid down before 1890 and conveyed from a number of Royal estates. Proceeds to the Prince of Wales' Hospital Fund.'

'Five thousand dozen,' Lestrade repeated as they entered the building.

'Defies belief, doesn't it?' Bandicoot agreed, 'and that's just surplus to requirements, you realise. I didn't know the old Queen was such a tippler.'

'Tsk, tsk,' scolded Lestrade, 'and you an Old Etonian.'

Bandicoot flustered. 'Oh, I meant no disrespect, Sholto, I assure you.'

Lestrade laughed. Fatherhood had not altered Harry Bandicoot one jot. He was still an idiot.

'Now there's someone who *is* a tippler. I thought he'd be here.' Bandicoot motioned to a corner of the crowded room. From his vantage point several inches lower, all Lestrade could see was a jostle of top hats. In his bowler, he felt decidedly out of place.

'Who's that?' he felt it polite to ask.

'Christian Barrett, the MP for my constituency. Drinks like a fish. Sherry?'

The policeman and the ex-policeman, retired, now of private means, each took a glass from the lackey's silvered tray. As they did so, a fanfare threatened to smash all the glassware in the place.

'That'll be His Majesty,' said Bandicoot, 'we'd better get upstairs. I hope the speeches won't be too interminable. Ah, Mr Barrett, how are we?'

The Member of Parliament for Bandicoot's constituency swung round, vaguely in the right direction.

'Ah, Mr . . . ah . . . er . . .'

'Lovely to see you. May I present Inspector Lestrade, an old friend.'

'Charmed, Mr . . . er . . . Charmed. Er . . .' and he pointed approximately to the stairs, 'the King.'

Lestrade wondered how long Barrett had been in the cellars,

sampling the olorosos. From the look of him, at least a week. They headed for the stairs, the fanfares still resounding in the chandelier-lit rooms above. The good-natured banter turned to something more alarming as a commotion occurred on the top flight of the stairs. Someone had stumbled, someone else went over him and a third plummeted over the rail to crash into a cask of amontillado.

'Not the best of years,' commented Lestrade drily.

'Look out there,' someone shouted.

'Have a care. That's my eye,' sobbed another.

It was a miracle Lestrade escaped with all his limbs intact, but then he wasn't going to admit to the fact that he'd already caught his teeth a sharp one on his sherry glass.

'Good God,' a voice rose above the hubbub, 'I think he's dead.'

'Dead drunk,' said another in one of those silences which always descend as someone puts his foot squarely in it. True to form, that someone was Harry Bandicoot. 'Make way. Mind your backs. I'm a doctor.' And another tippler fought his way to the stairs. The crowd surged back, clearing the area so that Christian Barrett lay alone on the steps, his head dangling over the edge. The doctor fussed around him and stepped back. Hats were removed as realisation dawned. Lestrade took charge, as he tended to in these situations. Of all the men in that fume-laden room, he was the one most accustomed to sudden death. He called up the stairs, 'Mr Christie!'

A frail white-haired gentleman appeared. 'Would you inform His Majesty there has been a tragic accident here. I fear the auction will be postponed . . .' He stopped in his tracks as he reached the corpse. He dropped to one knee, sniffing the nose and mouth as he did so.

'Good God,' someone said, 'what's he doing?'

'Gentlemen,' Lestrade straightened, straddling the stairs, 'I'm afraid the auction will be postponed indefinitely. Harry,' he summoned Bandicoot to him and whispered in his ear, 'get the keys from Christie and lock the doors. Then call the Yard. Ask for Gregory – he's marginally the better of two evils. He'll need constables. Lots of them.'

'Just like the old days, eh?' Bandicoot grinned.

I hope you've got brighter since then, thought Lestrade, though he would not have said so for the world.

'What's going on?' someone asked as Bandicoot made his exit. 'Who the hell are you?'

'I am Inspector Lestrade of Scotland Yard,' he answered, 'and as of now, you gentlemen are all suspects in a murder enquiry.'

The heckled band

Messrs Christie, Manson, & Woods made one of their great rooms available for Scotland yard. Bandicoot barred the main doors with his Etonian bulk, but he was having trouble with one gentleman who refused to accept the temporary imprisonment. Lestrade came to the rescue, having ensured the cellar was emptied and the doors to it locked.

'Is there a problem, Harry?' he asked.

'I want to know by what authority we are being kept here,' the gentleman snapped.

'By mine, as an officer of the Criminal Investigation Department, Metropolitan Police.'

'Well, my authority outweighs yours. I am Sir Frederick Ponsonby, Equerry to His Majesty. We cannot have His Majesty compromised by this matter.' He became more confidential, 'Did I hear you say a murder had been committed?'

'It has.'

'Good God, man. Don't you realise the implications of this? His Majesty's life may be at stake.'

'Now then, Freddie. What's going on?'

The knot of remonstrators at the door turned to face the stolid figure of the King, wreathed in smoke from his giant Havana. They bowed.

'This . . . gentleman, sir, is refusing to let Your Majesty's party leave.'

'Quite right. Do you know who this man is, Freddie? Inspector Lestrade – Lestrade of the Yard, in fact. I have every confidence in him. How have you been, Lestrade?'

'Well, Your Majesty, thank you.' He was amazed the King should remember.

'Let me see, when was it – 'ninety-four at Ladybower. Old Harnett's place.'

'I believe it was 'ninety-three, sir.'

The nerve of the man, fumed Ponsonby, correcting the King.

'You're right. It was. Well, well, where have the years gone, eh?'

'May I congratulate you, sir, on your accession?' Lestrade found it hard to grovel, but he could manage it from time to time. 'And may I crave Your Majesty's indulgence? The murderer may still be on the premises.'

How crass, observed Ponsonby to himself.

'If I may begin with you, sir,' Lestrade ventured, 'I won't keep you longer than I need.'

'Lestrade!' roared Ponsonby. 'Have you lost your mind? You are addressing the King of England!'

'Now, Freddie, watch your blood pressure.' The King patted his man on the arm. 'I've been through baccarat scandals and divorce trials. A few questions about a little murder aren't going to do any harm.'

'Thank you, Your Majesty. This way, please.'

But before Lestrade could begin his enquiries, there was a thunderous knocking at the front door.

'The Yard,' said Lestrade, 'they're improving. Harry, let them in.'

Uniformed constables swarmed into the main concourse, the auctioneers attempting to restore order to the scene with the odd judicious tap of their hammers, utterly drowned, of course, by the hullabaloo. Unfortunately for all present, or fortunately if they had something to hide, Edward Henry, not Tom Gregory, led the invasion, and promptly took over from Lestrade as the most senior officer present. Having bowed almost double before the King, he acceded immediately to Frederick Ponsonby's request to allow the royal party to leave. He continued to grant such concessions, his constables furiously taking notes of names and addresses, until the only people left in the establishment were the auctioneers, their staff and a huge crowd of policemen with nothing to do. Rather than risk losing his temper and breaking Edward Henry's nose, Lestrade retired to the cellar for a further look at the corpse. Bandicoot went with him.

'What makes you so sure it's murder, Sholto?' the younger man asked.

'Smell,' said Lestrade.

Bandicoot did.

'Sherry,' he said.

'And?'

'Other drinks?' Bandicoot guessed.

'Probably. But there's something else.'

Bandicoot shook his head.

'Bitter almonds. Cyanide.'

'Good God. I can't smell a thing.'

'Many people can't. That's why it's so useful. Actually, it's not a common poison, though I came across it in the Brigade case, in 'ninety-three. Look here,' Lestrade lifted the deceased's head, 'notice that froth on the lips? Classic symptom.'

'But how . . . the sherry!' Bandicoot expounded suddenly, with the triumph of a man who has found the lost chord.

'Yes, the sherry. But there are problems there. I can't see our new Lord and Master allowing us to test all five thousand dozen bottles. Not if his performance in the last few minutes is anything to go by. You know, Bandicoot, I still can't believe it. He almost certainly let the murderer walk out.'

'A man who plays things by the book. But isn't it likely that the murderer wasn't here at all? And why bother to kill old Barrett? He was harmless enough.'

'When I can answer your last question, Harry, I'll have my man. This is one of a pattern. Christian Barrett is the fourth Member of Parliament to die in mysterious circumstances in as many months.'

'Good Lord. Really?'

'In answer to your first question, the murderer had to be here. Barrett wasn't an accident. The man I'm looking for is careful and clever – very clever. He takes chances only when he has to. How could he be sure Barrett would get the poisoned bottle among all these thousands of bottles?' He began to sniff glasses lying where they had been left in the confusion. 'How could he be sure that only Barrett would drink the cyanide?'

'I give up,' said Bandicoot, uncomprehendingly.

'Answer,' Lestrade beamed triumphantly, 'because it wasn't in a bottle. That'll please Edward Henry. We don't have to confiscate the King's sherry and I've got a set of fingerprints for him.'

'Fingerprints?' Bandicoot was as lost as ever.

'Never mind, Harry, it's too long a story. But *this*,' he held it up to the light, 'is the poisoned glass. Barrett's glass.' He sniffed at it again. 'Bitter almonds.'

Lestrade came back on duty a day early. In fact, he travelled with his new chief in his very own cab, past the Houses of Parliament and on to the Yard. For the rest of the day, the two men were incarcerated with the scientific Sergeant Collins in the bowels of the building. Dew, Dickens and Jones were buried somewhere above in Hansard's volumes, trying to trace speeches by any of the deceased. It would not make light reading. With his test tubes, his Bunsen burners, his powders and his brushes, it was evening before Collins had finished.

'There,' Henry beamed, 'are the fingerprints of your man, Lestrade. Let the others scoff now. We've got him.'

'Who is he, sir?'

'Well, I don't know. We'll have to fingerprint all those who attended the auction.'

'How many were there?'

'Two hundred. Three hundred. Can't remember.'

'Can we insist on that, sir?'

'Insist? Lestrade, some of the richest men in England were there today. Not to mention ladies. You were all for interrogating the King this morning. You really must learn some discretion, you know.'

Collins stifled a chuckle.

'May I make a telephone call, sir?' Lestrade asked.

'Of course. What for?'

'Just an idea, sir.' And he left.

It was not a good line, the one between the Yard and Christie's auction rooms, but Lestrade got the answer he wanted. Or rather, didn't want.

'Collins, have you taken Christian Barrett's prints?'

'Er . . . no,' the sergeant admitted.

'You'll find him in the morgue. Jump to it.'

'Just a minute, Lestrade. What's your point?' Henry asked.

'I've just spoken to Mr Christie of Christie, Manson, & Woods.'

'And?'

'And, as I suspected, their staff wear gloves when handling items for sale.'

'I don't follow.'

'Bear with me, sir. The cyanide was placed in a glass. Correct?'

Henry nodded.

'That glass was handed to Christian Barrett.'

He nodded again.

'He drank from it. And was dead in five minutes.'

'So?'

'So the murderer evidently did not have time to wipe the glass, since there are prints still on it. I'll wager my next month's pay that Collins will find that all these prints are Barrett's.'

'Well of course some of them are.'

'*All* of them.' Lestrade was emphatic.

'How do you know?'

'Because the auction-room staff wear gloves when handling exhibits for sale.'

'Are you trying to tell me—'

'That our murderer was one of the auction staff? I suspect he was temporary, sir. I'll check, of course, but I think we'll find not a trace of the man by now. Of course, if I'd been able to question everyone this morning—'

'Impossible, Lestrade.' Henry was quick to defend himself. 'Anyway,' a vindicating thought occurred, 'you were probably served sherry by the same man. He was right under what's left of your nose, Lestrade, and you let him go.'

'Well,' Lestrade curbed his rising annoyance, 'we must see that it doesn't happen again, mustn't we?'

'It's a pity,' Henry turned back to the murderous glass, 'I'd just begun to work out from the patterns of the whorls that our man was a left-handed Irishman who suffered from gout. Ah well, back to the drawing board.'

Summer died. And it was autumn, raw and cold before any further headway was made in Lestrade's case. He and Bradstreet and Gregory gave each other wide berths, nodding in the corridor, exchanging bitcheries in the ghastly monthly inspectors' meetings which Edward Henry continued from his predecessor, who had continued them from his predecessor. It was December by now, skies dark with threatening snow and little cheer for the Christmas season. Enquiries at Christie's had come up with a name – a name that rang bells in Lestrade's head each time he re-examined it. But he couldn't place it. Messrs Christie, Manson, & Woods had taken on, the previous Friday, a man named Henry Baskerville. His credentials had been excellent, but he had vanished without trace on the day of the unfortunate incident, the day that Christian Barrett died. Surprise, surprise.

As for the other murders, little new was forthcoming. Lestrade interviewed Beales again, but he was able to offer nothing else on the brutal killing of his former master, Ralph Childers. Besides, now he was in the employ of Lord Rosebery and had strict instructions not to talk to the police more than he had to. Lestrade had met Rosebery before and knew him to be a man cautious to the point of hysteria. There was no fathoming Knights of the Garter. The friends and colleagues of John Deering clammed up. Just what the remaining Deering's involvement in the Army Remount scandal was or how much he wished to save family and regimental honour, Lestrade was not able to say. For a while, he had Dickens observe, from a safe distance, the rather attractive Lady Brandling, since Lestrade could not be sure, despite her logical protestations of the problematical murder weapon, that her story was quite straight. He had to admit that he was clutching at straws. Then another man died. The news was brought, curiously enough by that doyen of Yard detectives, the man who handled, entirely to his own satisfaction, but to no one else's, the Ripper case, Chief Superintendent Abberline.

'Chief Superintendent Abberline to see you, sir,' Jones announced him.

'Don't I know you, Constable?' The large man with the large gardenia paused in the doorway.

'No, sir. You knew my father, Athelney Jones.'

'Ah, yes. I never liked him.'

'Chief Superintendent,' Lestrade hailed him. 'Dew, where's that red carpet?'

'Talking of people I don't like, morning, Lestrade.'

'Chief Superintendent.' The inspector snapped his fingers for Dickens to make the tea. He was coming on well. One day he might be as good at it as Dew.

'I've got a case for you, Lestrade.'

'Oh?'

'You may know I've been looking for a gang of ruthless cut throats who stole a quantity of ping-pong balls.'

'I knew you were assigned to Serious Crimes, sir. I had no idea just how serious.'

Dew just managed to change his snorting laugh into a sneeze in time.

'I don't care for your attitude, Lestrade. Here I am, giving you a lead—'

'I'm sorry, sir. Please go on.'

'My enquiries led me to Sir Geoffrey Manners, Bart.'

'Would that be the Yorkshire Manners-Barts, sir?' Dew chipped in.

'Ignore him, Mr Abberline. He's been trying to better himself by reading Debrett. Geoffrey Manners, MP?'

'Well, I'm glad to see someone's awake in H Division.' He threw an accusatory scowl at Dew. 'He's dead.'

Lestrade's air of levity vanished. Dickens stopped with the steaming mugs in mid-air. 'Put them down, Constable, before you pour that tea all over the Chief Superintendent. When?'

'Yesterday, my inspector thinks. His men found the body this morning.'

'How?'

'He didn't know. My men aren't used to murder, Lestrade. That's your department.'

'Have you told Mr Henry?'

'I didn't think there was any hurry—'

'Chief Superintendent, you have risen in my estimation. Stay and finish your tea. What's the address?'

'Oh, no, Lestrade. I'm not passing it over to you entirely. I remember how you wormed your way into the Ripper case.'

Dew's tea trembled slightly in his hand. Lestrade leaned forward confidentially to Abberline. 'He was on Mary Kelly's beat that October. He was first on the scene. Never been the same.'

'Well, this isn't a pretty one, either. Shall we?'

'Dickens, you've had your tea break. Get back to those Hansards. Remember you're looking for a pattern.'

The officers of the Yard took a cab to Jermyn Street, the shady side, and were shown in by a stalwart constable of Abberline's division.

'He's in the Games Room, sir.'

They were shown by a uniformed inspector whom Lestrade knew vaguely to a large room at the back of the house, in the basement. In the centre, under the swinging electric light, was a large table, painted green, across which was slung a net.

'What's this?' Lestrade asked the inspector.

'It's a table,' the other answered.

'Obviously, man. The inspector wants to know what it's for,' Abberline rounded on him.

'For ping-pong, sir.' The inspector looked suitably chastened.

'I am not familiar with the game,' Lestrade said.

'It's all the rage, man,' Abberline told him. 'Two people play it. It's like tennis, but played indoors, with the table as the court.

'Tennis for midgets?'

Abberline ignored him. 'Sir Geoffrey was a devotee of the sport. Ruxton here was making a routine enquiry concerning the loss of his balls when the deceased's man came hurtling out of the house screaming there was a murder. Here he is.'

'The man?'

'The deceased.'

Lying slumped in the far corner was Sir Geoffrey Manners, Bart. He was wearing a dressing gown, thrown open to reveal an expensive nightshirt and his face was covered in lurid pink patches. The mouth was distorted and the eyes rolled upwards. Oddly, one of his arms was resting on an upturned chair, his index finger pointing towards his face. The other hand still clutched his throat.

'Fingerprints?' asked Lestrade.

Abberline took him aside. 'Look, Lestrade, it's not for us to criticise our superiors, but this nonsense of Henry's, well, I mean . . . Let's get down to some serious policework, shall we? You can borrow my craniograph.'

'Your what?'

'Really, Lestrade, I always thought you were abreast of scientific developments. A craniograph measures the skulls of murderers. It helps in the identification of criminal types.'

'Haven't we got to catch him first?'

Abberline apparently hadn't thought of that.

Lestrade lifted the bat. 'Do they always break like that?'

'They can,' the inspector told him. 'It's the vellum, you see.'

Lestrade sniffed it. Bitter almonds. 'Where are these things made?' he asked.

'This one,' Ruxton found the other bat, 'seems to have been bought from Hamleys of Regent Street.'

'Can I borrow the inspector, Chief Superintendent?'

'All right.' Abberline was not keen. He had been helpful once already today. Twice was painful for him.

'Ruxton, be a good fellow and get over to Hamleys, will you? Talk to Hamley himself. Find out how these things are made. I'll meet you at the Yard later. My office.'

'Any ideas, Lestrade?'

'Do you want a guess?'

'Why not? Of academic interest only, you understand.'

'First, sir, whose case is it? Yours or mine?'

Abberline pursed his lips. 'All right, Lestrade. It's yours.'

'Cyanide gas. I've read about it. Never seen it. It could be carbon monoxide, that leaves this pink discoloration too.'

'I take back what I said, Lestrade. Quite the budding coroner, aren't you? But how was it administered? No one detected a smell in the room. Wouldn't a gas affect anyone and everyone in the room? I assume Sir Geoffrey wasn't playing with himself.'

'It's not his solitary vices I'm interested in, sir. Not at the moment. Let me try another guess on you. I don't think Ruxton will have much luck at Hamleys. I think our man bought these bats and pulled away the outer cover of leather. Then he inserted a capsule of cyanide between the layers of vellum. If, as Ruxton says, the vellum is always breaking, it would only be a matter of time before it broke. A sudden rush of air may cause an explosion, which would account for the shattered bat and the look of horror on Manner's face. It's only a guess, but I doubt if we'll find much better. The murderer would have time, if he was quick, to leave the room. May I talk to the servants?'

Lestrade did just that. For the rest of the day he examined and cross-examined. And for the first time in a long time he felt he was getting somewhere. Twenty-four Jermyn Street was the town house of Sir Geoffrey Manners, his quiet retreat from the hurly-burly of the House. His family seat was not, as Dew had surmised, Yorkshire, but Devon, near Okehampton. Consequently, his staff were few. He had a man, and two maids. He had no cook, for he usually ate at the House or his club, and much of his time was spent riding in the Row or rowing on the river. He was known as a keen sportsman and excelled as a shot, billiards player, cricketer and oarsman. His study, Lestrade noted, was festooned with trophies going back to his school-days.

His man, who had discovered the body, had understood that a gentleman was due to call the previous evening, to engage Sir Geoffrey in a duel of ping-pong. The gentleman's name was, apparently, Sherrinford Holmes?

Lestrade rocked back in his chair.

'Did you say Sherrinford Holmes?'

'Indeed, sir, I believe that was the name Sir Geoffrey mentioned. I *could* have misheard.'

'Did Sir Geoffrey ever mention this name to you before?'

'No, sir, I don't believe so. But Sir Geoffrey had a host of friends and acquaintances, sir. I couldn't hope to keep track of them all.'

'Who let Holmes in?' Lestrade asked.

'It must have been Sir Geoffrey himself, sir. I was on an errand in the City and on returning went to my bed. I had a feverish cold.' Indeed, to be fair, the man still had.

'And the maids?'

'Annie is deaf. She would have heard nothing. Mrs Elkins was visiting her sister in Deptford.'

'Not very sensible, employing a deaf girl,' Lestrade commented.

'Sir Geoffrey used to say he liked the exercise of answering the doorbell himself, sir. Even when we were all in the house, he would race us to the door. He usually cheated by sliding down the banisters. He was very vigorous.' The man blew his nose and sat there, a martyr to catarrh.

'Lady friends?' Lestrade thought he'd better explore every avenue.

'Oh, yes, sir. Many. It's funny . . .' Lestrade thought he saw the beginnings of a chuckle, but it was only a trick of the light.

'What is?'

'Sir Geoffrey was very fond of the ladies, sir. But he was so outspoken against them in the House. He and Mr Churchill.'

'Churchill? Winston Churchill?'

'Yes, sir. Do you know him?'

'As a matter of fact, I do – when he was a cadet at Sandhurst.'

'Ah, he's come a long way since then, sir. His exploits in the war. We followed it avidly.'

'And now?'

'Why, he's Member for Oldham now, sir. Eleven constituencies asked him to stand, but he chose Oldham.'

'Yes, well, there's no accounting for taste,' said Lestrade. 'So it looks as though he will be Home Secretary after all.'

'Sir?'

'Nothing,' Lestrade broke out of his temporary reverie and made his farewells. He sent a message via a constable for Inspector Ruxton to present his findings at Hamleys to Sergeant Dew and he took the Underground train to Baker Street.

Lestrade had always promised himself he would never return to Number 221B. It had too many sour memories. But here he was, ringing the bell again and here was Mrs Hudson opening the door, as though there had been no lapse of time at all. She was rounder, shorter than Lestrade remembered. He was thinner, taller than she remembered. She showed him up the stairs to the study which had been that of Sherlock Holmes.

'Doctor Watson, it's Inspector Lestrade to see you.'

'Lestrade. My God, this is a surprise,' Watson shook his hand heartily, 'I was just putting a few finishing touches to my . . . er . . . our latest novel. Conan Doyle is so careless with his punctuation.'

Lestrade glanced at the papers lying on the cluttered desk. Mrs Hudson had scurried away in the time-honoured tradition to fetch a sherry. 'No thank you, Mrs Hudson,' said Lestrade on her return, 'I am less fond of sherry than I was.'

'You'll stay for supper, Lestrade?' Watson asked.

'Thank you, no.'

'Not a social call, then?'

'That name,' he pointed to the papers, '*The Hound of the Baskervilles* – your latest novel.'

'What about it?'

'How did you come by it?'

'Well, don't you remember? It was your idea. That hyena thing you caught in Cornwall. It gave me the idea of a monstrous beast that slaughtered men on the moors. Really, Lestrade, we had this conversation at the Diogenes Club the night old Hamilcar Waldo died.'

'Indeed we did,' said Lestrade, 'I knew I'd heard the name, now I know where.'

'What name? Look, Lestrade, you can't be suggesting plagiarism. I mean, I know Conan Doyle and I . . . well, Conan Doyle has been a little harsh on you, but . . . well, nobody reads the *Strand* magazine, anyway.'

'Tell me, Doctor, is there a Henry Baskerville in your book?'

'Why, yes, he's the central character. Apart from Holmes and myself, of course.'

'Who has read this book?'

'Who? Well, I . . . er . . . myself, of course. Conan Doyle. My publisher, some proof readers . . .'

'I shall need their names, Doctor. And the address of Mr Conan Doyle.'

'I believe he's still with his field hospital in South Africa. Rumour has it he's to be knighted, you know.'

'Bully,' said Lestrade, 'but it doesn't exempt him from a murder enquiry.'

'Murder? What has dear Arthur to do with Hamilcar Waldo?'

'Ah, my dear doctor, I am not, in this instance, talking about Hamilcar Waldo.'

'Not?' Watson now turned from his sherry to his brandy.

'Tell me something else. Did your erstwhile colleague ever use the name Sherrinford?'

'Conan Doyle? Never.'

'I was referring to Sherlock Holmes.'

'Oh, I see,' Watson swigged heartily, 'er . . . yes, I believe he did. As you know, Inspector, he was a man of many parts.'

'Indeed, although I seem to remember not all of them were working?'

'Have a care, Inspector. You are talking of a man who was closer to me than a brother. And a genius, to boot.'

Lestrade leaned one arm on the desk, so that their eyes drew level. 'I am talking of a man who was so deranged through the misuse of narcotic substances that he tried to kill you, Doctor Watson. And he was a detective of very limited ability.'

Watson poured himself another glass, infinitely larger than the first.

'Why are you using the past tense, Lestrade?' he asked nervously.

The inspector straightened. 'Doctor, I know it is your pious hope to keep Holmes' memory alive. And in view of your former friendship, I understand that.'

'His memory, Lestrade? Who's talking about his memory? I'm talking about the man himself. I've seen him!'

Lestrade narrowed his eyes and glanced at the decanter from which Watson poured another brandy.

'No, Inspector. It isn't the brandy. Mrs Hudson has seen him too.'

'Perhaps you'd better tell me about it,' said Lestrade.

'I've seen him four or five times now. Always at evening, out there in the street.'

The two men went to the window. 'Down there.' Watson pointed. 'He always crosses from right to left, pauses below the window and glances at the door. On two occasions he has lit his meerschaum.'

'What was he wearing?'

'The ensemble Paget usually drew him in – an Ulster and a deerstalker. It's funny, really,' though Watson clearly wasn't amused, 'Holmes very rarely wore that hat.' And he drained his glass again.

'Doctor Watson, you can't imagine that the figure you've seen *is* Sherlock Holmes?'

'Why not, Lestrade? Conan Doyle is a spiritualist, you know.' Lestrade knew.

'He accepts it perfectly well. A phantasm, he calls it.'

'Doctor, you and I are men of the world. So was Holmes.'

'There are more things in heaven and earth, Lestrade . . .'

Lestrade nodded. His old boss, Melville McNaghten, had said that to him once. *He* was a believer, too.

'But he was killed. His body was found at the foot of the Reichenbach Falls. You were at the funeral, man,' Lestrade persisted.

'Yes, I was at the funeral. And I saw what everyone else saw. A mahogany coffin complete with brass fittings. How do I know what was in it?'

That indeed was food for thought. 'All right,' said Lestrade, 'let's assume Holmes was not in that coffin – is not dead. Why should he fake his own death?'

'Who knows? International espionage, foreign intrigue.'

'Hogwash, Doctor – with respect. I want facts, not fiction.'

'All right, Lestrade. But my contention is the same. Holmes

was neurotic – he always had been. And towards the end, the cocaine finally got him. But did it? You'd better look at this.'

Watson unlocked a drawer in the desk and handed a letter to Lestrade. 'I received that a month ago. It's postmarked from Switzerland.'

Lestrade read the contents, 'Watson, old friend, will be home sooner than you think. S.'

'Are you telling me this is genuine?'

'It's his hand, Lestrade. I virtually lived with this man for ten years, I ought to know his handwriting.'

'Wait a minute,' Lestrade checked the postmark, 'the letter itself is undated – and the stamp a blur. What if this were sent before Holmes' death?'

'Ten years ago? Good God, Lestrade, I know foreign postal systems aren't a patch on our own, but even so . . .'

Lestrade returned to the window. Dusk was settling fast on the hurrying crowds, the evening newspaper sellers calling raucously to each other in the raw cold of another winter's evening.

'Let's assume all this is correct,' he said. 'Let's assume that Holmes for reasons of his own engineered his own death, engineered his own funeral and remained abroad. Let's assume he wrote to you, from Switzerland a month ago, telling you he would be home soon—'

'"Sooner than you think" are his words, Lestrade.'

'Quite. Let's also assume that he is now in London and that on a few occasions he has appeared in his familiar – though apparently not too familiar – garb beneath your window and has lit his meerschaum. I have one question for you, Doctor – why?'

Watson shrugged. 'And I have one question for you, Lestrade. Why did you come here tonight, asking about Holmes?'

Lestrade's eye caught the bullet holes in the wall near the door – the holes made by Holmes in some of his more half-hearted murder attempts on Watson.

'What if I told you,' the inspector said, 'that I am looking for a murderer who is a crack shot, who wears an Ulster and a deerstalker and gives his name as Sherrinford Holmes?'

Watson's glass shattered on the hearth, causing a minor

explosion as its contents hit the flames. 'Then you believe it too. That Holmes is alive?'

'No, Doctor. I believe that someone is trying very hard to make us *think* he's alive.' He made for the door. 'Even so, I'll check with the Swiss authorities. If you receive any more letters – or have any more sightings – you'll let me know?'

Watson nodded. He was a frightened man.

As Lestrade had suspected, Gregory had drawn a blank at Hamleys with the ping-pong bat. It was inconceivable that a cyanide capsule could have been placed into the thing during its manufacture – unless the murderer was of course a manufacturer of ping-pong bats, which was not beyond the realms of possibility. One curious little footnote to the episode was that Mr Hamley had written personally to Edward Henry complaining of the fact that Inspector Gregory had insisted on telling the said Mr Hamley a number of excruciatingly boring jokes, all of which Mr Hamley had heard before and did not wish to hear again. This was, of course, a confidential matter between Assistant Commissioner Henry and Inspector Gregory. Or it would have been, had not Sergeant Dew been waiting outside Mr Henry's office and accidentally dropped his half-hunter on the carpet, so that in picking it up – an oddly lengthy process – his ear chanced to be very near the keyhole.

Dickens and Jones however had come up with something – they had verified from Hansard a chance remark by Geoffrey Manners' man, namely that the same Sir Geoffrey was highly outspoken of ladies in society and seemed to work every speech he made round to the subject. Lestrade decided to renew an old acquaintance.

'Well, Lestrade,' said the Member for Oldham, 'how long has it been?'

'More years than I care to remember, Mr Churchill. So you decided on politics after all?'

'I suppose my father's death ensured that. Anyway, too much blockage in the army, Lestrade – especially in the cavalry. It's full of chinless wonders and people called Nigel these days. No hope there.'

'And in politics?'

'Ah, in the House, Lestrade, you make your own mark. Another muffin?'

Lestrade declined.

'If it wasn't for this infernal rain, we could have taken tea on the terrace. I've got a soft spot for Old Father Thames, you know.'

Lestrade had noticed Winston Churchill's soft spot. There was certainly more of him than when they met last. Churchill had been a slim young man then, a cadet awaiting placement with a regiment. The Fourth Hussars, the Malakand Field Force and countless clashes with fuzzy-wuzzies and Boers had certainly left their mark. He was now a national hero, a respected back-bencher and nearly three stone heavier.

'But, confess it, Lestrade,' Churchill lit the inspector's Havana, 'you didn't catch me before the Christmas recess just to relive old times.'

Lestrade smiled. Yes, the man would be Home Secretary one day.

'It's these murders, isn't it? I've noticed an increasing – what do you fellows call it – police presence in the House recently.'

Bradstreet, thought Lestrade. 'Sir Geoffrey Manners,' he said.

'Ah, yes, poor Geoffrey. A damned nice fellow. It's the Irish, I suppose?'

'Why do you suppose that, Mr Churchill?'

'Well, naturally I . . . Matters are coming to a head, Lestrade. You mark my words. There'll be a bloodbath.'

'And you think these murders are the start of it?'

'Stands to reason, surely? I don't mind telling you, everyone's a bit on edge. Do you know we're all searched, morning, noon and night. Policemen in the Yard – that's Westminster, not Scotland – policemen in the Chamber, I'm not sure that's legal. Even in the committee rooms. Only here in the dining room do we get privacy. Couldn't bear some flatfoot – oh, sorry, Lestrade – watching me eat me buns!'

Lestrade glanced round. Most of the diners had the air of rather worried Members of Parliament. But the man nearest the door, in ill-fitting topper and tails, carried all the hallmarks of an utterly bored copper.

'I don't think it's the Irish,' said Lestrade.

'Oh? Who then?'

'I gather that Sir Geoffrey was an outspoken critic of the ladies?'

'Well, yes, but who isn't?'

'Sir?'

'Well, Lestrade, if you must know, there's a little band of us who rather enjoy needling the female suffragists. Manners, myself, even old Lloyd George and Asquith aren't averse to the odd dig.'

'Does no one object?'

'Good God, Lestrade, you aren't a feminist, are you? I took you to be made of sterner stuff. Well, to be candid, we do occasionally have rather a rough time of it in the House, when Emily Greenbush or the Pankhursts are in.'

'Emily Greenbush?'

'Yes, a militant feminist. I'm glad there's only one of her.'

Realisation dawned.

'Lestrade, if I follow your devious mind aright, you're not suggesting that Emily Greenbush killed Geoffrey? No, it's too preposterous.'

'It's too preposterous that a handful of Dutch farmers should have taken on the British Empire, Mr Churchill, but until a few months ago, I wouldn't have taken any bets on the outcome of that one.'

Churchill looked suitably abashed. 'Point taken,' he said.

'Do you happen to know where Emily Greenbush lives?' Lestrade asked.

'As a matter of fact, I do. It's splashed all over the noxious handbills which she throws at Members as they arrive for a debate. It's Thirty One, Curzon Street. You know, I'm glad you're going to pay her a visit, Lestrade. It'll do her good to have her collar felt. She's a dangerous woman.'

Lestrade thanked his host for the tea and made his farewells. As he passed the all too cognito policeman near the door, he called cheerily under his breath, 'Give my regards to Bradstreet!'

*

At Curzon Street, Lestrade met his Waterloo – or very nearly. But first he met Emily Greenbush. From Churchill's description, he expected a fire-breathing dragon at the very least. Instead, it was a sylph-like creature who showed him into the drawing room as the lamps were lit. The room of candles sparkled in her eyes and shone on her long hair, the colour of fine-spun copper. She wore a long dress of claret velvet laced with threads of silver and her eyes were clean and blue.

'I've been expecting you,' she said, and held out her wrists as though for cuffs.

'Indeed, ma'am?' Lestrade was uncomfortable in the company of intelligent women. And beautiful ones. Emily Greenbush was both.

'Tell me, who is it who sent you? Winston Churchill? Asquith? Not that old goat Lloyd George – who before you ask, did not know my father.'

'As a matter of fact, Mr Churchill—'

'I knew it. Well, take me, Inspector . . . er . . .'

'Lestrade.'

'Lestrade. Weren't you on the Hyde Park case?'

'Indeed, ma'am. Why do you ask?'

'It's as well to know your enemy, Inspector. What is the charge? Heckling in a public place? Loitering with intent to pester a politician? Come on, my arms are beginning to ache.'

'I am here on a more serious matter, ma'am. The murder of a number of Members of Parliament, most recently Sir Geoffrey Manners, Bart.'

'Ah, yes,' Emily let her hands fall. 'Can I offer you a Scotch?'

'Not when I'm on duty, Miss Greenbush.' He checked his half-hunter. 'Ask me again in half an hour.'

To Lestrade's surprise, she poured herself a large one and swigged it back, pouring another immediately. Catching the look on his face, she offered by way of explanation, 'In a man's world, we women must learn to do what men can. Would you care to wrestle?'

'Thank you, no, ma'am. It's Thursday. I never wrestle with ladies on Thursdays.'

'Cigarette, then?' She produced a silver case.

'I prefer my own.' Lestrade produced a Havana, but Emily promptly lit it for him. Despite all Lestrade's prejudices, the cigarette looked particularly becoming between her delicate fingers.

'My dear!' The door suddenly crashed open to reveal three ladies of the Miss Lawrence school, not Roedean perhaps, but mannish lasses all. 'Rawlins tells me *this*,' the leading lady pointed with evident distaste at Lestrade, 'is a policeman.'

'Yes, Emmeline, he is.'

'Rotter!' And Emmeline fetched Lestrade a sharp one with her umbrella.

The inspector sprang more nimbly than he thought possible behind the sofa, keeping the horsehair beast between him and them.

Emily was giggling helplessly. 'May I introduce you. Inspector Lestrade, of Scotland Yard, this is Emmeline Pankhurst and her daughters Christabel and Sylvia.'

'Chauvinist lackey!' Christabel hissed.

'Despoiler of women!' Sylvia accused.

Emmeline threw herself bodily across Emily Greenbush. 'What are you accusing her of?' she demanded. 'What are the charges?'

'With respect, ma'am, we've just been through this. I am making enquiries into a murder—'

'Murder? Isn't that just what it's been for womankind for centuries? You see these?' Emmeline shook her fists at Lestrade.

'They're fists, ma'am.'

'No, they're not. They're chains, Inspector. Chains. Oh, invisible, I'll grant you, but chains nevertheless. Who put them there?'

'Er . . . your husband, ma'am?' Lestrade was beginning to see this madwoman's method.

'Mr Pankhurst, God rest his soul, was a sainted man. The *only one* of his sex to realise the injustice of the situation. Until all others are like him, we ladies of the Women's Franchise League will fight – *fight*, Inspector, to obtain our God-given rights. Christabel, Sylvia, with me.' And the trio advanced on the Chauvinist Lackey Who Despoiled Women.

'Ladies!' It was Emily who halted the advance. 'I think you can leave me to handle the inspector. Really, I am in no danger.'

Slowly, the assault dwindled. There was much whispering and flashed glances and scowls. Eventually, the feminist trio were womanhandled out of the door. Emily leaned her full weight against the door and roared with laughter. To his surprise – and annoyance – Lestrade found himself laughing too.

Emily patted the sofa and the inspector sat beside her. Her mood changed. 'Geoffrey Manners,' she said quietly, 'I was as shocked as the next man to hear of his death. Oh, we had our disagreements, Inspector. I may have shouted some unpleasant things – all quite richly deserved at the time – from the Ladies Gallery . . . Now, there's a *non sequitur*, Mr Lestrade.' He found himself looking on the carpet for it. 'A Ladies Gallery in the House of Commons. We should be down there on the floor.'

Lestrade looked again. Or perhaps this was an offer he would be hard put to refuse.

'Do you know what Edward I said?'

'Er . . . about what, ma'am?'

'About Parliament, Inspector. He said, "Quid omnes tangit, ab omnibus approbetur." Don't you think he was right?'

'Well, I –' Lestrade began to waffle.

'Oh, forgive me, Inspector. I spend so much of my time putting men in their place in public I find it difficult to desist in private. It's the legacy of a classical education. You see, the late Mr Pankhurst wasn't *quite* the only defender of the cause. My father too saw the injustice of the world, and saw to it that I received as good an education as any man, in the confines of my own home. Edward I said, concerning Parliament. "That which touches all, must be decided by all." I like to think that makes him the first advocate of female suffrage.'

'And Geoffrey Manners?'

'Ah yes,' Emily poured Lestrade his Scotch, the half hour being up, and blew smoke-rings to match his own, 'I really am sorry. Any theories?'

'Do you by any chance own a Martini-Henry rifle, carbine variety?' Lestrade asked. Nothing about Miss Greenbush would surprise him.

'No,' she answered, unruffled, 'but I have a Webley Mark IV, an old navy cutlass and a couple of cavalry lances.' The smile vanished from her face as she saw the darkness spread over Lestrade's.

'Forgive the question, ma'am, but do you, in your quest to equal men, to drink their Scotch and smoke their cigarettes, ever wear men's clothes? A deerstalker, perhaps? Or an Ulster?'

Emily laughed. 'No, Inspector. I'm sorry to disappoint you. I don't take things that far. You'll stay to dinner?'

'Ma'am, I—'

'You won't compromise me, Inspector, if that's what's worrying you. You see, I've had dinner with men before.'

For the rest of his life, Lestrade never knew how he ended up in Emily Greenbush's bed later that night. Was it the Scotch? The exhaustion of a maddening and fruitless case? Long years without a woman's touch? He could never say. Certainly, it was unprofessional. If Edward Henry ever found out, he'd have a fit – of morality, probably. She rolled on top of him, her breasts jutting defiantly from the fragrance of her long, auburn hair. She began to rise and fall on him, stroking and teasing his chest with those long, slender fingers, her powerful thighs bringing him to a sudden and shattering climax. She stretched out beside him, her arm across him, her face buried in the pillow. After a while, when he'd come to, he noticed that she was crying. He lifted her face and kissed her softly on the lips.

'What's the matter?' he asked. 'I haven't upset you?'

She smiled through her tears, shaking her head. 'No, Sholto,' she said, 'some of us have feminism thrust upon us. From the time I was so high, it's all I heard.' She choked back the tears, 'For twenty years I've been sharpening the argument, honing the wit, learning to give as good as I got. "Never let a moment pass, Emily." "You're as good as they are, Emily." Didn't they know? Didn't they realise all I wanted to be was myself? A little girl who was not a little girl. A woman who is not a woman.'

Lestrade closed her lips with another kiss. 'You *are* a woman,' he whispered, 'a lovely one.'

She looked at him in the lamplight. 'Tomorrow,' she said, 'I will deny that this ever happened. I shall be Emily Greenbush, man-hater again. But for tonight, can I drop the mask with you?' And she folded into his arms.

The Irish interpreter

It was the night before Christmas and all through the House not a creature was stirring, except for Edgar Bradstreet and Sholto Lestrade, officers of the Yard.

'Irishmen,' said Lestrade again.

'Absolutely,' Bradstreet was emphatic, 'or women.'

'Women?'

'You met Miss Greenbush?'

For an instant Lestrade's sang-froid slipped. 'In a manner of speaking,' he said.

'What did you think?'

'An interesting lady.'

Bradstreet stopped. 'Sholto, she is a member of the Women's Franchise League. Not to mention the Independent Labour Party.'

'And that makes her a murderess?'

'Perhaps not, but there are others. Millicent Fawcett, for instance.'

'Oh?'

'She's militant, Lestrade. Rabid, in fact. Good God, man, you and I are rational, liberal human beings. We're prepared for change. But these women are lethal. I fear what is to come. Just imagine,' Bradstreet became confidential, 'just imagine being examined by one.'

'In court, you mean?'

'No, Lestrade. I don't. Imagine the inner sanctum of a doctor's surgery. You go along ready to bare your . . . soul, and a *female* doctor asks you to cough. It defies credulity.'

'I understand there are a dozen or so of them already,'

Lestrade said – a snippet he'd picked up, no doubt, in the *Sun*.

'Well, there you are. It's not natural. You wouldn't want a son of yours to marry one, would you?'

'I haven't got a son, Bradstreet. But what I have got is a hot rum waiting for me at the Yard. And walking round this cheerless mausoleum, I could do with it. Why did you ask me down here?'

They took the stone steps into the stark medieval grandeur of Westminster Hall.

'Padraig O'Leary,' said Bradstreet.

'Who?'

'He's a Fenian leader, Lestrade. I've been after him for years. If it is the Irish, he's the one mixed up in it.'

'What's it got to do with me?'

'Well, I'll be frank. I've had him in the Special Wing at the Yard for a fortnight. I can't get through to him. He does his stage Oirish and that's all. It's not much better than name, rank and serial number. I can't hold him for much longer. If the Press find out, they'll have a field day.'

'So?'

'So I wondered whether you would have a chat with him, Sholto? I've tried all I know. The commander's been through his paces too. Even Gregory's tried.'

'Without success, I take it?'

'Totally. Gregory tried to wear him down by telling him endless Irish jokes.'

'And?'

'O'Leary didn't understand them.'

Lestrade sighed and looked at his watch. 'All right,' he said, 'I'll have a word in his ear, but I can't promise anything. And anyway, you're barking up the wrong tree. You know something, Edgar?' Lestrade threw it out across the hall. 'Don't take this personally, but I preferred you when you were a sergeant.' And he turned into the cold.

The caped constable on the door saluted him. The night was studded with stars, the river a slow-moving gleam of chiselled silver. Lestrade's breath curled back on him as he buttoned up the collar of his Donegal and buried his hands as deeply as he could in his pockets. What happened next was completely his fault. He was gazing idly at the statue of the Lionheart, head thrown back, sword in fist. His mind had left the chill of the House and the silent policemen who guarded it. It turned now to Christmas Eve and to little Emma, sleeping soundly, he knew, at the Bandicoots'. It would be dawn in a few hours. She would leap from her bed, bright eyed and morning fresh and scamper to open her stocking with the boys. She would find the present from Uncle Sholto. He hoped she would like it. He was still hoping that when he collided with someone walking in the opposite direction. The figure went sprawling across the pavement, to land heavily at the base of the Lionheart statue. It was only then that Lestrade saw the white stick. And only then that he saw that he knew the man.

'Mr Holmes?'

'Who is it?' the blind man asked, still recovering from the shock.

'Inspector Lestrade. We met at the Diogenes Club.'

'Ah, of course, Inspector. I never forget a voice. How are you?'

'Damnably sorry,' said Lestrade, helping him up, 'I wasn't looking where I was going.'

'Neither was I,' said Holmes.

Lestrade chuckled uneasily. 'Are you all right?'

'I'm fine. Fine. What brings you out on a raw night like this? Spreading Christmas cheer?'

'Duty, sir, I'm afraid. We never sleep, you know.'

'Ah, indeed not.'

'And you, sir? On Christmas Eve and alone?'

'Oh, night and day are one to me, Inspector. I often stroll late – fewer people,' he laughed brittlely, 'less chance of accidents.'

'May I get you a cab, Mr Holmes? You're a long way from Jermyn Street.'

'Thank you, Lestrade. By the way, my bumping into you like this is very fortuitous. I remembered something about the night Hamilcar Waldo died at the Diogenes.'

'Oh?'

'It's probably nothing, but when I arrived at the club and cousin Mycroft met me . . .'

'Yes?'

'We were crossing the lobby and I heard someone asking for Waldo.'

'Asking for him?' Lestrade hailed a hansom.

'Yes, whether he was there and if so, which was his table.'

'And that was all?'

'I'm afraid so. Probably of no importance.'

'On the contrary, Mr Holmes. It might be of the greatest importance. To whom was this addressed?'

'Ah, there you have me, Inspector. One of the questions a blind man cannot answer. I wonder Mycroft didn't mention it.'

The cab lurched to a halt by the kerb.

'Isn't it so,' Lestrade asked, 'that when a sense is lost, others are improved?'

'To an extent, yes,' said Holmes, 'as I think I told you at the Diogenes, my sense of smell has vastly improved.'

'What about your sense of hearing?'

'Eh?'

Oh, God, thought Lestrade, that doesn't bode well. 'I said –' he began.

'No,' Holmes laughed, 'I heard you, Lestrade. I simply don't follow you.'

'You said a moment ago you never forget a voice. What about that one? The voice you heard asking for Hamilcar Waldo.'

'Well,' Holmes frowned with the effort of remembering, 'it had a slight lisp. No, not a lisp, exactly, but some sort of impediment. And it was Irish, of course.'

'What?'

'I said—'

'Yes, I know what you said.'

'Look, guv'nor,' the cabbie leaned over from his perch, 'it's Christmas. I've got a family at 'ome.'

'Right, Santa,' said Lestrade, 'Mr Holmes, would you like to accompany me to the Yard?'

'Are you arresting me for walking without lights, Inspector?'

'No, I'm going to break the habit of a lifetime. And a few rules as well. I think you can help me.'

*

'A hot toddy, Mr Lestrade?' The desk sergeant raised a glass to him.

'Tut, tut, Dalgleish. Drinking again?' Lestrade took it and quaffed its contents. 'And one for my friend here.'

Holmes quietly collided with a column. Dalgleish, who had not seen the white stick nor the upturned, sightless eyes, motioned Lestrade to him. 'He's blind drunk already, sir.'

'It's all right, Sergeant,' Lestrade assured him, 'he's not driving.'

He gave Holmes the rum punch and led him through the labyrinthine corridors of the Yard. It was Christmas Day before they reached the relevant door in the seldom-seen wing of the building set aside for the Special Branch. Lestrade noticed the bunch of mistletoe blowing in the draught over the door. Singularly inappropriate he thought. A knock brought a constable.'

'Inspector Lestrade,' the visitor announced, 'with Inspector Bradstreet's permission to talk to the prisoner.'

'Which one?' the constable asked with all the cheer and festive spirit of a man who drew the short straw to work over Christmas.

'Padraig O'Leary.'

'Oh, him. I'll have to search you, sir.' The constable proceeded to do just that, producing keys, knuckle duster, handcuffs, cigars and handkerchiefs from Lestrade's pockets like rabbits from a conjurer's hat. Lestrade winced a little as the constable measured his inside leg with his forearm.

'Sorry, sir. You'd be amazed what some of them hide up there.'

'I'm sure I would,' Lestrade agreed.

'Who's this?' the surly constable asked.

'Mr O'Merle Holmes,' Lestrade told him. 'He's all right. He's with me.'

The constable took Lestrade aside. 'Did you say O'Merle, sir?'

'No, he's not a Fenian, Constable.' Lestrade was at his most benign, as it was Christmas.

Even so, the constable duly searched Holmes too, although

the contents of his pockets were rather less interesting. And there was less fluff.

'Mr Holmes, I'd like you to wait in the next room. The constable will show you a grille in the wall. Through it you'll be able to hear my conversation with O'Leary. Listen carefully to his voice. I want to know if you've heard it before. Constable, look after Mr Holmes, will you? We'll have you home before Santa arrives, Mr Holmes.'

Padraig O'Leary was a jaunty leprechaun of a man, sitting cross-legged on the bare iron bedstead in one corner of his grey, spartan room.

'Padraig O'Leary?' Lestrade had a knack of striking up conversations.

'Top o'the mornin' to yuz,' the Irishman replied.

God, thought Lestrade, it's worse than Bradstreet was letting on.

'You've led us all a merry chase, haven't you?'

'Ah, I have that, sor. I have that.'

'Why did you do it?'

'What would that be, sor?'

'Come off it, O'Leary. You've murdered five Members of Parliament and an officer of His Majesty's cavalry. I want to know why.'

'Ah, I refuse to answer that on the grounds of replenished responsibility.'

'What?'

'I didn't touch them, sor. As God is my witness.'

'With respect to the Almighty, O'Leary, you'll need a better witness than that.'

'Holy Mother of God, may yez be struck down for that, yer terrible blaspheming Englishman!'

'Don't give me that papist claptrap, O'Leary. I want answers.'

The Irishman twinkled and leaned forward. 'May I be knowin' who yer are, darlin'?' he said.

'I'm not your darling, O'Leary. I'm Inspector Lestrade.'

'Be Jabez, not the Lestrades of Kilkenny?' The Irishman sprang up with delight.

'No, the Lestrades of Spitalfields, Pimlico and Norwood.' A pause. 'Do you mean I've got relatives in Ireland?' He glanced at the picture of the Last Supper behind which he knew the grille to be. He'd have some explaining to do to Bradstreet because of this.

'Tell me how you poisoned Ralph Childers.' Lestrade sat on the only chair in the room, his legs astride it and leaning on its back.

'Ah, that would be with the terrible afflictin' stuff yuz English call beer,' O'Leary answered chirpily.

'And what about the blunt instrument you used on John Deering?'

'A policeman's wit,' the Irishman replied.

'Careful,' warned Lestrade, smiling now, 'you almost gave the game away there.'

'Did I now, sor?' The stage Oirish persisted.

Lestrade looked at his man. The Commander of the Special Irish Branch and his minions like Edgar Bradstreet had had this man inside for days. They'd got no further than this. Judging by the bruising around O'Leary's eyes and nose, they'd tried other methods too. Lestrade knew the jargon: 'Injury inflicted while resisting arrest.' What it really meant was 'Irish reprobate looked at me funny, so I hit him with my truncheon. Several times.'

'All right, O'Leary,' Lestrade got up, 'that's it. I was your last hope. Constable!' he shouted. The door unbolted and clanked open. 'A pity they've pulled Newgate down,' said Lestrade, 'but the prison yard at the Scrubs is as good a place as any for a hanging. And the shame of it is I know you didn't do it. What a waste.' And he made for the door, shaking his head.

'Wait a minute!' The leprechaun stood up. The stage Oirish had gone. Lestrade stopped. 'All right, Lestrade. May we talk alone?'

Lestrade motioned the laughing policeman outside.

'What do you want to know?' O'Leary asked.

'Why the change of heart?' Lestrade sat back on his chair. 'Collaborating with the enemy? Isn't that what some of your Fenian friends will say?'

'Probably. But I'm not made of the stuff of martyrs, Lestrade. I fear there are some coming up now, oh, mere lads as yet, but they'll lead you a merry dance, Lestrade. And they are the martyr kind. It'll be Phoenix Park all over again.'

'I'm not here to argue Home Rule with you, O'Leary. You're in no position to bargain. But I need answers. I need to eliminate you and your so-called cause from my enquiries.'

'You're not Special Branch, then?'

Lestrade shook his head.

'I thought the name wasn't familiar.'

'What about the Lestrades of Kilkenny?'

'All part of the act, Inspector, darlin'. But tell me, apart from avoiding the drop – and personally I don't think you'd have enough evidence anyway – why should I help you?'

'That's what this is all about, isn't it? Cause the maximum of bother. Be as difficult as possible. Well, I'll tell you why you should help me, O'Leary. Because there's a maniac going around killing MPs. And it's got nothing to do with Ireland. For all I know, an Irish MP might be next. Or perhaps that's what you want too? Perhaps that will further your cause?'

O'Leary shook his head. 'I've got alibis for the times those men died, Lestrade. All of them.'

'That's very pat,' said Lestrade, immediately wishing he hadn't.

'And that's an old trick, by the way – you feeding me the wrong cause of death a moment ago. Ralph Childers was beaten to death with your proverbial blunt instrument – and no, it wasn't a shillelagh. And John Deering was skewered with a lance. Your colleagues of the Special Branch have been over and over all this. And even before I was arrested, I read the newspapers avidly. Rather free with the details, weren't they? I'm surprised you haven't had people queueing up to confess.'

'Oh, we have. Two men who claimed to be King Charles I wreaking vengeance and another who swore on oath that he was Guy Fawkes and would get the bastards this time. I passed them on to another colleague of mine. I think you've met Inspector Gregory?'

O'Leary yawned.

'Yes, quite,' Lestrade concurred. 'Tell me, do you know the Diogenes Club?'

O'Leary shook his head.

'One last thing,' Lestrade rose to go, 'before you make a statement that makes sense and we let you go, would you say something for me?'

'Is it my brogue yuz likes, Inspector, darlin'?' O'Leary reverted.

'Would you say "Is Hamilcar Waldo here tonight?"?'

O'Leary shrugged and said it.

'Thank you, Mr O'Leary, and a Merry Christmas to you.'

In the adjacent room, Aumerle Holmes roused himself at Lestrade's entrance.

'I'm sorry, Inspector. It's difficult to tell. It was similar . . . but after all these weeks . . . I couldn't answer to it in a court of law. I'm sorry.'

'Not at all, Mr Holmes. Thank you for being so patient. Constable, get a Maria for Mr Holmes and see that he gets home, will you? I appreciate your help, Mr Holmes.' He took the man's hand and shook it. 'We'll be seeing each other soon, I hope.'

Again the brittle laugh at the badly chosen phrase. 'You can count on it, Inspector.'

By the day after Boxing Day, the Christmas spirit had left Lestrade, particularly when Sergeant Dew gave him the news. Padraig O'Leary had been released. Well, that was right and proper. Whatever the man was involved in in the cause of Home Rule, he was not guilty of these murders. What annoyed Lestrade was that Bradstreet had changed his tack. Unable to pin anything on the Irishman, not even a bunch of shamrock, he had turned his attention to the fairer sex. He had arrested Emily Greenbush.

'Why?' Lestrade had asked him in Bradstreet's office, a murky corner high in the Yard's eaves.

'Look, Lestrade, I'm grateful in a way – but only in a way, mind you – for sorting out the O'Leary business. I still think the bastard's free to kill and maim again.'

'So that's it. It's an eye for an eye, is it? I let one of your suspects go, so you grab one of mine?'

'You're taking this very personally, Lestrade,' Bradstreet observed.

Lestrade checked himself. Bradstreet was no fool. Play it gently. He began to do that by sitting down. 'All right,' he said, 'what have you got?'

'One,' Bradstreet resorted to the policeman's finger exercise, 'Geoffrey Manners was a raving anti-feminist.'

'Five other men are dead, Bradstreet. Were they all anti-feminist too?'

'From your report I'd say Ralph Childers and John Deering certainly were. They used women as sexual objects, Lestrade. You'll notice there are no females among the victims.'

'Yet.'

'There'll be no more killings, Lestrade. I've got my woman.'

'All you've got is a damned thin motive. It'll never get to court.'

'Two,' Bradstreet's second finger came into play, 'Miss Greenbush is an outspoken critic of the Government, and with the exception of John Deering, all the victims were members of the governing party.'

'But not the Government itself, Bradstreet. Not the Cabinet. If these are really political crimes, why hasn't the murderer had a go at Salisbury or Balfour? And John Deering is a pretty important exception, isn't he? He doesn't fit at all.'

'I'll grant you that,' Bradstreet concurred, 'and it's possible the Deering murder has nothing to do with this case at all. On the other hand, three,' but he was still using the same hand, 'Miss Greenbush owns a cavalry lance – a pair, in fact. Of the type used on Major Deering.'

'Motive?'

'Who knows? A personal thing perhaps. There may be a link between Greenbush and Lady Brandling. I'll find it.'

'You won't.'

'Four, Miss Greenbush by her own admission is a pretty fair shot. She could have killed Arthur L'Estrange with a Martini-Henry without too much difficulty.'

'So could a blind man on a galloping horse. It was close range in broad daylight – a standing duck.'

'Five, and this is the trump card, Lestrade. Two of them in fact—'

'You'd better call it five-a, you're running out of fingers,' said Lestrade.

'The late Horatio Greenbush, Emily's father, was a chemist.'

'So?' Lestrade chose to remain obtuse.

'So she may well have had a working knowledge of poisons.'

Lestrade laughed.

'*And,*' Bradstreet was undeterred, 'she bought a quantity of cyanide not six months ago. I have the chemist's log.'

'What was it for?'

'To kill wasps, she said.'

'Well, there you are.'

'Come on, that's what they all say.'

'I see,' said Lestrade, 'so she walked into a chemist's, gave her own name and address to obtain cyanide, made a compound, disguised herself as an auction-room attendant and poisoned Christian Barrett. Then she broke into Geoffrey Manners' house, doctored his ping-pong bat with the same stuff and challenged him to a game, knowing it would blow up in his face?'

'Precisely!'

Lestrade lolled back in his chair.

'All right, I know it's bizarre,' said Bradstreet, 'but murder is a bizarre business, Lestrade. Look at the Ripper killings, the Struwwelpeter case, that thing in Hanover Square—'

'All right, spare me the museum inventory. Let me pose one question. Ralph Childers. Where it all began. Where does Emily Greenbush figure there?'

'She knew his . . . inclinations . . .'

'And was a member of the reincarnated Hell Fire Club?'

'Ah, I've done research there. Did you know that the original Hell Fire Club had one female member? The so-called Chevalier d'Aeon – a woman in man's attire.'

'Have you read the coroner's report on Childers? And mine?'

'I have.' Bradstreet was triumphant.

'What would you say Emily Greenbush weighs? Eight stone, perhaps? Are you seriously implying she could have inflicted those injuries?'

'Yes, if Childers was manacled at the time and unable – or unwilling – to fight back until it was too late. Don't forget Lizzie Borden. She was little, but she still hacked her parents to death.'

'That was never proven, Bradstreet. Do your homework. Anyway, she was American.'

The two men looked at each other, all logic tried.

'Are you arresting her or her entire movement?' Lestrade asked.

'I'll get the Pankhursts later,' Bradstreet answered. 'For now, I'll stick to Emily Greenbush.'

The conversation was ended there by a furious pounding on the door.

'What is it?' Bradstreet asked.

It was Walter Dew who stumbled in. 'Mr Lestrade, sir, there's a telephone call for you. A man with an Irish accent. Says he knows who's been killing all these MPs.'

'Where?' Lestrade grabbed his hat.

'Mr Henry's office.'

'Wait for me.' Bradstreet snatched up scarf and Ulster and followed Lestrade along the maze of corridors to where a weak and pale Miss Featherstonehaugh stood holding a telephone receiver in a weak, pale hand.

'It's him,' she whispered hoarsely, covering the wrong part of the apparatus with the other hand.

'Yes?' Lestrade snatched it unceremoniously from her.

'Inspector Lestrade?' The Irish brogue crackled in his ear.

'Speaking.'

Bradstreet and Dew crouched as close as they could. In the silence a pin dropped from Miss Featherstonehaugh's mouth. Bradstreet looked at her. 'I travel home via the Strood tunnel,' she whispered by way of explanation. 'I might be kissed by a man.'

Fat chance of that, thought Dew, though now was not the time to say so.

'Go to the Houses of Parliament,' the telephone voice hissed, 'to the base of the clock tower. There's a surprise waiting for you. Is that imbecile Bradstreet there?'

'He is.' Lestrade passed the receiver across.

'Yes?' Bradstreet took it.

'I've got a surprise for you. Go to the foot of Victoria Tower.'

And the line went dead with a click.

'Hello, hello.' Bradstreet rattled the receiver. Nothing. 'Nothing,' he said.

Miss Featherstonehaugh fainted quietly behind them. No one noticed.

'"A surprise", he said,' Lestrade repeated.

'Yes,' said Bradstreet, 'at the foot of Victoria Tower.'

'Mine is at the foot of the clock tower.'

'It's a trap, of course.' Bradstreet rested against Henry's desk.

'Of course,' Lestrade did the same, 'perhaps it was Emily Greenbush throwing her voice over the telephone wires. Miss Feathers . . .' Lestrade noticed the grey lady down on the floor. 'Dew, get some water for Mr Henry's secretary will you? And find out all you can from her when she wakes up. I want to know *exactly* what the caller said. Get Dickens and Jones first. Bradstreet and I will meet them at the House.'

'You see, Lestrade,' Bradstreet chortled, 'an *Irish* voice. I told you, didn't I? I told you it was the Fenians.'

'So you'll be releasing Miss Greenbush?'

The inspectors made for the lift.

'If we survive tonight, Lestrade, yes. Otherwise—'

'Otherwise, I'll release her myself.'

Dew gave the orders to his constables and returned to pour water, none too gently, over Miss Featherstonehaugh. 'I wonder what made her faint?' he asked himself. 'Must have been the anticipation of the Strood tunnel.'

The Maria screeched and jerked to a halt outside the Houses of Parliament. It was dark now, another sharp, clear night made magic by the sparkling frost.

'You're the expert, Bradstreet, though it catches in my throat to say it. What do you think?'

'I think it's an explosive device, Lestrade.'

Dickens and Jones looked at one another.

'That's a bomb to you, gentlemen,' he said.

'Ever tackled one, Lestrade?'

The inspector shook his head. 'You?'

The inspector shook his head too. 'But I'm getting my men out. If this place is going to blow up, there's no point in half Special Branch going with it.'

'Dickens, Jones. Get round the building. Clear every copper out – Inspector Bradstreet's orders. Double up.'

The constables scattered.

The inspectors walked away from the Maria. Bradstreet checked his watch. Nearly half past seven.

'Of course, if I'm wrong –' he said.

'You?' mocked Lestrade. 'Surely not!'

'If I'm wrong and this isn't a bomb, but there are Fenians in there – we're playing right into their hands. Are you armed, Lestrade?'

'Only in the line of duty.' Lestrade slid out the brass knuckles and flicked the deadly blade upright.

'Likewise.' Bradstreet tugged free a Webley Mark IV.

'All regulation, of course. And above board,' Lestrade commented.

'Absolutely,' agreed Bradstreet.

They were gabbling aimlessly, somehow reassured by each other's voice. 'Damn, it's cold,' hissed Lestrade, burying his ears in the collar of his Donegal. As they reached the clock tower, they heard a constable call into the darkness of the public convenience nearby, 'Come along now, Mr Strachey, there's a good gentleman. Put that away and go home, will you?'

'Right, Lestrade. Here's your end. I'll get to mine.'

'Bradstreet, we'll try and work through this together. Whichever of us finds it first, if it is a bomb, that is, waits until the other has found his. Then we'll relay messages.'

'How?'

'Runners. I'll keep Dickens with me and send Jones to you. They can act as go-betweens. All right?'

Bradstreet nodded.

'Lestrade,' he called as the inspector entered at the side door, 'mind how you go.'

'I love you too,' grinned Lestrade and was gone. He'd lifted a bull's-eye from a passing constable and proceeded to flash it in every corner he came to, hoping that Mr Strachey had indeed taken the constable's advice and gone home. Security or not, His Majesty's Government had insisted on strict economy and the whole tower was bathed in the dimmest of lights. Lestrade's lantern threw eerie shadows on the Gothic walls, sharply faceted with corbel and ogee arch. But the niceties of Pugin's architecture passed Lestrade by. He walked as though on eggs, one hand gripping the lantern, the other cradling his switch-blade. There was no sound but for his footfalls, soft and steady like the snow that began to flurry outside. At first, he wasn't sure he'd heard it, but it got stronger. Footsteps. Behind him. He slid noiselessly round a pillar, extinguishing the bull's-eye as he did so and waited for the step to get nearer. Two of them, he'd say. He pressed himself back further into the darkness. Then his foot jerked out and his fist came down. The first caught the shin and the second the head of Sergeant Dew, who crumpled as one pole-axed.

A shriek from behind caused Lestrade to spin to face the second intruder. Constable Dickens stood staring with open mouth at the speed of the attack. He wouldn't have said the old man had it in him.

'Dew, Dew,' Lestrade was kneeling over the fallen sergeant, 'are you all right?'

'Yes, Guv'nor,' Dew struggled upright, 'just a bit of a headache, that's all.'

'Dickens, where's Jones?'

'Gone with Inspector Bradstreet, sir, as per your instructions. He met us outside the building.'

'Is the place cleared?'

'Yes, sir.'

'Right. Dew. Go home.'

'Sir?'

Lestrade looked at him in the rekindled light of his lantern. 'You're a family man, Walter. What are all the little Dews going to do if they haven't got a daddy by morning? Go home. And that's an order. Give my regards to Mrs Dew.'

The sergeant hesitated, 'I'll wait outside with the Maria, sir. See if I can't get you some tea for when you come out.'

Lestrade slapped his arm in appreciation and the sergeant vanished.

'Right, Dickens. Inspector Bradstreet believes there's either a bomb or a gang of roughneck Irishmen in here somewhere. It's my job to find out which. I could use your help, but I'm not ordering it. If you want to follow the sergeant now, there'll be no hard feelings.'

'What are we looking for, sir, exactly?'

Lestrade smiled. Nimrod Frost had been right. He *did* like this man.

'What do you know about the Houses of Parliament, Dickens?' the inspector asked.

'The present edifice was built in the reign of Queen Anne, of Yorkshire sandstone. A serious fire in eighteen thirty-four led to an extensive renovation under Sir Charles Barry and Augustus Welby Pugin—'

'Yes, yes. Never mind the history lesson. How big is the place?'

'It covers eight acres, sir, has eleven courts, one hundred stairways and eleven hundred apartments.'

'What about this?'

'The clock tower is at the north end.' Dickens looked up into the darkness above. 'Three hundred and eighteen feet. The bell above us, colloquially called Big Ben, although in fact many people believe this refers to the clock itself, was hung in eighteen fifty-eight—'

'Well hung, I hope,' observed Lestrade.

'It weighs thirteen and a half tons.'

Lestrade felt his throat tighten a little. Thirteen and a half tons plus a few floor levels and the roof cascading down on him should the thing blow up. Not to mention the clock. Time would indeed weigh heavily on his hands.

'All right, Constable,' Lestrade took command of his nerves again, 'you proceed in a clockwise direction,' he regretted the phrase, 'and I'll go the other way. Is that your watch ticking?'

'I don't have a watch, sir.'

The inspector and the constable looked at each other. They glanced to the floor. Dickens' bull's-eye shone on a small, rectangular box in the corner. Dew had missed it by inches when he fell.

'Dickens,' Lestrade whispered, 'I want you to take off your boots and walk to the other end of the building. Tell Inspector Bradstreet it's a bomb. And it's ticking.'

'Very good, sir.' And the constable gingerly unlaced his footwear and padded into the vast halls and chambers where their Lordships, their Graces and countless Right Honourables were due to be sitting in a few weeks' time. Lestrade sat cross-legged on the floor, alone with the ticking and the dark.

It seemed hours before Dickens got back. He crouched by Lestrade. 'I found Jones, sir. It's quite straightforward really. I worked out a short-cut through the Lords' chamber.'

'Has Bradstreet found his bomb?' Lestrade whispered back.

'Yes, sir. From Jones' description, it's identical to yours.'

'What's he doing about it?'

'Jones said he said, and I quote, "Lestrade is the senior man, so it's up to him, but it sounds like a time bomb."'

'Brilliant!' hissed Lestrade. 'All right, Dickens. Tell Jones to tell Bradstreet I'm going to open my box. There are . . .' he adjusted his bull's-eye, 'four screws. I'm going to loosen them one at a time, top right, top left, bottom right, bottom left. Can you remember that?'

'*Please*, sir.' Dickens groaned exasperatedly. It was like asking a man with a photographic memory if his plate was clean. Lestrade put the rather offhand reply down to nerves. He didn't tolerate uppity young constables ordinarily, but tonight he'd make an exception. He switched the blade clear on his brass knuckles as Dickens exited left. He felt the sweat form on his forehead and more trickle down behind his ears. He took off the bowler and the Donegal before tackling the other screws. The first and second were fine. But the third jammed. Cross-threaded, he guessed. Why was there always one? He leaned his full weight on it, unable to tell now whether it was the bomb or his heart that beat louder. It gave way and he was able to turn the blade. Number four followed easily. He sat back on his heels. His wrists felt like lead.

Dickens padded back, breathing hard now with the exertion of his run. 'Right sir. Inspector Bradstreet had difficulty with the first screw apparently, but by now he should have managed it.'

'Right. How long does it take you to get to Jones?'

'About four minutes, sir.'

'And about the same for Jones to reach Bradstreet?'

'I would say so, sir. We meet under the central tower.'

'All right. It's . . .' he checked his half-hunter in the lantern beam, 'sixteen minutes past eight, now. At twenty-four minutes past eight, I'll take off the lid. You wait with Jones. If you don't hear an explosion, tell him to tell Bradstreet to do the same.'

'Yes, sir,' and Dickens was gone again.

While he sat there, trying to stay calm, Lestrade thought of all the places he'd rather be. He thought of little Emma with her shy morning face. Of Harry and Letitia Bandicoot. Of Sarah, his wife. Dear, dead Sarah. Then it was time. He worked quickly, his face contorted in a manic frown. One, two, three, four, the screws worked loose. He wiped his sweaty hands on his trousers and prayed as he'd never prayed before. He teased free the lid and it came away cleanly. He looked at the contents of the box. A clock. Set for eight-thirty. No wires. No gelignite. No bomb. He found himself giggling hysterically, kneeling in a rumpled heap on the floor when Dickens arrived.

'Tell Bradstreet it's all right,' laughed Lestrade. 'It's a hoax. A bloody hoax . . .' But no sooner had he finished than there was a dull roar from some distance away, echoing and re-echoing through the empty halls. 'My God,' murmured Lestrade and he and Dickens raced each other for the Victoria Tower. Through the darkness they hurtled, the bull's-eye's beams darting and flashing in every direction. Through polished corridors, past silent statues they ran, Dickens still in his stockinged feet sliding and slipping in Lestrade's wake. The smoke and flames beat them back as they reached the base of the furthermost tower. What was left of Inspector Edgar Bradstreet lay against the far wall. Lestrade and Dickens grabbed the badly injured Jones and hauled him free of the burning building, out into the raw night.

'It went up, sir. Right in front of us.' Jones mumbled, shivering with shock and pain, 'Inspector Bradstreet . . .'

'All right, lad.' Lestrade mopped the blood from the boy's

head. 'It's all right. Dew!' Lestrade turned wildly to the milling mass of policemen, 'Get this man to hospital on the double. You there, get the fire brigade. The rest of you – there's a bloody river over there. Get some water and put this thing out.'

And the snow flurried in through the open door, spitting and crackling on the flames. Lestrade spent the rest of the night at Jones' bedside, hoping he would recover. Hoping he would regain consciousness. No one else slept.

The second stein

'So it's finally turned nasty.' Edward Henry tapped his fingers violently on desk, lamp and ephemera. 'How's the Jones boy?'

'The hospital were cagey, sir,' Lestrade told him. 'As well as can be expected, I think is the phrase.'

'It wasn't a very big bomb, then?'

'Big enough to kill one man and very nearly a second. No doubt the country will be delighted to know no damage was done to the fabric of the House.'

Henry was staring across the river where the last skies of the old year were full of unshed snow. He turned back to Lestrade and motioned him to sit.

'Your views, then,' he said, 'as one copper to another.'

'It's not only turned nasty, sir. It's turned personal. That phone call proves it. Whoever was on the other end of that line knows I'm on the case – and he knew Bradstreet was too.'

'Does that help pin it down?'

'No. The papers have had a field day with this one. My name, Bradstreet's, Gregory's. It's in all the dailies.'

'It certainly is.' Henry waved a bundle of that morning's at Lestrade. 'I insisted on total secrecy when I took over this job,' he said, 'and the gentlemen of Fleet Street have chosen to ignore me. Well, this afternoon I'm calling a meeting of City Editors. I'd like you and Gregory to be there. Before that, the commissioner wants to see us all. Best bib and tucker.'

Lestrade returned to the House later that morning. The whole area was heaving with coppers, uniformed and plainclothed.

There was a strange air of tension about the place; Lestrade had remembered a similar atmosphere before the Mafeking news had broken.

'We've got her sealed as tight as a drum now, Lestrade,' the Commander of Special Branch had told him. Yes, now, thought Lestrade, now a man is dead. He walked back along the smoky river to the Yard. The wind was biting as he crossed the square. Miss Featherstonehaugh had been no help. The man who phoned had an Irish accent. He had asked – no, demanded – to speak to Inspector Lestrade. He had been insistent. He sounded nearby. The local exchange had been less help still. Now it had become a personal duel, and Lestrade was pretty well where he had been at the start of it all, back with Ralph Childers in the spring. He barely acknowledged Dalgleish's salute as he entered the Yard and when the new swing doors hit him on the back of the head, he only gave a grunt, not at all his usual rejoinder when life's little foibles turned against him. He was mulling over how the pattern had changed. So far, it had been a careful, calculated series of assassinations. Whoever the madman was, there was an obvious method in his work. And all the targets, save one, had been Members of Parliament. Even that one had had political leanings. So why now had the pattern changed? Why had the chain been broken? Why should the two men in charge of the case be lured to what Lestrade felt sure Emily Greenbush would call the scene of innumerable crimes? And why was there death waiting for only one of them? And why should that one be Bradstreet, and not Lestrade? They were each directed to a specific tower, one loaded, the other not. Bradstreet had drawn the short straw. Why? Was it because the late departed Edgar had been on the right track? After all, the man on the telephone *did* have an Irish accent. And, after all, Emily Greenbush *was* still in custody. Well, it was Lestrade's case now. He knew the commander wouldn't waste another man on it. He'd be content to leave it to Lestrade. Now, Lestrade would keep his mind open. Deep down, his sense that this was not a political case was wavering. It wasn't easy for him to admit he was wrong. But having come this far . . .

'Miss Greenbush, you are free to go.'

Emily rose in the cell doorway. The po-faced wardress who

was with her scowled her disapproval. 'Her late Majesty,' she said, with an imperiousness above her station, 'was of the opinion these suffragists should be horsewhipped. I am of the same opinion.'

'Good for you,' said Lestrade and escorted the offending article up the steps to the daylight.

'What does this mean?' she asked him in the yard at the back of the Yard.

'That you are free to go,' he said again.

'Yesterday I was an accessory to murder,' she pointed out.

'That was yesterday,' Lestrade told her.

She looked at him with her pale, clear eyes. 'Sholto, what has happened?'

'A man is dead,' said Lestrade, 'a policeman.'

'I'm sorry,' she said.

'Are you?' His response was quicker, sharper than he had intended.

'Yes,' she said, facing him squarely, 'yes, I am.'

He smiled. 'Now it's my turn to be sorry,' he said. 'You'll know by the evening papers, anyway. It's Edgar Bradstreet. He was killed by a bomb last night.'

'My God,' Emily touched his arm, 'who?'

'About now I'd give my pension to answer that one,' he said.

'You look tired, Sholto.'

It wasn't something he had had time to think about.

'Come home with me,' she said.

He looked at her hard. Here was a would-be felon, whom only yesterday Bradstreet had sewn up for murder, inviting an inspector of the Metropolitan Police back to her house – and within the portals of Scotland Yard. On the other hand, it was nearly 1902; the world was changing. And Lestrade knew the charms of Emily Greenbush. Besides, she might yet provide him with some answers.

'Not yet,' he said, 'I've got to go to St Thomas's. One of my constables was hurt by the same bomb that killed Bradstreet. Besides, I've got more meetings today than Mrs Pankhurst has causes. Begging your pardon, of course.'

She laughed. The musical sound Lestrade had not heard

from a beautiful woman in a long time. 'Later then?' she said.

'It might be very late,' he warned her.

'Later.' And she held his hand.

The commissioner was terse. Never a happy man, he was, that afternoon, decidedly morose. The new electric light in the Yard's Assembly Hall dazzled on the wealth of silver braid and the draughts caught the gusting plumes of a veritable millinery of cocked hat. The hard-bitten detectives of the first floor and the second, together with the macassared sergeants of the third floor back, sat like drab damson jam in the middle of a plate of gleaming tapioca. At least it seemed so to Walter Dew, now with his recent promotion that much nearer his goal – his biographical memoirs. Edward Henry exhorted, cajoled, threatened. The eyes of the country, no, the world itself were on the Yard at that moment. There was to be an all-out effort. No stone unturned. All leave cancelled. And any officer found revelling in the fountains in Trafalgar Square at New Year was to be dismissed without benefit of pension. A tough line indeed.

Later that day, in the offices of the *Daily Mail* newspaper, Edward Henry made history. he held what was henceforth to be called a Press Conference. The gentlemen of the Press, wreathed in cigar smoke, sat in the said offices, clutching pads and pencils.

'Are we to understand, Mr Henry,' said one, 'that you would have us publish nothing on this case at all?'

'Correct.'

There were rumbles and guffaws in the room. Lestrade looked at Gregory. Gregory looked at Lestrade.

'Er . . .' another rose to his feet, 'T A Liesinsdad,' he announced with the voice of a circular saw, '*Daily Mail*. Are you trying to muzzle the Press, Mr Henry?'

'I am trying to save lives, Mr Liesinsdad. And to catch a murderer to boot. I can't do that without your help.'

'How can we help if we aren't able to publish our stories?' Liesinsdad persisted.

'That's exactly it,' Henry repeated, 'we're not interested in stories, sir. We are in the fact business.'

Roars and shouts drowned him out.

'You are scaremongers, gentlemen!' Henry accused them.

Lestrade and Gregory were suitably impressed. Even though the audience appeared rapidly to be turning into a lynch mob.

'Is it the Boers?' someone demanded.

'No comment,' said Henry.

'The Germans, then. Could it be the Kaiser?'

'Nonsense, it's the French,' somebody else chipped in.

'The whole thing has the smell of gelignite,' said Liesinsdad. 'It's the Irish.'

'No comment,' said Mr Henry.

'What about the Labour Party?' another voice bawled above the din.

'Or the Liberals?' And the whole meeting collapsed in uproar.

'We haven't heard,' said a stately voice from the back, 'from these gentlemen here.' He pointed to Lestrade and Gregory.

'Mr Harmsworth, isn't it?'

'Yes, the *Daily Mail*,' Harmsworth replied, 'I am right in assuming that Inspectors Lestrade and Gregory are in actual charge of the case?'

'Well, if I may say so –' Gregory began.

'I was hoping to hear from Inspector Lestrade,' said Harmsworth.

Lestrade untangled his fingers from the cradle he had formed over his nose.

'I'll offer you a deal, gentlemen,' he said.

'Lestrade!' Henry snapped.

'If you will stop printing rumour and speculation, I will give you your murderer on a plate within a month of the New Year.'

'That's no sort of deal,' Liesinsdad retorted. 'What'll you do? Give us *all* an exclusive?' And mocking laughter filled the room again.

'Unless you can give us facts, Mr Lestrade, we will have to publish what we can,' Harmsworth said.

Lestrade stood up. 'And unless you stop the fiction, Mr

Harmsworth, Fleet Street will have successfully spread a screen of smoke so thick across this case, we won't be able to see our hands in front of us. Mr Henry, with your permission, I have a job to do.' And he swept from the room amid cackles and screams for resignations.

Athelney Jones, Inspector, retired, of Scotland Yard, stood bareheaded in the corridor of St Thomas' hospital. He nodded to Lestrade, as he arrived, breathing heavily.

'Tell me one thing,' he said, 'did my boy volunteer?'

Lestrade nodded, 'Bradstreet I'm sure would have given him the option,' he said, 'and, knowing your boy, he chose to stay. Is there any news?'

Jones shook his head.

Lestrade patted his shoulder, something he would have said once he would never have done. Then he took a tram to Curzon Street.

'Is it done, Sholto,' whispered Emily, 'for officers of Scotland Yard to sleep with murderesses?'

'Murderesses?' Lestrade turned to her.

'Isn't that what Bradstreet thought I was?'

'He had no evidence.'

'And that's why you let me go?'

Lestrade nodded.

'Are you married, Sholto Lestrade?' she suddenly asked.

He looked at her in the candlelight, 'Not any more,' he said. 'She died.'

'I'm sorry.'

'Yes, so am I.'

'What was her name?'

'Sarah,' he told her. 'She died seven years ago.'

'And you've passed your apprenticeship without her.'

He smiled, 'Yes, I suppose I have.'

'Children?' she asked.

'A girl,' he nodded, 'Emma. She lives with friends. She doesn't know about me.'

'Doesn't know about you?' she repeated, lifting up on one elbow. 'Why not?'

'Bradstreet wasn't married,' he said, 'and he ended up in pieces all over Victoria Tower. That's bad enough, but how much worse if he'd been a father. What would I have said to his kids? I don't want somebody coming to tell my kid, one day. She's better off where she is.'

'Isn't that her decision, Sholto?' Emily asked.

Lestrade laughed, 'You feminists,' and he planted a gentle punch on her chin. 'Emma is seven years old. Would you have her voting?'

Emily laughed too. Then, as was her wont, she fell silent.

'Sholto. This case of yours. It's serious, isn't it?'

He nodded.

'Parliament reconvenes in five days' time. Let me help you. If your man is on the inside – if he's an Irishman, or a Frenchman or a Boer, I can help. I know more about that collection of misfits at Westminster than they do about themselves.'

'Really? I can believe that. But . . .' he took her hand and kissed it, 'I thought I was the enemy. Why the change of heart? Have you deserted the cause?'

She slowly shook her head. 'Never,' she said. She broke away from him, walking gracefully in the candlelight, her long copper hair swaying round her naked waist. She pulled on the frothy nightgown and looked out on sleeping Curzon Street. 'Oh, Sholto, haven't you guessed it yet?' She turned to him. 'I'm doing this for you because . . . because you need help, and I'm not the harpy the world thinks I am. But I'm also doing it for Geoffrey Manners.'

'Manners?' Lestrade sat upright.

She turned to the window, 'He and I were . . . lovers,' she said. 'Oh, we opposed each other in the House. As I would oppose you, if it came to it, in the street. But here, behind these doors . . .' And she hung her head. He crossed to her, holding her shoulders gently and pulling her back against his chest.

'Well, then,' he whispered, 'we each have our memories. And we each have our cause. Let that be enough.'

*

Lestrade began his assault as soon as Parliament reassembled. They were not due to sit again until February, but affairs of state brought them back earlier than usual. Back from their country mansions, back from their elegant town houses. Back to the business of Empire. There was a war to finish and a king to be crowned and a whole host of lesser fry. Security in Westminster had never been tighter. Members and their guests were scrutinised as they arrived and as they left. There was a special squad of men who spent most of their shift lying on their backs under carriages, checking for explosive devices. These men claimed to be able to grow marvellous roses in their tunics.

It was to the Irish question that Lestrade first addressed himself.

'And is that all, Mr Redmond, you have to tell me?'

The leader of the Irish bloc in the commons looked at the inspector from Scotland Yard. 'Do you see this?' he asked.

'It's a flag.' The years had not blunted the acuteness of Lestrade's mind.

'This particular part of it, Mr Lestrade, is the Harp of Erin. Did you know that the ladies of the Royal School of Needlework have refused to embroider it for His Majesty's coronation?'

'Indeed?' Lestrade clicked his tongue in mock disbelief.

'They claim, of course, that it's the nakedness of the human form they object to depicting, but I know – and my members know – that it's a deliberate snub to the Irish nation.'

'And that has driven one of your members to murder, Mr Redmond?'

'I have told you, Inspector,' Redmond was a man of infinite patience, 'we are pledged to reform by constitutional means. You have my word on that as an Irish gentleman. I cannot of course speak for the likes of Padraig O'Leary . . .'

'And none of your parliamentary people would stoop to planting bombs in the House of Commons and to murdering policemen in cold blood?'

'Never. But . . .' and Lestrade stopped as he made for the door, 'do you have any Gaelic, Lestrade?'

'I'm not partial to foreign food, sir.'

Redmond looked at him oddly. 'Sinn Fein, Mr Lestrade. It means "Ourselves Alone". That's what we intend to be, Inspector. The day will come. And when it does, I fear there will be blood.'

'Will it be on your conscience, Mr Redmond?'

The leader of the Irish party pulled himself up to his full height. 'No, sir, it will not.'

Most of Redmond's people agreed to having their voices recorded on the phonograph, each one of them asking the question which Aumerle Holmes had overheard at the Diogenes Club. 'Is Hamilcar Waldo here tonight?' Somehow, Lestrade was sure this was the clue to his man. But John Redmond finally complained to Edward Henry about undue police harassment, Lestrade had his knuckles rapped and the recordings stopped. When Aumerle Holmes heard them, he could not be sure. Two or three sounded right, but the phonograph crackled and spluttered and memory had by now well and truly gilded the lily. For all he knew, the Irishman at the Diogenes that night might well have been Miss Langtry. Sergeant Dew followed in his governor's footsteps and quizzed the Diogenes staff. It was slow going, what with their being able to give only three responses and Dew writing it all down in his less than immaculate copper plate. But it was all to no avail. No one remembered an Irishman asking for Mr Waldo and the only Irishman living considered intelligent enough for membership of the club was Mr Bernard Shaw – and he talked far too much.

From there, Lestrade ventured into the camp of the Labour Party, whose room was tucked away from the opulence of the rest and near enough to the river to give the whole place an air of mildew. At least here, the field was small. Two members who represented the labouring classes had been returned at the last election. One was a non-event named Richard Bell. Emily Greenbush had demolished him in a recent much publicised slanging match in the lobby of the Commons. Now he went in mortal fear of her. The other, Lestrade was intrigued to remember when he saw an election poster, habitually wore a deerstalker.

'You habitually wear a deerstalker, Mr Hardie?'

'I do, sir,' Keir Hardie answered in his soft-spoken Scots accent. 'Is that a crime?'

'Not yet,' said Lestrade.

'Let's get down to brass tacks, Inspector,' Keir Hardie closed the book on his desk, 'I happen to represent the people of this country. Not the gentlemen in their fine houses with their bank accounts and their carriages, but the people, Lestrade, ordinary men – and women too – people like you, in fact.'

'What is your point, Mr Hardie?'

'My point is that I haven't got the time to rush around the country killing members of my own Parliament. Good God, man, even laying aside the moral question, I've got an enormous opposition here. I'm forty-five years of age. I haven't got enough years left to finish them all off. There's still six hundred and fourteen to go! No, Mr Lestrade, you look to someone among the Conservatives' own ranks for this. That's where you'll find your maniac. Man, there are scores of them.'

Keir Hardie could not vouch, any more than John Redmond could, for his followers outside those hallowed walls. But something told Lestrade his man was not of the working class. The ease with which he passed unnoticed at exclusive gentlemen's clubs, at private school functions, in the mother of parliaments itself. No, his man was cultured, subtle, clever. And whereas such men, Lestrade knew, were to be found among the denizens of the proletariat (he'd read that phrase in the *Sun* only yesterday), he sensed that such a one was not guilty of the crimes in hand. He would have to look elsewhere.

'Still too cold for tea on the terrace, Inspector Lestrade.' It was Winston Churchill, the Member for Oldham, who hailed him. 'No matter, do join me here. Best fire in the whole damned place. Oh,' Churchill turned to a colleague, 'this is Mr . . . er . . .'

'Bonar Law,' said the colleague, 'Member for Glasgow, Blackfriars Division.'

Lestrade shook his hand before accepting Churchill's armchair and the tea and scones on the Commons china.

'I hear you've been bearding the bore in his lair.'

'Sir?'

'Keir Hardie, the redoubtable Member for Merthyr. Got enough to hang him?'

'I don't think we should make light –' said Bonar Law, but Churchill brushed him aside.

'Seriously Lestrade. What progress?'

'Do you want the political answer or the truth?' Lestrade tried the same line on the young Member that he had tried on his new boss at their first meeting. It was a useful yardstick, he found, in sorting men from boys and indeed, in more pastoral moments, sheep from goats.

'Well, they're never the same thing, are they?' mused Churchill ruefully. 'But there's an hour or so before the House reassembles. It'll make a change to hear the truth.'

'None.'

'But surely –' began Bonar Law.

'The trouble is,' Lestrade went on, 'it's rather like looking for a needle in a haystack.'

'Do you believe the murderer is one of us?' Bonar Law looked appalled.

'Do you mean one of you two, Mr . . . er?' Lestrade checked.

'Bonar Law. No, not precisely. I mean a Member of the Commons.'

'It had crossed my mind, sir.'

Bonar Law fell back in his chair with shock and with horror.

'Oh, come now . . . er . . .' said Churchill, 'logically speaking, it's quite likely. Who knows the moves of an MP better than an MP. Right, Lestrade?'

'I look forward to working under you as Home Secretary, sir.' Lestrade saluted Churchill with his tea cup, enjoying the luxury of a handle.

'Have a care, Lestrade,' Churchill leaned forward, 'walls have ears, you know.'

'Of course,' Bonar Law was summoning up all his powers to be profound, 'it could be someone in . . . the Other Place.'

Both men looked at him. 'The Other Place?' they chorused.

Bonar Law looked anxiously around, 'Don't forget the ears, Winston.'

'I'll try not to,' said Churchill and caught Lestrade's look of utter mystification. 'What Mr . . . er . . .'

'Bonar Law,' said Bonar Law.

'Yes, quite. What he means is the House of Lords.'

'I'll get to them eventually,' said Lestrade.

'Better hurry,' chuckled Churchill, 'some of them haven't got much time!'

And the silence fell as he realised the singular bad taste of the remark.

'Anyway,' Churchill sought to fill the embarrassed space, 'this thing has set us all on edge, Lestrade, I can tell you. I don't mind admitting my service revolver is never very far away nowadays. You know, just in case.'

Yes, Lestrade knew. He patted the brass knuckles in his pocket for his own reassurance before leaving the members to their tea. Then he bade farewell to Churchill and . . . the other one.

The shapely young lady bounced off the Honourable Member's knee, frantically buttoning up her blouse as she did so.

'Mr Lloyd George?' asked Lestrade. 'I hope I'm not interrupting anything?'

'No, no,' the Welshman beamed, 'nothing unusual anyway.' He casually flipped a photograph on his desk. The face of the young lady formerly ensconced on his lap disappeared to reveal that of his wife. 'So you are Lestrade of the Yard?'

'It's a little grandiose,' said Lestrade (another word he'd picked up in the *Sun* that week), 'but it's accurate.'

'And you want to know why I'm going around murdering my colleagues, is that it?'

Lestrade was still for a moment. But this was the Welsh Wizard. Emily had warned him about this one.

'I'm glad you can joke at a time like this, sir,' he said.

'Joke?' roared Lloyd George. 'Joke? My dear fellow, I am without doubt,' he slapped the ample rump of the secretary now returned demurely to continue some filing, 'the most detested man in England at the moment. The King dislikes me more than his mistresses' husbands. People like Kipling can wave their little Union Jacks, Inspector, but I happen to believe the Boers are right. My anti-war meetings have been broken up more times than you've had hot dinners. Tell me, what the bloody hell is there to joke about?'

'I'm not interested in the Boers at the moment, sir. I am trying to conduct a murder enquiry.'

'Aye, and not getting very far either, from what I have heard. Look, I'm not a Limp like Campbell-Bannerman.'

'A limp, sir?' Was this a gammy leg or a sexual complaint, Lestrade wondered.

'A Liberal Imperialist, Inspector.' Lloyd George was the model of patience. He crossed to his secretary and squeezed one of her breasts as she wriggled either with excitement or perhaps with embarrassment at the inspector's presence.

'But,' he wiped his hand down his waistcoat, 'I have been following these murders. Here,' he produced a sheet of paper from a desk drawer, 'is a list of the dates on which the murders took place. And alongside each one, where I was and who I was with in each case.'

'You've been very thorough, sir,' Lestrade remarked.

'The Most Unpopular Man In England has to be, Inspector. I knew you'd get to me sooner or later. After all, I am a Liberal and probably the most outspoken critic of the Government you will find in this House. And outside it. Sooner or later someone was bound to point the finger.'

Lestrade perused the list. 'I see,' he said, 'that Mrs Lloyd George's name occurs only once in this document. These other ladies—'

Lloyd George rushed to him, loudly drowning his sentence with fluster. 'Er . . . various er . . . members of my constituency er . . . friends of the Party and so on . . .' And he edged Lestrade to the door. 'Look,' he whispered, when the secretary was out of earshot, 'a little discretion, dear boy, there's a good fellow. I'm not yet in a position to pull any strings for you of course, but who knows, one day . . .' And he patted Lestrade's arm confidentially. 'In the meantime,' he reached behind the door and produced a cape and helmet of the Birmingham Constabulary, 'when I was at a meeting in Birmingham last year I was damned nearly killed myself. Had to escape dressed up as a bobby. You couldn't return this to them, could you, with my compliments?'

'No, sir,' said Lestrade at his frostiest, 'I think the Lost Property Department is at Paddington Green.' And he left.

It was the middle of the night when the constable hammered on Lestrade's door. In retrospect the inspector was grateful he wasn't in Curzon Street. A constable, all boots and bull's-eye, would not have understood the relationship the inspector had developed with the lady. In fact, Lestrade was not sure he understood it himself.

'You're one of Gregory's men, aren't you?' Lestrade pulled the Donegal over his pyjamas and stuffed his feet into the wrong shoes.

'Yes, sir. The inspector's compliments, sir. 'E says will you come double quick 'cos there's been another one.'

With a summons so gracious and precise, how could Lestrade refuse? The Maria hurtled through sleeping Pimlico and on into the West End, finally rattling to a halt on the cobbles outside the Metropole. Lestrade followed the constable in, was extra careful to avoid the polished brass of the top step and jammed his hand in the letter box on his left. He only lost one nail in his eagerness to reach the lift and not knowing the constable too well thought it best not to alarm him unduly by screaming. One death in the hotel that night was probably enough.

On the fourth floor, a pale and worried Inspector Gregory met them.

'Hello, Tom. This had better be important,' said Lestrade.

'It is, Sholto.' And he led them to the door of room 83. A trickle of blood, dark and congealed, ran from a point below the brass numbers to the floor where it formed a brown pool on the carpet. At the top of the trickle, a steel point projected. 'That's only the tip of the iceberg,' quipped Gregory, as always grotesquely inappropriately and he forced open the door as far as it would go.

Lestrade saw what was blocking it when he went inside. The body of a man in smoking jacket and pyjamas was pinned to the door by an ugly sword, razor sharp and slightly curved. It had been rammed through his throat with such force that the epiglottis was shattered and the blade must have penetrated the spine and the two inches of oak behind his head. A similar trail of blood had run down his chest to form another stain on the carpet inside.

'He's dead, Sholto.' Tom Gregory, ever the incisive policeman, had done it again.

'Who is he?' asked Lestrade.

'Reginald Cobham, MP for Kettering.'

'Where?'

'Kettering? It's—'

'All right, Tom. Never mind the geography lesson.'

'I called you right away, Sholto. Quite frankly, and I'm not too proud to admit it, you're better at this sort of thing than I am. What do you think?'

Lestrade surveyed the body, carefully peeling back the pyjamas. No other wounds. No sign of bruising or abrasions. He checked the fingernails. No signs of skin or other tissue under them. The room bore marks of a scuffle of some kind. A coffee-table had been overturned. So had a chair. All the lamps were still burning. On the floor lay two beer steins of the type Lestrade knew the Germans favoured – ornately carved cups with hinged metal lids. They were both empty.

'Has anything been touched in this room?' Lestrade asked. Gregory turned to another constable, who shook his head.

'No, Sholto. Bearing in mind how the brass is about fingerprints. Nothing at all.'

'Who found the body?' Lestrade asked.

'I did, sir,' the constable admitted, 'when I came on duty at one o'clock.'

'Who was on before you?'

'Constable Mason.'

'Why did he notice nothing?'

'Well, sir, Mr Cobham wasn't the easiest man to protect, sir. He said he refused to have . . . flatfeet . . . outside his room. Made us stay in the lobby, downstairs.'

'The lobby?' Lestrade was appalled. 'So anyone could have entered by a side street, the back way or for that matter through a skylight in the roof.'

'Don't be hard on these lads, Sholto. You know we're strained to the limit. Cobham was lucky to have protection at all.'

'Yes,' said Lestrade, viewing the corpse before him, 'he was very lucky, wasn't he?'

He checked the window. No sign of forced entry. 'Constable,' he called the man to him, 'get back to the Yard. Find out if Sergeant Collins is on duty. If he is, tell him to bring his bag of tricks here. If not, find out where he lives and knock him up.'

'Very good, sir.'

'What do you make of the sword, Tom?'

'I've been puzzling over that one. Chinese, isn't it?'

'The Tong?'

'Chinatown isn't my beat, Sholto.'

Lestrade found it. The lamplight glinted on it as he crossed to the door again. Gingerly, he picked it up. A glass phial with a needle at one end.

'What's that?' asked Gregory.

'I'm not sure, Tom. But I think I know someone who is. Finish up here, will you? When Collins is finished, get the body to the morgue. And leave that sword with Sergeant Dew. You might make the point to him that it's sharp.'

Gregory chuckled.

'The question is, Tom, who drank from the second stein?' And he disappeared down the corridor.

Pausing only to have his finger bandaged at the infirmary at Charing Cross, Lestrade made for Baker Street. He was only marginally better dressed than Watson at that hour of the morning and it took a while for the good doctor's eyes to focus on the glass object in Lestrade's hand.

'It's a syringe,' he told him.

'I thought so. What did it contain?'

Watson adjusted his pince-nez and turned up the lamp. He sniffed it, tapped it, removed the needle and licked the base.

'I'd say it was . . . cocaine, Lestrade. Where did you get it?'

'Wasn't that Sherlock Holmes' little vice, Doctor?'

Watson stared at him, 'I think you and I could both do with a drink, Lestrade.'

He poured quadruple brandies.

'Have you seen him again?' Lestrade asked.

Watson nodded, swigging back the brandy. 'Yes, three times. So now you believe it too. You *know* Holmes is alive, Lestrade, don't you?'

'The Swiss authorities were beautifully vague, Doctor. All they could tell me were the official facts as they know them.'

'There's one way,' mused Watson, 'we could check his grave.'

'Body snatching now, Doctor? Isn't that a little before your time?'

'I'm serious, Lestrade. If Holmes is not in that coffin, we'll know he's back. And that he means to kill me.'

Lestrade finished his drink.

'If Holmes is not in his coffin,' he said, 'it's not you he's after, Doctor. Shall we go?'

The copper's speeches

'Well, Dew? What do you make of it?' Lestrade munched his bacon sandwich, the doorstep that passed for breakfast at the culinary hands of the sergeant.

'It's definitely a sword, sir.'

And that had taken all Dew's powers of deduction.

'Remind me to commend you to the Assistant Commissioner, Sergeant,' yawned Lestrade. It had been a long night. The Home Secretary was not available in the early hours and an inspector of Scotland Yard ought to know that and ought not to ask. Application for exhumation of a body could be made to the local magistrate. Lestrade and Watson were told to pester him. They did. And were told by an extremely irate gentleman that such procedures took time. It was the early hours of Saturday morning and if the King himself asked, nothing could be done until Monday. Lestrade had filled in the necessary forms and there, along with the bones of Sherlock Holmes, the matter rested.

'That's a nice looking tachi,' was Constable Dickens' comment as he hung up his bowler.

'What?' Lestrade and Dew chorused.

'The sword, sir. It's a tachi.'

Lestrade and Dew looked at each other.

'Of course, Walter. I should have realised. Simply unlock our walking encyclopedia here and we've solved the case.'

'Would that be a tachi case, sir, bearing in mind the parliamentary nature of our enquiries . . .' Dew's voice tailed off into silence as he caught the excruciated look on his guv'nor's face.

'A tachi, sir, is the shorter of the two swords carried by the Samurai or warrior class of Japan. They are made by a process of tempering steel—'

Lestrade grabbed the morning paper and scanned the headlines. 'Dickens, I want a report – in triplicate. Everything you know and don't know about that sword. Come on, Dew, this is where you learn Japanese.' And the inspector snatched his Donegal and bounded from the room.

'It's the blow to his finger,' said Dew to the astonished Dickens and scurried after him for the lift.

What Sergeant Dew was about to discover and what Constable Dickens realised as he read the *Graphic*'s front page, was that there was a Japanese embassy in town. A whole host of grand-sounding Eastern potentates were in London on official high-level business of the first importance. But as the *Graphic* was furious to have to report, it was all very hush-hush. So was Lestrade as he tiptoed along the carpeted corridor of the Strand Palace Hotel. One thing the *Graphic*'s foot-weary hack had been able to discover and had printed without a qualm, was that the embassy was staying at that hotel. The words 'Scotland Yard' muttered in the ear of the officious desk clerk had, as usual, opened doors. In this particular case, half the fourth floor was given over to Their Excellencies.

Lestrade tapped the nearest door. It opened to reveal a wizened little man in saffron coloured robes who bowed almost double to Lestrade.

'I am from Scotland Yard,' said the inspector.

The little old man bowed again. Lestrade looked at Dew, who was clearly going to be no help at all.

'Scotland Yard,' Lestrade repeated, 'police.'

The little old man bowed a third time. This was becoming monotonous.

'Allow me, sir.' Sergeant Dew prided himself on Orientals. Had he not, as a young constable, walked his beat in Chinatown? And were not his shirts, even now, laundered by Mr Foo of the Mile End Road? It mattered not one jot that Mr Foo came from Peking, whereas the saffron-coloured gentleman was from an entirely different country. The niceties of the East were lost on Dew.

'Lookee,' Dew began, 'policee. Scotland Yard. You callee boss.' And with that brilliant entrée, he pushed the old man back gently into the room. No sooner was Dew inside than he found himself sprawling. From nowhere two men in armour had rushed the length of the room to the little old man's rescue. When Lestrade looked down, Dew was kneeling in a tight ball, the foot of one of the men firmly planted on his neck, and the tip of a sword in the middle of his back. The second man, with a series of snarls, advanced on Lestrade, his short, curved sword inches from the inspector's moustache. Lestrade found himself wondering how his four-inch bladed Apache knife was going to cope against that. He tried reasoned English, only louder than before, for one last time.

'Inspector Lestrade, Scotland Yard,' he said.

'Ishiro Yamomoto, Charterhouse and Sandhurst,' an impeccably English voice behind him replied.

Lestrade turned to see a young Japanese officer, with gold lace from cuff to shoulder and a chest full of medals. He growled something incomprehensible and both swordsmen sheathed their weapons with a frightening blur of speed and stood back from the crouching figure of Dew.

'You can tell your man to get up now,' said Ishiro. 'Ordinarily my man would have urinated on his back, but . . .'

He caught the look on Lestrade's face and chuckled.

'Yes, perfectly bestial, isn't it? I fear my country has a long way to go before we can hope to reach the sophistication of yours. Cock fighting and foxhunting and so on. Besides,' he returned to his former topic, 'it ruins the carpets.'

'Forgive me, Mr Yamomoto,' said Lestrade, 'may I ask your position here?'

Dew slowly unfolded himself as he realised that the hardware had been safely put away.

'Actually, it's Mr Ishiro,' the officer explained. 'In Japan we reverse the order of names. Another archaic practice. And actually, it's colonel. I am Military Attaché to His Excellency the Japanese Ambassador.'

'I told you, sir,' Dew whispered from the corner of his mouth, 'tachi. This bloke's involved up to his neck.'

'Tea, gentlemen?' Ishiro clapped his hands and led the

policemen into a second suite of rooms. The only furniture here was a series of wooden blocks on the floor and the carpets were missing. He sat cross-legged on the polished boards and invited Lestrade and Dew to do the same.

'I'm sorry about this, gentlemen. Personally, I should have thought "when in London . . ." but the wheels of progress grind slow.'

A white-faced lady appeared in a plethora of silk robes, wearing long pins in her jet black hair. She knelt before Ishiro and placed the tray before him. 'Saki or Darjeeling?' he asked. Since Darjeeling was the one he'd heard of, Lestrade chose the latter. Ishiro grunted something to the girl, who poured the tea into the tiny, handleless porcelain cups. Both Dew and Lestrade were at home here. The mugs at the Yard hadn't got handles, either. The girl remained kneeling, her chin on her breast, glancing up shyly at Lestrade from time to time.

Ishiro caught her glance. 'Oh, dear me, I'm forgetting my manners. When our business is concluded, Inspector Lestrade, would you like to have this girl?'

'Have . . .?' Lestrade nearly dropped his cup. He glanced at Dew, whose smile vanished at once.

'She is a geisha, Inspector. A lady of pleasure. It is her sole purpose in life to please honoured guests.'

'Would I be offending anybody if I declined?' Lestrade asked.

'In the days of the Shogunate you'd probably have lost your testicles or at least had your tongue split. But now we are a *little* more civilised. Despite the wooden pillows, we have come on no end in the last few years.'

Lestrade looked relieved.

'Of course,' Ishiro went on, 'it will mean that your subordinate will have to accept her favours.'

'Me, sir?' Dew nearly choked on his Darjeeling. 'I'm a married man, sir! What would Mrs Dew say?'

'The world is full of married men, Sergeant,' Lestrade observed, 'it's hardly the most onerous of duties. Besides, you'll be able to test the rumour for yourself.'

'Rumour, sir?' Dew looked aghast.

'You know the one.' Lestrade nudged him.

Dew looked at Ishiro. 'My dear fellow,' the attaché said, 'I wouldn't dream of denying you the pleasure of that particular voyage of discovery. But first,' he clapped his hands and the girl scuttled away, 'your business?'

'I am conducting a murder enquiry,' said Lestrade.

'Indeed?' Ishiro finished his tea. 'How can I help?'

'The victim was killed with what I understand you call a tachi – a warrior's sword.'

'Indeed?' said Ishiro again. He clapped his hands and the two swordsmen appeared again. Dew braced himself, wondering how, from a sitting position, he could possibly avoid being peed on this time.

'These gentlemen are *samurai*,' said Ishiro, 'knights I suppose would be your English equivalent of the term. They have less power of course in today's Japan and, to be quite candid, we don't let them wear their swords in public. Well, they're such a nuisance getting on and off the bus.'

'But you let them wear them in London, Colonel Ishiro,' Lestrade commented.

'Oh, the natives love it. No offence, Lestrade.'

The inspector waved it aside. He sensed that being offended by this man might lead to the loss of more than his dignity.

'This one,' he pointed to the longer of the two swords thrust through each man's waist sash, 'is the katana. The other, I fancy, is the one you're interested in, the tachi.'

He barked an order and the *samurai* sprang apart. Walter Dew nearly dropped his cup with surprise. With an astonishing flick of their wrists, both men drew the tachi and stood poised like marionettes on wires, waiting for the next command.

'They are the bodyguards of His Excellency the Ambassador,' Ishiro explained. 'One word from me now and they would kill each other or themselves.'

'Themselves?' said Lestrade.

'Yes. It is done by disembowelling. Using one of these.' Ishiro whipped a dagger from nowhere, a shorter replica of the swords now gleaming like arcs of light in the hands of the *samurai*. 'Shall I demonstrate?'

Lestrade noticed that Dew was beginning to look as yellow as their host.

'I'd rather see how the tachi is used, sir. Not for real, you understand.'

'Of course. Just as well, perhaps. Suicide – *hara-Kiri*, we call it – is usually a token of failure anyway.'

Ishiro got to his feet in a single movement and took the sword from one of the *samurai*. I'm a little out of practice, of course,' he apologised. 'Give me a Maxim, any day.' And he brought the sword up in both hands before letting it fall with an oath on one of the blocks of wood. The thing shattered on impact and Ishiro bowed before returning the sword to its owner. Lestrade picked up the pieces of wood, cut as though with a razor and handed them to Dew.

'This block must be four, five inches thick,' Dew muttered, feeling even more queasy than before when he remembered having one of them in his back a few moments ago.

'What you have there is a pillow,' Ishiro explained. 'You probably lose yours in the Chinese laundry. We slice some of ours for sword practice. Well, each country has its own little foibles. More tea, gentlemen?' He resumed his seat.

'No, thank you sir.' Lestrade spoke for both of them. 'Is the point of the sword ever used?' he asked.

'By a *samurai*, never. You see, we Japanese don't have the problem you English have; this extraordinary inability among your cavalry officers to decide whether the edge or the point of a sword is more effective. I suppose,' he scanned the middle distance while draining his second cup, 'I suppose it *could* be used that way, but if that was how your murderer struck, Inspector, he is not from Japan.'

'Thank you, sir,' Lestrade stood up, 'that was all I wanted to know. You have been most kind,' and he bowed low.

'My dear fellow, how admirably quaint, but do let me shake your hand. I've been bowing all morning.' And he did so.

As they reached the outer door, the man in saffron robes appeared again and motioned Dew aside, pointing to an open door through which the sergeant and the inspector saw the geisha, naked now and sitting demurely beside a bath of hot fragrance. Lestrade pushed his sergeant towards her. 'Come along now, Dew. You wouldn't want to offend these kind people, would you?'

'But sir, I can't—'

'Nonsense,' Lestrade slapped his shoulder, 'lie back and think of England. And don't worry. We don't make you stick a knife into yourself at the Yard.'

He stopped at the door.

'Not for that, anyway!'

Despite the massed resources of Mr Edward Henry, Head of the Criminal Investigation Department, and of Sergeant Stockley Collins of the Fingerprint Room, nothing from the scene of Reginald Cobham's demise produced much of interest. Both beer steins had contained beer. 'Three cheers for modern science,' applauded Lestrade mentally. There were no fingerprints on the sword hilt, the second stein or any of the furniture. The door had not been forced and according to Gregory's report, no untoward sounds had been heard either by staff or guests. In short, it was a typical brick wall. Except that Lestrade now knew his murderer was not Japanese (well, he now only had all the other countries in the world to eliminate) and either the murderer or his victim or both used, or at least carried, cocaine. Not content, as a good policeman never should be, with one man's verdict, Lestrade had the laboratory at the Yard, that curious little room that doubled as the Police Museum, check the contents of the syringe. Even though it was Sunday, he used his considerable charm in the form of a mildly administered hammerlock to persuade the boffin to carry out the necessary tests. Yes, the good Dr Watson had been right. It had contained cocaine and search though he might the cold dead arms of the late Reginald Cobham in his refridgerated drawer at the morgue, he could find no signs of needle marks. That indeed began to limit the field. A deerstalker, an Ulster, a tall man who used cocaine . . . But he was running before he could walk.

And before he could do anything, there was an urgent summons from the Foreign Office. It was signed by Lord Lansdowne himself. The lights were burning that evening in mid-January as the inspector entered through the side door in the building in St James's Square. The constable of the watch recognised him and he went unchallenged to the top floor as requested. He knocked on the oak-panelled door. 'Inspector Lestrade,' he tucked the bowler under his arm, 'CID.'

It was Mycroft Holmes who met his gaze first, but that gentleman moved aside to close the door and to reveal the seated figure of Henry FitzMaurice, the Fifth Marquess of Lansdowne. His fierce eyes smouldered in the firelight and the heavy, grey moustache twitched with irritation.

'What do you know about CID?' he barked, pointing an accusatory finger at Lestrade. 'That's top secret information. Holmes, do we have a leak?' His voice cracked in panic for a moment.

Mycroft was his usual laconic self. 'I believe Inspector Lestrade is referring to the Criminal Investigation Department of Scotland Yard, sir, not er . . . the other thing.'

Lansdowne gasped and flicked his fingers. Holmes poured his lord and master a stiff brandy, which Lansdowne clutched convulsively. 'Thank God,' he muttered several times, 'thank God.'

'Sit down, Lestrade.' Holmes was without the comparative bonhomie he had displayed at their last meeting at the Diogenes Club.

'Would you mind telling me,' Lansdowne had recovered, both his composure and his seat, 'why an Inspector of Police should call on a Japanese military attaché at an accommodation which was kept secret?'

God, thought Lestrade, Dew's performance couldn't have been that bad, could it? In fact, he rather thought the sergeant looked a little pleased with himself on his return to the Yard, but men like Walter Dew were pleased if they got out of bed the right side of a morning.

'In the first place, sir,' he began, 'the accommodation was far from secret. I read it in yesterday's *Graphic*.'

'*Graphic*?' Lansdowne quailed. 'Holmes, check the Editor. The man's in the pay of China, or I'm the Queen of Sheba.'

'Very good, Your Majesty,' Holmes answered him po-facedly. Lansdowne glared at him.

'As for my reason for being there, I was conducting my enquiries. The late Mr Reginald Cobham was murdered with a Japanese sword.'

Lansdowne took another gulp at his brandy. 'Yes, yes. Reggie. I know. Shocking. Shocking.' He paused. 'You can't seriously think a member of His Excellency's staff—'

'I can safely say that the Japanese are not involved, sir.'

Lansdowne and Holmes breathed a sigh of relief.

'But it looks as though someone went out of their way to make it look as though they were.'

'What do you mean?' Lansdowne asked.

'I thought you might be able to tell me,' said Lestrade.

'Us?' queried Holmes.

'Lestrade,' Lansdowne persisted, 'whatever your motives in this matter, you had no right to go trampling on Japanese sensibilities. They are a strange people, you know, fierce, proud. And they are here on a matter of extreme importance. I cannot, of course, divulge too much, but our entire position in the Far East depends on the outcome of their visit. One breath of scandal—'.

'Is that why someone killed Cobham with a Japanese sword? To make it appear as though the Japanese were responsible?'

Lansdowne and Holmes looked at each other.

'Reggie Cobham was . . . instrumental shall we say in working with the Ambassador's party,' Lansdowne said and, turning to Holmes, '*could* it be the Chinese, Holmes?'

'It could always be the Chinese, my Lord,' Holmes nodded, 'they've never forgiven us for the Boxer business, Lestrade—'

'That's enough, Holmes!' snapped Lansdowne. 'Walls have ears, you know.'

Obviously, Lestrade realised, Lansdowne was in touch with Winston Churchill. Perhaps even with the other one, whose name was on the tip of no one's tongue.

'Well, Lestrade,' Lansdowne steadied himself for the admonition, 'we'll say no more about it this time. But if I find you meddling in Foreign Affairs again, I'll have you out of the Yard so fast your feet won't touch the ground. Do you understand me?'

'Perfectly, sir,' said Lestrade.

'I'll see you out,' said Holmes, and they left Lansdowne with eyes and fingers whirling wildly.

'You must excuse Lord Lansdowne, Lestrade. He has a lot on his mind. What with the Japanese alliance . . . Oh, God, what a giveaway!'

Lestrade stopped in the corridor. 'Mr Holmes, I could use a little help round about now.'

Mycroft looked at him, 'I appreciate that, Lestrade. But I don't see—'

'This doesn't come easy for me, Mr Holmes. I understand, however, that you, as well as your late brother, have an interest and ability in solving crimes.'

Holmes chuckled. 'This is rather more than a three-pipe problem though, isn't it?'

'Let's start with the basic question. Who is killing our MPs?'

'You see that, Lestrade,' Holmes pointed to a map of the world, 'that little red bit is us. Great Britain. The other little red bits are our Empire. It's because of them nobody likes us, Lestrade. They're green, you see – with jealousy rather than the colour in the atlas. Was it not our great Prime Minister himself who coined the phrase "splendid isolation"? Well, take it from me, Lestrade, it's getting less splendid by the minute. You want to know who's killing our MPs? My guess, as a senior civil servant in the Foreign Office, would be the Boers – they're losing the war, you know. It will all be over in a few months, mark my words.'

Lestrade turned to go.

'Or,' Holmes stopped him, 'it could be the Germans. Yes, I know the Kaiser is His Majesty's nephew, but blood is not thicker than water, Lestrade, especially when most of the world's water is ruled by the Royal Navy. It's that that sticks in His Imperial Majesty's stiff-necked craw. There again, there's always the French. You remember Fashoda in 'ninety-eight.'

Lestrade didn't.

'Well, it was an obscure village on the Nile then, but tomorrow, who knows? They've never really forgiven us for Waterloo, you see. Or for buying up the Suez Canal. Then, of course, it could be the Americans. Tricky lot, the Americans. Lansdowne thinks it's the Chinese—'

'With respect, Mr Holmes, this isn't narrowing my field down very much.'

'Well, that's Africa, as they say, Mr Lestrade. Now, there's a thought. The Watusi. Your man isn't a seven-foot negro, is he?'

'Not unless he's a master of disguise, Mr Holmes. Which brings me to another point. Are you aware that Doctor Watson thinks your late brother is still alive?'

Holmes' demeanour visibly changed.

'Watson is a very sick man, Lestrade. Very sick. I've said too much already. Your way out is down the corridor and second left for the stairs. Thank you for coming.'

'But—'

'Good night, Mr Lestrade.' And Mycroft Holmes vanished behind double doors, disappearing into the corridors of power.

It was raining as they exhumed Sherlock Holmes on that Monday morning. Dr John Watson of 221B Baker Street stood bareheaded beside the grave, irrespective of the weather. Inspector Sholto Lestrade, of H Division, Scotland Yard, stood with him, but his deference to the rain was greater than his deference to the late Great Detective and he kept his bowler on. Constable Dickens did likewise and the long-suffering gravediggers toiled in oilskins. No one spoke. Exhumations were melancholy affairs. There were more jolly ways of spending a January morning.

'I'm surprised he wasn't buried in the family vault,' Lestrade observed.

'I didn't think it proper,' Watson was not his usual self, 'bearing in mind the circumstances of his death.'

The coffin was dragged to the surface by the grunting, cursing gravediggers.

'Open it,' said Lestrade.

They set to with crowbars and levers. It had been ten years. The screws had rusted fast. Watson braced himself. Dickens was wondering what state of preservation was possible after ten years in the London clay.

'Stop! I forbid it!' a voice roared across the silence of the cemetery. A tall figure, displaying less dignity than usual, was bounding over the graves towards them.

'It's Spring-Heeled Jack,' mused Lestrade, suddenly reminded of the tales of terror his father told him. And his father was one of those coppers who had seen the terror face to face.

'God, it's Mycroft!' growled Watson, wishing he was currently under any of the nearby stones.

'I didn't know he could move that fast,' Lestrade observed.

'This is an outrage, Lestrade, what is the meaning of this?' Mycroft fumed.

Lestrade handed Holmes the magistrate's papers.

'This is invalid,' Holmes shouted. '*I* am the next of kin. No exhumation can take place without my signature. Whose idea was this?'

'It was mine,' muttered Watson.

'Yours?' Holmes was speechless.

'If I may correct you,' said Lestrade, 'those papers are perfectly valid. They have been signed by Mr Edward Henry, Head of the Criminal Investigation Department.'

'On what grounds?' Holmes demanded.

'On the grounds that there is suspicion of a crime.'

'What crime?'

'Open it,' said Lestrade to the gravediggers, 'and we shall see.'

'No!' Holmes brought his cane crashing down on the hand of the nearest man, forcing him to drop his crowbar. He raised it again, but Lestrade caught it on his switchblade and wrenched Holmes' arm aside.

'That constitutes common assault, Mr Holmes. And I would urge you to refrain from using your cane as a weapon against me or it will constitute striking a police officer. It might also constitute a broken arm.'

Holmes was purple with rage, but he lowered the cane and glowered at Lestrade. The inspector slipped the knife back into his pocket and motioned the gravediggers to continue. With a jar and a squeal of timbers, the lid came loose. Watson was the first to peer in.

'Good God,' and he stepped back as though bitten by a snake.

Lestrade crouched by the coffin. It was full of rocks. If there had ever been a body in it, it was not there now.

'Can you explain this, Mr Holmes?' Lestrade asked.

Holmes was visibly shaken, but not for nothing was he the brother of the Great Detective, so the Great Civil Servant pulled himself up to his full height and said, 'No sir, I cannot.'

'Then I don't think we need to detain you, sir,' said Lestrade.

Holmes whirled away from the graveside.

'One thing more.' Lestrade stopped him. He turned to the injured person, 'Do you want to press charges against this man?'

The gravedigger looked at Holmes in his astrakhan collar and his gold watch chain and thought better of the whole thing. He shook his head.

Holmes stabbed the air with his cane. 'By the time I've finished with you, Watson, you'll be curing lepers in Tanganyika. And as for you, Lestrade, you won't just be policing the river, you'll be under it!' And he crunched away on the gravel to his waiting carriage.

'How do you suppose he found out, sir?' Dickens spoke for the first time.

'He's a member of His Majesty's Foreign Office, Constable. He only has to knock on the right door and he knows when any of us sneezes. Are you all right, Doctor?' He turned to the ashen Watson.

'I hadn't really imagined—' Watson began.

'Did you see Sherlock Holmes in this coffin ten years ago?'

'No. It came by train and steam packet from Switzerland, all sealed and signed for. I never dreamed—'.

'But you asked for the exhumation,' said Lestrade.

'Because I'd seen the figure that resembled Holmes in Baker Street. I'm a man of science, Lestrade. Like you I kept telling myself it's not him. It's someone dressed as him. But now . . .' And he took a hearty swig from his hip flask.

'Constable,' he turned to Dickens, 'see the doctor home. I shall need a list of all those you can remember who were present at Sherlock Holmes' funeral, Doctor. The constable will take it down.'

Dickens led Watson away, but hung back with Lestrade for a moment.

'Is it Tanganyika that's bothering him, sir?'

Lestrade looked at him. 'Something like that, Constable,' he said.

It was towards the end of the month that Constable Jones returned from death's door and hobbled into the Yard for duty. Bradstreet had caught the full impact of the blast and Jones had been lucky. No one breathed a heartier sigh of relief than Inspector Lestrade. After all, as he explained to Dew, if Jones had died, he would have the palaver of training another constable. That would constitute inconvenience.

'So, gentlemen, we are looking for a man who, for reasons of his own, is impersonating the late Sherlock Holmes of 221B Baker Street.'

'The Great Detective?' Jones asked. He received an icy stare from the others.

'He hasn't been well,' Lestrade excused him by saying.

'Forgive me, sir,' Dickens was clearly puzzled. Anxiety furrowed his forehead, 'But if the coffin of the late Sherlock Holmes was full of rocks, aren't we looking for Holmes himself?'

'There is that possibility,' Lestrade agreed, 'but there are things about that that I'm not happy with. First,' he checked himself just in time from counting on his fingers in the Bradstreet manner, 'there is the time lapse. Holmes went over the Reichenbach Falls ten – no, eleven – years ago now. Why has he been silent all this time? Why does he wait until now to appear to Watson?'

Dew was excelling himself. 'But perhaps he was in hospital, sir. Some sort of foreign clinic. I believe he smoked cocaine.'

'He didn't smoke it, Sergeant, he injected himself with it.'

'Hence the syringe in the hotel room where Reginald Cobham died.' Jones *had* been ill.

'Quite so, Jones,' said Lestrade. 'And, yes, Dew, your clinic idea is a possibility. Without the full co-operation of the Swiss, I doubt if we'll ever find that out. I've been saying for years there ought to be an international police organisation, but nobody listens.'

'Why else do you think it's not Sherlock Holmes, sir?' Dickens asked.

Lestrade bit the end off a cigar. 'Second,' he said, 'I can see a motive for Holmes sending shivers up Doctor Watson's spine. He hated him. But why kill Members of Parliament? From what I remember of the man, he had no particular political leanings.'

'How er . . . reliable is Doctor Watson, sir?' Dew asked.

'He's hitting the hip flask a bit,' Dickens observed.

'Do you think he *really* saw Sherlock Holmes?' Jones enquired.

'If you're implying he's more likely to see little green caterpillars all over his wallpaper, I don't think so. Besides, his housekeeper, Mrs Hudson, saw him too.'

'Ah,' said Jones, 'housekeeper. Can we rely on her to be impartial, sir? Could there be something between them?'

Lestrade blew rings into the air. 'Spoken like a true detective, Constable,' he said. 'You know, you're a lot brighter than your old man.'

'Thank you, sir.'

'Not difficult,' Walter Dew was heard to mutter under his breath, but he changed it at the last moment to a cough.

'There is one possibility, sir.' Dickens had woken up. 'From what you've told us, and from the stories of Doctors Watson and Conan Doyle, Sherlock Holmes had little time for the Yard.'

'For policemen in general,' Lestrade agreed.

'Isn't it the perfect motive for him then, sir? For him to use what he considers his gigantic brain to outwit us? To sprinkle false trails left, right and centre – and still to leave deliberate calling cards like the deerstalker, the Ulster and the syringe – just to bolster his ego?'

'Better and better,' said Lestrade, a man rarely impressed.

'I want to know where Mr Mycroft Holmes fits in to all this,' said Dew.

'Yes, Walter,' Lestrade pointed at him with his cigar, 'so do I.'

*

In accordance with Lestrade's orders, gentlemen wearing deerstalkers and Ulsters were questioned by policemen, plain-clothed and uniformed. Mr Keir Hardie appeared three times in as many weeks at Cannon Street and Clapham, and each time there were apologies all round and a certain amount of egg on Metropolitan and City faces. It was interesting, however, how the two London police forces were working together. Only four punch-ups had been recorded between officers. Not even the dark days of the Ripper had produced such camaraderie.

So at first, when Lestrade looked at *another* man who 'fitted the description etc.' he was cool. Another over-zealous constable looking for a stripe had grabbed an innocent passerby. But then, he looked more closely. The man below the deerstalker bore an extraordinary resemblance to the Great Detective – the piercing, intense stare, the hawk's nose, the gaunt features.

'You are?' Lestrade asked.

'Mr William Gillette,' the other replied. 'Why have I been brought here?'

'Routine enquiry,' said Lestrade and waved his fingers at the still desk-bound Jones to dig out his notebook and put pen to paper. 'Please sit down, Mr Gillette. May I ask your profession?'

'I am an actor.' And he said it in such a stentorian way that no one could argue.

'Indeed.' It was not one of those professions with which Lestrade felt immediately at home. 'May I know something of your background, Mr Gillette – home, family . . .?'

'No, sir, you may not.' Gillette produced a small glass bottle such as ladies use for scent and proceeded to squirt its contents down his throat. The policemen looked at each other. Lestrade gambled with his constable's encyclopedic memory.

'Jones?' he said.

'William Gillette,' the constable began, 'born twenty-fourth July eighteen fifty-five in Hartford, Connecticut, United States of America, the son of former senator Francis Gillette and Elizabeth Daggett. Educated at Harvard and Yale—'

'And the Massachusetts Institute of Fine Arts.' Gillette stood up, clearly peeved. 'Am I under arrest?'

'No sir,' said Lestrade quietly, 'you are merely helping us

with our enquiries.' He paused. 'You *are* helping us, sir, aren't you?'

'Who are you?' Gillette asked him.

'Inspector Lestrade. This is Constable Jones.'

Gillette burst into a fit of laughter and sat down again. 'Well, that's all right then!' he managed, between hysterics.

'What is it?' Lestrade was prepared to be amused.

'Perhaps I'd better explain. I am playing against you every night at the moment. In *Sherlock Holmes* at the Lyceum. I never thought I'd meet you in the flesh.'

Apart from Gillette's chuckling, one could have heard a pen drop in Lestrade's office. It fell from the astonished hand of Constable Jones.

'Do I understand you correctly?' Lestrade was first to recover. 'You are acting in a play called *Sherlock Holmes*?'

'Acting?' exclaimed Gillette. 'My dear fellow, starring would be a better word. I *am* Sherlock Holmes.'

Another silence.

'And the garb you are wearing?' asked Lestrade.

'Ah, a little conceit of mine. I must confess . . .' Lestrade and Dew both stiffened, 'I wear it as a little extra publicity. It does no harm, you know.'

'Are you ever in the vicinity of Baker Street?' Lestrade asked.

'221B, you mean? No, in fact, I've never met John Watson. Although of course I know Conan Doyle very well.'

'You do?'

'Why, yes, we wrote the play together. I wrote to Watson asking him to join us, but I don't recall receiving a reply. Look Lestrade . . .' Gillette became confidential, 'you haven't taken umbrage, have you?'

Lestrade wasn't sure what that was, but he knew he had not knowingly taken it.

'I mean,' Gillette went on, 'I had no intention of causing you embarrassment. That piece in Act Three doesn't make you look a *complete* buffoon, does it?'

Lestrade raised an eyebrow.

'Damn it, man, I got the characterisation from Conan Doyle.'

'Who in turn got it from Doctor Watson. Yes, I know. Your interpretation of my character is not my concern, Mr Gillette –

at the moment. What does concern me is that there is a maniac going around London wearing the clothes of the late Sherlock Holmes.'

'I beg your pardon?' said Gillette.

'And before you ask, impersonating idiots is not an offence under British Law. But this particular maniac kills people.'

Gillette visibly subsided.

'Now do you understand why you have been brought here?'

'God, yes, I do,' said Gillette. 'Inspector,' suddenly the arch actor lost his stage presence, 'I can assure you I had nothing whatever to do with this. I—'

'That remains to be seen,' Lestrade cut him short. 'In the meantime, my officers and I will wish to take statements from you and everyone in your cast.'

'Oh, of course, of course,' offered Gillette. 'I shall see to it that you gentlemen receive free tickets.'

'That will not be necessary, sir,' replied Lestrade, 'but could I ask you not to impersonate Mr Holmes anywhere else but on the stage in future?'

'Certainly, my dear fellow, certainly.' And he made gratefully for the door.

'Rather a close shave, eh, Mr Gillette?' said Jones as the actor exited left. 'Do you think he's got something to hide, sir?' to Lestrade.

The inspector took the unprecedented step of pouring his own tea. 'Probably only wrinkles and a few grey hairs,' he said, 'but we'll have to delve further.'

Dew and Dickens thoroughly enjoyed the show at the Lyceum and found themselves giggling helplessly as, on stage, Lestrade tripped over the furniture, collided with the hat stand and generally made a *complete* buffoon of himself. Lestrade remained expressionless throughout, watching Gillette intently. Every gesture, every word was so right. It was as though Sherlock Holmes had risen from his grave.

Backstage, instead of the usual adulation, all was very subdued and tense as the three policemen interrogated cast and crew. Dew wasn't altogether happy with W L Abingdon who played the fiendish Professor Moriarty. Anyone who played a villain so convincingly must have something to hide. But he could pin nothing on him and had to let it go. All in all, it was a fruitless evening.

'Have you read this, sir?' Dickens bounded in some days later, a paper in his hand and the doorknob in Lestrade's ear. The inspector had been bending over to tie his shoelace at precisely the wrong moment. 'Oh, sorry, sir.'

'That's all right, Constable,' Lestrade said through clenched teeth. 'What is it?'

'The latest edition of *Punch*, sir.'

'Don't tell me,' said Lestrade, 'they're getting at the Yard again.'

'No, sir, not this time. Look.'

Lestrade read the relevant paragraph. 'Arthur Conan Doyle, forty-two, surgeon, and William Gillette, forty-four, actor, two able-bodied men, were flung into the dock charged with the exhumation of Sherlock Holmes for purposes of gain . . . Professor Moriarty stated that Sherlock Holmes was never really dead, but merely in a comatose condition . . .'

Lestrade flopped back in his chair. Then realisation dawned.

'It's what they call a review, Dickens. They are referring to the play at the Lyceum.'

'But the exhumation—' Dickens began.

'A figure of speech,' explained Lestrade, reading on. 'Mind you, here's a sentiment I can't fault: "The magistrates dropped the case, saying that if Sherlock Holmes was not dead, he ought to be"!'

It was some days later that a cryptic note addressed to Lestrade arrived. It was from William Gillette. And its contents sent the inspector post-haste to Mr Henry's office.

'Let me see if I understand you correctly, Lestrade. You want to go undercover as an actor. Why?'

'Because there's *another* play about Sherlock Holmes afoot – at Terry's theatre. They're auditioning now.'

'And you think—'

'You know my opinion, sir. Our man is using the Holmes disguise. It's perfect. People see – if they see anything at all – the deerstalker and the Ulster. They don't see the man inside them.'

'And one of the cast of this new play—'

'It's a stone I can't leave unturned, sir.'

Henry looked at the inspector from H Division. 'I don't like undercover work, Lestrade. It smacks of melodrama.'

'But that's exactly what this is, sir.'

'Are you any good?'

'Well, sir, I was persuaded to take part in the police revue two years ago.'

'And?'

'Modesty forbids, sir, but my Sarah Bernhardt was legendary.'

Henry humphed several times, then reached for his pipe.

'Very well, Lestrade. But be careful. I've lost an inspector on this damned case already. And keep in touch with someone – your sergeant, what's his name?'

'Dew, sir.'

'Yes.' He plugged the tobacco in the bowl and caught Lestrade's look. 'Yes, it *is* a meerschaum, Lestrade. And no, I have not been going round murdering MPs dressed up as Sherlock Holmes. If you'd care to check my alibis?'

'Nothing could be further from my thoughts, sir.'

Early February and empty theatres did not go together. Lestrade tried to look as Bohemian as possible. Despite his legendary Sarah Bernhardt, he really didn't have a great deal going for him on the boards.

'Next!' a stentorian voice roared from the darkness of the auditorium.

'That's you,' someone hissed behind him.

He shuffled self-consciously into the limelight.

'Name?' the voice roared.

'Lister,' he replied, using the time-worn alias, and then to make it a little more theatrical, 'Roderick.'

'What have you done?' the disembodied voice said. It was a little lighter, more effeminate now. He glanced down wondering if he'd trodden in anything.

'I beg your pardon?' he said.

'Oh, never mind. What part are you trying for?'

'Er . . . Doctor Watson,' said Lestrade.

'Oh, God,' he heard the voice mutter, 'not another one. Look,' it resumed its theatrical level, 'you're about a foot too tall and three stone too light. Still, I suppose this is supposed to be a comedy. All right, Clarence.'

Silence.

'Clarence, dear, where are you this time?'

A tall, rather limp character drifted on stage and looked Lestrade up and down.

'Ah, Clarence, there you are. From the top, sweet. Page four.'

Clarence stood with one arm locked behind his back, and furrowed his brows. 'Well, Watson,' he had the enunciation of a razor blade and it positively ripped Lestrade's ears, 'what do you make of it?'

Silence.

'Roderick,' wailed the voice in the darkness, exasperated now, 'that's you. You're on, dear,'

'Oh,' mumbled Lestrade. 'Sorry.'

'Clarence! Give it to him again, heart, will you?'

'Well, Watson,' Clarence declaimed, 'what do you make of it?'

Lestrade cleared his throat. It wasn't easy to see the script in this light, but he did have the advantage of knowing what the real Watson sounded like.

'I didn't care for the man's tone, Holmes,' he said. 'In fact, I—'

'Thank you. Next,' said the floating voice.

'I beg your pardon?' said Lestrade. Clarence wandered off again.

'Look, Roderick,' the voice appeared before the footlights now, an overweight gentleman with a wig which looked as though it once belonged to Oscar Wilde, 'it's nothing personal dear. It's just not Watson, I'm sorry.'

'Another part then,' Lestrade suggested. 'What about the policeman?'

'The policeman? Oh, you mean Lestrade? Oh, no, you're all wrong.'

The voice caught the look in Lestrade's eyes.

'Oh, very well. We'll try. Page two hundred and twenty-one. Clarence!'

Clarence swanned back on and assumed the same stance as before, the brows beetling as though crumbling under the weight of the gigantic brain.

'Well, Lestrade, what do you make of it?' he read. It all sounded depressingly familiar.

'I haven't a clue, Mr Holmes. There is no one at the Yard who can hold a candle to you, sir.'

'No! No!' the voice fumed, slapping his thighs with the script, 'Roderick, darling. Lestrade is as common as muck. He lacks any finesse whatever. You make him sound too . . . well, too human. Do it again, Clarence, from the top.'

They repeated it. And although Lestrade nearly choked on the words, the voice seemed to like it.

'It'll have to do. We're running desperately late as it is. All right, Roderick. You've got the part, dear. Leave your address at the stage door, will you? I'll be in touch.'

'Thank you,' said Lestrade. 'Er . . .'

'Yes?'

'How big a part is it?'

'Well, you just read it, dear. Decide for yourself.' And the voice bustled off into the darkness, muttering something about prima donnas.

Lestrade walked back home that night. It was crisp and clear and he needed air. Time to think. He was on the right track. He was sure. The slowest yet surest method there was: eliminate all the possibles, work on the probables and you have your answer. But would the answer be there before anyone else died? He wrestled with it, worried it, turned it this way and that in his mind. Then he turned right instead of left, towards Curzon Street.

The Tintagel squires

Lestrade had been at the Yard all night. He was tired, very tired. Tired of staring at the board with its maze of chalked victims, places, times. He had known murderers before who broke the pattern, who killed by a variety of means, never allowing themselves to be pinned down to one method. But the difference with this one – and it was this which rattled Lestrade the most – was the man's coolness and his total disregard, and contempt, for the police.

'You and I have known cases,' Dew had said to him in an unusually patronising moment (the stripes having gone to his head), 'where the murderer was a woman posing as a man. Is that it now, I wonder?'

Lestrade was used to Walter Dew trying to better himself by ruminating aloud. Thought was such a strain for the man that he couldn't do it silently. Most of it was nonsense, but just occasionally there was a flash of something that approached reason. A woman. A woman? Bradstreet would have said that the obvious choice was Emily Greenbush. And even though Lestrade shared her bed and her innermost thoughts from time to time, he was too much of a policeman to let that cloud his judgement. All the same, it was a dangerous liaison. One that he would have to end – one day.

He was still wrapped in thought – cyanide gas, ping-pong bats, tainted wine glasses, Martini-Henrys – when Constable Jones hobbled in.

'Have you seen the morning papers, sir?'

Lestrade's eyes looked and felt like roast chestnuts on that February morning.

'Morning?' he grunted.

'Oh, sorry sir. Good morning.' Jones had forgotten his manners.

'Do you mean to tell me it's morning?' Lestrade unwrapped his feet from the desk top.

'Cup of tea, sir?'

'Music to my ears, Jones,' said Lestrade. 'It's your turn for the Bath Olivers.'

'Got 'em, sir.' Jones produced the biscuits.

'Good God!' Lestrade saw the headlines: 'Is Sherlock Holmes Alive?' He read the article. Speculation that Holmes had engineered his own demise, that he had been in hiding in Venezuela, that he was in the pay of the Boers, that his mind had gone. Well, certainly the last supposition made some sense to Lestrade. 'And where,' the article went on, 'does Professor Moriarty fit into this?'

'Moriarty,' snarled Lestrade, hurling the paper from him, 'is a figment of Doctor Watson's dubious imagination. When will these people in Fleet Street learn to sort fact from fiction?'

'There's a crowd of newspapermen outside,' said Sergeant Dew, brushing the snow from his Donegal. 'Filthy morning, sir.'

'Same to you,' grunted Lestrade. Dew and Jones exchanged glances.

'Bath Oliver?' Jones offered them to Dew.

'No thanks. I had one only last week. And don't call me Oliver. Ha. Ha.'

No one else laughed.

'What do they want?'

'Usual thing, sir. A comment from you. I told 'em you wouldn't be in until twelve. It didn't work.'

'It never does. What's Dalgleish doing about it?'

'Keeping them back, sir, as best he can. It's like Horatius and the bridge down there.'

'Horatius and the bridge?' Lestrade was frankly astonished by his sergeant's new-found culture.

'He features in *The Lays of Ancient Rome* by Lord Macaulay, sir,' said Jones. '"Lars Porsinna of Clusium—"'

'Thank you for that, Constable.' Lestrade cut him short. 'Dew, get down to Dalgleish and tell him to allow one – *one*, mark you – of the gentlemen of the Press to come up.'

'With respect, sir, that will cause a riot,' said Dew.

'Good,' said Lestrade, 'that'll give us a chance to arrest the lot of them. On your way.'

Dew and Dickens collided in the doorway. 'Sorry, Sergeant. Filthy morning, sir,' Dickens said to Lestrade.

'Don't tell me there's a crowd of newspapermen outside, Dickens,' said Lestrade.

'Well, yes, sir, how did you know?'

'Never mind. How far have you got with that list?'

'List, sir?' Dickens dived gratefully for the mug of tea Jones had poured for him.

'The mourners at Holmes' funeral.'

'Nothing of note, sir.' Dickens dug out his notepad. 'Two of them are dead. Or at least, everybody claims they are.'

'Well we can't go round exhuming all and sundry,' said Lestrade, 'even cynics like us must assume some people tell the truth. What about the living?'

'Eight have alibis for most of the murders, sir. One is inside.'

'Oh?'

'Defacing Westminster Bridge.'

'That hasn't been a crime since Robert Peel was Home Secretary – eighty years ago.'

'Ah, but he was trying to deface it with three pounds of gelignite, sir. Had a grudge against the Metropolitan Omnibus Company and wanted to make his point somewhere along their route.'

'Anything else?'

'Nothing untoward, sir. No one could shed any light on Holmes' death at all. Most of them seemed to be fond of him. They didn't have much time for Watson, though. I've got three more to see.'

He handed the list to Lestrade. 'All right,' said the inspector, 'I'll deal with these.'

'Mr . . . er . . . Lise . . . Lis—' Dew stumbled at the doorway.

'Liesinsdad,' said the reporter, '*Daily Mail*. Inspector Lestrade, it's good of you to see me at—'

'Let's get down to brass tacks, Mr Liesinsdad. Is this your article?' He waved the paper under the man's nose.

'It is,' he answered.

'How did you come by it?'

'Oh, come now, Inspector,' Liesinsdad crowed with that nasal problem so common among the mid-Welsh, 'you can't seriously expect me to reveal my sources.'

'How would you like to spend a term in Pentonville for obstructing the police in the course of their enquiries?'

'Well,' the icy smile did not vanish from Liesinsdad's face, 'this is brass-tacks stuff, indeed.'

'And it's not an idle threat,' Lestrade went on. 'How did you know about the exhumation?'

'So it's true, then?'

Lestrade was not at his sweetest at this time of the morning. He leaned across to the reporter and jerked the end of his scarf, so their noses were on a level.

'I learned a new word the other day, Mr Liesinsdad,' Lestrade said through clenched teeth, 'defenestration. Do you know what that means?'

'Er . . . yes . . .' blustered the Welshman, 'it means to be pushed from a window.'

'Quite so,' said Lestrade, glancing ostentatiously across at the sash. 'It's such a quick way down,' he said, 'saves all that fuss of catching a lift, don't you think?'

'You wouldn't dare,' said Liesinsdad, but there was an air of uncertainty in his voice. 'I am a member of the Press.'

'And I am trying to catch a maniac,' Lestrade released the scarf, 'and by printing this sort of thing, Mr Liesinsdad, you aren't helping us at all. Now once again, can we work together for a change? Who was your source?'

'Very well.' Liesinsdad sat down. 'I received a telephone call at the *Mail* offices. A man with an Irish accent. He told me all about the exhumation and said that Sherlock Holmes was bent on revenge . . .'

'Revenge?' Lestrade repeated.

'Yes,' said Liesinsdad. 'Another new word you've learnt, Inspector?'

Lestrade blew the smoke from his newly lit cigar into the reporter's face. 'Anything else?' he asked.

'No. The accent sounded genuine, but it might not have been.'

'Why do you say that?'

'We Celts have an ear for these things, you know.'

'I see. Thank you, Mr Liesinsdad, that will be all.'

'All?' said Liesinsdad.

'Yes. A new word for you, Mr Liesinsdad?'

The reporter stood up, '*Is* Sherlock Holmes alive, Lestrade?' he asked.

'When I catch him, I'll ask him,' said Lestrade. It was all Liesinsdad was going to get.

Mrs Hudson answered the door as usual.

'Inspector Lestrade,' she said, 'I'm afraid Doctor Watson isn't in.'

'I know, Mrs Hudson,' said Lestrade. 'It was you I came to see.'

'Me, sir?'

She showed him up to what had been the consulting rooms of Sherlock Holmes.

'I'd like you to cast your mind back, Mrs Hudson,' said Lestrade, 'to the time of the late Mr Holmes' death. You went to the funeral?'

'Yes, sir.'

'Do you remember anything . . . odd about it?'

'Odd sir? In what way?'

'In any way, Mrs Hudson. Did anything strike you as peculiar?'

'It was a funeral, sir, like any other. There was a huge crowd in the streets I remember, but the funeral itself was a very private affair. I provided the baked meats.'

'Of course. Was there anyone among the immediate mourners who spoke in bitter terms? Did you hear anyone talk of revenge?'

'Sir, it was over ten years ago . . .'

Lestrade sighed, 'Thank you, Mrs Hudson. Oh, by the way,

have you seen the figure Doctor Watson believes to be Sherlock Holmes?'

The housekeeper's face darkened. 'I have, sir.'

Lestrade leaned closer to her and stooped to look her in the eye. 'And it *is* Mr Holmes, Mrs Hudson?'

She returned his steady gaze and nodded. 'As God is my judge, sir. And I've heard his violin.'

'His violin?'

'The Stradivarius he played. I've heard it in this very room sometimes, after dark.'

Lestrade checked the locks of door and windows. No sign of a forced entry. 'Have you kept the effects of Mr Holmes?' he asked.

'Why, yes, sir. Exactly as Doctor Watson instructed.'

'May I see them?'

Mrs Hudson stood on her dignity for a moment; never, in Lestrade's experience, a less than painful process.

'If I may say so, sir, when Mr Holmes was alive, you were not exactly a welcome visitor here. Whatever he is up to, he has his reasons. You tell me why I should show you his things.'

Lestrade caught the tremble in the voice, the tear in the eye. He took Mrs Hudson by the hand. 'I do not believe,' he said, 'that Sherlock Holmes is still alive—'

'But the stones in the coffin . . .' Mrs Hudson interrupted.

'Someone wants us to think he's still alive, Mrs Hudson. Is that what you want? The Great Detective,' and he nearly choked on the words, 'to be branded a deranged murderer? A madman?'

Mrs Hudson turned to the window, then produced a large handkerchief, blew her nose with the force of a dreadnought and said, decidedly, 'No, Mr Lestrade. Please come with me.'

She led him into a darkened room, where the heavy velvet curtains had not been undrawn for years. The room was dry with cobwebs like a tomb, still and dead. Mrs Hudson caught Lestrade's arm. Had she suddenly realised how forgetful she had been? Or was this the usual level of her housekeeping?

'It's gone,' she whispered.

'What has?' Lestrade peered into the gloom.

'Mr Holmes' violin. It was here, on this cabinet.'

Lestrade threw back the curtains and the dust flew everywhere. Mrs Hudson recoiled from the light with a gasp. 'Is anything else missing?' he asked.

She checked surfaces, a wardrobe and drawers.

'His favourite meerschaum, his deerstalker and his Ulster.'

'Surprise, surprise,' mused Lestrade.

'He's been back for them,' Mrs Hudson clutched her handkerchief, 'here, in this very room.'

'This door is kept locked?' Lestrade asked.

'Yes. You saw me open it now with my key.'

'And where is the key kept?'

'Here, on my chatelaine.'

'Is there another?'

'Doctor Watson has one.'

'Anyone else?'

A pause. Then, 'Mr Holmes, of course.'

'Of course,' echoed Lestrade. 'Mrs Hudson, what you do with this mausoleum is up to you. If I can spare a man, I'll put him out there in Baker Street at about the time this Sherlock Holmes has been appearing. If I can't spare a man, or if my man should miss him and you see the figure again, I would be grateful if you would contact the Yard immediately. Will you do that?'

'Yes, sir,' said Mrs Hudson.

Lestrade found his own way out. He was making for the nearest tram when he suddenly became aware of someone following him. A youngish man, perhaps mid-twenties, shabbily dressed with the appearance of a coster. As Lestrade boarded his tram, the coster vanished, but the inspector became aware of a second follower, another young man who had caught the tram with him. He continued about his business and walked around the corner into Jermyn Street. The young man walked on as Lestrade rang the bell at the door of Mr Aumerle Holmes, the last but two on his list of mourners at his cousin's funeral. His man Blenkinsop ushered Lestrade into a study.

'What do you think of it, Lestrade?' Holmes arrived after a few moments.

'A delightful room, sir,' said the inspector.

'No, no, man, not the décor. The tapes. They've gone.'

'Tapes, sir?'

'Oh, my dear fellow, how silly of me. In my excitement, I'd quite forgotten you haven't been here before. Until yesterday I had cotton tapes all over the house, from doorknob to doorknob to enable me to get about. At last I don't need them. Brandy?'

'I shouldn't, sir—'

'Now, now, Lestrade. Don't make life easy for me. Let me show you how clever I am.'

He crossed with ease to the tantalus, unlocked it and rattled around until he found a glass. Lestrade stared fascinated at the sightless eyes. He had to knock his own hand down to prevent himself from helping the blind man.

'Two fingers, Lestrade?'

No need to be offensive, thought the inspector, the offer of help was kindly meant.

'Ah, I see,' he realised it was a means for the blind to measure the level of liquid in a glass, 'that will do nicely.'

Holmes brought it to him.

'Now, Inspector, delighted as I am to renew our acquaintance, I fear this call is not a social one.'

'I'm afraid not, sir.'

'Well, then, how can I help? Is it still those terrible murders of MPs? Blenkinsop reads me the papers every day.'

'Yes, sir, it is.'

'You want to know if my cousin is still alive.'

'Ah, you take the *Daily Mail*, Mr Holmes?'

'And *The Times* and the *London News*, Mr Lestrade. Just because I am blind does not mean I cannot keep abreast of current affairs.'

'I understand you were at Sherlock Holmes' funeral.'

'I was.'

'Do you remember anything unusual about it?'

'Unusual?' Holmes poured himself a brandy and edged his way into an armchair. 'Forgive me, Inspector. Blindness can cause inhospitality, quite unintentional, I assure you. Please, sit down.'

Lestrade did.

'Let me see. I had just finished at Harrow when news of dear Sherlock's death arrived. Doctor Watson informed us.'

'And what did he say?'

'I can't remember the exact words, Inspector, but the gist was that Sherlock had pursued an arch criminal to Switzerland and that they had both perished in a duel near a waterfall. Quite tragic. Sherlock was nearly the most brilliant man I have ever met.'

'Indeed?' said Lestrade. 'May I ask who was the most brilliant?'

'His brother, Mycroft, of course: It's no secret, Lestrade, that Sherlock would take his more baffling cases to him.'

'Would you say that Mycroft felt a sense of bitterness towards society?'

'Society? You mean the *haut monde*?'

Lestrade assumed that was a French breakfast, but stuck to his guns. 'I mean people in general.' It seemed to make sense.

'Why should he, Inspector?'

'Why should someone fill Sherlock's coffin with stones?'

'Yes, that was bizarre, wasn't it? Do I understand that you are asking questions of all those who attended the funeral?'

'Yes, sir, I am. I want to leave no stone unturned,' said Lestrade, and immediately regretted it.

'They were better days, Lestrade,' Holmes suddenly became wistful, 'lighter days. "When I consider how my light is spent . . ."'

'Sir?'

Holmes laughed. 'Did you know I once toyed with politics, Lestrade? I intended to do what this chappie Churchill has done. When I left the army, I—'

'You were in the army, sir?'

'Yes, didn't I tell you that?'

'I haven't asked before, sir.'

'No, of course not. Why should you? Yes, I served in South Africa. I joined Lumsden's Horse at the outbreak of hostilities. It was there I lost my sight.'

Lestrade looked up, 'Forgive me, Mr Holmes. I believe you once told me that you lost your sight as a result of a prank.'

Holmes laughed. 'What a memory you have, Inspector. You are quite correct. There was some tomfoolery with a Hotchkiss machine-gun. I was standing too close to the thing when it went off. You see these?' he pointed to the pale brown scars on his cheeks. 'Scorch marks, Inspector. Oh, they healed all right. But the doctors tell me my optic nerves are gone. I shan't be following Mr Churchill's success. Still,' he drained his glass, 'the way things are at the moment, it's probably healthier to stay out of politics, wouldn't you say?'

Lestrade would and did. He bade farewell to Holmes and was shown out by Blenkinsop.

'Blenkinsop.' Lestrade stopped in the hall.

'Sir?'

'Here is something for you,' he pressed a coin into his hand. Blenkinsop looked disparagingly at it. He hadn't seen so small a coin in years. 'I will walk to the end of the street. I want you to watch and see if I am followed by anyone. I will bend down to tie up my shoelace, that should make it easier for you. If you notice someone waiting, hanging back while I do it, when I get to the end of the street, I want you to pull down that blind. If you see no one behaving suspiciously, don't touch it. Understand?'

'Very good, sir.'

Lestrade buttoned his Donegal against the chill of the late February day. He noted the silent shuttered house that had belonged to Sir Geoffrey Manners, Bart, and he stopped to retie his laces. When he reached the end of the street he looked back to see Blenkinsop lower the blind. But by now, the street was empty save for a chestnut seller Lestrade had already noticed and who had not moved. But now he was certain he was being watched. The game, whatever it was and whoever was playing it, was afoot.

Mycroft Holmes was unaccountably unavailable to Lestrade. Or any other officer of Scotland Yard. He was away on business of the gravest international concern and was not expected back for some time. Further than that the Foreign Office was not prepared to say. This left Lestrade with only one remaining witness at the funeral of Sherlock Holmes: Dr John Watson. Deliberately, Lestrade had left the good doctor until last. The wheel had come full circle. It was from Watson that Dickens had obtained the list of mourners in the first place and it was to Watson that Lestrade now returned. After all, he said to himself on the Underground train to Baker Street that last day of March, wasn't it Watson who had seen *Sherlock Holmes*? Wasn't it Watson who paid Mrs Hudson, the only other eyewitness to the visitations? Wasn't it Watson who had a key to Holmes' personal effects? And wasn't it Watson who had demanded the exhumation, which seemed to suggest that the man was not dead after all? And who, apart from Conan Doyle, had a motive for keeping 'Holmes' alive? John Watson, MD. Lestrade had suspected Watson before. He had a knack of turning up at the right place at the right time, of being involved in cases where, by all reason, he had no right to be.

But for the moment, Lestrade was thwarted. Watson had gone to Tintagel, to the pageant. The man he had left in Baker Street had seen three men wearing deerstalkers. One, it transpired, was a retired bishop from the colonies. Another, a stockbroker's clerk who was obsessed with the idea that people found his ears funny and so wore the deerstalker, even in bed. The third was Mr Edward Henry, Head of the Criminal Investigation Department and what idiot had told the constable to accost innocent passers-by with the asinine question 'Excuse me, sir, where did you get that 'at?' On being told the order came from Inspector Lestrade, that seemed to Mr Henry to say it all. None of them was smoking a meerschaum. None of them was carrying a violin. The constable looked utterly wet and dispirited.

'Never mind, Braden,' said Lestrade, 'you stay on the beat.'

It was to be the first and most spectacular pageant of the season, a little ahead of schedule, perhaps. Several had been planned for what was to be a Royal Summer, culminating in the festivities of the coronation itself, fixed for 26 June. Lestrade took Dew, who needed some fresh air, and boarded the Great Western's morning train for Cornwall. The first-class carriages were packed with Aumerle Holmes' *haut monde* bound for exactly the same destination as the officers of the Yard, although their motives may have differed.

Dew had never been further west than Wimbledon and the experience clearly unnerved him. By the time they reached

Swindon, he was most homesick and consoled himself with the sandwiches Mrs Dew had made him. Lestrade liked tripe and onions too, but not between slices of bread.

'There are more coppers here than members of the public,' Dew observed as they walked over the springy grass towards the village of Tintagel.

'Protection,' explained Lestrade. 'There are four MPs here today in various capacities. You'd think they'd use their sense and stay home.'

They were directed to the officer in charge, the chief constable of the county, no less, hoping that the plumes and lace of officialdom would scare away an assassin.

'We're honoured, of course,' said the chief constable through the gritted teeth of barely concealed resentment.

'Don't worry, sir,' said Lestrade, 'we're not here to tread on toes. We are anxious to ask a few questions of a guest, Doctor John Watson, of London.'

The chief constable conferred with one of his officers. 'He's probably over there.' He pointed to a brightly painted pavilion beyond a broad, grassy concourse. 'He's on our guest list. Ticket holders are in those tents.'

Lestrade thanked him and the Yard men began to weave their way through the building crowd. Parasols against the watery sun, ribbons, silks and satins, it seemed that the whole of polite society had descended upon the ruins of the ancient Camelot, gaunt against the breathtaking backdrop of sea and sky.

'Sholto?' Lestrade turned to the direction of the shout. It was Letitia Bandicoot, sitting on one of the tiers of seats in the nearest pavilion. 'What are you doing here?'

The policemen tipped their hats. 'Oh, no, you'll have to do better than that, you know,' Letitia taunted them, 'this is the Tintagel Tournament. Knights Errant are supposed to doff their caps and pledge undying love to their ladies.'

Dew's lip trembled for a moment as he thought of Mrs Dew, so many, many miles away.

'We're on official business,' Lestrade explained, crouching on the stairs beside her.

'Uncle Sholto!' Rupert and Ivo 'Bandicoot, resplendent in

scarlet tabards, scrambled over their mother to pull the inspector's moustache and listen to the ticking of his watch. He ruffled their hair as their mother eased them back into their seats.

'They're so excited,' she said. 'They didn't sleep a wink last night, Nanny tells us.'

Little Emma, adorable in a hood lined with white fur and a long crimson cloak, squeezed past her brothers and gave Rupert a clout when he didn't move fast enough. She threw her arms around Lestrade's neck and hugged him. Letitia's eyes met his behind the girl's back and the look spoke volumes. He pulled the girl away and kissed the tip of her nose.

'How's my best girl?' he said, but her answer was drowned by a roar from the crowd nearby. Lestrade looked up to see a heavily armoured knight canter across the tilt yard towards the pavilion.

'Daddy!' Emma shouted.

The knight swung up his visor to reveal the beaming schoolboy face of Harry Bandicoot.

'Sholto,' he shouted, 'how do you like it? Knight of the Golden Chalice!' he announced himself.

'Very good, Harry,' Lestrade smiled.

To the roars of the appreciative audience, Bandicoot whirled his horse away to where other knights were taking position at the far end of the lists.

'What's he going to do, Letitia?'

'Shame on you, Sholto Lestrade. Have you no sense of history at all? This is a tournament, in honour of the coronation. Harry volunteered to take part at once. Look at my poor finger,' she held it up, 'it took me days to sew all those sequins onto his tabard.'

And I thought he made all his own frocks, thought Lestrade to himself.

'Business?' Letitia whispered in a dark brown voice in his ear.

'I do believe you're prying, Letitia,' Lestrade scolded.

'Right,' she confirmed.

Lestrade laughed.

A voice bellowed out that the festivities were about to begin.

The wind successfully drowned the speech that followed it, made by the Lord Lieutenant of the county; a divine wind indeed thought those who knew him. His lady wife looked less than pleased, but then the wind was not blowing in her favour. One by one, the knights who were to do battle trotted before the Lord Lieutenant's pavilion and were announced to roars and cheers from the crowd.

'I hope it doesn't rain,' Letitia scanned the sky. 'Harry's grandfather fought at Eglinton in eighteen thirty-nine, you know. The heavens opened. It was a shambles, apparently.'

It would be impossible for Lestrade to get to the pavilion where he would find John Watson. He would simply have to sit it out until this nonsense was over. Another announcement punctuated by a blast of trumpets – the Marazion Brass Band doggedly wearing their modern braided tunics without deference to the occasion. The crowd cheered and clapped appreciatively as, to the 'oohs' and 'aahs' of the ladies and the restiveness of the gentlemen, the Queen of Beauty was brought down the lists in a gilded carriage. Historians might have winced that the vehicle was mock-Elizabethan, but to most of the company – Lestrade included – it was splendid.

'Good Heavens!' Letitia fixed her field glasses on the Queen, a beautiful girl with long tresses of hair, plaited and swathed over her cloth of gold cloak. 'It's Mercy Alabaster. I haven't seen her since her engagement. Isn't she ravishing, Sholto?'

'Indeed,' said Lestrade, 'particularly her hair.'

'Oh, that isn't hers,' said Letitia, 'she's dark really. Aumerle loved dark-haired girls, she told me once.'

'O'Merle?' Lestrade's ears pricked.

'Aumerle Holmes. Her fiancé. He's—'

'A cousin of the Great Detective,' Lestrade beat her to it.

'Do you know him?'

'We have met.'

'Such a shame. I think it's perfectly horrid the way Mercy treated him.'

'Really?'

'She left him, you see. Oh, I'm sure she was very kind about it. He was heartbroken, apparently. A year ago she married a shipping magnate. They say Aumerle hasn't mentioned her since.'

The Queen of Beauty took her place on the central dais. The trumpets sounded again. Letitia consulted her programme.

'Harry's on first, Sholto. Oh, dear. I do hope he's all right.'

'If I know Harry Bandicoot, Letitia, he'll clear the field. Who's he fighting?'

'William, Lord Dymoke, the King's Champion. I'm afraid he drew the short straw. William has rather a reputation as a *beau sabreur*. They say he killed a man in a duel in Germany.'

'Let's hope he's off form today then,' said Lestrade.

Harry cantered across to Letitia's pavilion and thrust his lance tip towards her. 'Your colours, my lady,' he boomed through the iron visor. Letitia felt her heart rise and her cheek blush as she tied her scarf around the ash pole. He nodded to her and wheeled his horse away, the children bouncing excitedly. Lestrade noticed Letitia's eyes wet with tears. 'You must think me silly, Sholto,' she said. He smiled and patted her hand.

Harry's horse was lurching down the lists, the man on its back hunched in the saddle to meet the shock of impact. His lance was level, his shield high, and he and Dymoke sailed past each other, woefully wide of the mark. A groan of disappointment escaped from a thousand lips. The tilters wheeled again and drove home their spurs a second time. This time Harry's aim was better and his lance shattered high on Dymoke's shield, the King's Champion being catapulted backwards over the crupper to land in an undignified heap on the grass. Letitia hugged her children to her and the crowd went wild.

'Bread and circuses,' said Dew to no one in particular. The man was definitely bettering himself.

Harry sat his caracoling horse, saluting the cheers of the crowd, when a solitary horseman galloped from nowhere, riding straight for him. The rider swung a sack which broke on impact and showered the Knight of the Golden Chalice with flour. It hit him with such force that he pitched forward out of the saddle. The rider then swung away, spurring towards the pavilion of the Queen of Beauty and proceeded to hurl another sack at Mercy Alabaster. Another perfect shot and the ravishing Queen stood sobbing hysterically, running with what appeared to be mud from the bottom of a river.

There were screams and shouts of panic. A dazed Harry Bandicoot sat upright, coughing and spluttering, much to the amusement of William Dymoke who was grinning maniacally with a new-found gap in his teeth which the fall from his horse had given him.

'Catch him, Dew!' Lestrade shouted as the unknown assailant cantered past. The sergeant hacked his way with both arms flailing through the crowd and launched himself at the retreating rider. He mistimed it perfectly, snatching thin air as he leapt and bringing down two or three of the Marazion Brass Band, tuning up for the next bout. Lestrade's attack was better, although he had to use a few heads and shoulders as stepping stones to get there. He caught the horseman around the neck and both of them sprawled across the tilt yard. As he straightened, an army of burly constables encircled them and one of them snatched off the hood which covered the rider's head. The long auburn hair shook free.

'Emily!' Lestrade was truly astonished to see Miss Greenbush kneeling in the mud before him.

'It would have to be you, Sholto, wouldn't it?'

'Do I understand that you know this . . . lady, Lestrade?' the chief constable had arrived.

'In a manner of speaking, sir,' the inspector answered.

'What is the meaning of this outrage,' the chief constable rounded on her, 'ruining the enjoyment of these good people?'

'Enjoyment?' Emily looked at him levelly. 'This chivalric nonsense degrades womankind. It is a return to the bestiality of the Dark Ages. I am merely registering a protest.'

'You are disturbing the peace, madam.'

'If I may, sir, I'd like to deal with this,' Lestrade interrupted.

'Eh?' the chief constable looked irked. Still, this man *was* the Yard. No point in antagonising him. 'Oh, very well. Advise her on her rights, Lestrade.'

'Rights?' snapped Emily. 'Women have no rights. But you wait. The women of Britain will soon unleash such a campaign that every policeman in the country would be insufficient to cope with it.'

'Come on Emily,' and Lestrade dragged her out of the ring of policemen, towards the horse lines to the approving applause of the crowd. Out of sight of them, he swung her sharply round and she gasped. 'What the hell is all this about?' he hissed.

She shook free her wrist, 'Just because you share my bed from time to time, does not mean you can shake my resolve.'

'Resolve?' Lestrade repeated in disbelief. 'You sound more like Mrs Pankhurst every day.'

Emily stopped and looked at Lestrade. They both started to laugh. 'Do I?' she asked. 'God, how awful. I'm sorry Sholto, I've embarrassed you.'

'No,' he said, and brushed the grass from her riding habit. 'Have I hurt you?'

'No,' and she kissed him.

'The knight you hit with the flour is a friend of mine. I think I can persuade him not to press charges. But I'm afraid the Queen of Beauty may file a complaint.'

'It's all right, Sholto,' she whispered, stroking the gaunt cheek, 'I've been in prison before.'

A roar from the crowd told them that the jousting had recommenced.

'Dew!' Lestrade shouted.

'Sir?' the sergeant emerged inches from him, under a tent flap. It took the inspector unawares.

'You haven't heard this conversation, understand?'

'What conversation is that, sir?'

Lestrade slapped his back, 'Good man. Accompany Miss Greenbush to the edge of the field. We'll take her back to London with us. I'm going to see the Queen of Beauty and then John Watson. It's time we got out of this madhouse.'

The Queen of Beauty was sitting in an improvised shelter behind the pavilions, sipping cocoa. Around her fussed a number of attendants. Lestrade introduced himself and ascertained how the lady felt about the assault on her person. The attendants left at the Queen's command.

'I will settle for the cost of my gown,' she said, with a materialism which surprised Lestrade. She pulled off the long blonde wig and combed out her own hair, 'But that harridan should be horse-whipped.'

'Quite so, ma'am. Oh,' Lestrade turned back in the doorway. 'I understand you are acquainted with Mr O'Merle Holmes?'

Mercy Alabaster opened her mouth, glancing hurriedly around her, 'I *was*,' she said.

'He was your fiancé, I gather?'

'Until his blindness, yes, he was. Why are you asking me these questions?'

'You ended your engagement because of his blindness?'

She paused. 'Yes, Inspector, I did. Does that shock you?'

She swept past him as regally as her damp clothes would permit.

'A lifetime with a blind man. Imagine it, Mr Lestrade. I am young, pretty. He is a wreck. I should, I know, feel for him, but I do not, not even pity—'

'And all for a moment's carelessness with a Hotchkiss,' mused Lestrade.

'A Hotchkiss?' she queried.

'It's a kind of gun, ma'am,' he explained. 'It blinded Mr Holmes in the veld.'

'I think you must have been misinformed, Inspector.'

'My dearest,' an armoured man rushed into the tent, 'forgive me, I could not get to you for the crowd. Are you all right? That beastly woman. Who are you?'

'Inspector Lestrade, sir, Scotland Yard.'

'Ah, good. You've got the slut, have you?'

'No, sir,' said Lestrade with an unusually tart reply, 'you have.' And he left.

He was crossing the field in a last determined attempt to find Dr Watson when the trumpets blasted in his ear. Recoiling from them, he overheard from men nearby what the signal meant.

'An Unknown Knight,' said one, 'what fun! Just like *Ivanhoe*, what?'

Lestrade had heard that name before, but he couldn't place it and turned to watch the knight trot onto the field. He struck the shield of Dymoke where it hung on a brightly painted pole.

'What's his device?' another man asked.

'Three feathers,' came the answer, 'that's Bohemia, isn't it? How odd.'

The Bohemian knight cantered to the far end of the lists and waited for William Dymoke to mount again and face him. The crowd watched, eager and hushed as the trumpets sounded. Then Lestrade saw it. It was having Harry Bandicoot's lance-tip so near to his face when Letitia had tied her scarf to it that alerted him. This knight's lance had an iron tip. And it was sharp. He rode over to where the Queen of Beauty had resumed her place.

'Your colours, my lady?' the voice boomed out, Irish and fierce through the breathes of the helmet.

Mercy Alabaster bowed and handed him her scarf. He wrapped it around his lance and rammed his spurs home. Something in the man's movements, something cold, ruthless, made Lestrade move. He found himself running across the field, deaf to the 'I says' and 'bad forms' crashing around him. Those level with the central pavilion saw it most clearly. They saw the Bohemian's lance come up at the last moment, away from the shield of his opponent and straight for his head. The very observant saw the iron tip slide with a sickening thud through the sights of Dymoke's visor and into bone and brain behind. The King's Champion dropped lance, shield and reins and pitched sideways, blood trickling over the dark steel casque. The Bohemian knight galloped on to the end of the barrier and then swung round to race for the gap in the crowd. People were on their feet, shouting, screaming. Children cried, women fainted. Lestrade tried to grab the horseman, his fingers snatching the stirrup for a moment, but the knight jabbed a short iron mace down on his shoulder and the inspector somersaulted across the hard ground.

Policemen were running towards the knight, who slashed them with the mace and wheeled away, the snorting horse lashing out with steel-shod hoofs. Time and again, he drove for the blue lines before turning again and disappearing through a gap in their ranks.

Lestrade, dazed and bleeding, stumbled into Sergeant Dew.

'Are you all right, sir?'

'Dew. Where's Bandicoot? I need his horse.'

Harry was there in a second, 'My de Dion's faster, Sholto. Can you stand?'

Lestrade waved aside the fussing and the policemen and the Knight of the Golden Chalice dashed for Bandicoot's horseless carriage. They all leapt onto the gleaming machine. 'What happens now?' asked Lestrade.

'Oh, sorry,' said Bandicoot and tugged off his helmet. 'Sergeant Dew, grab that.'

'Right, sir.' Dew grabbed the helmet.

'Not that, man,' said Bandicoot, 'the starting handle. On the floor.'

Bandicoot snatched the thing from Dew and disappeared below the blunt end. Lestrade and Dew sat willing the engine to start. Once, twice, Bandicoot's shoulder appeared above the front and the whole machine roared into life, Dew and Lestrade vibrating like unmoulded jellies. Bandicoot pulled levers and switches in all directions and the de Dion sped away as the Cornwall Constabulary hurtled past them in a Maria. Bandicoot soon outpaced them, leaning forward into the wind. The Bohemian knight was a speck bouncing on the horizon.

'He'll cut across country,' shouted Lestrade, his coat flying out behind him. 'Can this contraption follow him?'

'To the ends of the earth, old chap!' Bandicoot beamed with pride.

Dew was clutching his bowler with white knuckles, his eyes tightly shut. 'How fast are we going, Mr Bandicoot?' he managed to ask.

'Ooh, must be twenty miles an hour, Dew,' and he turned smiling to see the burly sergeant slip backwards over the seat in a dead faint. He hit the bank and rolled into the road. Bandicoot reached for the brake.

'Keep going, Harry. Dew will be all right. There isn't a road made that can make an impression on that skull. Besides, the Maria will pick him up.'

Lestrade glanced back in time to see the Maria swerve around the prostrate Dew and keep going.

'Determined, the chief constable, isn't he?' observed Harry.

'I think he's more intent on beating us than catching our murderer,' said Lestrade.

Bandicoot pushed his foot to the floor and the de Dion hurtled off the road, bouncing out of control across the fields and slewing across the furrows.

'If he reaches the woods, we're lost,' said Harry, 'I can out-distance a horse, but I can't out-manoeuvre one.'

Their quarry was clearly visible now, the knight still in armour from head to knee, lashing his lathered horse as he raced for the safety of the trees. The de Dion was rattling with a vengeance, the pursuing constables invisible in the spray of mud and smoke.

'Get the other side of him, Bandicoot. Have you got your sword?'

'Steady Sholto. Are you up to this?'

Lestrade gave the younger man a withering look and jerked free his broadsword. It wasn't sharp, but it was heavy and could no doubt do a reasonable amount of damage in the right hands. Were those, however, the hands of Lestrade? Time would tell. He stood up in the bouncing machine, bracing his knees against the front bit and steadying himself against the bit that stuck upright, extending his sword arm in practice. Bandicoot swung right to avoid a tumulus and Lestrade sat down again, jarring his spine.

'For God's sake, Bandicoot, you told me you could drive this thing.'

He struggled up again and waited until the de Dion was level with the horseman. He was using his left arm, never his best, and the knight was pulling away, but he swung wildly, smashing the high cantle of the ornate saddle. Leather and studs crunched under the blade's impact but it acheived nothing. Lestrade hacked again, higher this time in an attempt to hit the man. The knight parried with his mace and the two men traded swings, the steel ringing together as they reached the trees. Bandicoot was wrestling manfully with the wheel, missing trees by inches and crashing through bushes. Lestrade took a blow from the mace on his forearm and using two hands in a desperate attempt to unhorse his man, drove the blade deep into a silver birch. The impact made him lose the sword altogether and the de Dion spun out of control, tilted at a crazy angle, then plunged into a hollow.

At a safe distance, the Bohemian knight wheeled his tired horse and saluted with his mace. Lestrade knelt in the bushes, fighting for breath, wondering what lay behind the dark steel of that helmet. Then the Unknown Knight rode away. By the time the lumbering Maria came up, Bandicoot and Lestrade had freed themselves of the tangle of de Dion and undergrowth and clambered wearily on board.

'Bad luck, Lestrade,' said the chief constable, 'we've lost the blighter now for sure.'

'Get us back to the village, sir,' said Lestrade, 'we can still stop him. An armoured knight on horseback is likely to turn a few heads even in Cornwall. This *is* nineteen-o-two.'

But the Bohemian knight had other plans. Beyond the woods he unbuckled his armour, let his horse run free and climbed into the seat of his waiting Lanchester. It had all been so easy.

William Lord Dymoke lay in one of the pavilions, his helmet and accoutrements beside him. The crowd had gone now and it was almost dark. The Eglinton tournament had ended in a downpour. The Tintagel tournament had ended in murder. There was a bitter taste in everyone's mouth. Lestrade stood bareheaded beside the body. It was the eighth murder of its kind, and once again the pattern had been broken.

'So Mr Churchill was right,' Lestrade said softly to himself in the candlelight, 'there has been a death in the "Other Place".'

'What's that, Lestrade?' Dr Watson forced himself out of the silence he had maintained for some time.

'Nothing. Thank you for waiting, Doctor. I came to ask you a question and found, or nearly found, the man I'm after.'

'What question?'

'Do you have a key to Sherlock Holmes' room?'

'Of course.'

'Who has the other?'

'Other? Mrs Hudson, I suppose.'

'And have you lost or mislaid yours recently?'

'Why, yes, as a matter of fact, I have. It was, let me see . . . the night Hamilcar Waldo died. A day or so later Boscombe brought it back. I'd left it behind.'

'Boscombe?' asked Lestrade.

'Yes, you know, Mycroft's man at the Diogenes.'

The devil's feat

'You don't want to come here any more, do you Sholto?' Emily Greenbush looked up from her book.

Lestrade was staring at the evening sky, heavy and dark with unshed April showers. He looked at her.

'Why do you say that?' he smiled.

'Because it's true. Because the only reason you came here at all was to – what's the phrase you policemen use – keep me under surveillance?' There was no malice, either in voice or look.

Lestrade crossed to her. 'That was so,' he admitted, 'at first. Now—'

'Now you care?' The impassive smile played around her lips.

He nodded.

'But not enough,' she said. 'Geoffrey was the same. Oh, Sholto, don't you see how it is? For all your fondness, you don't approve of me. Of what I stand for. And I . . . I shouldn't care for you, either.'

'And you do?' he asked her.

She nodded.

He lifted her face in his hand and planted a single, gentle kiss on her lips. He felt an iron lump in his throat, but he took the Donegal and the bowler from the settee.

'Before you go,' she said, 'do one thing for me. That little girl of yours, Emma. Tell her about you, that you're her father. I think she'd want to know.'

'Perhaps,' said Lestrade, shaking his head.

She stood up, sniffing away her tears, determined not to cry.

'If I see you again, Sholto, when I'm chained to the railings outside Number Ten, Downing Street, I'll pretend I don't know you. I'll never embarrass you again. But one day,' she stood erect, proud in the lamplight, 'one day, we'll meet each other in the polling station, my cross next to yours.'

'I'm sure we will, Emily Greenbush,' he said and walked into the night.

Curzon Street was quiet for a Saturday. The theatre crowds were not yet abroad and the teeming thousands had gone home to sleep in the suburbs – the Surbiton secretaries and the Norwood builders. Yet Lestrade was aware somewhere behind him of a shadow. Not one, he realised, but two, and a third. He was still being followed. Ever since he had visited 221B Baker Street, he had known it. He ducked left into an alley and waited. A dark figure crept past, followed by a second. Lestrade waited for the third then grabbed the man's collar and swung him backwards into the wall. He rammed the prowler's arm hard behind his back and forced him down onto his knees.

'Right, laddie,' he hissed, 'who are you?'

'Find out, copper!'

Lestrade hauled him upright so that his face scraped every brick on the way up.

He spun round and struck a match near his face. A man in his mid-twenties, rough looking, unshaven.

'Wiggins,' a voice called from behind. Lestrade clapped his hand over the lad's mouth and dragged him down to street level again.

'Wiggins!' said the voice. 'Where are you? We've lost 'im.'

'No, you haven't,' said Lestrade and kicked Wiggins so that the other two went sprawling. They struggled upright, clawing free heavy coshes. Lestrade tried the old ploy and thrust his finger into the pocket of his Donegal, so that it looked like a pistol.

'Drop them!' he snarled.

The three men looked at each other, gripping their weapons, sweating.

'Any trouble here, gentlemen?' the gentle tones of a constable of the Metropolitan Police growled behind the three. They threw down their coshes and Lestrade picked them up.

'No thank you, officer, no trouble. Is there, gentlemen?'

The three men mumbled.

'Now, Wiggins, tell me why you've been following me,' said Lestrade as the policeman moved on.

'Orders,' said Wiggins.

'Orders? Whose orders?'

'Mr Holmes', answered Wiggins.

'Sherlock Holmes?' Lestrade checked.

'That's right.'

'He's dead.'

'No, 'e ain't,' said another.

''E's alive as you are,' chimed in the third.

'Where?'

The three looked at each other.

'Dunno,' said Wiggins.

'How is it you know Mr Holmes?' Lestrade asked.

Another pause.

'We're his Irregulars,' said Wiggins. ''E called us so 'isself. The Baker Street Irregulars. I've been tailin' coppers and trassenos since I was so 'igh.'

'If Mr Holmes so ordered it?'

'Right.'

'And when did he give you these orders to follow me?'

''Bout a week back,' said Wiggins.

'You saw him, face to face?'

'Na. 'E's in 'idin', see. Moriarty's in England.'

This last was breathed in such reverence it was as though the King himself had just walked past.

'Is he now?' said Lestrade. 'So how did Holmes get the message to you?'

'A letter. We was to follow you until we 'eard different and report to 'im regular.'

'Where?'

Silence.

'Wiggins, I can get you and your friends two years apiece. And not even Mr Holmes can save you from that.'

The Irregulars conferred by a series of grunts and monosyllables.

'At the newspaper stand opposite of 221B.'

'And when do you next report?'

'Tomorrow night. Ten sharp.'

'All right. Keep your appointment. But I shall be there too. And Wiggins – all of you. One signal, one gesture and I'll have you inside so fast your arses won't touch the dock bench. Got it?'

'Yes, Mr Lestrade,' they mumbled and shambled off into the darkness.

'Roderick, love, can we have a word?' the disembodied voice whined in the darkness of the theatre.

Lestrade stumbled down the steps in its direction.

'It's no good, sweetie,' the producer was at his most acid, 'you're not getting it. The rugged quality of a policeman on the edge, a man hopelessly out of his depth. I just don't feel it. It's got to come from here,' and he patted Lestrade's waistcoat with his tapering fingers. 'And you *have* missed rehearsals, haven't you, Roderick?'

'What are you saying?' Lestrade asked.

'I'm afraid you're out, dear. I've given the part to Lewis Casson. Well, he's no Henry Irving, but he'll have to do. I'm sorry, Roderick. Don't send a telegram to us. We'll send one to you, dear.'

Lestrade wasn't sorry. That one line had given him more trouble than all the assassins and Bohemian knights put together. Besides, he'd had time during the endless rehearsals to ask questions and note responses. He was sure that no one here was impersonating Sherlock Holmes off stage as well as on it. Mr Roderick Lister, actor, could go back into the closet for a well-earned rest. And Lestrade swore he'd never touch a police revue again.

I've got it,' the little man chirped, waving sheets of paper at Lestrade.

'I'm sorry to hear that,' the inspector emerged from a pile of paperwork. 'What have you got, and who are you?'

The little man looked crestfallen, 'Bloom: Codes and Cyphers. I've broken your code.'

The cryptic notebook of the late Ralph Childers; Lestrade had all but forgotten in the hurly-burly of the past months.

'About time,' he said. 'What does it mean?'

'Not much, I'm afraid. It's a series of meetings, weekend parties and so on. I've listed them here. These,' he pointed to page two hundred and twenty-one, 'are the initials of . . . who knows? Friends, acquaintances, colleagues? This one's interesting,' he quoted, '"Ghastly time at the Grange. Felt guilty about it." And this one, "Scars beginning to heal." Or this, "Galley slave routine tonight. Very enjoyable. New cat arrives tomorrow."'

'Yes, well, I don't think we need dwell on all this,' said Lestrade. 'Thank you, Mr Bloom. Better late than never, I suppose.'

The little man exited.

'Jones?'

'Inspector?'

'What do you know about John of Bohemia?'

'John of Bohemia?'

Lestrade was used to these delaying tactics. Dickens used them too. It was an excuse to give the photographic brain time to go into action.

'The name given by the Unknown Knight to the Marshal of Arms.'

'John of Bohemia.' Lestrade heard the brain click into position over the staccato tap of Dew's typewriter. His finesse was such he might as well have used his elbow. 'Elected by the German nobility and reigned from thirteen hundred and eleven to forty-six. He was Count of Luxemburg . . .'

'Yes?'

'Forgive me, sir, but about this stage in my giving of information you usually stop me.'

'For myself, I would,' said Lestrade, 'but between us, Sergeant Dew is hoping for promotion and he needs all the culture he can get. Go on.'

'Count of Luxemburg,' repeated Jones, 'married Elizabeth, sister of Wenceslas the Third.'

'Ah, yes,' said Dew, 'Good King Wenceslas; I've heard of him.'

'Congratulations, Dew,' said Lestrade.

'He was killed at the battle of Crécy in thirteen forty-six and it is said that from him the Black Prince took his device of three feathers and his motto of "Ich dien", "I serve".'

Lestrade rubbed his chin, 'And all he served was death on a plate. You look constipated, Constable. What's the matter?'

'There's something else, sir, about King John, I mean. But I . . . I just can't remember.'

'Never mind, Jones. You can't win them all. It can't have been very important. Dew, Dickens. We're going to meet Mr Sherlock Holmes.'

It was a waste of time. The three of them left the desk-bound Jones for the basement changing room of the Yard and got into coster clothes before catching a bus to Baker Street. They busied themselves in various ways. Lestrade muscled in on a chestnut-seller's stall. After all, he had done the man on four separate occasions for shoplifting. The chestnut-seller was glad to slope off into the warm, spring night. Nobody was buying chestnuts at this time of the year anyway. Dew barked something incomprehensible after the manner of newspaper vendors and Dickens blacked more boots than he had seen before in his life. At the appointed time, Wiggins and his Irregulars strolled along. They waited. And waited. No one came. No Sherlock Holmes. No man in a deerstalker, smoking a meerschaum. No King of Bohemia thundering along Baker Street.

At midnight, Lestrade called the whole operation off. He might have guessed it was a fool's errand anyway. He glanced up at the windows of 221B. They were dark. Dr Watson and Mrs Hudson had gone to bed – together or separately made no odds. Three tired, dispirited policemen went home.

*

'You sent for me, sir?' Lestrade stood before Edward Henry.

'Sit down, Lestrade. Lemon tea?'

'Now, that's much better for you,' simpered Miss Featherstonehaugh.

'That will be all,' Henry said to her.

'Mr Frost used to—'

'Become as irritated by you as I am,' said Henry.

The secretary stood up as though there were a rocket in her drawers and left the room with all the bonhomie of a mantis shrimp.

'That woman has to go,' grunted Henry. 'Now, Lestrade – the case.'

'It's as I thought, sir. Bradstreet and the commander were and are working on the assumption that the killer is a paid assassin. That these murders are political.'

'And?'

'And the death of "Uncle" Deering worried me. It didn't fit the pattern. Here was a man who was toying with entering politics. He was still a serving soldier. The death of Lord Dymoke has strengthened my opinion. *He* wasn't an MP in the accepted sense, either.'

'Where does that leave us?' Henry sipped his tea.

'With the notion of revenge,' answered Lestrade.

'The revenge of Sherlock Holmes?'

'The revenge of someone pretending to be Sherlock Holmes. The question is, who and why?'

Henry leaned back in his chair looking at the inspector.

'It's not a question I can let you answer, Sholto,' he said.

'Sir?' Lestrade sniffed conspiracy in the wind. He had most of the nose for it.

'You're off the case, Lestrade. From now, I'm putting Gregory on as senior officer.'

'Gregory?' Lestrade almost choked on his tea.

Henry walked to the rain-lashed window. 'It's not my doing, Lestrade. I too have superiors.'

Lestrade could believe that. 'Mycroft Holmes?' he asked.

'Lord Lansdowne put pressure on the Home Secretary and hey presto . . .'

'Gregory pops out of the hat,' said Lestrade. He put his cup down. 'And if I refuse?'

Henry looked at him, 'Don't be an idiot. You've got a few years to go to your pension. What about that daughter of yours?'

'What indeed?' said Lestrade. And he went away to kick a few cats.

The Boers ceased to be beastly that May. An armistice was declared and, as the dust settled, accusations began to fly. Why hadn't the army been prepared? How was Krupp to be dealt with, supplying the enemy with all those guns? And who exactly *was* involved in the Army Remount scandal? Lestrade could probably have helped them there, but he felt disinclined to do so. The summer approached, warm and dry and all London began to buzz with the approaching coronation. Bunting by the mile fluttered from lamp post to lamp post. Ribbons and lace and flowers fluttered everywhere else.

No one thought of the maniac who had been reducing the elector's choice for the past months. No one except Tom Gregory, who was supposed to be catching him. And Sholto Lestrade who couldn't forget him. The Commander of the Special Branch had the Houses of Parliament sewn up, he said, as tight as a gnat's arse. Not a man of refinement, the commander. Miss Featherstonehaugh fainted when she heard it.

It was the night before the coronation that Lestrade received the summons. Two sober-looking men in top hats and scowls came to his bedside and spirited him away. It was urgent, they said. Of the gravest urgency. Two in the morning it may be, but he was to ask no questions and to go with them. Under the stars of the clear night, he saw the façade of Buckingham Palace loom as the carriage rattled down the silent Mall. In an hour, perhaps less, the crowds would begin to assemble, camping at the roadside. Bobbies patrolled the shadows already, ready for their stint of duty. It looked like being a long three days.

He followed the undertakers, for so they behaved, through a

maze of silent corridors, gleaming in gaslight and electricity. He was shown into a hall of vast dimensions with painted ceilings and marble columns and told to wait.

'Lestrade.' A curt voice made him turn.

'Sir Frederick.' Lestrade attempted a bow and realised his pyjama jacket was dangling below his waistcoat. He tucked it in as unobtrusively as he could. A second figure, frock coat flying behind him, dashed into the room.

'Is this he?' he said to Ponsonby.

'This is Inspector Lestrade. Lord Esher.' There seemed no time for greater ceremony.

Esher grunted at Lestrade.

'Know why you're here?' Ponsonby asked.

'I haven't a clue, sir,' said Lestrade.

'That doesn't bode well,' Esher grunted at Ponsonby.

'Lestrade,' Ponsonby took the inspector by the arm and led him to a table in one corner of the room, 'what I am about to tell you is of the utmost importance. It concerns . . .' and he paused to look around him, 'the Highest in the Land.'

Lestrade looked at him quizzically.

'The King is gone.'

'God rest him,' said Lestrade. 'His heart?' He remembered the sudden demise of the overweight Nimrod Frost.

'No, no, Lestrade. He's not dead, man. He's been kidnapped.'

'Kidnapped?' Lestrade repeated dumbly.

'Are you sure this is he?' Esher checked with Ponsonby.

'Gentlemen,' a female voice rang from the dais.

'Your Majesty.' Ponsonby and Esher clicked their heels and bowed. Lestrade did likewise, but his slippers clicked but poorly. At least it gave him a chance to check his pyjamas again.

Alexandra, Queen of England walked noiselessly and as elegantly as her hip would allow into their presence.

'This is Inspector Lestrade, ma'am,' Ponsonby bellowed.

'There's no need to shout, Freddie, I am not deaf.'

Ponsonby looked suitably chastened. She turned to Lestrade and held out her hand.

'Inspector Despade. How good of you to come.'

'Charmed, ma'am.' Lestrade kissed the outstretched ring. Didn't that make him Prime Minister, he wondered?

'You will help us, Inspector? You see, my husband is so dear, to us all.'

He looked at the fine face, dignified and wise, the lip firm but the eyes glistening with tears.

'Fear not, ma'am. We'll find His Majesty,' he said.

She patted his hand.

'Best you retire, ma'am,' suggested Ponsonby. 'Leave it to us.'

The Queen looked a little surprised. 'I don't know, Freddie,' she said, 'it must be about half past two,' and she limped alone into the shadows.

'She's taking it very well,' whispered Ponsonby.

'I'll say this for Her Majesty,' said Esher, 'she certainly calls Lestrade Despade. Ha, ha!'

The others looked at him. 'I'm not sure this is a time for levity, Esher.'

It was Esher's turn to know his place.

'Gentlemen, forgive me. I'll have to have some details.' Lestrade was bewildered.

'Of course,' Ponsonby explained. 'You know there was a banquet here tonight? Royalty and aristocracy from the world over. His Majesty retired shortly after midnight, when all the speeches were done. Just after one I went to his chamber to escort Miss . . . to see if he needed anything. And he was gone. His bed had not been slept in. Miss . . . no one had seen him.'

'You have searched?'

'Of course,' Esher snapped. 'Good God, man, you don't think we'd invent this business, do you? The whole world is waiting for a coronation in two days and there is no king to crown.'

'Besides,' said Ponsonby, decidedly the calmer of the two, 'there is this.' He showed Lestrade a piece of paper.

'It is the transcript of a telephone call made to me within the hour.'

Lestrade read it. '"I have the last of them. The big fish himself. If you wish to see Bertie again bring one million pounds in used notes to . . ."'

'Is that it?'

'The phone went dead. I tried to get him back, but it was hopeless.'

'What did the voice sound like?'

'An Irish accent.'

'What?' Lestrade rounded on Ponsonby.

'I said—'

'Yes, yes,' Lestrade began to pace the floor, 'I heard what you said.'

'Do you think it's a practical joke, Lestrade?' Esher asked.

Lestrade looked at the distraught courtiers. 'No, gentlemen. If I'm right, the man who made the phone call – the man who has the King – is the same man who has been murdering Members of Parliament in recent months.'

'God!' said Esher.

'So he *is* an Irishman? A Fenian after all?' asked Ponsonby.

'No, sir, I don't think so. That's merely a blind. The man is as English as you or I.'

'Well, I'm not so sure about you, Lestrade,' grunted Ponsonby. 'What the devil do we do?'

'Why did you send for me?' Lestrade asked.

'The Queen wished it,' Ponsonby explained. 'His Majesty often talks of you in the fondest terms. You were the natural choice.'

'Don't let it go to your head, Lestrade. Unless you can find him by morning, we'll all be out of a job,' Esher grumbled.

'That won't be possible,' said the inspector.

'God!' It was no more than Esher had expected.

The three men paced the room. 'What about . . .' Lestrade began.

'Yes?' the other two asked.

'An announcement that the King is ill, appendicitis perhaps, something sudden. The coronation will have to be cancelled, of course. But it will give us time to think and to act.'

'What do you think, Freddie?' Esher asked.

'It's brilliant,' said Ponsonby, who by now was praying for an earthquake, an invasion, anything to avert the publication of the truth.

'Right, consider it done. We'll have to take the King's surgeon into our confidence, of course. We'll get a sick room set up. Only ourselves, Her Majesty and the doctor can come and go. Hourly bulletins and so on. That sort of thing. It *might* just work, Lestrade,' said Esher.

'It will have to,' said Lestrade. 'Now, to the matter in hand. How could anybody have smuggled the King out of the building without anyone seeing him?'

'God knows. He is rather large, when all's said and done,' said Ponsonby. 'It must have been the very devil of a feat.'

'Very little has been said and nothing has been done!' Esher snapped. A pause, 'You know it's the Browns, don't you?'

'The Browns?' Lestrade looked up for an explanation.

'The family of the Highland ghillie, John Brown.'

'The attendant of Her late Majesty?'

'Attendant? That's a polite way of putting it!' Esher said.

'The point is,' said Ponsonby, 'it's common knowledge in court circles that His Majesty detested Brown. When the old Queen died, he personally ordered that everything which smacked of Brown, every memento, every keepsake, should be destroyed.'

'So it stands to reason. The Browns are wreaking their revenge. That's where you'll find the King.'

'With respect, Lord Esher, the man who has the King is the same man who has been killing MPs for the past year.'

'Yes, yes, Lestrade. You said that. But where is your evidence, man?'

'The telephone call. The Irish accent. I received just such a call the night a colleague of mine was killed in the Houses of Parliament.'

'I remember that,' said Esher, 'Broadstreet, wasn't it?'

'Nearly,' said Lestrade.

'What's your plan?' Esher asked him.

'To get some sleep.'

'Good God, man, the King of England's life is at stake and you're going to bed!' Esher was purple.

'I may be all that can preserve that life, Lord Esher. And if I'm going to do it, I want to be at my best.'

'Lestrade,' Ponsonby took him aside, 'there's to be no going to the Yard with this. Who knows how this maniac will react with policemen all over the place. Not even the commissioner knows. And Edward Henry is totally in the dark.'

'His usual place,' mused Lestrade. 'I can call in sick this morning,' he said, 'but I will need a man. My sergeant, Walter Dew.'

'Very well. But you and he had better operate from here. I want no leaks. Come, Esher, we have much to do.'

Walter Dew's mouth was not seen to close for twenty-four hours. He moved as if in a daze through the wing of the palace set aside for 'the gentlemen' and intrigued footmen and flunkies of all shapes and sizes wondered who these two furtive looking men might be. To Walter Dew fell the hopeless task of sifting through the coronation guest list, in case one of them, having dined with the King the previous night, had then smuggled him who-knows-where in the most audacious plot in history. What Lestrade needed was a thousand constables and all the resources of the Yard at his back. Instead, for reasons of State of which Ponsonby continually reminded him, he had Sergeant Dew. That illustrious example of the Metropolitan Police Force pored over the names at his disposal: the Crown Princes of Russia, Denmark, Portugal and Italy, Prince of Asturias, Prince Tsai Chen. When his crossed eyes alighted on the Japanese representative, Prince Akihito Komatsu, the memories of his experiences at the Strand Palace sent a shiver up his spine. When Inspector Lestrade asked him who he suspected, he said, 'All of them, guv'nor,' refusing to believe anything good of men with names like Ras Makunan, Mohammed Ali Pasha and Said Ali. When his guv'nor asked him which of them had butchered Ralph Childers, poisoned Hamilcar Waldo, shot Arthur L'Estrange, stabbed Reginald Cobham, gassed Geoffrey Manners and skewered Lord Dymoke and Major Deering with lances ancient and modern, the sergeant was at a loss for words.

Esher and Ponsonby had done their job well. The Houses of Parliament took the news of the King's acute appendicitis and the indefinite postponement of the coronation with a stoicism unusual in a collection of men damned by Nimrod Frost and Miss Emily Greenbush alike. The wires and the post office were flooded with letters and telegrams. Changes of plan, alterations of itinerary. Trains, yachts, liners and steam packets, not to mention trams, buses and hackneys, were in urgent demand. The invited noblesse were going home. No one had told the workmen, however, and they continued hammering nails and hanging bunting until the boys in blue, already exhausted with turning away crowds, sent them home too.

Frantic royal chefs fled this way and that and the palace was ringing with cries. 'What shall I do with two thousand five hundred quails?' Lestrade clapped a hand over Dew's mouth before he had a chance to answer. In the end, the bulk of the food was distributed in Whitechapel by the Sisters of the Poor. Lestrade and Dew got a chicken each and a bottle of exceptionally fine wine. Both of them declined the black stuff that looked like sieved rabbit droppings, and felt a lot better for it.

The King's surgeon came and went as though for a real operation and sent out bulletins with impeccable timing, being as non-committal as he could about the state of His Majesty's health. Then the letter arrived. It was addressed to Ponsonby.

'By now you will have called in Lestrade,' it read, 'I expected that. He really will do you no good at all. But he can serve a purpose. He is to bring one million pounds in used notes in a suitcase of your choosing to the Old Wharf, Shadwell, at midnight tomorrow. He is to come alone and unarmed. If any of these demands are not met or if anything should go wrong, the King must die. Do you see how clever I am?'

Lestrade saw. He knew the Old Wharf from his years with the City Force in his youth. There was one point of access now the new docks had been built – a narrow pass where one man could hold off an army if he wanted to. And beyond it, a labyrinthine maze of courts and alleys, running this way and that along and under the Thames.

'You think he has the King there?' Ponsonby asked him.

'If he has, it might take us months to find him.'

Lestrade reached Shadwell Stair with five minutes to spare. He carried a battered old suitcase as requested and took along nothing but his trusty brass knuckles with the switchblade. It was moonlight, the river bright and silver under the creaking timbers. He left the ghost of the Ratcliffe Highway behind and joined the water rats scampering and squeaking on the rotting jetties and green timbers. But he crept rather than scampered and he kept his squeaking to a minimum. A thin mist wreathed the river. He saw in mid-stream an anchored barge, laden with tarpaulins, roped and bound. There was a whistle along the quay, a signal he knew was used by the Bluebottles, the River Police. He ducked into the shadows and stopped breathing for a while. At least on the warm night air his breath was not visible. The last thing he wanted now was some oaf of a constable pursuing his enquiries all over Lestrade's beat. The whistle moved off and Lestrade heard the lapping waters and briefly saw a boat under the moon. Across the river the line of warehouses and wharfs looked dark and threatening. He kept his back to the walls and edged towards the Old Wharf.

'Hello, Lestrade,' the voice was cold in the warmth of the night. As if in answer, a ship's siren whooped a mile away and there was a bark from somewhere, probably the Isle of Dogs.

'Who's there?' Lestrade's knuckles closed white around the Apache knife in his pocket.

'Don't you remember my voice, Lestrade?'

'Sherlock Holmes?' the inspector asked.

'It's been a long time,' the voice answered.

'Where is the King?' Lestrade was peering into the total blackness of the doorway, desperate to make out a figure, something to give him the direction of the voice.

'The King is dead, long live the King,' said Holmes.

'Why are you doing this, Mr Holmes?' Lestrade asked, 'Oh, I can understand you trying to kill Watson, even me perhaps—'

'You, Lestrade!' the voice hissed. 'You flatter yourself.'

'Bradstreet then. Why did you kill him? Because he represented everything you are not? A good detective?'

There was a crash of timbers. Lestrade realised a block and tackle of heavy iron had splintered the wall behind him, showering him suddenly with brick and plaster.

'One of my many skills, Lestrade,' Holmes went on, 'is being able to see in the dark. Didn't Watson chronicle that in one of his infantile stories? Ah, I see you have the money with you.'

'It's all here.' Lestrade brushed himself down, rising to his feet now, but staying out of the moonlight. 'Why did you kill those men? Childers, Waldo, the rest? What were they to you?'

'Nothing to me, Lestrade. Nothing whatever.'

'And why the King?'

'That's my business. I have my reasons. But it's over now, Lestrade. Finished. And so are you. I have a Martini-Henry carbine pointed at your head. I want you to put that suitcase down on the jetty. No, to your right.'

Lestrade checked his position. He was still in the dark, the sharp shadow of the building was inches to his right. If he placed the suitcase where Holmes had told him to, he was in the moonlight, a standing duck.

'Now!' the voice bellowed.

'All right Sergeant,' Lestrade bluffed, 'call your men up. He's in there!'

A shot rang out as Lestrade rolled to the right. He saw, in that instant, where the explosion came from. The bullet grazed his forearm and he dropped the case, but the momentum of his roll had carried him too far and he somersaulted off the end of the jetty to splash into the water. He clamped his mouth shut. He knew a few gulps of this water was as deadly as the cyanide Sherlock Holmes had given to Christian Barrett. He let his limbs go loose and floated to the surface. He saw the moon and stars and kept his eyes open.

As the surface bobbed and the water in his ears drowned all sound, he saw as in a dream the Ulstered figure, tall and gaunt, saunter out onto the jetty. He saw the deerstalker and the rifle, cocked in one hand. Sherlock Holmes bent down and picked up the suitcase. Lestrade lay motionless, letting the rank water wash over him. He knew he was helpless in this position. That any minute, the late, Great Detective might finish him with a second shot. His only hope was to play dead, something Sherlock Holmes had done for eleven years. He gambled on the man's arrogance, that he could not bring himself to admit that he needed one more shot. He heard him laugh as he checked the suitcase and turn away. And there was something in his walk . . .

'You gave that maniac one million pounds?' Esher fumed as the royal surgeon patched Lestrade's arm.

'It's only a scratch,' the eminent man pronounced.

'Scratch be damned,' roared Esher, 'Lestrade, you've killed the King.'

'I don't think so, my Lord. And by the way, I gave that maniac three hundred and twelve pounds. The rest was paper.'

'What? You bloody idiot, you've signed His Majesty's death warrant!'

'What's this, Esher?' Ponsonby came in. 'Going for the record of saying the same thing several ways?'

'Ponsonby, you're damned casual! You know, of course, that Bertie's done for?'

'That's three,' said Ponsonby. 'Tell him, Lestrade.'

'Either His Majesty was dead before the ransom note was written, or he is still alive. That's the way with kidnappers.'

'But when he discovers he's been cheated?'

'We may call him a maniac, Lord Esher, but actually, he's very clever. He must be aware that even the Royal Family cannot raise one million pounds in used notes in twenty-four hours, not without telling the Bank of England and that's as good as shouting it from the rooftops.'

'What does he care for secrecy?' Esher bellowed. 'If the whole story is blasted over the country, why should that bother him?'

'Because if he wanted publicity, he would have gone to the newspapers. Northcliffe, Liesinsdad, somebody would have been informed. We know he's made such contacts before.'

'Then why—'

'Because he has the King in a public place. Oh, not the middle of Hyde Park, I'll grant you, but somewhere where he might be discovered, recognised.'

'I don't follow.'

'Put yourself in the shoes of a member of the public,' Lestrade explained. 'If you saw a stout, elderly gentleman with a grey beard and poppy eyes on the thirty-seven bus, would you assume it was the King?'

'Well, no, I suppose . . . Is it as public as that?'

'Not exactly.'

'You know where the King is, Lestrade, don't you?' Ponsonby suddenly realised.

'Let's say I have a pretty good idea. Sergeant Dew here carried out a great piece of detective work earlier. This paper . . .' Lestrade waved the ransom note, 'has a rather peculiar watermark. Hold it up to the light, Lord Esher.'

'So?' Lord Esher saw nothing of portent.

'So it is the type used by the Foreign Office.'

'The Foreign Office? Good God.'

'Could that explain how the King was spirited away?' said Lestrade. 'Not unconscious, drugged, gagged and bound, but of his own volition, because of an urgent summons from the Foreign Office which, on the eve of his coronation, could not wait? Once outside and in a waiting hansom, it was too late.'

'Are you telling me—' Esher began.

'Gentlemen, my arm hurts like the very devil. I must catch a nap for an hour or so. Trust me. The King will be safe and I think I know where to find him. If I may take my leave?'

Ponsonby and Esher had more questions than answers, but they had little choice. If the King's secret and the King's life were to be safe, they *had* to trust Lestrade, there was no one else. As he dozed, the inspector tried to keep his arm as loose as possible. It was stiffening and whatever the surgeon's advice, he couldn't run the risk of it becoming useless. There was too much to do. He ran his eyes again over Ralph Childers' cryptic book and the boffin's translation which Dew had brought from the Yard. It was nearly dawn in the great grey gardens of the Palace and Lestrade suddenly saw it. The link that had been missing. He rang the bell by his bed furiously. Ponsonby staggered in moments later, in nightshirt and cap, bleary from the half hour's sleep he had snatched.

'Do you have a diary of the King's private functions? Shooting weekends and so on?'

'Of course, but I carry most of it in my head. Why?'

'I'm talking about nearly three years ago, now. December, eighteen ninety-nine. Where was he?'

Lestrade ran with Ponsonby to the Equerries' Office. Together, they threw open ledgers, riffled through papers.

'The Grange!' thundered Lestrade. 'I knew it! Ralph Childers was there too.'

'It's the Dymoke country seat,' said Ponsonby, hearing, as did Lestrade, pieces of the puzzle falling into place.

'What do these initials mean to you?' Lestrade found another deciphered page in Childers' notebook, 'Alongside the Grange entry. People? Who are they?'

Ponsonby read them out loud, 'CR, MG, WH, BC . . .' he paused, 'God knows!'

'Probably,' said Lestrade, 'and so do I. What about this one?' he pointed to the last on the list.

'HM,' read Ponsonby, 'His Majesty! But, no, the King was still HRH in eighteen ninety-nine—'

'Precisely,' said Lestrade, 'but turn the initials around and what do we have? CR: Ralph Childers himself; MG: Geoffrey Manners, Bart; WH: Hamilcar Waldo; BC: Christian Barrett. Need I go on? The names of all those murdered in the past months.'

'And HM?' said Ponsonby.

'Ah, yes,' said Lestrade, 'I shall take great pleasure in turning those initials round myself.'

The return of Sherlock Holmes

Six men outside the immediate Royal Family knew that the stories of the King's appendicitis were lies. Two were royal aides, two were officers of Scotland Yard. One was the King's Surgeon Extraordinary. The sixth was the kidnapper himself.

And it was to him Lestrade and Dew made their way by hansom late that night. The clock was striking ten as they reached the Diogenes Club. It was in darkness and its imposing façade was encrusted with scaffolding.

'As I thought,' nodded Lestrade, 'a very convenient time for structural alterations.'

'Well, that's it then sir.' Dew was ready to go back to the Palace. It wasn't often a sergeant of the Metropolitan Police got to sleep in the same house as a king. But then, the King wasn't there, was he?

'The devil it is,' said Lestrade, dismissing the cabbie. 'We'll try the back.'

The back was as dead as the front, but there was a light burning in the attic of the building.

'Shoulder, Dew,' said Lestrade. 'I'd do it, but the arm . . .'

The Sergeant had been here before. 'Yes, sir, of course,' and he stepped back onto the cobbles of the yard. He mentally measured the door in the moonlight and paced the run up to it. Then he took several deep breaths, lowered his head and charged. This was how he must have tackled the geisha, Lestrade imagined. Expecting the thud of a Metropolitan shoulder and the corresponding splinter of oak, all Lestrade heard in the shadows was the click of a latch and an echoing cry as the door swung open as Dew reached it. Lestrade saw him disappear at breakneck speed down the darkened corridor and winced at the re-echoing clash of copper and aspidistrae.

'Can I help you, sir?' It was the cheery Boscombe, ever ready with a merry quip at times like these, who had opened the door at so untimely a moment.

'Perhaps,' said Lestrade, fumbling past the man and his candle, 'but first I think, my sergeant . . .'

Dew was groaning and bleeding profusely from a head-wound. It was nothing he hadn't received countless times from his mother-in-law.

'How are you, Walter?' Lestrade helped him to sit up.

'All right, sir, thank you. I'm just wondering where your twin brother came from.'

'Ah.' Lestrade pulled him back so that his head could rest against a wall. 'This is Sergeant Dew, Boscombe. Do what you can for him, will you? Why the candle? Are there no lights at the club?'

'All the power is off, sir, on account of the workmen. May I ask your business?'

'You may, Boscombe,' said Lestrade cryptically, lighting a second candle from Boscombe's, 'you may indeed. When Dew comes round, he will have some questions to ask you. And I suggest you are more forthcoming than I have been. Or is your three-word rule still in operation?'

'No, sir, not while the club is under reconstruction.'

'Good,' said Lestrade and, candle in hand, he made for the stairs. 'Who's up here?' he asked.

'Why, no one, sir. I am alone in the building. At least, I think—'

'When were you last in the attic portion of the club?' Lestrade asked.

'Not for a few days, I suppose. I suffer from vertigo, you know . . .'

At last Lestrade knew why he walked that way.

Boscombe was detained by Dew, manfully trying to clear his head.

'Now then, sir,' Dew fumbled for his notebook and pen, 'you were here on the night that Hamilcar Waldo was killed? True or false?'

'True,' said Boscombe.

'And you know the party who killed him. True or false?'

'False, Inspector Dew.' Boscombe was on his dignity.

'That's Sergeant, sir. Sergeant Dew,' he said and slumped forward in a faint.

Lestrade had visited the Diogenes only once before and in the dark orientation was particularly difficult. He passed the corner where Hamilcar Waldo had been silently stabbed to death, the room where he had talked with would-be witnesses to the murder. His hand slid along the polished rail, gleaming mahogany in the moonlight. The skylight bathed the stairwell in a lurid silver. All else was blackness. Below him, Lestrade could hear the ministrations of Boscombe, tending to the fallen sergeant. Above him, where every instinct told him his quarry lay, was silence. He took a leaf out of the book of Inspector Smellie whom he had met on the Childers case all those months ago. He remembered where he had seen the light in the attic and tried to navigate by the stars.

He found the door, the light shining beneath it, at the top of the house. The paint was peeling on the walls here. There was a smell of disuse, of decay. Perhaps even of death. Aware of Dew's débâcle downstairs he tried the door handle. It gave way under his hand and he kicked the door back. It crashed on its hinges and he ducked into the room. He found himself kneeling on bare boards. In front of him, a table, bare except for an iron helmet and a shield bearing the three feathers. But it was the figure beyond the table which held his gaze, silhouetted against the pearl of the night sky. The unmistakable outline of deerstalker and Ulster, the smoke ascending lazily from the ornate meerschaum.

'Mr Holmes?' Lestrade eased his right hand into the brass knuckles in his pocket.

No reply.

Lestrade rose to his feet, the candlelight dancing on the walls and ceiling. The figure beyond the table did not rise with him, as he had expected. He checked his position, the door still open to his left, the table and chair in front. Little room for manoeuvre. He could make out the gloved right hand in the lap but the left he couldn't see. What was in it? A pistol, cocked and aiming at the inspector's head? He decided there was no time to wait.

'Do you have nothing to say to me, Mr Holmes, after all these years?' He edged nearer the table. 'No cheery greeting? Not even a snarl?' And he suddenly hurled the helmet with all the force his arm could manage across the room. Somehow the candle stayed alight and the candlestick stayed in his grip and he saw the meerschaum fly to the left and the deerstalker to the right and the head pitch forward onto the floor.

For a second, Lestrade's heart stopped. He blinked in disbelief at the headless body slumped in the chair, then dropped to his knees again and let the candlelight play on the head. This was no dummy. There lay a skull, peat-brown, with gaping jaws and sightless eyes. Lestrade ran his fingers over the clothes in the chair and felt a fragile framework of bones. 'The body of Sherlock Holmes,' he said aloud. Nothing unusual in that. After all, he had been talking to himself for the last five minutes.

A sudden rush of air snuffed his candle. 'Damn.' He crouched in the darkness, the cranium that once housed the Great Brain, the grey matter so beloved of Watson and Conan Doyle and countless others, still cradled in his lap. He crossed to the window and looked out on the sleeping rooftops. He saw the silhouette of the Houses of Parliament, 'tight as a gnat's arse', and, by craning a little, the secret spires of the Foreign Office, lights still lingering under Lansdowne's regime. Had he been six stories higher he could probably have seen the round bastions of the Yard and the fleeting comfort of Curzon Street. He wondered, not for the first time in his life, whether he would see these things again, after tonight. There had been too many such nights. He checked the cobbles below. He had missed the room by feet. The one he wanted must be next to him. He pulled away from the window and chanced the naked corridor once more.

This time he did not bother with the candle. He had no means of relighting it anyway unless he could salvage something from the corpse's pipe. Better to trust to the wayward fancies of the moon. He gripped the knuckles again and let the blade click free in his pocket. He placed his boot against the door, prayed to his God for a second and then launched himself forward. The room was in darkness save for a single candle burning away to the right. It lit the rotund figure of His Majesty Edward, by the Grace of God, King of England etc. He was bound, gagged and blindfolded, but there was no mistaking the royal paunch and the astrakhan-trimmed coat. Even the Homburg was perched jauntily on his head: He turned, alarmed, to the direction of the noise, roaring as much as the tightness of the cloth would allow.

'You're late, Lestrade,' said a voice, 'and so discreet an entrance.'

Lestrade flung himself from the doorway. There he represented too open a target. In the corner away from the King he might stand a chance. Then he saw the gleam of the gun's barrel jutting from utter blackness. 'This is a Martini-Henry rifle,' said the voice, 'and will blow your head off your shoulders, rather as you did to my brother next door, judging by the noise.'

'Mycroft Holmes,' said Lestrade, in as matter-of-fact a tone as possible while staring death in the face, 'I arrest you for the kidnapping of the King. We'll get to the murders later.'

'Later?' queried Holmes and chuckled. 'I'll be charitable, Lestrade, and assume you knew it was me before I mentioned my brother next door.'

'You left a trail a blind man could follow.' Lestrade was playing for time.

'Indeed?' Holmes seemed content to play that game too. 'For example?'

'For example, the reporting of the death of Hamilcar Waldo. Not the first time a murderer has trumpeted his own crime. Yours was the Irish voice your cousin O'Merle heard asking for Waldo – presumably when the reception desk was unattended, only your cousin of course wouldn't know that.'

'Quite right. Go on.'

The King struggled against his bonds. 'Shut up, Your Majesty,' snapped Holmes. 'I have no fear of adding regicide to the list of Lestrade's charges against me. Assuming, of course, that he can spell it.'

'Then there was your over-reaction to Watson's exhumation of your late brother.' Lestrade felt for the wall behind him. 'Of course you didn't want us to find out the man was really dead, because by that time you'd laid a clever trail – the deerstalker, the Ulster – your resemblance to Sherlock was of course a vital factor. But you'd been there before us, hadn't you, filling the coffin with rocks? I should have noticed the grave had been tampered with. But I still don't understand why the scene at the graveside. Once you'd removed the body; that was unnecessary, surely? Presumably, that was for the honour of the family and all that?'

'Oh, of course.'

'Then,' Lestrade was trying to catch the outline of the man behind the gun, trying to think of a way to duck the bullet he knew was inevitable, 'there was the muscle you showed in getting me removed from the case, the ransom notes on Foreign Office paper – very careless. Above all perhaps I sensed I was looking for a man whom nobody else would dream of looking for. Who better to kill a cavalryman with a lance, a brilliant games player with a ping-pong bat and a king's champion in the lists than a man noted for his lethargy? A man for whom the effort of walking to and from his club was widely known to be too great – and his only – exercise. And, of course, a Foreign Office employee could produce any number of special passes to enable him to spirit himself past any police cordon ever erected. Hence the bomb that killed Bradstreet – a particularly pointless flaunting of power, that, I thought.'

'Yes,' Holmes sniggered, 'wasn't it?'

Lestrade heard the bolt slide back.

'Tell me,' he gabbled, desperate now to postpone the next sound it was said the target never heard, 'isn't it usual to grant a dying man a last request?'

'Oh, come now, Lestrade,' said Holmes from the shadows, 'you can't want a cigarette, surely?'

'Never touch them,' the inspector said, 'but I am fond of answers.'

'Fire away.' He heard Holmes chuckle.

'How did you get into Ralph Childers' house without his man noticing?'

'His man was paid not to notice. I was a member of his fatuous Hell Fire Club. It amused me for a while, but it was about as titillating as a cycle ride without wheels. As for Miss Fifi Labedoyere—'

'And you battered him to death and walked home with blood-soaked clothes.'

'No, I brought a change of clothes with me. I knew Ralph's proclivities. That night I pretended to share them. The nauseating misfit. He deserved what he got. They all did.'

Holmes' voice was rising with anger now. He didn't sound himself.

'And you were the rider on the grey horse who rode to hounds with John Deering?'

'Of course. Uncle was an idiot. A lecherous old bastard who got his come-uppance. In fact, his amorous intentions nearly undid me there. I was poised behind a tree when he suddenly pounced on poor Lady Brandling. I had to wait.'

'Shame,' said Lestrade, but the rifle muzzle lifted in disapproval of the flippancy and he changed tack. 'Hamilcar Waldo I know about. Your arrogance was such that you had to call me to test my abilities as a detective. And you had the perfect witnesses – a blind man and an idiot.'

'Tut, tut,' Holmes clicked his tongue, 'what a way to refer to Doctor Watson. He's truly fond of you, you know. I even did him the honour of calling myself Henry Baskerville after one of his characters.'

'I assume that's the gun you used on Arthur L'Estrange?'

'It was. A shame about Arthur. I really quite liked him. You realise of course that *I* was the waiter who poisoned Christian Barrett?'

'I know how you killed Barrett, Holmes,' said Lestrade.

'I was inches from you, man. You took the glass from my tray and looked straight through me. No one, not even an inspector of Scotland Yard, notices lackeys.'

'The cyanide gas in the ping-pong bat was clever.' Lestrade tried flattery to ease the trigger finger.

'Yes, wasn't it? Aumerle was kind enough to welcome me to his house in Jermyn Street, a mere ping-pong ball's throw from the home of Sir Geoffrey Manners. Geoffrey's face when I walked in was a picture!'

'Why the Japanese sword for Reginald Cobham?'

'A whim, nothing more. I saw these little yellow fellows going around and thought I'd litter the trail with a few more false clues. Like the letter from Switzerland. Actually, I wrote it in my office in St James's and smudged the postmark. Then of course there was the German stein. I thought it might send you racing off to arrest the entire staff of the Kaiser's embassy. Sure enough, you wasted time running up all those blind alleys.'

'And of course, you'd met the Japanese delegation in an official capacity.'

'Ah, yes,' said Holmes and gave an uncharacteristic brittle laugh. 'You're moving to the right, Lestrade. That won't do. You see, I'm going to kill you anyway. What matters is how slowly I do it. Move again and I'll blow off your kneecap. I'll have time to hit every limb and kill the King before anyone comes to investigate the noise. I, of course, shall be gone.'

'It was Childers, the very first one, who betrayed you, Holmes. He kept a secret diary. It contained the initials, reversed, of all the victims. It also contained yours. HM. And one final question,' Lestrade blurted out, seeing the muzzle rise again and hearing the tortured breathing of the King, now almost behind him, 'the obvious one, really. Why? Why these men?'

'Ah, yes,' said Holmes, 'I thought you'd get to that eventually.' He walked forward into the candlelight.

'O'Merle!' Lestrade literally staggered back as though from a punch.

'You see, Lestrade, my late cousin's opinion of you was justified, wasn't it? You *are* an idiot. Ironic really, you were actually on the right tack. You *were* looking for a man whom nobody would dream of suspecting. But not a smug, complacent lump like cousin Mycroft. Who would dream of a blind man committing the murders? And I led you like a lamb to the slaughter, Lestrade. The blind leading the blind.'

'So that explains Mycroft's indignation at Sherlock's exhumation.'

'Of course,' Holmes said, 'it was genuine. He didn't know I'd removed the corpse days earlier to give credence to Watson's obsession. A few appearances in Baker Street outside number 221B, the odd contact with those morons Sherlock called his

Irregulars and the picture was complete. The cocaine syringe merely framed it. Sherlock Holmes was alive.'

'But can you see?' Lestrade squinted at the clear, blue eyes.

'Better than you, Inspector, so no tricks. I really don't want to prolong the end for you. Sorry to spoil all that nonsense of dear old Ralph's diary. The reversed HM was ingenious. If only Mycroft had been your man. Besides, had you delved deeper you would have found that Childers habitually referred to the Prince of Wales as His Majesty long before the Old Queen died. It was something of a private joke between them. Weren't there any other initials there? HA, for example?'

'Well, yes,' said Lestrade, 'I couldn't place them. Presumably someone you have yet to reach?'

Holmes laughed. 'Dolt!' he said flatly. 'Don't they teach spelling at the Yard? *I* am HA.'

Lestrade chose to ignore the slur. He had never seen the name written down and in any case, Childers had given no indication that there was anything special about Holmes' presence at the Grange. He was wondering what else he and the boffin from Codes and Cyphers had missed in the diary.

'And the motive?'

'Yes, the motive. I think perhaps you were right all along. Revenge, not the revenge of Sherlock Holmes, but of Aumerle Holmes. Mimicry was always simple for me,' he lapsed into the crisp, curt delivery of Mycroft, 'wouldn't you say?' And then the Great Detective, 'Eh, Lestrade? Eh? A three-pipe problem. I was a dab hand too at forgery. I knew Watson would be totally taken in by "Sherlock's letter from Switzerland". Oh, I *was* blind, Inspector.' He came closer. 'Can you know what that is like? Total, unutterable blackness? And these fine fellows, these bastions of society caused it. It was a weekend shooting party. I was home on leave from South Africa. His Royal Highness was there. The big fish himself. All of them, laughing and joking. The toast of the Conservative and Unionist party, and Uncle Deering who was about to join them. We were at Dymoke's place when it happened. Horseplay, they called it. Playing silly beggars with a Hotchkiss Dymoke had bought. I knew it was dangerous. Deering, as a soldier, should have known better. The thing blew up in my face as I tried to stop them.

Blindness. Oh, they were all very sorry. Sorry!' He spat with contempt at the obese bundle of monarchy at Lestrade's elbow. 'I lost my sight, the girl I loved—'

'Mercy Alabaster,' said Lestrade.

'You know her?'

'I met her at the tournament,' he said. 'It's funny, she almost gave you away. When I mentioned you had told me you had been wounded in Africa, she said I must have been misinformed. I didn't listen.'

'You should have, Lestrade. Well, my sight returned. I fell downstairs one day when Blenkinsop was out. It was a miracle. A sheer bloody miracle. The jolt had somehow restored nerves the bang on my head had affected. And that very miracle gave me my chance. I couldn't have hoped for revenge as a blind man, but as a sighted man playing blind man's buff, well, it was easy! I got them all, Lestrade. You and Bradstreet got under my skin. So I killed him in a fit of pique. You, I was merely toying with. It amused me, just as it has amused me to go on playing the blind man for Blenkinsop and the world. As it amused me to choose the Diogenes, Mycroft's odd place, as the scene of your death. Because now you're going to die too. With the King dead, I will have had my revenge. Aumerle Holmes will leave the country after a suitable period has elapsed and take up a new, sighted identity elsewhere in the world. Which is precisely why I needed the ransom money. You owe me, Lestrade. But that's a debt I will overlook, because, you see, you won't be here to pay it.'

The muzzle came up for the last time. Click. Click. Lestrade's features were frozen in a maniacal grin. Holmes laughed his brittle laugh. 'Empty,' he said, 'how careless of me. And London's finest has been quaking here for half an hour under an empty gun. What would Mr Henry say?'

Lestrade lurched forward, only to come nose to tip with the rapier blade from Holmes' white stick. 'This, however,' Holmes hissed, '*is* loaded. The weapon that killed Hamilcar Waldo. You see, I *was* a cavalry officer, Lestrade. Lumsden's Horse, remember? You can keep your Martini-Henry, your cyanide. Give me the clean poetry of a blade. You see how clever I am.' He forced Lestrade back to the wall again and lapsed into the brogue which had haunted Lestrade almost since the case began. 'Goodbye, Inspector, darlin'.'

He lunged upward, the blade stabbing through Lestrade's collar, but deflecting on a stud and drawing a crimson line across his neck. In the same instant, the Apache blade ripped through Lestrade's pocket, up with a sickening thud into the pit of Holmes' stomach. The eyes rolled upwards and he hovered there, pinned to the wall by his sword stick. Then he pulled away, gurgling as he stumbled backwards. Lestrade fell back against the King and clutched out in vain as Aumerle Holmes crashed bodily through the moonlit window. All that was left in Lestrade's hand was a piece of torn cloth and the white-coloured lenses he had inserted under the eyelids – the perfect disguise for a man who could see in the dark.

He rushed to the sill and looked down. Five floors below, the body of Aumerle Holmes lay twisted awkwardly on the cobbles. Boscombe was already coming out to see what the commotion had been.

'That's for Edgar Bradstreet,' said Lestrade.

He staunched the flow of blood from his neck with one hand and with the other began to untie the King. His Majesty gasped and breathed in the chill night air with gratitude. When the feeling returned to his hands, he hugged Lestrade for all he was worth. Not many men could say they had been hugged by a King. Especially this King.

'Harlequin,' the older man growled, 'I owe you my life. Name your reward.'

Lestrade waved it aside. 'Every citizen's duty, sir,' he said.

'Lestrade, I'm going beyond the bounds of decency. You risked your life to save mine. And that's a lot. But I'm going to ask one thing more.'

'Name it, Your Majesty.' Lestrade stood to attention as well as the dizzying pain in his neck would allow him.

'Have you got a cigar?'

And the inspector and his King smoked together in the candlelight.

*

'I've got it, sir.' Constable Jones hobbled across to the bandaged inspector. 'Oh. You look as if you have too.'

'Thank you, Constable,' said Lestrade stiffly. 'I'll do the jokes. Now, tell me,' he collapsed gratefully into the worn old chair, 'what have you got?'

'King John of Bohemia, sir. There was something I couldn't remember about him. At last, it came to me. The man was blind. Does that help the case, sir?'

Lestrade glanced at Dew, 'Enormously, Constable, enormously.'

And he looked at Dew, Dee and Dum, a happy, smiling trio of coppers. And he started to laugh.

The rest is history. For his part in the case, Walter Dew was made a chief inspector. Never had there been so dramatic a rise at the Yard. Much to Abberline's disgust, Sholto Lestrade was made Superintendent. In addition, the King instituted a new order for him, the Order of Merit, and Lestrade was first to wear the ribbon. The reason for the honour was never made clear. To a world teetering on the brink, the news of the King's abduction could never be made public. When Lestrade returned from the palace, a gleaming new Lanchester awaited him. He called it Elsa. But old habits die hard. And at the King's coronation in August, as the feeble old Archbishop of Canterbury trickled holy oil down Queen Alexandra's nose, Superintendent Lestrade caused a scene by treading on Mr Balfour's poodle. He still had the feet of the unfortunate. Fame and promotion could not alter that.

'These are very popular now, sir,' said the anxious assistant in Hamleys toy shop, waving a pair of ping-pong bats.

'I'm sure they are,' said Lestrade, 'but I think this is what I had in mind.'

He picked up a lovely doll with a china face. Its hair was the colour of copper and its eyes were bright and clear.

'For a little girl, sir?' the assistant asked while wrapping it.

'Yes, my daughter,' said Lestrade. 'We haven't seen each other for a while. We're going to have a little talk . . .'